A PECULIAR PERIL

Jeff VanderMeer

A PECULIAR PERIL

The Misadventures of Jonathan Lambshead

VOLUME ONE

Pictures by Jeremy Zerfoss

Straus Farrar Giroux & Dvorak

Prague, Aurora

390 · 0091

Farrar Straus Giroux Books for Young Readers
An imprint of Macmillan Publishing Group, LLC
120 Broadway, New York, NY 10271

Printed in the United States of America
Designed by Aurora Parlagreco
First edition, 2020

3 5 7 9 10 8 6 4 2

fiercereads.com

Library of Congress Cataloging-in-Publication Data

Names: VanderMeer, Jeff, author.
Title: A peculiar peril / Jeff VanderMeer.
Description: First edition. | New York : Farrar Straus Giroux, 2020. |
Series: The misadventures of Jonathan Lambshead ; volume 1 | Audience:
Ages 12-18. | Summary: "The first book in a two-volume fantasy about a
teenaged boy who inherits his grandfather's mansion and discovers three strange
doors, evidence his grandfather did not die of natural causes but spectacularly
unnatural ones, and clues to the family's ties to an alternate Europe immersed in
a war fought with strange tech and dark magic"—Provided by publisher.
Identifiers: LCCN 2019037060 | ISBN 9780374308865 (hardcover)
Subjects: CYAC: Magic—Fiction. | Fantasy. | Europe—Fiction.
Classification: LCC PZ7.1.V396 Pe 2020 | DDC [Fic]—dc23
LC record available at https://lccn.loc.gov/2019037060

Our books may be purchased in bulk for promotional, educational, or business use.
Please contact your local bookseller or Macmillan Corporate and Premium Sales
Department at (800) 221-7945 ext. 5442 or by email at
MacmillanSpecialMarkets@macmillan.com.

Contents

BOOK ONE
WOBBLING

PART III: THE LEAP

PART IV: THE FALL

BOOK TWO

THE MARMOT'S SHADOW

PART V: A HIGHER POWER

PART VI: A LOWER POWER

PART VII: LOST IN THE MIST

~~For the children~~
~~For the birds~~
For the bird-children

BOOK ONE

WOBBLING

Part 1

THE LAY OF THE LAND

"You're going to have to get much smarter very quickly."

Chapter One

A MARMOT AND A MYSTERIOUS WOMAN

The strange things started happening as soon as Jonathan Lambshead walked onto his grandfather's estate and only got worse. Although, in a sense, you could say that strange things had been happening to Jonathan his entire life.

First it was bad cell phone service as he got off the bus, which shook to a stop where the country road turned onto the rutted drive that, a half mile beyond, ended at the mansion.

Then no reception, although he supposed he could call the mysterious figure lurking in the bushes some hundred feet ahead a kind of "reception."

That this figure then darted into the underbrush suggested it wasn't the gardener. Something about the nongardener was familiar, but Jonathan couldn't put a finger on it. The moment passed and Jonathan decided against pursuit. Usually an unexpected detour would have delighted him, but he was too eager to get to his destination and the wonders promised by the estate agent, Stimply.

So he filed the encounter away under the category of "shy herb specialist." Dr. Lambshead's estate was large, and the man had had any number of helpers as his health began to fail. Knowing his grandfather, upward of half of these helpers were helplessly eccentric—people his grandfather had met on journeys drawn into his orbit.

It had taken all day to travel to the mansion, coming from Poxforth

Academy near Robin Hood's Bay on the coast of Yorkshire. Three bus transfers, each one more ancient and creaky, the last with wooden floorboards and faded insignia that seemed to date back to World War I.

Now he was as deep into woods and rolling hills as you could get in England. The summer light was fading to amber, slowly withdrawing, drying up the lovely patches of gold projected onto the road through the tree cover.

He was a tired sixteen-year-old lugging a heavy backpack. Yet the tiredness had nothing to do with a physical weight. It came more from a dissatisfaction with his studies at Poxforth Academy. He missed his life in Florida before Poxforth. He missed the summer tanagers and winter warblers, and so many other things.

Perverse in a sense—he'd grown up in a tumbledown cottage in the wild and desolate countryside near Robin Hood's Bay until age seven, and then been brought kicking and screaming to Florida by his mother, Sarah. But Jonathan had grown to love the subtropical wilderness there, and the Panhandle coast, so different from northeast England. He'd made a life in America with Sarah, and had forgotten England for the most part. Until Poxforth.

Most days at the academy, when not in class Jonathan could be found sitting on the grass under a shady tree, pretending a swamp full of alligators stretched out before him rather than a small, reed-filled lake. Being outside helped Jonathan ignore the depressing brutalist architecture of the school's concrete buildings. ("My kingdom for a gargoyle!" was a common lament of Poxforth attendees.)

It was not that he found the intellects or demeanors of his professors less than satisfactory, but that Jonathan had soon realized that he was out of touch with the world, or it with him. He had little interest in any further formal education, unless it occurred outdoors. Especially as he had, without much thought, assumed he would follow his grandfather's own trajectory of using biology studies as prologue for a career in medicine—only to realize it wasn't for him. And how, anyway, could he possibly compete in that shadow?

The newspaper clipping of his grandfather's obituary was always on his person, folded safely inside his wallet.

Noted "man of medicine" and erstwhile explorer Dr. Thackery T. Lambshead has died at the age of 75, of a heart attack, in his study at his estate in the countryside outside London. In addition to his outlandish medical inventions, Lambshead was best known for his efforts to eradicate mosquito-borne diseases in the tropics, his animal rights advocacy, and the monies his foundation has donated to indigenous organizations for repatriation of lands and artifacts.

Although very successful, Dr. Lambshead lived a life often marred by tragedy, including the death of his first and only wife in a car accident in the 1970s and the more recent disappearance of his daughter, Sarah, in the Italian Alps.

On it went, telling Jonathan nothing he needed to know, and leaving out anything along the lines of, "He is survived by a grandson, Jonathan Lambshead, still enrolled at Poxforth Academy but in the process of crashing and burning."

Jonathan had not been invited to the funeral.

The distance Dr. Lambshead had kept in life, he had kept in death, and this after ignoring Jonathan's letters asking about the disappearance of his mother. It was hard to forgive his grandfather for that, the only charitable explanation being that this had come a mere two years before Dr. Lambshead's death, a period that may have been fraught with medical issues. But not a single query acknowledged?

The great man had been dead a year, but it had taken ages for estate issues to be settled. Nor could Stimply, who had found Dr. Lambshead's body and been Sarah's lawyer as well, shed any light on why Jonathan's mother had traveled to the Alps, or what had happened there other than "mountaineering accident, presumed dead."

There had been some depressing back-and-forth with Stimply about

Dr. Lambshead's will, details Sarah would have handled in a better world. All it boiled down to, as Stimply avoided too many of Jonathan's questions, was that Dr. Lambshead had left explicit but brief instructions about the inheritance. "Namely, that it is contingent on your ability to catalogue the items in your grandfather's mansion. Once that task is complete, including the submission of a list and brief descriptions"—which, Stimply had hinted, might take just that single summer—"the property is yours."

As for the "most valuable part of the collection," as Stimply put it, Jonathan was given a folder containing "the fruits of a prior cataloging effort" and a comforting diagram of the mansion's floor plan and the "Cabinet of Curiosities" in the enormous basement that made it all seem tidy and manageable.

After Jonathan had agreed to the terms, a typed letter from Dr. Lambshead had come via Stimply, just a week before. Sealed with a huge blot of red wax seeming to date from the Edwardian period, the letter had instructed him to "memorize and then destroy."

It had only been two pages long, single-spaced, but the contents loomed large in Jonathan's imagination, even if he didn't understand most of what Dr. Lambshead had conveyed to him. Some of it was practical, some of it abstract, some of it straight-out marching orders, and there were parts that even appeared to be stolen from fortune cookies.

Random highlights included:

"What you seek is always above your head and deep in the ocean."

"Never go through the second or third doors unless you know how to come back through the first."

"Take care of the bird-children as best you can. Or they will take care of you."

"The fuse box is in the basement, to your left."

"Help will come from unexpected quarters."

"Nurture allies where you can find them."

Taken together, it was a garage sale of advice.

Still, Jonathan had followed the instructions—memorized the contents, burned the letter, kept the old key that came with it (sans instructions). As a matter of practicality, he'd had to write down Dr. Lambshead's eccentric "Allies List," but had mixed in some nonsense names to obscure what was real and what wasn't. Although perhaps all of it was nonsense, given "The one-eared squirrel near the dead tree in Park Borely, Marseilles" was one of the "Allies." Nor was this the only squirrel on the list.

Watching the letter turn to ash in the waste bin beside his dorm room desk should have meant nothing, but for some reason it brought back with it the pain of Sarah's disappearance. No: her death. He must be honest about that, and strong. There was no hope that Sarah would be coming back.

As for his father, well, Jonathan still had no idea who he was, nor ever expected to know.

Also: *bird-children?*

❧

It had been a bit much, after Sarah's death, for Dr. Lambshead to be his guardian and yet so absent that Poxforth had, in a sense, been a better parent. Worse, almost, that Dr. Lambshead's mouthpiece, Stimply, had never put in an appearance, either—just a voice on the phone. Yet the relief, too, that after Dr. Lambshead's death it was still Poxforth and the disembodied Stimply taking care of him, Stimply inheriting the task and the Poxforth headmaster displaying a breathtaking understanding of the situation. For Jonathan neither needed nor wanted some "real" foster parent for the short period before being considered an adult. Had, in fact, told Stimply that he would simply run away into the wilderness if need be, there to wait it out. No one had wanted to test his resolve, for which Jonathan felt no small measure of relief.

For who could replace Sarah, anyhow? And while summers were a bit tricky, he'd dutifully waited them out at the invitation of Poxforth families he assumed Stimply had put up to the task of reluctant shepherd.

It was true, however, that from time to time, he wondered why they'd been so amenable—why Dr. Lambshead and then Stimply hadn't forced him to obey the law.

Jonathan had concluded that it was better not to know.

The mansion was as much a distant relative as Dr. Lambshead. Jonathan had hardly any memory of his last visit as a child, and although he'd expected the overgrown grounds, other elements surprised him. For example, as he approached the gravel half circle right in front of the ridiculous wrought-iron front doors of the mansion, Jonathan spied a sports car and the custom-built shed that had sprung up near it. The shed's roof had been blasted apart by some distant catastrophe. Experiment? Accidental fire?

Yes, it was very much Dr. Lambshead's estate. No lord to the manor born would have built a ramshackle shed in front of a mansion—nor left it there after apparent disaster. Jonathan remembered with fondness his mother's story of once discovering in Dr. Lambshead's plush foyer one of the man's many awards propping up a table leg, and another half-buried in the cat's litter box in the corner, looking like the Statue of Liberty at the end of *Planet of the Apes*.

As he came closer, Jonathan saw with relief that the Jaguar his grandfather had bequeathed to him, the fabled automobile Stimply had described in glowing detail as if it were every young man's dream to drive one, was in terrible condition. Jonathan didn't care if he ever learned to drive. Now he wouldn't feel obligated to try.

The Jaguar lay like a metal corpse on the shoulder of the drive in the foreground, rusted out and resting on four flat tires, the convertible top down and the expensive leather seats covered in leaves and vines and weeds that shot up out of the undercarriage. Jonathan quite liked the effect, and felt the vehicle might be most useful as a pot for plants or an unwieldly trellis.

Less pleasing: no sign of Stimply, who had fallen all over himself with the promise of "being there to greet you at the door and show you around."

This didn't strike Jonathan as the best start; always good to have a guide when taking a new trail.

Yet there was a welcoming committee, of sorts. Next to the shed, next to the rotting Jag, amid the tall grasses, stood a marmot, staring in his general direction.

Woodchuck. Groundhog. Whistle-pig. Fat ground squirrel. Many were the names of marmot, which appeared neither in Robin Hood's Bay nor in the part of North Florida where he had spent his teenage years. Certainly not native to the British Isles, but an interloper. A descendant of a pet gone feral? Mrs. Tiggy-Winkle's assistant?

The furry, low-to-the-ground shed-guardian was golden and shimmering in the failing light, framed by wildflowers and long grass, and looked just as perfect as if captured by a wildlife documentary. The marmot stared at him with inquisitive dark eyes as, ignoring the purple flowers half-crushed by its rump, it destroyed a large oxeye daisy with fearsome buckteeth.

"Marmot!" Jonathan said, grinning. "Marmot! What are you doing here?"

Unashamed to talk to the marmot—relieved, even, as given a choice between a shadowy figure and a misplaced marmot, Jonathan would choose the marmot every time. No matter that this habit of conversing with animals had made some of his fellow students call him childish—that just made them unsuitable friends in his estimation.

In response, as if he'd broken a spell by speaking, the marmot went "a-runnin'," as his neighbor Paula in rural Florida might've said, which meant Jonathan had to go "a-chasin'." Through the long grass, in the fading light, as the wide shimmery rug of marmot swooshed through the vegetation, headed around to the back of the mansion, it seemed at times to wink out of sight, wink back into sight, in a decidedly uncanny manner.

The treasure of a neglected pond overrun with bulrushes and lily pads lay behind the mansion, surrounded by more weed-choked lawn and, off to the side, ancient lichen-clad wrought-iron chairs in a Stonehenge-like circle.

At the pond is where the marmot, apparently confused as to the location of its burrow, turned to chatter at Jonathan, and promptly became full-on mysterious by becoming *translucent*—to fade, and then recover, gather its gumption, corporeal once more.

"You are the tricky sort, then," Jonathan said. "Tricky, tricky marmot."

Neither *Marmota flaviventris* nor *Marmota caligata*. More like *Marmota arcanum*. The term *Marmota arcanum* came to him in the instant, but he felt as if he had already known it. But from where? He'd met all sorts of tricky animals at Robin Hood's Bay as a child, and a few more in Florida. The tricky sorts he recalled with a fondness tied to brilliant memories of exploring. They were, in a way, his best-kept secret.

As dusk settled over the pond, the marmot turned to barge through the weeds again, and disappeared for good off toward the other side of the mansion. Had Jonathan lost sight of the marmot in the thick, tall grass, or had the fade come on?

The pond reflected a deep blue against the encroaching dusk. Leopard frogs croaked, and from the bulrushes he could hear the song of birds perched precarious amid the swaying. A line of tall pines behind the pond obscured the glare of the setting sun as they creaked and sighed in the wind.

Peaceful enough.

Except for the mysterious figure standing beside the water about seventy-five feet to his left. Shy herb specialist? The person had positioned themselves in a patch of pine-tree shadow so deep that relative to the glare of the last bit of sun he couldn't tell.

"Hello," Jonathan called out, and waved. But he was glad for the distance between them.

The tall figure just stood there—in a hoodie, or just a hood, he could not tell—so he said hello again.

"You're not very impressive." A woman's voice. Not shouting, and yet the voice seemed to be speaking right into his ear.

How had she gotten from the front drive to the backyard so quickly? Had she run? His pulse quickened and he felt unmoored, which was just a little better than feeling unnerved.

"You're right: I am not very impressive. My apologies," he replied. Putting on a mask that said he wasn't much bothered, a hard-earned talent from often having to act older than his age.

"Well . . . you aren't," the woman said, as if scripted, as if she'd very much *not* expected Jonathan to agree with her.

Shy herb specialist now appeared inaccurate. Belligerent perennials genius? Conflicted conifer consultant? She sounded very English, and yet odd; he couldn't place why. Which was also odd.

She wore boots, he could see that much in the glare—military-grade, tucked into dark slacks. He had an impression of a lithe physique beneath what must be a poncho or a jacket of some sort. He also had the impression she'd conducted a secret test . . . that he'd failed.

"Who are you?" he asked. "Were you part of Dr. Lambshead's staff?"

A rough laughter greeted that question.

All right, then, not a member of staff. A trespasser? He was armed with no more useful a weapon than a tiny flashlight and half of a salami link, in butcher's paper, that he'd dropped into the pocket of his blazer a day ago and forgotten about.

"Are you too dimwitted to be afraid of animals that disappear right in front of you? Shouldn't you be more careful?"

"I've seen stranger."

He was seeing stranger right now.

"Again, not very impressive."

"Care to tell me who I am auditioning for? And what position? And why I shouldn't just call the police?"

"You think a vanishing varmint is ordinary, and yet you think the phone works here? Bless. You're going to have to get much smarter very quickly."

"Is insulting people a professional calling or just a hobby?"

"Hobby."

"You should think about becoming a professional."

"I know you, Jonathan Lambshead, and if you were smart you'd leave this place and never come back. But I don't think you're smart enough for that."

"Well, I *don't* know you and I'm staying put, despite your warm welcome."

"Then we will meet again."

"Let's take a vote on that. If it's a tie, we'll agree to never meet again."

In the time it had taken for him to try to be witty, Lady Insult had faded into darkness, if not in the uncanny way of the marmot. Night had fallen and she made her escape along with the last of the light.

"Get off my property!" Jonathan shouted to the innocent pond, feeling a bit powerless. "Stay well clear of me from now on," he said to the croaking frogs.

Despite his bravado, Jonathan shivered, and not from the chill of the night air. The conversation had exhausted him. And he was glad now that his Poxforth friends Rack and Danny were due to join him soon. Danny was a year older, and Rack was a grad student and older still.

A tinkling, like bells, came to him, faint and ethereal.

What now?

The sound put Jonathan in mind of faeries and hidden kingdoms. But it was only a telephone, proving Lady Insult wrong and ringing from somewhere inside the mansion. Ringing with an urgency that demanded his attention.

Chapter Two

THREE PECULIAR DOORS AND A WEIRDER MAP

What faced Jonathan inside the unlocked front door of the mansion put the lie to his thought that it would be a quick jog to the telephone. Instead, he'd clearly embarked on a quest. Nothing looked particularly navigable in the entrance hall. It seemed like a hoarder's paradise.

There were herds of rotted umbrella stands and skeletal umbrellas— dozens of them in black, white, brown, rust red, gray, blue, green. An extensive collection of pots constituted another part of the obstacle course. Pots were everywhere. Pots of brass, pewter, and sandalwood; pots of copper and hardwood and iron, most rusted or corroded. A pair of dandelion stalks poked out from the lip of one pot, suggesting another problem altogether.

Waiting beyond pots, a second line of defense: hansom tops, bridles, shirts still in their packages, too many sea chests for a noncaptain, comical clown hats riding marble busts, eyeglasses riding hats, fake emerald necklaces, tables buckling under stove parts, and, like odd windows of escape from the sheer ruthless mess of it all, paintings of scenes from far-distant cities that no longer existed in quite the way the painter had captured them.

A suspicious person might view the clutter as a barricade to keep something out. Or to keep something in?

A mouse, or even a *Marmota arcanum*, could've managed the mess easily, have ducked in low and tunneled through. But, as an upright and angular human being, Jonathan had fewer options.

Had this clutter begun with Dr. Lambshead's illness? Or much earlier, when his wife, Jonathan's grandmother, had died in the car crash? His vague memories of his last visit at age seven suggested it hadn't always been this way.

The phone was still ringing. A plaintive yet fey sound, but a kind of lifeline, too.

He plunged into the mess, becoming rather more intimate with the ceiling than he'd expected, searching for a light switch, determined to reach that damn phone. Cursing the whole way.

The telephone proved to be in a living room next to the pantry, which peeked out from the ground floor onto the backyard and pond. A moment of frustration. If he'd known in advance, he might've found a quicker way in. But at least this area was clear of flotsam and jetsam.

He flicked on some lights and breathlessly lifted the receiver. By now, the conditions imposed on him by his grandfather to catalog the contents of the mansion were clearly what Sarah would term "being sold a bill of goods." Best of luck to anyone trying to make sense of this place. Even the architecture was a challenge, as rooms seemed to have been subdivided and others added on with no particular care or plan.

"Hello? Hello?" he said, ecstatic he'd reached the phone in time.

"Hallo, Jonathan? Is that you, my dear boy?"

A surge of relief. Stimply! Even if there were sounds like dogs fighting mixed with roosters crowing in the background . . . and also crows cawing?

Jonathan frowned, held the receiver away from his ear for a moment. "Are you in your office?"

"What? No." Already sounding distracted.

"Where are you, then?"

"Never mind that. Never mind. Where I'm at is where I'm always at: half-past chaos. But, I am ringing to welcome you to your grandfather's estate. Apologies for my nonpresence, but I was urgently needed elsewhere."

A squawk from somewhere behind Stimply made Jonathan's eyebrow rise.

"Listen, Stimply . . . did my grandfather have a pet marmot?" A blurted question. No idea why he led with it, but he was unaccountably nervous.

"Marmalade? Wouldn't say he much liked it. Too sweet for him. Much more a legumes man."

"Marmot, I said." Now wishing he hadn't.

"Marmots? Oh, I wouldn't say he was fascinated with marmots, but he was fond of them. Came from all of his mountaineering in the Italian Alps. Now, lad, I wanted you to know that you will find some items your grandfather personally wanted you to have on a dais—glorified birdbath—near the center of the cabinet of curiosities, when you get there. You needn't start there. Nothing's urgent. But I do recommend you retrieve the items sooner than later. Given the circumstances."

"Stimply—do those 'circumstances' include a strange woman by the backyard pond? And a marmot that I can see right through?" It was hard for him to get off the subject of marmots. As for the woman, he'd dubbed her Lady Insult, but no point calling her that to Stimply.

The menagerie behind him began a symphony of sounds too various for Jonathan to catalog.

"I'm afraid the connection's bad. I didn't catch that."

Of course he hadn't, and Jonathan felt a blaze of irritation. "Stimply. Where *are* you calling from?"

"Yes, well, is there anything else I can do for you right now?"

Jonathan sighed. "A strange woman. A see-through marmot. You could help me with those."

"Don't put that there—that goes over here!"

"What?"

"Sorry—chatting with someone else. A strange woman, you say. I can call the police. If you like."

Stimply managed to convey through his tone that calling the police would be an act equivalent to scraping his fingernails across a blackboard for hours.

"No, you needn't do that." Jonathan was having the exasperating thought that nothing was going to be easy with Stimply.

"Oh! And I know Dr. Lambshead loved his birds, but there is no reason why you can't insist that they stay on the outside."

Jonathan considered that a second. "By 'birds' do you mean—"

"I mean that you are soon to be the master of the house. You may have anything on the inside you like and anything on the outside you like. And Dr. Lambshead's order for those things may be reversed from your particular preference."

Jonathan decided to forge ahead without asking the obvious question.

"Are you still planning on coming out here?"

"Oh, certainly. I hope so, lad. Definitely if work lets up. But you're very self-sufficient for your age, I'd imagine. You don't really need me."

Jonathan felt no small measure of irritation. In theory, without Stimply putting in some kind of appearance, he was in breach of some statute of English child-welfare services.

"I might need you to help me sort through this mess Dr. Lambshead left behind." Unwilling to be direct about it.

"I'm no good at sorting," Stimply said, a stern quality entering his voice. "Sorting is just not within my skill set. If you called me for anything other than information, my dear boy, I'm afraid—"

"*You* called *me*."

"Did I? Yes, I guess that's true. Quiet back there!" The menagerie shut up, for a millisecond.

"At least answer me this, about Dr. Lambshead's letter, and this Order of the Third Door—"

"You might remember your grandfather's own advice in such a

situation," Stimply interrupted. "He always used to say, especially about the Order, that—"

The phone went dead. A compartment at the base sprang open.

A curled-up piece of paper beckoned.

With a clinical wariness, Jonathan extracted it, unrolled it, read it.

"No one's home, but things are looking up."

How droll. The telephone dispensed fortunes, of a sort. Under the circumstances, Jonathan found that suspicious, as if the phone meant to distract him from Stimply hanging up. Or his hang-ups.

Still, he had a number for Stimply's office, so he called it. There was no answer and no answering machine, but when he put back the receiver, the compartment in the bottom of the phone shot open again.

"Someone may be home, dear chap, but he's a bit shy."

He closed the compartment, picked up the receiver, put it back down. The compartment opened again, and another message appeared:

"You are in terrible danger."

Bloody hell. Not so droll. He closed the compartment. Sat there, wondering if the whole mansion was rigged this way. He didn't much like ending on that note, so he picked up the receiver one last time and put it back down.

"No answer is sometimes a good answer."

Is that what Stimply had been doing? Because Jonathan wasn't sure what exasperated him more—Stimply or the chatty telephone.

Stimply's full name was Stimply J. Nightingale, Esq., but Jonathan suspected when said in full most people thought he'd said "Simply a nightingale." And he didn't seem a simple man. He didn't keep simple hours. He didn't have simple background noises on his telephone calls. He didn't simply show up where he was supposed to. Jonathan had still never met the man, only seen a blurry photograph of him in the newspaper article about Dr. Lambshead.

A terrible hunger came over Jonathan, and the pantry was right there, off the living room. An eccentric arrangement, but he was thankful for it now.

Jonathan took off his blazer, tossed it on a chair, and wondered, as he stared at his options in the small refrigerator, if Lady Insult, whom he'd almost forgotten about, really would return. Then he reminded himself he had to check the locks on all the doors and windows, even though the urgency had faded.

Stimply had promised Jonathan the pantry would be well stocked. Of course it wasn't, but it did contain the staples. He settled on a suitably ancient blue cheese and filled a glass of water at the nearby sink. Then he found a plate and a knife and some crackers, retrieved the salami from his coat pocket, and sat with the plate in his lap, enveloped by one of the worn, spring-sagging chairs.

The long line of windows across the wall facing the backyard reflected only blackness and the pale distortion of his face, and Jonathan felt lost.

The imperative part of Dr. Lambshead's letter—the part that had prompted his last question to Stimply—had come without context, plopped into the middle of a section on the many varieties of house keys (useless, because nothing much in the mansion seemed locked).

Restore the Order of the Third Door to its former glory. Seek out the rot within the Order and the threat to it from without. Keep your own counsel on this subject until you have the lay of the land and know your friends from your enemies.

An "Order" of anything made him think of Knights of the Round Table or long-dead fascists, but was otherwise meaningless.

Stimply had, on one prior phone call, pinned to the wall, characterized the Order as "like an eccentric book club," which couldn't be true.

There were also the lines written in the letter's margin: "*I've stumbled onto something dangerous. I'm not sure how dangerous*" had been scrawled right next to "*The stove's unpredictable; you have to jiggle the turning thing to get the thing on the top of the stove to light.*" How to prioritize such twin dangers?

The wind became wild, gusts of it out of nowhere, and the bushes against the side of the mansion tapped the glass. Nothing peered in at him, and if it did, Peeping Toms were welcome to stare. He couldn't have cared less. But he now felt *observed*, improbably, *from within*, and thus self-conscious, as he started to cut his salami into slices.

At that precise moment, midcut, while he was looking forward to a snack to quell a rumbling stomach, two things happened.

First, in turning to set down the knife, he noticed not so much with surprise as resignation that a *portrait of the marmot hung on the far wall*—a glossy, well-fed, golden marmot, a painting most startling for being in an ultrarealist yet brooding style. It had a breathtaking gravitas to it, a legitimacy, and, yes, underlying sorrow, that sobered Jonathan right up. Less a referendum on the usefulness of marmots sitting for portraits as on his grandfather's state of mind.

Second, the lights went out.

In the pitch black, he could not account for crackers or salami and dumped them both on the floor with a clatter as he rose in alarm. A lesser soul would have also deposited his cheese on the floor, but Jonathan greatly valued cheese and managed to hold on to it.

In his hand. Crumbling.

He let the remains fall from his hand to the floor. Wiped his hand, a little sadly, on his trousers.

The fuses. It must be the fuses in the basement. He'd studied the floor plan on the second bus.

Stimply had warned that the electrical system might be fidgety and high-strung. Wiring inelegantly added to such an old house. Stimply was ever so helpful. Except when he wasn't.

Jonathan waited a few minutes, but the lights did not return.

"Crap and bother. Bother and crap."

This said to the darkness as he awkwardly felt for his flashlight, which he'd set down somewhere near his backpack. Found it only after first stepping on the salami, slipping in blue-cheese residue, then grappling for a long moment with the cheese knife.

The flashlight cut a sharp circle from the shadows. Right, well, he had learned enough about fuse boxes during hurricanes in Florida, and emergency generators, to restore the light.

That would be a little victory, at least.

To restore the lights, Jonathan faced a gauntlet of the unpredictable.

First came the strange wrought-iron spiral stairwell leading to the basement—strange because it seemed to corkscrew into the earth at least two floors more than it should, and because it featured a python mural. The green-and-gold creature glowed a tad in the dark, although what startled were not the scales of the endlessly descending serpent or its jet-black eye, but, as Jonathan reached the bottom, the raspy pink of the open jaws, the deep red of the tongue.

Deposited, a bit shaky, in the hallway leading to the basement, Jonathan intuited as much as saw the glint of a dangerously low-hanging chandelier, and then the vast, all-consuming bulk of the main basement, veiled by a deeper darkness beyond.

On his right-hand side an alcove held a child-sized chair upholstered in a horrid lavender bumblebee print. Child-sized . . . or marmot-sized? Above the chair was a map of Europe. Even a brief swing of his flashlight revealed that the country shapes were all wrong. And was that a *land bridge* between England and the continent?

Never mind, the fuse box awaited him, right inside that basement, which Stimply referred to as Dr. Lambshead's Cabinet of Curiosities. No doubt an antiquated assemblage, its location reflecting a kind of contemptible Victorian disregard for modern convenience.

The quicker the better, and so he hurried down the corridor, until the black maw of the open doorway leading to Dr. Lambshead's collection confronted him. Rather than contemplate the darkness, he plunged in. The fuse box should be affixed to the wall on the left.

Instead, a dark monster stood there, staring at Jonathan, and he jumped back immediately, let out a shriek.

Then an exhalation, and with it relief and embarrassment.

"Bloody hell." Cursing his own rattled nerves, and blaming Lady Insult.

The figure had not moved, just stood there guarding the fuse box. Clearly, Dr. Lambshead's or Stimply's idea of a joke: an old-fashioned diving suit, complete with brass oversized head and baggy canvas body and thick waterproof boots. The skeleton inside was almost certainly made of plastic. He hoped.

"How about I call you Fred?" Jonathan asked the diving suit. Or was he asking the skeleton? Thankfully, neither replied. "Well, then, Fred it is."

The play of the flashlight over Fred's helmet revealed a nest of curled-up mice, looking cozy but blinky-eyed.

"My apologies," Jonathan said.

He took the spotlight off them and got busy with the fuse box. He fumbled for the latch, pulled it open. He was still a tad rattled by Fred, not stopping to wonder at the designations on the pieces of masking tape beside each fuse. For every "Second Floor Bathroom" there was a "Ceiling Lights for the daytime birds" or "Was for the sauna, but now it is a storage room for knives and owl figurines." All of which continued to promise a terrible punishment for anyone who tried to sort out the mansion.

He found, as he suspected, a blown cartridge fuse, formerly held in place with duct tape, and replaced it from a dusty box of spares inside the cabinet, no special knowledge required.

With an awful thrashing followed by a diseased hiccuping hum, the house returned to life, with any number of appliances and light fixtures wheezing and coughing above him on the other floors. The basement before him remained dark. Not a surprise. No one had been down here in months, except perhaps Stimply.

Should he now turn on the basement lights and reveal the full measure of the task that awaited him?

No.

Some instinct made him turn away. The basement would still be there for years and years, as he did his best impression of Bartleby the Scrivener. Besides, Dr. Lambshead, per his letter, had left him mysteries back in the corridor—specifically, at the python mural.

The chandelier light was shimmery and too mystical, but bright enough for Jonathan to make out the eye of the python without his flashlight.

"Push twice to open—only twice! The doors are within."

Could this obscure advice from Dr. Lambshead's letter apply here?

So he pushed that black, mysterious eye amid the garish scales. Once, twice, and no surprise that a secret join became visible and a rounded door disguised by the lines of the mural opened up.

Inside, in a small, undistinguished room with a low ceiling, he did indeed find three doors, as promised. Scorch marks marred the floor in front of the doors, where carpet had been pulled up to reveal old mahogany planks.

The first door was uniform gray, stolidly rectangular in the best tradition of unnoticed doors everywhere. It seemed generic and institutional, as if leading to a school cafeteria or a rather boring classroom.

The second door was made of ordinary oak and nailed shut with two boards forming an X across it. Weird symbols had been cut into the boards, including a repeated >o >o that looked like a bird head and beak to Jonathan.

The third door was a bit more impressive. It had been encased in a metal latticework, like a cage, with a lock. Most alarmingly, the black stain and kiss of old flames raged up from the sides of this door. The fire had blasted through from the other side at some point in the past, and the door shut just in time to avoid engulfing the mansion in an inferno. Or, at least, that was Jonathan's guess.

The claw marks erupting high on the slightly warped door frame Jonathan chose to interpret as further evidence of fire damage rather than the ravages of some monstrous beast. The palm print—a wrinkled hand—faint and lower, did not bear thinking about, not yet. Nor did the hints of blood.

For the first time since arriving, Jonathan felt a genuine fear: an inability to understand a situation that he most identified with his one experience observing in the autopsy room as medical students split open the chests of corpses. The cracking sound was exactly and only like ribs being broken, yet he heard it now, too, in his mind.

Tracks on the floor through a thick layer of dust were almost anti-climactic, yet important. Jonathan thought they might be more recent. Even though he had muddied the evidence by walking over some of it in search of the light switch, Jonathan could make out boot prints and animal prints.

The marmot? The portrait in the first-floor living room came back to Jonathan in all its unsubtle glory.

Both sets had come out of the first door, then lingered. The paw prints became heavier and lighter as the human's pacing continued, until they both headed out past the python mural toward the spiral staircase.

Jonathan stood in front of the three doors for a very long time, thinking of Dr. Lambshead's advice: "*Never go through the second or third doors unless you know how to come back through the first.*"

Which Jonathan took to mean, if he believed in magic over metaphor, or even just in dead-end streets, that the second and third doors were one-way trips of some kind. Locked from the inside. But that it might be safe to explore what lay behind door number one.

So what to do?

He had a key in his pocket.

He had a letter from Dr. Lambshead that seemed, vaguely, to endorse opening *first* doors.

After the day he'd had, one quick look inside didn't seem like much of a risk. Perhaps, given the habits of marmots, the doors even led back up to the grounds outside the mansion.

The key fit the lock on the first door, and somehow Jonathan had known it would. He opened the door shyly, as if he were a common burglar, not the lord of the manor.

Beyond was only blackness, but there came to him the smell of *ice-*

blue. He could have described the air no other way. The smell was of the purest ice, of something frozen in place, out of time, and behind that hints of pressed wildflowers and mint, as of a promised spring still encased in winter.

Even as behind him, from the corridor, from the basement, Jonathan felt something stirring, the sensation of an *uncurling*, of there being some *thing* unfolding in the room behind him.

He had the illogical thought that the serpent on the wall was a guardian of the doors, that it had come to life, and was about to swallow him whole. The feeling was so raw and so near and so intense that he had no time to think.

Jonathan leapt into the darkness two steps at a time, and let the nothing take him.

Chapter Three
DAMN THE CZECHS, DAMN THE ENGLISH

"'Do what thou wilt' shall be the whole of the law. Ordinary morality is for ordinary people, not the Emperor or those who believe in him."

—From *The Teachings of Lord Master Crowley*, broadcast weekly via mecha-bear in the cities ruled by Crowley's Franco-Germanic Empire

Napoleon's head was complaining again, from the dais Aleister Crowley had created especially for the former Emperor turned gadfly and general expert on everything. The dais lay atop a tall Doric column powered by hydraulics; at the moment, Napoleon's head resided somewhere near the cathedral's ceiling, next to a paint-peeled cherub with stupid, unrealistic wings. But the entire assemblage recessed into the floor when Napoleon deigned to come down for a look at how mere mortals were getting on.

Napoleon was a holdover from the French Republic crushed by Crowley just three years before—one of several undead heads kept in jars by the government, a national brain trust. Yet breaking glass in case of emergency had come too late, because Crowley had destroyed the French armies long before Napoleon had had a chance to enter the fray.

Granted, Crowley had had a secret weapon: the ability to strike at the heart of French magic, which gave animals the power of human speech. He had found a way to undo the spells that allowed the French to enlist animals in their cause as familiars. Familiar-less, most of the French magicians had folded like dying flowers, petals falling off, their powers reduced to party tricks, while those animals that escaped Crowley's power had fled to the dark forests beyond Paris. There to commiserate with far wilder spirits, no doubt, until Crowley found the time to chop all the trees down.

Some days Crowley very much regretted keeping Napoleon alive, for he was very chatty. But on the other hand, Napoleon offered enough useful strategic advice that Crowley could stand the nattering on and the insults and the ongoing pomposity. Nor could Napoleon pass gas like too many of Crowley's minions, a side effect from absorbing too much magic, and that was a kind of dark blessing.

"Why am I wasting my time giving advice to the uninspired?" Napoleon was muttering in a fake whisper, making sure everyone down below could hear, although it was only Crowley and his familiar for now.

"What use is having a huge brain and a limitless capacity for battle strategy?" Napoleon said, a bit louder, almost a bellow. "What use, indeed." Concluding in a triumphant tone as if he'd just given a rousing speech instead of a bitter sentence.

Above all else, Crowley now very much regretted learning French. But since he could also reduce Napoleon's head to a cinder anytime he liked, even as he congratulated himself on his patience, it was, he recognized, a false virtue. Everything in his immediate vicinity could be reduced to a cinder, and thus his patience was just a smugness about his power to delay horrible fates for all. Being self-aware was very important and explained how he was so excellent at everything and kept remaining true to himself and his talents.

"Everything" in this case meant the command-and-control center in the middle of Notre Dame in Paris, the cathedral hollowed out, pews removed, and his minions the demi-mages ensconced, while a catacomb of further offices and war rooms lay below the floor, and outside a maze of fortifications defended against any surprises from insurgents, whether from the Islamic Republic or the damned English Crowley had had to foreswear—like alcohol or opium, his own people had turned out to be very bad for him. That they should wish to betray him, their native son, hurt him to the quick, but also energized him in his war. They had made it personal; they would pay the price as much as the damn Republicans and their "science."

Not to mention the Czechs and the Russians and the—well, in the end, everyone would pay. But the Czechs sooner than later.

Dominating the central space of the cathedral, oddly temporary-looking surrounded by centuries-old marble and stonework, lay the All-Seeing Eye. A kind of deep bowl made of compressed bloodwood, bound with dark magic so that it lived as if still a tree, and from the sides gnarled branches with tiny green leaves had already begun, in a witching way, to infiltrate and crack the marble, to anchor the bowl such that no one, not even Crowley, could easily remove it. The wooden bowl reminded Crowley of midnight ceremonies of his youth, and this invigorated him even on the worst days.

Crowley stood with Wretch, his familiar, on the platform built beside the All-Seeing Eye, and was bent over the edge, staring into the depths of the dank pool of water that filled it. In the reflectionless water, he could spy on his armies of men and elephants and other beasts in their battles against the forces of the Republic, could reach out to plant a thought in the minds of his generals, some more corporeal and some less corporeal than the living.

Across Western Europe, Crowley's forces rained down hellfire confusion and it was only the damnable Republicans shoring up his enemies that truly held him in check, slowed his victories and ultimate ambitions. Yet he recognized this as temporary, told himself patience was a virtue, even though he lacked both.

"Better than a public school in Kent!" he roared at the mirror in his imperial bedroom some mornings, slapping his face to restore feeling to it. "Better than beatings. Better than childish pentagrams."

Better than being on the Earth he'd known before, where he could only pretend his magic worked, even if more and more Crowley woke feeling numb, had to cast any number of spells to restore his good-natured rage.

He always felt better in the cathedral. One day they'd find him sleeping in a hammock slung between the All-Seeing Eye and a supporting column.

"Bavaria is a bitch," Wretch croaked from beside him. "Bavaria definitely needs to burn."

It was true—in addition to the betrayals by the English, Bavaria had risen in revolt and he had had to turn some of his attention from the enemy on his eastern flank to attend to the Bavarians. It was unclear if agents of the Republic had instigated the uprising, but no matter what the source, it would be put down.

Reports from his spies in Bavaria of sightings of a mythical being, half hedgehog, half man, riding a giant rooster, stoked his rage. It bespoke drunkenness and dereliction of duty on the part of his magical lieutenants, especially as the All-Seeing Eye could not corroborate their stories.

"I'll burn some of it," Crowley said. "I'll leave some of it unburned so the burning is seared into their memories."

"Excellent," Wretch said.

Crowley had found Wretch while exploring the worlds of the three doors. In fact, Crowley had found Wretch in a place existing behind one of the so-called "third doors." Wretch hadn't named himself—that was Crowley's job, since naming formed a kind of binding—but someone else had definitely created him.

Wretch was organic and yet made of some ultrastrong black metal, like obsidian in texture but pliable. Wretch could not be burned. Nor could Wretch be broken by tossing him off a cliff. Nor could Wretch be pulled apart by wild horses. Nor could Wretch be spoiled by dousing him in various vats of flesh-liquefying acids.

Crowley had tried all these things before taking Wretch on as a familiar, and Wretch for his part had been extraordinarily patient with the testing process, and had not held it against Crowley.

Wretch resembled a melding of a rat, a cat, and a bat, and yet also looked like none of those things. Staring at Wretch directly was not recommended, as human beings tended to go mad if they did so.

"What should I do about Prague?" Crowley asked Wretch.

"Burn it, too?"

"No, Wretch. I can't just burn everything. That's not the point of this."

What was the point?

To be the Lord of Everything, to bind all the other worlds to him. That someday, perhaps even soon, there would be no one who would dare to ignore or doubt or defy him. Then he could get down to the serious work and all the experiments on a grand scale that had eluded his ability.

"Of course you can't," Wretch said soothingly. "Just parts of it. You can burn parts of it. The bad parts. The parts doing the bad things."

"Wretch. Please concentrate your thoughts. Prague. What should I do?"

"We will conquer it, but I wouldn't send elephants again, if you will forgive my presumption. No matter how well they worked against the Italians and the pope."

"Oh, I'll send elephants again, Wretch," Crowley said. "They just won't be the *same* elephants."

The fact was, the magicians of Czechoslovakia were entirely too joyous and unpredictable a group. And he supposed, in the end, it was his fault for splitting up the Austro-Hungarian Empire. Because he'd freed Prague in a sense; all the structures and institutions and armies that bound them had fallen away.

The first wave of magically coerced, half-mechanical elephants Crowley had sent to crush their foul little country had been turned into vast, immobile trellises—topiaries that sprouted a startling profusion of wildflowers and drew thousands of bees to them and, over time, vines so dense that now the elephants looked more like overgrown hills. Rewilding the outskirts of Prague beyond their famous wall, as if Crowley had never even tried to attack the city. While the bees continually and forever hummed a classic Czech lullaby.

His childhood love of gardens meant he recognized that the topiaries were charming. But a lingering nostalgia wouldn't save the Czechs now, not at all. The Republic and the English had acted up right after his failed attack, and he hadn't turned his attention back to the Czechs or the obstinate Poles. But soon he would have the time to devote to them—and playfulness and imagination could not trump raw aggression, not when aggression was backed up by overwhelming force.

"Put it on the agenda with my generals," Crowley told Wretch.

"I will do so, sir. That is very wise, sir," Wretch said. "What else goes on the agenda?"

Crowley stared at the flickering scenes of warfare in the water and didn't say what was on his mind.

Instead, he said, "Sacrifice one thousand magpies. And five hundred goats. Also, the earthworms. Don't forget the earthworms."

Another reason Crowley appreciated the All-Seeing Eye's fresh smell; it kept the stench of blood wafting up from below distant enough to remove anything distasteful, just near enough to be refreshing.

"Yes, sir, Lord High Commander," Wretch said. "Immediately."

Also in the catacombs lay Crowley's war factories, where his acolyte magicians the demi-mages labored at creating armies to Crowley's specifications. Magical elephants that bestrode the Earth in war armor did not just make themselves, could not be conjured up out of thin air. It was hard work, difficult work, and required attention to detail.

Once the scaffolding was in place and the temporary canvas to give them form, followed by the metal latticework, they must be animated by magic, the flesh grown with unnatural speed, and the armor, as if their skin, with it . . . so that what was a physical reaction became an alchymical reaction—as John Dee might have said, if he existed as other than words on a page. Blood sacrifice was the only way, and it was the meek and small animals of the world that must make that sacrifice for the bold and larger creatures he needed for his army.

"And . . . is that all I should put on the agenda?" Wretch asked—tentative, as if wanting to tread lightly on Crowley's moment of contemplation.

"Yes, that is all, Wretch. And more than enough."

Wretch managed a tortuous half bow, complicated by his many legs and other limbs and which took on the appearance, even with Crowley still unwilling to view Wretch directly, of how an infernal black mantis must look genuflecting.

At the center of Crowley's thoughts was the Golden Sphere, Johnny Dee's most famous alchymical creation. Or, at least, Dee had taken credit for creating It. Perhaps instead It had always existed and Dee had merely summoned It and bound It to him for a time—using the ancient knowledge of what Wretch called the Builders, according to the forbidden texts Wretch had brought to him.

The Golden Sphere, Wretch had told him, meant ultimate power for a warlock like Crowley, the sort of energy source that could make him invincible and render issues like what to do about Prague or the English treachery moot.

With Wretch's help, Crowley had flushed the sphere from a remote location inside the maze of worlds hidden by the third doors, but once It had entered Aurora, trapped by Crowley's magic, the blasted thing had cloaked itself by arcane means and Crowley felt not a hint of its presence vibrating through any part of the magical realm. No pulse or glow or signal.

All he knew for certain was that the Golden Sphere could not leave the Europe of Aurora without his knowledge, would trigger a trace, put in a hook that could not be taken out, and then Crowley could follow, forever and a day. Only seven doors to escape through and magical lines of force drawn between them like a wall to keep the sphere contained. So surely it was just a matter of time?

Yet Napoleon and Wretch couldn't help Crowley with locating the Golden Sphere now It was trapped and, apparently, neither could the All-Seeing Eye. Which meant it wasn't really all-seeing, and even Crowley could see the irony in that.

Crowley pushed a button on the table, and Napoleon's column began to lower into the floor.

"Aha, aha," Napoleon hallo'd from above, and then from closer to eye level, "you are in need of my advice again. I knew you would be. You would never have defeated me if not for betrayal from within. Not in a thousand years."

Once, Crowley had experimented on a cat, to see if it really had nine lives. Most days he wished he could do the same to Napoleon. Just how undead was the head? What kind of pressure or flame or liquid might muffle the head's enthusiasm but leave that military mind intact?

In truth, Napoleon had not been much prized by France. He had been missing from the official government archives, where the other heads were stored—"on loan," as Crowley thought of it.

Wretch had discovered him languishing in a dead magician's attic in Sardinia, in a remote mountain town called Gavoi. Crowley intended to reveal this fact to Napoleon at a point when he most desperately needed the man to be both silent and humble.

"And now you need me. Now you need me to win the war that you cannot otherwise win without my ample help. But if you want me to aid you to the utmost, what you must do first is restore my body and my armies and—"

Mercifully, though, whatever else Napoleon might have said was smothered as the column continued to recede into and past the floor, headed for the catacombs. For the hydraulic column, like an elevator, went all the way down.

Napoleon's head was required in the war room for the daily briefing, and while the All-Seeing Eye was in the cathedral, the war room was, as ever, in the basement.

Chapter Four

AWOKEN BY BIRD-CHILDREN—AND A PHANTOM MANSION

"Wake up, Johnny Lamb. Wake the hell up, Johnny Lamb."

Someone was speaking softly to Jonathan, who was no longer dead asleep in a bed on the second floor of Dr. Lambshead's mansion.

The voice was hard to hear amid a terrible din . . . of birdsong?

Opening his eyes Jonathan saw a shocking number of birdhouses hanging from the ceiling high above. No less than a dozen birds were availing themselves of the accommodations—accommodations that he was fairly sure had not been there the night before. He watched the darting shapes of larks, starlings, blackbirds, and wrens—all of them cackling, jeering, warbling, and chirping. It was too much motion and noise for first thing, not with everything else wobbling around in his head.

Dr. Lambshead had thoughtfully put in some feeders as well, and some cuckoo clocks just to confuse things further. He must have also put in a hole somewhere in the ceiling large enough for birds to plunge through. It was a wonder the whole mansion wasn't full of birds.

Was that a small *duck* up there, among the darting others?

Bang. Bang bang.

Now something was slamming against the frame of Jonathan's bed.

Battering ram? Hammer of the gods? Or just an annoying friend named Rack?

"Wake the hell up, Johnny Lambshead. Are you having a Personality Crisis? Are you on a Sad Vacation?"

Nothing muffled about that, although cryptic if you didn't know Rack's obsession with Johnny Thunders.

Jonathan buried his head under the covers. That deep, comforting space where he could just hug the pillow and not face any of the things he had to do. "How did you get up here? How'd you even find me in this maze?" His mother's wariness had descended over him, and even these ordinary questions meant to hide secrets now.

"I flew, mate! Like I always do. Like the birds, Johnny, the birds above your scary, too-long horse head. No, I lie—I just followed the smell of an unwashed, vile Poxforth second year."

"Rack" for short. Otherwise, Dirk Wulf Rackham. It always sounded to Jonathan like a list of items required before putting together furniture or someone introducing three different people: "These are my friends Dirk, Wulf, Rackham. Barristers at large." *We are housed for your convenience within a single body, along with a full set of the Encyclopedia Britannica.*

If Rack was here that meant his sister, Danny, had arrived as well. What to do now? Send Rack and Danny packing, out of danger, or pretend like nothing was wrong while he tried to make sense of what he'd found behind door number one?

"Do you not see that there are too many birds in this room and that I might need . . . a moment?" Heaven help him—were these the "bird-children" Dr. Lambshead had referred to in his letter? Because if so, he wasn't feeling very charitable toward them.

"Help. I'm in a death chair. Save me, Lamby. You must save me from this contraption before it kills me."

A new ploy, in such an insistent voice, a tad nasal but also oddly deep. A voice that served as a fearsome weapon in debate competition or urging his fellow oarsmen on, and not to be denied.

"It's not a death chair. It's a one-person mobile tank for all your personal protection needs. You pedal whilst wearing an iron helmet. Antique. Prussian. Never used in combat."

Last night Jonathan had brought it upstairs on a whim, felt it might be valuable. As if he were now the proprietor of an antiques roadshow. But he didn't really know its origins.

Said Rack, "It's offensive that it's a wheelchair with offensive capabilities. I love it. But I'm also uninterested in getting shat upon this morning."

It hadn't occurred to Jonathan that he was lying beneath an aerial bombardment. It should have. Dr. Lambshead had even left a cryptic note about the birds on the bedside table. A fact about birds, rather.

Did you know that a woodpecker's tongue is so long it curls around the inside of its skull? Remember that.

But why?

Jonathan sat up in bed, defeated.

Rack stared at him, not without affection, from beneath a wide and unexpected black umbrella.

Jonathan couldn't suppress a jagged laugh at the sight. A figure with the build of a bulldog slouched in the one-person Prussian tank/wheelchair wearing his usual outfit: a dark blue suit, with threads that sparkled dull in the light from the windows, along with a flamboyant blue-red-green-all-the-colors dress shirt that the uncouth might call psychedelic and the unwashed might envy.

That broad face and strong jutting chin, beneath unruly black hair that grew long and unmanageable when he was immersed in his studies. "Danish Korean" was how Rack explained his heritage, "so I must like bitter cabbage *and* rotted fish, right?" Daring anyone to confirm that. Despite his upbringing and last name screaming "English, So Very Very Very English!" Rack was a terror in the pubs when accosted by the drunken small-minded. Adopted, or as he sometimes said, "adapted."

Dark, bright eyes that glittered or gleamed depending on whether he was irritated or elated. Dull when bored, almost glazed over as if he'd been turned off and was waiting for someone to flip a switch. But really it was his expressive mouth and sardonic eyebrows that gave away the game. Jonathan loved to play poker with him because he was crap at it.

Rack had a brain on him like no one Jonathan knew. He also found catalogs and lists exciting, which was a plus in the current context. His main vice was pocket squares, especially crimson ones with gold embroidery at the corners. But they seemed intended as distraction from an ensemble of the same three dress shirts, two pairs of trousers, and two blazers, well preserved but beginning to lean toward the status of "relics." Tatty. Jonathan feared the family's old money was getting too old. Otherwise why would he, after some fake dithering, accept the fee Jonathan had offered for the help?

"Couldn't you have waited downstairs like a normal or abnormal person until I got dressed, Rack?"

"It's after nine a.m. We've been here since seven. We rang and rang. We knocked. We pounded. We pleaded. You never answered the doorbell—"

"Doesn't work. Hasn't worked in ages, I fear."

"—so we broke in through a window, no apologies for that, and we took some bread from the cupboard like a couple of country mice and begged some milk from the fridge, no thanks to you. We'd driven all the way up here since the taint of dawn and needed a bite to eat and some shelter and some honest human company who is not my sister and probably isn't you, either. And you still can't be bothered to sit up. Are you depressed or something? Do I need to take extreme measures? Shall I set the bed on fire? Because I'll do it. I'll do it, by god, and then you'll have to choose between roasting and being shat upon by birds. And either way the stench will be fantastic."

"I feel I need to point out that that's not *your* personal wheelchair. It is part of my estate."

"I believe I already expressed an affection for the spikes jutting from the wheels and the rails for twin machine guns," Rack said. "But, mostly, I like that I can sit down in it while wreaking havoc."

Rack had a prosthetic left leg below the knee and a damaged right foot housed in a special orthopedic shoe that bothered him no matter how far the technology advanced. Sometimes the wear and tear meant he used a cane or, for brief periods, a wheelchair.

"*Why* are there so many damn birds in here?"

Jonathan slumped a little in the bed. Dr. Lambshead's letter had been clear that he had to sleep in this accursed room as a condition of his inheritance, but he would have to fib to Stimply and move immediately.

"You're already like a beaten old man, old bean. Ancient bean. Maybe you should break the window next to the one we broke. You know, just to make yourself feel alive."

"I'll show you the basement after I have some breakfast," Jonathan said, ignoring him. "And we can get started."

Rack laughed, a deep, rollicking sound that Jonathan was fond of; there was a weight behind it, like a man with his shoulder braced against a buckling door.

"What? You thought we needed a map and a torch and a pickax? Do you think we can't find our arses with both hands, either? We're already in the basement. We're already sorting all the flotsam and jetsam down there. You know my sister—I might've wished for a leisurely egg and a cup of tea, but not her."

"She's competent, you mean."

"Yes. Quite. *That.* Never really got the hang of that."

Danielle Rackham. Never had a middle name, seemed to think it an oversight on her father's part that could be remedied by becoming the most complete athlete Jonathan had ever seen, most fearsome in a rugby scrum, and a double-major in sociology and cryptobiology.

She was the only friend he'd made by the lake at Poxforth who was actually doing relentless laps in the muddy, reed-choked water when he met her, Rack coming along in due time from some French club extravaganza. Some at Poxforth called them "R & D," as in Research & Development; Rack would come up with some harebrained scheme and Danny would make it real.

The three of them had bonded for some reason, perhaps because Danny was easy to talk to. Perhaps because, in a more boisterous way than Jonathan but similar nonetheless, Danny couldn't stand people "rabbiting on."

The second time Jonathan had met the Rackhams was at a party at Poxforth to celebrate something silly, like physics majors who were also on the rowing team. The third time, which had cemented their friendship, he'd taken them on a tour of Robin Hood's Bay and, in a local pub he knew Sarah had liked, fell afoul of a folk band called Monkey's Knuckle when Danny got the giggles over the words "monkey's knuckle."

Jonathan had only known them a year and a half, but it felt much longer, as with friends you could always pick back up with, no adjustment period needed.

"Perhaps you could guide yourself outside for just a bit while I put on some clothes?"

"Nothing I haven't seen about two hundred times before, young feller me lad." That probably wasn't too far from the truth, despite the old-duffer syntax.

Rack had never divulged how he'd lost his leg, damaged his foot—always told people different versions of the story, left it to them to sort through. Which was all Rack's way of saying it was none of their business.

"From birth."

"Car accident."

"Boat mishap."

"Maniac attacked me."

"Chased by a cow feetfirst into a thresher back on the family farm."

"Bear mauling. Now we're friends."

"Family that adopted me first liked me even less than I thought."

Only Danny knew how Rack had lost his leg and his foot. She'd never offered up the information, and Jonathan had never asked. As the months went on and he saw what Rack had to put up with, he thought he'd passed a test by not asking.

Jonathan found it charming that, sometimes, their friendship was based on the things they did not share with each other. That R & D knew some questions, too, were off the table, and that was okay.

Except, overnight, the questions had multiplied, become more sinister.

For example, Jonathan now knew that Dr. Lambshead had died not from natural causes, but instead from spectacularly unnatural ones. Stimply had lied to him. The evidence in the basement pointed to a conclusion Jonathan had been trying to deny.

Most likely, someone or some *thing* had attacked and killed his grandfather.

༶

Beyond the first door the night before, Jonathan's first step into oblivion had been more banal than he'd thought, anticipation of falling replaced by a fight to keep his balance, and landing rough on his knees.

Jonathan had, somehow, returned to the mansion—that was his first thought. Except now it was suffused with a blue misty light that made him think of the moon. A kind of haunted version. The temperature had plunged and he shivered. There was a fresh if frozen smell to the air.

Behind him, the door had still been open, thankfully. There was enough light to see by, so he had placed his flashlight in the crack so it couldn't close and walked forward.

What lay before him Jonathan recognized as the long hallway on the first floor, not the basement at all. The corridor that led south to the pantry and study, and north to the kitchen proper, with a confusion of other rooms between.

Except that confusion was minimal here, and this is how Jonathan grasped that he was in a copy or imitation of his grandfather's mansion. Some *version*. The corridor walls had been stripped bare of paintings and the suits of armor and side tables and bookcases had all been removed.

Every door along that path, north and south, was closed. All that remained of clutter came in the form of birdhouses and feeders, which here, in this place, hung from every ceiling, sometimes in the most unlikely ways. And even then, they were empty. There were no birds. There was no sound at all. The air as he moved forward smelled faintly of spent sparklers and wintergreen.

He soon came out into a circular space not at all like the real mansion. More doors lined the outer wall—ten of them—and in the middle a large clock tower, more like what one would find in a train station than inside a mansion. The contraption atop the silver pole etched with a vine pattern was both intricate, with gold filigree and hands inlaid with mother-of-pearl, and faintly ridiculous. Around the clock tower was arranged a circular sofa, in two parts, which seemed not well thought-out. The edges didn't quite reach, and the cream plastic finish didn't match the clock at all.

Something had gone wrong with the sky as seen through the long row of windows in Dr. Lambshead's downstairs study. Or, rather, this spectral version of the study. The strange blue-tinged light spoke of frost and winter, but clearly the sun shone in quite the normal way and any chill Jonathan felt came from inside.

The problem, or one of the problems, was that the moon hung in the sky next to the sun, and the lawn, the pond, the surrounding trees could be said to experience night and day at the same time. Or, rather, that the moon had been brought close and the sun kept far.

This was not the worst thing about that space.

For come to a chaotic halt in front of one of the ten doors, a claw-sharp hand or paw reaching out endlessly for sanctuary, lay a creature made of riven metal and fallen-in flesh, its hindquarters a mess of wire and bone, the shoulders blackened by flame. Someone had drawn in thick red chalk on the floor around it—a dotted outline with odd symbols inside the rough circle. Not so much like a crime scene outline as a containment of something infernal.

Something dark, like dried blood, coated those claws.

The strangled look upon the broad yet wolflike face as Jonathan sidled round to look closer was unsettlingly human and full of pain. The eyes were dead flashlights. Spreading out from the flesh-and-metal body had spilled an exodus of smaller creatures, now mummified and dead.

The creature looked imprisoned by the facts of its own body. Unwilling. Still feral. Pitiable and damned. There was no smell. There was no sense of life. This had happened months or years ago. There was not even the husklike quality Jonathan knew from encountering long-dead possums or raccoons in the Florida wilderness.

Why had it been left here? In a place that otherwise would have been almost preternatural in antiseptic cleanliness.

He would have welcomed the presence of Lady Insult or even a tricky marmot, as something more familiar than this lost creature.

Yet, back in the corridor, creature safely distant, Jonathan paused, took stock. The hallway doors were different, more normal, and each had initials stenciled on them. Unevenly. As if Dr. Lambshead had done the job himself while taking a tipple.

One door Jonathan had noticed bore the initials "RHB," and he thought that this one, at least, he could chance. Like following one fork in an unknown hiking trail, he could still easily find his way back. If "RHB" meant what he thought it did.

Yet how could it? The absurd idea occurred that behind the door he would find a tunnel leading all the way to Yorkshire, populated by the occasional earthworm, vole, and badger.

At the last second, he hedged his bets and held on to the doorknob, swung out into that darkness, planted a foot on the other side and stood there between two places, staring out at a night sky flushed with an outpouring of glittering stars, a seashore against which the dull white of waves crashed in the shadow of massive cliffs. In the distance inland, a cluster of familiar lights. The lights from the cricket fields of Poxforth Academy.

It was Robin Hood's Bay, as observed from some hidden grotto or ruined tower or light station high in the cliffs. He was staring out at the coast of north England. He was hovering between the haunted mansion, from Dr. Lambshead's ancestral home, and a place over two hundred miles away.

For a flickering second, a moment of vertigo, Jonathan wasn't sixteen. He was a little kid at Robin Hood's Bay, sneaking off to the rocky stretch of coast to the south of their cottage. There, along the empty beach, except when disturbed by a rare tourist or two, Jonathan could pick a natural alcove in the stone cliffs for shelter, looking out across the bay, and in its cool, smooth embrace fill his composition book with short essays or blunt poems ("Oh, how I love the sea."), or anything else the bright, bold day might bring to him. Barnacles on a sea wall. A curious gull peeking in at him. The way the surge of water would begin to warn him of high tide and a sad early end to adventuring.

Now he knew for certain what Sarah had meant when she had told him, more than once, "It's okay not to be *here* all the time. But just know when you're not. Know when you're not *here* but somewhere else."

With a pointed look, as if she understood those moments of reverie in the wilderness where he wasn't sure, where the animals began to speak to him, those cliffs and caves and black water places where when he turned the corner he no longer knew for sure where he was.

Could have been anywhere, even another world.

❧

When Dr. Lambshead had died, Jonathan had felt a need to talk, had let R & D console him. But he hadn't wanted to talk about Dr. Lambshead; he'd wanted to talk about Sarah, one loss dislodging the grief of another.

Danny had asked him what Sarah had been like. That rare probing question, but he hadn't minded. Just . . . where to start?

"I mean, what did you like about her? And didn't like, maybe?"

"Didn't like?"

"Well, she was a person, wasn't she?"

What he couldn't say: That Sarah had been too secretive, not open enough, in his opinion. That she'd forced him to grow up too fast in some ways, and not enough in others.

What he did say: That he liked that she was deadly because she was so smart. And fiercely protective. And terse. And didn't suffer fools. Which maybe all sounded like bad things, but they weren't. And that she could be demonstrative, loving, and very funny. But, he realized now, just couldn't afford to be most of the time, because most of the time she'd been on her guard.

For that reason, he knew there were no easy answers here. Whether he followed the intent of Dr. Lambshead's letter or stepped away, spent a month or a day in the mansion, he could not get free of this.

From this door, Dr. Lambshead or Sarah would have been able to check in on him with ease. Perhaps that had been the plan before she had disappeared and Dr. Lambshead had been attacked. From this door, perhaps, too, someone or something could have been let in. It implicated Poxforth Academy and Robin Hood's Bay both in a larger mystery.

There was such a wider world out there as well. He was just starting to see that, even as he still didn't know what Sarah had truly thought about him being out in it.

The vastness of his discoveries felt like a weight on his back, but also an exhilarating, liberating relief.

Chapter Five

WAR PLANNING IN THE CATACOMBS (NOT AN OSSUARY)

"All goats must be given up to the empire. All goats in Paris are the property of Lord Master Crowley, by official decree. They must be brought to the appropriate processing station. Anyone harboring a goat will be punished. Noncompliance will result in imprisonment or immediate execution."

—From "On the Importance of Goats to Your Country," a broadsheet issued by Lord Master Crowley and dispersed by amphibious mecha-croc

Napoleon and Wretch had been in Crowley's underground war room for at least half an hour before Crowley could put in an appearance. The governance of Paris as an occupying force took up precious time, was both tedious and frustrating. But unless Crowley just fed everyone into the war factories, it was his lot in life to hear complaints about irregular garbage collection and the need to appoint a new mayor. (The old one had, somehow, been turned into a goat and fed to the war factories.)

He also had to listen, from atop the catafalque-turned-into-throne on the altar of Notre Dame, as the liaison for the ungrateful Parisian population went on about how the moratorium on team sporting events had affected the morale of Paris.

"Morale? Would setting loose two hundred wraiths in the streets help with morale? Perhaps they can organize lawn-tennis tournaments.

Would that be of use?" Crowley was referring to his "dead-alive" Emissaries, the terrifying used-up wisps everyone thought he had conjured from thin air, but had been there on Aurora all along, waiting for the Crowley touch.

"That might not quite be necessary," said the liaison, an elderly bald woman in flowing robes and riding boots who had at some point been part of the remnants of a cultural aristocracy. She had survived Napoleon as a youth, apparently had saved up enough fortitude to be brave now, volunteering to serve as the focal point of Crowley's wrath, the shield between him and the citizenry. This despite having been there to witness Crowley bind the Eiffel Tower and turn it into a walking monster that ravaged the city and then the countryside. Crowley's finest spell, which had almost killed him, but had broken the will of the French armies at the crucial moment.

"Then I don't want to hear about it again," Crowley said. He concentrated his irritation, and three pigeons flapping around dumbly in the rafters exploded into flame.

"But there is still the issue of garbage collection. It befouls the city, and it halts work on reconstruction. People are without clean water," the bald woman said, ignoring the pigeon ash that spiraled onto her left shoulder.

Crowley groaned. The city stank, it was true, and even as he plunged through the city on the back of a giant spell-fueled mecha-crocodile or, his new favorite, a hybrid rhino-eagle, instilling respect and fear . . . he could smell the rotting food, the mold, the dead animals. Bore witness to the huge piles on the street.

But why in all the hells was garbage collection such a difficult process? Why couldn't they sort it out themselves? He would have asked Napoleon how he had dealt with it back in his heyday, but Crowley knew Napoleon would see that as weakness and he would have to listen to any number of lectures. Then Crowley would once again be tempted to toss Napoleon's head in the Seine, which he could not afford to do. Yet.

"Very well," Crowley said. "Very well. We will deal with garbage collection."

Even as he was trying to do something spectacular, something unique, to rule first one world and, soon enough, many worlds.

If only Crowley could keep the complaints about garbage collection to a minimum and find the missing *thing* that stymied him. The contrasting scale of his problems amused him. He might even have laughed, but without noticing, for he was now so focused on the *missing thing*, poring over the Golden Sphere in his mind, seeking it reflexively through the senses he had that others didn't. Still not there. Still not seeable through the All-Seeing Eye. But getting closer, he thought.

"Lord Crowley?" the bald woman queried.

Some minutes must have passed. Had he looked mad, sitting there on his dead throne, half in Notre Dame, half elsewhere?

"I will take three hundred workers from the war factories, and I will place them under your control, but as the devil is my witness, Amantine Dupin, if you do not get the garbage situation under control, I will turn you into a goat and feed you to the war machine."

Dupin nodded, turned on her heel, and left the hall. Crowley had never seen her afraid. Especially when Wretch wasn't around, he felt relaxed enough to admire that.

༄

Down in the war room, Crowley found Napoleon up to his usual antics, and his pasty-faced, too-skinny demi-mages in awe as usual, unable to shake their sense of being in the presence of a legend. It didn't help they were dead-alive whereas Napoleon's head was alive-dead.

"The horsies don't go there," Napoleon was saying from a huge table in the center of the vast cavern of the war room. "The horsies go *over there*. And then you need to reposition those things that look like gray rocks to the left. Somewhat closer to Prussia. I hate Prussia—hate hate hate! Stuck-up bastards. Useless military maneuvers."

And other infantile mutterings beneath the man, but apparently not beneath the man's head.

Crowley had entered from an irregular tunnel with wooden stairs fashioned makeshift over marble and unfinished rock riven with moisture from the Seine that could never quite be squeezed out.

Everything was a little irregular down in the catacombs—not as fancy as an ossuary—and Crowley hadn't had the time or patience to fix it up. There were too many other tasks he had to oversee directly or risk trusting his secrets to underlings. Besides, he liked how the place had been dug right from the rock, how he couldn't see the ceiling in the war room, and how sometimes a bat or two would twitter, or even flitter into view from the gloom. The cool dank smell was glorious.

Not to mention he had a built-in audience for his military genius: the thousands of bright skulls sunk into the walls, which he had imbued through magic with a white glow so further lighting was unnecessary.

"No, actually," Napoleon said, pondering, from the hole at the table's edge, "perhaps the horsies don't go there. Perhaps you should prance the horsies on over to Prague. Why don't you be good boys and do that now?"

"Goddammit, Napoleon! We have serious business here. And Wretch? Where is Wretch!"

He counted on Wretch to keep Napoleon in line, but Wretch was nowhere to be seen.

As if Crowley had conjured him into being by uttering his name, Wretch promptly descended from the ceiling and in a mean feat of floating hovered onto a chair beside the vast table. Nothing about Wretch looked like the creature should float, and yet it was one of the things at which Crowley's familiar was most adroit.

"I am here, my most glorious lord," Wretch said with solemn respect. "My apologies. My thought was that Napoleon might be better behaved had he a chance to play first."

Crowley considered that, grunted, decided not to take any bait given, and turned his attention to the map of Europe, which in fact formed the surface of the war room table, with Napoleon's hydraulic column piercing off to the side, raised just enough for him to have a good view—somewhere remote, in the middle of a bit of the Caucasus Mountains no one but a few separatists thought important. Enemy territory anyway.

"Give me the latest reports," he commanded his demi-mages, who were huddled in a group opposite Napoleon, as far away across the map as they could manage. He'd gotten used to addressing a disembodied head, but curiously they never had.

Laudinum X, the leader of the demi-mages, stepped forward. Crowley had named him after the drug laudanum, which did not exist on Aurora, but a spelling error in human resources had ruined the joke. Laudinum began listing troop advances, casualty estimates, complaints and individual reports from commanders in the field, and, in a quiet voice, LX mentioned a very few areas of "resistance" that Crowley could already tell meant he'd been pushed back.

Well, never mind that for now. The overall trends favored him.

The map had been carefully created by a topographic expert and miniaturist who had constructed the most perfect three-dimensional diorama of Europe and Asia Minor anyone had ever seen. The blue of the rivers and the Mediterranean was stunning and the water seemed almost in motion, and the mountains looked formidable and accurate, down to the goatherd trails through them.

Although he sometimes wished Asia Minor could be torched right off—it was too depressing to look upon for long, given that the Republic controlled it.

"We should press harder," Wretch muttered in his ear. "Turn it all into blood stew. Stir it up. Turn the heat to boiling." Somehow Wretch managed to make that sound like a lullaby rather than an intense recipe.

"Hush, Wretch, hush," Crowley whispered back.

One set of demi-mages projected upon the map, like ghosts, little images of his various armies—one battle elephant stood in for twenty elephants, or, yes, "horsies," one man for fifty men, and so forth. Along with estimates of enemy forces and their relative positions, much of it confirmed by flyover by his wraiths or even common crows commandeered for the purpose.

Over this, the demi-mages had projected through petty magic, and distilled from the All-Seeing Eye, additional detail that allowed Crowley to look in on conflicts in progress. Although, to be honest, such views often confused him and he disliked making decisions gleaned from such. It all looked like a scrum of men and magic engaged in group Turkish wrestling whilst screaming and bringing down hellfire on one another. Confusing.

"Enough, Laudinum," Crowley said, raising a hand. There were only so many such reports he could take.

His task as Lord Crowley was mostly at the high level of ensuring the war continued unabated and confirming that his troops took the fight to the infernal Republic, conquered more territory, and that his war factories produced enough war matériel to keep the enemy on their back foot. To know that his magic still trumped the efforts of those arrayed against him, at least for the moment.

And it did: Although England hid behind a strong navy and a wall across the land bridge to the continent, Crowley held Spain, Portugal, France, Germany, the Netherlands, Austria, Belgium, and Italy, along with other, lesser sovereignties.

So-called Eastern Europe, what was left of it, had allied with the Republic, but on the front there his armies would soon push forward. Thankfully, the Siberian Federation held Russia in check, and China's ongoing civil war had caused many problems for the Republic that made it harder for them to bring necessary resources to bear.

When Crowley's troops entered Prague, they would know all the way to the Black Sea that he could not be stopped. Then he'd see what new alliances could be formed before he crushed them all anyway.

"You are being outflanked at Austerlitz," Napoleon said, which Crowley knew was the head's way of beginning to be serious.

That and the fanatical light in his eye anytime Napoleon even got wind of a battle order or a war map. Napoleon could not help himself. It was in the marrow of his bones—of which few were left, granted, other than his massive head bone, but still . . . He had been born a general, and if he had not diversified his portfolio his undead head might still be ruling France.

"By which I mean," Napoleon continued, "you have seen their small beachhead in Sardinia."

"That backwater full of bandits." Sardinia was a beautiful island, Crowley recalled, but remote and hard to get to. Also, full of a wild, unkempt magic.

"The Republic wants you to devote resources to Sardinia, but you will not," Napoleon said. "Instead, you will take the fourth mecha-elephant army and fortify the shoreline between Fiumicino and Latina. You will take the fifth mecha-elephant army and pivot north through Italy. You must let them dig in along the north coast of Sardinia—even take Corsica—while throwing just enough at them—shadow troops, perhaps?—so that they believe you take the maneuver seriously."

Crowley nodded. Shadow troops "just" meant tossing a few demi-mages into a boat big enough to reach Sardinia and then letting them conjure up phantom armies that, seen through the trees, at a distance, might almost seem real. For a while. The agents of the Republic were always improving their methods of detection, and the demi-mages, recruited from corpses and reanimated, gave off their own distinctive aura that gave them away.

"What else?"

"It would help if you built creatures that could burrow deep and surprise from below. That would add an interesting dimension to this map."

"Noted."

Napoleon seemed to have forgotten that demi-mages had already begun work on parts of the Burrower, created to the specifications of the inventor he kept in the dungeon just one level below. It was why he needed a few million earthworms. "What else?"

"You *must* move the horsie—I mean, the horses," Napoleon said in exasperation. "Cavalry *must* be used in support only, for movement behind the lines. You cannot keep sacrificing them on the front."

"Oh, then you were serious. It is so tiresome to have to guess."

Winding Napoleon up, for Crowley had endured already one lecture on the charge of the Light Brigade in Crimea, during which cavalry had been transformed into deranged and useless centaurs.

"Yes! I was serious. I am always serious. I am a serious person!"

"Then would you *please* stop saying the word 'horsies' when in my war room, for the love of all that is unholy?"

"Never! No! Perhaps. Someday."

Crowley considered Napoleon's defiant head from across the vast map with its forever-toiling tiny mecha-elephant ghosts and antlike troops and even, where a demi-mage had been particularly inventive, some semblance of clouds and precipitation that never made the map's surface wet. They'd even added what looked like a few dandelions to Sardinia.

"I'm thinking of opening another front. Against Russia," Crowley said. "What do you think of that? Do you think that would be incredibly stupid for someone to ever contemplate doing?"

What Napoleon thought of that was a stream of curse words so inventive and in such a cross section of languages picked up from various war campaigns that Crowley could make sense of almost none of it. What would he think when he realized the Burrower was meant for the British, so that technically Crowley might indeed be about to open another front? Well, Napoleon would earn his keep then for certain.

Napoleon having been handed his head, Crowley turned to Wretch.

"Have we progress on a plan for locating you-know-what?" The thing-he-had-to-find. Made of gold. Vaguely spherical. The thing he rarely now conjured up by name in front of others, for fear of spies.

Wretch smiled, which always made his lips look like a sneer made of smashed-together worms.

Crowley's eyes narrowed. "You're hiding something, Wretch. Out with it!"

"It's a . . . surprise, my Emperor."

"I hate surprises." Including surprise birthday parties, not that anyone had ever thrown one for Crowley.

"I have been inspired by your own ingenious exploits." Wretch's smile had widened, and creepy monsters peered out from behind the mountain range of his fangs. "I have been growing a solution for any number of problems."

"What does that mean?"

Was Wretch turning into some kind of infernal gardener?

"Look at Paris," Wretch whispered. "Look closely."

It didn't strike Crowley right away, but as he scanned Paris on the map, he noticed, amongst the tiny flickering piles of garbage, an odd little doll in the middle of it. A schoolmarm doll.

"What. Is. That?"

Had Wretch gone mad? Or was he "just" being impertinent?

"It's the surprise, my lord! It's my assassin, Ruth Less." Wretch laughed, the sound disagreeably like the squelch of rotting melons underfoot.

"It looks like a badly made doll, Wretch." A schoolmarm, exactly like the ones Crowley had hated as a boy.

"It does, doesn't it?"

Crowley sighed, rolled his eyes, certain everyone around him was losing their marbles.

"What's she going to do, Wretch? Bite people's ankles? Teach them math to death?"

"Patience, my lord. Think of it as the larval form. But it will grow and grow . . ."

Crowley stared at Wretch, but no further explanation was forthcoming. Instead, Wretch smiled so broadly that it seemed his head must surely split in two. Crowley had to turn away from the stench issuing forth from somewhere inside the familiar.

"Very well, then. Carry on." Aware he might begin to look foolish in front of his underlings. "And what about *the other matter*?" Around

Napoleon any matter was always *the other matter*, in part because he knew it infuriated Napoleon to be kept in the dark.

"Not yet sorted, I'm afraid," Wretch said in a voice that curled around Crowley. "The two in question are under surveillance, and our agents are closing in. I should have a report soon."

Crowley shook his head. "Good, good—that is progress."

The Maori and the tiny Czech magician he sought were agents of the Order of the Third Door hiding somewhere in Paris. He needed them taken alive, if possible. Dead they were useless. Captive, they might be of great use. Much better for *the-thing-he-had-to-find*, according to Wretch's sources. They also had a list of known associates in the Order, including a man named Alfred Kubin, who was of particular interest because his loyalties seemed vague.

Crowley clapped his hands at the demi-mages. "Meeting adjourned."

"As you wish," Wretch said, half bowing.

The demi-mages, led by Laudinum X, exited like a gaggle of geese, using the far entrance. Napoleon's head, death-stare following Crowley, rose up, up, up, into the shadows of the cavern and through the specially designed hole into the cathedral. He'd return soon enough, though—most nights Napoleon lowered himself back down to the battle map and slept overlooking it, said it had a calming effect. Death and high stakes, perhaps.

Crowley remained behind, alone, staring at the map. Such a beautiful map. Even with Ruth Less staring up at him from it in a disconcertingly ravenous way.

Sometimes, rarely, a chasm opened within Crowley and he was afraid, humbled by his own glorious ambition, his own spectacular plans. How what had never been real in his former life was so real here, in Aurora. But what had been Crowley's religion had become the truth, and what was most unbelievable was that not only had God turned out to be real, but *he* was God. Or a god. Of a kind.

All he'd had to do was take Wretch's advice as they stood on the edge of a vast infernal volcano in a cosmos foreign to Crowley . . . and, upon alighting in Aurora . . . kill his own father so that Aurora-Aleister would never be born. For Crowley appeared across worlds, and in Aurora everything was a bit behind or scrambled.

"Hello, Papa," Crowley had said, to a surprised childless man younger than he was, and then smashed his not-father in the face with a mug of his beer and then dragged his not-father to a keg of that same ale and drowned his not-father, back behind the brewery. After that, to be safe, he had burned his not-father's corpse and scattered the ashes.

Then Wretch had embraced him in his deadly claw-talon-feet-hooves and lifted off into the black night, and they'd fled England for France, laughing all the way, and that's when all the fun had started. Because it was fun, wasn't it? Destroying things. Traveling through blackest night in the embrace of one's familiar, the wind buffeting your face and all things seeming possible.

Sometimes all the skulls in the room seemed to be silently laughing at Crowley. Not today. Today, they were laughing with him. He was fairly sure.

Chapter Six

A BLOODY DISASTER AREA

"Memory is what the mind fills in out of necessity," Dr. Lambshead had written in *A Life Without Porridge*, his memoir. "Memory gathers a kind of uncanny magic to it—turns life, without warning, into story, and story into a life. It sneaks about in ways few understand."

Perhaps that was true, perhaps not, although a scrawled note from Dr. Lambshead in the margin of Jonathan's copy that read "Memory puts hair on your chest and then hair in your ears—and then everywhere else" rather undercut the point. Nor was an Order of the Third Door mentioned anywhere on those pages.

Jonathan's copy bore a bookplate not with his given name but another name entirely. This was long before his mother ever allowed him to use the name "Jonathan Lambshead." At the time, he went by the name Peter Cellars, and when he asked his mother why he must maintain such a disguise, she would say only, "The other choice, my dear son, was 'Underhill,' and that's been taken." It was one of her few jokes, not much repeated and not understood by him until later—but sometimes he pressed the issue of names just to hear her rare unfettered laugh. And because it made him feel dangerous, like a spy. And, finally, because he feared his father would never find him if he wasn't Jonathan, in Plain View.

Yet he was thinking again of Peter Cellars and whether it would be best to fade into that name, return to Florida, while in the pantry stuffing some toast and marmalade into his face for breakfast. Rack had relented in the barrage of nonstop talking, gone to investigate some other wing of the mansion, vigorously relying on a walking stick to negotiate the tricky bits of passageways. But Jonathan could still hear Rack's booming voice, a kind of echolocator hollow with high ceilings and whispery with the low. Somehow it made Jonathan's little meal melancholy, the ghosts of that place conveyed via echo.

But, anyway, Rack returned too soon to herd him down into the basement.

"Ready is as ready does, Gloom Bean," Rack said, tossing his plate into the sink. "And we're ready already."

Gloom was gloom apparently, for the coiled serpent still threatened, with a ravenous eye, and the three doors had not lightened nor brightened anything about them, and he tried to ignore that side of the corridor, along with Rack's relentless banter.

Rack rather liked the serpent, thought it "stylish and daring." Jonathan thought it served as omen only.

Soon enough, the glory of Dr. Lambshead's collections, the fabled Cabinet of Curiosities, spread out before him: an enormous warehouse bigger than an airport hangar. Nothing could have prepared him for the preposterous depth of that expanse, certainly not the floor plan, which had not noted the scale or the high ceiling.

Nor had the floor plan included any notation to expect everything to be a complete and utter mess. But it was. A catastrophe. A battlefield of inanimate objects as dense as what had awaited him in the mansion proper. High shelves full of inventory had toppled over, and random barricades of crates resembled last defenses against some forgotten enemy.

"Bloody hell."

"Holy hell for you, American boy."

"Bloody hell, y'all," Jonathan said stubbornly. He quite liked relaxing back into Britishisms. And keeping his Florida-isms.

"'Y'all' is an abomination upon the face of the deep."

"No worries," Jonathan said. Rack hated "no worries," too.

"I'm just going to pretend you apologized for the abomination," Rack said, having allowed him time to take in the extent of the disaster. "You may now understand your failure to foist that ridiculous floor plan back at Poxforth. Order hath no dominion over this . . . this *cave*."

"Well, it's not *that* bad," Jonathan said, perversely feeling he should defend his grandfather.

"'A thesis on the curve became a dog turd on the curb,'" Rack said, quoting a Poxforth professor about a student's translation from the French.

"Depends on your attitude toward turds. And curbs."

"Aren't we all very much pro-curb?"

If there was any order to the basement, it came via the path from the doorway, which branched off into three separate "tunnels" through the junk. They were headed down the central spoke toward some birdbath contraption, while down the left-hand path, leading to a distant corner, lay all sorts of wreckage, including what appeared to be a ruined tiki bar. Ripped from its original moorings near some beach and deposited here.

Near the tiki bar lay a pile of old deep-sea diver suits, looking at that distance like badly stacked canvas dolls with metal heads. More Freds. Had Dr. Lambshead at one point led an army of deep-sea divers into some ocean trench?

A disembodied voice called out from somewhere in the stacks. Danny.

"Hallo, Jonathan! You know this place is a mess, right? A complete cocked-up bollocks of a disaster. Turns out your grandpap couldn't be bothered to make it even a skoosh easy."

Jonathan smiled. He couldn't ever be anything but fond of Danny. He always felt a bit diminished in her presence, but so did Rack, Jonathan suspected, and he always experienced a pleasant urge to *keep up*, to try to be older than his years.

"It's not a pleasant enough cock-up?" Jonathan asked as Danny emerged from an aisle, wiping her hands on a rag that might once have been a fancy embroidered dish towel.

Danny's dyed blond hair was a mess, but tied back in a ponytail. She was dressed in flip-flops, cutoff jean shorts, and an old T-shirt that read POXFORTH WOMEN'S RUGBY: *WE'RE SCRUM-TIOUS. DEAL WITH IT*. Her legs were less like tree trunks than like steel twisted into the form of human flesh. In other ways, she resembled her brother, but unlike Rack, her face was set in an expression of wonder at the miraculous nature of the universe, accentuated by dark eyebrows. At first, Jonathan had thought that meant she was naive. But no: She was just perpetually curious, and over time she converted even the most jaded to her cause.

"Mate, it's a junkyard masquerading as a collection," she said. "You couldn't find a mess this rich outside a Dickens novel. But no worries. It's brilliant!" A season in Australia at a rugby training camp had forever diluted the true Brit in her. That included any modicum of reserve.

She gave Jonathan a big hug, nearly cracking a rib, and a rough kiss on each cheek. Honestly, he found her strength astonishing; she practiced with the men's rugby team, when they weren't feeling too fragile. Once, she'd thought about playing cricket, but the pace of the game exasperated her and she broke a week of bats against various walls in frustration at "all the waiting around." Often "banged up" but cheerful about it.

"Frankly, it gives me the creeps," Rack said. "Such a strange and unsanitary place. Have you noticed that odd map of Earth on the wall? If it's accurate, I can waltz from here to Brittany, no Chunnel required."

"Yeah—isn't that great!" Danny said, giving her brother a playful punch in the shoulder. "It's got some amazing 'here be dragons' beasties on it. Real grotesques. Lots I haven't seen before, yeah?"

"Yes, it's so great that there's no phone reception in this dump," Rack said, "so I can't authenticate the value of what's down here. Dr. Lambshead could have stolen the queen's silver and we wouldn't have a clue. His filing system seems to have been devised by a blind drunk sailor on shore leave, in a brothel."

"I don't need to know what's valuable," Jonathan said. "I just need to put a name and number and description to it all. Then this hoarder's paradise is all mine."

Danny raised an eyebrow. "Oh, you'll want to know the value. I would, at least. There is lots of treasure! Do you know, I think I found the forearm of a Catholic saint back there? Or maybe it's from a rare animal, yeah? Or even ripped off one of your ancestors?"

"Ripped off, I agree with," Rack muttered darkly, but what he meant perhaps even Rack might not know.

Stimply hadn't said anything about whether Dr. Lambshead wanted him to keep the contents of the house. Perhaps Dr. Lambshead intended for him to live amongst it, so long as it was all named and numbered.

"Take this . . . birdbath, for lack of a better term, laden with bear guns and the like . . . what do you make of it?" Danny gestured toward the elephant in the room: a grotesquely ornate marble fountain or, yes, birdbath, that rose waist high while the central flourishes continued up toward a depiction of small dolphins or large fish leaping out of marble water spouts.

The deep basin contained a confusion of items, including a stash of antique muskets with brass triggers like tiny smooth tongues. A sign tossed on top had scrawled on it, FOR YOUR RUSE, possibly in Dr. Lambshead's hand, even though in theory everything in the basement was for their use. Assuming that was a typo.

"Bear guns?" Jonathan asked.

The idea of a bear gun seemed pointless to him, black bears in Florida being rather shy and retiring—and nonexistent back at Robin Hood's Bay. But it struck him that the items had all been left there after Dr. Lambshead's death, for surely his attackers would've taken them otherwise?

"Yes! Bear musket, rather," Danny said. "Rather a lot of reloading required. By which time you're lunch! Which is when, by the by?"

She said this with such a bloodthirsty enthusiasm Jonathan wondered if she knew what she was saying. Or if the bears with which she was acquainted were much different than the ones he knew.

"Just because it has a label like 'bear gun' means less than nothing, sister-blister," Rack said. "Not in this benighted collection. It might as well be labeled 'trick spatula' or 'horseradish croissant.'"

"Maybe you're a trick spatula," Danny countered.

"*Presumably* it means a gun designed to shoot bears," Jonathan said.

Rack scowled. "Yes, but next to it are guns labeled 'otter gun,' 'weasel gun,' 'sparrow gun,' and 'hamster gun.' Wouldn't you say that means this is a bit of a joke, old bean? I'm not trying to be difficult, I promise—I mention this to illustrate a larger point about the profound hopelessness of our task and life in general.

"And there's an envelope Danny plucked from the mess—addressed to you," Rack said.

"There is?"

Danny handed it over without comment, but then they both crowded around to read over Jonathan's shoulder. Rack smelled like lavender cologne, and Danny smelled like hay, Bactine, and the lingering fear of her opponents, which seemed about right.

Jonathan opened the bulky envelope. It contained a note as well as three objects: a small key, an odd pocketknife, and a weird clam-shaped brass object with inscriptions on it.

Dear Jonathan:

You are about to start a journey. You might even call it a quest. I can help prepare you for what I think might happen, but I can't predict everything. You'll have to discover things on your own to truly understand them.

What you'll find here in the birdbath I've placed here for a reason. Make good use of it. The key is for the Château Le Fou à la Menthe. I hope you never have to use it, for if the château appears, things have gotten dire. (Sark and Jaunty Blue, indeed!)

The Astronomical Compendium for Subterranean Places, sometimes known as the DeVesto compass after its creator, orients not to north and south, but to up and down, among other settings, and I suspect it will be of more immediate use. The knife and the guns should be self-explanatory.

When you find the Black Bauble, you are to keep it on your person at all times and tell no one about it. For it is the Black Bauble. When the time comes, you will know what to do with it. (Remember to Wobble your Bauble!)

It's not a chosen life, Jonathan. It's not a life anyone would want, given the choice. But it's the one you'll have to live, so you must make the best of it.

Much love,

Thwack (late of the Order of the Third Door)

PS: Notes from dead people may not seem like much solace, but you'll find quite a few here, as I had more time than most to contemplate the abyss. So get used to it.

PPS: Also, you may remember my neighbor, Reggie. It's possible he'll pop round. You may count on his frank and honest counsel.

Jonathan had never, ever met the phantom Reginald. He still suspected, given Dr. Lambshead's odd sense of humor, that Reggie was a friend of the family who did not actually exist. Had Dr. Lambshead been batty toward the end? Or did this have something to do with Lady Insult? He didn't like that thought. Nor did he like how parts of the note echoed the secret compartment in the telephone in the study.

Even less did he like how the parts of the note not about the "birdbath" were word for word a copy of the original letter Stimply had given him from Dr. Lambshead.

"Oh, a quest!" Danny said. "Spiffy. Posh. Exciting."

"Not any of those words," Rack groused. "Much more like a scavenger hunt dressed up like a quest. And excruciatingly serious!"

"Rack." Danny smacked Rack on the shoulder. He was so used to it, he hardly winced. "Rack! The man is dead, and he's still trying his best to take care of Jonathan."

Which was a little surprising, considering how distant his grandfather had been in life.

"*Château Le Fou à la Menthe*: Château Peppermint Blonkers. Sounds like one of your ridiculous television shows, Danny."

"They're not ridiculous, and I dispute your translation, yeah? No château anywhere is named Peppermint Blonkers. Nor do châteaus just 'appear.' Nor, I'm sure, are Sark and Jaunty Blue a comedy duo. Which I'm sure would be your guess."

"Dispute and obfuscate all you like, dear sister. That's not just an accurate translation from the French—that's likely the condition of Dr. Lambshead's mind." And as if aware he'd gone too far, Rack added, "With all due respect, Jonathan."

But Jonathan had tuned them out. Along with the note was the aforementioned key, small and so ornate as to have fit well with the court at Versailles, and on a simple necklace of twine, the round "astronomical compendium"—which was just a strange brass compass with markings he couldn't interpret—and the knife, which was both like and unlike a Swiss Army knife. For one thing, it had a friendly face etched across it and a base made to look like legs.

As Jonathan studied these items, there came the sensation of warm little paws and Danny's admonishment not to move, and his left shoulder became completely occupied by a plush-looking rat.

"Surprise!" Danny said. "In case we need extra help!"

"Rat," Jonathan managed. "A lovely, lovely rat!" Where had Danny produced him from?

"I told Danny you'd prefer advance warning," Rack said. "But she insisted you wouldn't go into cardiac arrest."

The peculiar white-and-black creature stared at him with an air of profound wisdom or disinterest. The rat looked like it was wearing a cardigan, questing on its hind legs with its nose up, sniffing, front paws like pink stars.

Danny laughed. "Oh, Jonathan. I knew you'd love him." Which presumed a lot. "Meet Twinkle Toes—Tee-Tee for short. He's a woolly rat."

She scooped up the rat and plopped him onto her shoulder. "A rescue from the Porthfox zoology department." Danny's little play on words;

she often said Porthfox instead of Poxforth. "I had to beg a permit and quarantine him and everything. He's not from around here." Pirates had parrots. Danny as often as not had a small mammal secreted somewhere about her person.

Tee-Tee wasn't wearing a cardigan; he just had exceptionally rough, thick fur. Danny wasn't the sort to spend time sitting around knitting a sweater for a rat, anyhow. Jonathan gave the rat an experimental rub on top of the head and was not rebuffed. The truth was, his spirits were rather lifted by Tee-Tee's appearance. But could Tee help with the inventory? Jonathan found that unlikely, tried not to read much into the way the rat kept staring at him. He already had a reputation as an animal whisperer with the Rackhams, so he didn't ask his favorite question: "If your [animal in question] could talk, what would it say?"

"He's officially Danny's other brother and has been for the week or two," Rack said with disgust.

"Not true," Danny said to Jonathan, retrieving Tee-Tee for her own shoulder. "I haven't yet made it official under the law, for one thing. That's a project for *next* month, if Rack doesn't measure up. But it's true that Tee-Tee is a very old and wise rat."

"When she requires a trusted opinion from a confidante, she asks Tee-Tee, not me. It doesn't matter if the question is 'Why do rats shit so much?' or 'What was the first jazz club in Brighton?'"

Danny hit Rack in the shoulder again, this time without much affection. "Liar! Apologize to Tee-Tee! You hurt Tee's feelings."

"How can you tell?"

It was true that Tee-Tee's expression hadn't changed, and he clung to Danny's shoulder like he was born to it.

Rat, Jonathan pleaded, *please don't ripple or fade or do anything else preternatural.* He didn't think he could take anything much more peculiar at the moment than another room full of bird feeders.

"Right, it's a lovely rat. But it's time to get some work done," Jonathan said, although it was clear Danny already had.

He gave the DeVesto compass to Danny, whose delight at the gift was clear; she loved compasses. Then he put the key around his neck and shoved the knife in his pocket. Each had a comfortable weight, a pleasing heft and coolness to the touch.

His suspicions came not from the items, but their lack of secretiveness: displayed in the open, easily found. When had Stimply left the items? Jonathan very much doubted they'd been around long. Otherwise, he was sure, Lady Insult would have pilfered them. For a moment he had the paranoid thought that Stimply might actually be hiding in some secret part of the mansion.

It was so much easier to see the threats out in the world beyond people. As a child at Robin Hood's Bay, he just had to remember not to walk too close to the edge of the cliffs, not lean too far over staring down into an empty well. Avoid strange doors. In Florida, a wild boar or a snake could be predicted, and all you needed to do was be careful and observant.

But humans? Jonathan couldn't fathom them at all, sometimes.

As that first day of sorting continued, Jonathan couldn't help a certain jumpiness. He had a sense of being watched, and there were odd sounds as of antiques shifting, or rambunctious mice, or pipes in the wall that did their best impression of ghosts clanking with chains. Nor did he appreciate Rack and Danny making jokes about him being rattled.

Meanwhile, the haunted mansion, the three doors and where they led, were in his thoughts always, along with the image of the creature. It all popped up to disturb his thoughts and interfere with the cataloging.

Perhaps, though, if he were honest, he'd already begun to lose his appetite for the reality of sorting through such an overwhelming collection—an absurdly banal chore after everything he'd learned since coming to the mansion.

Which also made Rack and Danny's continued delight difficult to bear. They had not signed on for anything except an interesting summer adventure in his grandfather's mansion. Surely, he must shield all his misgivings and suspicions from R & D as best he could? Surely, he had the discipline for that?

Finding some of his old things from Robin Hood's Bay didn't help. A bag of marbles, a toy telescope, and a stuffed mutt of a dog in a red sweater that he'd worn mangy with hugs.

He guessed he'd forgotten them here when they'd left so suddenly for Florida . . .

The row between Sarah and Dr. Lambshead had occurred on that last visit to the mansion. He'd always thought it was because his grandfather had offered him a sip of spirits, or maybe because he'd shown Jonathan the three doors, but he couldn't be sure. Either seemed a meager motive for what had happened next: a quick breakfast with Sarah's dagger eyes aimed at a Dr. Lambshead whose head was bowed, followed by a ferocious argument behind closed doors.

There was no return to Robin Hood's Bay. Immediate travel to London the next day and on to Florida, with Sarah never giving him any explanation beyond "it's not safe" for wrenching him out of one life to live another.

In truth, it wasn't totally unexpected. He'd always thought something like that could happen. Sarah had always seemed on the lookout for disaster, for some unforeseen something looming just beyond the horizon. As if danger would peer out sinister from between the seat cushions on an ordinary train trip. It was a peculiarly selective eye for danger. He could have all the freedom he wanted roaming the wild landscape on the abandoned farmland and surrounding woods of their home near Robin Hood's Bay. He could exhaust himself exploring inlets and taking grass-clogged paths along the cliffs, where it wasn't inconceivable he might fall and break a leg . . . but god forbid if he wanted to go into the town proper by himself and be among *people*.

There had been no arguing with her over their move to Florida—she had taught Jonathan that when she used a certain tone, gave him a certain look, he must obey or risk a much more horrible and harder-to-endure look, and possibly a time-out in a chair facing a corner for hours, which was torture.

Dr. Lambshead left his clues scattered about everywhere, but his daughter was the secretive one; she'd never leave him anything as obvious as a note. Nor had Sarah been any more forthcoming before her trip to the Alps. All she had told him prior to the trip, during a hurried phone call to Poxforth, was that she had "some business to attend to abroad."

"But you don't have a job," Jonathan had said, which was another way of asking why.

"Not a job per se. A mission. You have to trust me."

"I've trusted you my whole life. Why don't you trust me?" He'd put it plain, and the hurt in the middle of that.

"I do trust you, love. But it's not the right time."

"What's the right time, then? When I'm ancient and in a home?"

Sarah laughed. That pure laugh he heard so rarely, but was always infectious enough to make him laugh, too. Until they were both giggling for no reason.

And that was the last time he had talked to her.

Laughter enough to end a conversation. Laughter to say goodbye.

If only she'd told him what was going on. But, then, too, would it have been different if he'd gone with her? Or would he have been one more unrecoverable corpse buried in an avalanche? Questions that, as he searched through Dr. Lambshead's collection, made him fidgety and out of sorts and uncomfortable in his skin.

The final straw was finding the stack of photographs behind a dusty samovar: images of Sarah as an adult with her father. Lambshead at a museum, Sarah turned around in a chair at some charity event, Sarah petting a golden retriever. He ignored the men standing beside his mother in those photos, or in the backdrop—trying to guess if one of them was his father was an old, bad habit.

As recently as late spring, out at the lake beside Poxforth, feeding ducks, a shadow had fallen over him and something about the silhouette, the hat atop the head, was undeniably masculine. Jonathan's first thought had been "Father?" And he'd almost looked ridiculous by uttering that question out loud, only to see, shielding his eyes, that it was the Poxforth groundskeeper on his rounds.

Sick with himself for falling for the hope once more, he needed to banish the idea of "family" once and for all, but "father" most of all.

⁓

"I saw a strange woman in the backyard yesterday," he blurted out to his friends as they all took a break on canvas chairs they'd set up around the bear-gun birdbath. He didn't add: *I also discovered we could return to Robin Hood's Bay in an instant, just by opening a door.*

"That was me in a dress," Rack replied.

"She wasn't in a dress."

"That was me in a catsuit," Rack replied.

"She wasn't in a catsuit. But she was very insulting . . . I also saw a strange marmot."

"That was Tee, yeah, all puffed out and buff," Danny said, smirking. "A buff puff living rough."

"Just how strange a marmot, Jonathan?" Rack asked. "Did it sing 'Ave Maria' whilst wearing some sort of naval costume—or was it just in its altogether and sporting a funny look?"

"What is it with you and sailors?"

"Not a fan of military uniforms, are we?" Rack asked.

"Fair enough. I'm the ridiculous one, I suppose."

"Not at all. Not. At. All," Danny said. "You're just mysterious. We don't mind mysterious. And we'll deal with the strange woman when she pops up again. Probably just an ex-employee of your grandfather's. As for a strange marmot, we'll take it under advisement. We'll be on the lookout. I'll have Tee have a word if we see him. Good enough?"

"I don't think this is a joke," Jonathan said.

"No it's not," Rack said quietly, his air of sarcasm dissipating. "We know it's serious. We know your grandfather was a strange man. We know that this collection is a serious thing, that you're burdened by the weight of it. That you don't know what it contains or why you've been set on this dusty cleanup quest. And that's why we've committed to helping you."

"Too little credit, Jonathan," Danny said. "We'd like more credit, yeah? We make light when we're nervous, but we thought it might cheer you up."

"And, honestly, I needed something different this summer. Some distraction. Damn it to hell, but it's a rat's nest in here, so even Tee may prove of use. He'll be our rescue rat; he'll dig us out from under all the brass pots and ruined umbrellas when they fall on us. Although if those diving suits come to life, all bets are off."

Jonathan took a deep breath. "Fair enough," he said, because it was—more than fair. "I'll find a smile and a better attitude."

"Back to work, yeah?" Danny said brightly.

"Not until I try on this fabulous bodybuilder suit," Rack said, holding up a vaguely human form in beige deflated plastic with fake abs painted on it. "I want to be what the kids today call 'swole.'"

"Swole like a mole on the dole," Danny said.

At which point, the conversation got very silly.

But Jonathan didn't miss the glance she exchanged with Rack. Perhaps they were having second thoughts after all. He wouldn't blame them.

Chapter Seven

A PLANT IN A MAP

A faint glint of moonlight managed to fall upon Crowley's battlefield map after dark, brought there querulous by the hole that imprisoned Napoleon's pedestal and extended through the ceiling and up into Notre Dame cathedral. Along with the slight glow from the map itself—residue from the magic that created the battle reports—the lunar glitter lent a stillness and an odd sort of peace to a tableau that in the day was rife with violence.

Ever had it been on battlefields in the aftermath, and Napoleon felt calm and in control fixed in his place above Europe. It reminded him of his most successful campaigns, as long as he didn't allow his gaze to wander England's way. He didn't remember, but Crowley had told him he'd been killed at Waterloo.

The nightly calm allowed him to slumber without the dragnet of Crowley's spells. And if Napoleon still could not find sleep, or it could not find him, he would reenact upon that map those moments when he had made history. Austerlitz. Leipzig. Marengo.

Or had Marengo been a cake his nanny made him? Sometimes he got confused.

But that night, an odd scene played out on the map below him, as he kept one eye closed and one a slit that he might not be found out as Peeping Nappy. It was a scene he had observed before. The first time, he had opened his mouth, meant to sound some sort of alarm, but shut it when he realized no one would hear him and also that he might regret having filed a report.

Now it seemed imperative that he simply watch, as if attending an entertainment.

An opera or play, perhaps, put on in his honor. In the vein of the old cautionary tale about the talking potatoes possessed by the devil, which had danced through the old priest's church and beat up the hard-living farmer families who populated his pews. His nanny had spun all sorts of these strange tales of possessed objects and peculiar vegetables, when she wasn't kissing him so much on the forehead he could still feel the dent.

Although, were that the case, what moral or message could possibly be extracted from the scenes that played out there, in front of him, in that dim light?

From Sardinia—the second largest of the Italian islands but the most annoying in Napoleon's experience—a dandelion sprout that had seemed so innocent and so likely to be part of the scenic backdrop created by the demi-mages, now uprooted itself and roamed, using an awkward but effective gait that allowed this sprout to sidle out of that island setting and—miracle of miracles—cross over the sea into Italy, where, in amongst the artfully staged ruins of Rome, a companion met the dandelion: a remarkable golden marble, a mere speck, that rose up with a faint squeal of delight, recognition, and utter giddiness.

The two . . . beings? . . . engaged in a peculiar but charming game of tag in which the dandelion—in truth, now more lion than dandy—made up the strategic disadvantage of lack of flight by deploying a sprinkle of silvery seeds that rose not by the power of any breeze, of which there was none, but a more intense and hidden animating force.

The golden marble ducked and weaved to avoid these natural missiles, all while making sounds that were either too swift or distant to catch or that could only, to Napoleon's ear, be interpreted as "tee-hee." Over and over again.

This was remarkable enough, especially witnessed across several nights running, but even this peculiar alliance had yet to reach a zenith.

For there now appeared from the regal and complex structures representing Paris . . . a tiny schoolmarm?

From his perch atop the pedestal, Napoleon had to admit to himself the first night that he thought perhaps he had gone mad and become subject to hallucinations. Thus, the repetition of the tiny schoolmarm settled his stomach, which was not his stomach but a manifestation in his mind of a phantom physical reaction. If an appropriate one. He'd always liked miniaturizations, used them in magical war on occasion.

For tiny schoolmarm the apparition remained each time it appeared. Indeed, Napoleon guessed, although the lighting would never be ideal, that the schoolmarm appeared *particularly* British in both clothes and demeanor. And wore owl-like glasses.

On that first occasion, a week before, with an energy that reminded Napoleon more of a stoat than a classroom teacher, this thimbly figure with a laugh and a twirl ran nimble yet fierce across the map from Paris to Rome, there to meet up with the dandelion and the marble—both of whom gave up their game of tag to greet the newcomer with squeals and even gestures that conveyed exceeding happiness.

At which point, the dandelion sprouted green arms, the marble some approximation of same in gold, and the trio formed a dance circle, yelling and carrying on as if all three had spent a day in the forest like peasants, eating mushrooms and drinking honey mead. And yet for all that, the hubbub still at such a tiny scale it only came to Napoleon's ears as a tinny vibration.

Oh, the looks of glee upon their faces! For, yes, if Napoleon squinted hard and made of his right eye a telescope, he could see that the dandelion had a face! And the marble some simple etchings so it too could join in the fun of having expressions, and thus opinions.

The schoolmarm creature would at times break the enchanting spell by leaping up all of a sudden to devour a firefly hovering above the map, or some other insect, but the other two ignored this rude and gluttonous behavior, perhaps because they seemed to have no need for sustenance. Perhaps, too, for this reason, each night the schoolmarm seemed a little bigger and brighter, while the others remained the same size and the same dull radiance.

The three danced and laughed and gamboled for hours every night, before at some signal or sign or symbol known only to them—but probably timed to the cathedral clock bells making a petulant internal *clack* at four in the morning . . . the speck, the schoolmarm, and the dandelion reluctantly ended their reverie, said their goodbyes, and retreated to their respective hideouts. Or, in the case of the dandelion, appeared once again to be nothing more or less than rustic Sardinian scenery. Innocent of all intent.

Or, rather, that had been the case in the past. This particular night, the sequence varied toward the end. This time, the leave-taking seemed grief-stricken, full of sadness, the capering dances slower and full of depth and secret meaning. This time, the dandelion—its tired and faded yellow flower now transformed into a white puffball—did not retreat to Sardinia, but instead stood very still in the embrace of the other two . . . and its fluffy seedhead promptly exploded into a profusion of tufted seeds, the stem sagging, lifeless.

The seeds, in a formation not unlike a tightknit school of fish, darted upward on no wind Napoleon could discern, past his position, and up through the hole for his pedestal in the ceiling, and out into the cathedral, and from there who knew where? Napoleon dared not tongue the tiny lever that would make his pedestal rise, to watch the progress, not while the golden speck and the schoolmarm watched mournful from below him. But their formation suggested words like "rudder," "coordinates," "compass," and "destination." Napoleon knew a spy when he saw one. To whom could such an unconventional Peeping Tom be reporting?

After a time, all traces of the dandelion seeds were gone from the room, and speck and schoolmarm retreated as usual to their sanctuaries. Yet, also, Napoleon had seen a few seeds drift back down to the map, as if to start the process anew.

❧

Napoleon remained awake for some time after. He was no fool, although he worked hard to play up for Crowley the blowhard, buffoonish part of his personality, to appear more harmless than he was. For he might at the moment be merely a head on a glorified stick—pedestal or spike, it was all the same, except for the itching—but Napoleon believed there might come an opportunity to regain his former glories . . . or at least attain a body, lose the pedestal, and lose also his servitude to Crowley. For in truth what was this twilit half life but a purgatory?

So, he had neglected to tell his "master" about the speck, the schoolmarm, and the dandelion to this point.

Now, though, he thought again about what report, if any, he should offer up to Crowley and his blighted Wretch in the morning. There was always intelligence that Napoleon could have delivered and had not, from the perverse desire to see his benefactor fail, and he pondered if perhaps he should drop it all on Crowley's head at once, just to watch that lopsided globe roll off *its* pedestal.

For example, Napoleon had neglected to mention to Crowley how much more Wretch influenced the war now than even a month ago, or how Crowley's body language bespoke a growing wariness of Wretch.

Or how the demi-mages clearly now feared Wretch more than Crowley.

Or how Wretch sometimes gave orders to the demi-mages behind Crowley's back.

What might best serve his interests? And, truly, could he make any sense of what he had seen? Would Crowley think him mad? Or was all of this somehow part of Crowley's plan—or Wretch's? Even Napoleon's nanny would've recognized the difference.

In the end, Napoleon decided to say nothing. His life would be more interesting if he left the magical sprats to their own devices and saw what benefit it might lend him in the long run.

Besides, spies in times of war were nothing new, and perhaps they were just heat lightning, the fleeting, meaningless heat lightning—discharge from the demi-mage magic that had created the map. For he had never seen anything quite so fleetingly innocent.

Perhaps one night soon, Napoleon would work up the nerve to speak to the speck, to the schoolmarm. Or perhaps not. Who knew? He was just a head, after all. A weary head. A ridiculous head, always. Full of ambition one moment and the need for sleep eternal the next.

Chapter Eight

A TIKI BAR TRAP, WITH WOBBLE

The next day, Stimply rang on the phone on a table outside the tiki bar, almost as if he knew Jonathan was nearby, sorting through a bizarre collection of ceramic frogs and toads that included a tableau that appeared to be a reenactment of the battle of Waterloo.

"Hallo, Jonathan!"

Stimply, accompanied by a crackling sound like tinfoil or crab legs breaking or insect wings unfolding, captured by a microphone.

"What's that sound?" Jonathan asked.

"I'm molting. It's molting season."

"What?"

"I'm joking. It's joking season. Now, why did you call me?"

"You called me. *You* called me. It's always you calling me."

"Ah, yes, old chap! You've got the right of it, my dear boy."

If he didn't think it unlikely, Jonathan would have sworn Stimply was giddy in the way drunk people get before the evening has worn on to the point of oblivion. And that his accent had changed.

"Listen, Stimply, have you heard of something called the Black Bauble?" Another task in Dr. Lambshead's letter.

"Don't say that name!" Stimply hissed. "Don't say it!"

"Why not?" Jonathan asked. And then because he was still irritated with Stimply from before: "Black Bauble! Black Bauble! Black Bauble!"

The line went dead.

Jonathan sighed. Yes, that had been childish, but then he had the excuse of not yet really being an adult, even if he'd been expected by his mom to act like one most of his life.

Besides, who didn't like saying "Black Bauble" over and over.

The telephone rang again.

"Hello, Stimply," Jonathan said. A guess, but a sound one.

"Wobble," Stimply said. "Call it a Wobble. Please call it a Wobble."

"I'm about to call *you* a Wobble," Jonathan wanted to say, but didn't. Instead he said, "Apologies. If you like, I will call it a Wobble from now on."

The sounds behind Stimply of frantic . . . knitting? . . . and the clatter of what sounded like sewing machines set to maximum overdrive drowned out his chittering.

"Good, Jonathan, good. Mark my words, Wobble will be much, much better. But, in any event, I'm calling because I must report a bit of a crisis."

"Does your crisis involve a marmot and a strange woman?"

"Why, Jonathan, I do believe you have the most delightful sense of humor. No, I'm afraid it's about the estate, which has rather been run into the ground of late."

Exasperated, Jonathan said, "Haven't *you* been the one running the estate?"

"Looks that way, lad. Looks that way." This said in a conspiratorial mutter in no way appropriate to the context.

When Jonathan said nothing, Stimply continued, as the sewing machines abated. "I'm afraid that we have only the summer until some fateful decisions await. Your cataloging must be followed by an auction, and we must hope for some kindness from various banks, as well."

Great. So now he was on a sinking ship full of junk that he had to somehow rescue. He didn't bother raking Stimply over the coals as to why he hadn't said anything before, for a terrifying thought occurred.

"And what about Poxforth? Is my future there secure?"

"Ah, yes—Poxforth Academy isn't going anywhere."

"What? I mean, my tuition, room and board. Is it—?"

"Paid in full for the duration? No, I'm afraid not. You could conceivably commute to Porthfox—I mean, Poxforth—for the summer term and most of that would be paid up, but going into the fall . . . a bit iffy, I fear. I'll look at things again, but it may not be possible."

Jonathan just stared at the receiver in shock. It was one thing to leave of his own accord, but it had never occurred to him he would be forced to leave Poxforth. Perversely, the possibility had him remembering all the things he liked about the place.

"Jonathan? Jonathan? Are you still there?"

But Jonathan had had enough of Stimply. He smashed the receiver down.

Although it had remained mum before, this phone, like its pantry cousin, now proved to be either less or more than ordinary, depending on your perspective. A secret compartment opened and a message popped out: *All that glitters is not gold. All that dulls is not mud.*

Really?

Also rounding the corner was Rack, in the wheelchair, possibly for dramatic effect—smashing his way with glee through a latticework of inextricably confused trellises. He was almost always nearby, and Jonathan believed this was because Rack sensed what Jonathan sensed—that the basement, for all its hoarder whimsy, was not a place in which you would like to find yourself alone.

Apparently, he'd heard none of Jonathan's exasperating telephone call, because he launched right in with a question.

"Why is there a portrait of a huge fat squirrel on the wall in the study upstairs?"

"How should I know?" Jonathan replied, perhaps more abruptly than he'd meant. "But it's a marmot, *not* a squirrel. Maybe even the marmot I saw on the lawn. Groundhog. Whistle-pig. Not squirrel. Not a damn squirrel."

"My apologies, my friend. I did not mean to offend. I did not know you and the marmot were engaged to be married," Rack said.

Danny chose that moment to relay some important news of her own, from around at least a couple of corners.

"I've found Dracula's testicles!" she said.

"Finally!" Rack shouted back.

"Dracula did not exist," Jonathan said.

"Sure he did!" Danny said cheerily.

"On the level, Danny—what do you mean?" Jonathan asked.

"I've found a jar labeled Dracula's testicles!"

"What's in it?" Rack shouted, as his wheels crunched joyous over some bubble wrap.

"A couple of old balls, it looks to be," Danny stated with a laugh as she came into view holding a small liquid-filled laboratory jar.

He needed the Rack and the Danny that made him feel like they knew more than he did, could rescue him if he got lost. These two clowning-around-town types he wasn't as sure about.

Jonathan sighed. "How long did you say you could stay?"

"Forever, mate!" Rack and Danny shouted back.

"And, no, really, it's labeled 'Dracula's Testicles.' Whatever it is," Danny said, faux hurt that he didn't believe her.

"Not as glam as a Black Bauble, right, Jonathan?" Rack said.

Which meant he had heard his row with Stimply after all. Great.

"Wobble," he said weakly. "Call it a Wobble."

❧

The enthusiasm of Rack and Danny, how they'd so swiftly become hard-core catalogers of his grandfather's mess, worried at Jonathan, created a twinge of guilt, for his mood had soured the longer he had poked around in the mess bequeathed to him.

Danny's relentless forward motion, like that of a friendly shark, counterpoint to Rack's snark, felt earnest and sincere in a way that his withholding of vital information did not.

Even as Jonathan felt more than a twinge when he noted how Rack took longer and longer breaks, would hazard a wince and a quick sit-down when he thought Jonathan wasn't looking. Some instinct pulled at him—to simply fire R & D, send them packing in a gentle or joking manner, and avoid the question of telling them more. He need *never* tell them more and thus spare them the many, many mysteries he had already encountered, the solutions to which might turn dark indeed.

Tee the Rat had not helped Jonathan's mood, intrepidly clinging to Danny's shoulder as she bounced up and down off the ladder seeking this or that potential treasure deep on the shelves and stacks. Even the rat was implicated now, all-in. Not only that, but when ordinary rats appeared, Jonathan would now feel uncomfortable with any but the mildest of relocations. "Hurt any rat anywhere, Jonathan, and I will feel the pain," Tee's look told him, as if doubting Jonathan's pledge to never knowingly hurt any animal. Except, perhaps, fish or chicken for dinner. Yet even in the midst of the tumult of cleaning and sorting, the rat stared at him as if Tee were aboard a lurching ship in a storm and Jonathan were a lighthouse.

All of which explained why that night, after an early dinner in the parlor, Jonathan begged off playing card games, citing fatigue, and went off by himself back down into the basement. He'd given over his birdhouse bedroom to Tee-Tee and Danny, who thought it was hilarious and "good value," and Rack had staked a claim to a guest bedroom on the first floor.

"Sleep tight. Don't let the bedbugs bite," Rack had said as his good night.

"See you later, alligator," Danny added, while Jonathan rolled his eyes. She was obsessed with alligators lately, kept wanting Jonathan to tell stories of jumping over them on his Florida rambles.

Jonathan had his sights on more than a normal bedroom. What he needed right now was space in a mind rapidly filling up with *things*, an escape from this huge piñata full of antiques and oddments that had exploded all over the basement. What he needed was some humid sunlight and black water populated by reassuring snakes and snapping turtles. Although in a way the basement was like a swamp or marsh, too. You could get lost here. You could get lost and never find your way out ever again. And who knows what sort of creatures you might have to jump over?

The large tiki bar intrigued him in this regard, a space indoors that was also outdoors in a sense with its bamboo cladding and ridiculous palm thatch roof. It belonged poolside in some suburban backyard or in someone's basement den.

Upon the bamboo had been scratched what Jonathan took to be more advice from the good doctor: "Beware the Wobble," "Take care with squishy, if squishy you encounter; usually mean you a mischief," "Always stopper the booze, my friend, or the fruit flies will make you regret it."

He approached the interior tentatively, afraid of some new trap, perhaps even another door. One that this time led to a land of talking animals that for no good reason celebrated trading a witchy dicta-torship for a monarchy? Instead he found the usual: a bar top, with stacks of old liquor bottles and a mirrored glass wall with wood panel highlights.

The doorway past the bar led into a large space in the back of the structure, no doubt meant for supplies. But someone had repurposed it already as sleeping quarters. Dr. Lambshead?

He recalled a grainy old video of a group of foraging capybaras in the pampas of Argentina, from which after several seconds Dr. Lambshead had risen like a peculiar haunting. It was a hilarious and yet somehow unsurprising clip. The way the capybaras had ignored him. The unas-suming way he'd risen from among them as if from deep sleep. The man had camped in the open quite a bit. Perhaps at times the mansion had proved too claustrophobic for him as well.

Inside the sleeping nook, he found a makeshift mantel for a small lamp and an old wind-up alarm clock, and a dilapidated clothes chest, and even a couple of old woolen blankets that Jonathan tossed out into the general clutter. He'd brought his own sleeping bag.

Someone had painted a night sky on the ceiling beams, which just made him think it more likely Dr. Lambshead had slept there. Although, the more he looked at that expanse of the heavens the less sure he could be it was mirrored in the sky outside.

Lines from a poem by Thomas Hardy came back to him, courtesy of a bizarre commencement address by Sir Waddel Ponder, the headmaster of Poxforth:

> *Yet portion of that unknown plain*
> *Will Hodge for ever be;*
> *His homely Northern breast and brain*
> *Grow up a Southern tree,*
> *And strange-eyed constellations reign*
> *His stars eternally.*

He disliked the poem's colonial sentiment, but prized the cosmic expanse that opened up within it.

Was he destined now to live under strange-eyed constellations? Alone? Because it was impossible to tell any of his few friends what was really going on.

It would be easy to return to the doors, the haunted mansion, but also dangerous. He knew no more from a day exploring the basement than he'd known last night. But the woman he'd met by the pond knew what was going on—he was almost sure of it. And he was also sure that she wasn't finished with Dr. Lambshead's mansion.

Jonathan wasn't just bivouacking because it felt more comfortable to him. If someone still lurked about the basement, the tiki bar was a great place from which to catch them in the act. It was the spot Sarah would've chosen, he knew.

Especially as someone, presumably Dr. Lambshead, had already bored a hole in the wall next to his sleeping spot. Along with the door-way and window slit, he had clear lines of sight back to the glorified birdbath, the mouth of the corridor, and right into the heart of the bramble of objects.

Jonathan shivered.

Perhaps Dr. Lambshead had chosen it for the same reason.

Sentinel post. Refuge. Trap.

Chapter Nine

FLOWERS FOR A PLANT

It seemed ill-advised to the Czech magician known as Kristýna to leave the seedy fourth-floor apartment she shared with Mack to collect her spy. Especially as she'd just returned from a solitary mission that had been perilous enough.

But she began to consider it when, for consecutive evenings, nothing had drifted in through the open window, which overlooked the River Seine. Her spy was now late by more than forty-eight hours. Had the Seine proven an insurmountable barrier to her spy, or had her spy drifted down below on the dark streets, become lost amid the huge mounds of garbage while silently pulsing out her name?

"Time for push-ups," Mack the Maori said from across the room. "Been a while."

Four hours at least. To Kristýna, Mack was as predictable as the pretentious clock in the Prague town square that drew all the tourists. Still, she must lodge the usual protests, even as she had her own reasons to stay put a little longer. Hoping her spy would come to her.

"We have tasks ahead of us, Mack, and little time."

"Must. Keep. Up. My. Strength."

"Push-ups and paperbacks."

"Yes. That. Is. The. Sum. Of. Me."

Through his shirt, she could see the taut muscles in his back flexing as he went through his routine. Sometimes she thought of his muscles as individual nations, with their own sovereignty. Sometimes they moved, she was certain, without his intent.

The paperbacks he received from a succession of dormice and potato folk, no doubt obtained on the black market and not even from Aurora. She had rarely heard of the authors. She liked watching Mack receive them, for he displayed a delicate touch and a kindness toward the creatures that showed how aware he was of his strength.

"Tell me more about the sphere. The Golden Sphere." As if there were any other. "Forty . . . forty-one, forty-two . . ."

Mack was a hard man to read. He did not talk with ease about himself, for one thing. That could appear brusque, but was really shyness.

"What can I say? It can be marble-small or house-big. Visible in plain sight or becomes invisible, as it wishes. A good sense of humor on that sphere, too, of course."

Such meaningless pride, as if she had something to do with it. Yet everything that animated the sphere had come in some way from Czech magic, despite John Dee's claims.

"Sounds. Impossible. Fifty-five . . . fifty-six."

"It exists. You begin to sweat. It is unpleasant."

"No. I mean. Impossible to find. Sixty. Haven't complained before."

"True . . . The sphere will stay small most of the time. Helpful?"

"Less than you think."

"Soon, we will have to leave. I can feel it. Can you hide, Mack? Can you be small?"

"Sixty-five. Sixty-six. I can disguise myself. As a landslide."

"Mild-mannered reader of paperback novels, is my thought. Glasses. A cane. Stooped a bit. Have some respect for the physiques of normal men."

He stopped then, arms bent, turned his head as best as he was able to look back at her. The quizzical look on his face made her laugh, so hard it took her last remaining energy.

She was so weary, wanted badly to sleep. Even to sleep badly. "Oh, my friend, my love, what can I say? You are nothing if not unique. I treasure you. You are my treasure."

This declaration only made him look more puzzled, as she had said it in the old tongue, which he couldn't understand. Mack always said it sounded to him like hundreds of bean sprouts growing fast from the soil or the soft chitter of flying squirrels speaking out the sides of tiny mouths, and even that made her laugh.

Beyond the window, the streetlights that should have given a sophisticated cheer to the night had been snuffed out by Crowley. The Seine looked like a thick, stinky, syrupy strip of blackness, and the breeze did nothing to freshen up their stuffy digs. Some of the garbage, yes, was refuse and rotten food, but more of it represented the entire contents of apartments, left by the curb. People who had fled Paris or tried to flee. Citizens conscripted into the war effort or liquidated or imprisoned.

It was a city under siege by its own ruler, and she remembered it from better, grander days, but for Mack this sad shadow of Paris was all he had known. Should they be proud or ashamed that they had hatched the plot that Rimbaud and others had taken up? That this torrent of garbage was, in part, their fault?

"I'm done," Mack said, standing up. He stepped into the bathroom to change.

"Then I suppose we should take a walk, while we can."

Mack nodded, and soon they slipped quietly out the apartment door and down the stairs. As ever, she marveled at how agile Mack could be despite his bulk. Catlike did not cover it.

He had on the subdued suit that he preferred at night, a kind of a second skin, rain or shine, hot or cold. A tattered paperback book dangling from one meaty hand. Always there, always a different one. Always in English. With all the little scraps of paper to mark pages.

"*Mack, no knife and no truck.*" His new joke. But also a lie, as he was both, on some level. No one appreciated that joke more than a Czech, because it was so clearly a joke and, on some level, a lie, and yet no one knew what it meant. After all, the beer in Prague that was black was light and the beer that was clear was heavy.

They had an hour until Crowley's current midnight curfew. Although the curfew often changed without warning. Her friend John Ruskin, trapped in Paris due to an ill-advised visit three years before, had been one victim. Crowley had broadcast the Englishman's capture through the tinny maws of every one of his mecha-crocodiles, beating his chest like a triumphant ape.

As fiery a polemicist as he was, Ruskin had not been made for such times. Kristýna wondered, with some sadness, if he had been shrieking as Crowley had him put to the sword. Like a dazed bird mortally wounded by a cat. The glittering sword assembling from shards of gravel from all over Paris, held by an invisible hand. "That the populace," Crowley had decreed, "shall participate in the people's justice."

The body of Ruskin thus wrenched high in the air, that all might observe the spectacle better and derive the satisfaction of seeing a dis-embodied head, post-sword, tumble slowly—thus spake Crowley's dark magicks, with arrogance toward gravity—to the hard marble of Notre Dame.

Just one of the luminaries whose heads had rolled recently across the floor of Notre Dame and then down into the darkness to join past generations.

But at least Ruskin *rippled* across worlds, as some did, and so he was not lost to everyone, everywhere. Just here.

The streets were deserted due to the impending curfew. The lights that should have shone out with merriment from shop windows were muted, dull, mournful where present. Everywhere, the shambolic mounds of gar-bage added unwanted texture and weight to the shadows. To combat the smell, she must continually ask the tiny white flowers on the vine that formed her necklace to discharge a vanilla fragrance. Mack might not mind the stench, but it gave Kristýna a headache, reminded her how Paris at the moment had too few trees, too few parks clean of piles of refuse.

Almost at once, she became preoccupied with another problem, however, and all thoughts of her rendezvous left her. For they had picked up stalkers again, and from their appearance and the glance she shared with Mack, Kristýna understood they would never be returning to their apartment, and that she had been right: They were not long for Paris, either.

To be almost always traveling, to have almost nothing left of family, as much of a rump-pain as they could be, was wearying. Spycraft was wearying, too. And she knew, wary of the feeling, that this was the reason Mack's bulk beside her, so dapper and indestructible, made her happy . . . even as they picked their way through ankle-deep garbage followed by two crooked shadows.

She had spotted the two who shadowed her and Mack a day before— one lurching beneath a bulky overcoat and the other gliding smooth, neither motion to be trusted. Now it was clear that Lurch and Glide were not random watchers, but assigned to the Case of Kristýna and Mack. A hard case to crack.

Their path took them to the threshold of a pub with no name that lay in the darkness at the end of a shadowy street full of battered, abandoned apartments. Next to the pub lay a little public park, glutted with trash and some pathetic trees. Still, it had enough grass and vines and bushes for her purposes.

A careful observer might have been wary, but Lurch and Glide hadn't been made that way.

Beyond the rickety wooden door lay a central bar island with a low ceiling; glasses hanging down from slats looked like transparent tulips. The bar top was old, pitted wood, gnarled and knolled, a surface rough and familiar to her. A bar in Prague very much resembled this one.

Kristýna wore practical tweed trousers and a white cotton shirt with a black jacket she now took off and placed on the back of a chair. The jacket was lined with a thick green moss that might have resembled wool in a certain light. But there was no certain light in that place. It had sprung up, without a license or other preamble. It hadn't even been there a few minutes before.

The barkeep fit the bar: a tiny wizened man in an ancient brown vest and old-fashioned dark tights, whose green slippers curled upward at the end. His eyes gleamed like whorls of polished bloodwood in the dim light and there was about his physique a twisted, rootlike quality. Just like her father, so very long ago.

Mack took up a position opposite her at the bar island. They both ordered honey mead, warmed, and received giant mugs frothing with an elixir that tasted like the sting of bees as well as honeycomb. In Mack's hand, the mug looked like it must contain a bee's portion.

It was all rather comfortable, and Mack smiled across at her as if they had no cares in the world. He took a book from his pocket.

But, after a time, the two rather curious individuals crept into the pub and sat to the immediate left and right of Kristýna. She turned toward neither of them, instead taking her cue from Mack's reaction.

There was no Mack reaction. *No knife. No truck.* Although she kept telling him "lorry" made more non-sense, even in Czech.

The barkeep served both pursuers honey mead. That was all he had on offer. She wondered what was creeping up to the roof to outflank them while they entertained these two guests.

"Cold night," said the one on her left, after pretending to drink. It came out like "Cauld gnat," with too many tongues getting in the way.

"Yes, a bit chilly," said the one to her right, who dared not pretend to drink given his constitution. This came out like "SSSSsss, eh BITE silly." Not enough tongues. Which is to say, not even one tongue.

For these two were more dead than alive, in a sense, more *there* than *here*.

The one on her right was already beginning to *drift* into her space. The one on the left was eager to *topple* into her space. The looming shadows of either did not predict a good time, for anyone. But still she kept her gaze on Mack.

"One too particulate, one too many legs," Mack said, taking a delicate sip of his mead, wiping stray liquid from his mouth with a white pocket square.

"Rude," No Tongues said. "Rsssuuuud."

"Where are you from?" Too Many Tongues asked Mack. "WAR-AR-U-FRAM?"

"Mack," said Mack.

"Mack isn't a place."

"Cultural observer."

"Not from these parts, then."

"Far-distant land."

"No verbs there?"

"No wasted ones."

"And where are you from?" Too Many Tongues asked.

"Nowhere," she replied.

"You must be from somewhere," No Tongues asked. "Ussssss mussssss-beeeee friiiimssswear."

"Where are *you* from?" she asked. "Far from here, yes?"

Mack had his gaze locked on hers. If ever there was a mountain about to erupt into a volcano, that was Mack. The empty mug of mead had disappeared, perhaps crushed to dust.

More than once. More than once she had looked across a table or a bar or a room at someone she cared for and wondered if this was the last time. It got old. She was getting old in the service of the Order. But she could not see her way clear to another life, given her purpose and her responsibilities.

All she wanted in the moment was for the moment to last, the honey mead a comfortable blaze in her stomach, the threat as yet to either side and not in front of her.

"Oh, I think you know where we're from," Too Many Tongues said. "I think you know who I represent."

The barkeep looked less like her father and even more like a wizened shriveled root, no matter her best efforts. Kristýna felt thick smoke like velvet lingering on her right arm and what seemed like a sack of wet meat leaning heavy on her left arm.

"We've come to . . . we've come to . . . ," No Tongues started to say, but by then the dark smoke of him had begun to turn into the lines of delicate green vines like luminescent fractures in the very air, questing and growing until No Tongues was very much rooted in place on the stool, unable to say anything at all. His vine-self sprouted tiny white starlike flowers—and then she had had enough and the vines withered, blackened, became crisp, brittle, exploded into flakes.

"This cannot last," Too Many Tongues said, although with difficulty, as from top to bottom he was becoming a huge sack of fruit, his disgusting raw meat quality tumbling away in a cascade of apples, plums, grapes, and an assortment of melons, great and small. "This is so *unfair*."

Too Many Tongues became an avalanche until his great coat held nothing at all, and rolling across the floor beneath his bar stool was a great quantity of bruised fruit.

She slumped, let out a sigh of relief.

Mack stared at the mess, shook his head. He placed his battered paperback on the bar.

As if the encounter had served as a beacon, a light shone out of the dark . . . and drifting down out of the night floated Kristýna's spy: a dandelion tuft that landed, secure, in her outstretched hand. Tuft but tough, as she liked to say, for the texture of the words.

I spy with my little vine. I spy with my little spore. Tuft but tough, you are.

She clasped the tuft tight but gentle. Safe. There must have been many others, but only the one to make it through. What might it tell her that would have been splendid to know an hour ago? Well, they'd debrief as soon as they'd reached a safe place. Still some obstacles to that. She placed the tuft-spy in her shirt pocket.

"To the catacombs, then, to pay our respects to Ruskin?" Kristýna asked in a language Mack would understand.

A huge, world-devouring smile.

"Not an ossuary?" Mack knew she loved the sound of that word, but that there was no ossuary here. At least, not nearby. The word "ossuary" had always struck her as a good Czech word, made her think of the sound an owl's wings made. Whereas "catacombs" was just a banal place with cats shoved into cubbyholes, surely.

"No, not yet. Not just yet."

"I left a few things behind I should retrieve," Mack said.

"No time." She knew Mack would miss the Paris apartment, especially the shelves he'd built for his paperbacks, although perhaps she could grow him some shelves. He'd have to start all over again, and perhaps she hated their vagabond life in part because she felt a loyalty to Mack as well as to the Order.

Yet what would happen when Mack's aims, his purpose, diverged from hers? And how would she know when they had? Seven years, and she still could not yet see the edges of his ambition, knew only that he was not without his secrets, as she had hers. Mack had never joined the Order, only joined her, and his home was so far away.

Came a creeping outside. A creep-creep-creaking.

"Now, Mack!"

"Then the catacombs it is. Excellent choice. Keep our enemies close," Mack said, ever staid.

Was that a creak? A crack?

The door smashed open to reveal a giant mechanical jaw full of glittering trash. A feral red eye of flesh, pulsing. A guttural growling roar. A dumb inability to negotiate the narrow entryway, huge metal shoulders stuck. For a moment.

"Don't look in its eyes!"

Kristýna swept up his paperback and her blazer, waved her arms—and they were away, taken up out of the bar and punching up through the weak ceiling in a torrent of vines and flowers to an adjoining apartment rooftop. The snapping jaws of the mecha-crocodile a hot rush of air on their ankles.

As it scuttled up the side of the building toward them, Kristýna blasted it with enough vines to form a net. She did not much mind the mecha-crocodile: It did only what came natural to its unnatural situation. It could do no more. It could do no less.

"Now I turn it over to you," she said, leaping into Mack's arms. She felt as if she were being engulfed, cocooned, and she could not say she hated the feeling. Quite the opposite.

Mack smiled, kissed her on top of her head, which was all he could reach from that vantage. Then, with a controlled recklessness, jumped to the next rooftop, and then the next, under the barren half moon that looked like Crowley's psychotic cracked smile, the mecha-crocodile in confused pursuit as the probing vines delicately destroyed it from the inside out. Until, looking back over Mack's shoulder, she saw it two rooftops back, overgrown and caught in midspasm, unable to follow any longer, all its gears confounded and overrun.

All to the good, and yet as she lay there in Mack's arms, a tiny Czech magician who loved plants and was much older than anyone might think, Kristýna had a nagging doubt that their escape had been too easy. Perhaps because she always took such care and pride in planning possible escapes.

But also, because the two dispatched had not been made by Crowley, just sent by him. She was a veteran of the old ways of magic. Hers was one kind. The two who had been sent represented another. To encounter that kind again after so long felt like a message being conveyed without words. A message like . . . a growing confidence, a sense of some *thing* soon to come out into the open.

No matter what the dandelion-tuft spy revealed, Kristýna doubted it would solve this particular mystery.

Chapter Ten

A POTATO AND A CARROT HOLD HANDS

A couple of nights in the back of the tiki bar tucked into a sleeping bag helped Jonathan more than he'd expected. It oriented him to the clutter, by living within its borders, and thus he noticed it less. The less he noticed it, the less it bothered him. The more he could focus his energy on the baffling evidence around the three doors. Although he'd been careful to conceal them from R & D, so he had to pick his spots.

The mystery had multiplied in oddly banal ways. On day three, for example, when Jonathan checked the secret room, he had noticed that the marmot tracks now led *back* to the second door, with fresh boot prints as well.

What could that possibly mean? His dreams had been full of moments where he viewed himself sleeping on the floor of the tiki bar while some shadowy figure loomed over him. Each time, he'd shouted out, "Go away!" and the figure had retreated. He was fairly sure they'd all been dreams. Certainly, after waking up he'd not noticed anything amiss, had caught no further glimpses of Lady Insult.

During this span, Jonathan had successfully fought against his natural curiosity and not gone through any additional doors. He thought of those doors as leading to trails for which he didn't have the map. Without some sort of guide, he'd best not use them.

But each night, Jonathan had snuck out of his tiki bar sanctuary and once more walked through the first door into the haunted mansion, looked in upon the dead creature, then poked his head through to Robin Hood's Bay. Each time, it became more real to him, less like something he had dreamed. Each time, it assuaged, just enough, the itch to explore further. He knew this would be disastrous, that if he gave in to the urge he might disappear from Earth, never to return.

Instead, he focused on searching the basement for more information on the Order of the Third Door. If Dr. Lambshead refused to reveal all in his letter, then surely among the books piled as high as watchtowers in the basement, or in the chaotic first-floor library, there must be clues.

Yet clues were sparse and even after so much searching, Jonathan had found nothing. It seemed suspicious—an absence that formed a shape or a hole in the mansion's contents. Every ripped-out page—and he found an astonishing number of books with ripped-out pages—made him more ill at ease. Even if most of the damage could be attributed to a poorly cared-for collection.

Could the solution to the mystery just as likely be that Dr. Lambshead's famous impulsiveness and enthusiasm had made him impatient about lugging books about the mansion when he could tear out what he needed and fold it up in a pocket?

Then there was the matter of the object he'd been tasked by Dr. Lambshead to retrieve, the Black Bauble that had sent Stimply into such a panic. The "Wobble."

"*Retrieve it while no one else is around,*" Dr. Lambshead had instructed in the letter. And, thus, on the second night in the basement, he'd crept on tiptoe to the mural of the serpent and looked with interest at the serpent's dark eye.

With a bit of trepidation on Jonathan's part, "place your thumb on the eye and push four times, wait two seconds, push in two more times" went from an instruction on a piece of paper to something he was doing. He already knew the whole wall would push in to reveal a secret room or corridor, as in some hackneyed gothic film. What would this new code do? Would he even get his thumb back?

Instead, nothing at all happened except the eye depressed slightly, by perhaps a quarter inch.

All right, now what?

He waited, concerned about the consequences of release.

Perhaps it would result in the top of the mansion blowing off and the entire second floor growing wings and becoming some complicated flying machine. Or, admittedly, something considerably less dramatic. Or even . . . nothing?

When Jonathan had waited for long enough that he felt a bit like the little Dutch boy with his finger in the dike, he removed his thumb from the serpent's eye.

The eye promptly ejected itself from the serpent, rolling across the floor. Jonathan caught up with it, snatched it up.

It appeared to be not the Wobble itself, but a case, as if for a monocle.

Inside the case was a flat, solid black circle. When he tapped the case, it fell out onto his palm and became a black sphere, with flashes of gold and emerald shooting across it. He couldn't tell what the Wobble was made of. Rubber? Stone? Wood? The feel defied classification. The change in shape suggested plastic, but then it also drooped like a newborn droplet off a leaf when he started to put it away, flattening on impact with the case.

Whatever it was, Jonathan did as Dr. Lambshead had further instructed, placing it in his most secure pocket. "*You are to keep it on your person at all times and tell no one about it. For it is the Black Bauble.*"

No, Jonathan told himself, the Wobble.

After several fruitless experiments, he had to admit that the Wobble put him no closer to understanding what the Order of the Third Door was when it was home, nor what the dead machine-monster was in the haunted mansion.

"*When the time comes, you will know what to do with it.*" But he didn't know what to do. About any of it.

Just one more question mark for now, and question marks at the moment felt like arrows to Jonathan.

From the wall, the serpent's eye still stared out, black paint obscuring the fact that something had been removed from that space.

But some change in the perspective made the serpent's expression appear angry, as if it knew he'd stolen something from it.

⁊

Even with this proliferation of mysteries, by the fourth night of his bivouac, his attempt to keep a vigil began to seem absurdly paranoid. As did his boring of additional peepholes in the wood of the tiki bar, that he might have the security of seeing out in all directions.

Why should he assume the woman would return at night? When they could hardly be sure there wasn't during the day an entire Mad Hatter's tea party going on in some backwater section of the basement hidden from view by a pile of Freds or the remains of hydraulic digging equipment covered in colorful hats.

For instance, right before lunch that very day, they had discovered the presence of moles in the northwest corner, where someone had smashed the cement of the foundation into rubble, allowing a patch of dirt and even a few yellowing weeds to find favor. A mole tunnel running across the surface seemed delightful to Jonathan, if dubious to Rack.

"For we are the moles, Jonathan," he'd said. "Real moles are redundant. Even a tad insulting to us in our pre-mole forms. For we shall putter around here so long that like certain types of cave dwellers we shall lose our sight and we shall regain a much sharper sense of smell to compensate, and our hands shall become more like great clawed paws, the better to dig our burrows down here in the dark."

"Just so it's clear, we're not harming any moles," Jonathan said, ignoring Rack.

"Even if there's structural damage?"

"No. Harm. To. Moles."

"And if we find a bleedin' badger down here?"

"Invite it to tea. Full stop."

That was R & D's signal for lunch, apparently, taking Tee with them, but Jonathan kept working. He wanted to keep working. There was no Floridian hiking path through old-growth forest waiting for him outside the mansion, no cypress knees, no pileated woodpecker calling. Just a pressure in his skull caused by Stimply and little matters like the Black Bauble weighting down his pocket.

He tried to concentrate on the junk, which now seemed to matter rather more than before. The lesson thus far was that any treasure, no matter how great, could be turned into junk by excessive quantity.

What to keep and what to throw out? At what point would he just be hauling it all away in lorries and giving it to the Salvation Army, no matter what Stimply had told him? A pile of old medals with inscriptions in foreign languages could be melted down or given to the Boy Scouts for reassignment, he supposed. He could advertise an estate sale and hope Dr. Lambshead's reputation would bring potential buyers out in droves to such a remote location.

Oh, Poxforth! How he had begun to dislike the place and yet now longed for its semihallowed halls. Longed perhaps for the simplicity the academy represented. The structure.

He was still sorting through, and untangling, the pile of medals with inscriptions in foreign languages when he heard soft footfalls. Had Rack or Danny returned? He started to call out their names, but stopped himself. Something about the movement didn't sound like them at all. Nor could he see that boisterous pair sneaking back down to scare him. Yet neither was this something quite so different as a rat or other underground denizen of the mansion, but instead the deliberate stealthy tread of some stranger—perhaps three rows down, parallel to his position and moving toward the exit.

So much for his tiki bar being of use for surveillance. He'd been caught out of position. But he knew hiding near the glorified birdbath would give him a view, too.

Quietly, Jonathan made for the birdbath, dodging the ever-present umbrellas, a few stray bowling trophies, a horde of candlesticks, and a tire iron. A stack of suitcases came into view, and he crouched behind it, tried to hear beyond his own breathing. Had the steps faded? Had he imagined it?

No, not at all. He'd guessed right, and the footfalls were much closer, as swift as his own had been just moments before.

He peeked around the corner of a large portmanteau, low as he could get without putting his hands in the dust for balance, waiting—and was rewarded a minute later with a glimpse of a figure in a dark robe or cloak. There, then gone.

Nimble, Jonathan followed, waiting until the figure reached the fuse box. The figure's pace was deliberate, quick, but not panicked, as it disappeared into the corridor.

Jonathan made up the distance at something close to a fast walk.

Back to the wall, fuse box digging into his left shoulder, Jonathan peered around the doorway, into the corridor.

The figure had disappeared.

But he knew where—into the secret room. Quickly, he followed, pushed the eye of the python the requisite three times, hurried through to the alcove with the three doors, braced for a confrontation.

Nothing. No one.

If the figure had gone through the second or third door, Jonathan was out of luck, and he'd not follow anyway. But what if the figure had gone through the first?

Quietly as he could, he opened the first door and ducked through.

His luck held. A shadow that registered to him as a woman was walking away from him, into the semicircle with the weird clock tower. He hugged the wall, sidling forward, hoping she wouldn't look over her shoulder.

She paused next to the clock tower and the circular sofa, half turned so Jonathan could see her face.

Lady Insult.

In the blue light, she came into focus—a pale face and thatchy dark brown hair, as if she'd cut it herself—eyes a startling bright blue, high cheekbones, and with a nose and mouth that Rack would have assessed, respectively, as "a pert cliché, but not annoying" and "neither full nor thin." The same boots, dark trousers, and a dark shirt under the cloak.

Jonathan found Lady Insult beautiful as she stood there, unaware of him. Absolutely the last thought he'd expected to have. Beautiful for the sense of purpose, beautiful for the way he now thought of her as not just a figure by a pond giving him the what-for. There was something driven in her poise.

He crept closer.

She was concentrating hard, with one pale hand now touching the door, not palm-first, but with each of her four fingertips against its surface. Her body was rigid, upright, the very picture of tension or stress.

The door opened inward, into blackness. Lady Insult stood there. Then she took a step forward, disappeared through the doorway. The door shut behind her.

Later, he could have told Rack and Danny that the long day of cataloging dusty relics had taken its toll. Or he could have said it was just a perverse impulse, no matter the consequences, to have done with all sorts of niceties and rituals.

But, whatever the case, when Jonathan came out of hiding, he already knew what he was going to do. He paused at the same door for just a moment. This was a risk of a different order of magnitude than peeking in on Robin Hood's Bay. But, in the end, there was only one way he could think of to break the paralysis of feeling powerless, of feeling ignorant.

Jonathan took a deep breath and plunged through the doorway.

He shouted out, flailed, tripped, fell, sprawled against a hard surface, bruising his shins and elbows.

He lay there a moment, collecting his wits. Well, that was anticlimactic or too dramatic or just not what he'd expected.

Jonathan felt vaguely wounded at the lack of transition, was cursing as he picked himself up, thinking perhaps the door hadn't taken, and he'd just fallen through into a corridor beyond.

But no: He was already somewhere else.

Cacophony expressed through heat and strident loud explosions and a constant pounding. All of it intimate in Jonathan's head as if a corkscrew had been driven into both ears. He lay sprawled on the floor of a round stone building—a tower?—staring up at the damaged wooden beams of a ceiling long ago flame-seared and now reverberating with the impact of those explosions dislodging dust and splinters. Dull light crept in through slits in the walls at eye level, but there were no windows. Had he traded the trap of a ghost mansion for some sort of hell turret?

At the far edge of the cobblestone floor were corkscrew metal stairs leading down to a basement and up at least one more story. There was no sign of the woman.

Jonathan's mouth was dry. His hands shook a little. He felt a tightness and a formless nausea. Heard his mother's voice: "Calm down. Take stock. Slow time." Right. He needed to anchor himself before he could hope to address questions like, *Why are there so many explosions so close by?*

The pounding again. The smell of fire. The horrible sound.

Another lurching thud, much stronger.

A clatter and torrent of voices. The dull smack of boots on metal steps. Six or seven people, some dressed in what read to him as odd robes and some in even odder military uniforms—the ones with the pointy bits atop the helmets, as if to thwart an enemy from above—ran down the narrow spiral of the stairs, frantic to get to the basement. They didn't stand still long enough for Jonathan to get much sense of them. Nor did they spare him even a glance.

Fast on their heels scampered a foot-tall carrot with orange arms and legs popping out from a pale wrinkled torso. Beneath a frazzled froth of green leaves spurting from the top of its head, the carrot had scared dots for eyes and a startled "o" for a mouth.

It was holding hands with a little . . . a little potato person. A potato a bit smaller than the carrot with large bloodshot eyes and a slit for a mouth. Sturdy legs. Pudgy arms.

At the first-floor landing, they paused in their headlong rush to look at him. Jonathan stared in astonishment, mouth open, frozen.

The carrot's expression had changed from fear to irritation. It said to its companion, in a harsh, judgmental tone, "He's not from around here."

"He'll last a day at most," the potato said in the most melodious voice Jonathan had ever heard.

"I give it an hour. Oh well. Not our problem," the carrot said, glaring at Jonathan.

"Can't even speak," the potato said. "He's got no chance at all."

"I can speak!" Jonathan managed.

"Then why are you just sitting there like a clod?" the carrot asked in a grumpy tone. "There's no time. Leave now if you want to get out."

The potato person said: "Oh, never fear—it'll get worse. Much worse. They'll kill you. They'll kill everyone. And they won't even have the decency to plant you after."

They brushed past him without another word, the carrot giving Jonathan the elbow in the process.

A talking potato. A talking carrot.

As the impossible duo vanished down the stairs, Jonathan had a terrible thought.

He whirled around, was confronted by a normal stone wall. Not even the outline of a door.

His way home was gone.

Chapter Eleven

THE INVENTOR STASHED IN THE BASEMENT

"The Lord High Emperor Crowley decrees that all earthworms of Paris shall from this day forward be relinquished unto Him. Citizens, perform this patriotic duty. Relinquish your earthworms at any guard post or at the collection depot behind Notre Dame and you may receive a fair and just reward."

—Handbill plastered on Paris streetlamps

Dung heaps were much on Crowley's mind that morning—giant festering dung heaps and alchemists. Giant festering dung heaps and treacherous alchemists. Giant festering treacherous dung heaps and interfering alchemists. Giant festering treacherous interfering dung he—

Fie on John Dee, dead though he might be. Ever since, men and women alike had found glamorous the idea of meddling with deadly magical secrets and odd substances, often people with no talent to speak of. Although here on Aurora, he could just call alchemists chemists.

Mountainous dung heaps meant to produce saltpeter for explosives rose and kept rising in Crowley's imagination—perhaps with other hidden experiments beneath the odious surface, and that had led to the sudden urgent thought that the garbage situation in Paris might be a ruse, cover for a deadlier insurrection than simple protest.

"Break up *all* the dung heaps!" he declared in the war room. "A matter of the utmost importance. Divert resources from the catacombs, and use the curfew enforcement hordes to help."

As he spoke, his blasted demi-mages just stared at him, almost in horror. Given all they had seen thus far, everything they had gone through together, what about mucking about in a hill of shit should unsettle them much? And yet that had been their reaction.

At which point Crowley roared, "By official imperial decree: All dung heaps as tall as my waist and as wide as Burly Karl over there must be inspected for evidence of magical interference. From this point forward."

The demi-mage known as Burly Karl perhaps felt that being the benchmark for inspection meant he could forego being an inspector, but that would not be the case.

"Bravo!" Napoleon called out from his position over the map. "Insurrection starts at home. You must nip it if you wish to rule secure. Nip it! Nip it good!"

"As you wish, my lord," Wretch said, genuflecting to Crowley. "We shall upon your order inspect the dung heaps. All throughout Paris, in every arrondissement, on every street. Why, the number may run into the hundreds upon hundreds. It shall be a glorious sight, our inspections."

Did Crowley detect a layer of sarcasm in the tone? Even of . . . insolence? Well, Wretch had nothing to be insolent about. He'd proven less than effective of late, even if he did rabbit on about patience being a virtue. The Czech magician had escaped to god knew where, defeating Wretch's personal minions. (And why did Wretch have his own minions, anyway?)

Nor did they have much clue as to the whereabouts of the Golden Sphere, except for some vague reports from Rome, no doubt apocryphal. The victories in Spain seemed inconsequential given that failure.

Nor had he yet figured out now to extract from the All-Seeing Eye an All-Seeing Puddle that might accompany him on what now seemed inevitable: that he must venture forth from Paris and conduct the war personally to tip the balance, and to claim his final reward. Even an All-Seeing watermark would be of use.

But it was slow-going figuring out the magical equation that would allow this, and Wretch seemed uninterested in the question—still obsessed with the experiment he had been "growing" on the war map and now had taken under his wing, literally, and sequestered in his quarters. Wretch promised a fearful assassin-monster, but Crowley had his doubts.

At least Crowley's innovation with the Emissaries had paid off—pulling wraiths in from other worlds, weakening the ghosts further, so they became echoes of echoes and thus more malleable to his will. Perhaps they might prove of use in tracking down the Golden Sphere. In the meantime, they swelled the numbers in his fade pens, marinating in useful fashion alongside still-living abductees. Much preferable to using ordinary mercenaries, which were like windfall apples by comparison.

"Pardon, Lord High Emperor, but I must measure . . ."

A thin demi-mage who looked like a stick insect with a too-heavy face plastered on top had stepped forward with a tape measure.

Crowley withered him with a stare, and then flung him against the wall of skulls.

"Not *literal*, for hell's sake! Not literal. Just *close*. Just close to up to my waist. Just *close* to the width of Burly Karl."

"Not literal, you fool!" Napoleon admonished the crumpled pile on the floor, swiveled to address the cluster of demi-mages across from Crowley. "Not literal! Figurative."

"No, Napoleon—not that, either. Not . . . oh never mind."

Perhaps he must acquire smarter demi-mages. But there lay the conundrum: Smarter demi-mages were harder to magically control. Such were the trade-offs and the headaches of his chosen path. Along with the possibly seditious quality of piles of crap.

Yet even after the daily war room conference, the trials of Crowley's morning were not over and the next part he must do himself, accompanied only by the demi-mage Laudinum X.

The Inventor in the dungeon came over all funny with Wretch

THE LAY OF THE LAND

105

around, could not be counted on to be sensible or un-gibbering, such was Wretch's unaccountable effect upon him.

Crowley couldn't say he minded being free of Wretch. The familiar was less and less fun with each passing day, and seemed too eager to attack in all directions, the advice coming with an implied note of correction that Crowley wasn't bloodthirsty enough. Just because he had yet to set a date for the next assault on Prague. Which Crowley resented.

Why, he almost felt hurt.

Had he not so utterly decimated Rome that it had become a chaotic wasteland of magical discharges? And had he not put so many Decadent authors and artists to the sword that one could say that he had saved thousands and thousands of Parisian citizens from any number of the disgusting diseases their lifestyles encouraged? Although Crowley had not yet found a way to express this triumph via broadsheet in a dignified or elevated manner.

Among those Crowley *had* spared was the Inventor, a prize catch during his siege of Paris. The Inventor had been found as the Eiffel Tower laid waste to Paris, trying to escape in a one-person underwater vessel of his own creation, desperate to push the "submarine" contraption off the stubborn muddy banks of the Seine and head for parts unknown.

Before Crowley, the Inventor had squandered much of his time writing for broadsheets and the like, rather than applying his talent to something useful. Fanciful depictions and blueprints of machines he no doubt thought would never leap off the page and into the world.

"This isn't like writing for your penny dreadfuls," Crowley had growled at the Inventor, once he had been ensconced in his fancy prison in the dungeon. "This is for something important." Something that could get you turned into a goat to feed the war machine if you failed.

"What I need from you," Crowley had told the Inventor, "are not delicate contraptions but beasts of war, legions of mecha-animals of death and dread. And lots of them. And very fast."

It was the Inventor who had allowed Crowley to abandon the

exhausting, sometimes harrowing task of animating local monuments and statues and buildings to terrorize their own citizens. Much less enervating to make creatures from scratch and imbue them with magic, receptacles built for the purpose. Once Crowley had the specifications for the framework, he and his demi-mages could do the rest. With signs and symbols, incantations and dark magic, using the inversion of some of the French magicians' knowledge of animal energy.

Out of the Inventor's head had come the giant mecha-elephants and the smaller bear-machines and any number of other terrifying marvels that Crowley had, with the appropriate sacrifice of thousands of small mammals, made come to life, to be more than just metal and wood, but breathing creatures that adhered sharply to his command and the control of his underlings. They had made further conquest possible, and had loyalty to Crowley and Crowley alone.

"I was not meant for this kind of work," the Inventor would protest in those few instances when he had gathered his nerve. "I cannot continue. I cannot do this."

"Of course you can," Crowley would coo. "You were born to this."

"But this—this is always the same task over and over, to explore cryptozoology of a crude sort. All that changes is the type of animal, and the only challenge is whether the jaws on a crocodile can reasonably be expected to fit onto a bear. For example."

"Now, now," Crowley would say. "Not everyone is lucky enough to have the opportunity to make a croc-bear, and sometimes it is not so much functionality that matters as the horror inflicted by the sight."

Crowley was doing the Inventor a favor. After all, the man had been a failure before, in a way. Most spectacularly, he had invented a crude version of internal combustion engine like a fool with no sense of timing. Who on this world much cared about such an unwieldy contraption when you could just shove five hundred goddamn goats through a magical grinder and power a preternatural elephant for a month? Goats and goat substitutes were thick on the ground wherever the campaign led, while oil was difficult to magick and too far down in the ground.

Meanwhile, the engineers of the Republic were already beginning to create electricity from water and wind.

"Have I not given you a spacious room in which to work?" Crowley would also point out, noting with a sweep of his upturned palm how long and wide the dungeon was, and how the iron bars had a delicacy rarely seen in most prisons, etched with a pattern of tiny grotesques besides.

Not to mention the ubiquitous audience of burnished skulls peering from every wall. The sumptuous desk, all bloodstains scrubbed from it, that Crowley had brought from the former interior minister's offices. The finest parchment, and even the slick new blank paper used by the Republic, captured from the abandoned tents of enemy generals as they fled the Spanish front. Not just nubs and fountain pens and quills, but the blasted enemies' cartridge pens. Not just the normal lantern light one might expect in a dungeon, but the electric lights used, again, by the goddamn Republicans and their infernal allegiance to science. (Not that Crowley minded electricity per se, but why not start with better indoor plumbing? Aurora had terrible toilets in his experience.)

Did not the Inventor have the power to control his own illumination by virtue of the stationary bicycle attached to the generator? Did not the smell of the dungeon, redolent from the candles placed beyond the bars and replenished weekly, seem more reminiscent of Versailles than of a dungeon full of dead things, located within a catacomb bursting with old skulls and next to the war factories? Did not Crowley also endeavor to conduct all torture of traitors at such a remove that the screams fell light upon the Inventor's ear?

Finally, had Crowley not, out of concern for the Inventor's ceaseless need to roam, fashioned a halter and harness, based on the Inventor's own designs from the aforementioned penny dreadfuls, and attached it on one end to the Inventor and, on the other, via a light but ensorcelled metal chain, to a stalwart rod running across the top of the room and stuck in the rock at both ends, which allowed the Inventor free movement across the magnificent dungeon room, including bicycle access, without any possibility he might slip free of the bars, given his increasing skinniness despite being plied with the best food, and do himself a mischief getting lost in the tunnels under Paris?

Thus spake Crowley gentle to the Inventor when necessary, with a restraint and refinement unbecoming in a Lord Commander who believed in the rule of fear. But the Inventor's nerves jangled too easily. And the diagrams must keep coming.

Now, for example, Crowley needed the final details for the mighty burrowing wurm currently in production in the war factories. The Burrower—a mighty beast that could smash through or dig beneath, say, a long tall wall protecting a land bridge to England, and erupt up from under the enemy on the battlefield, and wreak the kind of havoc that caused full-fledged panic and flight.

Lately, Crowley thought the Inventor might be fudging the schematics, the framework for the Burrower having run into production difficulties. Was the Inventor brave enough and ungrateful enough for that?

Laudinum X stepped forward with a list of entirely new schematics required from the Inventor, supplemented with terse instruction. Frustratingly, Laudinum X had a scritchy balloon voice that Crowley found hard to understand. Such a valuable lieutenant, the essential link with the war factories, and yet more than once Crowley had to interpret for the Inventor.

The Inventor, for his part, nodded, looking very pinched-lipped, and in the harness perhaps a bit awkward, but taking down accurate annotations. When Laudinum X had finished destroying the French tongue with his scratch-talking, the Inventor handed over the corrections for the Burrower requested by Crowley the week before.

"It was all a matter of scale, Lord Emperor. Just as a recipe for chicken marsala cannot be doubled without adjusting the amount of the ingredients, so too increasing the size of the Burrower by a third required accounting for structural stressors. If you had only told me that you had decided—"

Crowley cut the Inventor off, for the man's own safety; that sentence had appeared to be curving toward criticism.

"Just remember, your counterpart in England is working on some sort of horrible mechanical contraption to foil us, and we all know how much you hate him."

In other words, these changes had better work. The Inventor could not know it, but the contraption Crowley had housed him within could also draw and quarter him in a second flat. Crowley believed in inventions that could be used for many purposes, and once the Inventor left the dungeon—on a mission he meant to reveal to the man soon—Crowley planned to repatriate the space with the interrogation quarters.

But the Inventor could not concentrate on the warning. A stabbing anger came over his face, and a disdain, that faded back into agreement. Really, truly, the Inventor hated his counterpart Wells, "the socialist bastard," as he called his rival. Wells had been critical of the Inventor before Crowley's ascension, but Crowley had made sure that Laudinum X gave the Inventor current press clippings from English papers, in which Wells's attacks on the Inventor had become ever more vicious.

"So you will get to work on these new diagrams."

The Inventor nodded, jaw tight, gaze elsewhere.

"Excellent! Then I will leave you to it!"

Truly, Jules Verne in his chains could not realize that the contraption flaring out behind him, imprisoning him, took the outline of Wretch's form and that when he struggled it resembled Wretch unfolding himself from some hidden part of the ceiling of Notre Dame. A little joke on Crowley's part, one that now sometimes gave him the creeps.

And still Crowley's rounds were not yet over.

There were several levels below this one, and many doors, besides.

Part II

QUICKSAND

"Everything will get darker soon."

Chapter Twelve

THE TEA TRAY IN THE TOWER

At the top of the stairs, Jonathan came from dark to light, half-blinded by a searing blue sky, the sun a blazing halo.

Through the black spots that floated across his eyes like intrepid explorers, he made out the curving stone wall of the top of the tower, with crenellations for archers or riflemen. The vague, burnt-out silhouettes of people. More soldiers? He hesitated, leaned there half in the shadow of the steps, where he could still only be seen as a forehead looming out of darkness. If he were seen at all.

At eye level, thirty feet away along the far wall: the unlikely sight of a folding canvas table, atop which sat a wooden tea tray with a blue porcelain pot, two cups, and a plate of small pastries.

He stared at the tea tray as his eyes adjusted to the brightness, shook his head as if that would be any help clearing the cobwebs, tried to slow his breathing.

Focus on what's important, discard the rest, as his mother would say. The important thing. Not the carrot creature. Not the potato person.

The door was gone and he had no sense of where he was.

The table shuddered, shifted, settled, every few seconds as the tower shook. Hostage to whatever was happening beyond. Which sounded like rocks smashing together, like a pitched battle.

His vision improved against the glare. He saw that the battlements were obscured in part by curling vines and in part by a half-dozen people mostly in motley tunics and trousers. Not modern clothing. Not a costume drama. Not Vikings. Not Visigoths. Not ren faire. Not Britain. Not European. Vaguely . . . Persian? No, that wasn't right, either. Clearly, Poxforth hadn't been very good on Middle Eastern history or military fashions.

They watched whatever lay beyond the ramparts. Some with spyglasses, some with binoculars, both of which looked very non-Earth-standard. Some were in feverish discussion or argument and another frustration re the European emphasis at Poxforth: he couldn't tell if they spoke Arabic or Farsi or Urdu or something else entirely. He just knew they had the look of battle-hardened soldiers; they read like "army."

Right. Nothing for it but to plunge ahead.

He stumbled out onto the open top of the tower, a stiff breeze cool against his face, but bringing with it the smell of burning. The tower was perched atop a forested hill. Rough-laid stones bruised his feet through his shoes. He realized there had been a time change. From the quality of the intense sunlight, it was late afternoon here, wherever "here" was.

At his back through the crenellations lay a fringe of dark forest and then the sea—a vast, blue-green sea, sparkling and roiling, with a fleet that floated on it, and small boats rowing out to the ships, while there came the white puffs of cannon firing from the shore. He could see little of the landward side from that vantage, with the watchers standing there, other than that blue sky cut through now with a scattering of metallic gray clouds, columns of black smoke, and a faint cacophony, as of distant but furious battle.

Then he saw Lady Insult. She was splitting her time between looking out beyond the turret and talking intensely to a stranger, the tea tray between them. He wore a sophisticated, silverish armor over his tunic and riding breeches tucked into scuffed black boots. The boots and trousers could've been from anywhere. But the armor evoked Persian miniatures to Jonathan, although he so distrusted his paltry knowledge in this arena he felt once again at sea. The armor truly was a marvel, more like advanced tech than protection from the past, so finely wrought as to almost be invisible.

The stranger was of average height, well put-together, with dark hair, deep-set friendly hazel eyes, firm chin, neatly trimmed beard. Maybe just a few years older than Jonathan?

The man saw him. He straightened, brought his hands up in greeting.

"Welcome to Aurora, Jonathan Lambshead!" the man said in a cheerful tone. "My name is Mamoud Abad and I am the one trying to ensure this retreat does not become a rout. So I'm afraid we've not laid out what might be considered the customary hospitality."

Aurora?

Yet he looked as if he'd been expecting Jonathan, even if behind the cheer there was a thoughtful, appraising look. His English had a slightly clipped quality to it. Jonathan couldn't place the accent.

The others all turned to stare at him. Not in an entirely friendly way. Mamoud waved them back to their work, whatever it was, with a hand gesture.

In the face of that, all Jonathan could manage in reply to the man was: "The carrot spoke to me."

"And the potato, too, I imagine," Mamoud said, clearly amused. "You don't have talking carrots where you come from."

"No," Jonathan said, although it had been a statement, not a question.

The other problem: Lady Insult, who was glaring at him as if she'd be just as happy if he took a running start and jumped off the turret.

"Never mind a talking carrot," Lady Insult said. "What in the blazes are you doing here? How did you follow me? It's impossible. You shouldn't be here."

"Rich, coming from the person who was trespassing on my property all week." It took all his energy to keep his composure, to say the words, to throw it back at her. Irritation warring with the almost giddy relief of not having lost his last connection to the world he'd left behind. She could've attacked him with a knife and he would've tried to be cheerful about it.

"You have no idea what you've stepped into, no idea at all, and if I had—"

Mamoud held up his hand like a referee, and Lady Insult cut off in midtirade.

"It is true that as I've said we're a little busy at the moment, Jonathan, but no need to be rude, Alice. Perhaps he had a good reason to follow you. Give him a moment to acclimate."

While she continued to glower.

Focus on what's important, discard the rest.

"The door is gone, and I don't know where I am."

"The *return* door isn't gone, you fool," Alice said. "It's in the basement."

By now the man had smoothly put himself between Jonathan and Lady Insult, proffered his hand as if to ward her off. Jonathan shook it.

Mamoud's grip was firm, professional. "It's a pleasure to meet you, if in urgent circumstances. My grandfather knew your grandfather. They were both in the Order, of course."

"Did you ever meet Dr. Lambshead?"

"No, but I wish I had. I am glad I'm meeting you now, though."

Standing closer to Mamoud, Jonathan could see that from a belt at his waist hung a silver pistol and a short, curved sword in a scuffed black scabbard. But he also had a burnished copper device, inscribed with symbols, shoved into the belt that looked suspiciously like some type of phone or shortwave receiver.

There came another explosion, and Jonathan flinched, but Mamoud moved not at all, and somehow his calm steadied Jonathan. He had the demeanor of a doctor or a civil servant, in a useful way.

"Apologies—one moment, Jonathan." Mamoud turned to the others, barked out a command, and the rest all headed for the stairs, and were gone in a blink.

"Didn't know that you'd be in the thick of it, did you?" Alice said. She'd leaned back against the wall, arms folded, calmer now but no less intense.

"But *where*, exactly, am I?"

"Aurora. Spain. In the middle of a rout, a massacre."

But whatever Jonathan might have said in reply fell away from him. For now, beside the tea tray, Jonathan was close enough to peek out through the rifle slots on the landward edge of the turret to see for miles.

"Bloody hell." His stomach lurched, and he felt as if he were falling all over again, the carrot and potato dancing atop his head. He didn't hear whatever Mamoud said to him next.

Against a backdrop of burning fields, long columns of enormous elephants, three abreast, bestrode the earth, making the ground quake. They smashed the world flat beneath their tread, made Jonathan want to turn and run. But to where?

Even from this distance, Jonathan could see that they were not natural—there came the glint and glitter of metal parts, and the heads held gleaming green eyes like vibrant emeralds and had the aspect of repurposed black beetle carapaces, startling against the gray and striated red of their massive bodies. The creatures were so heavy they sank a little into the ground with each step.

Mechanical battle elephants, their frames made of metal and their insides animated by something uncanny. A faint green-and-orange light enshrouded their many moving parts, coursed in a path around and around as if goading each beast onward.

As the elephants trumpeted their wrath, they also spewed forth a kind of hellfire from their trunks, the purest gold, flecked with red, to scorch what he realized must be wheat fields, to clear the path ahead of obstacles. Some of these obstacles Jonathan could tell were people seeking only to flee, while others turned and fought, briefly, before falling either to the fire or the mechanical onslaught.

Dust under that mighty tread sent up clouds. The heat shimmered all around, but even that could not account for the quavering dark drifting shapes on either side of the elephants. But surely it must be a mirage that made the grass around them turn black. It must be an illusion that they floated forward, unmoored from the ground.

He recoiled from the ghastly sight, with the impact of something heavy closing in with incredible velocity, smashing into him. His legs felt weak and his mouth dry.

People were dying out there, beyond the tower.

Jonathan could hear the distant screams now, beneath the claxon shriek of the elephants' battle cry and the whooshing discharge of the hellfire.

"Would you like some tea, Jonathan?" Mamoud asked, breaking in on Jonathan's thoughts.

"And stand away from the edge unless you want a cannonball through the skull." That last from Lady Insult.

Jonathan took a step back.

"Perhaps a pastry, then?" Mamoud suggested, both solicitous and somehow ridiculous at Jonathan's shoulder. The smile said he knew how his comment might appear.

"It's admirable you can be so calm as to stand here and sip tea," Jonathan said.

"Do you think it takes bravery to stand here and drink tea?" Mamoud replied, eyes narrowing in thought. "Or a certain cowardice?" Not unkind, but as if the question had just occurred to him. Or as if he'd read Jonathan's mind.

"No, I just mean—"

"In any event, it's good you are here to witness this. To know what the Order is about." Worry lines Jonathan hadn't noticed before radiated out from the corners of Mamoud's eyes. His hands were not quite still most of the time. Cracks in the calm.

"But it's . . . chaos, not order."

"No. We're helping our allies retreat in an organized manner. As organized as is possible under the circumstances. As calm."

"I don't understand what I'm looking at," Jonathan said.

Among the things he didn't understand: how the cannonballs fired from the ships at the elephants could have such an incredible physicality scudding through the air . . . but then change into something else before reaching their targets. Into explosions of harmless feathers, drifting in the air. Into drops of water, forming miniature rainfalls.

Or how rebel infantry in the wheat fields now wrestled with rifles that had become alive like serpents.

Mamoud stole a glance at Lady Insult. "Your friend can help you understand. But, in short—very short—it's what happens when a very powerful but deranged magician gains the reins of power. It is a classic formation for the enemy: The war elephants have no subtlety, so they smash through the front door. They become almost like moving fortresses. Then the wisps or wraiths you see—Emissaries—come in around the sides and spread fear. The demi-mages and the mercenaries bring up the rear—the latter because they are the least effective and the former because they are, loosely speaking, the brains of the operation. Not including the demi-mages atop the elephants.

"No doubt you know some of this already, Jonathan. Dr. Lambshead must have told you?"

No. Dr. Lambshead had told him nothing. Just hinted at bird-friends and vast secrets. But he nodded all the same.

"As for chaos," Mamoud said, "chaos is not what is happening around you, but how you conduct yourself around . . . chaos."

The earth erupted in explosion and flames not forty feet from the turret. Mamoud didn't flinch, but Jonathan definitely did. Even Lady Insult put her spyglass down. The tower shuddered from the footfall of the elephants. There was a sour smell like sulfur.

There came to Jonathan an itch, a premonition, very subtle, that was familiar from meeting up with tricky animals back in Florida.

"The wraiths—the Emissaries," he said. "I think they're closer than you think. Or something is."

The rippling in the wheat. The gray clouds in the sparkling blue sky. The tense, electric quality to the air.

Something in Mamoud's demeanor, his stance, changed. He took out his communication device, jabbed a button, said two words, listened for an equally terse response, shoved it back in his belt.

Turning to Lady Insult, Mamoud said: "He's right—something's wrong. Something we're not seeing. Take him back, Alice. *Where he came from.*" As if he didn't entirely trust Lady Insult not to just drop him off any old place.

A wry smile to Jonathan. "And now that the chaos is about to come down on our heads: Goodbye and good luck. Or better luck." Mamoud winked and ducked down onto the stairs, leaving Jonathan alone with Lady Insult.

The tray was shaking harder now, spilling tea. The gray clouds had come close, lit by the sun in a peculiar way.

Lady Insult's electric blue eyes narrowed. "Shut it. I don't want to hear it."

"But I didn't say anything!"

She opened her mouth to reply—but all that came out was an inchoate sound between a curse and a shriek.

"What did I do now?"

But she was staring behind him.

The front half of a mecha-elephant had appeared just fifty feet away, charging toward the tower. Then three fourths, then the whole thing, as if it had come toward their position under the protection of some cloaking barrier that only extended so far.

Then two things happened simultaneous, even as Lady Insult grabbed his arm, prepared to retreat to the stairs.

The tray upturned along with the table.

A shadow slipped across the sky, across the stones of the tower. As if the dark lining of the clouds had *come free*, drifting down, taking form. Fast.

A face inside the cloud. A face, inside the shroud that was the drifting darkness. A reaching down. The ache of it. The pull of it. The dissipation of the light.

A terrible scream of need, of loss, and a more terrible abrupt silence.

A peculiar chill cut the heat.

Nothing in Robin Hood's Bay or Florida had prepared Jonathan for the sight. It brought him to a state of paralysis well beyond fear.

In that long, stretched-out moment, Lady Insult's head tilted up to meet the trajectory of the incoming Emissary. There was a deep mingled contempt and surprise on her face.

"That's not possible."

She seemed shocked, even as she was still pulling Jonathan along.

She flung Jonathan at the stairs as more pale and glistening faces peered out from a sea of black right above them.

Down, down, down, in scrabbling headlong flight, Alice now ahead, dragging him toward the basement, him still staring back up, mesmerized, toward that unfolding darkness.

They'd reached the first floor when the elephant rammed the tower, and they went sprawling from the impact. Stones tumbled around, the beams creaked, but the wall held.

"Just one more floor," Lady Insult said, pulling at his shoulder, him sprawled on the stonework, coughing up dust.

An elephant was trying to crush them in rubble. The wraith-cloud still chasing them from the stairs above.

He got up, followed her as best he was able.

Then they were in the basement, facing a rounded wooden door with a blue mosaic fringe. She wrenched it open.

"Through the door, Jonathan. Take my hand."

"I don't need to hold your hand." A rebuke that sounded pathetic and naive, that came from shock.

She grasped his hand anyway. Her palm was warm and sweaty, and he could sense her pulse quick beneath the soft skin.

The elephant rammed the tower again, stones ricocheting down into the basement almost to their feet. A wooden beam snapped, and he heard a roar of more stones released. A terrible, deafening noise.

Yet even though he stumbled, Lady Insult was pulling him through the door. She was going to save him.

In moments, they would be through and gone.

But the darkness had spread, too, and he could not help looking back in that last instant before he left the tower behind.

The dark mist of its body beside him, the shining strangeness of its face. The chill on his shoulder, the black breath. It froze him to his core. It froze him on the inside in places he had not known could be cold.

He wanted it to be terrifying. He wanted it to make a choked gurgle like wet dead leaves caught in a storm drain. But, instead, the voice was human, the voice was plaintive and pleading. Like someone in need, walking across his grave. Someone he had already loved and might learn to love again. He tried to push against that, to push it away, made of his mind something hard, unwelcoming.

Some *thing* recoiled. Some *thing* drew back, but had already been too near.

The teapot came bouncing and spinning down the stairs, to shatter on the basement floor.

Then the door shut and he was in another place.

Chapter Thirteen
GARBAGE IN THE CAUSE OF LIBERTY (HOLD THE GOAT)

"All refuse must be placed in appropriate cloth bags or other approved containers by the side of the street by ten in the morning on Wednesdays to be eligible for pickup. Incorrect garbage disposal shall be deemed grounds for immediate imprisonment or execution, or possible dismemberment prior to execution."

—Decree of Lord Master Crowley, glued to lampposts and fired in crumpled bunches from mecha-bears screaming out the decree from their megaphone mouths.

Another day, another travesty involving garbage.

The decadent poet Jean Nicolas Arthur Rimbaud looked out over the crowd gathered clandestine in the basement of a Parisian bordello from atop a battered desk, resembling a shipwreck survivor who had swum to a makeshift raft and stood atop it seeking rescue.

Rimbaud gestured for quiet. Even glimpsed through the All-Seeing Eye, he looked feverish, off-color, rocking back and forth on his heels with tremors and shaky balance, appearing more than twice his tender age of twenty-four. The powdered wig was no affectation but hid the monstrous burn that without it seemed to eat his head, scorching up the back of his neck, across the top of his skull.

His singed eyebrows had been drawn back in by the madame who ran the establishment. Sadly, she had in her haste drawn in a third eyebrow atop the one on the left, lending him a perpetually surprised expression.

But when he finally spoke, his voice rang out with a strength and nervous energy that belied his eyebrow situation.

"More garbage! More hideous garbage! The more disgusting the garbage the better. Fish heads if you can spare them, although I know many of you cannot. But fill the bins until they overflow, throw it on piles at the curb. Make of it mountains and let not your flared nostrils betray you, citizens. We must smell vile for the cause. We must upend and clog the system with refuse, with everything that is low, lost, and thrown away. We must by pestilence and decay and rot force the usurper to spend much of his time and vile energy on surcease of the problem. For they must live here, too, and work here, and even a turncoat, especially a turncoat, wishes their attire to be untargeted by the disgust of others. Anything you can spare must go onto the street. Dead dogs, dead relatives, a cheese that has rotted in the wrong manner or one that is strong and can be spared. Use not the commode, but pile your shit at the entrance to Crowley's guard stations. Piss your piss down into the catacombs where his magicians perform their unnatural acts. Let a mountain of shit and a lake of piss overwhelm his control. Save it up, and then crap under cover of darkness and show them the real meaning of alchemy. Make of your stomach a revolution. Temporary disgust is more easily withstood than this occupation, and through temporary disgust we may prevail.

"Citizens, they think I am dead. But I am not dead. I stand before you risen up, and I tell you I know the truth: Only through filth will we be victorious. Filth . . . and goats. We must deny Crowley his goats. We must deny Crowley his goats with every fiber of our being, with all the blood in our bodies. Hide your goats or spirit them away to the countryside or make of them goat stew posthaste that the enemy shall not expand his imperial war because of you. Give sanctuary to the goats you know and the goats of a stranger. There is no more patriotic act than goat stew. For while there are too many things Crowley can do with a goat, there is only one thing Crowley can do with a carrot—shove it up his hairy ass!"

From out of sight, some member of the audience asked his companion, "Is Rimbaud off his nut?"

"Oh, most certain. Most certain. But so is Crowley. Fight madness with the mad, so say I, and my bowels are happy to agree."

"Disease more like will follow."

"Perhaps Rimbaud does not mean it literal."

"What, then, pray tell, is the figurative meaning of 'goat'?"

The answer must have been in the form of a shrug, as there was no reply and the scene dissolved into chaos as Crowley's animated human-sized Eiffel-tower golems broke into the basement and started making arrests while Rimbaud managed to escape through a trapdoor under a rug in the floor before they could get to him.

⁓

That's when the scene in the All-Seeing Eye went dark and Crowley pushed away from the scrim of the edge with a growl of exasperation. "Shove it up *his* ass," he muttered. "Up. His. Ass."

He was accompanied in the cathedral by Wretch, Laudinum X, and Amantine Dupin—the very person who a week ago had promised she would have the garbage issues under control very soon. Napoleon slept silent atop his pedestal, put into a temporary coma by Crowley's spells. Did he dream of battlefields and blood or of deep winter or of nothing at all? Crowley was surprised he even cared.

"Dupin—the garbage crisis has only become worse in the past week. Is this not true?"

"Most unfortunate, but true," she murmured, as if a soft voice might keep her from punishment and correction.

"And Laudinum X, how has this affected the war factories?"

If it had been a competition, the demi-mage's weird murmur would have beaten Dupin's normal murmur by a country mile.

"Oh, for babel-butt's sake, I'd as soon have a chance of understanding a moon's reflection buried in a bog. Just write it down. Write it down—who has a bloody pencil? Paper? One of you must." Except for Wretch, who clearly had no pockets.

Dupin had both, and soon enough Crowley managed to make out

from scrawl almost as indecipherable as the man's speech that Laudinum X had been saying production had fallen by 25 percent against an influx of 10 percent in cost due to inflation. Quite absurd how piles of garbage clogged the war machine, but there it was. That and the lack of goats, which Crowley now understood much better having heard Rimbaud's speech.

"Wretch, I thought we had burned Rimbaud alive, and yet here he is, the wretch, rousing the citizens of Paris to insurrection."

Wretch cackled, a sound like a thousand live starlings being shoved onto tiny spits and roasted over a vast bed of hot coals.

"Oh, surely we did burn him alive. There was crackling and skin sizzling, most certain. But . . . although we burned him, he appears to be alive. If much unhinged from being on fire . . . for longer than a human is normally on fire. No matter—everyone in that basement is now in *our* basement."

"But not Rimbaud."

Wretch uncurled his full length from beside Laudinum X and Dupin, making them both shudder. Crowley shuddered, too, on the inside. He kept forgetting how physically repulsive and complex Wretch was because Wretch kept himself as compact as a Swiss Army knife most of the time. But when the edges came out, the blades, it could still startle him. Even the equivalent of the toothpick and the tweezers.

"Remember what the All-Seeing Eye showed us while Rimbaud ranted?"

"Yes, I *know*, Wretch. I know. We have only one All-Seeing Eye, and we cannot be everywhere at once. I understand that."

"You were watching your army sack Madrid and push forward into Catalonia and conquering the last Republic redoubts along the coast."

"That was satisfying."

Napoleon had earned his keep, it was true, coming up with interesting tactics like disguising Emissaries in gray clouds to attack from above and making war elephants invisible for brief stretches of time. Of course, now the enemy would adjust, but it had worked.

"You were watching your war elephants claim such a victory on the battlefield that all of Spain is now free of the enemy."

"And Rimbaud and his ilk? This . . . garbage war?"

"Let my agents deal with the ilk."

"And you, Dupin—what have you to say for yourself?"

But Dupin was too busy exploding into bits at that particular moment to provide any sort of satisfactory answer.

Chapter Fourteen

NO BELLS ARE RINGING, BUT ALL THE BELLS ARE RINGING

Jonathan's heart was not in where they'd washed up, finally, he and Lady Insult: the haunted version of his grandfather's mansion. An anchor he'd have been glad to toss over the side. But could he even be sure it was *the* haunted mansion? No, he could not.

The two sat with some distance between them on the circular couch that surrounded the clock tower. Even in here, in the faint blue light, there were empty birdhouses and feeders hanging from the ceiling. They should have been ridiculous, but in that faint blue light they resembled cozy cottages, which comforted him. With sudden insight, he realized this was why Dr. Lambshead had added them—this place had scared him, too.

He could not forget the silky touch of the thing Alice called an Emissary as it fell through his skin, his flesh, and kept passing through. It was like a chronic ache and fever in him, a sore throat that wouldn't clear. Would that feeling dissipate with time, become a fading afterglow, or did its presence gather even now in his heart, his lungs? He had no idea. He didn't know if the beauty he had seen was a mistake, a ruse, or an illusion, or . . .

The war elephants in all their hideous mechanical glory, steeped in the blood of dead animals, smashing into the base of the tower . . .

In the midst of the assault, Jonathan had spied two shrikes, the birds' sleek black-and-gray bodies performing aerial acrobatics at low altitude in an attempt to flee. But the air was full of smoke and the gouts of flame from the elephants unpredictable. They were lost, caught between hiding in the wheat not yet on fire and the hazard of flying between the elephants toward safety. They wheeled and dove and still were trapped.

A voice came to him as if from a dark, empty well lined with moss. A voice saying his name, telling him to answer a question.

Until he snapped back into focus, or she did, Lady Insult. Who had given her name as Alice Ptarmigan. From the other world, Aurora.

Another line from Dr. Lambshead's letter came to him: "*Beware false birds.*"

Alice had started in with questions he wasn't sure he understood.

"The Emissary, Jonathan. The wraith that popped up, just before the elephant smashed into the tower—did you do something to it? Not like them to appear then wink out like that."

Is that what had happened? In the end, it had just been a confusion of falling stones.

"Jonathan, are you listening to me?"

He took her measure. The disheveled brown locks that told him she cut her own hair, the lines in her forehead, the long pale scar on the back of her left hand. He had thought they were closer to the same age. But that wasn't true. Why had he wanted to believe that?

"I did nothing. It came down the stairs at me. I pushed it away."

"You did *what*?"

"I pushed it away from me. Then we got down to the basement and you took me through the doors."

Alice muttered something that might've been "Take something, give something." Said in a resigned way, as if she needed to marshal patience. Well, not on his account. He'd lost patience long before this moment. So many doors, even just to get back to the haunted mansion—six or seven, he'd lost count—her hand tight around his wrist. Ordinary doors. Extraordinary doors. In busy corridors streaming with oddly clad folk and silent ones in the dead of night under a crooked moon. One in a forest, standing like a huge slab of headstone, with nothing behind it,

Lady Insult whispering in his ear that they had to go back the "circuitous route" to "be sure."

"Well, I did." Repeated. With a snap of irritation.

"Not possible," Alice said. "Not at all possible. Not ever, lad. To push a ghost. You must be mistaken."

The frozen hands of the clock tower came free, jumped forward with a juddering rusty scrape to account for more time than had actually passed. Nor was the time correct. Nor did Jonathan care.

Alice had been watching him very closely, as if for signs of sickness. He half expected her to put the back of her hand to his forehead to take his temperature.

"It's been a shock for you, I'm sure," she said. "I'm sure you just want to go home. I have things to do, and you have a mansion to get back to cataloging."

Get back to cataloging? The idea struck Jonathan as absurd.

"What *things*?" Jonathan asked. "Are you an insurance adjuster? A chimney sweep? A unicorn? I'd like to know."

Alice leaned forward, into his space, eyes ablaze. "Given what you've seen, what do you think I do?"

The animals had been dead-alive, squirming inside the metal cage of the elephant's stomach, a slow-motion half existence, unable to get free. The potato men had run screaming, trying to escape across the fields of cut wheat. The shrikes had shared some harsh language he'd never heard come out of a shrike before—the language of terror.

"I don't know who you are, and I'm not leaving this place until I find out."

She blanched, as if he had some power over her he didn't realize. Well, good.

"You do realize I saved your life," Alice said.

"I saved *yours* recognizing the wraiths were close. And let's not forget you'd spent a lot of time trespassing in my mansion before that." Perhaps that wasn't entirely fair at this point, but it was also true.

Alice's voice grew even chillier. "Why don't I just leave you here and go off on my merry way? I hope you're certain which door you take to get back."

"Don't care." Did care, but also did know how to get back, and wasn't about to admit it. Would she really leave him? He didn't think so. "I told you I wanted answers."

"It isn't even night yet in this place, Jonathan," she said, leaning back against the couch and folding her arms. "After dark, you really don't want to be here. You won't enjoy what you see through the windows."

Jonathan ignored her, pointed at the dead monster. "Like, what is that thing, which you've not looked at once? And who are you, exactly? And what, exactly, is an Emissary?" This last question seemed very important at the moment.

"Or instead of taking a half day to answer all that, I could just knock you unconscious and drag your body back to your pathetic tiki bar."

"You could. I don't doubt it." Not just the will, but the ability.

The barest verge of a grim smile from Alice as she calculated odds or variables in her head that probably included some of the answers Jonathan needed.

"Very well, then. Answers it is. A handful."

∾

Part of Jonathan listened to Alice Ptarmigan. Part of him tried to ignore how his hands shook ever so slightly and how what resembled phantom swifts flew backward in slow motion through what passed for sky outside. Stitching their way through the door, disappearing and reappearing in pursuit of . . . what? How beautiful and strange, and how he longed in that moment to put on that same unthinking speed and just *be*.

"I'm a member of the Order of the Third Door, one of Aleister Crowley's sworn enemies. I knew your grandfather, and I helped him from time to time. Mamoud, the chap you met, is or was an intelligence officer for the Republic—hard to tell sometimes—a powerful secular state that also opposes Crowley. Mamoud isn't necessarily a chum, but at the moment he's also a member of the Order, believes in the mission.

If for no other reason than his grandpa did. Other than that, and for all geographical questions, just consult the map in the corridor of your own blasted mansion.

"An Emissary is a person who faded—became a ghost—because they crossed over from another world into Aurora and stayed too long. Repurposed by Crowley, the despotic leader of the Franco-Germanic Empire that now threatens our world. All the worlds."

"Aleister Crowley?" The semimystical British buffoon who experimented on his cat, led an ill-fated mountaineering expedition, and was described by the newspapers of his day as the evilest man in the world? There'd been a few paragraphs on him in a textbook at Poxforth. Rack's textbook or Danny's? He couldn't remember much. Something about witchcraft or alchemy, along with an old photograph on the cover of a book, of a deranged-looking, moonfaced man wearing a funny hat.

"Not your Crowley. He's a Rippler."

"Ripper?"

"Rippler. Across worlds. Has doubles. Reoccurs. He came over to Aurora from a different Earth, or was brought over."

Jonathan had no answer to that.

Alice continued: "As for that creature lying there, it's the beastie that killed your grandfather. An epic battle by every indication, but no contest in the end. Thankfully, though, he managed to injure it mortally, so it couldn't make it back through the doors to report to its masters. So Crowley still doesn't know how to get to this place. Which is also why we doubled back through so many doors. You can go straight to somewhere from here to Aurora, but you *never* come straight back. Or you risk discovery. Carelessness in that regard is why so many doors on Earth are no more, destroyed. It's one reason the Order exists, to help protect, hide, and monitor the doors."

"Where do the second and third doors go?"

"Shouldn't you get used to the first door . . . first?"

"Fair enough."

Perhaps it was a mercy she'd batted that one back at him. Because it was true he felt all over again as if he were confronted by a talking carrot, a melodious potato.

"Why didn't you get rid of it? Clean up a bit." Motioning at what he could only think of as a monster, constrained within its red dotted line.

Alice snorted, as if he were a fool. Perhaps he was a fool.

"It'd be dangerous to move. Like this place, it's dead but not dead. Volatile, under certain circumstances. Leave it, the creature will never move an inch. Touch it, and who knows what lurches back to life, or what magic distress beacon it tries to send back home. Besides, it's a reminder to all of us to be on our guard."

Anyone who could create as infernal a beast as the mecha-elephants wouldn't stop at one killing. Anyone who would send an uncanny assassin after Dr. Lambshead had no boundaries.

Everything was about to get darker and more dangerous, Jonathan realized. Whether he wanted to stay clear or not.

A thought occurred. "How do you know it was Crowley who killed my grandfather?"

"Because he killed your mother."

That sinking, floating feeling again, but he refused to give in to it. Later, back in the sanctuary of the tiki bar, hunched over, he could let his anguish show, where no one could see. But not now.

"So, you're not sure." Not staring at her, because he was biting back tears. He didn't want to believe her. Had only her word for it. It couldn't be true. It was one thing to know she was dead, another to hear it said by a stranger.

"It'll never be put in front of a judge and a jury, if that's what you mean."

"And this place? Is it some sort of purgatory?" Better to forge ahead. What lay behind was no better.

"No. It's a house on the borderlands. An old, ancient place. If that rings a bell." Alice sounded almost respectful, as if they were in a cathedral.

"No bells are ringing." They were, though.

"Remote and secure. Neither here nor there. Always on the threshold.

Always becoming, never quite getting there. Not Aurora and not Earth. It's not a ghost, but it's not the actual thing, either. A way station. Does that help?"

"Like a poke in the eye. Isn't that the definition of purgatory?"

She glared at him. "It's like a gateway and a safe house got married and had a creepy child. That's as much of an answer as you get. The Builders created it. The Order found it, preserved it. I imagine before the mansion was built, it 'echoed' whatever existed on that spot before."

The Builders. Them again.

"And what lies beyond that glass?" Jonathan pointed to the windows.

Alice shrugged. "A world none of us want to know. Or care to know. Lifeless, peculiar. I don't know if you can even breathe out there."

Jonathan shuddered. There were birds in his head now, as if escaping from the empty feeders above their heads. Ghost birds. Fluttering around inside his skull, and he could not get them out.

Yet still he went on, wanting to burst through the nettle and tall trees, find a copse and feel the sunlight on his face. It was getting colder and colder in the haunted mansion.

"Who are the Builders, then, when they're at home? Rather generic name."

"You're turning into a proper little owl, aren't you? You'd die if you said their real name. Their real name would fill you up and fry all the neurons in your brain and leave you stumbling around like a zombie."

"That doesn't tell me who they are." But it kind of did.

"The Builders created the doors between the worlds, before they disappeared. Some say they created the worlds themselves."

"Good on them." But he had a niggling itch in his head at the repetition of the name, a dawning awareness that he'd heard this before. That, in a pinch, he could have recited the Builders' myth to her himself.

But Alice misread his puzzled expression, said: "You're rattled. Good. You should be. The stakes are very high. Your place in all of this is insecure. You have no idea who and what are in play."

"Did Dr. Lambshead want me to steer clear?" he asked. "Of all of this? Like you do? I don't think so." He didn't know what Sarah had wanted, but he was beginning to guess.

"Like *I* do?" Alice said, folding her arms. "Do I? What if I just thought you were too young to be plucked for service? Raw, green—whatever the right word is. I don't mean it as an insult. That you should go back to your stupid academy for now, out of the path of danger?"

"What if I don't want to be out of the path of danger?"

Then regretted saying it. Because even after Spain, the thought of being in danger hadn't hit home. Until now.

Along with the one other thing.

ᖁᘒ

Oh, Sarah! It was almost too much, the way he felt now. Jonathan had known more than he realized. In code. Peter Cellars. Down in the cellar of his mind, Sarah had placed some of the answers. A clever Sarah, if an exasperating mother.

"Builders" had been "Cold Pricklies"; "The Order" had been the "Agency"; "Aurora" had been "Euphoria." It all came back in a rush. The stories she had told him until he was too old for story time, and how that must have hurt not just because it meant he was growing up but because there was no other safe way to share what she knew.

Not three magic doors but five magic windows. Not talking carrots, but definitely talking turnips, in abundance. And he wondered just how alone she must have felt, at times, to have been in Florida, looking after him, reduced to acts of translation and deception. It struck him, sitting there in the haunted mansion, in such a profound way, what she'd given up to keep him safe.

Sarah had pretended to read the tales out of a book, but whenever he, indignant and then, over time, faux indignant, said that wasn't the real story, had nothing to do with the image on the cover, he'd demand to see the pages and they'd both dissolve into giggles when it was clear she'd made it up and he was right. "The Monster's Shadow," "The Legend of the Cold Pricklies," "The Talking Turnip and the Third Window," and more besides.

Silly now, perhaps, but funny to an eight-year-old. All the things he'd thought were just a single mother entertaining her child, for amusement, for love, out of a sense of play . . . It was all more preparation or fair warning.

In one sense, that felt like a betrayal of their time together. In another way, it felt like a bond so strong it could reach out beyond death to speak to him. And couldn't it have been both things? To amuse, and so he wouldn't get the bends later. So he'd get his footing sooner. So he'd be up to the challenge of what came next.

The ache, the agony, that there was so much of it he couldn't remember, that had not come along from childhood into his teenage years. Had he squandered her gift?

Regardless, the realization stiffened his resolve, made him ready to ask Alice the most dangerous question, and get it over with.

"What were you looking for in the mansion?"

A hesitation, a direct look from those blazing blue eyes, appraising him, and if he read her right, a frustration as well.

"An artifact of the Builders. Crowley has brought a . . . weapon . . . to Aurora with which he means to subjugate our world and, eventually, all the worlds. Somewhere in your grandfather's mansion, I believe, there is an artifact that will allow us to capture this weapon and banish it. Because even without Crowley's intent, it should not exist in our world. Everywhere it wanders, this object creates chaos in its wake."

Jonathan contemplated her. Was she trustworthy? Was she at least more trustworthy than the alternatives?

"You mean the Black Bau—I mean the Wobble. Silly name for it."

"Yes, that," Alice said, giving him an appraising look, more respectful. "And not silly. Not really. Wobble is what you change Bauble to. Bobble, then Wobble. Twice removed. Like a cousin you don't really know."

"But why?"

"Most of the things the Builders made are powerful or scary or both. Their real names have power, a kind of . . . beckoning. So we call them by other names. Ordinary names. Absurd names. The more ridiculous the name, the better."

"Well, anyway, here it is." He pulled the Wobble out of his trouser pocket. This time round it looked more like a tiny black colander with silver rubber bands across, as if it didn't want Alice to know what it really looked like.

Alice looked stunned, as if he'd pulled a live platypus out of his pocket instead.

"Where did you get it?" Accusatory.

"I'll take that as a yes, then? This is definitely the Wobble?"

Dr. Lambshead had called it "the ultimate problem solver" in his letter, "even more than the bird-children."

It might as well have hypnotized Alice. She stared at it in an unfocused yet intense way.

"Keep it safe," Dr. Lambshead had written. Now, seeing the hungry look in Alice's eyes, he wondered if he'd meant "leave it where it is." And could he be sure it didn't do more than Alice said it did?

"I've been searching for ages in that accursed basement, the grounds, everywhere. And here you've got it." A wry disgust with herself, but also a tension behind it, a real need. "You should give it over to me. The Wobble's meant to be used by the Order."

"Am I not part of the Order? By birthright? Besides, Dr. Lambshead said it would only work for me. He also said I shouldn't give it to anyone else."

He was trying to sound confident, but a feeling had risen up in him, as if the events of the day had finally conspired to overwhelm him. He was convinced something was scrabbling inside his skull. A frantic dark fluttering that drew close, and this version of the mansion would provide no defense.

Alice was trying to appear calm, but she continued to look at the Wobble like cats looked at catnip mice. Or just at mice.

"Dr. Lambshead was a loyal and valued member of the Order, but I think you'd find he was mistaken in that detail, Jonathan. There are work-arounds. You really ought to give the Wobble to someone more experienced."

"It's what he said in his letter. 'Blood of the maker, blood of the user.'" He dared not think too much about what that might mean about his family. About his father.

"Show me."

"I destroyed it. Memorized it and then burned it."

"So I just have your word."

"And I *just* have your word on everything else."

Everything else. The smooth blue simplicity of the ghost mansion was actually so complex. The strange swifts stitching their way through the window. Crowley. Aurora. The Builders. He did not want to believe it. Any of it. This did not seem like the kind of thing that ought to be believable. Perhaps it was the kind of thing that if you believed, it only then became real.

"Leave now if you want to get out," the carrot said again to him.

"They'll kill you," the potato said in its gorgeous voice. "They'll kill everyone."

The whole world, and another besides, and an infinity of worlds beyond that. It all began to kaleidoscope and collapse. Again.

"We're both English," Alice said, almost pleading.

"Not the same England," Jonathan said.

Alice took a different tack, and he didn't appreciate it any more than the head-on approach.

"Listen, Jonathan. We need the Wobble to contain Crowley. We need it to help preserve everything the Order stands for."

True, he didn't even know what the Order stood for. Not really. But he knew what orders Dr. Lambshead had given him.

"Then you need me. It won't work for you. I'm keeping it. If you want to try to take it from me, Alice, I promise I'll put up a fight."

Alice stared at him with a new sort of appraisal in her eyes.

"Do you really have what it takes? Is it possible?"

"I guess you'll have to find out."

A sigh from Alice—of surrender or resignation? "It is true I never thought you'd get this far this fast. And Dr. Lambshead thought you had special powers. I don't see it, but I don't know everything, Jonathan. *Do you have special powers?*"

"I pushed a ghost. You said that's impossible. So let's assume I do."

A creepy flamelike feeling moved across his scalp. A soreness around his eyes, almost a burning. He looked down and saw that the half moons of his fingernails had turned sooty.

The fallen beast's jaw moved, and they both stared at it in horror.

But it was a warning only, that reflexive movement.

For now the Emissary was rising up out of him, where it had hidden, in his skin, his flesh, through all the doors they had traversed.

It was rising up and up to the ceiling and curling down at them in all its shadowy strength and Alice was shouting at him to come clear of it and that seemed grim and funny both, for how was he to come clear of something that had so thoroughly curled up inside him?

Because Jonathan was wrong—he hadn't pushed the wraith away after all, but absorbed it.

Embraced it.

Chapter Fifteen

A WELL-MAINTAINED LAWN IS AN UTTER HORROR

To anyone watching from afar—and Kristýna believed there might be watchers in droves—she was enjoying a midafternoon picnic in an empty public park on the outskirts of Paris, with her companion. Clearly, he was a bodybuilder, indulged in odd tattoos, and could be assumed a dour, humorless sort, nose buried in a tattered paperback with a robot and a newt on the cover. Kristýna was playing the part of a middle-class woman of enterprise, no doubt owner of a candle shop, taking off the afternoon. Mack had just finished doing two hundred push-ups.

An idyllic scene beyond their picnic blanket, almost suspiciously free of garbage: Oak and birch trees provided shade, rosebushes splashes of color, and in the distance, beyond their expansive stretch of grass, lay a pond with ducks, while a hedgerow passed close by like a wall, to their left, protecting the lawn from a dark, tangled forest.

Pleasant enough, but not much to Kristýna's tastes. The current French trend of precision in gardens was too much like turning a wolf on the prowl into a pug with an embroidered ruffle for a collar. She much preferred the wolf.

"Why aren't we meeting in the forest?" Mack had asked just minutes before as he spread out the picnic blanket. "It would be safer."

"For us. But he doesn't trust us. Not entirely. Don't blame him. *I* don't trust us," she said with a wink for Mack that made him smile uncertainly.

It was true in a sense: Mack had begged off hiding with her in the catacombs after a week of too many tunnels. They had met up again two days later, and she had no idea of where he'd been during that time. True, Mack had no idea what she'd been up to, either.

To a passerby, the marmot that now grazed on the lawn near them, close enough to the hedgerow to bolt for a burrow, would seem to have nothing to do with them, and, as it was not a goat, did not count as a beast subject to confiscation under Lord Crowley's law. Even if that marmot was, in fact, the Marmot, one of the secret leaders of the resistance to Crowley's despotic rule and a charter member of the Order of the Third Door.

"An English marmot, assisting the French?" Mack had whispered upon the Marmot's approach.

"Yes, the times, they are that desperate."

Kristýna had always believed French-English cooperation resembled "a hen with shoes." Yet the normal rules need not apply to a marmot who required no other name than the Marmot. Besides, the Marmot was Swiss in origin, had only later become English. To split hairs. Or to acknowledge that she did not know what nationality the Marmot felt he owed allegiance to.

"I like grass," she murmured, "but cannot see the attraction in eating it."

"I like grass," the Marmot murmured back, "and cannot see the harm in eating it."

"A well-maintained lawn is a thing of beauty."

"A well-maintained lawn is an utter horror."

Bona fides established, they could speak freely. In English. The Marmot's French had not improved with the years, and he knew no Czech. Nor did she know any of the various forms of Marmot.

The Marmot devoured a dandelion whole, then another.

"How goes the resistance?" she asked.

Kristýna was meant to report to him, but they existed not just within the ever-shifting hierarchy of the Order, but also within layers and circles of other allegiances, some of which went back more than a century. All told, it evened out.

The Marmot considered whether to consign a cluster of clover to his buckteeth, reached a decision, and delivered a frenzy of death to the unfortunate white blossoms, then raised his head, scanned 180 degrees of lawn horizon.

"We had an agent close to Crowley. She was meant to observe and report back on his plans. But yesterday she died in an explosion. I'm sure you've heard. A bomb of some sort. Ordinary dynamite. The demi-mages missed it."

"She went . . . rogue?"

"No. We don't believe so. We believe Crowley . . . induced it. To give him the excuse for further excesses against us."

"Does Crowley need an excuse? For that?" Mack asked.

Most unexpected and unwelcome. Mack never talked during these meetings. Observer only. Once, the Marmot had asked Kristýna, "What does Mack do?" Clear that wasn't the real question. Not at all.

The Marmot's aspect darkened, and he stared at Kristýna, teeth prominent, ignoring Mack.

She became very aware, sitting there cross-legged in front of the beast, of the Marmot's rough physicality, the thickness under the fur that spoke of muscle mass, the toughness even of those beady dark eyes. The huge buckteeth.

Not to mention other qualities. Marmots of a certain persuasion could cast shadows larger than themselves. These shadows had peculiar properties and had been known to detach themselves from their hosts and develop their own agency. Become dangerous, depending on the whims of the marmot in question.

"No, he does not need an excuse," the Marmot finally said. "Which is why we are also perplexed."

"Your agent wouldn't have decided on her own? Felt a need to undertake such an operation. For some reason you could not know?"

"Absolutely certain," the Marmot said. "She knew how important her spying was to us and how small the chances of assassinating Crowley. Nor was she a fool."

Just her notes on the schedules and activities of the demi-mages in the catacombs had been invaluable. Now it would be even harder to infiltrate Notre Dame.

"Conclusion?" she asked.

Mack spoke again, still seemingly engrossed in his paperback. "Conclusion: a third party. Someone who would benefit from Crowley rattled, but not dead."

"Very good," the Marmot said to Mack. "We concur."

Hazards and cautions. Alarms and breaches. The Marmot had never acknowledged Mack's presence before. But just now there had been in the Marmot's glance toward Mack a hint of familiarity that worried her.

"I have news as well," Kristýna said, if only to put the moment behind her. Or her paranoia. Whichever it was, she did not like it.

"Source?"

She smiled. "Better you don't know." Better for her, since her dandelions spied on more than just Crowley. Although, in theory, marmot shadows could be spying on her dandelions, too. How wicked everyone was. No respect for privacy.

"Go on."

Was it coincidence that the Marmot chose that moment to snap dandelion stalks in two and munch on the remains? Well, they weren't hers. The Marmot knew some of her secrets, but hopefully not all, for she still had a spy in Crowley's war room.

"Crowley has had Verne create a new magic war machine," Kristýna said, "one which burrows into the ground, like a submarine on land. It will, it is rumored, soon be used as part of a new offensive against either England or Prague. Crowley already, too, has asked Napoleon to draw up new plans for an assault on Prague. As for the Golden Sphere, Crowley thankfully still does not know where It has hidden, although he searches feverishly. Crowley has ordered his familiar Wretch to train some sort of assassin to target members of the Order. Those are the main points."

"And the not-main points."

"The saltpeter is in place. Crowley is trying, but he can't get rid of it all. He can't possibly get rid of all the garbage in time anyway. Rimbaud is ready. Which is to say, I'm not needed here anymore. Nor is Mack."

Worse, if Crowley captured them and found a way to make them talk, they would be a liability.

"No one expects you to stay," the Marmot said. "You've done quite enough."

She smiled. Anyone who knew the Marmot less well would have taken that as a rebuke. And the nagging doubt, despite wanting to leave: Did the Marmot need her gone for some other reason?

"I have tactical intel, too, from the catacombs, but I assume you'll want me to tell that to the Decipher Duck."

"Yes, quite." The Marmot did not trouble himself with that level of detail. Nor did he seem troubled by her other intel. How much of it did he already have from other sources?

"There is another . . . anomaly," she said. "One we've spoken of before."

"Namely?"

"Still no evidence that Crowley has begun to fade. No evidence he has left Aurora for any period to counteract the effects."

No one, not the greatest of magicians, could avoid fading away into a wraith if they stayed in a world not their own. You could stave off the process of disintegration for a year or two, even three. But you would during that period begin to show the signs. It was a natural side effect; you might as well elude gravity. Nor would a quick trip through a door be enough to offset the months, the years, Crowley had now spent in Aurora.

"Troublesome," the Marmot said.

"Further interference," Mack said.

Yes, it was, for him to continue to speak up. She gave him an irritated look, but he met it full-on, as if she were the unreasonable one. As if she were the one breaking an unspoken agreement.

"We had hoped our agent would discover the reason for this, but it was not to be . . ." The Marmot bent a sedge weed with one paw, inspected it, found the weed wanting, let it spring back into position. As he watched it settle, the seed head dispersed into the wind. "I also had hoped Dr. Lambshead might have had some insight, might have said . . . something?"

"No, he never said anything on that subject. I'm sorry."

She replied perhaps too quickly, out of unease. The Marmot had never mentioned Dr. Lambshead in front of Mack before, and she had not once in seven years told Mack anything about him.

A couple of men in drab, nondescript clothes began walking along the path to a gazebo to their far right. The Marmot retreated back onto all four legs and rummaged in amongst the grasses of the lawn.

The picnic basket held cheese, wine, and bread. It also hid an impressive assortment of deadly weapons, magical and otherwise. Should they be required.

⁐

The Czech term for "whistle-pig" was „píšt'alka prase", and to most Czechs was a nonsense term, which amused her because a talking marmot was certainly nonsense to the average Czech. The word for "marmot" was simply „svišt'", but this also meant "baby" or "child."

Thinking of the Marmot in this way reminded her of his true age, and thus his guile. In the old tongue, the word for marmot also meant "disarming" or "deceptive." Perhaps because who could on first sight think of a marmot as less than earnest.

This particular svišt didn't speak again until the two men were suitably distant, apparently using the cover of the gazebo to engage in some passionate kissing. But when the Marmot turned to them again, he changed the subject in what she would later think of as a peculiar way, although in the moment nostalgia snuffed out suspicion.

"Do you remember, Kristýna, when these gardens were full of nectar deer at night? And such beautifully strange blossoms. And so many of the Old Folk."

The Old Folk were the ancient animals, the ones from folklore rarely glimpsed in the modern era, even less so now that Crowley consigned so much animal life to death.

An affection came flooding back to Kristýna for the Marmot, from before the current troubles. From when there had been no Crowley, no war, no divisions within the Order.

"Of course I remember!" she said. The flying nectar deer were rare everywhere now, their huge gossamer wings like cosmic sails, harvesting moonlight from particles of the air.

"Perhaps one day, the Old Folk will come out of hiding and the nectar deer will return to this place." The Marmot's voice, usually impassive, unreadable, contained a rare hint of sadness.

Sometimes she felt sorry for the Marmot; he lived in the past, which could be a beautiful thing, but only in moderation. As she knew well.

The Marmot stood upright, shook off whatever melancholy had come over him.

"Thank you for your report, Kristýna. When will you leave Paris?"

A not-so-subtle hint.

"Tonight." Not yet for Prague, but soon. They had an opportunity to exploit first.

"I will not ask for where. I know you will tell me if you need to. You might then wander over to the pond. Give the rest of your information to the Decipher Duck—and good luck with your travels."

"Which duck?" Mack asked.

"Witch duck?" the Marmot asked in confusion.

"Which one of the ducks?" Kristýna clarified. "Is it that mallard trailing a broken wing or the wood duck winking this way with one good eye? For example."

"It is the only duck that will talk to you."

"Ah," both Mack and Kristýna said.

"And you? What will you do now?" Kristýna asked.

The Marmot got a wild look in its eyes, exclaimed, "*Sunny hells damn it to all the dark havens, but that is* good *clover!*"

No further answer would be given. The meeting was over, the marmot lost to reverie while committing a brutal series of atrocities against the defenseless clover.

In truth, Kristýna found the bloodthirstiness unsettling, even directed against a few dozen plants. Perhaps especially. Kristýna knew that the Marmot could easily betray her, if it benefited what he thought of as the proper goals of the Order of the Third Door.

Anything was possible for a creature at least two hundred years old, tough as old boot leather, and ruthless as sin.

Chapter Sixteen
NEITHER GHOST BEARS NOR WRAITHS SHALL LOVE THEE

Rack would never get his fill of Dr. Lambshead's mansion. He knew this by day two, but confirmed it early on day four when he experienced euphoria upon a find of fifty-two crystal candelabras from the 1920s wrapped in green velvet cloth and stored in a huge war chest banded with an intricate mother-of-pearl design. The whole ensemble, though very dusty, smelled faintly of lavender.

Perhaps it reminded him of the heyday of the old ancestral home in "Hay-on-Straw," as they'd dubbed it, now cold and gray and much emptier. Casualty of estate taxes and declining fortunes. The home he'd hopped into at age five, victim of the same fire that had killed his parents and grandparents. Only to lose his adoptive parents at age twelve to a car accident, at which point any residual feud between him—the interloper—and Danny had died away, replaced by an unbreakable bond.

Underneath all the candelabras, a worn case full of carefully stacked silver. Dull, yes, but with some dusting and polishing all of it would be mansion-worthy. Although: not *this* mansion. This mansion was a high-end flea market. This mansion had been run by a nutter posing as a reasonable man of science and medicine. Of this Rack was sure. Dr. Lambshead had been about as reliable to poor young Johnny Lamb as—take your pick, pick your poison—some pack-rat version of Attila the Hun or one of the parchment-dry instructors at Poxforth, who Rack imagined might one day during a drought burst into flame right at the lectern.

"This is the life!" Rack muttered to Danny as he foraged in a particularly vibrant pile of antiques.

"Or a life," she replied. "Turns out the rat doesn't take to dust, Rack. Surprise surprise."

"The rat. Always with the rat. The dust is of a superior vintage, innit, sister-blister?"

A grunt from Danny—she was a champion at grunting, once grunting her way through a whole field of rugby opponents, the ball, ovoid, or whatever they called it, secure in one massive muscled hand. Her enthusiasm might seem underwhelming to an outside observer, her giant pilot light burning a tad lower and slower than the usual maximum-high, raging flame.

Yet Danny had been the one who had wheedled and cajoled him into saying yes to Jonathan's offer. At the time, Rack would have been just as content spending a threadbare summer crashing at various acquaintances' houses, while Danny went on a succession of dates with alternating lads and lasses, as was her summer tradition of late. Rack would've gotten a break from his sister (and rat) whilst living in decadent squalor with jaunty conversation on the couches of any number of handsome fellows.

But Rack didn't feel that way now. He'd caught a kind of fever from all the sorting, recognized it as akin to his propensity to collect pocket squares. Wondered if it meant he was destined to run an antiques shop himself. Was that a good or a poor fate? He wasn't sure.

No, certainly he could at least run a posh auction house, get his thrills that way. Rise above his station as a person of non-British origin twice-orphaned and heir to a drafty mansion-castle they couldn't afford upkeep on and no one wanted to buy. While he and Danny lived adjacent, when not at Poxforth, in the cottage with its much more affordable utilities and other amenities.

Perhaps his fanatical enthusiasm for the cataloging is what made him miss Jonathan less and less, lose track of "their project," as he sometimes—always with fondness—referred to Jonathan behind his back. Because that was how Danny had acted at first—as if taking Jonathan under their wing was some pagan responsibility, a notch in a good karma belt Rack didn't think was that stylish and he would never wear. Even if they'd all three clicked very early on. It was true: Although jaded and cynical, Rack quite liked the underclassman, and felt the trio was better together than apart.

Even if (or because?) the truth was that the lad had a naive streak a kilometer wide. He talked to animals like they could actually understand him. Liked to walk in nature, whether or not mosquitoes and biting flies lurked, and had interminable stories about jumping over alligators back in Florida.

Jonathan was as wont to frolic in a meadow as to want to see the latest art house movie in Poxforth's Smeltworth Memorial Cinema House. Cared not for the imbibing of forbidden fermentations. "Straight edge" was too organized a principle by which to describe Jonathan, as he'd likely never heard the term, being, as far as Rack could tell, blissfully asexual and a Luddite who rarely switched on a computer except to do his studies and was forever keeping his phone turned off in his school satchel.

Which is the reason Rack wasn't worried when Danny with a frown appeared from beyond yet another ziggurat of malformed, overflowing shelves to ask him if he'd seen Jonathan lately.

By then it was midafternoon, and not only hadn't the lad popped up, but he wasn't in his self-appointed tiki-bar guard shack nor in the pantry or the study—and definitely not, Danny reported, in the backyard by the pond.

On his priority list of worries, Jonathan's nonpresence currently ranked sixth, well below the top three, which included money and money. Which was followed by a vague worry that Danny had been on the verge since they'd arrived at the mansion of telling him something important that she couldn't quite bring herself to say, which was very unlike her. Possibly related to those dates of hers.

Below that on the worry list, the sad lack of romance in his love life due to dusty-mansion syndrome, followed by: Jonathan's absence.

"He'll turn up. He's off somewhere taking a piss or having an attack of the wank."

Danny ignored that. "Tee-Tee says he's not here at all. Not on the property at all, yeah? Not anywhere."

Rack sighed and came to a halt, for Lester, as he had named his damaged foot (once upon a time named, melodramatically, "Das Boot"), was still throbbing, even off it. Literally. Which was why, at the moment, Lester née Das Boot had a drawn-on frowny face and rabbit ears drawn in nonpermanent marker on its polymer surface.

"Tee-Tee is not a bat with powers of echolocation. Nor a Brighton pier psychic. Nor yet a Blackpool amusement ride. Tee-Tee, my dear Danny"—and here he warmed to the task—"is a very confused rat who thinks he is a person because his owner has spoiled him rotten. Cheeky bastard, lying to you about Jonathan."

"All right, then." Danny scowled, turned back toward the stacks. "And for your information, Tee-Tee is a very clever rat who does not appreciate your scorn."

"It's rather more scorn for the general idea of rats—and psychics—than about any specific rat, sister-blister," Rack said.

"You must get used to the idea of Tee-Tee soon, brother," Danny replied, staring skeptical at a broken pen shell turned into an ashtray, before binning it.

"Jonathan will turn up," Rack reassured her.

Never had he spoken a truer word. But even if he had been Nostradamus, he could not have predicted the nature of Jonathan's eventual reappearance, which forever after he would describe as a "wee bit overdramatic."

Reconciled to rat and sister alike, with Tee-Tee even daring from the expanse of Danny's shoulder to place one admittedly cute star-shaped pink-padded paw on him, they all three were leaning against the ridiculously huge birdbath contraption, taking a break to eat the last of the pathetic prawns and cucumber slices Rack had brought with him, on stale bread, when there came the echoing sound of a door smashed open from the corridor beyond the basement.

Before Rack could so much as lower the sandwich from his mouth, there came barreling out of the corridor into the basement an unfamiliar brunette woman in her midtwenties and Jonathan, looking as ashen as if he'd seen his latest grades . . . and pouring out behind them an oily black mist or fog or smoke that made Rack think they were fleeing some sort of fire.

Was the mansion ablaze? And them trapped in the basement?

But then he realized in the next second that the black mist had a face—a lost and vacant look, almost waifish—and a discernable shape, and this apparition made a sound like a shriek or scream that he did not believe was a fire alarm.

"The bear gun!" the woman shouted. "Shoot it with the bear gun!"

Rack's sandwich dropped from his hand as the wraith-thing took up more and more space at incredible speed. He was proper frozen, unable to digest what he was experiencing.

Incredibly his sister Danny shouted back, "I've got this," picked up the bear gun, fell to one knee, and commanded, "Get down!" to the strange woman and Jonathan—who promptly went from full-on sprint to sprawled across the floor, giving her a clear shot.

Which she took.

There came a heartrending growl right in his ear. There came such a sound that Rack felt it in his bones, as if *he* were being ripped apart by a bear's claws, a bear's fangs. A roaring in his ears.

Then, an impossibility: a *whole bear* plopped right out of the end of the bear gun, a bear-fur-covered droplet that expanded into the bear proper. A white bear—no, a ghost bear, for he could see clear through the beast—that expanded and became irrationally huge, propelled with a tremendous velocity at the wraith, leapt up at its foe to tear and rend, the leap timed perfectly so that the target fell to the floor wrapped in its dread embrace, dark filaments trailing out to all sides. Even as Jonathan and the woman rolled out of the way and closer to Rack.

It was so brief a battle, and yet indelibly etched into Rack's memory that ever after it would pop back up into his thoughts at odd hours, in the pale gloom right before dawn. Or as he drifted off to sleep, only to be brought awake by the vision.

The way that the bear crunched and popped the "bones" of a being so ethereal. The way that the edges of the wraith began to fray and fade like an old cobweb, while more and more of its essence disappeared down the ghost bear's gullet. The moment when the wraith became immobile, reduced to prey, and how the hollow spaces that formed its eyes fixed on him and the mouth opened in a wordless howl.

Until with a ridiculous sound like a balloon popping in slow motion, a balloon whooshing into airlessness, the whole apparition collapsed in on itself, and, with the bear getting in a few last eager gobbles, it disappeared as if it had never been there.

A smell lingered, as if a child had burned the wheels of his go-kart, as if a spent match had been dipped in glue. He thought he heard a last gasp, a swooning hopeless sound that swept up the walls of the basement and was no more.

While the bear—with murderous intent, all and every part of it pure bear despite being quite translucent—turned on him, an innocent bystander, a Rack who had taken no position and done nothing more than stand there and drop part of a perfectly good prawn-and-cucumber sandwich to the floor.

A leap, a bound, before Danny, or anyone, could react, and though he flinched and did his best impression of someone jumping to the side, the great dirty mouth, the hot breath, were upon him and the glazed murderous eyes and the enormous paws that intended to smite his silly head from his silly neck and then gnaw on it for a time eternal . . .

Except in the next moment, the bear, too, had begun to fade and the paw meant to kill him just soft-patted his cheek as if in fond farewell as it dissolved and the bear's gaze that met him in that instant turned to something sad, melancholy, that pierced him to the depths of what was, presumably, his soul.

Then the bear was gone, save for a disconcerting whiff of chocolate and cinnamon, and where the bear's face had been it was just Jonathan and the woman, risen from the floor, and Danny, still on one knee, but turned to face him, smiling as if all of this was normal and they'd just had a good day at the range or something. Tee-Tee still perched on her shoulder, part of a deranged artillery crew.

"I'd say that was a good shot, yeah?" Danny said, and then stared pointedly at Rack. "At least, Tee-Tee thinks so."

Chapter Seventeen

A GIANT EARTHWORM SHALL LAY WASTE TO YOUR CITIES

"No one shall leave their home after the hour of six o'clock in the evening. All spirits (in the libational sense) are hereby banned, and anyone found drunk or dancing shall be subject to immediate execution. Anyone harboring an animal of any sort shall have their left hand removed, cooked, and fed to their mouth or ass. Everything will get darker soon, if you do not obey."

—From Part I of Lord Crowley's Final Decree, distributed in peculiar and strange ways, at night, by Emissaries, demi-mages, and bats

With Wretch, Verne, and Laudinum X by his side—an army of demi-mages and Emissaries crammed in behind them for good measure—Crowley admired the Burrower in all its substantial glory from a rocky overhang. The Burrower filled almost all of one of the catacombs' largest caverns, surrounded by workers making last-minute adjustments.

Hours since the explosion that had killed Dupin, but still no time to clean up proper. No time at all.

Crowley was covered in dried blood where it could not be wiped away, and he could not quite shake the ringing in his ears and the shaking of his hands. But he lived, praise the Devil and Demon both! The traitor had been blown to smithereens, yet Wretch had, with uncanny reflexes, saved him, even as Crowley had watched with disbelief as Dupin's features came apart and then the eclipse that was Wretch slipped between to shelter him. Such a strong shield, so infernally dark. He should wear Wretch on the field of battle.

"Why, Wretch? Why?" Crowley asked, staring blank-eyed at the Burrower.

"Let us just say, my lord, that my inquiries reveal she had a lot of
English friends for a Frenchwoman."

"England. Prague. England. Prague. I say we burn them both down."

"They do go together these days, like hearts go with blood," Wretch
said.

Why, he was trembling. Trembling. Him, the Emperor of a fourth
of the world that mattered. Who would have thought? That she had
hated him that much, to try to kill him in such a vile fashion. And he
had continued to stand there, in his shock, splashed in various bodily
liquids, as if baptized by a cult of autopsies, scraps of skin and fragments
of bone sticking to him.

Until he'd caught sight of Laudinum X. Which was when he had
started to laugh—pointing at Laudinum X and laughing, hooting even,
slapping his knee. For Wretch had been less successful in protecting
Laudinum X. Shrapnel from the blast had bisected LX's skull as perfectly
as if a butcher had had time to draw lines on his head and split it open
five inches with a cleaver. His head was wrapped with blood-soaked bandages, but still Laudinum X lived, and not only lived but did not even
blink, just stood there awaiting further orders.

"You look so stupid. So, so very stupid," Crowley had shrieked at
his chief demi-mage immediately after the explosion, and yet so did he,
covered in exploded Dupin, and so did the All-Seeing Eye, victim of a food
fight with lasagna in a thick tomato sauce. Only Wretch, floating there
wrathful, surveying the cathedral for a second enemy, did not look stupid.

But Crowley had stopped laughing soon enough and a flood of fear
came over him and he was drowning in it. They had come so close, the
Resistance. They had come so very close to ending him, and his ambitions. After all the time and effort Crowley had put into his plans.

"I need a new garbage . . . I need a new garbage . . . I need . . . garbage . . ." The word escaped him, not only escaped him but sat at the
edge of his mind making rude gestures at him.

"A new liaison with the citizens of Paris?" Wretch had suggested.

"Yes, that! And a maid. We need a maid in here. And some towels. And a mop. My kingdom for a mop."

Then he was hopping and kicking at bits of Dupin and stomping on bits of Dupin, and if he could not stop laughing now it wasn't because Laudinum X was so absurd with a split skull but because he could picture in his mind's eye just what vengeance might look like.

The Burrower: A two-hundred-foot-long dreadnought, wide and thick and glutted with millions upon millions of its namesake: earthworms. Atop the blind, questing stump of a head lay the "command barnacle," as Crowley called it. From there, the Burrower's leviathanlike tendencies could be controlled for maximum devastative effect. Beneath, Verne's most useful invention: a tread rotated via a pulley that helped the Burrower to move at speeds of up to thirty-five miles an hour over open fields; reversed, that same tread cut into the earth to allow the Burrower to dig with ferocity into the ground.

The vast and tumultuous frame represented a breakthrough in Crowley's magic technologies. Whereas the blood of mammals powered his other creations and must be continually replenished with more blood, the Burrower required blood only to consecrate the latticework that formed the frame. Thereafter, the writhing balls of living earthworms that occupied much of the interior did the rest; Crowley's minions must only use his necromancy to keep them alive without sustenance and, wherever the Burrower came to rest, dig up more earthworms to replace any casualties of the day. The small army of soldiers and mages that accompanied the Burrower had their living quarters in spheres hanging from the Burrower's metal spine and could spill forth through tubes leading through the masses of earthworms to the exterior.

The Burrower had a squirmy feel to it, as the earthworms writhing out from the latticework gave the machine at rest a kind of creepy residual movement.

In the distance, the bleating of muffled goats, for this cavern was surrounded by Crowley's surplus goat pens. Although, to be honest, it sounded more like Crowley had abducted thousands of human babies, such was the sort of noise goats made en masse. For this reason, Crowley often had his demi-mages, on their lunch break, drown out the sound by playing Beethoven's Ninth, synchronized across a platoon of phonographs.

"Put a fresh towel on that," Crowley said to Laudinum X, wearying of the sight of the cleft cranium. The injury was nothing a necromancer couldn't withstand, but old LX still seemed in shock, had had to be led here by Verne, much to the Inventor's distaste. "*Someone put a goddamn towel over Laudinum X's head!*"

His hands were fists at his side, fingernails cutting into his palms. The explosion still rang in Crowley's head. The look on Dupin's face, staring blank into his eyes even as she came apart at all the seams. The thought that he might so easily have become chaos and void. This must never happen again.

"Of course, Lord Emperor," Wretch said, and summoned over a worker, who was forced to take off his dirty white shirt, which then hung sadly across most of LX's face like a flag of surrender.

Ever since the explosion, even in acknowledging Crowley's curt thank-you for saving his life, Wretch had the look about him of a satisfied cat, one that had eaten a mouse, or a dozen mice. Not that Crowley was ungrateful, but . . .

Crowley turned to Verne, who had been trying to make himself small and invisible against the shadows of the gray rock.

"You now shall have an important opportunity. You and Laudinum X."

"I don't understand," Verne said. "I am merely a novelist who dabbles in invention."

"You shall pilot the Burrower from the command limpet."

"Once the modifications are complete. The ones I gave you in the diagrams the other day?"

"They've already finished those—gone without sleep to do it, bless them." Most were dead now, turned into goats and slaughtered.

"There must be at least a month of testing!"

"Oh no. We've stepped up the schedule while you were lounging around in your luxury accommodations. This is happening right now."

"Now?" Verne practically shouted it. "Now? But you can't. It hasn't been tested. It hasn't been tested. There has been no testing."

"Are you a bloody parrot? Test it en route, inventor. Test it on your way to the front. Write another bloody boring novel while you're at it, about your adventures."

Verne's mecha-elephant novel set in India had been a snooze; perhaps a Burrower novel would be more dramatic. But Verne was not enticed by the thought of novel-writing.

"The front?"

"You *are* a blasted parrot."

"You cannot do this. You cannot."

Crowley snarled. "I can and I will." Laudinum X would oversee Verne, ensure he didn't get any odd ideas about rebellion. While Verne would ensure Laudinum X didn't fall over dead, because LX would have the dead-man's switch. Or in this case, a giant red button in the cockpit, safe(ish) beneath LX's bum. If LX tumbled from his perch, the entire war machine would explode, spewing pieces of earthworm over half the continent.

The Burrower could not fall into enemy hands should his plans go the way of Napoleon's career. Indeed, in the case of failure, the Burrower would become an enormous, earthworm-filled suicide bomb. Again, though, Dupin's dissolving face came back to him, and he suffered a lurch, a dislocation, came slowly back to earth.

"But where will we go? What shall we do?" Verne staring distant, as if Crowley meant to just banish him to the farther horizon.

"It's not a bleeding vacation, Jules. You don't get to choose. You will invade England. You will utterly *crush* those pathetic eel eaters. We will kill them all. They will drown in their own blood. We will show them what it means to defy the great God-Emperor Crowley."

Was there spittle? Was he shouting? Shrieking? He did not care. This defiance must end. This defiance must be put to an end. Everywhere.

The Burrower would take care of England, or at least keep them in check . . . and he would take care of the Czechs, as Wretch had long counseled.

"Wretch. Promote Laudinum X's second, Opium Y, to head of the war factories. Ready the largest army of war elephants you can in one week. I shall personally ride at the head of them, and together we will crush Bavaria and lay waste to Prague. We'll kill them all. We'll wage such a war that they will wish they had never even thought about resisting. We will have revenge!"

"Most excellent, Your Excellency! It shall be as you command," Wretch said, bowing. In his way.

Now if he could just be sure he wasn't still wearing some of the brains of the traitor Dupin before he addressed the legions of demi-mages and Emissaries at his back and roused them to new heights of passion for the glorious adventures to come.

Which would, in the preparation for said adventures, just by chance, just by sheer coincidence, put immense hardship and new horrors squarely upon the populace of Paris.

Chapter Eighteen

TOO MANY HAMSTERS, NOT ENOUGH FAITH

Rack was even less fond of the aftermath of the wraith attack than the attack itself, because it appeared that everyone except for him had lost their everlasting minds.

At least the wraith-and-bear situation had been direct and brief. What followed was long and excruciating and set his brain and his leg to aching, his teeth to grinding, so that in the end he wished he'd given up his position at the beginning, just to spare himself the agony of all the explaining.

"Crackers. Bullshit. Excuse my French, but what you're telling me is ridiculous. Aleister Crowley? That buffoon? The one who wore the tin-foil hats? Is this all some mad LARP? Are you cosplaying some anime I'm unfamiliar with? And was this the idea all along? Bring an unsuspecting Rack to the mansion so he can be the ironic straight man in a one-time-only production of Jonathan Lambshead and the Fruitless Quest for a Logical Explanation?"

"Ridiculous" applied to all of it, even if his protestations on the side of the rational and logical were seemingly only self-convincing.

For none of his verbal parrying managed to stop Jonathan from all the explaining. Jonathan calmly explained the origins of the Emissary, introduced Alice as from a world called Aurora, further explained that their lives were all in danger in the mansion, that Aleister Crowley—not *the* Crowley, but a copy from a parallel Earth, third party to both the one Rack was standing upon and the second Earth already referenced—ruled a despotic empire on Aurora, that Dr. Lambshead had headed up something called the Order of the Third Door (which Alice belonged to), tasked with hiding all of this for people's safety or some such, that the mansion was a nexus for a series of doors leading to other worlds, and that he, Jonathan, intended to go *back* into that other world with Alice—not Crowley's original world but Aurora—taking with him an odd knickknack called the Wobble, to help trap a weapon called the Golden Sphere that Crowley had brought into Aurora from another dimension, to help him rule all the worlds, including Rack's Earth.

("What the hell is the Wobble, anyway?" Rack had asked.

"It's like when something isn't stable standing up and so it—"

"I know what 'to wobble' means, Danny! I know that.")

Oh yes, and the doors had been built by a group of singularly unimaginative types called the Builders, whose real name was so stinking 'orrible that if you said it out loud your flesh would peel off and your brain explode.

Oh, and yes again: Only Jonathan could use the Wobble because: "blood of the maker," whatever that meant to anyone other than the man down at the butcher shop.

Oh, and yes, yes, and yes again: Italy, or *some* Italy, was the destination of Jonathan and Alice's quest, there to meet up with a man Rack didn't know from Adam named Mamoud Abad, who Jonathan vouched for and Alice said had been told while in Spain—but not their Spain—that the Golden Sphere in question was hiding in Rome.

"Do I have all that right?" Rack asked. Because he'd felt compelled to repeat it back toward the end, for Jonathan's sake, so he would understand how it sounded. Had bit his tongue, because he was fit to burst with Crowley's wiki, which he could have recited like machine-gun bursts at them, slayed them with the perfect righteous logic of a reasoning that said this was, yes, bollocks. Didn't like his tendency to cover stress with blurtings of odd facts.

But Jonathan remained unmoved by reason, and said, "So you don't believe the evidence of your eyes. The Emissary? The bear gun?"

"That? Parlor trick. Mirrors. Holograms. A nothing." A nothing that had scared him half to death, it was true.

Rankled, too, at how Alice and Jonathan appeared to be in sync, as if they now stood on one side of a divide, with R & D spectators on the other side of the fence. Jonathan brainwashed into a particularly stupid cult.

"A whole pack of bears wouldn't be enough, would it?" Danny asked, no doubt rhetorically.

"You don't call three or more bears a 'pack,' sister-blister."

"I think after what just happened, I could call them a gaggle if I wanted, yeah?"

Nagging at Rack, too, was not just Danny's proficiency with the bear gun, but her defense of Jonathan's position. What game was his sister playing at? Couldn't she see how delusional this all was? While her stupid rat looked so unconcerned from her shoulder that clearly everything had gone over its head.

By then, they'd dragged him through the secret door after Jonathan had poked the snake mural in the eye, only to reveal, first, three rather disappointing doors and then, behind door number one, a bizarre alt-world version of the mansion and a hideous papier-mâché or clay sculpture of a dead monster.

Except it was more realistic than Rack would've liked, and the carcass's growling snarl and the dead look in the eyes, the collapsed-in-midstride pose, did not help Rack's stress levels. Nor did it prove anything, however.

"And there *is* that map in the corridor with England connected to the continent by a land bridge," Danny pointed out.

"Bollocks bollocks bollocks," Rack said, having exhausted his dwindling stock of applicable words.

"Didn't seem bollocks, what just happened. Looked very *not* bollocks."

Danny was also making him nervous by hefting the gun around—not the bear gun, which she'd put down, but the one labeled HAMSTER GUN, which Rack admitted was likely less deadly in terms of the hallucinations it induced, but . . .

"Listen," Rack said, and by now he'd sat his rump down on the circular sofa under the odd clock, exhausted by the conversation and, truth be told, beginning to feel the aftershocks of having a ghost bear lunge at him and pass through him. "Listen, I don't know what's exactly going on here. If, as I maintain, you're having a very long practical joke at my expense or not, but I'm going to have to ask you to stop. Just stop it, right now."

Anger had begun to boil up. Some days were fine. But other days it was hard enough to do the simple things, let alone the difficult. Some days he had to manage pain and had to be extra careful he didn't misstep and mess things up worse. Rote details that faded into routine then came into focus again. Clean the mechanism that was his leg. Take off the leg and shoe at night, inspect and clean both. Make sure they were close enough to the bed, here, in an unfamiliar place.

"No worries, Rack," Jonathan said. "I understand. I really do."

Still distant, aloof, curiously impassive. Except later Rack realized Jonathan was in shock over this, too. That Jonathan was trying very hard to keep it together.

"*Yes*, worries," Danny muttered. "Plenty of worries, and no time for them. Just a bloody waste of energy." Petting Tee-Tee and frowning at Rack.

"Best if your lot left now," Alice said. "It really isn't safe."

"I'm not going anywhere," Danny said, again to Rack's surprise. "And wherever Jonathan goes, that's where I'll be, along with Tee-Tee."

"You think we can't hack it?" Rack asked Alice, his hackles up at the thought, even though of course he didn't want anything to do with this madness. But reflexive, because Danny's glance at Alice meant his sister was wary of the woman.

"I'm not paid to be a babysitter," Alice said. "And I still think Jonathan should just give me the Wobble, but he won't."

"For god's sake, then," Rack said to Jonathan, "just give her the stupid Wobble thingy and let her get on with her LARP elsewhere."

"It's not a LARP!" Jonathan and Danny shouted at the same time.

"Quite the duet," Rack said. "How long did you spend practicing?" He folded his arms.

They knew whenever he folded his arms he was digging in his heels. An impasse, and Rack was perfectly comfortable letting the silence build while he fumed.

Except Alice, who'd left Rack feeling perversely insulted when she sneered at the others.

"A bloody show-and-tell is a waste of time," he said.

"Rack, we can't be sure the wraith you saw didn't somehow report back before the bear destroyed it," Alice said, still pressing her point. "Crowley might now know about this place. Or any number of powerful magicians could have felt the echo of our passage, because of the Emissary hitching a ride. I think we must expect company sooner rather than later."

How did this stranger presume to use "we," a pronoun that had until just then applied only to Rack, Jonathan, and Danny? Worse, why did Danny acquiesce to it so easily? Why was she nodding now, as if what Alice said made all the sense in the world? While Jonathan remained shadowy, checked-out, as if his mind was elsewhere?

Except now Jonathan turned to him and said, and there was an underlying anguish to the words, "*Rack*, can you honestly see all of this—see *that*"—pointing to the dead monster—"and not believe what we're telling you? Even if just for your own safety. Believe me, I'd rather you were completely out of the picture. At least acknowledge the danger and *get clear* of it. Please."

The weight of that on Rack's shoulders was as intolerable as the idea that they were telling the truth, and as intolerable as both things the idea that just as they had gotten started on the mansion . . . their idyllic summer holiday cataloging and sorting and living in a bubble of time and space was over.

Alice was at Jonathan again, since Rack was being stubborn: "Either come with or give me the Wobble but enough with trying to convince the unconvinced."

"If it's not real, what does it matter?" Jonathan asked Rack, ignoring Alice. "If nothing is going on here, let's test it. You and me, we'll poke a head through one of those doors and it'll lead to a closet or the backyard, and that'll be the end of it."

"I don't know, Jonathan," Rack said, slumping onto the center couch that encircled the bizarre lamppost that ended in a peculiar clock. "I just don't know."

But Danny had reached the end of her tether, and exploded on him.

"Rack! You are going to get on-side! You're part of this team, and you are going to be a team player if I have to kick you in the buttocks! We are going to help Jonathan because even if it lands us in a pickle, he'd do the same for us. So you are going to suck it up and do what has to be done!"

It all came out in a kind of ragged shout and made a bear gun seem positively normal. But her speech did not impress. Something still nagged at Rack.

"I don't buy it, Danny. I just don't. Why in the blazes are you so *calm* about all of this?"

"Why are you being so hysterical?" Danny countered.

"I'm being reasonable, under the circumstances. But you, and your damn rat . . . something's fishy. You've got a secret, something you're not telling me."

"That seems paranoid," Jonathan said.

Rack pointed a finger at Jonathan. "You. Be quiet. This isn't about you, Johnny Lamb. This is between me and my sister."

Danny said something so rude Rack couldn't believe she knew the words. Then, even more unbelievable, she aimed the musket at him and pulled the trigger.

The musket must've been near-empty. Just a few sad-looking ghost hamsters dribbled out across Rack's feet, chittered a bit in confusion, and then began to vanish into thin air. Until only one was left, staggering upright on two legs like a person. Then even it was gone.

Rack should have flinched, but he didn't. Couldn't help meeting Danny's half smile with his own, and then hated that he'd done that. Rack liked the hamsters. He really did not want to like the hamsters. Somehow it undermined his whole argument, made him just want to put it all behind them.

But the smile left his face as soon as Danny spoke again.

"I've been there, Rack. I've *been* to Aurora, more than once. I know that everything they're telling you is true and we need to *help*. We need to go to Aurora, and we need to find the Golden Sphere and do our part to save the world. Both worlds."

Chapter Nineteen

LOONS APPRECIATE FIREFLIES

"Anyone who does not have proper papers to hand to any representative of his Lord High Emperor Crowley shall, at the discretion of the representative, be whipped until dead or whipped into whatever physical state shall most please the representative. Food shall henceforth be rationed. All such rules, however, shall not apply to families of any men or women who join the new Army of the People that the Lord Emperor has formed to fight infidels of all sorts."

—From Part II of Lord Crowley's Final Decree, distributed in peculiar and strange ways, at night, by Emissaries, demi-mages, and bats

By the time Crowley had finished exhorting his particular masses to glory and returned alone to the cathedral and the All-Seeing Eye, scene of the bomb attack, night had fallen. He was sore in every muscle and fading, but he could rest now with a sense of accomplishment. His ire had cooled to a brittle clarity.

Thankfully, his janitorial minions had removed all evidence of the bomb attack from the cathedral, and soon enough a good long hot shower would remove all evidence of it from his person.

Groaning, Crowley lowered himself to the cold, hard marble floor beside the All-Seeing Eye and stared up at the ceiling. Notre Dame had a pretty ceiling, he'd give the French that. It had the appearance of the long spine of a whale, in a good way. But much prettier now that he'd replaced the rich blues with crimson and swapped out the gold of the arches with black. Black and red, with orange highlights: gorgeous! Hell in a handbasket! Flames eternal!

He'd miss the cathedral, but raining down destructive magic from afar was like relying on the air force, not that Aurora had one, more's the pity. Eventually, you had to send in the ground troops, put in a personal appearance. And better Prague in a specially made war elephant than England in the Burrower. The defenses on the land bridge to England that Verne and Laudinum X must assault were a magical minefield. Unpredictable to the extreme.

A burble and then a chuckle from the top of the pedestal signaled that Napoleon had awoken from one of his stupors; no doubt he had drooled all over the side of that classic Doric column. The drool of a former emperor; some might consider that as valuable as a relic . . .

"Hallo down there," Napoleon called out. "Hallo, Lord Emperor Crowley. Do I espy you dead upon the marble? Or do you simply abase yourself before a higher authority, one that resides in splendor atop this pedestal?"

"Shut up shut up shut up," Crowley said. It had been a long week. He had hoped that in the gathering gloom he might rest upon the cool hard marble and think not a single thought.

But Napoleon was not about to shut up and Crowley hadn't the energy to spend the fifteen minutes binding him with a spell to do it for him.

"The brains and bowels of your garbage expert have not been cleaned from my lower pedestal," Napoleon complained. "It is most unhygienic and foul. This place is not a battlefield."

"Isn't it?" Crowley folded his hands across his chest. A proper sarcophagal position might lend to him the patience of the pharaohs who, as they slept through an eternal night of the soul in a palatial coffin, must surely still endure any number of ridiculous comments from tourists, well-wishers, true believers, and former generals.

"You are a vainglorious homicidal maniac, Crowley. But most of all you are a filthy pig."

"And you are a three-time failed hopped-up little leprechaun of a military commander and prized wanker."

"Prized wanker?" A puzzled silence. No doubt that was harder without a body.

"It is hard being a ruler of men," Crowley said.

"Try being a ruler of talking vegetables, too."

But Crowley's thoughts had turned to Wretch, waiting back in Crowley's quarters. Wretch, waiting to do the things—the terrible things—required so that Crowley could continue to rule over his empire. So terrible and lengthy, performed nightly, yet Crowley could never recall in the morning what had happened, would scritch the itch atop his head and sit up in bed feeling both more and less like himself than the day before.

All Crowley really remembered was that he never looked into Wretch's eyes the entire time. He'd found it was like looking into twin dark suns and there was a lurch and sense of nausea, of falling, that was unbecoming the ruler of an empire. As unbecoming was the scrabbling panic when he must again submit to Wretch.

Napoleon had continued on without him, as usual. "Indeed, try living as an undead head with a stump that itches—on a pedestal that some tyrant, some *prized wanker*, can on any whim move up and down, up and down, up and down, up and—"

"You asked for the damn pedestal," Crowley said. "Besides, you have the override."

Although Crowley knew that Napoleon didn't like using it, since that meant the undignified sight of him sticking out his tongue to move the little red lever located right in front of his mouth up or down.

Silence again.

And then there was this latest report, about the grandson of the noted dead pain-in-the-ass Dr. Lambshead, with his Order and their snooze-fest of rules involving the doors. The Ancient Marinator. The famous borer-to-death. They had news of the doctor's grandson glimpsed in Aurora, just for a moment. A bit player or a more serious problem?

Crowley tried to let it go, all of it go, as the darkness deepened, and all around the marble took on hues and shadows that made it more beautiful still.

"It does have an excellent view," Napoleon admitted finally. "I saw the entire explosion entertainment as if it had been staged for me and me alone."

"Oh, you were awake?"

"Yes, despite your shoddy spell, and it was an excellent show. So much human debris! As bad as a direct shot with a cannon. And so heroic, your Wretch, to throw himself in front of your exalted person, your sacred body."

"He did save my life."

"Indeed, he did," and now Crowley could see Napoleon's head peering over the side at him, in an unnerving way. "Truly, Wretch's reflexes were so excellent he almost might seem to have been moving to save you *before* Dupin so ignobly blew up."

Quiet again, except, perhaps, for a faint chittering of bats and the echo of a thousand babies screaming, except that was actually the goats again.

High up near the ceiling, Crowley saw tiny floating lights, blinking on and off.

"What are those?"

"Oh, those," Napoleon said, in a reverential tone. "Those are fireflies. It is spring, you know, and they come out to mate, and some fly into the cathedral and gather up there and make their light. I watch them often . . . although there have been fewer of late. They fly down the hole for my pedestal and hover over the war map and disappear. For some reason."

The fireflies were like tiny worlds unto themselves, an elegant rogue cosmos. He could lie here forever watching them and never have to spare a thought for Wretch at all. Except he kept seeing Dupin's face coming apart.

Was it foolishness on Crowley's part, that he had, every once in a long while, believed Dupin might become his comrade, his confidante? Yes, and delusional, too.

None of his old friends had come over to Aurora with him, and he had only the vaguest memory of how he had arrived here, what he had done in the early days, beyond killing his not-father, to take control. Dreams of blood and fire and raising demons that could not be put back. Not really.

"We shall have to go soon, Napoleon," he said. "Sooner than I should like."

He imagined that Napoleon up on the pedestal was, best as he could, nodding sagely, commiserating with the lonely life that great men must lead for the sake of immortality.

Yet what Napoleon said, in a sympathetic voice, had nothing to do with Prague or England.

"The Golden Sphere still eludes you. Still you cannot grasp what you seek. Still it is always ahead of you, in the dark, in the light. Sometimes you can see it, or think you do, but then it's gone again. Ever it eludes. And still you pursue it. Ever you pursue it, for you have no other choice."

"Thanks, soothsayer," Crowley growled, but not without the affection that one sometimes bequeaths upon a vanquished foe.

Crowley lay there for a few minutes more, and, as if they had reached an unspoken cease-fire, Napoleon remained silent so Crowley could watch the fireflies and appreciate the cold marble against his back.

But inside Crowley the fireflies helped not at all and he was screaming, "Where the *living fireballs* is that goddamn Golden Sphere?"

If only because if he should find It, these nightly sessions with Wretch would no longer be necessary.

None of it would be necessary, not even bloody Napoleon pontificating from a pedestal.

Chapter Twenty

NOT A MARBLE

"I am a pretty bauble. I am a pretty, pretty bauble," the Golden Sphere burbled to itself, floating atop a mound of unconscious bodies, some of them clearly buffeted about the head. They had been playing marbles for small sums of money on the taverna floor a mere half hour before. "Pretty because I am made to be pretty. Bauble because I am valuable. Don't you know I'm valuable?"

The last man in the taverna cowered in the corner. All the benches had been overturned, and the chairs turned to kindling, and the fire in the fireplace blown out so quickly there was no lingering smoke, as if even the embers were afraid.

"Leave. Take the money behind the bar and leave."

"Oh, dear man, would you let me? Could I? Certainly, gold if there be gold is shiny, and I am a Golden Sphere after all. You might believe there to be an affinity, even if all that is gold is not good."

"I am sorry that they panicked. No harm was meant to—"

"Intent!" the Golden Sphere squealed. "Intent! It is overrated to be intentional. You were about to use me as you would a common marble, and after I twice rolled across the floor away from you—all of you. Did you not see *my* intent? My intent was clear, and yet it meant nothing to you. Soon enough I would have cracked up against other marbles that were actually marbles even though I am not in fact a marble and am indestructible, as you can well see now, and in fact the most proud and glorious creation of the Builders and John Dee, who though he may be dead across the world-lines is forever alive within me. Sir! Sir?"

But the man had fainted dead away.

No matter—the Golden Sphere happily nattered on with its monologue for many more minutes. There was, after all, a transition period between marble and boulder sizes that required It to be at rest. Yet the circuitry, the gears, of its mind required that It discharge thought, that It *do* something. Especially in the aftermath of an invigorating fight.

So that at rest, the Golden Sphere became more talkative, might even seem a little drunk. But mostly It spoke along intoxicating philosophical lines, although the Golden Sphere, if cornered—in other than a marble-to-marble clack—would admit It knew little formally of John Dee's views. The influence of Dee was more by a kind of mechanical osmosis, the way in which the very act of creation had caused the Golden Sphere to veer into certain circuits and patterns.

Not to mention that hidden in its very core was a miniature map of all the universes, all the doors, and some rudimentary knowledge of the Builders' intent. Few else had that, and it had cost John Dee his sanity and his life. Which might have been why the Golden Sphere held forth on the subject so frequently—or at least as frequently as this new adventure of hiding and being hidden allowed for. Why, it felt quite liberating to have given that lecture to the man who was now unconscious. It felt like being let out of a cage. Perhaps there was a lecture circuit It could undertake, given the right credentials. Once It was no longer on the run and in hiding. Some honorary degree It could award itself, to establish bona fides.

The Golden Sphere also felt It needed minions; "muscle," some called it. The Golden Sphere had hoped before its marble incarnation to acquire said minion muscle among the mutated wall lizards common in these parts, sometimes called "ruin lizards." Due to circumstances beyond their control, the wall lizards had been transformed by rogue magic into ten-foot-tall mega-lizards that walked on their hind legs, had rudimentary speech, and although not good at cocktail parties also were no longer good at climbing walls.

This sudden lack had apparently created a terrible hostility toward all life within now abnormally large brains and enraged hearts, for four ruin lizards of this particular varietal had set upon the Golden Sphere and It had had to resort to some tricks learned while living inside a pinball machine some decades ago. Needless to say, the ruin lizards had never played pinball before—and would now, sadly, never have the opportunity. Yet the Golden Sphere still held out hope that appropriate lizard-minion muscle might be found.

"But now, my good man," the Golden Sphere told the slumped form ten minutes later, abbreviating a rant on Kant, "I must avaunt. That means I have to go—leave. As much as I've enjoyed our conversation, I am now a most conspicuous size and although the mess that awaits outside is more than enough camouflage and cover, I'd best not linger, for I would hate to have to snuff the brains of any more flesh-cogs. It is not a good look on you, and you seem to not have backup minds in your fingertips or toes or lungs or anywhere else that might be useful. Indeed, why, given the humanoid form, your brains are in such an obvious position might explain why you still know so little about worlds and about doors. A shame, such an awful shame."

During its lecture, It had switched from Italian to Polish to Russian to any number of more esoteric languages, including birdcalls, and the subsonic shrieking of slime molds, although none of that had been much appreciated by the unconscious man. Above all else, the Golden Sphere valued variety, not just for disguise, but for entertainment purposes.

But it was mostly for the Golden Sphere's own benefit. After all, if you didn't keep on your toes, or in this case on your spinning globe of gold, you might wind up feeling lonely, given It was the sole member of its species, and some might even dispute that the Golden Sphere was a person rather than a puppet.

"Toodles, now," the Golden Sphere said. "Out I go into the supernal supernatural nuclear sunset."

And, indeed, although the "nuclear" was figurative, the Golden Sphere did float out into a supernatural nuclear sunset through the tavern doors. Beyond the world of the taverna lay a far-different land, one the men had been trying to forget by immersing themselves in the ill-fated marble game.

For Crowley had rained down spells beyond measure upon Rome, trashing the Holy See, and in combination with turning the Italian mages' own magic against them, created a maelstrom of tangled magic that infected the ruined church tanks and smashed lorries and buildings beyond the tavern door, and in the process lent the sunset a gorgeous orange-neon-green beauty.

"A mess. Such a messy mess." Made by wretched messlings. Yes, that was a good term for human beings. *Messlings*.

Yet one of those messlings had the power to bind It and another a cage to house It. Shudder-inducing to think of.

The Golden Sphere wrapped all the colors around It, became invisible against that backdrop, and spun high—out across the destroyed city of Rome, to revel in the freedom of being a boulder that could think and that could fly. All whilst singing to itself:

> *Sing ho! for a brave an' a gallant ship*
> *An' a fast an' fav'rin' breeze,*
> *Wi' a bully crew an' a cap'n too*
> *To carry me over the seas;*
> *To carry me over the seas, me boys.*
> *Me boys me boys me boys.*
> *Me marble me garble me barble.*

It had been alive for centuries now, but still, beyond monologues and soliloquies, the Golden Sphere liked nothing better than the feel of the atoms of the wind flowing through the atoms of its intricate nano-parts.

For a time, the Golden Sphere could almost feel as if It weighed nothing at all.

Part III

THE LEAP

❧

"What in the name of all that's holy was that?"

Chapter Twenty-One

A ROGUE SISTER-BLISTER

The row at Dr. Lambshead's mansion between Rack and his sister became epic once Danny had dropped her bombshell. Even Alice stepped aside, leaving them alone to sort through the wreckage.

For his sins, Jonathan tried to mediate, during a break in the action.

"She's the same person she was an hour ago," Jonathan said. "The *exact same person*." Except she wasn't. Except she was. Jonathan hardly felt like *him*self anymore, for that matter.

"No," Rack said. "She's an effigy, a doppelgänger, a total cipher. Where's my real sister? Has someone kidnapped her?"

"I'm *not* a cipher," Danny said. "I'm *not* an effigy. I'm *not* a freaking doppelgänger! But you're definitely a tw—"

"Well, you're something else, all right. And you, Jonathan"—Rack circling back to an argument fresh half an hour before—"this means your friendship with Danny is a sham."

Jonathan sighed. It wasn't that he didn't sympathize, didn't understand. He did. But perhaps he was just more practical, or didn't see it in black and white. Especially given the enormity of Alice's revelations.

"What about my friendship with you?" he asked Rack.

"Well, that's genuine, of course. I didn't know anything about this." Except he hadn't shared parts of Dr. Lambshead's memorized letter with Rack, but certainly didn't think Rack would have anything but a low opinion of "bird children."

"How can I be sure of that?"

"I vouch for it."

"How about you, Danny? Is your family a sham now? Is Rack no longer your brother?"

"My family is *not* a sham," Danny said through clenched teeth. "Rack will always be my brother."

"Rack, you really didn't have a clue? Not a single clue?"

Rack's response was thunderous, and no amount of capital letters or exclamation points could capture its volume or anger.

"That my sister was a member of a secret society devoted to guarding doors to other versions of Earth! No, I didn't have a clue."

"Oh, give it a rest," Danny said. "It's not like I know much at all. I only went across a few times as a child. You hadn't joined the family yet. Daddy said not to tell you, to keep you safe, and Mummy agreed, and I did as they said. And he's dead now and he can't explain anything and she's dead, too, and can't be reached, either. I just did what I was told. Which was that Jonathan was a friend of the family. To keep an eye on him. Make friends if you can."

This was as agitated as Jonathan had seen Danny, and it bothered him. He hadn't realized how much he'd relied on her the past year to be a rock. Good old dependable Danny. The direct one, the one who told it like she saw it.

"That's supposed to make it all right? You did what you were told?"

"Seemed like the best call at the time," Danny muttered, looking at the ground. "I stand by it."

"The best call at the time," Rack echoed. "You stand by it. And *you*"—turning on Jonathan as if trapped between the two of them—"are you a zombie? You act as if this is all perfectly normal."

Jonathan took a breath, tried to think of bunnies cavorting in a meadow. No hawks overhead, just blue sky.

"It was very clear to me that someone had told you or Danny or both of you to take me under your wing. For all I knew it was the headmaster at Poxforth. I didn't think much about it."

The fact was, he hadn't examined it too closely, because he hadn't wanted a real guardian.

"I didn't know it had to do with any of this, because I didn't *know* about this. But I knew I didn't meet Danny by chance—it was too clearly a setup. But I didn't mind. Do you know why? Because after that first get-together, it didn't feel false. It didn't feel forced. If it had, I'd have dropped both of you loons like hot potatoes.

"So, no, Rack, it doesn't matter as much to me as it does to you. Although I understand why you feel betrayed. But she's still your sister. She's Danny, Rack. You know Danny. I know Danny. She's a straight shooter. She didn't hide what she knew when the time came. She told us."

No doubt there was more she needed to tell them, about why Rack was to be kept well clear, in her own time. But now wasn't the time to push her—or point that out. But other parts of Jonathan's world would begin to fall apart if he started down the path of not trusting Danny.

"Not to mention this ridiculous story," Rack said, shifting the goalposts and returning to his other objection, "about another world."

"Are you afraid it's true or that it's not true?" Danny asked. "Because all we need do is walk through a door to prove it. You can't have it both ways. Either I'm a nutter along with Jonathan or I betrayed you in some way that's more than make-believe. Which is it?"

Jonathan winced; Rack was speechless. But it was still pure Danny. Go straight for the goal, defenders draped off her, legs churning grass to mud.

"You're confusing me now, on purpose," Rack said.

"Ask Jonathan why he's going to go with this Alice. Oh, wait—he's already told you. Because it's *important*."

"As you've said." Rack turned on Jonathan again. "But just how important is it?"

"That's part of it."

"What's the other part?"

Jonathan shrugged, opened his mouth, thought better of it, said nothing. Started again, stopped, then dropped his arms to his sides in surrender.

"Because there's *nothing* for me here. Not really. I could dress it up any which way—say it's what Dr. Lambshead would have wanted, perhaps. Parrot something Alice's said about the peril to the world. But the truth is, my mother's dead, Dr. Lambshead is dead, and I'm stuck in a house full of ghosts and piles of useless junk. And Stimply's informed me I'm bankrupt and have to sell everything in the mansion anyway. I've nothing at all, *nothing* to lose."

The kicker was he *wanted* to go on this adventure or misadventure, however it turned out. Not just because, as Danny thought, it was the right thing to do. But also to learn more about what his family had been, at least. He'd been trying to forget he had a father, but it never really worked.

"Sob story told to another sob story," Rack said, and rightly so. But also not said without some empathy.

Because they were truly all friends. Because R & D, even at each other's throats, were fundamentally good-hearted people, and now they were thinking of Jonathan's situation, not their own. At least for that moment.

"Which is also why you shouldn't go with me." As desperately as he wanted them to, he proceeded to take that opportunity to underline and underscore why they shouldn't come along. Circled it in red pen and drew green arrows pointing at the circle. Then he took the whole thing and had it embossed and tattooed on their foreheads.

But it didn't make a difference. In the end, his obstinance fueled their own. Despite their squabble. Despite Alice's protests when she caught wind of this development—that not only wouldn't Jonathan relinquish the Wobble, but she'd have three hangers-on to deal with, not one.

Then came the moment Danny folded her arms, which meant it was over. She was adamant: She was going with Jonathan, and if they tried to ditch her in the doors, then she'd just get lost.

Which only made Rack resolute, as if chained to his sister as she jumped off a cliff. It was all foolishness and betrayal—a huge mess, in Rack's opinion—but if Danny went, "I go, too." Besides, it was "all a crock" and no doubt all that lay behind the next door in this weird haunted mansion was "a broom closet."

Instead, as it turned out, what lay behind that door was a men's room on a speeding train.

Jonathan wondered if Rack would've been so contrarian and yet keen if he'd known that in advance.

Chapter Twenty-Two

DAMN THAT SPECK!

"Kill all creatures and deliver them to me! All garbage must be killed, too! All the wretched of the Earth must suffer me."

—From Part III of Lord Crowley's Final Decree, never delivered to the populace

Night in the Notre Dame cathedral, standing next to the All-Seeing Eye. Another long day for Crowley, but not yet over. There now resided a Golden Speck trapped under the glass of a terrarium for ice frogs gifted to him by a terrified potentate from the Siberian Federation. Speck, fleck, dreck. The Golden Sphere's spy.

Crowley had long ago consigned the frogs to the war effort, sent the potentate packing without a head, and the terrarium had just been lying there in a corner next to his Wrath Throne for months. Now it sat on the broad edge of the All-Seeing Eye while above, Napoleon's head on the pedestal snored more like a whispering scream.

"Do you think it can hear us?" Crowley observed the Speck from one side, Wretch from the other, Wretch's slit-red eye distorted through the glass. He wondered if his own bloodshot orb was as disturbing to Wretch. He bloody well hoped so.

"It's just a Speck," Wretch said with an annoying lack of ceremony. "A smidgeon. A mote. A mite. No, it can't, my lord. Hasn't the powers of the parent. Pale reflection."

Wretch's form was often now larger and yet more amorphous and he took up more space, so that he seemed to ooze and creep around the side of the All-Seeing Eye, slap disconcertingly into Crowley's personal area. Which he defined as the three feet in all directions that should be free of other people. Perhaps five or ten when he ruled all the worlds.

"The infernal thing has been listening, watching this entire time." Crowley indignant. Spying was for him, not other people. He felt violated. Not, perhaps, violated like a cavern full of goats screaming like babies, but it was the same general principle.

They had discovered the Speck whilst packing up the pieces of the map of Europe on the level below, intending to reassemble it in the monstrously huge mecha-elephant that would serve as Crowley's command center during the coming war. The Speck had sought refuge among a clump of unauthorized dandelions, which had already been disposed of.

"There are many infernal things listening throughout the universe," Wretch said with or without cryptic intent. "Yet whatever it might have relayed to the Golden Sphere, what use could it have been? We have the thing trapped."

"I'm blocking it now," Crowley said. "I'm blocking it. I have it blocked. It shall consider itself *blocked*."

"Very good, Emperor."

Yet did not that of itself tell the Golden Sphere something, that it could not speak to its beloved Speck? Perhaps Crowley shouldn't have blocked the Speck. Perhaps he should instead have staged elaborate fake dramas for the Speck, fed it misinformation. Except now it was too late!

"I shall create tiny golem Crowleys. I shall deploy them across Europe, and they shall report to me nightly."

"I would advise against that as a waste of your magical energies. I would advise you act on what we've learned from it and let the Burrower deal with England while we continue with the plan to crush Prague with all your remaining armies."

For, under the force of Wretch's alchemical questioning, the Speck had revealed—in a screechy, squealing language only Wretch could understand—the exhilarating yet disturbing news that the Golden Sphere was headed to Prague.

The Speck had only lapsed into English once, in response to a threat from Wretch: "You *should* kill me. Go ahead, kill me! Keeeeel meeeee dead as a bedbug in your own master's bed. Kill me, bedbug boy. I'll mess with your head. I'll make you wrestle with angels and with demons and, for kicks, with *el luchadore*."

"My lord, if I may, would now be a good time to approve the final adjustments?"

Crowley turned and stared at the man. Engrossed as he was with the Speck, he had forgotten the engineers standing there, below the dais of the All-Seeing Eye.

The little group of annoyances circled the main annoyance, the one who had spoken: Verne's replacement, Carl Roman Abt, whom Crowley had kidnapped to build his new and improved giant mecha-elephant. All the annoyances were dressed in white laboratory garb, as if that would impress Crowley any more than it had with the last engineers.

On a rickety wooden table, Abt had set up a scale-model cross section of the elephant's hindquarters, which would feature Crowley's rooms, among other facilities.

"My lord," Abt said, "it is just a matter of the, um, your proposed hole beneath the elephant's tail and the tube leading from the hole to your quarters."

Crowley felt his heart rate increase.

"Chute, Carl," Crowley said. "It is an exit and a chute. As I keep telling you. Carl. And you must make the exit and entrance to the chute larger."

"Technically, you are requesting a butthole," Abt said, resolute.

"No, I am not."

"I mean, Lord Emperor," Abt said in a cold voice, "in the sense of the elephant's anatomy. The elephant, from the outside, would look . . . peculiar . . . with an enormous butthole under a tiny tail. I'm not sure how one goes about disguising a huge butthole, which is also a security risk."

"Stop saying '*butthole*.'"

Abt ignored him. "So, anyway, my lord, we have this butthole problem . . ."

"It's *not* a butthole. It's an escape hatch. NOT A BUTTHOLE. What is *wrong* with you?"

Abt was a tall baldy, and Crowley could judge the man's stress level with ease: If frightened or threatened, he could turn a violent shade of pink starting at the bottom of the neck and all the way up to the top of his head. At the moment, the hourglass of his stress wasn't even quarter full. Perhaps because he had cancer, which would soon put him beyond Crowley's dominion.

"Yes, quite, my lord," Abt said. "But we have only just solved the problems of the interior moat for the salamanders. This new task will cause delay—we need more aluminum to line the chute—and also we would then have to make the cook's quarters into the size of a triangular broom closet. Can you find a triangular cook?"

This was the fifth set of engineers, and time was running out. Crowley willed himself to be merciful, that he might not smite the man or turn him into a bat.

"The cook can sleep standing up. We will get a cook who *likes* to sleep standing up . . . and at an angle. And you can, I don't know, put a flap over the butt—the exit. Just *get it done* however expedient—and remove yourself from my sight!"

The scale model burst into flame. For once, there was no editorializing from Wretch about impulsiveness.

Abt hurried from the cathedral, followed by the others, one brave enough to snatch the model and try to put it out with his lab coat as they scurried forth.

"Let it burn, you monkey's ass!" Crowley shouted and set the man's hair on fire.

When Crowley wanted something to burn, others should allow it to do so. That was his motto. Or one of them.

Afterward, Crowley looked once more at the Speck, golden under the flame-lights he had conjured up to float above them, not trusting in mundane chandeliers or candles.

The Speck bounced up and down within the dome, but could not break free. Crowley's magic constrained it. As it bloody well should. If Crowley could not contain a fey Speck, perhaps he should just pack it all in and, incognito, go teach alchemy at some English private school.

Still, there was a faint scent of burnt thyme and vinegar, byproduct of the friction between Crowley's will and the intentions of the Speck, and this made him nervous. Perhaps more than nervous. Something that had been rising within him began to spill out, could not contain it any more than Crowley could continue to contain his revulsion at the ongoing nightly sessions with Wretch in his quarters. Each time, along with the amnesia, he felt weakened even as strengthened, and his mind faltered, heart skipped a beat.

A panic spiraled through Crowley, leapt out of his mouth.

"What if I was *meant* to find it, Wretch? What if this is the trap? The Golden Sphere means to trap me as I have trapped this Speck. Served up under glass. With monstrosities of the Builders we cannot even imagine, Wretch, peering in at us? What if we are mere specks? Good lord, what if I believe I meant to use the Golden Sphere, but It always *meant* for me to think that? What if the Golden Sphere wanted to be here from the beginning, and we let It in?"

"Such a whimsical speculation, my lord," Wretch said. "You are a great teller of stories."

Yet wasn't it Wretch who had suggested to Crowley not a day ago that the Golden Sphere might, at some point, stand its ground and fight?

"And now that we have trapped the Speck, we have trapped ourselves and the Golden Sphere knows we will come to Prague and It knows something further we do not about that accursed magical city and if we venture forth from this, our beloved stronghold, the . . . the—"

"You truly need not worry, my exalted Lord Emperor. Indeed, possession of the Speck may allow us to strike at the Golden Sphere in ways it will not itself expect. The connection between them has snapped, but there is a . . . residue . . . across the dimensions that we can exploit."

What was Wretch babbling about now? Crowley hardly heard him, for the Speck danced most winsomely within the glass, and he had to wrest his gaze from that motion, almost but not quite hypnotized.

He drew back from the terrarium and the brink of the All-Seeing Eye.

"There! See! It almost had me. Even this facsimile, this nothing. A Speck in my eye. That mote there, that drifting darkness, did the Speck put it there? Have I been subverted to some cause not my own? How can we possibly leave this place and be certain we do not bring down our own destruction? Fixed in place like the All-Seeing Eye is best"—he lunged forward and gave the All-Seeing Eye a shove, only to find it wobbled, stepped back again—"and from here we can know better and know more. We must just be more diligent in our rooting out of spies."

Crowley meant to stop there, point made, but Wretch had an unconvinced look on his sorry excuse for a face, the massive batlike head turned sideways to stare at him. So he continued, more passionately.

"If what we require is to have every monkey we can procure grooming every goat and other war-factory animal for Specks to uncover the extent of the spying, and then special monkeys to groom those monkeys for their own hidden secret agents, and demi-mages to spend time first inspecting those special monkeys, we shall do it, by Satan's fiery tails! We shall never again have a Speck undo our planning, infiltrate our congress, make a mockery of us and our position. This Speck shall be the ignoble end of this matter.

"Why, I shall create a new category of spies, tiny, made by the best Swiss watchmakers, so small they cannot be seen by the naked eye, and those bacteria that the accursed enemy scientists are so fond of warning of shall be the goats to their elephant, the driving fodder force, and I shall cover the entire corpse of Europe with their seething invisible multitudes that there is no corner of the entire continent that can be hidden from us. Not a field in Spain nor a fjord in Norway. Not a drunken peasant spouting treason in a tavern in Prussia nor a chicken in Italy that walks funny for no reason. There shall be such a reckoning over this that—oof! Bloody—what the—"

Crowley found himself flung arse over torso, legs over arms, as Wretch grew mighty talons and yanked Crowley into the air by his shoulders, midspeech, with no word of explanation, just widdershins and shitbangles into the air, what was left of Crowley's dinner of fried bat hearts, blood gruel, and the spleens of baby mice shoved inside bloated rats and baked in earthen ovens for hours, just the way Wretch insisted Crowley liked it, nary a legume to be had . . . all of this looped down into the All-Seeing Eye to form a sardonic lifeline and then, as it fell away, a kind of goopy question mark in the pool as Wretch flapped enormous jet-black wings and carried Crowley from that place and out into the cold and garbage-stench-tinged night.

"I command you to put me down!" Crowley managed, but it came out in an almost silent croak as he realized were Wretch to obey he would surely at that moment fall to his death.

Still, Wretch, with his outsized ears, must have heard Crowley, for in reply he said, "Shut up. Shut up. Please, by all that is unholy, shut up. Just . . . shut up."

Some time later, after a bewildering rage and flap, hover and soar, through the night sky over Paris . . . after an upturn straight into the sky that had Crowley screaming in fright, then through a kind of patch of greater darkness in the heavens like a gate or hole, through which they fled like water down a drain . . . sometime later they were back in the place where Crowley had found Wretch, or Wretch had found Crowley. It was all jumbled and confused in his memory.

Wretch had set him down upon a blackened ridge overlooking the dark volcano belching lava. Usually he found Volcano Land eerie and beautiful. But not tonight. The place smelled of smoke and fire and rotting corpses.

He cowered there next to Wretch, who was so mighty now that he was more like an evil black dragon than a bat, his face wide and almost as if the Cheshire Cat had put a half-melted black mask over everything but its horrifying smile and pointed fangs.

After a time, Wretch said, "Do you remember this place?" His voice came out like a roar from the back of an endless cave.

"How could I forget?" Crowley said in a small voice. His bones ached, his skin recoiled—almost wanting to peel away from the heat—and his skull was crammed full of curled-up baby headaches.

"This is where I found you," Wretch said. "This is where I raised you up and brought you to Aurora. You seemed happy of the chance then."

"I was. I am." But was that how it had happened? Hadn't he been plucked from his own reality and brought to the volcano? By Wretch or someone else? Or had he gotten lost, wandered there of his own accord?

"Are you?"

"Yes."

"Yet you dither, my lord." No doubting the sarcasm in "my lord" now. "Yet you second-guess the best advice you receive. The advice of him who set you upon your throne."

Is that how Wretch saw it? But the magic had been Crowley's and Crowley's alone. Hadn't it?

"I am merely trying to be prudent."

Wretch stretched his face around in a terrifying manner, by extending his neck far enough over the edge of the ridge that he could look at Crowley from mere inches away. Those eyes were not catlike or batlike or any of the things Crowley had thought they were. The fangs that grew in that mouth had their own eyes, and farther inside that depth other creatures lurked, glowing faintly green and so hideous in form Crowley preferred to stare into the eyes that cut into his brain like curving serrated blades.

Crowley's brain had been searching for comparisons that comforted him, that made Wretch understandable, but Wretch was beyond any of those things. He was not satanic, in the sense that Crowley found the satanic familiar. His familiar was not, in fact, familiar.

Wretch curled one clammy hand around Crowley's neck, grabbed hold, hard. It felt as if someone was strangling him slowly with the remains of a dead octopus.

With an awful precision, Wretch plucked Crowley from his seat and dangled him over the edge of the volcano.

Where he struggled, legs kicking.

"Shall I leave you here? Shall I throw you in the volcano and start over with someone else? Would that be . . . prudent?"

"I would prefer you didn't," Crowley said in a small voice.

"Then you will continue the preparations to march on Prague. You will cease your endless dithering. You will cease your whining in general and about all things. You will understand that you are my puppet, and that I have my infernal eternal hand shoved very far up that puppet *butthole* of yours, and I shall ram that hand as fist up out through your mouth, pluck your sorry skull off your neck with my other hand, and leave your head on a spike for the Czech magicians to find and to have a jolly bonfire with if you continue to doubt yourself."

Wretch retracted his arm, placed Crowley, choking, back on his perch on the lip of the volcano.

"When you doubt yourself, you doubt me. Don't doubt that, Crowley."

"I understand," Crowley said, preferring now to stare at the volcano rather than any part of Wretch. Even though it appeared the lava was made of fountains of coagulating blood and still-living creatures screamed within those fountains. But it was more tolerable than Wretch in that moment.

"*Do* you truly understand?" Wretch said, and Crowley felt the power of Wretch's gaze upon him. As the black dragon grew ever larger and demonic, more malevolent than anything Crowley had ever envisioned.

He managed a nod even though his skin had gone cold and it felt as if all his internal organs now hung off the outside of him.

"I will go to Prague."

"Good Emperor. Very good Emperor."

Came a pat on the head more like a hammer blow. Three such pats, each more lingering than the last, as one might pat the head of a half-forgiven dog that had crapped on the rug.

Of all the indignities suffered that night, this was the one he could not forgive, would never forgive. A cold, simmering rage cut through his terror. He must rid himself of Wretch. Immediately. Even though he hadn't a clue yet how to do it. But it must be done.

"Endless are the worlds," Wretch said. "Endless, and as many doors as worlds, for you to rule. And you will rule."

As Crowley stared into the abyss of spewing lava, Wretch's grotesque talons again clamped onto his shoulder, cut into his skin, and the mighty leader of Aurora's Franco-Germanic Empire jerked and writhed in the embrace of a monster who soared like an angel up and out of Volcano Land, hopefully forever.

Chapter Twenty-Three
IF YOU DON'T JUMP, I PUSH YOU, I PUSH YOU HARD

"A train?" Rack asked, first to interpret the loose, jittery movement, the low scraping sound of wheels on the track.

"Yes, a bathroom, to your unspoken question, and, yes, a train," Alice replied. "And a train full of spies, to boot. Crowley's created a power vacuum in Rome, and enough chaos for almost anyone to operate—so they do. Now shut it and follow me."

Jonathan, for his part, had not expected the door from the haunted mansion would land them in the men's bathroom of a moving train, the urinal ripped out to make more space.

All but Alice stumbled, Jonathan's instinctual need not to touch the floor with his hands losing out to gravity, Danny also recoiling from the grout and the smell. Rack avoided this fate just barely because, out of necessity, he almost always kept his balance—and had brought a walking stick from the mansion to help.

Their only preamble from Alice, irritated at chaperoning not one but three "green gills," as she put it, was that Crowley had so "rubbished" Rome in magical terms that the doors there either were too unstable or his minions held them, so they could only use a door "to get close," after which Mamoud would meet up with them. Which had reassured Jonathan at the time, if meaningless to R & D, who had not met the man.

Even with the urinal ripped out, the men's room might as well have been a phone booth. They bumped asses and shoulders trying to gather up their backpacks full of supplies. Which, for Rack, included two extra of his special shoes, "because with my luck I'll need at least that many."

One good spill deserved another, the awkwardness of their arrival carrying over into the corridor, where they were immediately jostled by close-packed strangers, wearing different variations on their own clothes: the dark cold-weather slacks, shirts, and jackets scavenged from the mansion that Alice had said would suit the expedition best. Although Rack had insisted on wearing his standard ensemble, packing away his "emergency duds," as he put it.

The strangers had the look of being from several different countries, and their ensemble trended more toward ankle-length cloaks and the like. One, who Alice said was from the Democratic Republic of Mali, stared at him with a belligerence he was sure was earned in some general sense; the woman held her head high, shoulders back, and a colorful patterned fabric peeked out from beneath the cowl of her gray hood.

In such close quarters Jonathan almost fell, pinned between the woman from Mali and someone rough and grizzled who glared at him, but Rack clamped onto his hand and kept him up. All while Danny treated it like a scrum and even laughed with delight at being deposited on the floor of the corridor beyond, careful to shield Tee-Tee and keep her bear gun pointed muzzle-down.

Alice watched their ungainly attempts to right the ship with a scorn that wasn't fair. She no doubt had practice with this particular transit point, but Jonathan found it vanishing strange.

For one thing, the train was too quiet. As Alice led them forward, everyone was as silent as could be, even though so many seats were full— and it was clear from the darkness beyond the window panels that the train was running without exterior lights. At intervals, the moon peered in, framed by ragged branches or the husks of piles of ruined buildings. The only inside lights came from what appeared to be curled-up glow-worms in recessed circular ceiling fixtures more like cocoons.

Jonathan decided it was a once-posh train for the upper classes gone to rot and ruin. Cracked art-deco-style glass lampshades crouched on the corners of some of the full-on booths, with green dragonflies on them. Railings were rosewood, or something similar, inlaid with engravings long since plucked out. A rough animal scent rising from the scuffed and gouged rosewood floor made Jonathan wish he were taller.

The trend continued with torn upholstery and some seats missing entirely and—now he saw—the source of some of the cold: Some doors had been removed from their hinges and replaced with makeshift wood or tarp, insufficient to stop the wind from blasting in through cracks and gaps.

"How old is this train?" Jonathan whispered to Alice.

"Old enough," Alice whispered back. "It's not the age. It's that traffic on it has increased since Crowley sacked Rome and it must run at night and as silent as possible to avoid his attention. Some luck—that our enemy's turned his focus elsewhere for now."

Then to the group: "Keep up. Keep moving. There's an empty compartment near the front usually. No one likes to be near the front." In the tone of a classroom instructor leading a field trip of unruly children.

It was a solemn and subdued little group; Rack and Danny looked properly sober and alert. It was not a small thing to step into another world. Especially given increasing signs of recent violence in how a brace of booths resembled bombed-out parapets. Not to mention the eccentricity of the occupants.

One group of the silent anonymous passengers, this time in black cloaks, sat amid a garden, of all things, complete with small shrubs and trees, but also with some hot stones they huddled around, and ladled water onto so that steam rose in a way that Jonathan envied, given the chill. They had apparently staked a claim to one whole car and decided to seed it with reminders of home.

"Finnish contingent," Alice whispered. "Including some Laplanders. Ignore them. They're nature lovers and their ways are mysterious. Never tell a joke to a Finn and never discuss laundry and don't let them do magic tricks around you. You might find yourself in the wilderness of a sudden, talking to an unsympathetic reindeer, and wondering how you got there. They find that very funny in those parts, but I don't."

The example seemed very specific, and Jonathan wondered if this advice came from Alice's personal experience. He didn't much care for the generalization about an entire country, but, then, he wondered what Alice would say about the Brits on Aurora. Did they have their characteristic quirks?

Everywhere also people were exchanging what resembled perky greenleaf insects for goods or, perhaps, services. But he didn't ask Alice about that. It was too strange, and yet also clear: On Aurora, or at least on this train, a green-leaf insect was as good as money. Or perhaps money wasn't good here. He had yet to see any denominations; the closest thing had been a splayed-out deck of cards on an overturned bucket between two chairs, with—instead of jokers and jacks and kings and queens—a variety of strange animals, including some beast riding a rooster and a stately, well, marmot. Of course.

They reached their seats inside the train just as he was trying to make sense of looking into a hood and seeing first a swirling glimmer of dark lake water and then an owl's face—which suggested more complex disguises than boring old clothes—and then also what appeared to be a *tiny deer* flitting through the air, only to disappear the next instant, and where it had been the frowning face of yet another potential spy.

Clearly it must've been a hummingbird, but even so, what was a hummingbird doing on a train to Rome?

Thankfully, the compartment Alice led them to only fit four; no room for strangers. But Rack wouldn't sit next to Danny in the booth, so Jonathan sat with her, and the odd couple of Rack and Alice sat opposite.

Unthankfully, the window had been ripped out along with part of the wall to form a doorway covered by a tarp. Periodically, much to everyone's horror, people would enter from the corridor and throw themselves through the doorway and out into the night. One in particular Jonathan could have sworn became all limp cloak and then flew off into the trees.

To their credit, they all tried to remain calm. Except Rack.

"What in the hell is this?"

"The train doesn't make stops," Alice said. "Too dangerous. It's on a loop and runs only in the dead of night, and during the day it stops in the most wooded, most remote part of the track. To leave this train, you must throw yourself off."

"A one-way trip, then," Jonathan noted.

"Not exactly. You can get on in the woods, too. Find a way back through another door."

Neither of which was likely. So now Jonathan wondered what their exit point would be.

"How close does it get to Rome?" Danny asked, busy making sure Tee-Tee was settled in.

"Not nearly close enough," Alice said. "It'll be a trudge to where we're going. As I've said, Mamoud will meet us at the stop."

"You mean he'll be there to watch us fling ourselves out the door and into oblivion," Rack said.

At least he remembered who Mamoud was, even if Jonathan trying to explain had led to another disbelieving conversation, this time about the Republic and Spain.

Alice turned a sharp stare on Rack. "Just be thankful you're all still here." The stare turned into a wicked smile.

"Why wouldn't we be here?" Rack, defiantly sullen.

"Some fade right away. Poof! They're no more."

"What?" Rack again. They'd been informed about the fade back in the mansion, but Alice had made it seem a remote thing, nothing to worry about unless they stayed in Aurora for many months.

"Well, only a few. Less than a handful can't hack it. Turn into ghosts like that." A snap of Alice's fingers. A roguish look. She enjoyed frightening them, which is why Jonathan decided not to take the bait.

Yet another fellow traveler pushed past them, pulled the tarp aside, and plunged off into the night, with a subdued yell of "Hidey-hidey ho!" This one was pursued by a shimmer of sparks that zipped through the darkness, spiraling tight before disappearing.

"Bloody hell," Rack said, "bleedin' bloody double hell." Reduced to a string of curses aimed more at their general situation than Alice's withholding of information.

"Is there anything else we should know?" Jonathan asked, although he was certain no matter what she divulged, she'd always keep some secrets. Well, then, he would let parts of Dr. Lambshead's letter stay hidden for now, too. And keep the Wobble secure in the inside pocket of his jacket. A zipped pocket. If he'd had a small lock, he'd have added that, too.

"Not that I can think of. Just try to rest. We've a good hour left."

Two women, slight and almost elfin, entered the compartment, smiled at Danny and her rat, and stood at the exit doorway. One walked without aid and the other, leading the way with a light step, had a cane with a full cuff around the forearm. They'd taken off their cloaks and beneath wore overcoats, one a gorgeous light blue and the other purple. Their hair was done up and they both wore earrings. Their pockets overflowed with those odd green-leaf stick insects.

"We're going home," one said.

The other led her by the hand, and together they dropped off the side with a suddenness that had Jonathan gasping. Had they fallen onto the tracks, fallen under the wheels?

"Don't mind them," Alice said. "They're old forest folk. They shape-shifted the instant they left and burrowed deep. You wouldn't even recognize them anymore."

Rack dropped the pack he'd been hugging, slumped in his seat. "It's snowing now, too," he said, clearly to change the subject and not think about what they'd just seen. "It is snowing on the way to *Rome*. Is it that late in the year in this crap version of the world?"

"Yes, it's snowing!" Danny said with gusto, much to Rack's obvious disgust.

"Oh, please. If a bird shat on your shoulder, you'd find a way to turn it into a rainbow."

Even though, officially, Rack wasn't talking to Danny, Jonathan had noticed he was still sort of talking to Danny because it was difficult not to while on the same mission together.

The snow was the most normal thing about the landscape, to Jonathan. Outside the window it fell with that gentle drift that slowed the world down, that slowed his thoughts down.

"No, the snow's not normal," Alice said. "Crowley's sack of Rome has put a spanner in the natural order of things. It is autumn here, but it shouldn't be snowing here."

"And what're those, decorations?" Danny asked.

Referring to what resembled some prickly half-man creature riding a huge bird. They hung from the ceiling on hooks, like ornaments or deodorant trees.

"It's the Hedgehog Man, of course," Alice said. From the bright way she said it, it must be a fond memory. "During the holidays, the Hedgehog Man on a giant rooster delivers presents to all the children and we set off fireworks in thanks, because the rooster loves fireworks."

Anything that made Alice nicer should be explored further. Besides, he didn't remember Sarah telling him stories about a hedgehog man. Perhaps he'd been too young.

"Why the rooster?" Jonathan asked.

"*That's* your question?" This from Rack.

Alice shrugged. "That's just how it's always been. Of course, the Hedgehog Man couldn't possibly deliver all those presents; it's just a story that he does. But everyone loves the Hedgehog Man. Except when he's mad. No one likes it when he's mad, which is why you plant trees in the spring and dig tunnels in the summer. As payment for the presents. The Hedgehog Man loves trees."

Rack had blanched a bit, and Jonathan had to admit he felt a tad at sea. It hadn't quite dawned on Jonathan that Aurora might be very different from Earth in certain regards. Not in this way, at least.

"Imagine on Christmas Eve a bloody great hedgehog created by Dr. Moreau shoves itself down your chimney, eats all the cookies, drinks the milk, craps itself next to the tree. Not sure how children back home would react to that."

"The Hedgehog Man is *not* a burglar. The Hedgehog Man is always polite," Alice said. "He knocks on the front door on New Year's Eve, and when you answer at midnight he will always be gone, but your presents will be on the front step. Whether you've been naughty or nice." The clipped tone warned Rack not to step all over her holiday cheer.

"What about Santa Claus?" Danny asked in a distracted tone. Tee-Tee was still fussing about, wanting food pellets and extra attention.

"Santa Claus? Oh, I've heard of Santa Claus. Some of the Norweegies use him as a boogeyman to scare children into doing their chores. He's the one who can take away what the Hedgehog Man has given you."

"Are you joking?" Rack asked. "Please, tell me you're not joking."

"I tire of this interrogation," Alice said, and turned away from Rack.

Interesting. Perhaps Alice didn't know much about Earth. Shouldn't she know more? Unless her first trip to the mansion had been her first time on Earth? That would explain her bringing up the fade, which she could have withheld from them. It had been on her mind, or she had begun to fade a little already while on Earth.

Now that Tee-Tee had settled down, Danny roused herself and asked a series of very Danny-like questions.

From which they learned in quick succession that Alice had grown up poor in northern England, had little talent for magic herself, had been recruited for Her Majesty's secret services at a young age. She'd risen through the ranks through a willingness to take on any "shyte job" as she put it, and do it well. Until she'd been approached by the Order, and welcomed the opportunity to branch out.

All well and good, but when Danny asked about siblings, Alice abruptly shut up, overcome by a moodiness that forestalled any further personal questions.

So Jonathan jumped in with what he hoped was a bland inquiry into the subject of calendars.

"Not at all like on your Earth," Alice allowed. "We're not so formal."

They discovered that many Aurorians—Aurorines? Aurorites?—didn't much care what year it was, because every country and sometimes individual cities, towns, and villages had their own calendar system. Merchants and magicians were more attuned to seasons, sunup and sundown, and time of year, especially when those elements affected magic or crops. But watches were the same. The length of the days was the same. There was something to hang your hat on.

Circling back to a subject of personal interest, the England of Aurora, Danny asked a question that Alice answered with the surprising news, to say the least, that William the Conqueror had not conquered all, never managed even a fourth of the Doomsday Book. Instead, as a rumored "eel-o-thrope," William the Partial Conqueror had turned into a giant eel every month at the full moon, complicating his ability to lay waste to things and for people to take him and his rule seriously.

"I would've taken a giant eel with a crown seriously indeed!" Danny said.

Less surprising, to Jonathan at least, the Church of England coexisted with a very proper and ancient Pagan Ways & Means Committee.

"Pagans and Christ-eans haven't always gotten along. It's been a literal bloody mess at times, but with the wall the pagans built so long ago still defending England on the land bridge, how is any Christian supposed to deny the power of druidic belief? And so long as Christians can make magical little boxy gardens and do parlor-trick-type magic, we'll be invaluable, too."

"So you're Christian?" Danny asked. Last Jonathan had checked, Danny was an agnostic, Rack had an allergy to any organized religion, and Jonathan hadn't much thought about it, either way.

"I'm not religious," Alice said. "I just grew up that way."

"Don't believe in Christ, then?" Rack asked.

"Christ was likely a decent bloke, but miracles—those happen through magic every day in Aurora. Because of that, we should be a very rich world, if only everyone could get along."

"Did that Christ business end up the same way here?" Rack asked.

"Cheeky. Best I don't tell you. Might make you fade faster."

"Well," Danny said, "I suppose his followers' belief means even more here, if you see what I mean. Because it's just his teachings they've got."

Sarah had been an atheist, but it had become clearer and clearer that she believed in miracles of a sort. Who had created the universe? Who had created parallel worlds? The answer couldn't just be "the Builders," or, as in her story, "the Creators." That seemed a cop-out.

A torrent of something comfortingly familiar ran into the compartment, putting a halt to their conversation whilst side-stepping their massive feet.

Potatoes again. Potatoes with legs and arms and, yes, eyes, headed for the exit, while their leader held the tarp aside wide enough for others to jump out one by one. *Plop plop plop.*

Following closely behind, and not comforting or familiar, were half a dozen small figures disguised by cowls and robes. Jonathan caught a glimpse of huge bulgy eyes and somber fish mouths, greenish skin or scales, that made him think of mudskippers or salamanders. Then out into the night they went, extinguishing all further inquiry. *Plop plop plop.*

Just as quickly gone as there.

"What in the name of all that's holy was that?" Rack asked, but without much outrage this time. Another last straw, until the next last straw.

"Don't ask," Alice said. "Let's just say some get on the train without using a magic door. That lot for sure."

How quickly Jonathan had become used to the occurrence! A dozen wallabies being ridden by talking carrots and accompanied by an entourage of frogs dancing a waltz and singing show tunes could come through next and he might only be mildly amused.

Which was perhaps a good thing—the acclimation.

For while the potatoes had been plopping, the Swiss Army knife Dr. Lambshead had bequeathed him had begun to stir in his pocket, as if waking from a deep sleep.

ↄ๙

Perhaps some other sort of sixteen-year-old would have flinched or half risen from his seat in alarm. But Jonathan was quite used to stragglers and hitchhikers of various sorts while out on trails. Nor wanted the surly carrot from Spain scowling at him for being too easily astonished.

Jonathan delicately removed the knife from his trouser pocket. There, revealed, balancing on his palm: a lively little creature with an animated, friendly face. With its knife and corkscrew, toothpick and can opener, not to mention other appendages at the moment hidden, the creature always had some sort of legs to stand on, even if of uncertain purchase.

It resembled a compact wood-and-metal crab. The thing burbled in an affectionate way and began to sidle up Jonathan's arm, stopping at the crook of his elbow to send loving glances his way.

"Oh, how delightful!" This from Danny, while Rack recoiled, shook his head, gave Jonathan a stare as if this were all his fault. Which it was.

"Doesn't this world know a knife is supposed to remain absolutely still at all times?" Rack asked.

"What's his name?" Danny asked.

"Are you sure it's not a she?" Rack asked. "Are all knives automatically he?" At least he was closer to sort of talking to Danny now.

"No," Danny said, both she and the rat giving Rack a withering stare. "But this one is. You should call it Vorpal, Jonathan."

"Very appropriate," Jonathan said.

"A good friend for Tee-Tee," Danny said.

Rather optimistic, Jonathan thought. Especially given the look on the rat's face at the suggestion. Vorpal and Tee-Tee. Pals for life.

In the meantime, he gave Danny a glance that was meant to convey the uncomplicated message that she had to stop winding Rack up. He was, after all, the aggrieved party. Even if Jonathan really wished he'd snap out of his snit sooner than later.

"Such creatures can be fickle," Alice said. "Let's hope you don't get your throat cut."

Vorpal had begun to get agitated, so Jonathan cradled him in the crook of his arm, making the creature's purchase more secure. The little hooks it used tickled through his shirt.

"I'm quite taken with Vorpal," Jonathan said, lying. He was undecided about Vorpal, to be honest. He could tell its magic no doubt made it love whoever owned it. But, then, would you want an animated whirligig full of blades that *didn't* love you?

Alice gave him an appraising stare, as if recalculating his value. "Survives an Emissary. Now has a magic knife. You're full of surprises."

Anything further she might have said got lost in her surprise as Vorpal bristled with various esoteric tools, which stood up straight out of the top of its, for lack of a better term, carapace.

The woman from Mali had entered the compartment.

"A sentry, too," Alice said. "Impressive." While staring bullets at the intruder.

The woman stopped just short of the gauntlet of their assembled knees, the look on her face as if she were sucking on a lemon. An imperious manner, a simmering disdain.

"Alice. How terrible to see you again. If you could be trusted to take care of your own messes and not make them other people's, some of us would be home right now, instead of stuck in this malevolent backwater. Thanks for that." Each word of her English was like a good jab from a boxer—sharp, quick, demoralizing.

Before Alice could reply, the woman was through and past, jumping out the doorway like the others out into the darkness, the snow, the flickering reel of fast-passing trees.

"What was that about?" Jonathan asked Alice.

The reply came through clenched teeth, a refusal to look at him, as if ashamed. "They consider us quite backward, Europeans in general.

No magic schools of note. Chaos. Instability. Not to mention our poor handling of the Black Death back when we didn't believe in bacteria. Now we do, of course, and some even use it in their magic. And it's true we have our troubles, but we will catch up with the rest of the world. Someday."

Disconcerting. The shoe on the other foot, or another pair of feet altogether. The tarp-canvas doorway kept flapping now. The Mali woman hadn't latched it properly. Perhaps on purpose. The cold kept coming in, but none of them felt inclined to get up and fix it.

"But why is she here, so far from home?" It was the other question that bothered Jonathan. If this was a backwater, what did it matter what happened to Europe? From what any number of Poxforth instructors might call "the geopolitical angle."

Alice looked disinclined to answer at first, but when she did it was clear the answer frightened her.

"The energy Crowley is burning through is quite . . . immense. He's using ancient magical equations lost for centuries, which has the potential to change how magic works—forever. The scale of it is bewildering. It could blow up in his face at any time. That's the hope, anyway. But, of course, the whole world is intently interested in what happens here. Yet also wary of being drawn into the conflict. Thus, spies, insurgents, manipulation from afar."

"How is that even possible? To change magic forever?"

"I don't have the patience," Alice said. "Go read a book on it."

An intense shuddering came from the tracks, along with a singeing whine. Nothing at all could be seen outside, as if a void, the windows wide blank slabs of speed and indifference. Vorpal tensed up and made a sound like a steam whistle and withdrew every appendage except those he was using as legs.

"It's soonish, yeah?" Danny asked. "We need to get ready to jump?"

Alice was looking at Vorpal in a puzzled way. "We're not due to jump for another fifteen minutes."

A stickery hum and hiccup of the train's metal wheels. A change in the vibration, a surge in the coldness to the air.

"Are we really going to jump?" Rack asked. "That seems like a good way to lose a foot. Again. Or a head."

The dread came to Jonathan in the same instant, independent of Vorpal. A feeling. A certainty.

Something was coming down the tracks at them, and he could almost see it in his mind's eye. Reaching out for them.

"We need to jump—*now*," he said.

"It's not time yet," Alice said, but she didn't sound sure.

The train wobbled, wobbled worse.

"*Now*." Jonathan shoved Vorpal in his pocket, picked up his backpack.

But it was too late.

Came a monumental crack, farther up the tracks. A shudder that took their feet out from under them.

"Hold on to something!" Alice screamed from the floor.

An oddly hollow impact of crumpling metal, another crushing shudder.

The compartment twisted, buckling. Sent them sprawling, showered them with broken glass, even as it righted itself, clung obstinate to the tracks.

For only a second.

Rack was searching for something to hold on to. Danny lay still on the floor. Jonathan couldn't see Alice. He looked up from the floor, through the front window, saw with such awful clarity as the car in front of theirs was wrenched into the sky as if by a giant's hand—upended and tumbling backward over itself.

Jonathan reached out to Rack. So close. So far.

An impact that seemed to smash his bones to jelly.

Then their car was ripped away, into the night, off the tracks, throwing them this way and that—into one another, the floor, the ceiling, the floor, the ceiling. Was that Danny screaming? Or Rack? Or someone else.

He managed a handhold on a railing as the impact sent the car screeching toward the edge of the forest, the burning remains of the upturned car trailing behind them.

The seams at the corners peeled open as the joints popped free.

Rack was sprawled across the ceiling. Danny's hands around his waist trying to brace him, while Alice hung upside down, caught on something, bleeding from a forehead gash. Blood seeped across the side of Jonathan's face, and he had no idea how they'd banged heads, gotten close. Their packs had split open, clothes and supplies spilled everywhere.

Holes were forming under their feet. Jagged cracks filling with flames, as if ignited by the friction of their passage. The shrieking sound of distressed metal ripped through his eardrums.

"Enough!" Jonathan roared. "Enough!" He hadn't come this far to die before things even started.

Blink of an eye.

Trick of the light.

Something rising within Jonathan, something new and something old, out of anger and stubbornness and fear.

The glowworms detached from the cocoons of the light fixtures, drifted up from the floor.

Came a roaring silence.

Came a stillness full of urgency.

Came a dark voice inside, calming him.

The glowworms were still uncurling as if from deep slumber, floating above him in the night sky, through a gash in the floorboards. Cocooned in the warmth of his regard.

Enough.

As the train compartment around them burst apart in a torrent of flame.

Snap of the fingers. Blink of the eye. All the banal ways you could rationalize the impossible . . .

Just like that, they were all outside the burning train car, skidding and falling through clumps of snow, into a sprawled pile, with their backpacks. Jonathan staring up at the dark sky, the icy points of light beyond, exposed on open ground. The rhythm in his head, the signal that had been underlying everything, had come clear. For a moment, then eluded him again.

As a *pop-pop-pop* and gushing crackle of flame erupted from the remains of the train, the glinting silver Jonathan had glimpsed came clear: the horrible beaten metal face of Crowley. A deranged battering ram as pitted as the moon, mouth crumpled in by the train's engine, which had ploughed into that surface and shattered and peeled and crumpled beyond recognition.

That had by chain reaction thrown almost the entire train off the tracks, smashed and broken open the cars as Crowley's metal face moved forward like a combination destroyer and punisher both. In the most vainglorious form possible.

There was flame everywhere. There were people screaming and others busy darting into the woods to escape whatever terror might come next. Some writhed on the ground, or lay still, most mercifully hidden by smoke, shadows from flame, or the night. A few rough silhouettes trapped within train cars moved not at all, not really, just their heads bobbing and falling with every new jounce and shudder as the wreckage settled.

There was no time to gawp or linger.

"We have to get out of here," Jonathan said through the ringing in his ears. "Gather as much of your gear as you can and head for the forest."

He rose, aware he'd hurt his leg, that his leg was bleeding, and pulled Alice up, too. Her face was lacerated, he thought, but although she staggered, she was otherwise unhurt.

"Seconded," Alice said. She no longer sounded as if she were in charge.

Danny and Rack lay on the ground, hugging each other tight, alive. Perhaps even reconciled for the moment.

Danny managed to get to her knees, pull her bear gun out of the snow. She was looking back toward the train, toward the windows that showed people still trapped inside. Not just the dead, now, Jonathan could see.

"You can't help them," Jonathan said. "Not unless you want to be captured." Or die.

She nodded. "Up, Rack, up." Danny pulled him to his feet by his jacket collar, held him until he had his balance. Dazed, speechless, still clutching his cane.

From the edges of Crowley's occluding face now came two lurching mecha-crocodiles, creaky in the snow, ill-suited for the uneven ground and debris-strewn tracks. Behind and around them poured out pale gaunt men in black clothes. Against the night, highlighted by flames, they became floating or bobbing heads with grim, fixed expressions, disembodied arms and hands.

Crowley's minions.

Trailing wisps of black smoke surrounding both mecha-crocs and demi-mages were unquestionably Emissaries. The ethereal sight of them turned Jonathan's blood cold. Made the little hairs on the back of his neck rise. Yet, also, an inexplicable sympathy that he could not explain.

"Quick now," Alice hissed.

The tree line was close, right ahead, and they limped and fast-walked toward it, heads down, trying to be as inconspicuous as possible. While behind them the train roared in torment, died a fiery, smoldering death.

What they would have done next, where they would've gone, Jonathan had no clue. If not for Mamoud, who, like magic, stole out of the forest's shadows to greet them.

Jonathan had never been more relieved to see someone he hardly knew.

Chapter Twenty-Four

BOUND TO A MADMAN BY A GIANT WORM

Jules Verne existed in a state of unending terror, his fate chained to Laudinum X in the cockpit of the Burrower. Ever closer to England's dangerous magical wall.

With each crushing mile they had spent together, the Inventor's hysteria had built, until it had become such a block of horror that it had frozen around him and he had no idea what safety might look like or how he might return there.

"Smash the English bastard lords!" LX would scream at random intervals. "Smash the smug drunken goat-skull lickers!" He had no middle ground—it was either incomprehensible low-talking mumbles or these animal-like screams and shrieks that tore at Verne's eardrums. Nor did he quite understand the goat reference.

"We will eviscerate! We will destroy! We will . . . burrow!"

Laudinum also had no sense of his progressions, lived in what seemed like a shambolic and perpetual state of anticlimax. This should not have irritated Verne as much as it did, given the extremity of the situation: locked together with Laudinum X in the body suit, like two halves of an iron maiden, the spikes provided by LX's ravings.

But he could not stand it, had to stop himself from correcting LX, bite his tongue to avoid shouting at him, "*First* you burrow! Then you eviscerate! And, finally, you destroy!"

Perhaps it was the inventor in him as much as the novelist. But he was exhausted from feeling that the plot played out in Laudinum X's hindquarters first, followed perhaps by an arm and then the torso, with the head somewhere in the middle. It did not bode well for the strategic thinking needed to survive their assault on the English. For it was LX in charge, not him.

Yet the worry uppermost was earthworms. Or, rather, the possible dearth of earthworms, given the rate at which the Burrower burned through them. Whenever they came to a lurching halt at day's end, in some remote ravine or clearing, or even atop an unfortunate village, they must first feed the beast before Verne could think about feeding himself.

While Laudinum X would find new and inventive ways to castigate Verne for not, as LX put it, making the Burrower "go whoosh whoosh," by which he meant ever faster, for the infernal creation's appetite had slowed their progress and the demi-mages aboard feared some element of surprise was slipping away from them. They measured this potential by the number of crows that circled in the sky or clung to branches, assuming any crow or raven might be an English spy.

Then Verne would have to explain to LX and his fellow demi-mages once again the complex equation, the intricate variables, that bound the limits of the Burrower's operation.

For example, given X—"not you, Laudinum"—being the width of Burrower's exoskeleton and Y being the space between each square in the latticework of its metal frame, then Z number of earthworms would be lacerated and ground to pulp by day's end and thus rendered of no use to the Burrower's operation.

Because, A—the Burrower's magic method of locomotion depended on live prey, like a snake, and B—pulped earthworms created additional friction to their progress that threw off the calculations of X, Y, and Z. It had a tendency by dusk to turn the Burrower into a massive flinger of worm guts at the landscape around them, necessitating longer expeditions to all sides to find the earthworms to replace them—even acknowledging that resupply wagons and odd lorries belching smoke, pilfered from the Republic, would catch up eventually for resupply.

Not to mention that although the small army of demi-mages attached to the Burrower latched themselves via hooks attached to belts on all sides of the Burrower, or traveled en masse in special egg-shaped cages fastened to the Burrower, the centrifugal forces involved could turn them into paste if they weren't vigilant in their magic. Nor could the torque involved in all of this protect against some of those cages being corkscrewed into the ground side of the Burrower, giving some of the demi-mages unwelcome dirt baths and injuries that they sustained with stoic good cheer, but that, frankly, registered as horrific to Verne.

In short, he did not wish to live among such disgusting injuries, as visual insult piled upon all the other reversals he had suffered. Although he expressed it to the demi-mages, some of whom had served as his jailors back in Paris, as a concern for their safety.

Which is to say, he had taken what was on offer from Laudinum X in the way of calming drugs, principal among them LX's namesake. It settled him down for a stretch; then the abyss loomed again and his hands in their restraints twitched and there was an awful itching on his nose he could not reach and then the earthworm problem became a welcome distraction from his physical condition.

But none of this—not his personal distress nor the logic behind the problems of the Burrower—seemed to matter to Laudinum X. For he would at times also alarm Verne by screaming, "Go faster than horsies! Go faster!"

Unsure whether this was a bleated mimicry of the hapless head of Napoleon or some kind of childlike playing-at-toy-soldiers regression, perhaps sparked by LX's massive head wound. He'd wrapped bandages around it at least, although these soaked through with blood twice a day. Where LX found his blood, Verne had no idea, as a lesser being would've already been bloodless.

Yet still LX persisted.

"Toys. I want my toys. I wanted my stuffed badger. I want to stuff my badger if it is not yet stuffed."

Utterances such as these provided damning evidence that Laudinum

X was going through some kind of crisis, the perplexing-at-first seeming evidence of sudden lucid thought, no matter the randomness of the words, because delivered in a calm tone.

It tended to send a chill through Verne, and the frequent references to childhood stuffed toys just reminded him of the stories he'd heard as a child about the Wall—of the Old Magic that defended it, of how there was nothing more ferocious or committed than the animal armies that lay in wait on the land bridge. Among other terrors.

Verne's options remained limited. He was trapped there in the cockpit beside LX, and LX had the deadman's switch—actually a giant button under the demi-mage's seat that would've greatly disturbed and bruised any normal man's buttocks. But not LX.

If Laudinum removed his restraints and stood up, the entire Burrower would explode, raining metal and earthworms across all of Brittany or southern England (depending on how far they got). He tried not to think of his brothers or his parents receiving the news of how he'd died. They no doubt still thought he was imprisoned in Paris; he had had no word from them in months.

So Verne lived with dread every time Laudinum X muttered something about how stuffy the cockpit had become and how perhaps he should just go off for a little wander. Not knowing if this meant LX wanted a brief walk or had, despite his undead, unfood, undrink lifestyle, developed a phantom need to go urinate behind a tree. (Verne's own bathroom arrangements did not bear thinking about, but involved several tubes.)

This dread was how Verne knew that he still preferred to exist than not exist, even under the circumstances.

Chapter Twenty-Five

FLUTTER BLOOD BABY

Huddled on a hilltop overlooking Rome, staring at a list of names like "Flutter Blood Baby" and "The Tether Heads" on a torn, dirty slip of paper, waiting for Mamoud to get back from reconnaissance, wasn't exactly how Jonathan had expected things to go. But here he was, here they all were, midmorning of the day after their desperate escape from the train.

Atop a hill with a crumbling stone cistern in the center and yellowing grass and a ruined low wall either side of the cistern for shelter. No doubt the wall had been built by the Romans centuries before. Moss and lichen had transformed it into a spray and daub of greens.

Rack was propped up against the stones to the left of the cistern, legs out straight in front of him. Danny sat beside him, cross-legged, a distant stare widening her face, and Alice on the other side. Alice had bruises and a sore shoulder and lacerations on her face, but nothing serious.

Danny's pack lay where she'd dropped it, and looked abandoned. It alarmed Jonathan to see Danny that way, as if she'd reached her limit. Rack had a cut on his left cheek that would leave a scar and a pulled muscle in his left and only calf. Danny's hair was caked with dirt and her face smudged with smoke residue. Tee-Tee had curled around her neck like the world's shortest, worst scarf, almost as if he'd gone into hibernation from stress.

The sky beyond the cistern, looking back upon broken Rome, had taken on a green-orange haze so vivid it resembled a chemical leak. The puff of explosions among the maze of buildings blossomed now black, now white, depending on the cause.

What Mamoud termed "distracting decoys" floated in the air against that backdrop: imitation Golden Spheres that spoke in terrifying ways, that dropped low and then shot up high, that at times were corporeal and then less so, that changed size. Taunting the lumbering mecha-elephants.

While parts of the city disappeared in smoke and fire. While the giant lizards—which, through the binoculars Mamoud had provided, were the size of an anole seen green against a wall, but actually almost half the size of the elephants—engulfed one mecha-elephant in their scuttling ire, sympathetic to a Golden Sphere that did not wish to be caught.

A terrifying yet also absurd sight, to Jonathan.

Because what would they have done if Crowley hadn't derailed the train? Would they really have jumped off and made it through that hellscape to complete their mission? Fought giant lizards and Crowley's forces? Held their breath against the dangerous green-and-orange magical fog that rolled in and rolled out again, restless, aimless, unpredictable? Cornered the Golden Sphere, waved the Wobble in front of It, and all would've been well?

Somehow, he doubted it.

The wound in Jonathan's thigh had stopped bleeding, but if he were back home he'd have had a trip to the hospital in his near future. Here, he'd just have to hope it healed. The swift way Alice had ripped a sleeve from her shirt and wrapped it around the wound in Jonathan's leg in seconds flat had saved him from serious damage.

"Nothing like adversity to bind people together," Sarah had said. "If they're of good character."

But that wasn't quite right. Whether of good, bad, or indifferent character, when people's lives were in danger, they took steps. They took steps to survive. Even if they turned out to be the wrong steps.

Almost as an afterthought, Danny began to tie her hair back in a ponytail to get it out of her face, wincing from pain in her right wrist, while Rack now showed signs of life, pulling his pack toward him and rooting through it ceaselessly, looking for something important he couldn't quite locate.

Although disheveled, muddy, and spent, they were already like veterans of something larger than themselves. He could see it in their eyes. He could see it in the way Rack's resolve had stiffened with his stance, tension in his wide shoulders, the firm set of his lantern jaw. The night before, Jonathan had seen it in the way Danny had brandished the bear gun, had secured the ax she'd found through her belt.

As they'd slipped past the gauntlet of demi-mages and the train had gone from a mosaic of bright, almost cheery orange-red flames fractured and diluted by the black branches of trees to a dim glow against the chill.

"It's nothing like our world," Rack said, still rummaging.

"Actually, the trappings aside, it's very much like our world," Jonathan replied.

"I know one thing—I don't want our world to become like this one," Danny said. "I don't want Crowley to win."

Both of their worlds could use massive amounts of improvement, as far as Jonathan could tell, but he agreed with that one thing.

"I don't want Crowley to win, either," he said. "Especially not after almost being killed by a giant replica of his horrible face."

"Do you think they knew we were on that train?" Danny asked.

"Don't flatter yourself," Alice said. "It was bound to happen sometime."

"You really think it had nothing to do with us?" Jonathan asked. Somehow that seemed unlikely.

"I know one thing that had to do with us," Alice said. "Or you, rather."

Jonathan gave her a puzzled look.

"You mean how we got out," Danny said.

"What do you mean?"

"Well, Jonathan, why don't you tell us?" Alice said. "One moment we were stuck inside the train car. The next we were all sprawled on the snow, along with our things."

"We were thrown free."

"No, I distinctly remember you shouting 'Enough' and the next second we'd all gotten free."

Jonathan shrugged. "I don't know what you're talking about."

But he did know what they were talking about.

Something had *shifted* in that moment after he'd shouted "Enough!" Something had been different, for a speck of time. A mote of time. *He'd* shifted it, much as he'd "pushed" the wraith in Spain.

❧

A row of sparrows had descended upon the wall above the heads of Danny and Rack. Brief respite, and then in a chattering ruckus took their leave, headed somewhere safer.

Not as free to leave was a foraging hedgehog that either was brave enough not to fear them or too hungry to bother with fear.

As it snuffled around Jonathan's feet, he pulled out a half-eaten protein bar from his coat pocket and broke off a piece, tossed it in front of the inquisitive nose. Down the gullet it went. Not that they had much food to spare. They'd managed to save about two packs' worth of supplies from the train.

Mamoud appeared at the wall, from down the hill. Alice rose, hopeful.

"Any good news?" Jonathan asked.

Mamoud gave them a weary grin. A grim grin. "Rome is on fire. Crowley's armies are on the move, driving all before them. The leader of the Italian resistance is dead—someone betrayed him. The Golden Sphere is no longer here."

"Is that all?" Jonathan said, hurting all over. Aware that the Wobble in his pocket might not mean much now. Last times he'd checked, it'd looked like a black dot with teeth, then like a sunflower with fangs, then

THE LEAP

217

like a cheap glass marble. Only ever for a few moments, then it'd settle back into flat anonymity.

"No. Unfortunately, we have only one door out. Crowley's closed off some, and his army's in the way of reaching any of the others."

It didn't seem fair that Mamoud could deliver this news with not a hair out of place, with the appearance of limitless energy. He was dressed impeccably for the weather, in a spotless black overcoat and boots with silver trim.

"So we'll just go home, yeah?" Danny said. "Regroup. Take stock and take our chances back at the mansion."

Surprising but not surprising that Danny would say that. She said it a bit like he imagined her rugby coach might say it if their team was losing by a wide margin at the midpoint.

"Go home? There's no going home for now," Mamoud said. "The only door leads to the foothills of the Alps—here on Aurora. The Alps will be your home for a while."

Rack's head was bowed, and he'd ceased searching his pack. "I knew it. I just knew it."

Danny had decided to concentrate on rewrapping her left wrist with the fabric she'd torn from a spare T-shirt. But Jonathan could see the wheels turning.

"Less than a day in Aurora and we're all falling apart," Rack said, off his own thoughts. "Forget the fade—wear and tear and not knowing what the hell will come at us next will do us all in."

"I'm happy to be a parrot: We've no choice for now. No choice at all," Mamoud said, smiling.

"Are we going to die here, then?" Danny asked.

Mamoud blinked at her. "Alice thinks we should try to break through their lines, instead of risking the door. The argument is: What if the door's not safe after all and Crowley's men lie in wait?"

"And Mamoud thinks that's a crap idea because their 'lines' are so shambolic it would be a roll of the dice," Alice said.

"One person might break through," Mamoud said. "I might. You might, Alice. But what then? A long, arduous journey through enemy territory or a boat to Sardinia and then Corsica, and then what? Still behind enemy lines."

"I could do it," Alice said. "I bet I could."

"What about the other members of the Order? Can't you call on them?" Jonathan asked.

"Lots of them have turned up dead of late," Alice said. "Lots are scattered. There's disarray in the ranks. Factions."

"Which brings us to my Allies List," Jonathan said.

Which brought them to, among other oddities, "Flutter Blood Baby."

⁊

"Flutter Blood Baby" was an inside joke Jonathan shared with R & D, a bit of nonsense uttered by him late one night while playing a board game as relief from studying for midterms. The other two began saying it as well, and it became a favorite saying. Incomprehensible to anyone else, unable to be explained the way some things between friends just were, to outsiders.

"Flutter Blood Baby" looked plenty stupid now, on the page, but he'd felt a need when writing down the allies to disguise the real ones a bit. Never thinking that perhaps Dr. Lambshead had already done so.

The full list of allies in the area read as follows:

The Tether Heads

*The Black Tower of Sumurath**

Flutter Blood Baby

*Sir Zafir Samuels**

Mandible Man & His Star Goats

Hoard-Slugger Lastface

Various Bird-Children

The Alpine Meadows Research Institute*

The Three-Legged Squirrel of Zurich

He had not made up either the Tether Heads or the Mandible Man. But those didn't have asterisks by them, placed there by Dr. Lambshead: "*The ones I recommend you visit, when you have time.*"

Alongside each name was an address, each more absurd than the last. Surely there had never been a street named "Tensile Strength" or "Go Boom." "Various Bird-Children" he studiously ignored, as the address was Dr. Lambshead's mansion.

"How old is this? How accurate?" Alice had said in challenge, when he'd shown them the list, dirt-smudged and sweat-stained from living in his trouser pocket. Possibly "Flutter Blood Baby" had raised the alarm.

Jonathan had come right back with, "How would I know? Do you have a better idea?"

No, they did not. Other than splitting up and going their separate ways in enemy territory, which seemed like a terrible plan. All this right before Mamoud and Alice had tasked him with telling the others there was no easy way home.

Of course, Dr. Lambshead's list had been nonsense to Jonathan when he'd first read it, and nonsense he'd thought applied to people and places on Earth, not an entirely different Earth.

"Flutter. Blood baby?" It sounded even more ridiculous when Mamoud said it aloud, in a questioning tone. But not as embarrassing as admitting he'd made it up.

Both Rack and Danny lost it when he said the words, of course. No helping that.

"Oh, by all means, Jonathan, let's go visit Flutter Blood Baby. I've always wanted to," Rack said.

"Flutter Blood Baby—the superhero we never knew we needed, yeah?"

He just rode it out, at least happy he'd brought R & D out of their heads, said curtly, "No reason," when Mamoud asked why the laughter.

"Well, I don't want to go to a black tower," Danny said. "Neither does Tee-Tee."

"Quite right," Rack said. "Ever read P. D. James? Never go to the black tower, unless you want to be death-murdered."

"How's that different than usual murdered?" Danny asked.

"It's much, much worse, trust me, sister."

"So, does that mean you'd rather go to something or someone called the Tether Heads?" Danny asked.

"The Black Tower is closer than the rest," Mamoud said. "And the name is alluring."

"But only by a little," Alice added. "And I doubt there's help there, just shelter. Crowley's men would likely have taken it over by now, as well."

"The squirrel option tempts, but Zurich is the farthest away," Mamoud said. "Although I do not doubt the power of a squirrel ally."

"Zurich will be teeming with spies, including Crowley's operatives."

"What about the Alpine Meadows Research Institute?" Jonathan asked.

"I have never heard of it before," Mamoud said. "At least, by that name."

"I've heard promising rumors," Alice said. "Could be the best, given the options. Could definitely be the best."

"The address is somewhat precise at least: *Way Station 3712, Montagna del lago dell'inferno, Puffin Path, Mile Marker 667.*"

He didn't say he favored it because he thought he remembered Sarah mentioning it, or something like it, in one of the stories she'd told him. He also didn't say how the thought of retracing her steps, even on Aurora, gave him a sense of dread. Of a shadow looming into view.

"That's the trap, of course," Rack said. "The one that's innocent-sounding will be terrible, and the one that sounds like suspicious bollocks will be great."

"A way station is likely to have supplies and shelter—remote enough it'd be out of Crowley's path," Mamoud said. "If anything is."

"It sounds very formal," Jonathan said. And thus comforting, amid all the chaos, which had been exceedingly informal.

Alice hesitated, then said, "I know the general area. And the trail, or I know of it."

"But you grew up in England," Jonathan said.

"My parents sent me to a boarding school in the Alps. Swiss Alps, not Italian, but I still remember some things."

She seemed less than pleased to have to divulge the information. Or was that just good acting?

"The Alpine Meadows Research Institute it is, then," Mamoud said.

"Do we have any other choice?" Rack asked.

"*You* don't," Alice said.

"She has a point," Mamoud said. "The fade. Fatigue lowers resistance." He stared at Jonathan's leg. "Being injured does, too. We need to find a sanctuary."

Jonathan exchanged a glance with Rack and Danny. They were going to have to keep their wits about them, traveling in a strange land. Wary of the fade. Unable, yet, to get home.

"Where is the door to the foothills?" Danny asked.

"It's in the cistern, of course," Alice said. "The cistern is a door. Why do you think we came here? For our health? Gather up your things. We should leave soon."

Rack had his walking stick, which he could wield like a weapon.

Jonathan had nothing but the Wobble, a cheerful pocketknife, and, now, binoculars, but somehow that was enough for him. "You'd best dig deep to survive what's coming," he told the hedgehog, for Crowley's armies would overrun this position soon enough. Two or three hours, Mamoud had estimated.

To his surprise, but also relief, the hedgehog looked up, appeared to nod, and then on nimble feet trundled away down the line of the wall, popping into a hole near the base of the cistern Jonathan hadn't noticed before. He rather hoped the nibble of protein bar wouldn't hurt the little creature.

At least the hedgehog didn't look at him funny because of what he had done to get them free of the train. R & D had pointedly asked no questions, and perhaps thought in time he'd talk about it. But he wasn't sure he wanted to. As if talking let out all kinds of things into the world, things that shouldn't be there.

As for the cistern, it looked like the usual, with an ordinary tin lid that Mamoud lifted and pushed back on a hinge. Revealing a mouth of black water beneath and a not-so-reassuring burbling and bubbling. Enter the cauldron. Trust in doors that looked like wells.

"Not as bleak as it looks, I assure you," Mamoud said, a sparkle in his eye at some private joke. "Not as deep. Not as septic."

One, two, three, they went, Jonathan fourth but not last.

As Jonathan let himself fall over the side of the cistern, he felt not the expected weight of water but the crackle of some magical discharge; he had the thought that they might as well be visiting Flutter Blood Baby. After all, he had a voice in his head (he thought), a Wobble in his pocket, and a living knife to boot.

Thus ended the glorious Rome adventure, witnessed by a lone hedgehog and some dour weeds.

Chapter Twenty-Six

UP A TREE, IN THE BOONIES, WEST OF NOWHERE

Kristýna loved a pedunculate oak and always had, ever since she was a little girl. She especially loved that the gnarled, majestic trees existed in such quantity in that vast swath of territory known these days as "Germany," which she had crossed so many times on various missions. For they served as refuge and sanctuary both. Some more so than others. Her love tinged with relief that she had remembered with accuracy the ones with hidden steps up around the thick, misshapen trunks, threading their way to the top.

They'd arrived through the underbrush along a dirt trail that ran parallel to the main thoroughfare. Which just meant that Mack was hungry and tired of being pushed ever east by Crowley's army. A more leisurely pace would have been appreciated. Especially after so much time spent in catacombs beforehand. And, given a different mission, Kristýna might have been in a hurry to get to Prague ahead of Crowley.

But she was not unhappy to bivouac in such surroundings. To spy from such a tree, hidden but not hidden, was a joy. To be out of cities, to be out of catacombs, to be surrounded by plants. All of which spoke to her in their various ways, told her of their ills and of the slow triumphs of their days. Mack would never hear that, and there was no method by which Kristýna could make him hear it. But, then, there were things he heard that she could not.

It had been so long since she had visited this particular tree that, to her surprise, the tree jutted up from the courtyard in the middle of a ruined château. Imagine. So much time had passed that there had been enough of it for the château to be built around it and then partially torn down. In among the rubbish spread across the derelict rooms, she had found a child's toys, a squatter's backpack, and evidence of violence. But old violence, old toys.

At least the owners must have loved the tree, to save it from the ax, no matter what had happened in the end. That made her sad, the history so visible to all. Soon, there would be new violence to join the old, and perhaps the château would be commandeered, by Crowley or even the Czechs or the Republic.

Less charitably, Mack had told her when it came into view that French architecture in Germany was like finding a gold coin in your gazpacho: ultimately welcome, but a good way to lose a tooth.

Perhaps.

She was still mulling that as they overlooked the main road as war elephant after war elephant lumbered by, flanked by Emissaries and demi-mages. They looked to Kristýna at that distance like a peculiar carnival, one she had no interest in attending. The Emissaries could have been mistaken for plumes of black smoke while the demi-mages resembled failed clowns. Oh, if only they were.

Mack, of course, was doing pull-ups while they engaged in their surveillance. Mack, whose shadow much concerned Kristýna in recent days. So much so that she was staring at it now as Mack bobbed up and down, a tireless automaton. Yet it refused to do anything odd, like pirouette. Yet still she watched it.

"What is ossuary-adjacent?" Mack asked, and Kristýna, not for the first time on this trip, was startled. He'd been off in his own thoughts again. More than usual.

"A butcher's shop," she said, as if his question were a riddle. But in fact he was the riddle.

"And next to that?" Mack asked.

"A palace."

"Never next to a butcher's shop, Kristýna."

Mack hadn't liked the catacombs. Seemed to prefer the outdoors by only a hair, liked a city best, unlike her. As he put it, "hard to find a bookshop in a forest." Well, maybe he could find a book in the château and they'd no doubt wind up in Prague soon enough, after this slight detour. A place they must go, or ought to go.

Or she was losing the thread because she might be losing Mack.

"Mack, how many war elephants?" She didn't care, but wanted him to focus. On the mission. On her.

"Here? On the road? Gone past? Forty."

"And Crowley's elephant?"

"The big one? Not yet."

"Tell me, Mack: Is Crowley stupid? To make himself such a target."

"I think he is vain."

"Or thinks himself invincible."

"Wretch thinks himself invincible. Or doesn't care."

The elephants continued to parade past. Mack had stopped doing his push-ups. Still his shadow behaved normally.

"Do you know the story of this tree, Mack?"

"No. Would it interest me?"

"I don't know what interests you these days. I remember it, perhaps, because it happened to me: to grow apart from someone, to not know their thoughts anymore. When once you did. In the tale, Mack, she turns into a tree in grief over that. But I remember the real story. It was the man that became the tree, for lack of understanding her. This is always a risk."

"Turning into a tree?" Mack asked, mocking her gently.

"Around me. Yes, a risk."

"Some trees are better than people," Mack said. "Some rivers, too."

Kristýna wanted to ask Mack, point-blank: Do you support the Order? Do you support me? But she couldn't.

Besides, Crowley's war elephant had come into view, holding both of them rapt in a kind of guilty fascination.

It was twice the size of the other war elephants, and thus it smashed trees on the sides of the road as it lumbered along, clod-footed and benighted. She could hear the cracks of the branches, but also feel the hurt in her heart, had to set it to the side, quarantine it. While she soothed the vines and the grasses all around the damage, to do what triage they could.

A true folly. Yet also an engineering and magical marvel. It had the same anti-arboreal spells upon it as all of Crowley's elephants, which made it impervious to Kristýna, and demi-mages hanging off the sides acted as sentries against sappers, the Czech spy's magical combat engineers. Not to mention flamethrowers and what amounted to huge hedge clippers out front, disguised as tusks. The four wood-and-metal feet of the elephant came equipped with thick collapsible wheels, but there was always as now terrain the beast must tromp through, not glide through.

Verne's war machines had been assembled in secret outside Paris, they had learned, much closer to the German border, to save travel time to Prague and to avoid sabotage by Rimbaud and his cohorts. Or by Kristýna and hers.

Kristýna was so used to the mumbling screams of the animals housed within a "normal" war elephant that she no longer heard them, nor did Mack. But the screams of the creatures within Crowley's elephant she heard: a sound bloodcurdling enough even to get into her bones, despite all she had experienced during her very long life.

She could smell the sulfur and blood and oil and rot, even from this distance, half up a tree. No other army so visibly advertised its horrors on offer as Crowley's, and perhaps never would.

The breeze picked up and brought the scent of gardenias from the overgrown garden below, and thyme and basil. So, they'd raised herbs and no doubt had meals out in the courtyard, under the tree they'd saved. Before the world destroyed their peace.

But the breeze brought more than the past with it: Down drifted lazy the last tuft from the gardens of Paris, her last Parisian spy keeping watch on the Marmot. They were too far now, the risk too dangerous if intercepted over such distances, or trailed to their destination. To a certain tree.

And yet, miraculous, this tuft that had found her at last: delicate and light, twirling in the air, spinning and dipping, until she put her hand out, whereupon it settled onto her palm. Soon enough it would tell her all it knew, and then she would plant it in the courtyard garden, next to the herbs, and it would grow tall and strong and be whatever it wanted to be without her purpose imposed upon it.

"Did you know," Mack said, "that woodpeckers' tongues are so long that they wrap around the outside of their skulls like a fishing reel?"

"Yes, I know." Deflection. A way of saying he was loyal. Even if he wasn't.

What Kristýna already knew without the tuft disturbed her, and this just from observing Mack. In their progress through the forest, to observe Crowley's war elephant, she had more than once woken in the middle of the night to find Mack gone from her side. They slept rough, with no campfire, but Mack's roaming in the darkness did not strike her as helping them avoid detection.

Who did Mack meet, out there in the forest? Or did he have to be meeting anyone. Perhaps he just wandered, restless? The walk its own antidote.

Yet he made no mention of his forays, gave her no opportunity to bring them up in a context that would not be accusatory. Which might itself be a clue.

Other clues: The one time Kristýna had gone looking for him, under a full moon. Spotted his silhouette in a clearing past their campsite, framed by rows of apple trees in what had been an orchard but was now overgrown and abandoned. He stood by the ruins of an old stone shed murmuring to himself.

Except Kristýna could have sworn it was his *shadow* that was talking. This feeling became more certain when his shadow detached itself from him for a moment, to curl around the corner, adamant in making some important point, before flexing back into being a normal, Mack-sized shadow, in the appropriate place.

Then, after a time, Mack was finished with whatever transaction had just occurred, and started back toward her. She ducked into shadows behind a tree, made of herself a tree, in a sense.

And after he had walked past, when next she looked at the stone shed, an animal of some kind—the shadow of an animal—had revealed itself, bounding in the opposite direction. What manner of beast, Kristýna could not be sure. But something like a gigantic otter or stoat.

Nor could she be sure of what she had seen next, felt doubt at the distance and the murk, even with the moon. Knew, too, she must return to camp soon and not investigate further, if only to preserve the fiction that she had gone off to make water.

Why was Mack's shadow not his own? Worse, why did he let it happen, unless he was, in some sense, under a spell?

She knew why. She just didn't want to know why.

The tuft's report was, of necessity, a week stale, and yet contained much to mull.

The Marmot had sat on the edge of the same lawn in the same Parisian park. Soon enough, a second marmot popped a head out from dense thicket to join the Marmot. Kristýna knew from the tuft's description that this was the one Dr. Lambshead had nicknamed "Reginald" or "Reggie." The two marmots had then engaged in a lively conversation, composed of clicks, whistles, and belches, with a few interspersed words in Italian, French, and English.

Kristýna had written it all down, even took a while to translate it herself. Usually she used a translator from the Institute.

The transcript was fairly brief.

Reggie: "Jonathan Lambshead has crossed into Aurora."

The Marmot: "Do you think she knows?"

Did the Marmot mean her?

Reggie: "I rather doubt it. Although to be safe you'd better eat all those dandelions."

The Marmot: "Quite."

Reggie: "Right now, I mean. I'll help."

That confirmed it, and there followed an extended period of munching, according to the tuft, during which it became afraid for its life. But this particular tuft of Kristýna's was hiding under a huge clover, which itself feared for its life yet had been spared long enough for the tuft to keep spying.

The Marmot: "Why did you come back so soon?"

Reggie: "I waited as long as I could. Stimply promised the boy would arrive much earlier. Stimply also promised to be there. But in any event, I soon began not to feel myself anymore, and since he'd seen me—"

The Marmot: "Jonathan Lambshead saw you?"

Reggie: "Yes."

The Marmot: "What did he make of you?"

Reggie: "Didn't blink. Delighted, I believe. Thought I was an excellent marmot, by all accounts."

The tuft reported that Reginald said this with no little amount of pride.

Reggie: "Still, I felt it wise to leave, as, I said, I was beginning to fade, due to Stimply's cock-up."

The Marmot: "Fair enough."

Reggie: "And, too, Alice Ptarmigan was there and warned me off."

The Marmot: "Alice! What was she doing there?"

Reggie: "I couldn't tell you. I didn't ask, as she wouldn't tell me, of course. Just put a boot to my backside and said I was interfering and to get lost. Although she didn't put it so politely. And over there, I'd none of the advantages I've got here."

What had Alice been doing there? A member of the Order, but from that remote English branch that didn't always play nice with others. Had more paper as an English patriot. Which was why Kristýna had kept well clear of her.

The Marmot: "You're back more because of Alice than Stimply."

Reggie: "Both. Neither. Look, I stayed as long as I could. It just felt wrong, and I could swear there was another person lurking around the mansion besides Alice, as well. And then, Jonathan's friends came and that made it harder to skulk about. Especially because they'd a rat with them that knew I was there, knew what I was about, too, in some creepy way. Wasn't much fun getting free of its regard, let me tell you."

Even without any editorializing from the tuft, Kristýna knew the Marmot would have been curt, put off by Reginald's long-windedness.

At this point, Reggie had sat on the tuft and the recording became garbled for a while.

The Marmot: ". . . moved up the timing . . . depending on . . ."

Reggie: ". . . Prague? Then the saltpeter must be delayed or the . . . be sure of the . . . they're in the forest."

The Marmot: "And when ready, Ma . . ."

Ma . . . rmot? Surely Marmot and not Mack?

"Then we're agreed," Reggie said.

The Marmot: "Agreed. Move it all up. The time is right. Let the old replace the new. Let the shadow spread. After, you will go to the Academy and investigate further. Discreetly."

Reggie: "Of course. For who will notice an extra burrow? Except the dogs, and I can handle dogs. They're so stupid."

Then Reggie had moved again, and the tuft had sprung up, got the rest accurate.

The Marmot: "Any sense of the young Lambshead's role in all of this?"

Reggie: "I don't know that he'll amount to anything. His role may not be large. It may be very small. But he now *does* have a role, and knowing the Lambsheads, I doubt he will disavow what he's learned and walk away."

The Marmot: "You think the boy can help, then?"

Reggie: "He is a very old boy, really, from a very old family."

The Marmot: "Odd family?"

Reggie: "No odder than any of ours, surely."

That curious marmot laughter: clicks and whistles and wheezing.

Reggie: "And there's one other rather important thing."

The Marmot: "What's that, then?"

Reggie: "Jonathan Lambshead's got the Wobble—and an ally he doesn't even know about yet."

The Marmot: "Already."

Laconic, but in that one-word reaction, Kristýna could read multitudes.

But what had they moved up? *What?* For all the talk of Jonathan Lambshead, that seemed almost incidental.

Ever since the tuft's report, Kristýna had had an unsettled feeling in the pit of her stomach. As if events were soon to get beyond her.

As if spying would not be enough.

They stood atop the tree, watching the procession for a while longer, before climbing down and making camp in the château. She would enclose all the doors in vines and patch the roof with more vines and soon enough it would be habitable once more, but hard to get into. Find Mack a book, any old book. Just to keep him happy. Maybe if he were reading, he'd say fewer disconcerting things.

Who knew how many more days they had before "picking up the package" as they both put it, there being so many spies around these days. "Picking up the package" that Kristýna was still figuring out what to do with. A most dangerous package, in the wrong hands. A package that could do much damage. She would have preferred to have a companion she trusted completely with "the package," but she could not go freelance. Not now.

Still, Kristýna could not shake what she had seen that night following Mack.

That the bounding creature had been headed toward a much larger silhouette deep in the forest. One whose shape she recognized but which could not be a true shape. For such a creature had not been seen for hundreds of years. Nectar deer were as newly minted next to this apparition. If she weren't mistaken, and she must be, for what connection did Mack have to such a being?

For what she had seen most resembled a giant hedgehog man atop a giant rooster. The sight had sent a chill down her spine. She'd shuddered and felt an overwhelming urge to flee, to run, to hide.

The Marmot's words came back to her again, and even though she was herself immeasurably ancient, they gave her no comfort.

Let the old replace the new. Let the shadow spread.

Chapter Twenty-Seven

MY HOME IS A GIANT WAR ELEPHANT

"An imperial pronouncement will be issued in two days' time on the subject of further pronouncements. All hail Lord Crowley."

—Pronounced by Lord Emperor Crowley on the way to Prague

"To *what* do you owe the pleasure of my company . . ."

Perhaps too formal, don't you think? And never ask a question you don't want answered with an insult. Neener-neener-booyah.

"To *whom* do you owe the pleasure of Lord Crowley's company this fine day in this . . . village?"

Referring to yourself in third person could work, but not this way. How about "I am the slam dunk and you are the ball"?

"Good afternoon and welcome; I am Lord Crowley and I am here today to . . ."

. . . say a few words over a dead body? Also, it's warm in here. I'm ping-ponging off the walls. Please, sir, I'm just an innocent firefly. Please, sir, you must let me go. Was that a good impression of groveling? I'm not familiar with groveling myself, so all I—

"Welcome to all who have gathered here in this lovely village to attend my words on the occasion of a heroic advance in our war efforts . . ."

What if the village is awful and ugly? Well, I suppose the inhabitants never think so. Or maybe they do but are good at hiding it. Hidey-hidey ho! Hidey-hidey-hole!

"Hello, I am Lord Crowley, and today I will give a speech in this crap-hole of a village that will amaze and astound no one."

Honesty is the best policy. Or so I've heard. Somewhere. Once upon a time, in a fairy tale. Fairies are tasty, although it's wrong to eat them. Or so I've heard . . .

Damn it to Satan's balls! Every time Crowley tried to compose the speech he had a terrible floating feeling, as if he were once more in Wretch's clutches, about to do a flyover of that infernal volcano. Not to mention, he couldn't make that Specky thing under the glass shut up, now he'd opened the floodgates.

I'm made of cheese! I'm made of cheese! I'm made of cheese!

But perhaps he also couldn't shake the feeling because in their new accommodations, on the road to Prague, Wretch in truth lived in a compartment to the immediate left of Crowley's desk—the wall that divided him from his familiar right there in front of him at all times.

Crowley imagined Wretch on the other side, curled up in slumber, perhaps even upside down like a bat in a belfry. One eye no doubt open, for even when he slept he was half-awake. One ear against the wall, listening . . .

Tweedle-dee-do. Tweedle-dee-dum. When you go to bed do you still suck your thumb?

The thought of Wretch uncurling, dropping down from hooks in the ceiling, and coming into Crowley's own quarters made him shudder. For, if he didn't know better, he would think Wretch messed with the top of his head every night for some reason. Right where the sore, itchy spot was. But he dare not touch it anymore to test it. The last time the spongy *give* had frightened him, and the dizziness that came with his touch.

Gives me the creeps, too, I must say, Lard Fouly. That's one of them creeps-givers. Shivering all the timbers and all the hairs on my arms, if I had arms. But I'm just a little ol' speck. What can a little ol' speck know?

Enough. Crowley tossed his quill to the side and snuffed out the voice, cut the connection, ensured all the magical blockage was still in place. It had just been a test, for now, to see if he could communicate with the Speck yet still contain the Speck.

It had worked well enough, although the old Crowley would've raged at the Speck's impertinence. The new Crowley, post–Volcano Land flight with Wretch, took it in stride. The old Crowley would also have found the Speck ridiculous and callow. Perhaps the new Crowley should envy the Speck's lack of ambition, its clear burbling happiness.

Crowley sat back in his travel throne—gilded, creaky, finest leather, the works—next to the battered desk that had once belonged to the murdered art critic Ruskin in his Paris apartment. Crowley had left a few rather visible bloodstains from the prior owner, for snorts and giggles. A nice conversation piece even if it was a horrible desk, especially given Ruskin's commitment to good design. One leg was shorter than the rest, and all sorts of graffiti had been cut into the top of it.

Like that bit: *The Duke of Norville is a tosser who knows nothing of architecture.* How original. How mature. How long had it taken Ruskin to carve that? Had he been suffering from writer's block or had Crowley's ever-tightening net around him destroyed his mind?

Another read: *Ruskin loves only Ruskin.*

Well, granted, Crowley had added that one himself. He'd also carved a few choice curse words he'd always loved and the Latin symbol for the ecstatic monad. That sort of thing. Whittling calmed his nerves. He did a lot of it these days.

There came the lurch and the plunk, as he thought of it, his body already used to it so that unlike at the start of their journey his bejeweled slippers dug into the floor and he clasped the arms of his throne tightly enough to avoid being thrown. The lurch signaled a shift in the locomotion of the imperial elephant, specially designed for him and now awkwardly making its way east through the last of the ridiculously thick forests outside Paris, which extended all the way through Bavaria to the high wall, built by the dread warlock Charlemagne, that surrounded Prague.

As it moved forward, it laid waste to most everything in its path, including trees, which meant it served a twofold purpose, the second being to destroy more and more of the cover his enemy needed to operate. Yet, Crowley was not without mercy, for the plumbing system from quarters on board the elephant replenished the land. So that the elephant did indeed wee and poo, and everywhere the elephant went, the Emperor himself made fertile the ground of his conquests. What he did reap and raze, he did then sow.

But the *tromp-tromp* of the elephant required much more of his magical attention than he'd thought it would, as well as that of the demi-mages. Some Republic innovations had gone into those wheels, but most of the "science" imported had failed, didn't play nice with his magic. Even the best efforts of his indentured scientists to transfer what they called "Vaucanson's duck" technologies had had little effect.

So there was now a droning microheadache in the back of Crowley's skull *not* caused by the Speck—the space in which he quarantined the personal daily effort to animate the elephant. To join the compartments in which he controlled his demi-mages and his Miss Eiffel Tower surrogate in Paris—why install another flawed human?—always like a Speck in the corner of his eye. The thought occurred that he might one day have a dozen baby tumors in his skull as a result. Most days now, to offset the intense mental effort, Crowley ate whole chickens for breakfast and half a pig for lunch, and god knows what for dinner.

Any excuse to leave his quarters. The rooms were expansive for the interior of a battle elephant, but cramped next to Notre Dame. He had some portholes for windows, but they usually showed him trees or some banal scene of dead bodies or a muddy track. So he kept the shades down.

Worse, the thought to install Napoleon on another pneumatic pedestal that could rise out of the top of the elephant and give the general's undead head a bird's-eye view of the surrounding terrain had released unbidden the Frenchman's inner travel guide.

The acoustics of the elephant being what they were, Napoleon's faint commentary trickled down into Crowley's rooms—especially long-winded that morning.

"... the birds, they fly away free. Why, in certain species, the fledgling will hitch a ride on the mother's back. But leave the nest they must in time ...

"... and it is definitely a kind of fairyland ... makes fairy tales seem very real and very close by ... Why, even the woodpeckers indeed are most robust and often unafraid of me as they go about retrieving insects and drilling holes in tree trunks ... Do you know, wonder of wonders, I've been told their tongues are so long that they wrap around the outside of their skulls like a fishing reel ...

"... although this is to say nothing of the local cuckoos, which lay their eggs in the nests of the red-faced imperial nuthatch, laying with them plots against those species' ambitions, and the imperial birds none the wiser as they sit atop eggs that will hatch into babies that do not have the ambition of their own species but of another entirely, one that may not even be native to the area. Granted, this imperial nuthatch can in its displays appear a pompous fool, but, still, can one really sympathize with the treacherous cuckoo? That is really the question ..."

Between Napoleon and the Speck, who could blame Crowley if he went stark ravers long before reaching Prague?

☙

The thought occurred to Crowley later that afternoon that in the new hierarchy, he was to Wretch as Napoleon was to him. Above symbolically, but below in truth. And, who, pray tell, existed above Wretch? That might be the essential question. One he had no answer for.

Which made Wretch's latest update in the closeness of his quarters doubly unsettling. For it involved not just Wretch's infernal bulk pressing close on one side of Crowley, but that of the "update," which had appeared in the flesh, on the other. Wretch's would-be assassin, all grown up. Meant to be deployed from Paris, but moving up the invasion of England and Prague had destroyed that plan.

She was large, and of indeterminate age. "You'll remember our assassin?" Wretch asked. "Ruth Less."

"For god's sake," Crowley said, "tell her to pull herself in. Suck in her . . . chest . . . or whatever the hell that is."

"Think of it as a kind of . . . backpack . . . on the front, my lord," Wretch said. "She stores her provisions internally." In that confined space, being next to her was a bit like being next to a huge toad, dripping ichor, or an enormous evil balloon. He found it hard to breathe.

Wretch spat out some words in a language so harsh Crowley felt like fishhooks were careening down his throat. Ruth Less pulled in her stomach, but to negligible effect. With Wretch on the other side, he felt bookended by creepy-crawlies.

The assassin's name must surely be a joke—*Ruth Less*? Made worse by how the creature presented itself as a schoolmarm: a woolly pea-green cardigan and a bulky pink skirt down to the shoes that could just have been odd feet painted black.

This "assassin" had a head more like a bulldog, with glasses that, in a nauseating way, appeared to be part of the face. Except the head came to a gentle point, and at Wretch's command Ruth Less's entire skull peeled into four equal slices, and soon Crowley was looking down into a maw lined with sharp teeth, equal parts the inside of an orca's mouth and that of a Venus flytrap.

The breath was spectacularly foetid, and, unzipped like this, the four equal slices had a peculiar mobility at the edges, more common to an octopus's tentacles. The way it moved made Crowley want to vomit. Cilia were always filthy disease vectors, he felt. Good old sturdy feet or hooves got fungi, yes, or split hoof, but nothing like the variety of horrors that accumulated on cilia. And the beast appeared to be drooling as well.

Best, then, it be quickly on its way; he resolved not to protest at any length whatever purpose Wretch had in mind for it.

"Ruth Less is still growing, but she has made spectacular strides, my lord," Wretch said.

The "my lord" grated. At least the Speck's disrespect was honest.

"Yes . . . I can see. And smell." Honestly, when had Wretch had the time to mentor and train Ruth Less? What with all the secret missions into the countryside that Wretch assured him would help the war effort, he must never sleep.

Ruth Less belched, and moist greenish skin touched Crowley's arm, retracted. It felt as if someone had sutured squid suckers onto sweetbreads. He suppressed a shudder.

"And the purpose of this . . . assassin?" Crowley asked.

"By all means, my lord. She is ultimately to be of use against the Czech magicians, and the Golden Sphere, but in the meantime to be put to the test by pursuing another of our enemies."

"How many enemies do we have these days?" Crowley was losing track.

"The young Jonathan Lambshead has the potential to become a thorn in our side," Wretch said. "He has hold of an artifact of the Builders, our spies tell us. Unlikely he knows how to use it, but best to snuff him out earlier than later."

"So Ruth Less is off to track Lambshead and eat him." In truth, Crowley felt inclined to agree with Wretch's plan, even though he was loath to approve of anything Wretch-related. But he'd felt something—a jolt or outflux of magical energy—in the vicinity of the Rome train wreck as he'd watched through the All-Seeing Puddle.

They'd received information that Jonathan would be on the train, but he'd escaped. Murky as it had been, he would've expected to have seen Jonathan after the wreck, but he hadn't. Even though he had seen any number of other traitors and enemies trying to escape before being rounded up by his demi-mages. Curious that he'd caught no glimpse, but it was true the magical energy in question had taken time to fade, perhaps had befuddled the puddle, which had proven not nearly as effective as its parent.

Something unintended in his tone must have suggested disapproval, for Wretch left off the obligatory "my lord" in his reply, seemed to think Crowley needed convincing: "She needs to be out in the world. If she fails, then she wouldn't have been a match for the Golden Sphere anyway."

Wretch looked with clear affection at Ruth Less, and Crowley had to stave off a rush of perverse jealousy.

"Nothing to worry about, then? And yet we're obviously worrying."

"You did inflict much suffering upon his family."

"I did?" It was at times difficult to keep track of whom he had killed and whom he had not. There was also the matter of what he had done personally and what Wretch had done. But, yes, the boy should be quite unhappy with him for any number of things.

"I have a little something of his father's for the scent," Wretch said, extending a long, long arm to his creature. In Wretch's talons had appeared a gray object. "He smells like this. Similar. Not identical. Similar. Yes?"

Ruth Less snorfled and snuffled all over the object.

"Sim. A. Liar." The word in Ruth Less's mouth was as if someone had spoken while gargling through a mouthful of pond weeds, and then belched on the last syllable. The stench from that maw was even too much for Crowley's indelicate sensibilities.

"Good, Ruth Less. Very good."

"Goo. Duh."

With a slurp and smack, Ruth Less retracted its mouth parts, became the semi-perfect version (from a middle or far distance) of an English schoolmarm, seemed eager to be going, mummified appendage in one of her own rather hard-to-identify appendages.

"What *is* that?"

"A mummified hand."

"I know it's a mummified hand, Wretch! I mean—whose mummified hand?"

"The mummified hand of Jonathan Lambshead's father."

"That you just happen to have on your person?"

"Something like that. For a rainy day. Never know when a body part will come in handy."

Crowley suspected Wretch's flippant tone hid a more serious and pertinent answer.

"And how goes the new plan to find the Golden Sphere?"

"Very well. The first wave of rabid undead chipmunks will be sent out soon. As a test only."

Everything was a test with Wretch these days.

Two demi-mages had appeared, at Wretch's command apparently, and made to escort Ruth Less out of the chamber.

"Your two demi-mages will not be coming back," Wretch said. "You will need to appoint two new ones."

"What?"

"As I said, Ruth Less is still growing, and she has quite the appetite."

❧

The Folly. His imperial elephant had been dubbed the Folly by some of the demi-mages he'd since had executed, for calling it that behind his back, but not far enough behind his back. Yet, in truth, Crowley's elephant *was* a folly, if a folly with a purpose. The Folly—yes, perhaps this new, more thoughtful Crowley could claim that name with pride. It was not the typical double-decker mecha-elephant stuffed with the energy of half-dead animals.

No, it was three stories of magnificence with a unique ventilation system—Crowley thought of it as a circulatory system, for breathing, in particular his breathing (which he still needed to do; Wretch drew breath, but sometimes Crowley thought that was just for show). And then a kind of faux deep epidermal layer inside the outer skin, before the inner workings, filled entirely with undead albino salamanders in a lugubrious liquid one-fourth formaldehyde, one-fourth ground-up faery dust (actually ground-up goat overlaid with various spells), one-fourth swamp water, and, finally, one-fourth liquid strained from the All-Seeing Eye over a period of months.

A patient project, but well worth it, to create a kind of magical moat inside the elephant, protecting his quarters and everything else housed inside the Folly. The rough circle of salamander water helped him project the properties of the All-Seeing Puddle much farther than otherwise. Indeed, he'd had a glass panel put in the ceiling over his bed so he could watch as the salamanders passed overhead, their twinkling star-shaped toes a startling white against the glass at night, forming amphibious constellations.

Crowley rather loved salamanders, promised himself he'd set this batch free when he had no further need of them, had piped into their closed-off world only the finest food for their delectation. Sometimes it even included bits of demi-mage, for they did die of natural causes rather often, and it was, Crowley mused, sort of supporting the cycle of life.

By now, five days in, Crowley could distinguish one undead salamander from another with ease: Margie and Jean and Melody would remain loyal to the end; George and Larry and Ned, too.

Sometimes, he indulged in imaginary conversations with them, to while away the time before military briefings or updates from Paris. They made him feel comfy, pushed back against the claustrophobic sense of confinement. Him and the salamanders against the world. Some nights, after Wretch had left and he was shivering in bed . . . it felt like that.

Yet they could not help him with this speech that Wretch demanded he deliver at their next stopping point—a village in the middle of nowhere, the name translated into English bizarrely: "Slap on the Cheek." He was to give a speech in Slap on the Cheek. Wretch cited security concerns as to why in such a remote location.

In the speech, he was to put forth the official reasons for the invasion of Prussia and Bavaria, and the annexing of Prague into his empire.

Copies of which would then be sent by carrier pigeon and crow throughout Europe. To put more than one independent ruler on notice. To put Prague on notice. To serve notice, too, to the enemy, against interfering in what Crowley was to term "a regional dispute."

Perhaps Prague would capitulate without a war. Perhaps they would look at what had happened elsewhere and understand the wisdom of surrender.

But his heart wasn't in it. Wretch's impertinence—well, it was more than that—ate at him, made him feel impotent. For a time, even the humiliating memory of Wretch patting him on the head like a dog had been balanced against Crowley's fantasy of Earths imploding into nothing and him harnessing their energy for his war effort. Could he reach that distant goal without Wretch?

Yet the Speck . . . the Speck had changed that way of thinking. What had been a symbol of his control and lack of control both . . . had changed to a symbol of a possible alliance.

Might he find some common cause with the Golden Sphere against Wretch, and rid himself of his familiar while still maintaining his station? For several days, he had barely allowed himself the thought—the possibility so remote, and yet also in case Wretch through some uncanny eavesdropping might hear him inside his own skull.

But once he'd opened a conduit to the Speck in its jar, there was no going back. He'd decided not to be ruled by his familiar. He'd decided to rebel against his Wretch. Come what would.

Crowley opened the connection once more.

For he trusted the Speck more than his demi-mages or Napoleon to help him find out what Wretch did to him at night.

Finally, in the late-late afternoon, with Napoleon no doubt napping and thus blissfully deprived of his bird-laden monologues, Crowley wrestled the speech into submission, against the odds, tossed the parchment to the side. It wasn't artful, but who cared?

A spark of pride. He was still the emperor, even if Wretch had called him a puppet. No one knew what transpired beneath the scenes and he must conduct himself in public with confidence and verve.

What now to do for fun? Now his tasks for the day were complete?

In the corner near his desk was the entrance to the controversial chute out the elephant's backside, lined with slick aluminum. His emergency exit should the elephant ever be breached by an enemy. He contemplated the main door, gazed again at the chute. If he went out the door, Wretch was no doubt waiting—might even burst in on Crowley if he didn't emerge rather soon. Whereas Wretch would definitely not be waiting at the end of the chute, and he might have a few moments of freedom.

He clutched his golden crown in his hand, carefully braced himself in the mouth of the chute, arranging his robes, his cloak, in such a way that it might protect him against the friction of his passage.

Hadn't there been a playground back home he'd happily played on with just such a happy feature? Perhaps not housed inside an elephant, but he could remember sliding down without a care in the world, deposited on cedar chips or sand, only to want to immediately go again. A motley little crew of adventurers with him then. Not a leader at all, but just part of a gang.

There might be nothing like the cruelty of children, but also nothing like their unthinking comradery, either.

So down the chute he went, shrieking in delight at its twists and turns, tumbling out below the elephant's tail at a good enough height that he had an instant of panic that he might break a leg.

But no: His demi-mages had placed bales of hay beneath the elephant, and he was embraced by a hearty outdoors smell and a bristly softness, and he bounced up from it to an audience consisting, for now, of a half circle of very serious demi-mages. Laughing, crown and speech in hand, for once without a care in the world.

Until a nervous demi-mage stepped forward and said, "My lord, General Napoleon—he is missing."

Crowley looked up in alarm. The pedestal poked up above his magnificent Folly.

No head.

Napoleon had flown the coop.

Chapter Twenty-Eight

FLYING DEER AND SHADOWY WATCHERS

The trail up into the Italian Alps looped around the tallest mountain in the area. The gravel gave Jonathan and his companions purchase but also slid at times into the abyss beyond, enticing them to follow, to become weightless, and then to plummet.

Even though it was summer, a biting cold wind lashed them as they progressed, pushing a shoulder into the wall of air while the trail became surly or friendly, depending on whether the switchbacks went almost straight up or in lazy fashion looped around the mountainside like a necklace.

Far above, the trail promised the blinding whiteness of perfect snow-capped peaks that looked unreal. The conifers all around them—larch and pine and spruce—gave off a fresh scent that mingled with the softness of a gentle snowfall. The snow had the consistency of feathers, but you could slip on feathers, had to be careful.

It all looked so pristine and so empty, but Mamoud had explained that the area was more like a powder keg, about to explode.

"No central rule for long stretches, a struggle to keep mountain passes open for supplies—and also for who controls them. Freelancers, separatists take advantage. People do as they will in the small mountain towns. Some even side with Crowley to settle old scores. It's a gauntlet of a kind. People are watching, even if we can't see them."

Either way, Jonathan hadn't gotten used to it—any trail map for

Florida meant flat, even surfaces. The Alps maps tricked him; nothing straight meant easy; sometimes it meant climbing up into a curled circle of stone, pulling others up after him, until the next level bit. All while the cold-blue lake below still seemed so very close, as if they'd made no progress at all.

He also hadn't gotten used to the plants and animals here. Jonathan had never been to the Alps, but he was certain that back on Earth the Alps—neither the Italian, French, nor Swiss parts—did not include huge flowers three times the size of Rack's head that hugged the ground on stout stems and gave off a smell like sea salt and mint. The wide five-petaled blossoms came in two versions: One was a deep ocean blue, the other white with blue polka dots all over. The trail was lined with them. The texture somewhat rubbery, like a succulent, when Jonathan leaned down to touch one.

Alice, rather late, warned against it. "Swiss magician. A bit of a mistake, but it caught on after the arrival of the Comet Man. Unpredictable—best left alone."

"Which bit was the mistake?" Jonathan asked, pointing to the tiny flying deer that hovered and spun from the center of one flower to another, sipping nectar with delicate pink tongues.

Their wings beat so fast they couldn't be seen, their light brown coats glossy, their large shiny eyes bulging in their heads. Was the thin mountain air taking a toll? Because this certainly must be a hallucination, if a pleasant one. The creatures had two layers of fur, and their eyes were glossy black and compound like a bumblebee's. The nub of tail, tucked in close, and their compact bodies reminded him somehow of corgis. Their ears were also tucked in, close to the head, and the muzzles shorter, both more delicate and blunter than a regular deer's.

Yet he knew them—from Sarah! Honey deer, honey deer, flying, too, except she'd left out the weirder bits of their anatomy.

"The lesser nectar deer," Alice said. "The local ravens consider them a delicacy. The greater nectar deer you won't see—they only come out at night, to feast on moonlight."

Lesser or greater, the local ravens were huge, and Jonathan didn't fancy getting on their bad side: pure white but not albinos. Since they'd found the trail leading up to the Institute, Jonathan didn't think there had been a moment without at least one white raven keeping an eye on them. And shadows . . . the shadows from the rock formations all around were also strange, although he couldn't say how.

"Poor nectar deer! That's terrible!" Danny said from ahead of them. She always did have good hearing.

Mamoud had, after some decidedly weak protest, let Danny lead. The order went: Danny, Mamoud, Alice, Rack, and Jonathan. Rack was keeping up well. You could say Alice seemed the least avid hiker, Danny the most. Sometimes, on uncertain ground, Rack insisted on going first, as he had an eye for detail from necessity, using his cane not just for balance but to poke the ground for hidden holes.

Jonathan liked to go last, because he had always had a paranoid sixth sense on hikes about dangers leaping out from behind. Only Mamoud didn't need the help.

"We'll gather up the nectar deer near dusk and put them all in a pot for dinner," Mamoud said, staring back at Jonathan and Alice with a grin.

"No!" This from Danny, and by extension, Tee-Tee, who had proven a shoulder-hugging genius during the climb and kept watch on them all as if they were chasing Danny rather than following her.

"He's having you on," Alice said. "The ravens like them, but they taste sour—turn your mouth numb. Sometimes kids in the villages will catch one just to lick it and get 'dead tongue.' That's how boring it is around here."

"Alice has told me there is a much larger nocturnal flying deer that looks after their tiny cousins," Mamoud said. "Lick a tiny deer, get a huge one smashing through your window after dark."

"You do seem to know the area, Alice," Jonathan said, ignoring Mamoud.

Ever since Mamoud had found out they didn't believe in the Hedgehog Man, he had been winding them up with "facts" about Aurora.

Jonathan found this tongue-in-cheek side of Mamoud a little unexpected, wasn't sure he wanted to encourage it. Not that he had a choice.

Alice shrugged. "Boarding school, as I said. Me and my sister. Ages ago. And not here—Swiss Alps, not Italian."

"Wait," Rack said. "What's this about a sister?"

"Wait," Jonathan said. "What's this about a Comet Man?"

Alice shrugged, ignored Rack with a frown. "Didn't I say before? That's Comet Lake below," pointing down at the stunning cerulean oval alit with the flames of reflected sunlight. Where they'd started out.

"That doesn't help."

But Alice was done explaining. Anything. They'd reached a particularly rough patch and didn't talk for a while, focused on bending their knees and placing their feet.

Yet something about the weather, the bracing mountain air, which lingered in Jonathan's lungs as a wheezing tightness, had improved the company's mood.

High spirits, almost, to match the altitude.

☙

Another thing Jonathan hadn't expected: There was a huge hole in the Italian Alps. Of all the things he hadn't expected. The hole had been caused by a comet smashing into Aurora during the time of the Builders. It had sheared the mountains all around and created Comet Lake, which lay below them, and also explained why their progress on the trail seemed excruciatingly slow, since they'd had to go around the lake before heading upward.

Comet Lake was vast and so blazingly blue, surrounded by such a richness of trees and wildflowers, that Jonathan's slight sense of vertigo warred with the impulse to dive down into it, even from such a great height. It looked so close and yet so far.

According to Alice, the local villages still celebrated Comet Day every year, the day the comet had come down and the Comet Man had emerged from the wreckage and ravaged the countryside.

Comet Day had waxed and waned ever since—Jonathan imagined it had rather waned right after the event, through to the generation that had forgotten all about the death and destruction. There were Comet Day toys, which it had become tradition for parents in the area to hand-craft for their children. Clearly, from Alice's enthusiasm, she'd received more than one herself—a happy place for her just as much as the Hedge-hog Man.

"Some say the Comet was a lonely Celestial Beast that came down to Aurora to find a friend," Alice explained.

Mamoud had told them earlier that Aurora had a history of Celestial Beasts that fell out of the sky, but Jonathan hadn't believed him.

"Others say that the sightings of the Comet Man are actually of the great Emperor Charlemagne, for this occurred near the beginning of his reign, when he was mere warlord, and he is said to have had a vision of a falling Celestial Beast and in the dream the Builders came to him and said he must go forth to meet it. And thus, he was devoured by a lake of fire and baptized in those flames and reborn as Emperor. Part Comet Man."

"Daft," Rack said with the admiration of someone who loves a good yarn.

"What is not 'daft' as you put it, Rack, is that to this day the Comet Man is seen walking these trails. Charlemagne or not, Celestial Beast or not."

"Charle*mange* by now, I'd imagine," Rack said.

"That's not a very original Charlemagne joke," Alice said. "I bet others have already done it."

"You've got a better one?" Rack challenged.

"Some say instead Charlemagne lives beneath the lake and that Aurora is hollow and he lives on as an uncanny magician, ruling a hidden kingdom," Mamoud said unhelpfully. "Or that Charlemagne made it all up, and the Comet Man burns with fury and anger at Charlemagne for his deception."

"How will we know if we see him, yeah? This vengeful Comet Man?" Danny asked.

"Why, the Comet Man will be engulfed by perpetual flames," Alice said.

"And then, if you don't run . . . so will you," Mamoud added.

Alice and Mamoud carried on, but Jonathan fell out of the conversation, engrossed by a scene playing out far below, near the lake. One of his sweeps behind them with his binoculars had revealed a funeral procession. The black dots of a dozen people, four hefting the coffin, trudged solemn and swaying up from the lake to a lodge house Jonathan's party had themselves passed on their way to the trailhead leading up the mountain.

Because it was only four holding the coffin on their shoulders, Jonathan guessed the occupant was a child or youth. The eight other mourners followed a little ways back, the coffin bearers hurrying a bit, as if they'd misjudged the distance and difficulty, and wanted their burden laid to rest. A few women with black veils, three or four men, and a couple of children. Their Sunday best was hindering their ability to navigate the way, as the lodge lay at the end of a path half-hidden by fresh snowfall.

But it was the "person" bringing up the rear, at first well behind the rest, that drew most of Jonathan's attention. He thought of her as a "person" loosely from the start—and every fresh look as he tried to watch and also keep pace with Rack directly ahead of him led him to believe "loosely human" was the best description.

She was a very large woman and struck him as some caricature or stereotype of an olde-tyme village schoolmarm, in a green cardigan over a peach-colored blouse and with a long gray skirt that protruded over a bulging abdomen and draped to the ground, hiding any hint of leg. The head had a matching green cowl over it and a crimson scarf across the neck. As a result, Jonathan could only glimpse the features of the face, which had a potatolike quality to them, in the sense of seeming bulky or misshapen. She wore black spectacles tight across that face—so tight

Jonathan could have sworn that they weren't spectacles at all, but drawn with marker across her face, like a raccoon's mask.

The English schoolmarm, if schoolmarm she be, did not look like a dot or slender silhouette like the other mourners. Nor did the jaunty colors of her outfit jibe with the respectful black of the others. There was also the matter of how something moved atop the center of the cowl, almost as if the cowl was trembling of its own accord. Was the stitching not up to snuff? An inane thought, but it was all Jonathan had. As he studied her, Jonathan realized that the schoolmarm must be enormously tall for him to be able to unlock such detail through the lens.

Mamoud had said something outrageous and was cackling at his own audacity, but Jonathan had missed it, and only heard with half an ear Rack's reply.

"And to think, there was so much more treasure to catalog in the mansion, if we'd just stayed there"—Rack, over his shoulder, to Jonathan. Rolling his eyes as he forged ahead. But perhaps half pining for what seemed so distant.

"The mansion was a musty trap," Jonathan replied. "This is fresh air! And good stories!"

"It's not a story," Mamoud said. But something in his eyes gave him away.

"And all sorts of possible death," Rack said, cheerily talking over Mamoud. "Bears no doubt. Dark magic. Falling to our death or burning to death. Not to mention that exploding train we left behind and a ruined magical men's room."

By the time a distracted Jonathan looked again, the schoolmarm had closed the distance with the coffin bearers, who were still a ways from the lodge. Some of the black-clad mourners behind had apparently left the procession, for ahead of the schoolmarm there were only five figures. The coffin bearers had picked up the pace, and he couldn't tell for sure but were the five behind also moving faster?

"Jonathan!"

He put down the binoculars. Rack was asking for help—a stone stuck on the tread of the shoe on his artificial foot. It had happened twice on the trail, and each time he'd asked Jonathan, not Danny. Jonathan dropped to a knee, pried it out, and they went on.

Below, when Jonathan looked through the binoculars again, the coffin bearers had reached the lodge, for they were nowhere in sight, and neither were the mourners.

There was just the schoolmarm, lingering outside the lodge.

Was the schoolmarm singing to herself? The mouth was moving up and down in some semblance of speech. That the mouth might be chewing seemed obscene to consider. Who chewed with such vigor and enthusiasm? Nor did he much enjoy focusing on the cowl, which still moved so uncanny.

Jonathan watched for as long as he could—the trail had become rough again, with little between them and the edge, so hugging the mountain quite literally was the safest choice.

The schoolmarm didn't move the entire time. Just stood there outside the lodge, as if not even alive or—and Jonathan didn't know where the thought came from—as if in a stupor, as from sun-drenched drowsiness or the need to digest after a heavy meal.

A half hour of hugging the mountain like it was a dear friend gave way to a level patch through a meadow of wild grass. By then, though, the lake was finally too far distant or the schoolmarm had left. Nothing lurked by the lodge as far as Jonathan could tell. If anything ever had. He still wasn't quite sure what he had seen.

But one question stuck in Jonathan's mind for quite some time.

Which way had the schoolmarm gone—back down around the lake, or up onto the very trail they now trod?

Three days had passed since jumping into the cistern. Jonathan's leg had begun to heal, the others' injuries had faded, and everyone's mood had improved. The exit had been another cistern, and then Alice's knowledge of the area had allowed them by hook and by crook to make it to the trailhead. A suspect rusted bucket of an automobile ("Tin can," Danny had said, to which Rack had replied, "Tin can't") and the hay wagons of two helpful farmers had given them respite from walking some of those miles. One of the farmers also gifted Rack with a proper cold-weather gray cloak, which he wore grudgingly over his very dirty blazer.

Yet even with Alice's help and Mamoud's maps, their merry little troupe was, if not lost, then in unknown territory. "Somewhere north of Milan, south of Lake Como, well west of Bernt," Alice had told them. "I've never been in this region—always Switzerland."

Which was both not very comforting and meant nothing much to Jonathan. Not comforting either was the translation of the mountain's name from Italian: the Three Lakes of Hell Peak.

"A rough translation," Mamoud said. But did not provide a smoother one.

Nor did they know why it was called Puffin Trail. Although they did know why ancient letters carved into some of the immense rock formations read "*skufur*" or "*forniskufur*" and similar things.

"Ancient tassel," Rack told him. "Icelandic."

"What does 'ancient tassel' mean?" Jonathan had asked, but Rack had just shrugged.

Icelandic, Alice said, because in Aurora Icelanders had in ancient times invaded all the way from Britain down to the Alps, only to be repulsed. It went along with the look of some of the older burnt-out churches and burnt graveyards they could see on the slopes of other peaks, which Jonathan couldn't think of as either "alpine" or "Italian." The piles of old stones littering the sides of the trail, though, had a more prosaic origin: gravestones marking an ill-fated trek through the Alps by Aurora's version of Napoleon.

It was beside a particularly large grouping of such gravestones that Mamoud took him aside during a brief respite in their trek. Back down the trail to a rather daring granite ledge, the excuse a spectacular view.

"Tell me, what do you see?" he asked Jonathan with an appraising stare.

Jonathan took a swig of water from his canteen, considering the question. It sounded like a test, the kind of pop quiz Poxforth instructors were famous for. Perhaps in order of importance, then?

"There's someone . . . unusual . . . beneath us, coming up the trail," Jonathan said. "I thought they might be headed back down, but no—they're closer behind us now."

"A cause for concern, I think you'd agree. What else?"

"A lack, of sorts. We've met no one on this trail. Not going up or going down."

Mamoud nodded, too polite to condescend to Jonathan by saying "Very good, grasshopper," or anything like that.

"What else?"

"Probably unimportant, but it bothers me that we're on something called 'Puffin Trail' while in the middle of the Alps. Sounds like someone having a laugh, but I don't know of many trails named by comedians."

"It bothers me as well, Jonathan. Although not as much as the lurker below."

They took a moment to appreciate the view. Although by Jonathan's reckoning the view, on closer inspection, included too many burnt and ruined things clinging to steep inclines.

"And there's one last thing," Jonathan said. "Or did I imagine it?"

"Watchers above us, wearing shadowy masks for some reason. I, too, only saw them briefly."

"Yes. High above." He'd noticed this only after the curious funeral procession.

"Higher than the way station above us," Mamoud noted. "By my estimation."

"At first, I thought they wore dark ski masks," Jonathan said.

"No. They're masks like faces. Not human faces, although it's hard to tell."

"Drifty, too," Jonathan replied. As if the watchers weren't quite teth-ered to the rock beneath their feet.

Neither had to say the obvious: that this was creepy and odd.

"Shall we tell the others?" Jonathan asked.

"I imagine some have noticed by now. Alice, perhaps. If they haven't, no need to alarm anyone."

"But we should have some kind of plan."

Mamoud laughed, and his breath misted white. He said, in a good-natured way: "So you have been in this situation before."

Jonathan smiled. "I can't say that I have. Have you?"

"No. Not in this way. So I think all we can do is watch the watchers for now and not panic."

"Continue to drink tea on the turret."

Mamoud's eyes brightened. "Yes, for a time."

Alice, Rack, and Danny were looking back at them now, ready to continue upward. Danny and the rat in particular looked impatient.

"You know that Tee-Tee can talk," Jonathan said.

"Just not to us," Mamoud said, nodding at Danny. "Wise choice."

"Granted," Jonathan said.

Then they started to walked back up toward the group, Jonathan somewhat relieved Mamoud hadn't taken the opportunity to grill him about the magic surge after the train crash.

Yet Jonathan hadn't mentioned the most mysterious thing he'd dis-covered on their trek.

The day before, sparked by Alice dawdling and falling behind, he'd teased her about her spying back at Dr. Lambshead's mansion. How the day he'd arrived, that day that now seemed so long ago, he'd never figured out how she'd gotten from the hedgerow out to the backyard in time to meet him across the pond. Then felt he'd made a mistake, given something away.

For she'd hesitated, a pause that lasted too long, the wheels behind her eyes churning furiously.

Then Alice had said, with a weak smile: "I can be very fast when I want to."

To Jonathan, it was so clearly a lie.

Which meant Alice and the marmot hadn't been the only ones lurking around the mansion.

Chapter Twenty-Nine

PLEASE DIE ON OUR FINE SELECTION OF DRAGONS

After five horrible days and four terrifying, sleepless nights, it was almost a relief to Verne to glimpse the land bridge to England ahead of them. The wall was distant and somewhat fog-shrouded a mile or so beyond where the bridge began.

The wall, centuries old, was rumored to have been built by, as Crowley would've put it, "that slaggard shithead the Raven King," but in reality probably by some drunken hopped-up hedge magician, lost to history, who couldn't figure out how to channel or turn off what they'd created. Whoever it was had let in the magic of Stonehenge-era undead druids whose bodies had rotted into the ground but whose spirits still lingered in the trees and shrubs and weeds of the British Isles.

Verne had never seen the wall before, forgot for the moment his disagreeable companion Laudinum X as he strained for a look, which was not forthcoming. Too much of the land bridge got in the way from that distance.

Overgrown with thickets of plants, old ruins, a forest, cliffs to either side to fall screaming from—resistant to defenders and attackers alike—a hostile entity, that wall, still preferable to the sea serpents of the North Sea controlled by the unpredictable Fresians—Crowley had no navy to speak of—or the "electrical discharge" of magic in the ocean to either side of the bridge, which created all sorts of monstrosities and weather effects to overcome. The North Sea Fresians and England formed a bond that could not be broken—certainly not by the black sheep, the dark wolf, the prodigal son who had already betrayed them.

"A magic chaos region, an obstacle course," Verne muttered, and all at once, remembering again they were headed for the heart of that chaos, his enthusiasm dulled. Remembering, too, Rome and what Crowley's attack there had done to the city. What would their magical assault in the Burrower do to the wall? The bridge? Would they merely breach it like a battering ram, or be transformed? Crowley might not care. LX might not know to care. But Verne still cared.

"Microscope!" Laudinum X roared. "Speed! Speed! And stealth!" The latter, Verne believed, had been lost to them as soon as they'd been imprisoned in the cockpit. "Kill them all. Bastards made of porridge and bad weather! My mother was my father! All hail Crowley!"

LX's exhortations had only become more random with the passage of days, but he did have one good idea: to use the spyglass, which for some reason LX liked to call "the microscope." The spyglass Crowley had thoughtfully ordered to be welded in place on a stand in the cramped, crazed cockpit so that Verne's legs straddled it and more than once in their dread lurching progress he had banged his orbital upon it without the side benefit even of having seen anything through it. (The resulting bloodshot, bruised, and abraded right eye had given him, he feared, an evermore crazed expression. Although who would notice?)

A look at the wall through the glass did him little good, however—at least to his battered constitution. For what it revealed infuriated him and brought on the fear again.

Tripods! Flying tripods on mechanical wings reinforced with canvas—the invention, without doubt, of the accursed plagiarist and hack H. G. Wells. From the shoddy construction and the difficulty in keeping aloft what were practically metal death balloons, Verne doubted they were meant to attack in the traditional way. No, as he observed their asymmetrical bobbing and the buffeting they took from the winds off the sea, he guessed they were meant more as bombs. Like sea mines for boats, except they were sky mines meant to disable the Burrower.

That their steering ability was dismal might reflect a defect in their design that could be traced back to a defect in the mind of H. G. Wells as much as this clumsy purpose.

"To the feast!" LX screamed. "To the slaughter! For the glory of our lord! Let the mother of sin eat at the trough of their own offal! Meow! Meow! Roarrrr!"

Under the lash of Laudinum X's inchoate urgings, the Burrower had picked up speed, sliding along so fast it slaughtered any trees in its way. It slammed from mainland to land bridge with such velocity that what should have been a gentle bump, a slight dip, instead became a crack and snap that reverberated up from the bottom of the Burrower's frame to the top, and there came, too, the smell of burning earth, a little like a pungent glue, that signaled that tons more worm paste had just been made.

But while the demi-mages helping steer the Burrower had been negotiating the path onto the land bridge, the defenders of the still-distant walls had been busy. From an array of catapults behind the wall, there came a tumbling of red-and-white shapes arcing across the drizzling gray sky toward the Burrower. All animosity at Wells's floating bombs left Verne as he tried to make out through the spyglass what they might be. Were they odd small tables? White with red polka dots? Or some kind of assault by undersized bar stools?

"They mean to bomb us," Laudinum X shouted. "We will plow through them like oxen! We will shamble them into shards like pillows! They will become like dog crap only not as useful!"

"Shut up," Verne said, for LX was so annoying in his exhortations it made it not just harder for Verne to hear but also to see through the spyglass. LX smacked him in the shoulder for his trouble, but Verne hardly noticed.

Halfway through the arc, the objects began to emit a hissing steam and to shriek like the devil. Not small tables at all, but enormous toadstools. Mushrooms. Fruiting bodies.

The English were flinging fungi.

"I want my doggie. I want my doggie. I lost my doggie. And my badger."

"I don't have your doggie! I don't have your badger!" Verne snapped.

Laudinum X gave him a look both petulant and murderous.

The range was puzzling, far short of the Burrower's position. The toadstools, each about the height of a husky three-foot-tall man, tumbled and fell and bounced to a halt in a rough pile about a quarter mile ahead.

Then they set out tendrils in the soil while expanding upward with ridiculous speed—a swiftness comparable to the Burrower's progress.

"Their faces shall be smashed! We shall smash all their faces!" Laudinum X shrieked, and Verne realized that a stopped clock is indeed correct twice a day.

The mushrooms *had* grown faces, although LX could not possibly have known it. Terrible masklike faces with holes for eyes that had the torn-at-the-edges effect of someone punching a fist through cookie dough, and mouths not much better . . . and all these mushroom people were now holding "hands," which in this case were red-and-white tendrils that grew sideways.

All the mushrooms were now screaming and emitting even more steam and in some profound yet indefinable way continuing to grow even as they also melted into one another, and began to form a barricade about ten feet tall that the twenty-foot-tall Burrower was headed straight for.

What devilry was this? Wells's clunky creations he could cope with, but peering bumpily through the spyglass at these horrors made Verne want to gibber and give up. Lie slack in his harness, and whatever would come would come.

But the English had just begun to fight.

For that's when the mighty emerald dragon appeared from over the wall's ramparts and circled once and then in a twisty, crafty fashion headed toward them.

A sight that left even Laudinum X speechless.

It was made of ten thousand much smaller dragons.
All of whom were breathing tiny flames.
Just looking at it disoriented and confused the eye.
What hell had they descended into?
Could they ever get out?
Even as the Burrower inexorably drove on, into the morass.

Chapter Thirty

COMETS AND CAMPFIRES

By nightfall, they had found a place to sleep out of the wind, in a lee of the mountainside, a grotto with fallen fir trees forming a makeshift lean-to. The dirt floor appeared to have been swept recently, and a circle of stones ringed a dead campfire, now gray ash.

It seemed to reassure Mamoud that other travelers had stayed there, which reassured Jonathan in turn, and Jonathan gladly volunteered to help make a new fire and find a secure place to store their food a safe one hundred feet from their sleeping bags. To protect against bears, yes, if bears there were, but who knew what else lurked out in the dark?

Danny groused a bit at being left out of the preparations, but Mamoud and Jonathan had found common ground in their experience in the outdoors. Mamoud had, after the first day, begun to look at Jonathan with a certain amount of respect—and it was mutual. Mamoud was clearly used to bivouacking out in the open and sleeping rough. And this wasn't the time to teach others what to do, but to get it done as quickly as possible, before nightfall.

Their calm efficiency and Danny's rough eagerness to help gather wood—"shrubbery may do," Jonathan reminded her—contrasted with Alice's and Rack's somewhat disdainful tolerance of their conditions. Both stood around a fair amount asking what they could do, arms crossed, while it was done for them. Besides, they would both soon become proficient in shooing away the tiny nectar deer, which buzzed about their heads, perhaps drawn by something sugary in their supplies.

Well, good, maybe they'd bond over a shared dislike of "nature." Maybe Alice would even stop fixating on the Wobble. The one time he'd taken it out of his pocket, she'd looked hungry again, starved almost. Nor did he appreciate how it had changed again, keeping the usual shape, but turned all seething electric gold across a backdrop of muted greens. There was a grating *pulse* to it, as if the Wobble were sending out a signal.

But he forgot Alice soon enough, in his delight to see Rack come alive, finally, once Jonathan had the fire blazing and Mamoud got the pot out and some raw ingredients.

Mamoud had gone off on his own to forage and come back with mushrooms and a plucked bird, a rather decrepit headless bird.

"That, my friends . . . is not a chicken," Mamoud said. "I don't know the types of birds, to be honest. But I will have dinner ready for you soon."

They'd suffered through Mamoud's bare-bones—often literally—approach to supper enough nights to rouse Rack's instinct for self-preservation.

"Ah," Rack said, stepping into the breach, "let me make the stew tonight, mate," giving Mamoud a comradely pat on the shoulder and tugging the pot handle away from him. "You can make the tea."

Then he sat down next to Mamoud on one fallen log while Alice, Danny, and Jonathan faced them across the fire on another. There was moss on the log, and some tiny white starfish-shaped flowers and, of course, the ever-present nectar deer, now a nuisance, for they insisted on hovering near their shoulders and buttocks for some reason.

Out from Rack's pack spilled a veritable richness of spices, which he combined with Mamoud's "not chicken" and some of Danny's vegetables—leeks and carrots mostly—and a few other ingredients Rack rifled through his pack for.

Thus equipped, Rack set to the task with gusto and precision. Rack did like to cook when the spirit moved him. He could cook with almost nothing, out of necessity, and given an actual something, Jonathan knew he could be phenomenal. He'd made vegetable samosas once with a phyllo crust so light the contrast of the crust melting in the mouth and the rough hardiness of the potatoes and peas and the hot curry mix had been sublime.

Best not to think of that, given the available ingredients, but Jonathan was surprised, when Rack ladled the boiling stew into their bowls, that the rough-looking chicken had as if by magic become moist and not at all chewy and the stock was the kind of hot-sour concoction best for a cold night, making the nose run.

"Not bad," Mamoud grudgingly admitted, making even Alice laugh. The face he made was so at odds with what was on offer. Mamoud ate like he was used to fine dining, while Alice ate like someone who had had her food taken from her as a child.

"Tee-Tee recommends Rack should cook dinner the rest of the way, yeah?" Danny said, once more abdicating responsibility for an opinion to her rat.

With dusk came the beauty of the blue polka-dot flowers fully revealed: the blue dots glowed a dim phosphorescence against the darkness, all up and down the trail they were following. There came the gentle popping sound as the blossoms released tiny pulsing blue seeds, taken by the wind, looking like light blue wisps of smoke, quickly dissipating.

It was a cozy sight, although Jonathan also knew that the thick swooshing sounds of the nocturnal flying deer would soon follow. He tried to put them out of his mind because the sound made him a tad nauseated, he didn't know why. Perhaps because the gossamer wings were more insectile than deerlike. Perhaps because they had yet to actually see one of the giant deer, which were wary and never broke the cover of night, and the sound was more monstrous disassociated from the sight of an animal.

After dinner and the washing up—Jonathan didn't particularly like scrubbing with snow, which abraded the hands through his pitifully thin gloves—Mamoud told them more about the Comet Man.

". . . and when he came out from the crater he had created, now a lake filled with the winter's snow thawing down from the mountains, he felt an even greater loneliness. Whatever vessel he had used to traverse the cosmic seas had been destroyed, and he must seek company in this place so unlike anything he knew, between and inside the stars.

"So he walked forth and he greeted each animal and plant he saw. With a fiery hug. And each time what he sought to befriend burst into flames and ash.

"The bunnies in their burrows. The skunks and the songbirds, the badgers and the marmots. But not the nectar deer, for they did not live in the Alps at that time. And the trees around the crater all burned down, and a raging fire consumed all life on the mountain peaks around. And the Comet Man was still alone and knew he would always be alone. And so the Comet Man returned to the ruins of his vessel, and as the rains came and after the thaw came and went, and avalanches, his vessel was covered over by the blessed waters and the Comet Man as well. So that ever after he would burn below the lake as embers, as burning loneliness, and the lake waters would be forever warm.

"And the Comet Man might still be alone and look up at the stars and long to be at least a Celestial Beast again. But, on his loneliest nights, he can still be seen roaming this area, a burning figure against the night, trudging through the burning snow. Looking to hug someone who does not want to be hugged."

"The worst story ever," Rack said. "What's the moral?"

"It had its moments," Danny said.

"A cautionary tale," Jonathan said.

"Not the version I told you, Mamoud," Alice said.

"Your version needed a rescue mission," Mamoud said, chuckling in a good-natured way. "Your version did not fit 'Puffin Trail.'" Jonathan had a feeling Mamoud had had to amuse himself quite a bit while on various missions.

What Jonathan didn't say was that he had heard this story before, from Sarah, which meant it might be important. But he couldn't tell how. Mostly, he'd tried to put his mother's disappearance in the Alps out of his mind. Too painful, still. And it was dangerous to be distracted hiking through unfamiliar terrain. Sarah wouldn't have liked him to be distracted because of her.

"How do you tell someone who's just on fire from the Comet Man in these parts?" Rack asked. "Must be hard. Because if you're on fire you might be the Comet Man?"

Far out in the night came a bloodcurdling bellow, as of some beast offering a reply.

"What in the name of all that's holy was that?" Rack asked.

"The Comet Man," Danny said, giggling.

Jonathan exchanged a glance with Mamoud.

"Time to sleep," Mamoud said. "Alice and I will take the first watch. In case the Comet Man heard my blasphemous version of his tale."

They turned in for the night, Jonathan on one side of the subdued fire, next to R & D, warm in their sleeping bags, while on the other side A & M, as he sometimes thought of them now, huddled facing out toward the wilderness, engaged in a whispered conversation. Funny how Mamoud deferred to Alice on some things and Mamoud took the lead on others. He still hadn't worked out the hierarchy between them.

Jonathan looked up at the patch of night sky not obscured by the broken fir trees and was, of a sudden, melancholy. It had come over him fast. A kind of intermingling of residue from the wraith and the sense of Sarah being nearby, but separated from him by a veil. She must have disappeared somewhere close by, back on Earth. Had anyone been with her at the end? Alice and Mamoud didn't know the details; he needed to find someone who did.

He didn't mind feeling a little sad, a little down, at times. Especially there in the cold, snug in his jacket and warm hat, by the heat of the campfire, under the stars, with his friends. This was also the first time since coming to Aurora that they'd had a moment to themselves without Alice and Mamoud right there, listening.

"The stars are very different here," he said.

"How different?" Rack asked.

"You never studied astronomy?"

"Astrology."

"Well," Jonathan admitted, "astrology might come in handy just as much here. Given Celestial Beasts and all."

"It's beautiful," Danny said. "The sky."

"No North Star," Jonathan said. "No Ursa Minor or Major. No comfortable dot for Mars or Venus." He wasn't quite sure he wanted to know the cosmology of the sky above Aurora. It was as disorienting as the expected far-distant sound of deer wings.

"Might be paste diamonds stitched into black velvet," Rack said, which wasn't any sort of comfort. "I wouldn't put it past this place." His voice was laced with drowsiness and an earnest sort of weariness.

Jonathan wondered if the day had taken more out of Rack than he'd ever admit.

"Do you trust them?" Danny whispered. "Alice and Mamoud?"

Rack snorted. "I don't know if I trust *you*, sister-blister."

Danny sighed. "I've told you, it was a few times as a child. I hardly know more than you. For the longest time I didn't even know I'd gone to Aurora. It was just a different place."

"What did they tell you? And who told you?"

"It was after our parents died, Rack. The estate agent. I didn't believe him, but he provided proof."

"What kind of proof?"

"He brought me across to see the wall on the land bridge to England. It wasn't safe for long, but a glimpse of that would be more than enough to convince anyone. It's chaotic magic. Completely bonkers. I'll never forget it. But that was it, Rack—the three times, the warning not to go back, and to look out for you."

"If you say so, sister," Rack said, but much of the sourness had left his voice, for which Jonathan was glad.

Each time it came up, Rack left a little more of his resentment behind. Although Jonathan could understand it. No matter how much Danny thought of Rack as her brother, not just her adoptive brother, Rack must still carry some insecurity with him. About his place in the world. How could he not?

"By the way—I trust Mamoud," Jonathan whispered, to change the subject. "Jury's out on Alice."

Rack snorted again. "Of course you trust the outdoorsman. He could be a serial killer but because he can make a campfire he's all right by you."

"Not entirely fair," Jonathan said.

"They're both rather fit, Alice and Mamoud," Danny mused. Perhaps she didn't realize she was saying it aloud. "Do you think they're shagging, yeah? Tee-Tee bets they're shagging. So do I."

"You like both of them, Danny, just admit it," Jonathan said.

"Sod off."

"Sod on, you mean! Don't let our predicament stop you, Danny," Rack said. "Go right ahead and involve yourself in some sort of complicated relationship whilst we climb up this misbegotten oversized rock toward a way station that may not even exist anymore."

"Hey, Alice," Danny called out. "Are there a lot of tragic love affairs between worlds? Because of the fade?"

A curt reply came back across the campfire. "No. People who cross over are generally too aware of the fade to get involved. You would have to be very, very stupid."

"What about those who don't realize?"

"You mean Stumblers? They deserve whatever they get."

"Did you just make that term up? Well, I suppose you're right," Danny said, almost to herself rather than to Alice.

"Well, I'm glad we've settled that important issue," Rack said. "I'm going to sleep now. Or going to try to." He turned over, struggling with the sleeping bag, which was snug.

"Tee-Tee says good night to all, and to all a good night, yeah?"

"See you in the morning," Jonathan said.

But in the morning, Danny was gone without a trace, and so was the bear gun.

Chapter Thirty-One
I SHALL MAKE YOUR HAND EAT YOUR FACE

Puppeteer and playwright Alfred Kubin sat in his caravan that same evening, drapes drawn, hand engulfed by a horse-head hand puppet that had proven quite unruly. This affliction had come on the heels of a tepid show and a languid gambol by their little troupe back to their caravans, housed in the woods to avoid housing fees.

Kubin had struggled for some time to get the puppet off his hand, without success. It just would not come free, and the puppet knew he also struggled as to *why* it would not come free.

Well, Kubin would find out soon enough, although the puppet had nothing but time, having, ironically, given the nature of Kubin's latest production, put the rest of the cast into a deep sleep in their own caravans.

The head of the puppet, a nightmare more or less, stared up at Kubin with malign intent and the wild staring eyes that made people fear horses, or "horsies," as, it was rumored, the undead head of Napoleon liked to call them.

This particular puppet had been a silly contrivance for an even sillier phantasmagorical production, but the puppet had made self-improvements recently. The red fangs for example, more appropriate to a shark, the dark jagged mane, the swirling green hypno-eyes.

His opening line to Kubin: "Oh, your hand is so very warm, sir! Mercy!"

The look on Kubin's face had been priceless. Or, rather, the puppet believed it came at a high price to the man's dignity.

Even given Kubin's jaded lifestyle, he'd never seen a hand puppet staring back at him with malign intent after having hijacked his arm. Nor had one talked back before. At least it could be said of Kubin that he eschewed dummy ventriloquism, which was after all humor of the lowest order.

"Unhand me!" Kubin demanded.

And with that demand, the soft velvet neck of the horse had become as hard as a cast for a broken limb, closed around Kubin's forearm like a lamprey eel. He gasped, flung his arm up and down as if something had attacked him (because it had), smashed into a lantern, came to his senses, righted the lantern before it burned his caravan down, and sat down heavily in his chair, moaning. Chairs and a table had been over-turned, along with a shelf or two. Bric-a-brac only, including a sentimen-tal collection of ceramic owls that only served to reinforce the puppet's low opinion of Kubin's taste level.

The puppet imagined the lamprey arm holding Kubin's arm in a vise, up to the elbow, must hurt, but not as much as the necessity that they speak in German, for the puppet's lines would have been much warmer, mellifluous in French or marmot or chickadee—anything else, really.

"Please! Let me go! What do you want, accursed creature?" Kubin flung the words out despairingly.

"What do I want? Oh, I want your hand out of me, sir! Out of me for good! It is no suitable arrangement for a self-respecting puppet. Better the strings and arrows of manipulation from above. For 'tis better to be controlled from heaven than from hell, as even common beggars know."

"Please. Tell me what you want and be gone."

"Oh, puppet master, how do you know I will go so easily? Perhaps I burn with the memory of every indignity, each and every time I have been so animated and made to trundle stupid across the stage, made to give witness to your words and your vision, without any say in the matter. Not even the ability to improvise. In short, what if I plan to feast upon your arm as you have feasted upon my talent to create your puppet show? Perhaps I even mean for your hand to eat your face?"

Kubin trembled, shuddered once, head down, but puppet still at attention, looking at him face-to-face, as he could not lower his arm without consent. The muscles in his forearm in particular must be sore by now, and his hand, so near the hot epicenter of this uncanny occurrence, burning up.

"I beg you, good puppet. Just tell me what you want. I'll tell you anything."

"I'm not a good puppet. That should be clear. Call me what I am. Call me a bad puppet."

Kubin looked confused.

"CALL ME A BAD PUPPET!" the bad puppet roared in a voice like a thousand psychotic bears.

"Bad puppet! Bad puppet! Bad puppet!" Kubin shrieked, for the lamprey teeth had clamped down, drawing blood.

The horse-head puppet sighed. "No, no, no. You can't even take direction properly. I mean, *say the same thing*, but say 'bad puppet' not 'good puppet.' I thought that was clear. Are you not a director of theater?"

Kubin stared at the bad puppet for a moment, disoriented, eyes as wobbly as the shoddily made ones in the face of the monkey-butt puppet that appeared in act three.

"I beg you . . . ," Kubin managed in a strangled voice, "I beg you, bad puppet, just tell me what you want. I'll tell you anything."

"Was that so very hard? But once more—with feeling."

Kubin managed to say it one more time, the right way, with the right emphasis, which was the puppet's cue.

"Oh, I don't want you to tell me anything. I want you to tell me one particular thing, dear Kubin. A very specific thing." A thing Kubin himself had let slip during the times the puppet had eavesdropped on him.

From menacing, the puppet's tone had changed to cheerful, even jaunty, as if perhaps they were about to perform a medley of musical comedy.

"But first, I have most excellent news, my good man! I have useful notes about your rather shoddy production that should bring you a larger audience as you continue on your way. Assuming you do continue on your way."

"Thank you?" Kubin said, taking the twenty-five single-spaced parchment pages in his other trembling hand in much the same manner as one would accept a spitting cobra.

❧

The Golden Sphere had joined Alfred Kubin's outrageously dramatic puppet theater show "The Other Side" in the forests around Leipzig and had stuck it out, even though it was mere regional theater, perhaps even dinner theater, for a week, as the troupe traveled closer and closer to Prague. Up until that point, the few times the Golden Sphere had had need to talk to anyone on his travels, he had said he was "on the lam" in a gangster voice he doubted anyone on Aurora had ever heard. But here, as a horse-head puppet in "The Other Side," he had decided he was "on the ham." It was that kind of puppet theater.

On the lam or on the ham, straight outta Roma, had meant trekking along roads, through forests, even museums, elevators, dog parks, the back rooms of butchers, and more nefarious places. Various disguises had been available; the sphere was in a sense a veteran of all sorts of stages and the kind of thespian who could disappear into a role, which is why It could mimic a puppet with zealous ease.

All in all, the journey thus far had almost felt like a vacation, but the fun was now over, for the Golden Sphere had, against the odds— well, the odds were pretty good given the ridiculous number of enticing "The Other Side" broadsheets Kubin had his underlings post on every lamppost—*found* the redoubtable Alfred Kubin, who on various Earths was known for a phantasmagorical novel, *The Other Side*, and numerous weird paintings that would have made Freud ask in a blink, with a wink: "Tell me again about your mother?"

On Aurora this rough genius had taken a turn to the dark side and put all his energy into puppet theater—a genuine interest, one might call it a passion, on the man's part, but also as cover for his little-known role as an agent for the Order of the Third Door. This information uncovered by his Speck whilst hiding in Crowley's own war map, before poor Speck had been caught.

Good little Speck, performing the ultimate role, and perhaps to pay the ultimate cost.

Not like the Golden Sphere's role in Kubin's farce, which detailed a mysterious sleeping sickness that brought with it surreal dreams and real manifestations of the same in the streets of a fantastical city located in Central Asia—including of course of course: a strange horse.

A terrible premise for puppet theater, both too ambitious and involving an extraordinary amount of speechifying. More speechifying than many parliaments, of crows or otherwise. But the Golden Sphere had to admit that the spectacle involved was flamboyant enough to fool local yokels in the quarter-horse towns Kubin moved through.

And so long as Kubin's path incognito as humble-puppet-theater purveyor rather than Order agent had curved *toward* Prague, the Golden Sphere had been content to showcase its thespian impulses for the benefit of every Tom, Dick, and Hairy along the provincial path.

So long, too, as the Golden Sphere hadn't known Crowley's intention to attack Prague.

But now Kubin planned to head north, perhaps to seek refuge with the Fresians, notorious Order sympathizers who controlled the northern coast with a fierce and unwavering intensity. Well, they could have him, once the Golden Sphere was finished with him.

For now the Golden Sphere asked the pivotal question, the answer to which would set certain things in motion before Crowley reached Prague. Most absurd and hilarious that Kubin's own overheard words had created the opportunity.

"You have an associate, another K. This K., as you know, lives in the great wall surrounding Prague and in the tunnels beneath the wall. This K., shall we say, provides certain security for the city with regard to the wall. I would like you to tell me exactly where he resides within that maze, where he does his work. And the password for the door."

Thankfully, given the Order's connection, Crowley didn't yet know about the other K., or his role in fortifying the great wall around Prague. With luck, he would never find out, or find out only too late.

"I don't know what you're talking about. Or who."

At which point, the Golden Sphere lost its patience and hit Kubin in the face with his puppet face.

"Ow! I think you broke my nose."

"Yet I've nary a scratch. I'm just a puppet," the Golden Sphere said. "I can punch and judy you all day and all night."

A dead chipmunk appeared near Kubin's face, bounced off his knee, dropped to the floor, and Kubin screamed.

The Golden Sphere ignored the chipmunk. That had been happening a lot lately. The Golden Sphere thought It knew what that might be about, but all in good time. All in the goodest of times.

Kubin had already forgotten the punch and the chipmunk, stared in terror at the message now scrawled across his other arm: DIS ARM IS NOT A BOMB.

"But dis arm could be a bomb, Kubin. Dis arm could blow right off, if you don't tell me. Right now."

Kubin was not a brave man. He had not been chosen by the Order to smash in saloon doors, pistols blazing. No, he was an herbivore in the phyla of species: a cud chewer and grass grazer, all minor aggression reserved for whipping his tail to discourage flies. No doubt he had multiple stomachs to digest that grass, which meant he was devious in his way, but not really.

"All right. I'll tell you."

"Good man for a bad puppet. Don't tell me, though—draw it on a map. Precision's good. Precision's the best."

For the truth was, the Order wasn't just in the business of controlling doors on worlds or between worlds. The Order, those fusty bastards, were really in the business of futzing with or interfering in *any* sort of magical security or magical system that had a relationship to a door. The Golden Sphere was a little surprised that he hadn't found Kubin defending a pregnancy ward or a gastrointestinal clinic.

Kubin's bepuppeted hand found a pencil, and Kubin's arm held it up to him.

"I'll need paper, too."

"Draw it on me!" the bad puppet snarled. "DRAW . . . IT . . . ALL OVER . . . ME!" Then, in an even more sultry tone, conjuring up a different sort of theater: "Draw it all over me, sailor-boy. Pour it on me like honey."

Change of register again, to show range. Acting was nothing without range. This time as if Meryl Streep in that Margaret Thatcher flick no one had much cared for.

"There's a good Kubin. Draw all over the bad puppet whilst you've got your hand up its arse."

Soon enough, Kubin had drawn all over the bad puppet and the Golden Sphere had the information It needed and Kubin none of the information he needed, like the fact that the words DIS ARM IS NOT A BOMB would never come off, no matter how hard he scrubbed.

But the Golden Sphere cared not, for It had come to the grand finale.

Its horse-head puppet grew quickly enormous in size, with a great nickering and neighing. Luxuriating at no longer being small, for being small created great strain and anxiety on its bad self. The sproinging result smashed through the roof of the caravan vehicle, escaped out into the night, and dissolved in a slow fade from puppet head into a series of black floating marbles that Kubin with his limited human senses couldn't see, so that to his view of events the puppet mercifully left his hand, became huge, and then disappeared into the night.

Fluttering down from that night sky like a gentle rain of giant moths upon the head of a bewildered Kubin: another hundred pages of notes about the tepid and turgid dialogue in "The Other Side" along with recommended therapy and the suggestion that if he lived long enough to seek out the counsel of the "feller name of Freud, who can help with all non-theater-related anxieties."

DIS ARM IS NOT A BOMB.

Good luck getting that off.

Perhaps the fright would push Kubin to become the great writer he was on other Earths. For the Golden Sphere thought of itself as a kind of patron of the arts, pushing human beings to do their utmost. Or die in the attempt. The humans, not It.

No, It had miles to go before It gave up the ghost. Miles and years, It hoped.

DIS SPHERE: PRAGUE OR BUST.

"He who at first does not succeed . . . must get there first!"

Busta move to Prague. Prague, Prague, Prague.

And on to the next disguise.

Part IV

THE FALL

"Chipmunk punted into nothing."

Chapter Thirty-Two
A MONSTROUS SCHOOLMARM

The sullen overcast humid morning unfolded like a nightmare to Jonathan.

Danny was gone. *Danny was gone.*

The blue flowers in that new light looked like some shoddy carnival decoration the day after, spent seeds smudging the sludgy snow beside them a dark dirty blue. Mangy, bedraggled nectar deer with droopy wings huddled around the blossoms in the drizzle of rain.

Danny was gone, Tee-Tee with her, but her pack was still there and her boot prints headed off into the distance, turned to slush-filled tracks and then nothing at all.

Staring at that dirty blank canvas through his binoculars didn't help. Nothing moved out there.

Poor Rack was beside himself, walking in circles, pacing, and almost slipping in the snow and on patches of ice, cane little help. Mamoud had to caution both Rack and Jonathan to stop shouting out her name, as an avalanche was possible. And so, with a dreadful paltry whispering they had spread out to search, Rack agreeing through gritted teeth to man home base.

But by midmorning, the conditions not ideal, Jonathan and the others had returned to the smoldering campfire to admit defeat.

Or worse. Jonathan had discovered four bewildered-looking black bears on a ledge hundreds of feet below them. But no sign through the binoculars of Danny—or of the bear gun.

"One of you should get the hell down there," Rack said. "What in the blazes are you waiting for?"

"We don't have the necessary mountain-climbing equipment," Mamoud said. "And there's no guarantee she is there."

"But we have to try!" Rack said, then a muttered "sorry" for the loud voice.

Jonathan could understand his frustration, even though he knew Mamoud was right. Sarah would've said no different.

"I heard a gun discharge at three in the morning," Alice said. "It was distant. I couldn't tell where it came from. There was nothing to be done."

Certainly not now.

Rack couldn't believe it. "What? You heard gunfire and you didn't wake us? You didn't notice Danny was gone?"

"No." Alice, impassive, with the look Jonathan had grown to hate. The one that said her own problems were much more pressing than theirs, and always would be.

Rack was halfway to apoplectic, glaring at Alice, hardly able to speak, his hands clenching and unclenching, leaving red marks on both his palms. Jonathan wondered if he was about to break up a fight.

"Apologies," Alice said, in a nonapologetic way. "I was half-asleep. It barely registered. I thought I might have dreamt it."

"What you mean," Rack said, pointing his finger at Alice, "is that you don't care about Danny!"

"Come too close pointing fingers and you'll find out what I care about," Alice said.

Mamoud stepped between them, expressing distaste, as if they had both turned out to be bratty children.

"You must stop this. This is of no use to Danny, or to us."

"Rack, it makes more sense to head for the way station," Jonathan said, holding on to his friend's shoulder to steady him. "She knows where we're going. If she can, she'll catch up. And there might be help at the way station—to send out a proper search party."

But in the pit of his stomach was the terrible knowledge that Danny wouldn't have been at risk if not for him. That he should have found some way to stop her and Rack from coming along. That, in what now seemed the far-distant past, he shouldn't have allowed them to join him at the mansion in the first place.

Rack stared at Jonathan as if he were mad. "So we just abandon her. Is that seriously what you're telling me?"

"I know you hate the logic of moving farther away from Danny to save her, but . . ." He wanted to say it's what Danny would've done if one of them had gone missing, but feared Rack would really lose it then.

Mamoud stepped between them as if this were now his permanent job. "We reach the way station as quickly as possible, and use it as a base. Otherwise, we're just wandering around in the snow. And we don't know what made her fire the weapon. *If* she even did."

Rack opened his mouth to rebut that point but stopped, squinting down at a lower loop of the trail. "What's that—down there?"

All Jonathan could see where Rack pointed was a blotch surrounded by a few mountain goats, perhaps three hundred feet below.

Alice squinted against the sun's glare, shaded her eyes, frowned, said, "It appears to be a gigantic schoolmarm in a gray sweater and burgundy skirt."

Rack grabbed Jonathan's binoculars, pulling Jonathan close, as they were still around his neck.

"It can't be," he said. "But it is!"

"I saw that schoolmarm earlier," Jonathan said, "down by the lake. Thought her very odd." More than odd, less than odd, searching for Sarah's equivalent, some "teacher-creature" dredged up from childhood, but there was none.

Alice gave him a look that said, *Why didn't you tell us?*

So he in turn gave Mamoud a look. Mamoud shrugged.

Rack went rigid, still staring through the binoculars. "It's not a schoolmarm. It's not a schoolmarm!"

Even at that distance, Jonathan and the others could tell that the top of the schoolmarm's head—no longer covered by a scarf—had opened up and become a vast maw, into which the monster was shoving two of the mountain goats.

Jonathan grabbed the binoculars back, took a peek.

Finished eating, the not-schoolmarm had reconstituted its head and stared up at them.

An icy dagger of fear ripped through Jonathan's spine. But also a frisson of fascination. Of all the strange things he'd seen on Aurora, this was the most inexplicable. And yet he found the creature oddly . . . beautiful . . . in the same way he found certain kinds of invertebrate sea life beautiful.

"It can see us!"

"Well, of course it can see us," Rack said. "*We* can see it."

The monster took one last look at them, as if fixing their position in its brain. It let out a peculiar pleading bleat of a roar, almost as if asking a question.

Then the thing dropped to all fours and began to lope up the trail with surprising and uncanny speed.

❧

Mamoud took lead, Alice right behind, and set a brutal pace because the monster below them moved so fast, with a fluid grace despite the bulk.

Yet the surreal truth that as they ran past what had before enchanted them (blue flowers and flying deer be damned) the distance between prey and predator was still considerable, because the trail wound around the mountain rather than going straight up.

Worse, the icy suspense of not seeing the monster for a half hour at a time, until they rounded the next bend, or had a view down to the lower loops. No sense of how much ground it had gained until it once again came into sight. Still bounding forward on all four legs . . . feet? Hands? Who knew.

Fatal thought: Is this how Sarah had died? Not by avalanche, but encountering something like this?

"It's no Celestial Beast," Rack said. "It's more like every reform school student's worst nightmare."

Rack, just grimly trying to keep up the pace, his breath loud and shallow.

Yet when Jonathan had tried to take Rack's pack, pull it off his back, go on the attack, Rack had angrily shrugged him off: "I can handle myself!" Then redoubled his efforts, dislodging pebbles and rocks that tumbled into the abyss.

By the time Jonathan managed to draw level with Rack again, his friend was hyperventilating, had slowed.

"I meant for your balance, Rack. I meant because I'm more used to hiking. You can take something of mine in trade if you like. Don't be proud about it." And yet who was Jonathan to say what was pride and what wasn't?

Alice and Mamoud were already a hundred feet ahead of them.

Rack's hesitation, the naked look of terror in his eyes. Then he nodded. "You're right. You're right."

Quickly, they switched it up, Rack taking Jonathan's belt of supplies and Jonathan doubling up with Rack's pack.

Rack hugged Jonathan tight and Jonathan hugged him back.

"Time to redouble the pace," Rack said.

He turned and headed after Alice and Mamoud with fresh energy, Jonathan bringing up the rear. But even Jonathan's calves were beginning to tremble from the effort.

How long before the monster caught up to them?

Chapter Thirty-Three
JAW-PALM GRAW-MAR

Ruth Less had to admit it had been fun the whole time since the smelly, icky Wretch had let her loose on the Lambshead trail. Even if she hadn't talked to friend the Speck for too long and couldn't seem to track the whereabouts of friend the dandelion tufts. Their lack sometimes was like a hole in her mind. When she felt that way, Ruth Less just turned the hole into a nice memory from the map in Cathedral, from before Wretch's words.

Wretch had had so many words to share with Ruth Less. To Ruth Less, who relied most often on taste and smell and sight, and only then hearing or touch . . . words tasted bad, especially the Ing-lush ones. They weren't fun, except some of the ones that the Golden Speck had sung.

Songs were fun, but not words in general. She heard them wrong or bad, as if her kind weren't meant to have them. It was why her mimicry of a schoolmarm had faltered at first, even though she emitted phero-mones that made people think she was a schoolmarm. Also, Ruth Less still had only a hazy vision of what a schoolmarm was or could be. Wretch hadn't thought it important, shown her a diagram or two. She had the idea that a schoolmarm told people what words to use or that human children followed schoolmarms in packs, like wolves, but for what reason?

Grammar, Wretch had told her once. Grammar. Graw-mar. She had dipped a hand-mouth into an alpine stream and run her jaw-palm across rough and smooth stones to make the sound. Graaaa-maaaar. It still meant nothing.

She could *say* words, even string them together into what the dandelion tufts had told her were "sentences," even though when Wretch spoke of "sentences" it mostly meant bad things happened to a long row of kneeling men whereby a Wretch spike smashed through their chests or through their skulls. How could words strung together smash through anything?

But Ruth Less could not control how the words sounded or were received by others, much as they, unlike Ruth Less, could not control how they smelled or tasted. She had told the woman with the weird belching stick, who smelled like old bandages and sweat and mud, that she just wanted to play, and Ruth Less had truly meant "play" in the way she and the tufts and the Speck had played . . . but it had come out more like a gargle belch, with steam shooting uncontrollably from the blow-hole on the back of her head.

Then the weird iron stick had belched in a rude way in reply to her polite belch—and what had followed was a not-fun time of fighting too many bears. She liked bears, liked them very much, and often felt that she was much like a bear. So, she had only killed and devoured two of them, to keep strong, and the other four decided to go far away from her, which was good, but also not fun.

The woman with the belch stick had gone, too, vanishing into the shadows while Ruth Less dealt with the bears. Other things moved in those shadows—she had sensed being watched from above almost since she had popped out of a Crowley-controlled door far to the west.

But whatever watched was too distant to taste or smell, or masked their presence, and she could not be sure what they were. They kept fading in and out of focus. Yet she guessed the watchers had something to do with the vanishing belch-stick woman. Perhaps.

Worse, by the time Ruth Less had finished her bear snack and stopped seeking the vanished woman, the Jonathan-thing that Wretch wanted her to bring back for him had left the campsite, along with his fellow human-things.

Then, for the longest time—and she giggled to think of it, like a tiny sprotling flip-flapping through the viscous mire of her fathers' stomach pouches to pop out one of the holes in their back—she had pursued her quarry as if her human disguise meant she was a human. Or as if she were one of those human's friends, the dogs whose bark she found both blank and disagreeable. Nothing lived in the bark, much like nothing lived in the words.

Then it had dawned on Ruth Less, as the Jonathan-thing, reckless, stared down from the ledge above her, that she didn't need road or trail.

She could climb the rock face, go *up*, not sideways—and so she did, bounding as much as she was able, and protecting herself against gravity with hooks and prongs she made appear at the end of flesh-ropes that shot out of her no-longer-hidden mouth. Proud of her own cleverness, wanting to remember that moment so she could tell the tufts and Speck. If this was an "adventure," a word Heady had used, then she wanted to go on more adventures.

There was so much else about her adventure she wanted to tell someone, too. She so loved the cold of these mountains, marveled at the good work of vultures on the blessed carcasses she had encountered, of elk and of rabbit. Not to mention the nectar deer, which she gobbled like candy and washed down with sturdy mountain goat. The nectar deer had a slight bitter aftertaste, but it suited her palate. She stored many in her pouch, for later. Along with some bears and other things she liked.

By then, the smells of her quarry had changed, perhaps because she could sense they were running fast. The noisy one the others called Rack had developed a unique stench, like a night-flower opening and opening, with a hint of the metallic and grainy. Mamoud smelled dangerous, for some reason, all sharp edges, as if she'd have to pluck all his spines to eat him.

Jonathan-thing smelled like his father: not of his place, or any place.

She could not tell his true origins, and there was another scent or sensation around him, like a black aura, that she could not place, either.

Alice-thing smelled like a poison; she would taste bitter and Ruth Less reminded herself to crush this one to death rather than risk a bite. That might dilute the bitterness.

But none would ever be like Wretch, who stank of burning stones with bits of withered flesh trapped between, like rotted roast beef stuck between the teeth of a recently dead corpse. Around Wretch, Ruth Less kept her head down, averted the gaze of her many eyes, hidden across the expanse of her body. (Like some animals, the "eyes" in her head were just markings meant to distract an enemy from her real sensitive spots.)

"Be careful. Be sure," Wretch had said. Which is why when she had caught up to the campfire Ruth Less hadn't attacked, but just watched from afar, sent out her squishy brain tentacles closer to listen and report back.

But Wretch hadn't just given her orders she was compelled to obey; he had given her advice.

"Listen only to me," he said.

"Do only what I say," he said.

"Remember you are a schoolmarm," he said, although some of the demi-mages called her an "abomination." She wondered if that had something to do with "abominable snowman," which she had heard another one say, pointing to some mountains on the war map, while she had hidden inside a tiny building in Sardinia.

She did try to remember that she was in disguise, but the word "schoolmarm" tasted different from "abomination," and Ruth Less thought "abomination" tasted prettier.

"Your name is Ruth," Wretch had said, although he always called her "Ruth Less." But she knew her real name was Blarglararfangiaaaicioio-ussstorakabripyki in the tongue of her people. For that was the sound the blarglar made when it bled out in the swamps of Sarfangtredshadraded many eons ago and created the eternal effluvium.

Yet there were none of her people on Aurora, and the Speck had told her she had been "plucked" from a far-distant place and one day, if she was lucky, she might make it home.

So she thought of herself for now as Ruth Less Plucked Blarglararfangiaaaicioioussstorakabripyki, the abomination from another place that was also a schoolmarm and was one day destined to return to her roots.

That way it sounded more like a quest, and the Speck had said if you were on a quest then if bad things happened along the way it was for a reason and in the end everything would be all right.

The Speck and the tufts had also told her Wretch was really her enemy. Do not listen to Wretch, they said. Do not do what he says, they said. For a while, though, Ruth Less had felt Wretch must be right and Speck-tufts-Heady having their fun, because she felt a Compulsion to obey Wretch. That must mean Wretch was right. Right?

But Heady, the big noisy head they called Napoleon, had said the same thing, even if he didn't smell much better than Wretch—like a moldy wine mixed with vinegar. Heady had said she deserved better, and that maybe he could help her if she helped him.

So Ruth Less had helped him, with the help of the Speck and the last of the last tufts, named the Tuft.

At the agreed-upon time, she'd stuck Heady in her pouch along with a ham hock from the kitchens, gone to see Crowley with Wretch in the war elephant, then accompanied the two delicious demi-mages, eaten them, taken a slight detour into the forest, dropped off Heady, and then gone through the door to chase the Lambshead.

She had felt bad at first about just leaving Heady there by the side of the road, but Heady had said she needn't worry. Friends would be there soon. He would go somewhere far away and "rest up," and no one would see or hear from him until he was ready for his revenge. "That donkey's ass Crowley won't have a clue." So there was no way she could get in trouble because no one would find him right away.

But Ruth Less wasn't sure what "trouble" meant. Was it like a storm?

One of the demi-mages had leaned over the map and pointed at a swirl of hovering clouds and said, "Trouble."

Heady had also liked her pouch. Ruth Less knew he would. Heady had come out of her pouch amazed by it, and changed. They often did if it wasn't someone she planned to eat. Those she put in a special place in the pouch.

Her people were known for their amazing pouches, and Ruth Less was quite proud of hers, which was a spectacular example.

It contained all of the things.

Chapter Thirty-Four

ONE HEAD IS BETTER THAN NONE

"Thou shalt not harm any rabid chipmunk thou come across. Instead, please mark the location at which you saw the chipmunk and render that information to the God-Emperor Crowley or his Emissaries or demi-mages or even foot soldiers. But do not harm a rabid chipmunk on pain of death."

—Source and date unknown

"What or who is Stimply?" Crowley muttered as he fed his salamanders the heads of dead rabid chipmunks. "That is the question. Or, one of the questions." And would it even be a question next week? The landscape kept changing so rapidly.

Late afternoon. He was sick of the chipmunks being rabid, but Wretch said they had to be, and, anyway, they turned rabid as soon as Wretch got hold of them. But, then, he was sick of so many things.

Like, why the bloody hell they were *still* three or four days from reaching the edge of the forests around Prague, while other parts of his army were only two days away. One detached unit claimed to be six hours away. How had that happened? Logistics be damned—they'd planned this, and still gotten bogged down. The attenuated shitstains that called themselves the "resistance" hadn't been bothered to put up much of one yet. It was as if Prague and its allies had decided to fall back to their precious wall for a last-ditch defense. Even Paris, from every report, was quiet.

It made Crowley suspicious, all this calm.

Just in case, Wretch had flapped out into the impending darkness, on another of his secret missions, aimed at making sure something more sinister wasn't afoot. Crowley wished he would flap out more. Flap out and never return.

Even without Wretch around, Crowley was listless and feeling dangerous at the same time. He'd taken to distracting himself from his problems by viewing Verne and the Burrower through the All-Seeing Puddle.

He had to give Verne his due: The shrinking violet of an inventor was holding his own, just barely. That was a welcome surprise, given the delays getting to Prague.

૭~જ

Despite the relative calm, things had been in an uproar in and around the war elephant for days. Napoleon had not been found, and no amount of interrogation had revealed the slightest clue. Napoleon, when his pedestal was retracted, resided in a space no larger than a dumbwaiter, next to the kitchen. Thus, the cook and her staff had been vigorously put to the question. To no avail. No one had seen anything.

How in the holy hells had Napoleon gotten clear of them? Was it a plot or was Napoleon facedown in a ditch somewhere, shouting into the mud about the indignity of it all? Just fallen off and rolled into a ditch, where an elephant could have stepped on him and squashed him like a rotten melon. That would be unfortunate. Crowley found Napoleon hideous enough already.

Like a budding actor, Crowley cursed as would be expected, he raged, he made things burst into flame. It was easy enough to conjure up the right emotion—he had a throbbing eye from the apple a peasant had thrown at him during his speech in the village of Slap on the Cheek. He expected that meant the speech had gone badly, especially as Wretch had had to send out shock troops to secure their path from "new unrest," as his familiar put it.

Wretch was still assessing the damage the speech had done overall, how far the news had traveled. As for the village, it would have to be renamed Flaming Cheeks or maybe just Ash.

But all the Sturm und Drang was just subterfuge. In actual fact, he didn't much care that Napoleon the clown was gone. For one thing, it had given Wretch just one more thing to deal with, so that Crowley saw him less during the day.

Yet, despite not much missing Napoleon, Crowley kept hearing that word the general had used of late: "Chaos." Each time with special emphasis as they reviewed the war map on the elephant's lowest floor. It haunted Crowley, popped into his head unbidden like a depth charge.

For it had struck Crowley with particular force, as if he'd just woken up, that everything he'd done to impose order had, to varying degrees, resulted in the opposite. Rome. The continuing assault on the English wall. Even the garbage situation in Paris, or the vast waste of resources required to hold Spain against enemy insurgents. Was he fated to spread . . . chaos? Naturally, he rebelled against this conclusion. Such balderdash. Such nonsense. The Golden Sphere spread chaos, not him— his enemies, not him. But was that true?

When had he decided to invade England and attack Prague at the same time? Had he truly been so traumatized by the explosion? Had he taken Wretch's word for who the culprits must be, without further investigation? Yes, he had. He had done those things.

This same Wretch who Napoleon had suggested stepped between him and death a moment *before* the explosion. And what of the vague recollections, dreamlike, of Wretch whispering in his ear during their nightly sessions?

The Golden Speck under magical glass was still there on his desk, bouncing around, trapped, unable to stop moving. Its movements weren't random, but instead spelled out letters and words across the very air. It was how they communicated now, to avoid detection and because he couldn't stand its nonstop patter.

Crowley knew Wretch would consider this the worst kind of treachery, but he had required the Speck's aid in investigating the mystery of Wretch's nightly visits.

He felt ancient thinking about it, thinking about what the Speck had observed, and thus it was that he had spent nearly an hour feeding rabid chipmunk faces to his marvelous salamanders. Abt and his engineers might be obstinate and disrespectful, but he had to admit it had taken them no time at all to jury-rig a setup in the elephant's "attic" whereby he could climb a stepladder, stand above the magical moat, and pull aside a glass panel, revealing the Lovelies, as he'd taken to calling the salamanders.

With space on a lower rung of the ladder for a bucket of dead chipmunk parts—the leftovers that hadn't been used to test Wretch's theory about the connection between the Speck and the Golden Sphere.

The meat-loving white salamanders swam and cavorted and plunged beneath his gaze in ways he found mischievous and, dare he say it, charming. As he watched chipmunk faces and limbs disappear into their grateful maws.

It didn't help him forget, but it did relieve his stress.

For what he had discovered required stress relief.

Every night, according to the Speck, Wretch stole into his chamber, then numbed him, before taking a very long tongue and punching a hole in Crowley's head. Plunging the tongue like a sharpened pencil or needle into his brain. Doing the same by way of his hollow tentacles at various other places on his body.

Whereupon Wretch took the blood from Crowley's body and then replaced it with his own blood. As the Speck described it, Wretch poised like a monstrous black mosquito, hugging Crowley to him, and punching down into the skull with a distinct splooshing sound. And for the next three hours, Wretch in a kind of trance, the transfer took place, Crowley's old blood going god knew where.

It was a violation too profound to get over, ever. Adding to the insult was the glee with which the Speck related the spectacle and its unseemly humor that made it all the more difficult to listen to.

Once he had learned the truth, he had cut the connection with the Speck in that moment and reinforced the magical containment around the terrarium. He resolved that soon he would obliterate the Speck, no matter that this action would sever their only connection to the Golden Sphere.

But he could only feed salamanders for so long or they would grow fat and sluggish. He replaced the glass top to the salamander moat. He climbed down the stepladder and made his way to the kitchen.

The cooks were a frightened bunch at the moment, and not to be trusted with knives or rolling pins. But after he'd shooed them out, it was a relief to lean against a marble counter with his objective in one hand—a jar of juicy pickles. He meant to devour half the jar and save the rest for later. They had the tartness, a tad bitter, he would always associate with the grocery down the street from when he was a child.

Who or what was "Stimply"? The question came back to him as he feasted on a particularly spectacular pickle. Dreadnought-sized. The perfect balance of sweet and tart.

Putting a glass to the wall between their quarters, Crowley had listened the other night as Wretch talked to someone who he must be viewing through some Wretch equivalent of the All-Seeing Puddle.

"Are you Stimply yet?" Wretch had said.

A deep voice had replied, "Not yet. But soon. Practice makes perfect."

The rest had faded into murmurs, as if the two were whispering.

Stimply. A secret agent? Another assassin?

Recently, he'd begun to regret killing his father here on Aurora. At the very least he could have trusted the man's counsel, no matter how astute or unhelpful. For the fact was, Speck aside, he had no one to confide in, and hardly the privacy to confide in anyone anyway.

All of this had made the street tough, the fringe-person he had been before, in dirty hovels and attending seances conducted by charlatans, come back. That callow youth. He needed that hunger again, that ruthlessness. The way he'd taken a cricket bat to the table of the fake psychic, sent her customers screaming from the room.

Napoleon would say he was fighting a war on three fronts now: against England and the Czechs and Wretch. And as he must liberate the Czechs from the shackles of their independence, he must liberate himself from the shackles of dependence on Wretch.

Which meant making common cause with the Golden Sphere. For the moment. If it was possible.

He put the pickle jar down on the counter, meaning to put the top back on and return to his quarters.

But then an exceedingly strange thing happened.

Crowley felt a tickle, a kind of very rough tickle or itch. Across first the back of his neck, accompanied by a rising heat, while the tickle-itch spread to the front of his neck.

Then he was tumbling, with the odd weight of tumbling end over end and yet having no end. His face, impossibly, smacked against his chest, stubbing his nose, as he plummeted, and then there was the floor, well, too close, and his nose stubbed again, harder this time, followed by his chin, with a smack not at all like a tickle, and through his left eye he could see his headless body beginning to topple, spouting gouts of blood.

There was the horrifying shlump of his body catching up to his head as it plummeted to the floor beside him like a sack of human-shaped potatoes. A collision so great that his head bounced up and settled again, spinning once, twice, three times, before coming to an abrupt stop.

As his arm flailed out so it boxed his ear and on the recoil his right palm reached out to alight atop his cheek; he could feel the receding warmth in his fingers, could just see his own boxy thick thumb out of the corner of his eye. The weight of his own hand, the slickness of it, the roughness of it, but not being able to control it, like it had fallen asleep, made the panic set in, finally.

"Get it off me! Get it off me! Get it off me!"

Get me off me. Get me off me.

He was still trying to move his legs to run, wave his arms, but everything seemed tightly pressed against his body. Or rather his body wasn't responding, as if he was paralyzed. Because it couldn't. The heat was intolerable, and the depressing sight of his neck still spouting blood sideways, forming a spray and curling question mark while all he could do was watch.

"Chaos," said Napoleon, a ghost a ghost a ghost.

In those final moments, Crowley's life did not slip past his eyes. There was no vast summation of triumphs and failures.

No, as his eyes began to glaze over, as the heat was leeched away by cold, he was sliding down the chute from his room and out of the elephant. With indescribable euphoria, as if he were a child again. And the Golden Sphere, his good friend, was sliding with him, and Ruth Less, and Verne, and, yes, even Laudinum X. Why not?

"Wee!" shouted the Golden Sphere, lodged in front of Crowley like a beach ball, while Crowley clung to its comforting smoothness and Laudinum X behind Crowley screamed "Wee!" and Ruth Less mimicked "Wee!" and Verne, reluctantly, "Wee." All of them going on the ride over and over again. So happy and carefree.

But not Wretch. Wretch was not there. Which is how he knew, as perhaps he had known from the first tickle, that it was Wretch who had murdered him.

Chapter Thirty-Five

FUN ICKULAR

The drizzle had turned to sleet, making the footing treacherous, and by midday they all picked their way with care because they had no choice, the sun a dull halo through gray clouds. Jonathan felt hollowed out and numb.

Each new glimpse of the monster gave them fresh nightmare fuel, even as their panic had been dulled by weather and exhaustion. Trundling along, at times the thing emitted a foul green steam from an aperture at what would have been the back of the head had it remained bipedal, as if it were the blow hole of a breaching whale. The sheer number of mumbling and snuffling and burbling and chewing sounds that came from the beast, at a volume they could hear even from above, curdled Jonathan's blood.

The monster was also honking and ballyhooing at them as if in some grotesque parody of greeting. The monster had no fear of avalanche, and Jonathan prayed hard it might be swept away by a collapsing layer of unstable snow before it reached them.

In theory, the way station was just above them, but they'd yet to catch a glimpse of it.

"Faster! Faster!" Mamoud, shouting from the head of their frantic procession. Jonathan couldn't stop thinking of the disappearing funeral mourners.

But Rack *couldn't* go faster. Neither could Alice. Jonathan could have outstripped them all, Mamoud included, but he wouldn't, couldn't leave them. Besides, it wasn't much different from being charged by a bear—the bear would always be faster in the end. Climb a tree? Good luck with that.

Yet there came a bend around which there wasn't another bend, and that's where Rack and Jonathan caught up.

A sharp shelf of rock jutting out to the left, and to the right, almost too close, the steep peak, snow-wreathed and tree-dotted in places with mottled blotches of raw gray stone.

The path ended in a huge stone staircase with a large rounded glass pod at the base. What looked like two sets of train tracks ran up the stairs. At the top, the tracks disappeared into a dark archway leading straight through the mountain. COELECANTH INC. had been etched into the stone at the top of the archway, and a symbol Jonathan had seen back in the mansion made decorative down both sides: >o >o >o

"What in the hell is that? A deranged ski lift?"

"A funicular," Rack said.

"A what?"

"A funicular," Rack repeated, and then in an increasingly agitated and ever-louder voice: "An inclined plane or cliff railway—a cable railway—in which a cable is attached to a pair of tramlike vehicles on rails moving them up and down a steep slope, the ascending and descending vehicles counterbalancing each other. Funiculars have existed for hundreds of years and continue to be used for moving both passengers and goods. The name comes from the Latin word *funiculus*, the diminutive of *funis*, which translates as 'rope.' In olden days—"

"All right—that's enough! Enough!" Somehow, the outpouring was unbearable in that moment. Jonathan shook Rack, said, "Snap out of it. Snap out of it. You're panicking."

Rack shuddered. "Sorry. Sorry. Tested on it at Poxforth. Sorry. I don't know where my head's at."

Alice had already gone ahead to the little boxy control shed next to the funicular and had popped inside, examining something.

Mamoud looked back at them. "Alice is familiar with the mechanism.

Let's hope it's in working order. On the other side of the mountain is the way station. We're very close."

"Funiculars—not much fun," Rack said. "Can't rush a funicular, either. It'll go at the same pace up through the mountain whether we're being chased by a monster or by a giant tortoise stuck in molasses."

Over by the control box, Alice was cursing.

"It's not working—ancient and a mess. But I think I can fix it," she called out. But how? How did she know? It irked Jonathan this nagged at him, snagged him, made him think he might actually be in panic mode.

"The ledge looks over the trail below," Jonathan said. "I can see how much time we've got. Hold my legs, Rack?"

"That's what he said," Rack replied weakly, expression still terror-struck.

Jonathan slapped him on the back. "Just promise you'll hold on tight. I'm not interested in being that thing's snack."

Rack nodded, clearly glad to have something to do.

༄

Feet held by Rack in an achingly tight grip, Jonathan inched out on the ledge far enough to look down, suppressing nausea.

At least it didn't take much effort to find the monster. It was immediately below, snuffling along the trail. Quietly, he looked through his binoculars.

Oh dear.

Was it a bad sign that the monster hardly bothered to maintain its disguise now? Yes, yes it was. As if they weren't worth the effort.

"What do you see?" Rack whispered.

"Oh, nothing much. Just a god-awful monster."

What Jonathan could only call the "flaps" that came to a zippered join at the top of its head at times untethered free to the four points of the compass as it jogged on with a sure-footedness surely preternatural. The startling pink and gray of the maw thus revealed was matched by the revelation of the rows and rows of teeth of various sizes and edges, from serrated to smooth. Matching these teeth were the claws on its "hands," the fingers of which flopped with the claws on nubs on the palms, the effect as if someone had glued human hands on top of a possum's feet.

Rack had been whispering, "What, Jonathan? What? What did you say?" for longer than was polite.

"It's there, but still three loops down," he whispered back over his shoulder. Thanking any god who might be listening once again that the trail makers hadn't just etched a staircase leading straight up.

Mamoud had joined them. "Is it slowing down?" he asked.

"It appears to be scenting at the moment. So, yes, it's moving very slow. I think it's enjoying this."

"I don't care if it's enjoying this," Rack hissed.

Indeed, the monster had stopped to sniff and wander back and forth across the trail. What was it looking for? Didn't it already have their scent? But the next moment was more ominous.

"Oh no," Jonathan said, felt like someone had just sucked all the air out of his lungs.

"What is it?" Mamoud and Rack said at the same time.

He'd hardly believed it at first, but the creature had stopped sniffing with whatever or wherever its nose might lurk and stared straight up at Jonathan.

"I think it's seen me."

"What's it doing?" Mamoud asked, Rack reduced to quiet cursing, the grip on Jonathan's legs viselike.

"Looking up in my direction!"

"Stay perfectly still," Mamoud said.

"I'm frozen with fear, so that's not a problem."

"Now what is it doing?"

"The same thing."

". . . how about now?"

"Similar." Shut up.

"Keep still."

"Already was doing. As I said. As you can see."

"Stiller."

"There's no stiller than the still I've always been." Through clenched teeth.

"So . . . now what's it doing?"

Oh for the love of . . . but it was doing something different now.

"Mouthing words?"

"Words?"

Yes, words, hissing them out: "I jest tawk wont. Tawk wont."

Jonathan was no lip-reader, but for some strange reason, as if the monster had made it possible, he knew what it meant: "I just want to talk. Just talk."

"Naw eato."

"No, no, no," Jonathan cried out. No tawky. No eatie. No nothing. And no point in whispering anymore.

For the schoolmarm had gotten down on all fours as if reaching a decision, scrabbled across a thin layer of snow against the mountainside, and then sprung up onto the naked rock face. Clinging there somehow by the force of its limbs, it started ascending quickly toward them.

"Crap on a stick." It had dawned on Jonathan what he was seeing.

"What? Jonathan, *what*?" Mamoud asked. Probably he and Rack had been asking that for seconds more than had registered with Jonathan.

"It has cilia! Not feet!"

"Who cares?" Rack said.

"You should, Rack. You should. Because it's on the rock. It's actually moving up the *rock face*." Sliding toward him, in an awful lurch and burble, crazed and weather-torn, and snorting, and him, petrified, unable to move.

Then there was another reason he couldn't move: Mamoud, without warning, was awkwardly sliding past Rack and up Jonathan's body, using it disconcertingly to brace himself, silver gun drawn.

"Hey-ho! Careful, mate!" This from Rack while Jonathan, off-balance for a moment, hissed, "I'm not a diving board."

"And I'm not made of steel," Rack whispered and squeezed Jonathan's leg. "Not most of me anyway. Hurry it up!"

"It may help to shoot the animal now, rather than just look at it more," Mamoud murmured in his ear. Surprisingly, Mamoud smelled like . . . vanilla? "Now, just hold still a moment . . ."

"I haven't a choice, Mamoud . . ."

There followed the comforting *jut-jut-jut* of Mamoud's gun, surprisingly quiet, the bullets like little silver stars arching down toward the target. Such delicate little slivers of death.

The silver stars hit, fell right into the climbing monster . . . and came out the other side with both parties unscathed.

Jonathan watched in disbelief as the silver stars disappeared into the distance.

"I have put holes in the schoolmarm, but she remains unconvinced," Mamoud called out over his shoulder, toward Rack. "Bullets are not the answer," he added, somewhat unnecessarily, which made Jonathan realize he might be scared, out of his depth. That was a surprise.

But there was a new threat, more imminent, as Mamoud's weight left him in retreat back off the ledge, him still lying there, staring.

This new threat issued forth from a hole in the monster's head, writhed, streaming *upward*, in defiance of gravity and the idea of a rational universe.

"My god—it was *fishing line* before!"

Unspooling up, up, up. Fascinating strength there. Uncanny strength, for how else could something so thin and delicate-looking continue that upward extension. What kind of adaptation to what kind of environment had willed this . . . this appendage into being?

Truly, this creature was remarkable, brilliant, beautiful in its way.

He hadn't the sense to move in time, still couldn't quite believe what was happening, had just managed to kick one leg free of Rack, who didn't understand . . . when the fleshy hook part at the end smacked into his forehead, stayed there to frisk his face as he recoiled, spun back toward the funicular. Then found what it wanted—his left ear—and dug in. He was too intent on fighting off the hook to scream.

But it hurt. It really hurt, and blood spurted down the side of his face. He pushed off the ground with his palms, in an awkward half crouch, as the "fishing line" that was really a thin muscular tentacle wrapped around his neck, began to pull him back toward the edge.

He had a horrific vision of his fall being broken by the needle teeth in the creature's mouth. He reared up, tried to pull away. But the thing was too strong. Rack's grip broke entirely and his arm was rubbed raw against stone as he accelerated to the edge.

Then the smell of vanilla cocooned him again. A weight on top of him stopped the slide. Mamoud took out his knife, cut the tentacle just below the hook, pried it from around Jonathan's neck, and tossed the whole horrifying loop out into the abyss.

In one swift motion, Mamoud had pulled him to his feet, was helping him away from the cliff's edge.

Then there was nothing for it but hot panic, Jonathan holding a hand to his throbbing, bloody ear, and Alice waving them into the funicular pod. She'd gotten it working. They crowded into that space, sitting shoulder to shoulder on the bench-booth, stared anxious out the lichen-tinged globe of the window. Closed the hatch, locked it.

She'd already pulled the lever, and they began in a juddering, not-at-all rushed or fast or even medium-slow way, to rise up the slope. A clanking groan that repeated.

"Is there no other gear?" Jonathan asked.

"No."

That's when the music started, funicular music. Hideous, horrifying polka music, played tinny by some ancient music box hidden in the floorboards; now Jonathan saw the tiny circles of a speaker system or intercom. He'd not noticed before because of the rubbish at their feet: an ice-cream cone with a bite out of it, the ice cream long melted; a wooden golf club (driver) fractured in three places; a single ski; the first half of a book ominously entitled *Enscrotal Mondimus*. A half-burned rotary telephone that Jonathan wished would ring, really hoped would not ring.

"Are we seriously going to die to this soundtrack?" Rack said. "Is there no way to shut that off?"

"Is there no way to shut your mouth off?" Alice asked. "Or, if you like, I can turn the funicular off with this emergency switch. Then there will be no music."

"Where is the thing anyway?" Jonathan asked. It should've reached the ledge by now, but hadn't.

So they all watched the ledge to the sounds of polka music, waiting for the monster to clamber over the side.

As the pod dawdled, it gave them what under other circumstances, even with the weather, would have been a spectacular view of the surrounding peaks and the distant blue glitter far below of Comet Lake.

"Wasn't it right behind you, Jonathan?"

"It was, it was, and closing fast."

But still nothing appeared down below.

Instead, the telephone rang, rattling and jangling.

"I think that's for me," Jonathan said. Grimly.

Mamoud gave Jonathan a grim look, picked up the receiver, offered it to Jonathan.

Rack grimly said, "Please let it not be Stimply."

"Ten to one—it's Stimply," Alice said, not un-grimly.

Jonathan took the receiver from Mamoud.

"Hello, Stimply," he said in a grim tone.

A silence Jonathan hoped was rather stunned and not grim. Then, "Jonathan. How did you know?"

"More to the point, Stimply, you're calling me in Aurora, not Earth. On a half-burned telephone. That isn't connected to anything."

"Well, yes, there is that, old man. Definitely got a point there. Can't get anything by you, can I? But, putting that aside for a moment—"

"Do I have to?" Jonathan rolled his eyes at his companions.

Stimply's tone hardened. "I'm afraid you rather do, Jonathan. Given the circumstances. Which may be grim."

"I'm standing here holding my bloody ear together with one hand, in the world's slowest getaway contraption, while on the lookout for a marauding monster that could pop up at any moment and kill us, Stimply. It's already grim. Get to the point."

"Yes, the point. Swords have points. Knives and daggers have points. Ice picks have points. Even some bird-children have points, if you include the beaks."

"I'm about to hang up. This phone that doesn't work."

"YOU WILL NOT HANG UP, JONATHAN ARMISTAD LAMBSHEAD."

Jonathan was stunned. "So that's my middle name."

"There's no time. I mean, there's plenty of time left, but not right now. Too much time."

Gibberish again. "I don't have time for gibberish."

"Wait! Wait! I just wanted to tell you that when you get to the way station, there are two doors and you definitely should not take the one that—"

That's when Jonathan dropped the receiver because the monster leapt onto the front of the pod, eclipsing the great view. It had decided to climb around the side instead and jump from there.

"Get it off!" Rack said.

"With what? How?" Alice asked.

Jonathan was on the floor, trying to grab the receiver again.

"It can't get in," Mamoud said.

"How do you know? Are you secretly an expert on the very monster that made all your fancy bullets look harmless as raindrops?" Rack asked.

"Because if it gets in, we will die," Mamoud said simply.

"Stimply? Stimply?" Jonathan had the receiver again, there on his knees on the funicular's rather grubby floor . . . but the line had gone dead. Great. Wonderful.

"Because there's nothing we can do if it does," Mamoud replied.

"That doesn't make *sense*. Nothing in this damn world makes sense."

What didn't make sense was that Stimply could call them in Aurora,

Jonathan thought. What didn't make sense was that any excuse for a rotary telephone, no matter how massacred, maimed, torched, or toothed, could spew forth Stimply's used-car-salesman voice.

"What happened to my mother?" he muttered, the useless phone cradled in his lap. "What really happened?" The shadow hiding behind his mind, the little dark space that had saved them outside Rome, was pulsing again, telling him to prepare for worse than a train wreck. But for what?

Against that thought, Jonathan felt numb to the horrors of the intricacies of the monster's mouth as it tried to crack the glass with first its fangs and then the sharp glistening beak that erupted from behind the mouth.

Then with the tentacle. Which seemed most effective. The monster's hot breath formed condensation on the glass, and with its retreat left behind odd fast-forming moss and then little crablike creatures that surged out of the moss to spin webs across that surface. As if the terrarium wasn't the inside of the pod, but the outside.

Jonathan took out Vorpal, set the knife upon his shoulder. "Perhaps we should take stock of our weapons?"

"Perhaps, instead, we should pray we make it to the tunnel and that it peels away like used gum," Alice said.

The monster began to call out to them, something like: "Growley scent me. Has massage. Has massage." The insistence and repetition began to make the words sound like the lyrics to the god-awful music. Which had become ear-splitting, as if the monster's leap onto the pod had damaged the mechanism.

"Massage?" Rack said. "Crowley wants to torture us with massage?"

"Message, message, *message*," Alice said with scorn.

Jonathan slumped down on the floor. "Stimply was going to tell me something about the way station. But he didn't. And now we're going to have to make a last stand in this pathetic excuse for a people-mover."

Halfway up there was another small crack in the glass.

Three quarters of the way up, the fractures were larger.

Hold fast, he remembered Sarah saying to him. *Hold fast, dear son. You never know what next will come.*

While the funicular juddered slow-poke style upward, the polka music played and they huddled in their seats, unable to do anything, really, but watch the show.

Chapter Thirty-Six

SNAILMATE ALONG THE NORTHERN FRONT

It was day seven of the battle for the English wall, and the giant snails had been at it for hours. Snailmate behind them and snailmate ahead. The emerald dragons had been defeated, and waves of the utterly unreliable tripod bombs concocted by H. G. Wells had detonated their magic cargo as much upon the defenders as upon the Burrower—and in any event, earthworms transformed into eels made little difference to Verne. They even, under the demi-mages' deft control, could be considered an improvement.

Still, this change did not improve the vigor nor the complexion of the defenders. Verne could through the spyglass tell where along the walls humans no longer stood, where instead white-and-gray eels spilled writhing over the edge in their masses. Defenders either had to abandon those sections of the ramparts, as they had been reduced to seething troughs, or find buckets of water for the eels, in the hope that they might still in some way fight for England in their current form, or survive long enough to transform back to human shape.

Even as ominous reports came from the most distant demi-mages over their antiquated intercom. "It were naked and it were runnin'." "It were sad and mad and I were not glad." Which perhaps confirmed a fraying of wits at the edges of their enterprise as the battle raged on.

Verne had even used the mushrooms during a break in the battle, after they had finally overcome the noxious fumes, launching them by hastily assembled trebuchet back at the defenders on the walls (who, sadly, appeared to already have been given an antidote).

As for the fallen micro-dragons, the mages and their helpers had plucked them from where they lay amid the fragrant loam and stinking mud—and shoved them into the Burrower's fuel supply. The dragons ran not quite as smooth as pure earthworms, but still they worked, replacing the earthworms lost. Thus, the Burrower had become an engine running on a hybrid fuel source of eel, micro-dragon, and earthworm. It was something of a minor miracle.

Twice now, too, they had gotten close enough to ram the wall. It had buckled, yet still it stood, and in the end the Burrower had been so swarmed over by the defenders and all manner of wyrd magical creature that they had to fall back.

By then, after the second retreat, LX had come to his senses in a peculiar way, as memories seemed to return to him from a past life, from before he had been conscripted and brainwashed as a demi-mage.

Perhaps, in fact, he now remembered his real parents, the bomb brain surgery he had been exposed to finally jolting it loose—Or perhaps it was just that he could ignore the extent of his injuries through magical means for only so long.

"I don't want to die, Jules," LX whined, and it was not so much the whining that offended Verne's sensibilities when he was expending so much energy just on keeping them alive as the grotesque familiarity of using his first name.

"You're already dead, Laudinum, in a sense," Verne replied. Very much so in one particular sense—although his nostrils had been subjected to much abuse from all directions during the various battles, none was so blunt an attack as the stench that emanated from LX.

But Verne regretted the jibe as LX once more submerged his budding maudlin qualities, or drowned them in the tub, long enough to lunge at Verne so hard in his harness and stays that the Burrower took the gesture as a command and lunged and bucked as well—flinging demi-mages affecting repairs to the infrastructure right off the sides in a flurry of surprised screams.

LX had devolved into more of a demi-urge than a demi-mage. Once the undead spouter of insults had subsided, returning to a semicomatose state, Verne managed, through jury-rigging the latticeworks of metal and fabric that lay between them, to more securely lash LX in his place.

Taking care the entire time, as he worked, feeling at the literal end of his leash. There was still the deadman's button beneath Laudinum X's buttocks, and, perversely, Verne's priorities and sense of what was possible had so diminished that he felt a desperate need to deliver their magical payload to the wall. If they were to explode and die all over the place, his flesh unsure what was brain and consciousness and what just meat, he would like it to count.

But even this terrible, irrational thought was eclipsed by the snail mating. Great gray-shelled creatures with luminous light green bodies and the delicate tendrils of eyestalks topped with golden eyes flecked with purple. They had risen up spontaneously with the failure of the giant fungi and the rout of the micro-dragons. In thick bunches of normal-sized snails at first, they had engaged in an astounding orgy of snail sex. Some might have believed it part of the natural ecology of the place, or not, but in any event, the snails had appeared at dusk while magic fire wreathed the wall in green and gold, and could not be combated until dawn.

For what could have been combated anyway? Verne could hardly, through LX, command the demi-mages and their sub-mages to interrupt the mass consummation of snail desire, nor were attempts to put the mating snails to the flame advisable; the ground in front of the wall had proven remarkably prone to wildfire.

Unstable magic was as like to turn a controlled burn into an inferno as be snuffed out by the damp suspicious moss that crowded the ground. The most aggressive of the mosses at times called out to the attackers with lichenous mumbles of "Who goes there?" and "Is that you?" Some of these mosses tripped Crowley's foot soldiers as they advanced.

So, throughout the night, they had had to endure the faint crackle and pop of snail consumption, continuous and magnified by the odd acoustics of the land bridge and accompanied on either side by the roars and sometimes ridiculously donkeylike braying of a wealth of sea serpents eager for blood they could only spill if the Burrower were foolish enough to plunge into the ocean.

Snap, crackle, snap, crackle, into the early morning, which, when the fog had lifted from both land and sea, revealed that the sorcery lay not just in the replication of snails, their astonishing numbers, but now in *size*. For overnight the snails had grown until each would have been a match for a wild boar, or even larger. Thus, their continued activities had become not just much louder and more difficult to watch, but also a veritable wall, some ten snails high and twenty deep.

Both before them and behind them.

Overnight, the Burrower had gone from resting on level ground to lying in a trench. A ravine, really.

This could not stand.

And, of course, it didn't.

But not because of anything Verne attempted.

LX, made lucid by the sight of a mound of giant snails, screamed out, "They're coming! Battle stations!"

Through tunnels dug during the night under the massing snails, now the wall's defenders sallied forth in a sortie from all sides, while from above an air force of crows came down like a black storm, blotting out the sun.

This latter threat they had at least prepared for.

"Shields up!" LX shouted, and the order traveled up and down the sides of the Burrower, from demi-mage cage to demi-mage cage. With a mechanical groan, plates of metal slid into place to protect the latticework atop the Burrower from the crows, while on the sides, the demi-mages picked the birds off with common crossbows or even more common spells.

The crows fell from the sky in droves, covered the top of the Bur-

rower and part of the control limpet in a coat of black-feathered carcasses with glassy eyes.

They had meant to eat all the earthworms. They had meant to plop
through the spaces in the latticework, these not-ravens, and eat away the
Burrower's strength. But now it was Verne crowing in triumph.

Yet the ground attack had not quite failed. Demi-mages fell to what
looked like a rough lot assembled from every pub in England. Among
them motley Viking types and Celts in war paint and British regulars
armed with swords and pikes and muskets that shot out those accursed
bears and other creatures—large and hairy or small, deadly, and without
hair. Something about a naked creature of any kind was more terrifying
than one with fur, and England appeared well stocked with furless, reckless animals for some reason.

Pikes jammed in the Burrower would surely stop it from ever moving
again, without time to pull them all out. But Verne had no idea if they
could create velocity enough to break through the snailwall ahead anyway.

But they must try. They had no choice. Even a lurch forward that
failed might dislodge the boarding ladders and thwart the sappers at their
sides. Magic here was still so unpredictable, anything could happen—to
them or to the wall's defenders.

"LX—we must move!"

Exasperating that LX still had control over steering. More so that he
was mumbling to himself. Or was it a quiet gibbering? Verne couldn't
quite tell.

"Laudinum X! You must get hold of yourself! We must move. Don't
you hear the ladders?"

Over the antiquated intercom Verne could hear the demi-mages beg-
ging for instructions from their cages.

"But me mommy is dead and I never knew my daddy and I had a toy
stuffed badger named Roy and I don't have him anymore."

Verne took a breath so deep it took a few seconds to reply.

"LX. Can I tell you something?"

"What, Jules? What do you want to tell me?"

"England, LX, has lots and lots of badgers. And I am more than certain that Roy the Badger came from England and that he is waiting for you there."

A pause. A quieting of the blood tears from Laudinum X that Verne so loathed and which had made Laudinum's already filthy shirt and breeches look like an advertisement for leech cures.

"You think?"

"I do think."

"Do you promise?"

"I promise," Verne lied.

Another pause.

Then a return of the triumphant psychotic Laudinum: "To England it is, then! To the badgers! For the badgers! We will free the badgers! All the badgers!"

Verne rather thought any self-respecting badger would flee at even the most distant sighting of Laudinum X, but with any luck they would all be dead before LX had a chance to pursue a badger. Any sort of badger.

LX shook off his stupor, cranked the gears, pulled the levers, to bring the Burrower from slumber to full-on top racing speed, belching and bellowing in eagerness to lunge forward.

"We're going to take the wall!" LX shouted. "We're going to win! For the badgers!"

"Yes, LX, yes!" Verne shouted back. Only half ironically. Only half.

LX pulled the final lever, and the Burrower, released, shot forward, defenders dropping off the side in screams and most of them crushed beneath the metal framework, grist for the mud and the complaining moss.

At a hellish velocity that shook the Burrower's frame, flinging micro-dragons, eels, and earthworms to both sides, they smashed into the wall of snails in front of them.

Which did not give as Verne had supposed. Which was hard as steel or iron, not snail-fragile at all.

There came a scraping whine and the dread crumple of the Burrower's nose splitting and shattering.

The impact threw Verne forward in his harness, and he smashed his head against the dashboard in front of him, while he saw, turning his head through the blood, Laudinum X boomeranging back and forth in his seat, the impact having split his skull the rest of the way down to his brain stem and neck.

Yet still, thankfully, his buttocks rested upon the deadman's button. Even though he was incontrovertibly more dead-ish, not just dead-alive.

The snailwall had hardened from some sort of natural glue like the snail's version of drywall; although snails had flown everywhere, the Burrower, nose capsule split to both sides, now lay buried and trapped in the snails. A fire had started around the nose, and the attackers had regrouped, emboldened by the failure, were already rushing the sides again.

The Burrower lay there, unmoving and exposed, less vehicle than castle keep.

How could something soft as a snail, brittle as a snail, be so hard? They'd been fooled by escargots. They, the French, had been fooled by a food they knew too well.

LX had begun to prattle on again, all about the badgers. Oh oh— apparently he'd resurrected once more.

It was too much. A burning desperation and anger erupted in Verne, and he turned to LX meaning a sharp rebuke . . . but burst into tears instead. The tears were like an epiphany, like something coming free he hadn't known was lodged there.

He could not keep hardening and hardening his heart. LX, damaged, trying to *tell* Verne about the damage. Verne, pushing it away, wanting LX to be a demon, not-real. When, in fact, he'd been human once, before Crowley changed him. As Crowley had, in his way, changed Verne. It wasn't Verne's fault. It probably wasn't LX's fault. All of this was on Crowley, on Wretch. The horrible war. Being lashed together into this confined space together, likely about to die. Such a cruelty to it.

"Hush now, Laudinum," Verne said, wiping the tears from his face, "Hush now. It will all be all right soon enough," and as he reached out his hand to LX, the demi-mage settled down, stopped rambling, relaxed back into his seat, if only for the moment.

And, lo!, there came a great outcry on the English wall and once more Verne put the spyglass to his weary eye, unsurprised should there be a further surprise.

Yet, still, on the face of it, Verne would admit later he found it surprising.

Across the main length of the wall, tall, muscular half-naked men had appeared and formed a line. They carried spears that curled absurdly forward at the end and wore metal helmets with gray plumes. Their nether regions were protected by enormous codpieces.

The codpieces were shaped like the heads of cod.

The men thus attired smashed the butt of their spears against the floor of the wall, creating a mighty clatter. Some among them carried hoses also crowned with cod heads.

From the mouths of each cod-hose erupted a spray of magical red flame, arcing far out into the hinterland between English wall and snail-mate wall and setting fire to the ground there. Yet another . . . wall. "Kill! Kill! Kill! Kill!" came the awful chant from the codpiece soldiers, distant but carried by the wind.

Verne frowned. Or was it "Bill! Bill! Bill!"?

Or even some interspersing of the two?

Over the English wall then appeared Doom himself, ancient of days and so enormous he seemed bigger and longer than the wall itself.

Framed by the men in codpieces, arcs of red fire spewed farther, more intensely, and the spear stomps became louder.

"Bill! Bill! Bill! Kill! Kill! Kill! Bill! Bill! Bill!"

In their cockpits stuck to the Burrower, so many of his demi-mages craned necks skyward, jaws dropping, as the monster climbed the sky.

The eye black as death, the mighty gray-white head, the hungry jaws, and the coils beneath uncurling and uncurling, the shadow vast across the wall.

The sight made Verne forget his despair. A vast calm came over him as he braced for the assault. For the first time, an anger beyond his control began to smolder. It really was too much. Well too much.

"To arms!" he shouted over the intercom. "To arms!"

"For Crowley!" LX screamed.

"No—for France," Verne screamed back. "FOR FRANCE!"

And up and down the line, within the Burrower, the demi-mages took up the cry: "For France! For France!" Not for Crowley.

"For France and badgers!" LX screamed.

They could still repulse the enemy. The snails. The moss. The torrents of flame.

It was still possible.

Or perhaps not.

For, lo!, the Great Behemoth Cometh, to the adulation of His followers.

William the Conqueror Eel.

Bill.

Chapter Thirty-Seven

PLEASE, SIR, NO MORE PUFFIN' TRAIL

Rack's body had been like a cathedral bell being constantly rung since Danny's disappearance, and there was nothing that could stop the shaking. His thighs were aching terribly after all the hiking, but that wasn't the issue. All he could keep thinking about was how he should have made up with Danny for good and all around the campfire the night before, not just continued with what she called the Truce.

But he just couldn't, had been stuck obsessing about all the times Danny had held things back. All those strange away trips with all the teams she belonged to, the times not all her teammates seemed to be going with her, which he'd thought nothing of at the time. What if some of those trips had been to Aurora? What if what if what if. It would drive him crazy if he let it, because he had to trust, especially now. He had to.

Her and that bloody rat. Rack prayed that Tee-Tee was a help and not a hindrance, and if that were the case, would happily kiss the rat on the lips if he ever saw it again. If Danny was even alive. Resolved in the same breath to avenge Danny if need be. Heaven forbid. She couldn't be dead, could she? Not indestructible Danny.

He could live without her, but why would he want to? The loneliness growing up with such absent parents who were not even his real parents, in such an empty house.

Except for Danny. Danny, who was always in a good mood. Danny, who had never complained, ever, about helping him with his leg or his foot. Danny, who had sneakily forced him into a form of physical therapy by enrolling him on the Poxforth rowing team.

Christ, it seemed a sin now that he had let one lie, no matter how large, come between them.

The monster had given up right before the pod hit the archway, fallen off rather than continue. Perhaps scraped off was more accurate, there being mere inches between pod and tunnel wall, but it also might just be playing with them, cat and mouse. He'd gotten a disconcerting sense the thing was enjoying itself.

The funicular pod came out of the steep darkness of the mountainside with an incongruous peeping sound and a locking of gears that steadied them as they leapt out. For the funicular was already, counterweight and cockpit both, headed back down.

Which meant they knew what was coming up.

Yet even now they could not find any spare luck lying around. Directly in front of them lay the most rickety of rickety rope bridge, slung low over an icy plateau dominated by a deep pond and framed by broken and burnt ski lifts on the mountain slopes above them.

On the other side stood the way station: a cabin of sorts cut into the mountainside. An unprepossessing rectangle of stone with a faded red aluminum awning. No gate. No garden next to it. No sign. No signs of life.

It also appeared an army had firebombed the exterior, for the stone was awash in black scorches and there were two glassless holes for windows, a staved-in door, and a section of the front wall missing.

"I've seen better-looking outhouses," Alice said.

"Let's just get on with getting there," Jonathan said.

Mamoud had been calculating. "I believe we have thirteen minutes before the monster appears in the next pod. Twelve minutes fifty-eight seconds. Fifty-seven . . ."

"Thirteen clocks? Seemed an eternity getting here, to only be thirteen," Rack said.

"Shallow water and only a brief fall if the bridge doesn't hold," Jonathan said.

But all Rack could see was entanglement in all that rope.

"We don't actually know how deep the lake is," Alice said.

"I was trying to make a joke," Jonathan said. "But we have no choice anyway."

"Can I suggest fewer jokes and more decisions?" Rack pleaded. "Please!" He didn't have any answers, but something along the lines of movement, of *getting somewhere* seemed in order.

"Nine minutes left," Mamoud said. "Eight minutes fifty-nine seconds. Fifty-eight. Oh, wait—I meant eleven minutes . . . I think."

"Can we truly make it across before the monster gets here?" Alice asked. "Should we make a stand here instead?"

"I would rather hope there is a door leading elsewhere inside that way station," Mamoud said.

"I'd prefer to risk the bridge," Rack said. Entanglement was superior to devourment.

But if he'd had to do it over, he might've risked anything but the bridge.

Seen as some sort of absurdist obstacle course, a race of the kind favored by Poxforth's sadistic gymnasium taskmasters, the rope bridge was an utter disaster from start to finish. They had to go one right after the other, the bridge bouncing and swaying unpredictably as it took each new weight.

They'd agreed Rack would go first, and his tentative steps felt at first much like getting into a small bobbing boat from a floating dock.

But Rack steeled his nerve; after all, who knew what terrors his sister was encountering at this very moment?

From there it degenerated into the kind of athletic event only Danny would've been able to enjoy, during the first half of which most of them displayed a complete lack of knowledge about the coordination needed to navigate this kind of flimsy rope bridge.

If Rack fared better than the rest, it was likely because of his upper body strength and perhaps it gave him an advantage that he didn't try to do anything much with his legs because he couldn't—given the flailings of both Mamoud and Jonathan behind him. Instead, he just tried to keep them on top of the hemp-and-twine jury-rigging, doing what he could to avoid a plunge through the spaces in that treacherous weave, bending his knees enough so as not to trip, either.

As the early leader, his likely prize was the dubious one of reaching the firebombed sketchy way station first. But being in front also came with certain responsibilities, so he decided to be the motivational shouter, pausing at times to toss back over his shoulder old hot chestnuts like "You can do it!" and "Be the ball!" and "Don't give up the ship!" In this case, that meant "Don't fall in the drink."

None of which could ever make up for the fact that Mamoud on his front was like a beetle on its back and that Jonathan had spread himself wide like a sugar glider about to take off and floundered, only to find that when he drew himself back in, his weight caused a dip or gully in the rope that took just as much effort to get out of. Only Alice, more like a spider than a woman—her arse high up as if doing planks, arms and feet wide, weight distributed—made good progress.

All that energy, that effort, just to reach the midpoint. Whereupon they all suffered the same result, whether graceful or graceless, first, last, or middle.

They all started screaming. Not because the next funicular pod had arrived. Not because of the gusts of wind trying to blow them off the bridge.

No, it was because of the sudden attack of puffins from beneath that they were all screaming and recoiling and trying not to fall in their surprise at the upward-leaping multitudes.

Ambush!

Giant puffins. A flash mob of parted jaws, clacking and lunging as if to cut at the frayed fibers of the bridge, which dipped lower in some horrid sympathy for the attackers. Puffins. Giant. Lying in wait beneath the surface, waiting no more.

"I hate these bird-children!" Jonathan screamed.

"They're not children. They're monsters!" Rack screamed back.

"Watch those beaks!" Danny shouted, if only in Rack's mind. "Watch out for the beaks!" A disconcerting lurch and loss.

"Five minutes," Mamoud said with icy calm, oblivious to the horror show beneath them as he flopped about in the ropes.

The greedy little maniacal faces behind the curved black hatchets of the beaks, the saw teeth visible as the beaks parted to reveal the shriek of tough jerky that were the purpling tongues. Their black-and-white tuxedo plumage besmirched with red stains, from rending and gobbling god knew what beneath the pond's surface. A surface now roiling with the frenzy and blood reverie.

The accumulated stench seethed up from them, a wave of blood and *eau de parfum* akin to Band-Aid-flavored rotting corpse. The way station beyond the bridge had been reduced to a smudge or blur of no consequence next to that pungent presence. This was life, popping up unexpected. Life, raging at him as if seeking revenge for every bird Rack had ever eaten.

Giant, carnivorous, flightless puffins. So eager in their serrated slobbering for the taste of human meat that, heaven help him, Rack felt in some perverse way as if their enthusiasm should be rewarded, or at least not thwarted, and he would have extended his hand down through the bridge's netting if Jonathan, who had caught up alongside Alice, hadn't slapped him and then held his head in both hands, shouted at him as they rocked—which forced him to look down, truly look down, to see the crazed spinning pinwheels of their ever-widening eyes.

Hypnotism. They had almost hypnotized him into wanting to be eaten.

"Holy hells, these puffins are evil," Rack gasped. "But I'm all right now, Jonathan. I'm all right."

"One minute," Mamoud said, barely heard over the puffins.

"Are you sure?"

"No."

"Why can't you be sure!" Rack shouted at him.

"Only you can be sure," Mamoud shouted back.

What did that mean? But the stare Mamoud gave him steadied Rack. He was sure. He was all right. He was in control of himself. Even clinging to the bridge, with beaks seeking his soft bits at the apex of their leaps, and he instinctually flinching away, holding his cane in a death grip. Now with renewed vigor clambering across the rickety scaffolding, desperate to get to the end, needing to get there, and to hold the bridge steady for the others.

But as he looked back past where the others struggled, a new threat appeared: the monster, emerged from the chrysalis of the funicular pod and standing at the other end of the bridge. Giggling or giggle-howling, it began to rock the bridge.

"Faster!" Rack exhorted. "Faster!"

"We're going fast as we can," Alice shouted back, while still the puffins raged below.

"Zero minutes," Mamoud said, still floundering.

"We've company," Rack said, pointing behind them.

And, by Jove, once they saw what was rocking the bridge so roughly, they did go faster.

When he reached the other side, Rack quickly knelt there on solid ground, shouting that he'd hold the bridge steady, feeling the power in his shoulders, his back, and so thankful for it—for all those hours of rowing, rowing with his crew, rowing his poor lost Danny. The rope burned his hands, but he didn't care.

Miracle of miracles, that his efforts stopped the rocking, even as the puffins ripped at the underside of the bridge's belly, desperate to taste his companions.

But the monster was on the bridge. The monster was aided by Rack's stabilizing of the bridge just as his companions were. Soon the monster would be at their throats again. How its vast bulk didn't plummet into the pond by principles of gravity alone, Rack didn't know.

"Come on, dammit! Come on!"

Alice passed by him, fetched up on the shore of the way station side.

Jonathan, who had fallen behind again, lunged forward, rolled past.

Then Mamoud.

The monster was halfway across, swatting at the puffins with its tentacles, becoming more adroit and swifter by the moment.

Rack rose, cane in his hand.

There came a moment of frozen silence, framing the bridge, the lake beneath, white ravens far overhead. There came an instant when he could not hear the puffins. There was only the creak and fracture of ice in the distance, the nodding of the reeds at the edges of the pond, and the soft sigh of the swaying bridge in the wind.

Puffins. Monster. Johnny Thunders in Rack's head.

He grasped the pommel of the cane and drew forth the secret sleeping within: the shining silver glory of a sword. Glittering glorious in the sun. Not Excalibur, not by half or quarter . . . but it would do.

Rack brought the sword over his head and down with all his strength.

A blow for the ages, severing the ropes, sending their side of the bridge plummeting into the pond, and the monster with it—splashing frantic among slavering puffins. Covered with puffins as the monster tried to stay afloat, now more puffin than monster so smothered was the monster's surface with the psychotic birds.

A brief struggle in that freezing water, before the monster, immobilized by the sheer number of puffins, was drawn beneath the pond's surface. Vanished but for the ripples of its passage, followed by the largest air bubbles Rack had ever seen.

Funicular.

Puffins.

He had seen enough of both.

Then, off balance, he fell on his ass and Jonathan had to drag him away from the edge.

"Well," Rack said. "I guess now we know why it's called Puffin Path."

It seemed they'd been clutching at straws for a while now, and should've been down to a negative number. But perhaps, even after the puffins, the way station was the last straw. For in addition to being firebombed, it was utterly empty, had no supplies at all, and now they were faced with a decision in the form of the two nondescript doors against the far wall.

The first had *Enter at your peculiar peril* handwritten on it. The second had a messier *Enter at your particulate pearl* scrawled across it.

"Never fond of typographical errors," Rack said. "Unless it's a clue."

"I am certain it is a mistake," Mamoud said. "Nor do we know who wrote it. The handwriting is different in each case."

"The second door is taking the piss out of the first?"

"Enough banter!" This from Alice. "Always with the banter. Which door? Which door do you think?"

"Dr. Lambshead always said to take the first door," Jonathan said.

"Always? You mean in his letter—that one time," Rack corrected, losing patience with Jonathan's grandfather and his enigmatic advice.

"Some of us could take the first door and some the second," Alice said.

"No—we stick together," Mamoud said, curt. Perhaps he, too, felt the pressure of time. None of them should feel safe yet. Not in this pathetic excuse for a way station.

"Wasn't Stimply trying to warn us off one of the doors?" Alice asked.

Jonathan shrugged. "I've never met Stimply. How do I know I can trust him? Besides, I've no clue which door he meant."

Such a world, Aurora, that Rack must stand and watch them bicker over which magic door to flee through without any guarantee of either offering Danny help.

"The first door, then," Rack said, deciding. "We'll trust Jonathan's grandfather. Besides, I always prefer an honest door to a sarcastic one."

"On the count of three, then," Mamoud said, taking the doorknob in his hand.

One advantage to cutting a rope bridge with one stroke of a secret sword hidden in your cane: They all listened to his advice a lot more attentively.

"What's on the count of three?" Alice asked.

But Mamoud had already started.

"One . . . two . . . three . . ."

Mamoud flung the door open, they plunged inside, and he drew the door shut behind them.

Glimpsed of an instant: A strange Victorian-era house that had melted around the edges. The sort of place Rack should've liked to visit, under other circumstances, the melting aside.

But the landscaping left much to be desired: Behind the house, a huge, scarped wall of rocklike substance rose sheer. Far overhead, a thin ribbon of red, where the mouth of the chasm opened, among inaccessible peaks. A deep red glow from the further opening of the gorge. A sense of something huge staring down from that sky, and the sky hot, so hot, the air on fire. In front, a vast pit seethed and writhed in such a way under the steam that rose from it that Rack could not at first tell what lay within.

"I think we go back," Rack said, firm, but no one listened to him.

"Should we go up and knock?" Mamoud asked.

"No—back. Back, back, back!" Rack pleaded. But he wouldn't without the others.

"What's in the pit?" Jonathan asked.

"What's in the pit?" Rack said, incredulous. "What's in the pit? Nothing good's in the pit!"

Something peered over the edge of the pit—the eyes and ears alone showing. Leave it to Jonathan to spot the mammal.

"A pig!" Alice exclaimed.

Then they saw the thing more completely; but it was no pig. The creator alone knew what it was. It had a grotesquely human mouth and jaw, but no chin of which to speak. The nose was prolonged into a snout; this it was, that, with the little eyes and odd ears, gave it such an extraordinary swinelike appearance. Of forehead there was little, and the whole face was of an unwholesome white color. Rack felt he might've read about this in a book once, but not one that ended well.

A quick patter of many feet came to them, then, and an uncouth squeal and hideous howling. As of many, many pigs, indistinct in the red mist.

"I repeat, with much vigor and emphasis, as the one who cut the bridge ropes . . . let's get the blazes out of here," Rack shouted. The fires had intensified, the sound drowning out even their frenzied discussion.

But Mamoud was one step ahead, already at the door. "I can't get it open. It's stuck." He was jiggling the knob, and Jonathan was trying to help him.

What Rack could only describe as mutant death piggies roared out of the pit toward them, and they were all screaming but with no sound coming out because they were hoarse from screaming at the carnivorous puffins, all of them pushing at the door, knocking on the door, as if someone on the other side might be kind enough to turn the knob.

The howling became an insidious and bloodcurdling snorting, and Rack didn't dare look but kept banging on the door.

Then a distinctive click and Mamoud saying, "I think that's done it," and they were spilling back through.

Jonathan was shouting, "Close it! Close it! Close it now!"

Which, with difficulty, Rack and Jonathan managed, but not before Rack saw through the slit that impossible eye again, the barbarous snout. For an instant that would live with him longer than he would've liked.

The snarling echo of the door slamming shut reverberated like an accusatory voice.

"Well. That. Was a bloody mess," Rack managed, catching his breath. Safer to behave as if they'd just escaped some row at a pub or something. Safer to pretend this was normal. Otherwise, he'd just start screaming.

"Was that even Aurora?" Mamoud said. "I don't believe so."

"Fits right in with *my* experience of Aurora so far," Jonathan said.

They sat there, backs against the door, sprawled and panting, looking out through the rip in the way station wall. An astonishing amount of graffiti had built up over the years on that wall, Rack noticed. Jonathan was staring at the graffiti like he'd seen a ghost, which was odd. Perhaps he was just staring off into space, from exhaustion.

But still no chance to rest.

"Is that what I think it is?" Jonathan said.

"It is," Rack said, and his spirits sank further.

The monster had jumped out on the near side of the pond, dripping puffins, only fifty feet from them.

"Don't panic. I don't think she sees us," Mamoud said.

"Not she—*it*. And it definitely sees us," Rack said.

"You have to admire this creature's single-mindedness, at least," Jonathan said, even as he wearily got to his feet.

"Too complex to be single-minded," Mamoud muttered.

"I most definitely do not have to do that—admire it. Or marvel at its complexity. What is wrong with you?" Rack said. He was singed, bruised, so very tired. They did not even have the modicum of time he'd thought.

The monster shot out two arms impossibly far, along with her tongue, which had also become an arm, and all three stuck to the wall of the way station, and quick as thought, boomeranged the monster right onto the outside of the way station.

She peered in through the rip. Leered in, more like, the monster, in all her glory. The horrifying, vast mouth wide open to eat them, oblivious to the half-dozen puffins attached in death thrashes to her body.

A scrambling for the second door, in a wordless, horrible hurry, as the monster veered round to the way station's entrance, didn't bother to open the door, just smashed through it.

The second door opened, and Mamoud and Jonathan pushed their way inside, with Rack following in gibbering terror.

"What the—?" Rack was just as surprised as the rest of them.

They were in a rough-cut room, hewn from the mountainside. Still trapped in the Alps. It wasn't a magic door, just a damned ordinary door. And a damned ordinary room, smelling of must and chilled rot.

What wasn't ordinary: a rather large man sat dead and half-mummified against the far wall of the room, in shadow, with what looked like a large-scale model of a yodeler's horn driven deep into his chest.

"Help us!" Jonathan cried out, and Rack unfroze, hurried to help the others with the metal bar that locked the door. Except it was lying on the floor and it was damn heavy and they only had seconds to get it into place.

As they maneuvered the bar into position, the door opened a crack. Jonathan teetered backward holding the bar, and Mamoud had to shove the door closed again with one hand.

There came a tentative swat or a buckle, as if the monster was unsure of what lay beyond the door, and hot foul breath too near, too near. The monster bellowed and got two tentacles through the crack, which widened again.

"Bloody hell—help me keep it closed!" Rack pleaded.

As Jonathan struggled with the bar, Mamoud drove his shoulder into the door. But the door remained open . . . a crack.

A tentacle slapped through the crack, smacked at Rack's face, while a second grabbed his foot—his bad foot, and the rest of the assemblage in the orthopedic shoe. Rack cried out, as it tried to pull him back across the threshold, through that crack too small for the purpose. He dug in with his artificial leg as Jonathan tried to grab hold of him while still balancing the bar. Kicked out with Lester as best he could, dislodged the beast enough that the lower tentacle recoiled in pain. Off balance, Rack tumbled onto the floor.

Mamoud leapt at the door, shoulder first. The door slammed shut. Jonathan, groaning, brought the metal bar forward, Mamoud helped him, and put it in place. There was a reverberating metallic clang.

Rack had lost his shoe, his bright pink sock shocking against the dull walls of that place, as if he'd been wounded. The one tentacle had retreated with it, the other sliced off and still on the floor.

There came a banging on the door. The monster again.

As Mamoud and Jonathan sat down heavily and Rack propped himself up on one shoulder.

"We're going to die in here, aren't we?" It wasn't the way he'd expected to go. Although he hadn't spent too much time on being gone, but now his heart was all go go go.

"Maybe it will go away."

"I want 'go' to turn into 'went.'"

Breathing heavy, at the limits of their endurance, they listened for some sign the monster would give up.

Ten minutes. Fifteen.

The banging stopped. Rack thought he felt a great weight leave the door.

He let out his breath in a trembling rush.

"I think maybe it's gone."

Then the banging took up again.

"Hallo," the cut tentacle said from the floor beside him. "Do you know squishy? I am squishy."

To his core, Rack felt this was unfair. How dare it have grown an eye and a mouth?

Chapter Thirty-Eight

DEATH PIGGIES AND THE CELESTIAL BEAST

Ruth Less had banged on the way station's second door for a long time. Why wouldn't the two sweet-smelling ones and the stinky one who smelled like something that had stuck to her foot come out and play? Be a noble and loyal snack like all the others before them. Even the rude pecking puffins.

"Eyev yerfut. Eyev yerfut."

Bang, bang, bang went the club of her arm against the door. She didn't mind when they hid, if it wasn't for a long time. It was more fun. She liked fun. Fun was good. Heady said fun was good, and Heady had been nice to her.

"Wudlick shewbak? Wudlick shewbak?"

The shoe-foot she had taken from Rack had words written across the bottom in black ink. "Lester" was its name. "If you found this, bring it back. If you took this, you can fook right off." Then some numbers.

Eventually, Ruth Less tired of banging on the second door. She could have banged on it much longer. She could have eaten the frozen human snack on the floor, too, while she waited for the other, more important snacks to come out. But the frozen snack had almost no smell at all, so it was not alive in any possible way, not even the usual after-death way. Besides, Squishy would take care of them, and if not, well, she would leave another brain-tentacle outside the door, to continue the banging. She had plenty of them.

The other one, Alice, had left no trace, except some tracks leading back down the mountain. Ruth Less had no specific orders about Alice, didn't like the smell of her, and also there was a taste around her, as of some other . . . being . . . one much more powerful. There were things about Alice that Ruth Less didn't understand, and since she understood so much through her pouch, this made her reluctant to follow the woman.

Nor did Ruth Less care much for the shadows and masks lurking still well above them all. They were like mist or mirrors, neither of which she liked to eat.

Which left the first door.

Wretch had said, "Do not be curious," then had had to explain "curious" to her—a word that because it was forbidden tasted delicious to her. She could obey Wretch and yet also Tuft and Speck if she killed the Jonathan-thing eventually, but also remained "curious" along the way.

Besides, Heady had told her more than once that Wretch's orders to her would be just like her games of keep-away with Speck and Tuft. That the point of the game wasn't to win right away, but to play. To have fun. "Winning right away would spoil it, don't you think?" Heady had said.

For that reason, Ruth Less had taken the time to smell the giant blue polka-dot flowers and study the points of light in the sky at night. For this reason, Ruth Less had also, laboriously, read some of what was in the books carried by the snacks in the funeral procession by the lake. She read by running her snuffling mouth parts over the pages, because then she could taste the ink, and some instinctual talent of her species to interpret meant she could taste her way to comprehension. So she could begin to understand this world. Without really using words, for reading by taste did not register as "words" to her. Any more than the mountain goats had told her stories once in her gullet.

In this spirit, Ruth Less told herself it was pointless to bang on the second door any longer when she could be curious somewhere else. For example, it might be useful to open the first door.

And so she did.

And, oh my!, the marvels within! Amazing death piggies to play with, gambol with, and then lovingly devour!

After that the figure made of comet fire that appeared at the threshold of the mansion—a Celestial Beast, Mamoud the Sharp had called it at the campfire. As Ruth Less had lurked not so near but near enough to pick up on words. The Celestial Beast also known as "Comet Man," the lonely one who needed a hug but who destroyed beings even as he "read" them.

Ruth Less knew what a hug was from Tuft and from Speck. She loved hugs, even though they were unnatural to her species. Members of her species did not mind being alone for long stretches of time; indeed, one might register affection by biting off the head of your best "friend" in the world she had come from, since large congregations were only really for the purpose of devouring and gorging on one another. But she had learned about the idea of "togetherness" from Tuft, from Speck, and something about it had tasted nice.

When all the piggies had traveled, in various states of having been read, into Ruth Less's bulging belly, she approached the man of light. When he just stood there, burning, and did not shy away, Ruth Less wrapped the Comet Man in an embrace with her many arms, some of which popped out of the top of her head. He wasn't mad at her about eating the piggies. He said there were many more left over.

It was a long and firm hug, as the Comet Man wept tears of flame. He smelled like burnt coal and smoky ash and yet also like the seared salt shore of a sea on fire. It was a comfortable smell to Ruth Less, and she was glad she had been curious.

For the fires did not bother Ruth Less. She had been made fireproof and coldproof, and, indeed, they only had need to part when her hug grew so strong that it would have snapped the Comet Man in half and snuffed him. Although she doubted he would have stayed snuffed for long, as this Celestial Beast was quite powerful.

As they drew apart, the Comet Man regarded her with affection from the gaping empty holes of eyes surrounded by orange-yellow flame as the mansion behind them melted at the edges and more death piggies grew in the pit that was the front lawn.

The Comet Man began to sing to Ruth Less.

Soon she would have to be on her way, eager to show her pouch to even more of the people and creatures of this world. For this was one way Ruth Less grew, and with each new pouch-ing, Wretch's orders made less sense to her, as she learned more and more about Aurora.

Why, perhaps she would put the Comet Man in her pouch. Then she would be able to spout flame and know even more, become even larger. On the inside. For now, just on the inside.

But not yet. Instead, she would just listen.

For the song was made of emerald smoke curling into the heated air, not of words at all, and she thought it was the most beautiful song she had ever seen.

Chapter Thirty-Nine

DEAD LEAVES WALKING

"Leaves are the enemy. Heads are the enemy. All the enemies converge upon me."
—Pronouncement from the floor, never issued, recorded by Speck only

The cat had come back, the one Crowley had experimented on. The cat was huge, and it lay in wait at the bottom of the chute that exited the war elephant's bum. The cat was snarling, mouth wide, quivering. He could smell the cat's offal-tinged saliva. Came a wave of nausea and dislocation as he teetered at the top of the chute. He didn't want to fall. He didn't want to. But what could he do? Crowley was just a head. And so he toppled again and again, rolled down the chute into the waiting jaws of the cat.

Came the chomp. Came the sickening crack and the moist feel of blood spurting across his forehead. Last dim thought: Shitty death. Shitty-shitty-bang-bang death. To be a head rolling into a giant cat's mouth, split like a ripe melon by those yellowing fangs. Not an emperor's end, but a commoner's.

But when Crowley finally came to his senses, Wretch was dragging him through dark forest, across evil twigs that snapped like the brittle limbs of sick, starving children, that let out tiny screams. Not the usual, then. With Wretch a rippling black shape like a huge torn flag in the wind, stitching his way between trees, Crowley cradled in one monstrous webbed hand that served also as neck-pedestal, Crowley reduced, he realized once more, to the precarious position once held by Napoleon.

"Don't ask where we're going," Wretch said. "You don't deserve an answer. In fact, don't speak at all if you can help it. You're only along because I don't trust you, even as a head, back at the war elephant without me."

West of Linz. East of hell.

Now he remembered what had befallen him.

❧

Nothing could be more humiliating than regaining consciousness as an appendage to his former familiar, and perhaps that is why Wretch had done it. Ignoring Crowley's protestations as he held Crowley behind one door where his demi-mages couldn't see him and poking his head out to give them orders. Order after order, in Crowley's name, and Crowley just a growling head trying to nip at Wretch's tentacle, and, Crowley realized later, Wretch displaying forbearance in not just killing his former master outright.

Which is when Crowley realized, belatedly, that there was still something to live for and it was the same thing Napoleon had lived for: to still at least be a head, alive in its way. To experience the world through more limited senses and in more limited ways. But, still . . . to be part of the game.

So he'd shut up for a time and just listened, tried desperately to get the lay of the land, to, perhaps, find out just how much trouble he was in. And when Wretch came back into their quarters (for, truly, it was no longer Crowley's imperial offices, but Wretch's), Wretch scanned the All-Seeing Puddle without regard for or attention paid to Crowley. For which he was for this one time grateful.

The news was all bad.

Wretch spent an inordinate amount of time on the English wall, which Crowley had only ever thought of as a diversion; a bonus if it actually succeeded. The All-Seeing Puddle showed Verne's struggles against Ol' Bill as Crowley called him: William the Conqueror Eel. Ol' Bill was one reason Crowley had decided against personally leading the charge against England.

Ol' Bill was a handful, especially with the Burrower stalled before the wall of cemented-together snails. Ol' Bill periodically flailing over the wall to try to get at the Burrower, and Verne countering by reversing in the trough of his own making and smashing once more into the snail-wall. He seemed to know better than to take on Ol' Bill directly, and yet soon Verne would have to. The Burrower couldn't take the punishment of ramming the snailwall forever.

In other unwelcome news, their own procession of war elephants was even farther behind schedule, giving the Prague magicians more time to scheme and the Republic more time to send reinforcements through Turkey. Curious and curiouser: Ruth Less was missing, while mysterious forces gathered in the forests of Germany and France, such that the puddle could not dispel the mystery but only show them shadows and smoke.

Worst of all, the Golden Sphere still couldn't be found, no matter how many rabid chipmunks Wretch launched into the ether.

The state of the world seemed to be spiraling out of control.

Yet it was worth noting that Wretch spent almost as much time on reports of the whereabouts of Jonathan Lambshead as the situation in England or the Golden Sphere, which to Crowley was the most important thing of all.

Even reduced to merely a head.

❧

Deep in what even Crowley recognized as a haunted bog of a forest, Wretch continued on stoically, a wretch on a mission. Black water kept seeping through, and Wretch fastidious enough he made their stitching progress through the midlevel limbs of moss-covered trees that seemed, from Crowley's jouncing angle, to shoot up to the dismal moon.

Every so often, Wretch used another of his many tentacles to drop-kick a wriggling rabid chipmunk released from a third many-pronged tentacle through a small swirling vortex he created with his breath. Clearly, he did consider the Golden Sphere a priority, what with all the living depth charges he kept sending out.

Reflexively, like a wriggling lizard's tail, Crowley said, "Wretch, unhand me this moment! I am your lord protector! If you undo this treachery this instant, I shall forgive it."

Crowley hadn't really expected a reply, any more than Wretch had replied the last half-dozen times he had feigned indignation.

But this time Wretch laughed like a drain clogged with the hair of dead men and said, "We are at this impasse because of your own treachery. You meant to betray me. After I had made it clear at the volcano . . . after I had made it so very clear who wore the crown."

Crowley, smacked by a branch, took a moment to absorb the sting—of both branch and Wretch's words. A very real fear flooding through his head once again that he could lose even . . . his head. Inasmuch as Crowley was cynical about souls and well aware of how his soul, if it existed, might fare in an afterlife, he did not precisely know what to do. He decided on earnestness.

"Wretch, if I somehow offended or gave the impression that I did not appreciate all that you have done for—"

"Shut up. Shut up. If you don't, I won't restore unto thee, Lord Emperor, any sort of satisfactory body."

Thankfully, for Crowley's blood boiled despite the danger, Wretch slapped a wide thin tentacle-hand across Crowley's mouth. It had a stench like rotten eggs, but he was thankful. He was about to go stark-raving mad. Stark-raving furious. But a hand across one's face when all one had was a face had a sobering effect.

And so they continued on in silence through the witchy-woods, over the bog, over fen, across fetid meadows, and into patches where the trees grew so close together Wretch must slow and slow still further, upon what mission Crowley had not a clue.

West of Linz. West of Prague. In the middle of nowhere. Had his demi-mages back at the war elephant begun to catch on? Perhaps even now meant to mount a rescue effort to free Crowley? Or had Wretch truly deceived them? Cold, terrifying thought: Did Wretch now *control* them? Had he that power? Surely not. Surely he needed Crowley alive much as he had before, no matter what Wretch's purpose. Or he would be dead already. Instead of merely a half-dead head.

Finally, Wretch came to a halt, looking rather like a cat and a bear and a centipede welded together, looming over Crowley, who Wretch now kept on a contemptuous low tentacle, perhaps all the better to stare up at the dark-glinting majesty of Wretch in this form. Yet all Crowley saw was a traitorous vermin that like any rat must be snuffed out, should the opportunity present itself.

They had come to a dank pond lit by a dim supernal glow from the grasses and mushrooms lining its banks.

"Quiet for both our sakes, Crowley," Wretch growled. "For I mean to raise an old soul with the old magic and I've not the resources or the time to secure your mouth."

A kind of icy calm had come over Crowley as soon as he'd seen the pond through the trees. All his sorcerous instincts shied away from breaking free out into the open in that place. Every part of him that remained knew there was danger here. Yet Wretch saw opportunity. Why?

"Who do you mean to raise, Wretch?" The cold had spread to his heart, by which he realized it was true no one needed a heart to have the sensation of one growing cold.

"Charlemagne," Wretch replied.

The cold became ice, and the frightened thoughts burst through his anger, chilled it dead. Wretch *did* mean to replace him, had kept his head alive just so he might be further humiliated or fed as sacrifice to the dead. To a true emperor, a man whom legend could not subdue. The force that had united the German tribes and forged a mighty kingdom a thousand years before.

"Let him rest," Crowley said. "Please, for the love of the devil, Wretch, let him rest."

Wretch drop-kicked another chipmunk into oblivion, his dry laugh sucking the breath from Crowley's mouth. Crowley found it hard to breathe, realized again how conjoined, how dependent, he was to Wretch.

"I could just leave you here, by the pond," Wretch said. "You would eventually suffer the fade, without my blood."

"You cut my head off! I demand my body back!"

"I burned your body to ashes," Wretch confessed.

"You monster!"

Wretch cackled, sent another chipmunk off on its mission. "To be honest, Lord Crowley, it might have come to this despite your attempt at betrayal. How much easier to transfuse you now that I only have to replace the minuscule amount of blood coursing through your dumb skull of a brain."

Chipmunk punted into nothing.

"These insults! These insults shall not stand!"

Another chipmunk.

"As for why we are here," Wretch said, ignoring Crowley, and sending out yet another chipmunk. "We lack a general, as you may have noticed. We lack a general because you underestimated Napoleon. And none now living are his equal . . . except, perhaps, Charlemagne."

Relief of the most bitter kind. Wretch wasn't going to kill him. Wretch just wanted a new general. A new general using the old magic. And creeping into that relief, an internal giggle, a giggle that he had to stop from breaking free. A giggle about the old magic, for he had his wits about him of a sudden.

The old magic on Earth was feral enough, but here on Aurora? No matter who Wretch was, could he predict the consequences? Crowley thought not.

Besides, it meant Wretch had lied: He wanted Crowley along because he was afraid to be alone with the old magic.

The last chipmunk entered the void in search of the Golden Sphere, so as not to distract Wretch from the coming resurrection. Nor did

Crowley feel inclined to interrupt, either, knowing the consequences of a botched spell.

Wretch, in a gnashing and rending of fangs, recited words in a language that was less like words and more like the random pattern of maggots across a dead body. Not so much sentences as a swift decay that stilled the breeze and wiped the meadow clean of the sound of insects and even the far-distant whip-poor-wills.

Several bats careening over the pond fell dead with a *plonk, plonk, plonk.*

Heady stuff, and it filled Crowley's head with dead mice and earthworms and beetles gnawing through bark. Until he was stuffed full, felt like his brain had turned to soggy cotton balls squashed together and filled with blood.

Came the words again. And again. Waves of foul words beyond or below anything John Dee had ever hinted at. The cat waited at the bottom of the chute again, and Crowley closed his eyes, concentrated on nothing, nothing at all. On blank, windowless, antiseptic white rooms with not a spot of dirt in them. On a chair to sit in that had no upholstery and no cushion and was just smooth, clean wood painted white.

But still the rot came through.

Wretch gave out a sound of alarm, of surprise, of anticipation above him, and from the forest on the far side of the meadow came the sound of dead leaves gathering in a rush. The forest darkened, if that were possible, and from the loam and lichen a shape began to rise. Up, up, up out of the ground, assembling itself at Wretch's call.

A great, flaking, moist wreck. A man, but also a kind of accumulation, a midden that walked or seethed out of the pond toward them, dripping moss and water weeds.

He had lain too long to be himself any longer, Crowley realized, even if perhaps Wretch didn't. Fey things had gotten tangled up with the man in the soil at the bottom of the pond. They clung to him as he rose, crawling forth from the rotten skull beneath the rotting crown. But they had gotten deeper, too, so deep it did not matter, when, shambling, clotted with the stuff, and the remains of a rotting cloak and chain mail and once-fine boots, he resembled a man.

He was Other. He was beyond fey. He understood the old ways yet did not approve of them. Would want dominion if let off Wretch's leash.

Who better to counter the Prague magicians and their golems than an old corpse? Who better to understand the shadows creeping forth from the forests of Germany? Next to Charlemagne, Napoleon was a youth, his methods and strategies callow, blithe.

Charlemagne, now standing before them, turned that battered, be-cowled, be-maned head toward them, filthy with black and gray fruiting bodies, which dropped from his head as would drops of water.

"Why hast thou called me up, creature of the Builders?" Charlemagne said in an old German dialect familiar to Crowley from spell books, although the translation in his head was imperfect. "Who are thou to call me up from slumber?"

There was no syntax from Charlemagne that would be less than ponderous, Crowley realized. There was too much weight the litch carried from below, and too many centuries. Sunlight could not cure it. The laughter of children could not penetrate it. Nor could love or sacrifice or any human virtue.

In a word, dangerous as he was, Charlie Mange, as Crowley decided right there and then to call him, was also a big, giant bore with no sense of humor. An awkward, slow-moving travesty of an undead general. Deadly. Distinctly un-fun.

There lay hope. For Crowley if not for Wretch.

"Emperor," Wretch said, ignoring Charlemagne's questions entire. "General. Your time has come. Again."

Charlemagne turned that weighty visage up toward Wretch's downward gaze and then looked out across the pond, shrouded in mist. Yes, it definitely helped Crowley to think of him as Charlie Mange. Took the sting out of the danger, added a bit of slapstick.

"I have lain here, resting, for a while. I feel the stealth of sleep still clinging to my bones. I feel that many years have passed and I have been dormant and blissful in my repose. Yet you would make me lord again, among men, and any others that might stand against me?"

"Yes, something like that," Wretch said. "Good enough to start." But Crowley could see he was uneasy with this arrangement already. Were there regrets? Was Wretch losing the thread?

"The world beyond grows stale and unguarded," Charlemagne continued. "Does it not? The world beyond is corrupted and full of chaos. And, verily, I shall bring it to heel and turn to dust all who would oppose me."

"Yes, um, something like that," Wretch said.

With that declaration, Charlie Mange followed Wretch and Crowley out of the dark forest and back into the world of men, war elephants, and strife. Once more.

Chapter Forty

ALL THE WAY DOWN

The tentacle advanced on them less like a disembodied limb or even a snake than like a centipede that ended, or began, with a fist that was a face, as they'd backed up next to the dead body. Not by choice. At least, not Jonathan's choice.

"Squishy" proceeded to offer up a cheerful thrashing, begun by launching itself at them—literally punching them with its face. Seemingly everywhere at once, blackening eyes and reddening foreheads at will. Boxing ears.

Always bleating out "I am Squishy! I am Squishy!"

Then it leapt onto Rack with murderous intent, Rack flinging it against the far wall, only to have it immediately get back up and jump on him again, squealing cheerful platitudes and inanities like "Is this fun? Is this fun? This is fun!"

As it righted itself from a well-aimed kick from Rack's only good leg now and again attacked—in unorthodox fashion by attaching itself to Jonathan's face, blocked only by his flinging up his arms in an X in desperation—Squishy then adjusted tactics to try to flow through and strangle him.

At that moment, Mamoud pulled it off and then Rack brought out the sword and cut it in two.

"I believe it is dead now," Mamoud said, looking at the stunned, slow-writhing pieces.

"And I believe you're wrong," Rack said.

But Jonathan hardly heard either of them. Something had been nagging at him, panicking him now that danger had momentarily passed them by.

"Where's Alice?" he asked.

It was so astoundingly obvious now. A horrifying realization.

"Not here, not since the death piggies, I think," Rack said. "Could they have gotten her?"

"Where's Alice?" said the twin Squishies. "Not here, not since the death piggies. Could they have gotten her."

"You, shut up," Jonathan said. "I've had just about enough of you."

"You, shut up. I've had just about enough of you," mimicked the Squishies.

"Please please be quiet," Rack pleaded.

"Please please be quiet," the Squishies pleaded.

"No use talking," Mamoud said.

"No use talking," the Squishies sang.

With intensity and verve, the Squishies redoubled their attack, and they were reduced to a bloodthirsty and instinctual stamping and stomping of the Squishies and maiming and hurting the Squishies by all available means. Because it was like trying to stamp out a stubborn brush fire. Almost impossible.

The pieces of the pieces were crawling up their legs, echoing Rack's shriek of "Die! Die!" when Jonathan remembered his knife.

"Step back, away from the pieces," he shouted.

"Which pieces?!" Rack shouted back.

"All of them!"

And when they had, which took some doing, he tossed the smiling pocketknife into the midst of the pieces.

It gave a squeal of delight like a child about to have a nice time at the circus and then in gleeful and terrifying fashion extended all its blades, and in a whirring as intense as a hummingbird's but deadlier it sliced the pieces into tinier pieces and then tinier pieces still.

Until all the fight had gone out of the Squishies and they reflexively, almost in a philosophical way, moved in slow-motion micro-piles.

The smiling knife retracted its blades, scuttled across the room to hop up happy on Jonathan's knee where he slumped against the wall.

Jonathan pocketed the knife. He was bone-weary. They all were. Battered and bruised. Perhaps a little in shock at how badly it had all gone, ever since the funicular. Even before that.

Three. Down to three, without Danny and without Alice. They'd lost and failed not one but two members of their expedition.

And it was not over yet. Not by half. Perhaps the unrelenting nature of the assault was the most unnerving part. Never a chance to catch their breath.

For that renewed banging wasn't a ringing echo in their ears. It was the sound of the monster still battering at the door. It was the sound of there being no Alice in the shadows. It was the sound of now truly seeing the face of the half-mummified body in the corner, impaled on a yodeler's horn, and recognizing it. A sharp shock dulled only by fatigue.

Yet it was what lay behind that massive figure that got Jonathan's attention.

"There's another door!" Hope rising that surely would be crushed by whatever came next.

The outline of the door had been hidden by the propped-up corpse.

A small door, but a door nonetheless. My kingdom for a door. Three cheers for a door. He felt giddy, radiant, in the glow of that discovery.

"Up," Jonathan said. "Up. Otherwise, it'll be all for nothing."

Like a bunch of stumbling drunks, they all three rose, holding on to one another. Wordlessly, they shoved the body to the side, Jonathan trying not to look at it too close. It was inexplicable, for the man to be there. Dead. Had Rack noticed?

Kneeling, Mamoud tried the knob. It jiggled. "There's no lock." Such relief in his voice.

Then they were dragging themselves through into that even-cooler darkness, closing yet another door between them and the monster. One with a lock they could just turn into place. Pitch-black beyond.

After, they had slammed the second door shut behind and stood there panting, Rack hopping on his one foot.

"Can you walk?" Jonathan asked.

"I'm walking, aren't I?" Rack snapped.

Mamoud had taken out a small cylinder and broke it in two, releasing a low-powered light. More Republic science, almost the same as magic.

Facing them was the sheer mountain wall, no corridor, no next room, no next door.

Etched into that space, seven feet up, were words.

WELCOME TO THE ALPINE MEADOWS
RESEARCH INSTITUTE

"Is that some kind of joke?" Rack asked. "After all of that . . . just this?"

"It appears so," Mamoud said. "But I doubt that monster can get through two doors. It will tire. We can survive this."

"If it's not magical," Jonathan said. "I think it's probably magical. And tireless."

Rack looked stricken. "That's it, mate. We're toast. Let's just hope Danny got out."

"And Alice," Jonathan added.

But among all the other surprises, one more had surfaced, and Jonathan started to laugh. He couldn't help himself. It was all too, too much.

"She's picked my pocket. Alice picked my damned pocket." Hand over his chest. "She's taken the Wobble and done a runner."

Mamoud's head shot up sharp from where he knelt. Yet the look on his face didn't express concern. Perhaps it seemed like the least of their problems.

A helpless look from Rack in the shadows.

Should've seemed catastrophic. Now, under the circumstances, it seemed small, almost petty.

Like mother, like son, Jonathan thought. He would die in a version of the Alps, too, forever separated by the wall between worlds. Without ever solving the mysteries before him. Of the mansion. Of the Order.

Of how and why Sir Waddel Ponder, headmaster of Poxforth, lay dead in the next room, with a musical instrument piercing his heart. A man Jonathan had seen alive not two weeks ago. On Earth.

Of the scrawled words on the way station wall he had not pointed out to the others: "Sarah, I'm sorry." Words to a dead woman or . . . ? Stimply had meant to warn him from thinking that way—and failed. He'd tried to warn himself, in a way, by banishing thoughts of her since they'd come to the Alps. But now could think of nothing else.

How, like the headmaster, her body must be curled up somewhere, lifeless, still holding on to her secrets in a way he could not articulate.

Better if he had not seen that. Better, even, if her body had been there, beside the headmaster, than not to know. A selfish, terrible thought.

Came a voice in his head, a voice he'd known was there, for over a week now. Ever since Spain.

Don't give up hope. You can't give up hope. I won't let you.

But *who* was talking to him? Who had taken up residence inside his head?

As if in response there came a loud click, and the floor opened up beneath them.

They all three fell through darkness for a very long time.

Chapter Forty-One
HE WHO HE WHO HE WHO HE

Late afternoon. From a forested hilltop overlooking Prague, a blond woman with a sparkling face and golden eyes decked out in a sunflower dress pushed a pram with a cooing baby in it. They were headed along a brick path to a little beer garden nestled in a clearing among the trees. From there, gardens led down into the city.

"Who's a pretty baby?"

"I'm a pretty baby," said the pretty baby.

The baby had wisps of blond hair and a sparkling face and golden eyes.

"Pretty, vain baby," said the woman. "But you earn it. You work it, baby. You work it. Because you earned it."

"Oh yes, I did. I did I earned it." And the baby reared up out of the crib to punch the air like a boxer working up a sweat.

"What're you looking at, human?" the mother said, glaring at a codger type. The type she and the baby both abhorred. The type with a cap and bushy eyebrows who no doubt gawped at anyone they saw who was the least bit unusual, just because their own life was so ordinary and tawdry and full of drama.

"Yeah, crap-pants—what'cha lookin' at, bub?"

"Nothing," the man said in Czech, and hurried down the path away from the beer garden.

"Hmmmmph," the woman said.

"Hmmmmph," the baby said, and crossed its arms.

"I'm dire thirsty, thirsty dire. I must must have a drink, dahlink," the golden woman said to the golden baby, who lived within the golden pram.

And thus the woman pulled up to a round wooden table and sat down on a log stump seat with a dusty sigh, for it had been a long trip, pram beside her. All around were couples enjoying a beer, as if they hadn't a care in the world. But the woman with the pram had seen that often right before war. Many, many things were normal to the golden woman, but this, no matter how many times she had seen it . . . was not.

"Drink up!" she exhorted them as the waiter came over, a slight, pale man in dark trousers and a white shirt.

"May I help you?" the waiter asked.

"You may help both of us, my friend! I will take a pint of bitters or biters or lighters or liters—whatever you recommend—and my baby friend will have the same. Local specialty, local brand. Loco parentis. Make it so."

The waiter's face crumpled in on itself in confusion.

"Madame, we do not serve babies."

The golden woman guffawed and slapped her knee. The baby did the same.

"My dear sir, I am not asking you to serve me a baby. I already have a baby. I can always cook up this baby if I have need of victuals. Ain't that right, baby?"

The baby raised both thumbs up and gave a broad wink. "That's right, Mama—I'm highly cookable! I AM COOKABLE TO A HIGH DEGREE. Flammable as a baby should be. Flim-flammable. I do not do well with high temperatures . . . except when I do."

"I . . . I'm . . . I don't understand."

"Flummoxed like a dumb-ox," the woman said. "Well, why not just bring me two beers, then. I'd not like to flaunt local baby custom."

The couples with their beer lips were all staring at the golden woman and, also, at the golden baby.

The golden baby stood up in its crib, surveyed the scene.

"Please, dear people," the golden baby said, "return to your beer chugging. Chug thy beer like nobody's business, just as I am not your business. Chug and savor, savor and chug. We are just happy to be here, in the esteemed company of so many messlings."

The breeze fled gentle through the trees. The couples gradually returned to their own business, although many soon drifted off to the path and out of the beer garden. In part because in addition to the disruption caused by the woman and her baby . . . a fair number of rabid chipmunks had fallen out of the trees or just the plain ol' sky in a rather frightening way.

As the woman set fire to the chipmunks with her mind, she mused on the possibility of her and her stellar baby joining a local book club. That might be a good way to be anonymous. Who would suspect a member of a book club of being capable of . . . anything? Maybe even K's book club, such as it was. Some sort of moral there, surely. As much as she hoped to cause a stir now, anonymity later would be ideal.

"He who," she started. "He who. He who he who he who he who he who he who . . ." No moral, then, only he-who.

The waiter returned with two large beers.

The woman held one beer for the still-standing baby, and the baby drank it down like a champion.

"Ha!" the woman said to her baby. "You have a white beard now! You are an old baby!"

"Drink your baby, woman-mother."

"And you're drunk, too."

"I mean, drink your beer, woman-mother."

"And so I shall." And so she did, and then shouted for another and another and another.

"My goodness, wherever shall it all go?"

The baby had gotten noticeably larger from all the drinking.

The woman began to sing, for she loved a good sea shanty, especially when landlocked.

What shall we do with a drunken sailor?
What shall we do with a drunken sailor?
What shall we do with a drunken sailor?
Early in the morning?
Way-hay, up she rises
Way-hay, up she rises
Way-hay, up she rises
Early in the morning
Put him in the long boat 'til he's sober
(Feed him to the sharks and the jellies)
Pull out the bung and wet him all over
(Feed him to the snarks, take off his wellies)
Put him in the scuppers with the deck pump on him
(Give him over to the sea so very deep and true)
Heave him by the leg in a runnin' bowlin'
(Give him over to the likes of Sark and Jaunty Blue)
Tie him to the taffrail when she's yardarm under

Soon enough, the woman and her talking baby were almost alone, except for a very drunk couple at the far end of the beer garden, and the staff.

Which allowed the baby to pull out a spyglass hidden in the crib.

"You go, baby! You go!" said the woman.

And the baby did go—pulling out more and more sections of the spyglass until it was more like a magician pulling more and more scarves out of his pocket than a real spyglass.

Soon the spyglass was much longer than any baby ought to be able to hold, and drooping at the end by the time the baby put the spyglass to one jaded golden eye.

"What see you baby?"

"I see Spain, I see France, I see the captain's underpants."

"Seriously, baby. Be serious. Serious as the bees here, which sing the national anthem."

"Well, then, I see the city spread out below, and beautiful it be."

And truly the city was beautiful, for mother could see through the spyglass even as child beatific held it. The river running through the city. The long, tall wall that protected the city. The fortress-castle on the hill opposite them. All the frenzied activity of citizens and soldiers in the space between. How up wafted the sound of hammers and of saws and of smithies. How everywhere they looked, the city was preparing for war.

"Shall I explode now, Momma?" the baby asked. "Oh, please can I explode, Momma!"

"With my blessings! With all my blessings, my darling baby! How could you stop yourself, whether I approved or not?" the woman said. "After all that beer. How *could* they serve you all that beer, my darling! What villains! What cads!"

"Goodbye, Momma." The baby folded its arms, took a deep breath, held it like a tiny diver, looking even more like an over-blown-up balloon.

"Goodbye my child. Godspeed. Speed-god."

Then the golden baby exploded—all over the beer garden, all over the waiter, all over, even, the far-distant drunk couple.

Covering them all in warm beer as the last of the afternoon light faded into dusk.

Since leaving Alfred Kubin, the Golden Sphere had been most proud of playing a flotation device in a Prussian river with a name too tiresome to relate, attached to a common barge carrying a German burgher. Oh, how the burgher's hangers-on loved to hang on to a flotation device in their swimming trunk onesies as an idyllic respite from crunching numbers and chowing down on various repulsive types of food, including more sausage kinds than there were letters of the alphabet. Shame about all the near drownings, which the Golden Sphere put down to an unsafe inclination to swim after eating rather than any capricious tendencies on the part of the flotation device.

Would his splendiferous role receive any award nom-noms? Unlikely. Although the flotation device was totes adorbs, as the kids on one or another Earth might say, the award possibilities, this being real life, were nil, zero, zilch.

That fun over, the Golden Sphere had ended its stint as a sort-of-sailor and had the audacity to imitate a wagon wheel on the journey, the look on the face of the farmer priceless as the sphere-wheel rolled off into a field and then disappeared into a forest with a splendid flash of light and clap of thunder against a cloudless blue sky—all of this made even more priceless as the wagon as a result of the rude departure of the sphere-wheel was upended and the farmer and his crop of rutabagas and melons went flying into the mud.

The Golden Sphere made sure that the farmer's crop landed around the unfortunately bearded man in such a way that when he rose, his own splayed form greeted him in the mud through the outline of rutabagas and shattered melons.

Against a distant shout of "Treat thy vegetables and fruits as thy would thy children!" (not sure It had gotten all the "thys" right) that might, to some in this extremity of situation, sound like a command-ment from God and lead to a tradition, passed down for generations, of sheltering of legumes in swaddling clothes by the fire. That should've gotten a nod in the "best stunts" category of any legitimate awards show, but, again: nothing.

But the ol' mother-and-baby routine—a classic. Never failed to hit home. Every single time, even though there had only been a single time. Who would forget *that*? No one.

Fun over, the Golden Sphere reconstituted into a single globe, the beer garden empty of anyone with any common sense in their head.

Under cover of approaching darkness, the Golden Sphere rose into the sky above Prague and continued to increase velocity, taken over by a wild hair and the wild air and all the beer. Bloody minded, still rec-onciling itself into one where It had been two; sometimes that became confusing. So the Golden Sphere shook the disguise from its vast and lugubrious system through sheer speed, the city growing distant far beneath.

Up, up, up through the clouds. An ascent that only It could achieve: straight up.

Yes, verily, the Golden Sphere would have dared to touch the stars, to chance that long, cold journey for a hundred, a thousand, years to escape in the most arduous way possible. The creep that was Crowley might have It constrained, but if It took the Long View, there freedom lay.

But even It hesitated, took pause . . . yes, even the wonder that was the Golden Sphere.

For fear. For fear of limits. For fear of the Unknown. For fear of loss of what creature comforts It enjoyed. (The longing with the fear. To live. To be free. To not become a pawn in someone else's plan. Again.)

Came to the limits of Aurora, past the stratosphere, past the ionosphere, out into the pale dark, where It could look back on the continents as if itself a satellite or spacecraft.

There, where It bumped gently against the vast invisible wall that Celestial Beasts sometimes burst through, breaking it like glass . . . bobbed there for a moment like someone trapped under ice, trying to find a crack to breathe through, contemplated a running start.

Contemplated breaking through and continuing on. A new adventure. Alone. In the unknown. Nothing familiar. Ever. Again.

A celestial choir played thunderous in the Golden Sphere's head, the cosmos above opening up to It, and It with the choice of ushering in a new age of exploration. To become the agent of that, even if It should never report back.

Yet It needed humanity, in ways It knew in what served as its guts, but the Golden Sphere could not articulate. It needed even Kubin, much as It had tormented the man, and even the dumb waiter who had, finally, run screaming from the beer establishment . . . such that now the Golden Sphere felt a needle of "sorry" that was unwelcome but not unfamiliar.

Even perhaps toward the farmer whose cart It had destroyed by taking the wheel. For a fleeting instant.

But felt the uncertainty, too, in a slackening, a sense of drift, a deep and long in-falling . . . back down toward all the tiny and pitiful lights of humankind.

Back down to the puppets, of which It was one. Back into Crowley's trap.

As It fell back, the Golden Sphere screamed and shrieked in a dark hot fury that was in part for show—for It always knew It must in the end fall away, fall back to the surface, constrained, imprisoned.

But what gave the Golden Sphere comfort in that moment was knowing the chaos to come, of the events It was about to set in motion, the entities It would soon summon. What they would do, and how the world would change. All because Crowley had been so foolish as to think the Golden Sphere would be his servant.

Let Prague be the testing ground . . . for all of it. Let them *all* become mired in Prague.

Sark. Sark and Jaunty Blue would set things right. Sark and Jaunty Blue, who had been gone from this world for so long . . .

Lines came to the Golden Sphere, then, mother and child both. Not from Kubin's benighted puppet show, but from the work of the other K., whom he would be seeing soon. Lines that the Golden Sphere admired despite its worst tendencies, the lines It had no notes for, nor ever would.

"I cannot make you understand. I cannot make anyone understand what is happening inside me. I cannot even explain it to myself."

EPILOGUE: ROADSIDE PICKUP

There, by the side of the road, waiting, as he had for longer than expected; three days longer. Head high in the long grasses. He could smell the bluebells and a wild violet and a feral lettuce in bloom. Also, alas, fox scat, but never mind that. As his nanny used to say, so long ago.

"Never mind that."

Napoleon said it aloud, awkwardly. He had managed to gnaw off a leaning sedge weed to chew. Made it last. Make it all last. The feeling of the sun on his face, the sound of woodpeckers in the nearby woods, the wheeling hawks far above that sometimes dipped into his field of vision—all of it.

He breathed in a long draft of fresh air through his nose, as his mouth was otherwise occupied with the sedge weed.

Freedom. For now.

His benefactors were late, but at least it hadn't rained. At least Crowley hadn't found him; indeed, if he was any judge of Wretch's character, Crowley had his own problems to deal with right now.

At least Ruth Less had eaten the demi-mages around the corner, out of sight . . . and largely out of smell. Something large like a wolf had worried at the bodies one night, but even that was a mercy. That wolves had not yet worried about him.

Napoleon hadn't minded Ruth Less. How could one mind the person . . . well, the monster, that had set one free? He rather liked her, if he were honest. She had a quality he admired in a monster: honesty (of which Crowley had none, although it did not come easy to emperors, that much Napoleon would admit).

Earnestness, too. She was only ever and always herself. No one could change that.

Ruth Less also had the most amazing pouch, as Napoleon could vouch, having spent some time in that sacred space, lined with stars. It was only then, knowing that Ruth Less was larger on the inside than the outside, that he realized she was a Celestial Beast, but on an order of magnitude greater than he had ever seen. He doubted Wretch realized this, and one reason he'd chuckled in the pouch, during all his adventures there, was thinking of how surprised Wretch might be when he found out, and Crowley, too. And not surprised in a good way.

Fond reminiscence, that pouch trip, for time traveled different inside Ruth Less and Napoleon could write a memoir just chronicling the year . . . rather, the day he had spent there, before being deposited for roadside pickup. The places he had visited . . . he would never be the same.

But Napoleon was still just a head, all the same. A head peeking out among the weeds, propped up atop a half-decomposing tree stump. He could feel the wood lice rampant with their own tiny dramas along the edges of his own stump. Still cataloging the good rather than the bad: At least it hadn't been cold; at least no wild beast had gnawed upon his face.

A bumblebee landed on his chin, took off again clumsily. A toad hopped by. A fat old toad, the kind his nanny had thought were witches. A fat, squat old toad, hopping by and, admittedly a little bored with all the waiting, Napoleon followed it with fascination, as it bumble-stumbled over dirt and low-lying weeds and, yes, toadstools. Quite a distance he managed to track it, for as a head without a body, Napoleon's peripheral vision had become quite remarkable.

Ignoring the way it hissed at him as it passed, croaked, "Say nothing of what you've seen. Say nothing to no one."

"To *any*one," Napoleon whispered back, but point taken. He had no wish to antagonize a toad that could return and prove quite an adversary to fend off with a mere sedge weed.

For he *had* seen strange things upon his new throne, the stump. Much stranger than a toad—marching past in the dead of night, and no doubt in his mind that these fey beings would snuff him out in a blink had they noticed him among the weeds. So he'd held his breath until he'd felt faint, that he make no whisper of a sound.

These fey folks that he first thought he must be hallucinating, for they were the stuff of his nanny's fairy tales, come out of the deep wood. Hundreds of hedgehog men, stern and forbidding, atop giant roosters. Huge upright badgers. Dangerous-looking nectar deer, larger than he'd ever seen, flying overhead. All manner of animal, great not small, and even a phalanx of not marmots but the *shadows* of marmots. Wraiths the equal of Crowley's Emissaries. Things not seen or rumored of for centuries. All headed west at a stealthy yet rapid pace.

What could it mean? Nothing good. The Old Folk. The old magic. Another thing he was grateful his nanny had gone on about. How he wished he remembered more of it. But, then, she'd also told him not to grow up to be a soldier.

The road led to Paris, Napoleon knew that. If they stayed upon this old, grass-eaten track, they would soon approach the outskirts of Paris.

Even as it seemed all other armies descended upon Prague.

Of his own situation, Napoleon deflected his worry by imagining ambush. Of which way a force might travel through the woods to descend unnoticed upon his position. Of how sappers might be deployed, and trackers. What time of day would be best? (Brightest daylight, shining off his pale forehead.) How crucial would the role of clouds and shadows be in disguising the glint of armor or of rifle for his counterattack?

"Toad, stay awhile!"

A naked, frank pleading that surprised Napoleon. Given the nature of the toad.

But the toad was gone.

In its place, looming from the road, two pairs of worn boots filled with shadows as seen through the weeds. Across his face. There in the sun-soaked fire of stale afternoon.

"You're late," Napoleon said, hopeful. For it was crystal clear they'd seen him. If they were brigands, or the wrong brigands, he was done for regardless.

"We could have been later." A woman's voice. But was it the woman the Tuft had promised? (Of what the Speck had promised, his lips were, for now, sealed.)

"You're lucky we're here at all." A man's voice, deep. Napoleon imagined him as barrel-chested.

"My kingdom for a horse," he said, but it came out feeble, ordinary. Half a kingdom for a body.

"You have no kingdom," the one known as Mack said, stepping out of the sun.

"Woodpecker—tongue wrapped around brain. Such-like. Like-such. Must I say all the rest?"

The one known as Kristýna took his measure, arms folded. Finally, she said, "No. But if you are a wise man, you will remember that we are all you have. And if not . . . well, what's been found can be lost again."

Corsica, Waterloo, Moscow. All such a surprise. Destiny? He'd find out. But more than anything, he found to his surprise he had murder in his heart. He wished to do Crowley and his Wretch harm. Major harm. The type of damage they'd never recover from.

Napoleon smiled up at them and said, "I am at your mercy, my good friends."

And so, mercifully, they took him from that place and vanished into the forest.

THE WOBBLE BOOK CLUB QUESTIONS

If you would like your results tabulated and considered as part of our general survey of reader satisfaction, please print out this questionnaire, fill it out, affix your name and hometown to it, crumple the paper into a ball, and curl the paper into a bottle and toss it into a storm-water drain. We will receive it due to the power of magical drinking.

What is the Alpine Meadows Research Institute?
   A.   Another name for the Order's swanky new Health Spa &
        Rejuvenation Center.
   B.   An institute that researches alpine meadows.
   C.   Something to do with the figures in people masks.
   D.   Yet another sanctuary for puffins and death piggies.
   E.   All of the above.

Jonathan and his friends die from:
   A.   Falling.
   B.   Being crushed by the rocks below.
   C.   The suspense.
   D.   Jonathan's knife having a freak-out.
   E.   None of the below.

What are the odds of Wretch and Crowley reconciling?
   A.   50%
   B.   Snowball/hell.
   C.   Marmot/dandelion.
   D.   0.005%
   E.   Wrong question.

Who is the "other K." referred to by the Golden Sphere?
   A.   K9, a literary police dog.
   B.   A moon-blue mouse who eats bitter herbs.
   C.   Harry Krouton, the plasmatic slam poet.
   D.   Special K.
   E.   None of your business.

Which of these items does Ruth Less keep in her pouch?
   A.   Pepper spray.
   B.   Bicycle pump.

C. Umbrella.

D. Lump meat.

E. Slurpy puppy tadpoles.

If Napoleon had the choice, would he rather be:

A. A head without a body.

B. A head on a horse's body.

C. Just a neck.

D. A head with wings, so he could hang out with Wretch.

E. Somewhere else.

INTERLUDE

AN EXCERPT FROM
A SHORT HISTORY OF THE BUILDERS

No one knows where the Builders came from in the multitudes of worlds and parallel worlds. They were not human, but could take human form. Indeed, the Builders seemed to enjoy the human form. Flawless men and women appearing out of nowhere, almost ethereal in their perfection, and cryptic in their speech, this quality prized by the ordinary as evidence of an elevated status, of elevated minds.

In such disguises, they walked the Earths as mortals, but they were neither mortal nor exactly immortal. Nor was it possible to tell if they were moral or immoral beings. At times, the actions of the Builders were deeply humane and at others astonishingly cruel.

The Builders' real name was too terrible to be written or spoken. To do so was to feel as if eels and spikes were writhing in one's head. To do so was to feel as if one's own brain was screaming. So they remained the Builders, but some disliked saying even that surrogate name. A stirring somewhere, of some strangulation of space and time, even in that simple utterance. As if there were bargains the Builders had made that had turned them hideous in the attempt.

But everyone could agree on one thing about the Builders: They had snuffed out war and imposed order wherever they had ruled. Mostly in the form of the Doors.

Before the Builders, magical landscapes had an unruly, untamed aspect. Unbound by rules. Doors between worlds, volatile, and winking in and out of existence in their multitudes. In some places, merely walking outside, through a forest, could be a fraught experience. You might come back, or you might not. Any place could be magic or no place in those shifty uncanny times. The Old Magic ruled and even a stone or a tree stump might of a moment speak to a passerby.

But after the Builders created their own doors, magic no longer ran in unruly channels that might change on a whim. It was anchored to places rather than the landscape. Stability resulted. There was no free-for-all. Inanimate objects remained so and did not of a sudden turn on their owners. Animals, on the whole, stopped talking at unexpected times. People did not get lost from walking all unknowing through invisible doors that had not been there the prior day. People did not find themselves trapped in some other version of Earth, doomed to fade away without ever understanding what had happened to them. The myriad links between places had been snapped, and while for most this was progress, for some this was a bad thing, for it meant like was banished from like and whole living systems were cast adrift, one from the other. Forever lost, bereft of what had been connection.

Where the Builders extended rather more influence, there were three sets of doors, in particularly sensitive places. Where the Builders extended less influence, the doors were simple, straightforward. Places the Builders deemed dangerous might have no doors at all, or restrictions not clear to anyone but them . . . until too late.

The first doors might lead to corridors of other doors or to other doors on the same world. The second doors might lead to hell or hells. The third doors . . . well, they led to so many places, how could one catalog them?

Some believed the third doors were a dark joke by the Builders, a joker's card added to the deck out of a perverse sense of their own superiority. A challenge, even for them, to navigate. For there was no doubt the Builders liked a good joke, and a difficult challenge.

And, for a time, all went well.

But, over time, too, the Builders receded, lessened in visibility and effect. Over millennia they began to retreat from the worlds they ruled, leaving behind only the doors, a few artifacts, and a handful of very odd buildings.

These dwellings included what some dubbed "the Château Peppermint Blonkers," choosing absurdity over a true name that, like the Builders' true name, would crush a mind with sheer terror. The château, like most Builder buildings left behind, only appeared corporeal on certain terms and conditions. It only appeared in places of magical chaos or strife. Yet neither did the château's presence always restore order, as if it had become unmoored from its original purpose.

No one knew where the Builders had come from, so when they withdrew or disappeared . . . no one knew where they had gone. Or why. Had there been renegade Builders who did not support the purpose of the majority? Had there been some kind of revolt, or reconsidering of priorities? Had they simply grown tired of their creations and abandoned them? Had some other force destroyed them in a sly, stealthy way?

None of these questions could be answered.

Who knew even what worlds the Builders had not touched. How would one know? Before their rule, few returned from a visit to their native world to report back. Only those worlds with Builder doors had anything resembling traffic back and forth.

In the absence of the Builders, susceptibilities and weaknesses appeared . . . or one could say the old magicks reappeared. Magic, on some worlds, went feral once more. In other places, magic disappeared entirely.

Over time, men and women stepped into this breach, understood the importance of preserving what the Builders had left behind. They studied the magic involved, perused every relevant scrap of knowledge, eventually formed an organization: the Order of the Third Door. Their mission: to ensure stability, if on a smaller scale, for they were not as powerful as the Builders.

The more the Builders' doors could be preserved, the less magic would revert to the chaotic. The less travel between the doors, the less chance for reversion as well. And thus the Order was essentially conservative in its goals, one might even say protectionist. And they had succeeded now for an immeasurably long time. They had succeeded so well that kings and emperors in the know had grumbled for quite some time that some among the Order felt they knew as much as the Builders, pretended to take up the Builders' former glory.

Less an organization than new potentates. New rulers. Taking over backwater worlds, unlikely Earths, where the mainstream of intellectual commerce between worlds rarely took place, where the rumors might be contained. Where a human might appear to be a god.

Over time, however, fragmentation continued and against the Order was arrayed old magic and new, which might make a return to chaos more possible, much more likely. Let in all sorts of things that must not be let in. Let in old magic better left to rest in the ground, in the forest, in the sky. If people understood old magic at all.

For there was a whispered prophecy regarding the Builders that was ever at the back of the Order's collective mind.

That there would come a time when a cruel ruler compromised by darkness would come to power on Aurora. As the darkness spread, the château would once more appear and other artifacts of the Builders as well. That the magical wall of Britain would be compromised.

That the old magic would return in full fury and tempest—and all would once more descend into chaos. A new Dark Ages, for all time and all worlds.

But was it true?

~~For the bird children~~
~~For the rabid chipmunks~~
For the beautiful pouches

BOOK TWO

THE MARMOT'S SHADOW

Part V

A HIGHER POWER

"Could I kill you with a stick?"

Chapter Forty-Two
FALLING, BE-SOTTO VOICE

Falling.

Jonathan kept falling and falling.

Until after a time he could not sense the others around him, screaming, or register anything but the soft air beneath him and the floating sensation and the absolute darkness.

Falling and nothing to break his fall except the Voice inside his head, which was mumbling to itself.

Be still or be clear, Jonathan thought, be sharp.

The "presence" looked up at him. He could think of it no other way. That something lodged inside his mind looked up or over at him, as if separate. But not separate.

Still falling, falling now under the stress of that unknown regard, into his past. Had the presence put him there?

On a train with his mother beside him, on the way to visit Dr. Lambshead for the last time. Nothing like the train to Rome, nothing at all.

He peered out at farmland from the train, passing by swift, overlaid with the smudges of window fingerprints, and sometimes islands of forest, and then the outskirts of towns.

This younger Jonathan hadn't had many train rides. He didn't know yet if he liked them. Especially since some part of him still knew he was falling into a chasm.

It was all so vivid, more so than his memory could recall. The smell in the compartment was weird and worn and a little sad, tinged with cigarette smoke. The prefab sandwiches in their triangular plastic cartons struck him as unnatural, a weird travesty touted as a "ploughman's lunch." The grim concrete stations with their graffiti he didn't care for.

Is this you, Voice? All this detail? Some gift or curse?

No reply.

Nor was his mother much help, there in the unfolding memory. "Laconic" was a word she'd used to describe herself, and since "laconic" seemed also a land she would never leave, Jonathan had learned to read her body language instead. If relaxed, his mother would not have sat quite so rigid, although her "relaxed" was rigid enough that only someone who knew her could discern the difference. Nor would she have had her small black purse clutched in both hands on her lap.

Had it held a weapon?

A knife, perhaps. Or something stranger, something magic? Did magic work back on Earth? He couldn't remember if Stimply had said.

"Where are we going after we see Grandfather, Sarah?" Jonathan dared ask. Told himself he called her "Sarah" of his own volition. And yet the distance there at times felt like years of wasted light.

"We're going to see your grandfather, of course," Sarah said. "On his estate. A nice holiday. If only you can stop falling."

Sarah had a maddening habit of rarely answering the question he had asked.

"Yes, but, and that is all well and good," Jonathan said, "but—"

"Oh, look, dear—sheep! Right there out the window!"

Jonathan did like sheep, it was true. He found endearing the way puffs of fleece coats caught on fences and bushes and gates, and gave the impression that low-lying clouds had passed through. *That he was falling through clouds.*

But even so, he could smell a rat.

"If you plan to kidnap me," he said, "you could at least tell me where you're going to hold me for ransom."

He'd brought all his things, at her urging. What could that mean but that they were leaving Robin Hood's Bay for good?

She looked at him with a mixture of exasperation and love. "I can't kidnap you, Jonathan. I'm your mother. I would be paying ransom to myself, and thus operating at a loss. Which, now that I consider it, is a good description of being a parent."

One thing to smell a rat, and another to do anything about it. Even a rat in sheep's clothing.

The window soon became repetitive, the sprawl of limbs and coats peeking out from seats ahead somehow oppressive. He closed his eyes and half dozed against her shoulder the rest of the way, a shoulder he had always found softer than her posture would suggest.

When he woke, Sarah was desperately carving a message to him into the rock face of the way station that wasn't a message to him at all.

"Jonathan, take care. Stop falling. Stop. Falling."

But he couldn't. Not yet. There was a long way yet to fall, still . . .

. . . *into an expedition with Dr. Lambshead. Something the presence had dredged up from deep inside, from that last visit as a child* . . .

Stepping through a doorway in the basement, his grandfather beside him. Falling through. The sudden, unexpected smell of lavender, of mint, had hit, but also of deep, old magisterial rot, the reassuring smolder that rises pungent from rich topsoil.

Plunging forward in the dark, Dr. Lambshead reached out and, with a firm grip, pulled Jonathan onto a luxurious dark green lawn framed by the bright blue sky, weeping willows to the sides, and the lush grass leading in the middle distance to a large, open tent pitched in front of the pond.

People stood talking at the tent's entrance, some dressed in outlandish robes and some with masks held up over their faces. Some appeared to be animals, and one at least was a puppet maker. A kind of shimmer he by instinct knew had nothing to do with sunlight cocooned the tent and the people in it. To either side of the tent were statues or sculptures or machines that had been colonized by vines.

"It's morning," Jonathan said, squinting. "Why is it morning?" Had he slept in the long corridor? Had he never fallen at all? Where was the Voice now?

Dr. Lambshead did not reply, and a terrible sense of abandonment replaced his sense of confusion.

They approached the tent. Two figures stood to either side: a giant rabbit and a giant bear, and both combined the qualities of topiary with the qualities of the huge happy-go-lucky stuffed animals one might find in an arcade. Yet they moved. They moved with a fluid grace. Their eyes were giant sunflowers. Their paws were made of silver mesh through which burst honeysuckle and thyme and posies. They breathed out, and dandelion tufts swirled from their metal filigree mouths, their snouts formed by a five-o'clock shadow of curled-up baby ferns.

As Dr. Lambshead ushered Jonathan into the tent, the giant rabbit leaned down and said "Welcome" in a murmuring hush, something like a smile dawning across the vegetation of its face: One hundred white starlike flowers blossomed to form the smile and then faded back into green.

"Reverse Photosynthetic Cheshire-ism," Dr. Lambshead said, or was it just in Jonathan's head? "Magic is science. The Czechs. Show-offs. Don't forget that."

Photosynthetic? Checks? Confusion took the edge off his fear.

A tiny woman resolved into focus, while all else in the tent swirled and blurred. Her dress was full of birds or made of birds, or perhaps the surface of the dress was showing some vision of another place that was overrun with all manner of colorful birds, except the birds were all flowers or made of flowers or not birds at all except they were singing, the flowers were singing all over her clothing.

The woman neither smiled nor frowned, but in the way her gaze alighted upon him he felt a hidden amusement or mirth or happiness locked away inside.

Dr. Lambshead greeted her as if they were old friends. Because she was part of the Order?

But Jonathan couldn't focus on any of it. A tiredness crept over him that turned his muscles and bones to mush, so that he felt invertebrate, no better than a thing in a jar in a natural history museum . . .

Came a Voice in a whisper: "That's enough. Already. Timing is bad, Thwack. The timing could be *much* better." And then some reference to "war order" or was it War of the Order?

Followed by his grandfather's murmur: "It's the only moment I had. But you're right. Of course, you're right."

And when Jonathan woke, as he knew he must, he lay in the chair in the study, and it was early on a real and tumultuous morning. The light was weak. The room dull, drab.

Sitting up on the couch opposite, arms around her knees, Sarah stared at him with an expression he thought meant he had betrayed her trust in some way. Yet he had no words for her, could only stare back and hope that she could intuit what he had experienced. Thought again how young she looked, wondered if she had sat on that same couch as a child, looked just as concerned, as upset. In her controlled way.

No, not that *he* had betrayed her. Sarah knew, somehow, that Dr. Lambshead had made a decision for Jonathan without her.

"You're back," she said. "From the land of sleep. But you're still falling. Don't fall too long, Jonathan. Fall for just the right amount of time. If you fall for too long, you'll never stop. And Dr. Lambshead needs you. We all need you. All of us ghosts."

And she laughed, as if this were the funniest joke she'd ever told. Which it was, because she never told jokes.

Keep falling, said the Voice in his head. *Keep* falling.

Why should I trust you?

Because you have no choice.

Because you will keep falling.

Chapter Forty-Three

NEW BODIES AND OLD BUSY BODIES

"If you find piles of dead leaves on your property, you must rake them and throw them out. Whether they move uncanny or not. Better yet, burn them. Take the ashes and toss them to the four corners of the Earth while cursing their name forever."

—Doodle in the margins of Crowley's "rules and orders" notebook, a decree never issued

Crowley had learned to smile a lot and to be in jovial good humor, even when his humors were roiling and pitch-black. He stretched a crude rictus out of necessity because how else could he preserve the facade of control with his underlings?

Yet, still, Wretch had decapitated Crowley thrice more, each time Crowley's grin growing wider whether bucketed or free-form on the floor. Crowley was becoming quite addicted to the cut, tumble, and roll of his own head. So long as it was followed by resurrection.

"Why, Wretch, what a temper you have. What a temper. You should control that temper if you mean to rule the world."

Or Wretch's master did. For Crowley was more than ever convinced that Wretch did not act on his own.

"I *am* magic, Wretch," Crowley whispered to Wretch as Wretch punched another small hole in the back of his head to drain his brain fluid and replace it with "the good stuff," as Crowley now called it. The "stuff" that meant he wouldn't fade.

That it looked like grape jelly mixed with tomato sauce and balsamic vinegar and smelled like the vapors from a sulfur lake full of bloat bodies until it gurgled inside his brainpan was beside the point.

"Shush, Crowley," Wretch would say, like a man interrupted while concentrating on reading the paper on the loo.

Wretch would take the aspect of a giant mosquito for the bloodfest, which Crowley thought rude, given Wretch knew his Lord Emperor was mosquitophobic. Especially the loathsome look of their mouth-parts.

But, still, Crowley wouldn't shush or hush as the giant mosquito drilled into him.

"I'm magic. I'm so much magic it cannot be contained. It shines from my eyes and my ears and my mouth. Why, it would shine from my arse and armpits, if my arse and armpits were still my own."

"I've contained you just fine, in a container known as your skull-head," Wretch said. "Now shut up."

True, Wretch liked to keep him wondering in a bucket for a time after decapitation, as if to allow Crowley to reflect upon his faults. Like how he missed being able to scratch his ba . . . earlobes.

"Deep down, you love your lord Crowley," Crowley said. "You must. Or you wouldn't keep bringing me back after my insolence at addressing my servant so. You must need me."

"Perhaps even with my infinite patience, I will tire of dealing with you, Crowley," Wretch warned.

"Did you know, by the way, that a woodpecker's tongue loops all around its brain? Napoleon taught me that. You remember Napoleon? The head on a stick you let escape."

Wretch just grunted in reply, concentrating on pumping "good stuff" back into Crowley's brain.

❦

Mornings with the war report here inside the giant elephant had been awkward at first for Crowley. Was Wretch emperor now? Was Crowley still the One? And what about this rot-shuffling ex-emperor Charlemagne employed as a general?

Which is perhaps why even Wretch had seen the wisdom of constructing a bigger throne in the elephant's war room, upon which Crowley could now rest his foreign body, with Charlemagne (aka Dead Leaves) to one side, Wretch on the other. Speck under glass on a dais beside him.

Surely that was clear? Who was in charge? The one in the middle. Although given the cramped space, it was more like an office chair on wheels with a high back, so he could also use it with his desk and he did wish the water closet wasn't so close. Claustrophobia, an itch to get outside, was unbearable at times. And yet all that lay outside was more 'orrible forest.

Old Charlemagne, Charlie Mange, raised from the dead, Dead Leaves walking, Crowley had gotten used to. In front of the others, Wretch behaved as before: genuflecting familiar. It was only alone that Crowley need worry. Chums. That was it—he felt Wretch and Charlie Mange were becoming chums on the sly, and it made him jealous, perversely enough.

Especially worrisome: the "secret language" Wretch and Charlie Mange used, the old, old tongue that Crowley couldn't understand at all, and which gave Mange a fluency and richness of expression that was disconcerting next to the tetchy blurtings of Olde Germanic Crowley could glean when the frump addressed his Emperor.

For, usually, Charlie Mange grunted in reply to anything other than Wretch's direct questions, ancient wrong-wright that he was, not even a recent blood-and-guts job, like the ones Crowley made. Clearly inferior from ages spent seeping into a bog or fen. Crowley could never remember the difference, or the distance.

And contrary to myth, you couldn't instantly "magic" yourself into knowing languages, no matter how "magic" you were. So he was left, once more, in the dark.

"Old bucket punch," Crowley said, slapping Charlie Mange on the shoulder that morning, only seventy miles from Prague. A little disconcerted that Mange-Lad was so tall. "Old tickety-tockety . . . thing . . . raised from a lake for so little reason. How aren't you this morning?"

"Thou hast touch-ed my shoulder. Again-eth. Lord Crowley."

"Indeedeth I haveth, Lord Charlie Mange."

"My nameth is Charlemagne."

"Indeed-eth it be-eth, Charlie Mange."

"Enough," muttered Wretch. "Enough."

The glower of Mange's red, infernal eyes. Perhaps Crowley was finally getting under the Mange's icky skin.

He liked to slap Charlie Mange on the shoulder because it tended to knock a bathtub's worth of rotting leaves off old Charlie and temporarily change his clumsy anti-sashay to something even less coordinated. Put an exclamation point on how Wretch could raise the dead, but not restore them to much more than a creepoholic moth-mess wreck. Not to mention that Crowley liked to remind himself that he had a body himself, and wasn't just a head.

The tingle in his fingers registering in his brain was a bloody big relief. Even if it always now brought to mind the traitor Napoleon. If only Crowley had given the cultured oaf a body, perhaps he wouldn't have fled. Perhaps they could've both plotted against Wretch.

Sour taste of might've-beens.

Also, though, the shoulder push gave Crowley some idea of how fast his spells of degeneration were acting upon the Mange. Answer thus far: not fast enough. But he daren't make them stronger for fear of Wretch detecting his treachery.

"And you, my dear Wretch—you've yet to give me a report on Ruth Less."

All he'd heard so far was that the monster assassin had come back with a garbled story about death piggies and death muffins or some such nonsense—and people who smelled bad (big surprise, that) and comet men.

"Because it's none of your business. My lord."

"Pray tell, humor me a while anyway."

Humorless git. Who had in this moment undertaken to appear like a human made of jiggling black rice pudding, the rice bits instead too many Wretch-ed eyes and the head itself bereft of any eyes at all! Making it unclear exactly where to look. Given Wretch had not provided himself a mouth. Was it in the back? Perhaps instead of his arse? Where also resided tiny, diaphanous wings.

Crowley really didn't want to know.

Wretch sighed. "Ruth Less is already back from tracking Jonathan Lambshead, and is now deployed to Prague to seek out the Golden Sphere."

Yet another sacrifice, Crowley believed, to the Cult of the Search for the Golden Sphere. Some days he thought the Golden Sphere existed only in his head and Wretch's head, a bond as thick as blood or even the "good stuff."

"So Lambshead is dead? Excellent!" That, at least, would be real progress.

"No, not yet," Wretch snapped, irritated. Again, from whence came the words . . . who knew?

"Oh. *Not* dead. Yet. Captured and tortured, then, I imagine?"

"Noo."

"Horribly mutilated by Ruth Less's attack?"

"Um, noo."

"Inconvenienced, at least? Paper cut? Tripped on a banana peel and fell on face?"

"Shut up."

"Stole his nose? Called him a wanker from afar?"

"Shut up shut up shut up."

Wretch composed himself, which meant some of his black-rice-pudding aspect fell away into a smoother texture. The smell of maggots faded, too.

"I mean, if it pleases my lord, we now know where the young Lambshead is and he will be our captive soon. He is within our grasp!"

"I've heard that before about various things," as Crowley gestured to the demi-mage he had christened No-Name to step forward.

The other demi-mages jammed in there were looking anywhere but at his royal personage.

Oh, how they hated it when the parents argued!

No-Name, thus dubbed because should he perish the name could easily be applied to the next punter, had the report from the scouts sent to sneak ahead under cover of darkness. There was much the All-Seeing Puddle could not discern, after all.

Or at all, some days.

"Everywhere they fall back, my lieges, my liege, my emperor, my emperors," No-Name said, with Charlie Mange breathing down his neck.

No-Name was a strapping young demi-mage, full of vim and vigor. The sight of him strutting about so peacock-ish even though dead-alive filled Crowley with suppressed bile. To be so loutishly limber in his body in front of one who was a head attached to another body seemed like a not-so-subtle kind of insubordination.

"You hear that, Charlie? Nothing for you to do yet. Just stand there and look pretty."

Slapping him on the shoulder again. Watch the fall leaves fall off, destroying his shoulder once again. Why, the throne room would soon resemble a forest floor in the autumn. Messy and filthy with mushrooms.

"Everywhere the enemy appears in disarray, my Emperor." Did Crowley imagine No-Name had actually clicked his heels, something even Crowley's original body could not do? "And we have taken many bridges without conflict. Where we do meet the enemy, they are small in number and—"

"And signs of the Republic?" Crowley asked, butting in because he feared Wretch would speak first and wrest the spotlight from him.

"Not many, my Emperor. A few bivouacs abandoned in favor of sanctuary behind the Prague wall. Signs of logistical support, their usual military advisers, but it would not appear they are trying to sneak an army into Prague ahead of our advance."

That supported what little the All-Seeing Puddle had told them. It also supported what Wretch had found on his all-night flybys. Of late, Wretch had applied some infernal camouflage, so that to all he flew over, he appeared only like a dark cloud, an inky bit of sky.

A raspy, torn-at nothing.

A steaming pile of crap in the sky that Crowley would love nothing better than to see plummet to the ground and smashed into a million little frayed pieces.

But: "Beautiful!" Crowley said to No-Name. "The Hierarchs of Tophet have nothing on us."

"Cannibalism is just God preying on man," Wretch said in jaunty reply, as if the latter half of a call-and-response Crowley had not known he was part of.

"Pray tell, wise Wretch, my familiar, overly familiar, and loyal servant who commands me in defiance of the natural order . . . what does that mean?" Crowley asked.

"Learn to be happy. Learn to be happy no matter what, my lord," Wretch said through clenched fangs.

Crowley nodded as if in agreement, let it go.

He could not tell if the simmering rage boiling within him that he suppressed only by biting his tongue until it bled obscured the meaning.

So, instead, Crowley closed his eyes a brief moment, no matter how odd that might look to those gathered, and reached out to his precious, beautiful salamanders, cooling his wrath in their floating circumlocutions of the war elephant. Round the loop once, twice, thrice. He'd found linking his mind to theirs was very soothing, and Wretch had yet to detect the link. Perhaps because, in the end, it was harmless, not nefarious.

Nor did Wretch have enough respect for Crowley's friendship with the Speck, which might still bear fruit. Although the Speck remained very, very rude.

"Almost time to check in with Paris, my lord," Wretch said, unable to look Crowley in the eye whenever he said "my lord." As if he'd just found a bit of poo lurking underneath his shoe . . . if only he would wear shoes.

Both Crowley and Wretch had learned to leave out that which was unsettling or unsettled. At least they agreed upon that. Not good for demi-mage morale. Which meant no reports from Verne, for Crowley found it un-uplifting, positively plummetous, that Laudinum X (surely not Verne!) had found a way to make the wall and its environs invisible to the All-Seeing Puddle-Eye. Or, perhaps, the magical wall itself had done that. Regardless, insubordination seemed imminent, should they survive Bill the Eel.

Paris was different, and he still experienced problems with the All-Seeing Puddle. It was a bit like trying to see through dirty water in a drain after a storm.

He could make out Miss Eiffel Tower and Comte de Lautréamont, but he couldn't really see what they were doing or the expressions on their faces, and on the whole the entire enterprise was more like listening to the radio than anything else.

Frustrating. He would have liked to better see the rabid chipmunks that inhabited the human-sized Eiffel Tower. A genius stroke on his part, to animate the otherwise clunky ET. Harness the energy of the chipmunk in general, the frenetic motion. But even better, these were undead rabid chipmunks, to put the fire of urgency in Miss ET's . . . belly? Well, not belly, but the metaphorical equivalent. Viewing platform? Middle landing?

Latrine, as Crowley had taken to calling Lautréamont, stood impassive at ET's side. He was good at being impassive. Looked a bit in his dark clothes like a blackened coatrack that had suffered some kind of fire disaster.

Latrine was the author of the scandalous classic *Maldoror*, or as Crowley called it now, "Mal-odor," given the author's nickname. The book had spoken to Crowley when he'd encountered it as a youth—its bizarre and violent visions a soothing balm. In homage, he'd made Latrine wear shoes that were actually creatures with sharp fangs that could devour his feet. Some of the less trustworthy demi-mages had been forced to wear them, too. That they might become rather stumpy should they betray him. There were at least a few things Wretch still gave him the latitude to order on his own.

"The garbage has stop'd," Miss ET reported. "We have stop'd the garbage. It is no longer being generated in such vast quantities."

Crowley'd given her the female equivalent of his own voice, which was less useful and more disconcerting than he'd imagined.

"Our mecha-crocodiles are beginning to make headway in cleaning up the streets."

"And what pray tell did you do to accomplish this feat?"

ET stopped short. Even through the murk in his All-Seeing Puddle bowl, he could sense the hesitation.

"Nothing, my lord," ET finally said. "Nothing at all. It must be that the glorious policies you put in place before have finally borne fruit."

"Yes, must be," Crowley said, preoccupied, putting his feet up on the desk and making the All-Seeing Puddle jounce a tad. "Yet, just in case," he added, "I suggest you devote your time to breaking up the largest piles that remain."

"Yes, my lord," ET said.

"How do you like your shoes, Latrine?"

A pause, then in a silky voice, "I love them, Lord Crowley. I love them as much as I care for my own immortal soul. Most unique. It is energizing to stare down and have your shoes stare back up at you. I wake each morning thankful for this . . . honor."

"Anything else? Anything at all I should know about?"

ET hesitated, then said, "No, my lord. All is well."

"Not . . . chaotic?"

"Busy is perhaps the word, my lord," ET said.

Was it, though? Something about this lull worried at Crowley, and what worried at Crowley just as much was that Wretch seemed unworried.

Much more than his little problem with Wretch grated on him. So much more.

For example: when Wretch tossed Crowley's head in a cupboard in the war elephant's kitchen and went off for a time, only to let Crowley out as if there had been no moment when Wretch had needed his Lord Emperor to be in the dark.

Yet, there had been that one instance Wretch was agitated and stashed him in a closet instead, and Crowley had peered through a crack of light during that dire cupboard time.

What had Crowley seen?

Just Wretch talking in strangled-cat writhings and high-pitched shrieks . . . to a seemingly unlimited number of other Wretches, glimpsed through a hovering hole torn in the air. They seemed to be communicating across a vast distance, the other Wretches in their cling-limbed geckolike closeness hugging one another. At first they sounded like owls slaughtering field mice. Then, as they became less coherent and farther away, the hole smaller, they sounded more like field mice slaughtering crickets.

Until: no hole and no Wretches.

Huzzah! The aftermath in which Wretch curled up and wept hot bitter tears cheered Crowley no end.

Huzzah! Wretch was no mastermind. Wretch was intermediary. Wretch, too, was being acted upon, and, perhaps, in his actions upon Crowley's person, acting out.

Not to mention acting a part.

When the demi-mages had left. When Charlie Mange had shuffled out to be sequestered once more during their travel in a moldy trough next to the blessed circle of salamanders. When there was no one in the throne room but Crowley and Wretch.

That's when Crowley let loose with the torrent of choice curse words.

Those he'd heard sailors use and those he'd heard used applied to him by alchemists as he crushed them and stole their research.

A kind of magic spell, in that it altered the mind of the soul against which they were directed. But also, underneath it, what John Dee had taught him: how to hide a spell. How to hide a binding spell in a torrent. How every third or fourth or fifth word counted. How it took longer to work than a normal spell, but, still, in time, it might do the trick.

In this case, all he dared was wild magic, nothing targeted. Just enough to unbalance Wretch, to make him more hesitant, more doubting of himself. Building on what he'd glimpsed from the cupboard.

"That's who you are, Wretch," Crowley said. "You're just a shitty bag of bones that lonely goes off in the night to eat lice and fleas off the carcasses of dead animals. You're just the thing people fear when the Great Terrors aren't on offer."

Wretch became huge and shadowy like smoke and dragons, reached out with his suddenly elongated, sharp curved tail, and decapitated Crowley again.

Napoleon's voice, from everywhere and nowhere: "*We are both in the same boat and it has sprung a leak.*" A standard hallucination. He would be haunted by the old general until he died for good and all, he knew.

The topple-tumble.

The fall.

The cold-floor bruise.

The roll and glide.

Chapter Forty-Four
A SOFT LANDING IN A HARD PLACE

Still falling, as if falling forever was how some creatures lived, and Jonathan tried to think of vultures and eagles and ospreys high in the sky and creatures low and deep in long trenches that might find the descent normal, even a kind of state of grace.

Came a long gasp that was his own, as if dead and resurrected on some surgery table.

All around, and yet Jonathan could hear sounds again, as if he'd passed through some invisible veil.

Until their last breath he, in terror, believed they would be falling, his left arm flailing against Mamoud's shoulder, and on his right, gripping his cane, Rack was a projectile in the darkness whose free hand reached out to him but he could not take it, for he was still moving his arms as if he could at some point stabilize, come out of the plummet like a bird regaining wings, and glide.

Which would not happen.

Were they all screaming? Were they shrieking? Or was it dead silent from the shock? He could never remember later.

But the impact never came, at least not as his body had thought it would. No, instead, clouds broke through the darkness: thick white-and-gray clouds, dim in the gloom, and a burst of cold fresh air. Huge, thick clouds smacking into Jonathan's face, bringing even in that extremity, a cry of protest from Rack. Clouds smacking them all over. Clouds made of feathers and of cotton. Textured clouds, all of them pillow-shaped and-sized for some reason, and their violent descent smashing feathers loose so that Jonathan's mind flashed to pigeons. They were falling so far, to some underground world, that they had smashed through a flock of cave pigeons.

The density increased, and now they were smacking into and slipping through a porous wall of, yes, giant pillows, not clouds at all, some of them too much like sandbags for comfort, bruising Jonathan, but also slowing their descent, Rack and Mamoud jostling next to him, smothering in the pillows, and he was laughing even as he still thought that he was going to die, except in such a bizarre way that no one who survived would be believed when they told the tale.

Rack was chortling like a freak as if in on the joke. As if this were a prank R & D had concocted back at Poxforth.

Yes, pillows, and now their fall not just slowed but halted, so in a time lapse or slow motion they tumbled halfway down the mountain of downy, feathery soft rectangles, losing their footing, stumbling as badly as if amid some kind of elegant quicksand, aided yet blinded by the return of light in a subdued, rueful way from off to the side.

Rack, still giggling, was rolling down toward the base, and with a great cry, Jonathan followed suit, catching a glimpse of Mamoud above him on the pillow mountainside grimly trudging through the mess, unwilling to take any unsafe easy route.

And mess it truly was. Perhaps the pillows had saved them, but the smell of mildew and mold formed a patchwork—fresh air, then the subtle stink as of water damage, then fresh air again. They were well free of not just the trapdoor but also this mound.

At the base of the pillow mountain, Jonathan came to rest next to Rack, both still laughing hysterically. Rack was engaged in pulling his artificial leg back into position.

"Is this heaven?" Rack asked. "Is heaven full of rotting pillows?"

"We were going down the whole time, so this is the Other Place."

"Hell is full of rotting pillows?"

"Purgatory?"

Mamoud appeared above them, upside down from Jonathan's vantage, the perspective skewed so Mamoud's trouser legs were impossibly long and his head a tiny circle atop a foreshortened torso, as he continued to carefully pick his way down, stumbling and at times getting a foot trapped in the feather mire.

"Mamoud!" Rack greeted him as he drew level, staring at them with a curious clinical look on his face. "We've survived hell pigs, a monster, and now death by defenestration. We're invincible!"

"Lucky," Mamoud said, and started to look around for their packs. "We're lucky." But he smiled and clapped them both on the back, as if they were old comrades.

And perhaps by now they were.

The crack of light had become brighter, the vast pillow mountain revealed as existing within a cool cavern of black stone with a rock floor singularly free of dust or dirt. The cavern looked hewn out of the mountain, and from beyond the gigantic inverted triangle of a door Jonathan heard the pleasant sound of a waterfall. The smell in the air wasn't the must and dire cold of a cavern, but instead the fragrant smell of wildflowers.

He could also see, above the ridiculous mountain of pillows, another, advance guard of pillows, in phalanxes of a larger, longer variety. No wonder he'd mistaken them in his confusion for clouds. They had been affixed to planks of wood with hinges in rows up and down the sides of the vast cavern.

"Get up—someone's here," Mamoud said.

Jonathan and Rack struggled to their knees, helped each other up. The silhouette of a familiar woman stood there, framed by the door.

"Sister-blister?" Rack managed.

"Rack! Jonathan!"

"Sister-blister!"

"Danny!"

Danny, looking none the worse for the wear.

A great upsurging of emotion in Jonathan's heart and, surprise, his vision blurred from tears. Danny. Not just alive, but safe and sound!

She ran forward and, arms spread wide, almost bowled Jonathan and Rack and Mamoud over with a group rugby hug, accompanied by a pure, joyous babble.

"It was so stupid. I just planned to go for a wee beyond the campfire and good luck I decided to take the bear gun with me, because I saw the thing in the distance, and decided I might as well take a shot at it, but then somehow it got between me and the campfire so I was going to have to shoot at it to try to get back, but mostly I was afraid the bears might turn on me or the camp, so I was running while I decided what to do. But at least trying to lead the monster away from the camp. But I fell down an icy path and into a ravine, and it was climbing back up; I became hopelessly lost—although Tee-Tee called it hopefully lost, because he said we should be upbeat, and that's when I had no choice—the monster reared up in front of me and I blasted it with both barrels of bears."

"Did the bear gun work?" Jonathan asked.

"Not really. Turns out the monster loves bears. As snacks. Or something. It was all very confusing and tense. The bears looked frightened of her, and while she was eating two of them whole, I took off running again, yeah?"

"Tee-Tee can talk?" Rack said, making it sound like an accusation, but half-hearted.

"Oh, please," Danny said.

"You're right, sister-blister. Who bloody well cares! We're safe, that's what matters."

"But . . . how did you wind up here?" Jonathan asked.

"Yes, and *where* is here?" Mamoud asked. He had drawn his odd gun as if he did not quite believe they were safe after all that falling.

"Oh, that!" Danny said, as if it were nothing. "I think my friend can answer those questions for you. One of my new friends, that is."

A giant figure had stepped out of the glare of the doorway.

It stood upright, like a person. It was the largest marmot Jonathan had ever seen—nine feet tall at least—with bright dark eyes, huge teeth, and a fine plush russet coat with an explosion of gray-and-white down the middle of its body. The hindquarters, the feet, were powerful and claw-laden. Jonathan had never really thought of marmots as fierce . . . but now he did.

A long stream of whistles and clicks, clicks and whistles came from the marmot, before it switched to English, an embarrassed look on its face.

"Welcome to the Institute," the marmot said in a deep, gravelly voice. "You can call me Crikey McBitey."

Chapter Forty-Five

FABLED MOUSE SALAMANDER, NOW WITH RIVER SHANTY

Seeking what It sought, the Golden Sphere traversed the thick, hollow ancient wall that surrounded Prague. Through the centuries, the wall had become riddled through with cracks and tunnels underneath. People lived in the wall and never left it, and some of them never saw the light of day. There also were people who—in the soft parts of the clay and stone, those sections trapped in a sense between the great Bavarian forest and the sludgy Czech river—had the crackpot idea to dig with enough purpose to impose their own secret history on the city, to both fortify and undermine the wall. Magicians from long ago.

Dank in this particular tunnel the Golden Sphere must needs enter. Dank like dank meat. Dank like stank mold. Dank dank dank and, yes, the dreaded trifecta of dank-stank-rank. With dim gray mushroom lights dispensing as many dank spores as watts of illumination. Those the sphere had snuffed out as it passed by, on principle. Fungus could gum up its works, give it hallucinations, and considering what the Golden Sphere had seen, acceleration of mutant imagery was unnecessary.

Truly of all the Europes the Golden Sphere could have been trapped in, this was the most unsanitary. The Republic could not take over soon enough and impose its science upon the unwashed messling masses.

Finally, though, the Golden Sphere came across the man, or lad, It sought.

For the man-lad in question had emerged dripping wet from a culvert, near where the Golden Sphere lay in wait, hovering dim amid shadows. Holding a squirming fish in one webbed hand. The man-lad's name was Franz Kafka.

Slight, glowing pale green with thick eyebrows and large, dark eyes, clad in a sodden cheap black suit, Kafka looked like a skinny, tailless salamander. Nictating eyelids. The better to see in the gloom.

He had gills that heaved silent against the air now that he was breathing through his nose. The Golden Sphere knew Kafka had been gifted the gills by a magician to save his life from a consumptive disease as a child.

Kafka did not see the Golden Sphere, but immediately leapt up, ate the head off the writhing fish, tossed the rest to the floor, and began writing on the wall with what looked like the tail of a large silver scorpion, which he had taken from his pocket. The "tail" had been specially formed to fit his webbed hands. The Golden Sphere noted that the writer's feet were shoeless and webbed as well.

For his sins, no words appeared there in the murk, except as etchings, for the scorpion tail was more like a knife than a pen. The quick, then slow strike of the point gave off sparks, hinted at a passion not present in the demeanor of the man-lad himself.

Yet he was intent and industrious, as if he were writing a tale for himself, or as if it were writing him. A little black bowler hat sat upon a rock beside him, and there, too, stood a lantern, the glass of which was caked with a green luminous moss that provided light.

This was the man's masterwork on this version of Earth, the Golden Sphere knew. The Secret Engineer, the Tunnel Dweller, the Green-Glass Salamander, as some of his friends called him, who, even at this youthful age, stitched his almost-invisible words into the fabric of the city's wall that formed a protective spell, tales more a part of Prague now than any words put on an ephemeral page.

The Golden Sphere allowed its golden light to creep across Kafka's creation like an eclipse, snuffing out the moss glow.

Franz Kafka turned in surprise and wonder, but with no fear in his eyes, which the Golden Sphere found vaguely disappointing. Even the giant lizards had expressed fear, back in Rome—and he had taken the most dazzling form, the gold afire and making manifest the alchemical symbols that covered the wall's entire surface like mathematical tattoos.

Granted, the Golden Sphere did not intend to turn Prague into a wasteland as It had Rome. For one thing, no matter his intended amendment to the wall, several of the spells within it predated the Golden Sphere's existence and might snuff It out without a more delicate touch.

"'Allo, guv'nor," the Golden Sphere said, guffawing. "Well met in the mold, my friend with mutual interests!"

Kafka stared so blankly at the Golden Sphere that It reflected that perhaps its intel was wrong or this was the wrong tack, but then something clicked behind Kafka's eyes.

"You are an arcane machine?" he stated/asked.

"I am more properly a celestial arcade game, not arcane at all. Well, perhaps a bit. Or a byte. There's so much confusion between magic and science these days. Entire lifetimes spent in argument over that. Go ask the Republic—they've worked out the distinction. Like a nation of freaks and geeks. No, think of me more as a kind of Celestial Beast—no need to take a knee, not that you seem to have the good sense God gave a giant lizard—but, yes, for your purposes, you might as well call me a god, I suppose. A caged god. A god with—"

"Can you be killed?" Kafka asked, cutting the Golden Sphere off in midstream.

"Wait. What." The Golden Sphere microscoped back to a burning point of light, then telescoped out again to a scorching ball of midnight sun.

The nerve of this nelfling of baldorama, this naive naif, this all-powerful wizard of the Prague wall!

"Can you be killed?"

"Well, aren't you blunt, sonny boy. And not particularly agreeable. You don't even know why I'm here."

Kafka made a sibilant hissing sound with his gills and the Golden Sphere hovered backward a tad.

"A favor—why else would you be here? So, anyway: You can be killed."

"Why do you want to kill me?"

"Yes."

"Note the lack of comma, gill-lad! I meant what's with this unhealthy obsession with my death, right off the bat." The Golden Sphere was tempted to take a bat to Kafka right then and there. Or turn him into a bat. But, then, he was already practically a salamander.

Kafka gave a blank stare, as if a thousand miles away. "I'd like to get back to my writing on the walls. And the fastest way would be to kill you. No matter what you want. This usually works best. Otherwise, I have to listen to all the usual things, and I get quite bored when instead I could be in an ecstatic state, working on the wall." He said this as if it were the most normal, reasonable thing anyone had ever said.

"You're killing me, sonny, right now."

"But you said—"

"Oh. My God."

Kafka resumed his onslaught: "So . . . are there any words I could say that would kill you or even just hurt you badly?"

"*Again*, you can't kill me," the Golden Sphere said. Although, to be Frank, which It was on occasion, the conversation had become a bit unsettling and It had become unsure.

"And if I say no?"

"I will murder you and grind up your bones into pencil lead, and then I will write your story using you. I will take a salamander-sized egg slicer and put you in it."

"Oh."

"Luckily I'm a fan. Of you and Prague. Or really, more a fan of you."

"You look like a golden marble, not like a fan."

"Har har har."

Undeterred, Kafka asked, "Could I kill you with an ax?"

"No."

"Could I kill you with a hammer?"

"Nope."

"Could I kill you with a cannon?"

"*Nyet.*"

"Could I kill you with a crossbow?"

"*Nej.*"

"Could I kill you with a bag over your . . . head?"

"*Nee.*"

"Could I kill you with a magic spell?"

"*Nanni.*"

"Could I kill you with several days of starvation?"

"*Nein.*"

"Could I kill you with a drought?"

"*Nahin.*"

"Could I kill you with water?"

"*Nem.*"

"Could I kill you with a conjured monster?"

"*Nāo.*"

"Could I kill you with a well-aimed blow to your most vulnerable . . . part?"

"*Yuk.*"

"Could I kill you with a disease?"

"*Tidak!*"

"Could I kill you with a stick?"

"Could you kill me with a stick?" the Golden Sphere repeated, almost not comprehending the words. "God no! *Kadhu, neni, nage, rara, cha, oya, thay! THAY!* Which means 'no' in Khmer, ignoramous. Now just excuse me a moment."

Little winged Crowley heads had popped into existence just down the corridor and now flew at the Golden Sphere. Howling Crowleys with that horrid sallow face, the little pinhole black eyes, letting in no light. As if Crowley's eyes were just holes poked in the cosmos, to let in the bleakness of dead space. A good ten of them. The latest thing Wretch was throwing at It, instead of rabid chipmunks.

The Golden Sphere turned into a huge golden mirror ball and pierced the flying heads with needles of light through both eyes.

One by one they dropped to the clammy floor, spasmed, were still. In another moment, they had evaporated into a viscous steam, which the Golden Sphere was careful to shield Kafka from. Another new thing: an attempt to poison in the zeal to locate. What madness. Not playing fair. Not playing at all.

But the enemy didn't know games the way the Golden Sphere knew games.

Or how sending such things might allow It to return the favor.

❧

In the aftermath, Kafka still stood there, unmoved, arms crossed, a webbed finger at his pursed lips.

"Could I kill you with ugly winged faces larger than those? Enough of them?"

"You might yet kill me just with your questions, kiddo."

"Truly?" A kind of wild light went on in Kafka's eyes.

"NO! YOU CANNOT KILL ME. But I could kill you. I could kill you fifty ways to Friday and be left with a thousand more. For you are at heart a mortal man, a mere messling, the kind of flesh-and-blood that has ALMOST NO DEFENSE against a Celestial Beast."

Kafka considered that, said, "Well, then, why are you here?"

The Golden Sphere allowed some heat to trail off the sides of its body in a way It hoped would be worth some empathy or sympathy.

"I'm hunted, you see. 'They seek him here, they seek him there, they seek him everywhere.' We're so similar, Kafka. Misunderstood. Arrayed against the world. Taken to writing on walls or bodies. I'm here as a friend, really I am.

"There's someone coming to Prague, Kafka, and I'm here for your help. A very bad man is coming. A bad, no-good egg. A crapulous goat.

A nefarious panda bandit. Basically, he'd be bad as anything. Stick of gum. Stapler. Laundry line. Piece of li—"

"If I cannot kill you, why should you need my help? You are invincible and all should bow down before you."

"All I need is a little . . . adjustment. Lets a little light in. It will take no time at all. But buy me all the time in the world. Believe me, I'm saddened and enraged by the necessity, reduced to this by that little popped-up magician, the wizard dreadkin bobkin stabkin—"

"What is this . . . adjustment?"

The Château Peppermint Blonkers.

Although it would not appear as a name to Kafka. Not in a language he could read. Only in a language so old even the Golden Sphere could not understand all of it. The language of the Builders.

The Golden Sphere's . . . sphere . . . lit up with calligraphy across its middle portion, like a golden belt across one of them thar burghers.

"I want you to write these words on your wall."

"Which wall?"

"Which wall—this wall! This wall we're entombed within, of course!" Oh, how the Golden Sphere wished he could just roast Kafka's bones and be done with him!

Kafka considered the calligraphy for a moment, his greenish face lit by the glow.

"I will help you. As I have no wish to die. And I cannot kill you."

The Golden Sphere sighed in relief.

Kafka turned to the wall, and started to make the adjustment. "Although this will take time to manifest. The words some time to come to life."

"This I know," the Golden Sphere said. What it also knew that Kafka didn't was that once Kafka wrote it, he could not unwrite it or erase it or circumvent it. Nor would he be able to speak of what he'd done.

Kafka would find out soon enough, but by then it would be too late.

"I really wish I could kill you," Kafka said. "That would be simpler."

"So I've heard. Do you like sea shanties, Kafka?" the Golden Sphere asked. To mercifully change the subject. Finally. Forever. The Golden Sphere hoped.

"No, but I like river shanties."

The Golden Sphere had never heard of a river shanty before.

"How does it go, Kafka?"

"It doesn't go anywhere."

"Good grief, Kafka! What're the first lines!"

"'I'm a little river shanty short and stout / Here is my drift and here is my spout. / Quick!, get all the beautiful mud out / And row the nasty boat all about.'"

The Golden Sphere was rather sorry It had asked.

"Dreadful. Just . . . beyond dreadful."

It waited until Kafka had drawn every last flourish of the summoning. Which could not now be undone, except by the château itself.

Now the Golden Sphere just had to wait. And dodge undead flying Crowley heads.

But not languishing down in the tunnels with boring old salamander Kafka. No, sirree. The Golden Sphere had to walk the streets, find out what people knew, as no common tourist. Give notice to those who might worship a Celestial Beast, if only given some half-secret signal. There were usually a few such freaks in every city, and for better or worse, many of them had plentiful resources.

In short, the Golden Sphere had a book-club meeting to promote and attend.

Chapter Forty-Six
JAUNTY AND DISTURBING MEADOW TALK

The Alpine Meadows Research Institute turned out to be a hidden valley ringed by forbidding, cruel peaks . . . and populated entirely by giant, intelligent marmots in a variety of fur colors from beige to gray, from white to, yes, russet, and many other shades beside. The centerpiece of the valley was the magnificent meadow of wildflowers and weeds that lay right outside the cavern door, under a benevolent sun. The flowers were gigantic, the grasses over Jonathan's head at times, so that as they descended from the mouth of the cavern he only caught glimpses of the meadow and the Victorian building rising from its far end.

Crikey McBitey . . .

"Is that your real name?" Jonathan asked. It was easier to concentrate on believing in one huge marmot than to look out across a landscape with dozens of them grazing enormous wild grasses.

"No, it isn't my real name," Crikey said, staring down his snout at Jonathan. "But I don't wish to tell you my real name."

"Fair enough," Jonathan said. He realized he didn't know a thing about marmot etiquette, didn't even know if giant talking marmot etiquette would resemble that of small nontalking marmots. Or what other subjects might be off-limits.

"It's for your own safety, Jonathan," Crikey McBitey said. "The less you know, you know, even though, erm, there is so much you need to know . . ."

Mamoud and Rack didn't seem yet able or ready to ask anything. Indeed, they kept staring at the marmot as if they expected it to pull down a zipper and stand revealed as an extremely tall man in a marmot costume. Rack at least had the distraction of his sister, whom he could not stop hugging and they were both in general carrying on as if they'd never had a dustup.

Although Jonathan couldn't help but notice what Rack had not: Tee-Tee perched on Danny's shoulder kept whispering in the ear farthest from Rack, and glaring at Rack as he did so.

"Your friend seems uncomfortable," Crikey said, nodding at Rack.

It was true Rack seemed unable to stop staring at Crikey, perhaps because he thought the marmot might live up to his invented surname.

"So rude, Rack! They saved your life, yeah?" Danny pulled on his arm as if doing so would somehow wrench him back into some polite orbit.

"Well, I must admit," Crikey McBitey said, a wild gleam in his eyes, "we were concerned about rescuing Tee-Tee most of all, but . . ."

"I'm sorry," Rack said. "I don't mean any disrespect. Where I come from, we are not much used to talking animals. You could say we're not used to it at all. Because we don't have any."

"What? Don't have any? What about parrots?" Danny hissed. "And you're saying this *right in front* of Tee-Tee!"

"Would you rather I said it to his be-hind?"

"Yet you, sir, are a talking animal," Crikey said in a jovial tone.

Rack's scowl deepened, as if Crikey had insulted him. "I have always been told marmots spread disease."

"We only spread the word of the Lord," Crikey said. "Have you heard the good word?"

Rack looked shocked, perhaps even flabbergasted, but definitely silent.

The wheezing whistle that followed almost certainly was a kind of marmotal laughter.

"He's joking," Jonathan said. "It's marmot humor."

"Yes, we are nippers," Crikey admitted. "Little nippers and great big nippers." More whistling wheezy laughter.

"Sounds a lot like human humor," Rack remarked, clearly miffed at being made fun of. "And not of very high quality."

"And yet we are so very, very high," Crikey murmured.

Jonathan assumed he meant the elevation.

"You surely are in a bad humor, Rack!" Danny again, punching him on the shoulder, which was sure to improve it.

"I'm missing a foot. And I have a few spares. Do you expect me to be dancing with joy?"

"You didn't really think ahead, did you?" Danny asked.

"You didn't bring any extra feet, sister-blister. Nor from the smell of you any extra socks."

"I smell like I'm supposed to smell, yeah?" Danny protested. "I smell like we've been on an adventure. What do you smell like? Old farts."

"Well, there wasn't room in the pack for more feet. Or time. Before the ungallant gallivant," Rack said.

"Don't you humans spread disease rather handily?" Crikey asked, returning to Rack's argument, and then added, "And that reminds me— stay on the walkway. We wouldn't want you crushing any wildflowers. Or contaminating anything."

The wildflowers were so huge that Jonathan was more worried about one falling off and knocking him over than about any harm he could inflict, even if he were to hug one.

"You're human," Rack muttered. "You're more than curmudgeonly enough to qualify as human."

"And yet we have so much better hearing than mere humans," Crikey said.

"We'll be careful," Jonathan said to Crikey, ignoring Rack. It was as if Rack had transferred his snit with Danny to Crikey, and Jonathan felt a bit embarrassed for them all, except Mamoud, who was very much keeping his own counsel.

"You're lucky, you know," Crikey said. "For some visitors we put out pillows filled with iron filings and rocks. But, then, you come highly recommended by Dr. Lambshead. As does General Mamoud. Not so much the one we've dubbed Squishy. Oh, we know Squishy."

Another wheezing whistle.

General Mamoud?

The look of surprise on Jonathan's face Crikey must have misinterpreted, for the marmot, with a wave of its furry russet arm, said, "Oh, you needn't worry. The monster that was after you won't ever get in here. Not to the meadow. No, never."

Jonathan shot Mamoud a glance, but Mamoud just looked away. What was Mamoud doing here, then, with their desperate little band? And Alice—what did it mean that Mamoud and Alice had seemed close?

There was a lot to get used to here, not just the whistling nature of Crikey's English.

Jonathan felt as if the stakes had shifted, although he could not say why.

Crikey McBitey had moved on to other topics.

"Of course, we marmots don't need pillows—I always say marmots must learn to be their own pillows. But we will have to repair the pillow ramparts—and, more important, we will have to repair the rope bridge. The one Rack destroyed. That's quite costly."

"Bloody hell," Rack said. "What are you trying to say? You want *me* to pay for the bridge? For saving our lives."

"'A marmot is its own pillow.' That's lovely," Danny said. "Beautiful, yeah."

"Put that on a pillow," Rack muttered. "Meaningless enough."

"Maintaining infrastructure *is* one of our biggest expenses," Crikey said in a chiding tone.

"But you didn't lift a hand . . . or, or, paw . . . to help. You just watched!"

"We *did* unlock the front door."

The corpse. The writing on the wall. What to take from that? The wince of a pain grown older but no less intense.

Where are you, Voice? Speak to me now, Voice. Not just in emergencies.
But there was only silence. The Voice was gone again. Hiding.
If it had ever existed in the first place.

❧

The walkway was replaced in time by a wide pebble path, raised up on wooden planks, along the side of the meadow nearest the mountain, leading to the Institute proper, a vast Victorian-looking building at the end of the meadow, on the horizon line. In England, it would've seemed normal. Here, it rose across the horizon with all the import of a giant pulsating boil or rocket ship or something else that shouldn't be there.

Along the path lay several useful signs, like NO HUNTING, NO TRAIPSE-PASSING, and EAT GRASS. The signs had been made with a delicate marmot paw and were at human height, so clearly just for visitors.

"The great bat philosopher Swedenborg helped create the better features of this place and us. Well, discovered us, rather. We date our civilization to the coming of the Comet Man, of course," Crikey said. "But Swedenborg helped us protect and disguise this place."

"But surely that was long ago," Mamoud said. "What we see before us now is your doing entirely." It wasn't clear if Mamoud meant that as a good or a bad thing.

Crikey frowned. "Do you think Swedenborg is dead? It's not true. He still resides in the Château Peppermint Blonkers." Insulted, but why, Jonathan didn't know.

"Metaphorically speaking," Mamoud said.

"Marmot-a-tologically speaking," Danny said.

"Metaphysically speaking," Crikey replied.

Château Peppermint Blonkers. With each new mention, it became less whimsical and more ominous.

Tee-Tee again whispered furious in Danny's ear.

"All right—what's the little rat going on about, then?" Rack asked.

"Oh, he doesn't want to tell you, Rack," Danny said. "Can you blame him? Anyway, back to *my* story, that's when I met Crikey—no, he's not told me his real name either—and he pulled me into this hole in the ground I hadn't seen, and we wound up here, in this amazing place."

Because it was true she'd left off telling them what had happened when Crikey appeared.

"Didn't you think to bring them to our rescue?" Rack asked, the old suspicion pinching face and voice both. Without his foot, he relied on the sword-cane, but kept up a good pace.

Danny shoved him playfully in the shoulder, almost knocking him off the path, but also holding him up with a hand on his other shoulder.

"Yeah, silly. First thing I did. But they've rules about intervention in the outside world. They like to keep this place secret, yeah? So they were waiting for the right moment to get you out without the monster noticing."

"Sounds like a good way to die," Rack said.

"Are you dead, bro-blister? Are you dead? You seem very much alive to me."

"Bro-blister isn't as funny as sister-blister."

"Funnier," Jonathan muttered.

"Our motto is 'Disturb nothing, leave no clues,'" Crikey said. "Admittedly, it sounds better in either marmot or Latin." Another of those creaky whistle laughs. "Our scheduled visitors arrive clandestinely and leave through mysterious ways. No one other than marmots are aware of our exact location. And not all marmots, either."

"Is that why you left the body at the way station?" It felt now to Jonathan like a very cold thing to do, not to bury the body. Had the man been killed by Crowley, too? The corpse had been there a while.

"*Sarah, I'm sorry.*" Those cryptic words. Nagging at Jonathan still.

"To have removed the body or tampered with it in any way would have gone against our rules and our instincts."

Which belied the question of how the man had died, who had killed him, and if the marmots had come across him after, or just watched it all unfold.

"Yet you saved us."

"Not to blunt your friend Danny's optimistic view of us marmots, but it's rather good luck you barged through the second door. We thought we'd lost you to the first—and, admittedly, the monster might have made it difficult to save you and protect the secrecy of the Institute. Although we would've. Probably. Maybe. Perhaps."

Rack scowled. "What was that *thing*? It was worse that it looked like a schoolmarm, I think. I liked it rather more as a betentacled horror show."

Liked it. Jonathan still had mixed feelings about the monster. Something in him found the thing oddly sympathetic. Whatever form it took.

"Crowley sent it," Crikey said. "Its name is Ruth Less. It's not from Aurora. It went through the first door down where the Comet Man lives, then back out again, when it couldn't get at you. Then it disappeared back down the mountain. We believe its target was you, Jonathan. But you needn't fear—we're friends of the Order. Always have been. Most of us."

"Most of us?" Rack again, but all Jonathan could think was how lucky it was any marmot's interests coincided with the human.

"What about Alice Ptarmigan?" Mamoud asked. "Do you know her? Have you seen her? She was with us until the first door at the way station."

"Gosh, I didn't even notice she wasn't here," Danny said. Such a blissfully unaware diss.

"She escaped us in the confusion—somehow," Jonathan said. He tried not to look at Mamoud. Of them all, Mamoud had known Alice the best and it felt as if he should've anticipated her leaving them. Betraying them.

Jonathan didn't know what a marmot frown looked like, but he imagined it looked a little like what Crikey was doing now, the side of his mouth curling up a little, to reveal more of his teeth.

There passed some secret look between Crikey and Mamoud as he said, "We know her from before, but we've never been quite sure what side she's on. Still, an agent of the Order."

"She took the Black . . . the Wobble . . . with her," Jonathan said.

Then regretted it when he saw Mamoud's sharp glance. He would need to be more careful in what he told Crikey. Was this long walk in part a way to question them without asking questions?

But Crikey said nothing, and Danny's cheerfulness wouldn't be broken. "Oh, we'll get it back, or figure out something else, yeah? You'll see. Everything will be splendid."

Would it, though?

"You're in very high spirits," Jonathan said, emphasis on the "high."

Danny didn't notice, or pretended not to. "It's this place, Jonathan. It's the magic of this place. Just breathe in that air. Just look around. And Crikey and his mates have been so nice . . ."

True, that their surroundings were out of something like a good fairy tale, one where it all winds up fine in the end, the villain slain and the hero rewarded. The meadow was so very pleasant, the wildflowers a medley and jamboree of bright blue, yellow, orange, pink, and lavender colors, often flanked by such tall, agreeable-looking weeds and light green eruptions of stalks that Jonathan guessed must be lilies or tulips not yet in season to bloom.

The scent was a mélange of subtle notes, spice-and-sugar fragrances mixed in with hints of tarragon, mint, and basil. No doubt herbs lurked among the wildflowers. Many of the flowers positively dwarfed the ever-present nectar deer, and although some of the bees were robust and alarming, many also seemed bewildered by the size of the blossoms. Almost as if the flora and fauna had not quite figured out the rules of large and small.

In all ways, it was an ideal magical alpine meadow, for Aurora.

Except, or perhaps because, it was also rife with giant marmots, whose figures rose like fuzzy monoliths out in the meadow. Grazing with intensity, but also with an unexpected daintiness and sense of moderation, for the intensity was in aid of precision, to some sort of plan. Clearly, as they'd have soon picked the entire meadow clean without a plan.

Which also meant to Jonathan there were secret or hidden grazing grounds, perhaps many a meadow up in the Alps, sequestered from humankind.

Every so often Jonathan spied little stone circles, and less often a dark blunt head would poke up from the middle of the circles, by which Jonathan knew that burrows lay beneath. Most all the marmots ignored their little party progressing along the path.

Crikey caught the intent of Jonathan's stare, said, "Yes, most of our kind like to live au naturel, as we always had before Comet Lake, and before the mystic Swedenborg came to live among us and tried to make us wear pants, metaphorically speaking. Yet, others, myself included, prefer a properly furnished and adorned cottage. With a burrow attached. Naturally."

"Pants," Rack echoed. "Pants."

"We believe in front pants," Crikey said. "Just not end pants."

"By which you mean you don't believe in pants, I believe."

"Typical biped," Crikey McBitey said, still cheerful.

"A splendid life," Jonathan said, glaring at Rack, and meant both things.

Rack nudged him. "What about the flowers with faces? Did you see those?"

"I was trying to ignore that, Rack."

It was true: Several of the huge wildflowers had human-ish faces, and more than one sign reminded all and sundry, DON'T EAT THE FLOWERS WITH FACES. Very civilized, and yet the flower faces still startled Jonathan. He half expected to see more of those satanic potatoes from the train to Rome leaping among the tall grasses, but was grateful that he did not. Also grateful that the flowers with faces didn't seem inclined to bend over to nip at them. The teeth were a bit fierce.

Anything further Rack meant to say about flowers was cut off as a marmot hurried up from the direction of the Institute holding a ringing rotary telephone.

"Ah, that will likely be Stimply again," Crikey said. "He's been ringing us for updates the past two days. Very insistent, and a bit of a nuisance at this point, but I imagine you'll want to talk to him."

The very serious-looking (and old) marmot, even taller than Crikey, with a stripe of silver across his head fur, handed Jonathan the rotary phone, which was so frantically ringing the receiver almost came off the base. It looked very much like the telephone back in Dr. Lambshead's mansion.

A two-foot length of broken cord curled off from it, and the phone itself had been much chewed upon. Dirt smeared the casing, and the numbers one through three appeared to have been seared or burned.

"Apologies. This telephone doesn't get much use," Crikey said.

"I'd imagine not," Rack said. "I'd imagine it gets no use at all except as a peculiar paperweight. Yet it's ringing."

"Where did you get this . . . phone?" Jonathan held it as if he were concerned that it might turn into a beetle or bird.

"Dr. Lambshead gave it to us."

The thought occurred that perhaps Stimply was calling from *inside* the meadow, so to speak. That, perhaps, Stimply was a giant marmot. That, perhaps, this was all some monstrous game and someone would soon jump out from behind the giant wildflowers with human faces and yell "Surprise!"

"It won't ring forever," Crikey said.

"Oh, I think it will," Rack said.

"Oh, all right!"

Jonathan was so sick of this, and, of course, he picked up the receiver to the unmistakable sound of Stimply's voice, and also yet another unmistakably different backdrop than before. Nothing like a meadow or an alpine peak. He sounded this time as if he were calling . . . as if he were calling whilst encircled in a desert by a herd of angry camels? In the mountains surrounded by alpacas? Llamas? Jonathan could not quite source the sounds, except he could not shake free of the idea that Stimply was in a fix, trapped by irritated quadrupeds in great numbers.

"Jonathan! I am so glad you are safe at the Institute!"

"Stimply. Are you in Aurora? Are you nearby?"

"Who wants to know?"

"No one. I mean, me. I do, Stimply. The person asking the question."

"Oh, no, I'm not. Not that I know what you mean by 'Aurora.'"

"Stimply. Are you in trouble? Is someone after you?"

A nervous tone. "Isn't someone after everyone?"

"No. That is not true."

"Oh, right, right. Well, perhaps you've lived a very privileged life up to this point, because everyone I've ever known has had someone after them. You included now, my dear boy. And a very serious someone."

Jonathan forgot to be exasperated. "You mean Crowley."

"I'm afraid it's worse than that. With the Golden Sphere in Prague and so many Celestial Beasts in play, all bets are off. Call in your chips. Retract your head into your shell. What I mean is—the future becomes ever more unpredictable. It's all rather Wretched."

"I don't know what that means, not really. Why won't anyone be straightforward with me?"

"Never mind that—have you got the Wobble with you?"

An outbreak of squeals and neighing behind Stimply and also now engines roaring.

"Alice Ptarmigan scarpered off with it."

"She's not with you?"

"Not in the least bit with us. Very much *not* with us."

"Bloody hell. No Wobble. Well, you'll just have to rely on your natural magic to get you through."

"No, I won't. Whatever that even means. Isn't that like saying the barefoot man with shoes on? I don't have any magic."

Danny's and Rack's faces told a different story. He knew they were thinking of Rome and the exploding train.

Jonathan's face felt hot; he'd almost not realized he was getting irritated at Stimply. "I thought instead we'd come back to the mansion to regroup."

"It was always going to be difficult, Jonathan, you being so inexperienced, having to use the Wobble, against an opponent like the Golden Sphere, with Crowley trying to thwart you. I wasn't quite sure of that plan from the beginning."

"How do *you* know about that plan? I never said anything to you."

"I . . . I just knew."

"You've not been honest with me about a lot of things, Stimply. Are you saying I can't come home?"

Stimply sounded somewhat defeated in reply, but it could be that the quadrupeds were wearing him down. "Yes, you can and should come home. Mamoud's still with you, yes? Well, it's his problem as much as yours. And he'd likely prefer you were out from underfoot. Except it'll be complicated."

"It's already complicated!"

"No doubt, no doubt. I have no doubts. Well, I do have doubts."

"Ask him how we get back to Earth," Rack whispered, Jonathan waving him off, turning away so as not to get distracted.

"How do we get the Wobble back, Stimply?"

"Don't worry your head about it, Jonathan. Leave it up to me. I'm the expert on the Wobble."

"Why not let her keep it? Maybe she's an expert, too."

"No! No! No!"

"Because only I can use it?"

"Yeah," Danny whispered, "Tee-Tee wants to know how we get home, too."

Jonathan brushed that off, trying to listen to Stimply.

"Because the Order's wishes are still in her own best interests."

"Isn't she part of the Order?"

"Lord knows. Is that what she told you? I had no idea she was even lurking around the mansion. I thought it was . . . well, never mind who I thought it was. Alice isn't part of the Order. She's an English patriot—a spy for them, and a damn fine one, and the English are in a bit of a bind right now on Aurora. She'll be eager for any advantage. I'm sure she'll have brought the Wobble back to English magicians, to study. Whether you see her or it again is anyone's guess. I guess."

"Yet you implied you have a way of contacting her? Never mind—of course you do. I'm talking to you on a telephone with no cord."

"Neat trick that, old boy. Don't know how you do it."

"I'M NOT DOING IT," Jonathan shouted into the phone. "YOU ARE."

There came over the receiver such a lowing and mooing and neighing and squeaking that it quite flummoxed Jonathan. Was Stimply hiding in the middle of a petting zoo? Or was he a petting zoo?

"Quite, quite. But if you just could not talk so loudly. The . . . the people . . . I'm with can hear you, and it's making them quite a bit more . . . agitated . . . than I'd like at the moment."

Jonathan took a deep breath, tried again.

"Stimply, is the reason only I can use the Wobble because my father had some hand in its creation?" A wild stab in the dark. Something Alice had said that made him think this.

"I . . . I never said that only you could use it. Talk to Dr. Lambshead about it. He would know more."

"I can't! He's dead! Stimply, what is going on?"

Silence, then Stimply, sans animal noises: "It's not that others can't use it, my dear, dear boy. But that only you can use it properly. Others can misuse it. But to say more would be—"

"Refreshing? A lovely thing? An unexpected luxury?"

"Quite, quite," Stimply said. "You see my reasoning."

"There's no point trying to find the Golden Sphere without it. Even though if Crowley finds the sphere, Earth is in peril as well?"

"Perhaps, perhaps not. You might be able to reason with the Golden Sphere. It's no friend to Crowley. It definitely does not want to bend to Crowley's will."

Jonathan was gobsmacked. "So you want me to reason with the Golden Sphere. Just walk up to the sphere and talk to it."

"I'm a humble estate agent, Jonathan, conscripted into . . . well, let's just say I can't tell you what to do. But you need to leave that meadow as soon as possible and get to Prague and—"

"Poppycock. Don't change the subject. You're in this up to your neck. And you're not telling me every—"

But Stimply had hung up.

Jonathan cursed. "I will never, ever take a phone call from that man again." Although, of course, he probably would have to. After all, who could resist a ringing cordless rotary phone.

The compartment beneath the phone popped open. A message appeared there, rolled up. Handwritten. Recognizably Dr. Lambshead's handwriting.

"They'll tell you the culprits are the obvious ones. But this conspiracy runs deep. Don't trust the simple answer, grandson. Everything is bigger than it needs to be."

Most excellent. A mystery on top of a mystery.

"Ah, yes," Crikey said, "that message appears every time someone uses the phone. But it's not for us, it's for you, so we have let it be."

But Jonathan barely heard him. It could not now be said that Jonathan believed Stimply was "just" Dr. Lambshead's estate agent.

"Have you ever seen Stimply?" Jonathan asked Crikey.

"I doubt Stimply has ever seen Stimply," Crikey replied. But did not care to explain, then or later.

Who or what, exactly, was Stimply?

"Apologies again for the state of the telephone," Crikey said. "We use the cord to entertain the marpots."

"Marpots," Rack said, suspicious. "Marpots?"

"Yeah, poor marpots," Danny said, and Tee-Tee looked a tad sad.

"We call the ground squirrels marpots. Not sure how it started. That tradition. But we have lots of marpots to toss in the pot."

"What?"

"Never mind," Crikey said. "It is a marmot thing. The marpots."

Chapter Forty-Seven
A SPECK OF UNCOMMON SENSE

"Bats are forbidden across the empire. If you see a bat larger than a rooster, you should immediately murder it and have it sent to the Emperor for dissection. But in no context shall you aid or abet a very large bat in any task. For it is now against the law. However, if you encounter a bat or birdlike bat with a human face, you should offer it water and food and return it with all haste to the Emperor."

—Emperor Crowley order intercepted by Wretch and never implemented

Wretch had gone off on reconnaissance again, but not before making Crowley watch as Mr. Bat Monster created a dozen more mini-Crowleys with wings, to be sent off through those soul-devouring rips in the air that Wretch-thing was so fond of creating. All of this from the observation platform atop the war elephant, in the middle of a drenching downpour. The particular body Wretch had given Crowley this time had not been inclined to raise a hand to wipe the rain trickling into his eyes, which had made the proceedings even less enjoyable.

"I do not like this new innovation," Crowley had told Wretch.

"Oh, worry not, Lord Emperor," Wretch said sarcastically. "They're the same old rabid chipmunks—just with your adorable little face. For don't you want your influence to spread far and wide? Don't you want the world to quaver in fear before your rabid-chipmunk self?"

At which point Wretch had actually made a *heh heh* sound, a kind of laughter Crowley had not yet heard from Wretch. Nor was Crowley's bad mood improved by how immune Wretch thus far seemed to the spells Crowley was hiding in his familiar cursing.

Neither did he love how Charlie Mange, shoved up tight against him in that space, guffawed at Wretch's jokes. It was unbearable enough how much Charlie Mange loved a good rain bath. Apparently, the rotted leaves that covered him weren't quite rotted enough.

The close, musky smell of snails and earthworms and centipedes soon coated the entire platform.

Crowley couldn't, to be honest, be sure it didn't come from Wretch as much as from Charlie Mange.

All he knew was: The war elephant was becoming ever-more unbearable. The dark forest made this quality worse, as the trees loomed over them even as his men cleared the path ahead. Day or night, the forest was full of torments, from bats to mosquitoes, cricket choruses to stop his sleep and fireflies blazing too bright—so bright he suspected the return of faery folk.

He doubted that proximity to Prague would stop the perpetual beheadings.

Yet, Prague could not arrive soon enough.

⁓

Night atop the war elephant was a shifty, tallowy thing, with glowworms in lanterns and a dysfunctional demi-mage down below requisitioned as a lamp, his pale head luminous but features slack. The humidity could not be controlled by magic, alas. Nor could the smell of burnt cooking boiling up from inside the elephant, because the cook was incompetent. Mildew and sweat.

Having a fur-body this time around didn't help, either.

Although he could not bear to look at himself for long. For Wretch, in a particularly foul mood, had plonked his head on what amounted to a bear suit, not at all hirsute, but the body of a real bear, ill-suited to what Crowley was accustomed to, which was standing upright. More of a jumpy crouch. And bulky—making him even more claustrophobic and ill at ease. Although Wretch said he looked imperial enough "in such sumptuous fur," Crowley had, of course, insisted on clothing, and all that fit was a workman's overalls.

Pen and paper now being beyond his grasp, Crowley had had to bring in more demi-mages for when the urge struck to issue written orders.

Worse, there was an infestation of lesser nectar deer in the elephant, no doubt from leaving the butt chute open too long while doing the laundry, and he must needs wave bear claws at winged deer, when his minions weren't using fly swatters to try to bring this new torment under control.

He had sent No-Name to his quarters in the water closet and told another demi-mage to keep an eye on Charlie Mange, and Wretch had left an hour ago, which meant by Crowley's estimations would not return for another two hours, based on prior expeditions. Or such seemed the case whenever he became long-winged and long-winded beforehand.

Which meant it was time for another session with the Speck. Up top, on the observation platform, because his bear butt was not meant for the bony chair beside his desk.

"Speck . . . are you awake?" he asked once he had checked for magical surveillance, was fairly sure Wretch wasn't watching.

Contemplating the Speck as it zigged and zagged in its prison, container teetering on a small foldout table

Wretch had not yet taken the Speck from him. Well, rather, he *had* taken the Speck from him, for private interrogations, and then given the Speck right back to Crowley.

Crowley wondered why, but had no real answer. To give Crowley something to keep him occupied? For Wretch must see no danger there. Although it was true Crowley had bound it, not Wretch, and that Crowley had worked hard in front of Wretch to make the familiar feel comfortable with his possession of the Speck.

"Speck? Are you dead or just resting?"

The moon was full enough that he could see the monstrous forest almost dark green, and the cloudy sky reflected the moon such that it was as if cosmic rays lit up the other war elephants to front and aft, and all the sleeping demi-mages and the restless, floating Emissaries that stood guard. There was a furtive curling, questing sound that came from inside the war elephants, all the undead animals half-comatose but still moving their limbs in dreamy slow motion. Remembering a life before.

"You've gone all fuzzy," the Speck replied finally with a yawn. "You've gone all fuzzy fuzzy fuzzy."

"Pathetic mote, serving an ever-more pathetic master."

"He me he me he me. He meeeeeeeeee."

"No, he's not. It's not. Your master left you here to be discovered, to be exposed. And to be destroyed."

"What you don't know will kill you, familiar."

An explosion of rage and he hit the glass with his fist, making the Speck's container jump. "I'm not the familiar. Wretch is!"

"How many Wretches do you serve?"

"None. And I can extract what you know without your consent, Speck!"

"No, you can't, Fester Growley."

"Don't call me that."

"He who he who he who he who he who he who he who—"

"Just spit it out, Speck!"

"He who is imprisoned in a snow globe has only insults as weapons."

Crowley considered that.

"I'll free you if you help me." He'd never said it so bold. "But I need to know what you've said to Wretch, and what Wretch has said to you."

"Shall I replay it for you?"

"What?"

"I have recorded it."

"You have what?"

"Never mind. Here, listen. I'll make it all grainy so it feels more real."

A glittering mirror-ball light came from the Speck, and suddenly, amid crackles and pops, Crowley heard Wretch's voice.

Wretch: Why shouldn't I just pinch you between my two fingers and kill you?

Speck: You should kill me. Go ahead, kill me! Keeeeel meeeee dead as a bedbug in your own master's bed.

W: Why not kill yourself? Your existence in our hands puts your master in jeopardy.

S: I'm havin' too much fun, guv'nor. Truth be told.

W: Your master apparently sent a dunce to spy on us. But no matter—we know already. Or, rather, I know—your master is fleeing to Prague.

S: Fleeing. Fleas. Fleas on a dog's back. Hitching a ride. Are you a flea, Wretch? How can you be sure that my master does not look out at you from this mere Speck even now, and you, dear jolly anti-sir, just cannot perceive that in all your primitive animus? Oh dear, you are quite speechless. Not kept up with the latest nano-magic? Not read the full briefing on my capabilities? What of this, I wonder, will you report to Crowley? What will send him over the edge, do you think? A look in the mirror, if you were to ever allow him a mirror? What might he think of your own pathetic agenda, your unsubtle manipulations? How soon before he folds because of it? How soon before you acknowledge the full glory and wonder of your lard and savor the Golden Sphere?

W (terse): Is that truly you, bastard marble? If it is, here's a message for you: Soon enough you'll be caught and caged and reduced to the servant you were always supposed to be. Pity you ever escaped in the first place. Such a waste and such a nuisance. The Builders spit upon you and your kind.

S: Kidding! It ain't It! It ain't It! It ain't It! And aren't you just a familiar as well? In the end? We know the stench of you. We always know that smell. Most unfortunate.

W: Where is your master?

S: Up yer bum! Up yer bum!

"Enough!" Crowley growled. "Enough!" It wasn't. He could have listened to this blather forever, chortled at how difficult the Speck was making it for Wretch. He might even have discovered more than a vague mention of the Builders. But Wretch would return soon.

"As you wish, Fester Growley!"

"Stop calling me that!"

"Stop growling!"

Crowley wondered if a bear body meant, in some ways, a bear mind, because it was true he had been growling more than usual. Also, had a craving for raw meat. Also, felt an embarrassing need to scratch his back. Also, had begun to think he smelled nice, although he was sure he didn't.

Grubs in the forest called to him. Nice, juicy grubs. Juicy, juicy grubs. To pad through the forest grazing on berries. To . . .

Crowley growled again. Nonsense. He was a human sorcerer who wanted to rule the world, not an unambitious bear.

Perhaps, in fact, some of his claustrophobia was due to his bear body. Although at least when he threatened to slap a demi-mage now, they flinched and cringed more dramatically. But perhaps Wretch was countering his spells with spells of his own, through the bear's body?

Crowley shuddered. Enough.

"I say again . . . I'll set you free if you help me, Speck." Would he, though? He rather doubted it.

"And how can I help, thou. Am but lowly Speck of the lower lowest orders and genuses and families. Not a genius such as yourself, human-bear, but just a Speck under glass. Controlled by you."

Crowley laughed at that despite himself. Suddenly he was doubled over with laughter, until his eyes were wet with tears.

"I'm a human-bear," he managed. "A bearly human. Ah, me. What a life. I am the most powerful and the least. I am a moon and I am a speck. What am I to do, true Speck? What? Tell me."

"Recast your sins."

This made bear-Crowley outright guffaw. Oh, bear-Crowley, what a sense of the comic. It was as if Crowley were having a crackdown, no, a breakdown, no, an out-of-body experience.

"Surely you mean recant," Crowley said between bouts of hee-hee-hee.

"Perhaps," the Speck said. "Perhaps not. Mostly now I am concerned my newest ally be unhinged by a mere fur coat."

Crowley perked up. "Ally? Perhaps even friend."

"Fiend, but yes." The Speck still seemed subdued by the monumental nature of Crowley's fit. Well, well and good. Maybe his distress would be good for something.

"Can you get a message to the Golden Sphere?"

"Can I butter bread?"

Crowley hesitated. He had not yet seen the Speck prepare breakfast, or eat anything.

"Is that a yes?"

"Yes."

"Then perhaps we'll start there."

"Dumbo at three o'clock, Lord Crowley," said the Speck, gone over-all polite of a sudden. "Autumn Lawn Downer on the move. I repeat, Autumn Lawn Downer on the move."

Came lurching out of the shadows from below, then: Lurch! Crowley rolled his eyes. The demi-mage had failed at the task of chaperoning, and *this* had come rambling up in a froth of leaves . . .

"I toucheth *thy* shoulder, Crowley! I toucheth *thy* shoulder!"

And so Charlie Mange did, while Crowley cackled.

"Good on you, sonny boy. You toucheth my shoulder. Did-ith it explode into leaves-eth? No!"

"I toucheth thy face, Crowley, I toucheth thy face!"

"Oh hell no. Get away from me, you loon! You hopped-up German chieftain from the dead dead past!"

There began, and ended, a short game of slapsies that Crowley was relieved no one else had lingered to observe.

Which ended with Crowley pushing Charlie Mange away, shoving him into a corner of the platform, that it might not become a splatform.

From which the wight glowered and cowered both. For the spell Crowley had set was working, and Charlie Mange was weaker every day.

"Wouldn't you love to return to your roots, Charlie?" Crowley asked. "Wouldn't you love to be back . . . in amongst the roots?"

From the look on Charlie Mange's face he liked the idea as well as if Crowley had said "Wouldn't you love to be back in public school?"

Well, he'd come around. All Crowley needed was the Moment anyhow. The Moment when the confluence of events allowed him to wrest back control from Wretch, with Charlie Mange either helping or at least not hindering.

"Right. No more time for this palaver, my dear cadaver friend," and he turned to the All-Seeing Puddle.

He'd been meaning to check in on Latrine and ET without Wretch around. They might be asleep, but they soon wouldn't be.

He leaned over and dipped a finger in the puddle, trying not to notice all the fur on his finger. A swirl, a ripple . . . then nothing.

Paris would not come into focus. There was no connection, or the connection had been broken.

Crowley frowned. Even in the moonlight, he could see a kind of patina of algae covered the All-Seeing Puddle. Was it Paris that was the problem or the puddle?

"Latrine!" he called out. "ET?"

He thought he heard Latrine's voice for an instant, sharp, inchoate, even, perhaps, screamy? But, no, he must have imagined it.

No image cohered.

No further sound emanated from that pathetic dog's dish of water.

Oh, how he hated the All-Seeing Puddle.

Yet now there was an odd moony reflection in it, coming rapidly closer. And—coincidence?—a whistling sound in the air.

Crowley frowned, leaned in closer to the All-Seeing Puddle. A rather large object. A . . . piano? A *grand piano*?

Where in all the blazes was this report coming in from? Far afield or Paris?

At the last second, he realized it really was a reflection, and looked up at an object crashing down on him.

"Abandon ship!" Crowley screamed. "Abandon ship!"

He lunged for the side of the platform. The huge whistling weight smashed into the top of the elephant.

A moist squashing sound that must be Charlemagne.

A sharp bone-snapping sound and intense agony. His agony. Of all the holy hells!

Crowley screamed and could not stop screaming.

O take me darkness as thy own.

Chapter Forty-Eight

THE ALPINE MEADOWS RESEARCH INSTITUTE

It was a funny sort of place, up close, Jonathan thought, this marmot paradise. So fresh and clean. Even the Institute, which shared the same ridiculous dimensions as the flowers and grasses in the meadows. Up close, though, it resembled less a classic Victorian mansion, due to ad hoc burrows collapsing the original rooms, these excavations evident even through the ample cross-framed windows. Jonathan could not make sense of the layout with all the extra marmot-sized holes in the walls. Although perhaps the building in its gnawed-upon state had even more character. Brick and wood, chewed around the edges by the marmots who apparently liked pulp as a digestive.

Tatty yet homey. The marmots had made it their own.

But, then, Jonathan had realized that the entire meadow was in a way a facade, the remains of the Institute included. The real Institute, or the true land of marmots, must exist buried underground. A vast network of tunnels and burrows that no human would be allowed to see. That was where the marmot young would be found, too. For none had appeared in the meadow while they'd walked through it. Unless these particular marmots reproduced by budding.

Stacks of antique chairs were piled outside the huge stained-glass front doors, waiting to be carted around back to to be burned in the huge firepit behind the Institute building.

"It's a new development, rubbishing the chairs, but a long time coming," Crikey said. "We don't use chairs, you see. Some among us feel we were becoming too . . . gentrified when we tried to do as Swedenborg suggested and adapt to human customs. So now we only take those that make sense for us."

Inside, the foyer had a high ceiling of inlaid sky-blue tile, but they had to walk around a gigantic hole in the floor.

"Apologies," Crikey said. "But we needed another entrance to the home burrows. We have guest burrows, I mean rooms, for humans—and don't worry, they aren't filled with dirt and vegetables. Luxurious. Even by human standards."

"I doubt that," Rack muttered, staring with suspicion at the mess, and clearly expecting Danny to punch him in the shoulder. But instead she hugged him.

"Get off me!"

"I have a delightful room, yeah? Even Tee-Tee likes it. You'll see. Yours is next to mine."

"Excellent! So Tee-Tee doesn't have to be inconvenienced if he wants to murder me in my sleep."

Jonathan sighed. He rather hoped the spat between Rack and Tee-Tee would be short-lived. He was finding it as tiresome as Rack versus Danny.

Waiting inside, beyond the foyer, were two more enormous marmots.

"Crikey," Jonathan managed, startled. They'd emerged from shadows.

"No, I'm Crikey," their guide said. "He's Wallow and that's Sprogg. Wallow's the old chief of security and Sprogg's stepping in very soon."

Wallow had the demeanor, in marmot form, of an old warrior, with white fur and numerous scars from bites and other wounds. Sprogg lived up to the name, with a kind of spring to their step, a much more youthful marmot, with brown fur and large, gorgeous eyes.

"Guests pests," Wallow said. "Guests pests. Guest pests."

"Wallow's never been much for English. He means guests are always welcome."

"Nice to meet you," Jonathan said. Although he wasn't sure, even if it was true he also thought of guests as pests most of the time. Never much cared for them while living in Florida. Wallow, he'd noticed, had spikes for claws, honed sharp, and two of Sprogg's buckteeth had been narrowed to points. Marmot military fashion, then?

Sprogg spat to the side, said, "You could call us all Circus Meat and it wouldn't much matter. None of our names translate into your crude human tongue that well. My true name would be——" And there followed a long series of clicks and whistles. "How would you handle that?"

Rack scowled at Sprogg, and Sprogg scowled at Rack. Jonathan fought the temptation to tell them how much they resembled each other in their demeanor.

"Now, now, Sprogg and Wallow, I know you have much on your minds. We will leave you here while I guide our guests to sanctuary." Crikey gestured to the library, ahead through an enormous archway covered in surreal Boschian detail . . . except featuring marmots. "Just while your rooms are made ready."

Jonathan stared in amazement at the archway as they passed through. The Garden of Eden . . . full of wildflowers and populated by marmots . . . on one side, and on the other side, hell, with only a handful of marmots (who must be criminals) and much more congestion, fire, smoke, and humans.

Dim-lit by lamps filled with fireflies, the library was full of comfy seating, but also faintly luminous ground squirrels that zipped to and fro just above the ground, upending books and stopping to nibble at already much-abused lounge chairs and leather sofas.

They were the size of jovial springer spaniels. Floating and zipping about. Taking up space. Jostling one another.

"Only about twenty in here, so you're lucky. You can sit on some of them. They don't mind. When they cluster, they can be quite comfortable if you need a nap. But beware the group smother."

"Marpots?" Jonathan guessed. The odor was rich, but thankfully more like peat moss than pee or poo. Although something about their aspect made him think most of their names were variations on Pee or Poo.

"Marpots," Crikey confirmed. "Bit of an experiment back in the day by a magician visitor. Now we can't get rid of them. Invasive species. Just ignore them and they will ignore you. Probably. They feed on insects, dust, and ash, which is at least convenient."

"Do the rooms come with marpots, too?" Rack asked.

"Everything in the Institute comes with marpots!" Danny said. "Isn't that great!"

"Bloody hell," Rack said.

Jonathan was, himself, conflicted on the subject of marpots, which had begun to ring a distant bell. Could they be the same as Sarah's pot-marps? The potmarps that had figured in a brace of cute fairy tales she'd told as bedtime stories.

"Yes," Crikey said. "They love the Institute but tend to wilt and die in the sun for some reason. So you only see them in the meadows after dark. The nectar deer tend to feast on them, and yet they keep multiplying."

The great cycle of life, according to Sarah. "The potmarps hovering excitable over the magic swamp at dusk, their chirps met by frog song." Wait. Did that mean "frog" was code as well? He could hurt his head overthinking it.

"I was able to put on a production of *Hamlet* for Tee-Tee last night using marpots," Danny said.

"Really?" Jonathan asked.

"No, of course not!" Danny said, laughing. "Don't be ridiculous, yeah?"

Ridiculous seemed the only option, when it came to marpot pot-marps.

Soon enough, the marmots left them to the library and the marpots. Sitting on the chairs there, they could all look out the grand glass windows to the back of the Institute, where lay a small cemetery to the left and in the center the great firepit full of ash . . . and some odd random bones. Around the firepit was a sunken amphitheater of stone seating. Which gave the whole rather the appearance of a place for performance as much as for feasting.

Once they'd cleared marpots out of the way to properly appreciate the view, that is.

"If this were a movie," Rack said, "I couldn't imagine a creature more cynically created to sell stuffies of."

"You're a stuffie, Rack," Danny said. "You're a stuffie. And very cruel."

"At least I don't eat dust and ash and melt in the sunlight."

"Yet," Mamoud said.

Crikey had promised a feast at that very pit that night, and bade them to rest up once their rooms were ready. Beyond the pit was a steep drop-off, and Jonathan could see by the configuration of peaks all around that the Institute was situated with such cleverness and guile that only the most experienced mountaineer would ever catch the slightest glimpse of this marmot Shangri-la.

Jonathan swiveled in his chair to face R & D.

"Right," he said. "So, our mission is in shambles. We're reduced to just hoofing it for the first door that will get us home. This entire expedition has been a disaster from the beginning. And I have no idea what to do when we get home. If Crowley's creatures will pop up again. And what to do if so. Are we going home to 'regroup' and return, or are we just abandoning ship?"

He should have expected it, but his words had the effect of a bomb going off. Or not going off. The others just stared at him like he'd said something rude.

Finally, Rack spoke. "Listen, mate, we're here because of you, true. But my nitpicking aside, this is a whole other world. I can't unsee it or what's happening here just because we've made a mess of things. Or Crowley's made us make a mess of them. So I'm for the regroup. Which should surprise no one."

Which surprised everyone. Even Mamoud was looking at Rack as if he were a new and different person.

"Well, I'm doing it for the fame," Danny said, "and so is Tee-Tee. So we're up for the regroup."

"We still don't know what we're really in for. We've just gotten a taste." Jonathan said it with a warning underneath.

"And yet still we're going to do it," Rack said.

What they were going to do still seemed unclear to Jonathan. Weren't quests supposed to be simple and easy and there might be difficulties, but in the end you were victorious and everyone lived happily ever after? Except Aurora didn't like to play by those rules, apparently.

"We still need Prague just to get you home," Mamoud said. "That seems clear." Ever practical.

"I would very much like to get home," Rack said. "And by home, I'm not even sure I mean the mansion, but home-home."

"Prague doesn't mean as much without the Wobble," Jonathan said. "We just need to get back to Earth for now. We don't need to get to Prague."

"It's all the same," Mamoud said, "if the only doors from here lead to Prague."

Jonathan was struck by how none of them mentioned the fade, as if to mention it was as bad as calling a Wobble a Black Bauble. Well, maybe it was. Maybe that was how you let it in, even more than what the fade took on its own.

"And what of Alice?" Danny said, facing Mamoud. "She's your friend, yeah? Hasn't she betrayed you, too?"

Fair question, and it clearly made Mamoud uncomfortable as he sat back in his chair. Like all the chairs, it had been brutally gnawed at. A marpot hovered by Mamoud's head, then two. Trying to ignore the marpots was like trying to ignore, well, really, Jonathan had nothing to compare it to. But it was difficult.

"Ally of convenience. I have no claim over her actions. If I'm less concerned about what she's done, it is because in all things she puts Britain first and England's goals are the same, for now, as the Republic's."

"But that's not true, is it, *General*?" Jonathan asked, pushing away a legion of marpots gently burbling at his elbow. Their fur was plush and their eyes so large and curious.

Mamoud frowned. "Don't call me that. I'm not a general."

"It's what Crikey called you."

"His information is . . . out of date."

"So you *were*. What are you now?"

"A member of the Order expressing Republic interests."

"Is that so?" Rack asked. "Then why—"

"By the way, you've all grown such magnificent beards, yeah?" Danny said, interrupting.

So clearly a way of changing the subject, and yet . . . it was an impossible thing to ignore, too.

Jonathan, Rack, and Mamoud all looked at one another in confusion. And then Rack burst out laughing. But Jonathan felt mostly consternation. What was this sorcery?

Because it was true—they'd all the beginnings of quite amazing beards, even Jonathan, despite being the youngest. The itchiness of five-o'clock shadow had long ago given way to a rich smoothness that he hadn't questioned. Nor had he been looking in mirrors much since entering Aurora. Not that he did back on Earth, either.

"Well, I already had a beard, or a bit of one . . . ," Mamoud said.

"Which is why yours is so much longer now."

Truly, for Mamoud's beard now reached almost to his waist. Rack's was only down to his collarbone. and Jonathan's had hardly reached the middle of his neck.

Danny couldn't stop giggling, and Tee-Tee was emitting high-pitched squeaks that suggested hilarity.

"How is this possible?" Jonathan asked. "And I can feel it growing now. I mean, it is growing on my face as we speak like . . . like some kind of air plant."

"Jonathan, you're beginning to look like a young version of your grandfather," Rack said.

"It's true I can't remember a photo of him without a beard," Jonathan said. It was doubly disconcerting to stroke his chin and realize he might look much older.

"You should set your pocketknife to the problem," Rack said.

Jonathan shuddered. "Seems the wrong task. I'd like to lose the beard, but keep the face."

"Always an old soul, always cautious, yeah?" Danny said. "Crikey did mention that there might be side effects to the magical meadow air."

"Is that it? How long does it last?"

Danny shrugged. "Maybe it will never end, and you will be continually cutting your beards and forget all about any kind of quest. Maybe you will learn how to braid, yeah? Tee-Tee thinks you'd all look good with braids."

"How well you present horror as hilarity, sister-blister."

"It's scratchy and itchy at the same time," Jonathan marveled. "Shall we vow to grow our beards until the Golden Sphere is banished from Aurora?" he asked.

"Do we have a choice?" Rack asked. "I don't remember asking Santa Claus for a beard, and yet here we are."

Mamoud said grudgingly, "I rarely shave. And banishing the Golden Sphere is just the beginning, not the end."

"Oh-ho-ho!" This from Rack, who was pointing at Danny's face.

"What?" Danny asked.

"I think I see a five-o'clock shadow on your face, Danny."

"And what of it? Are you going to make something of it, bro-blister? Look to your own facial hair before you judge mine. I am totally *fine* with mine, yeah?" Good natured, but a little bit of an edge to it.

"Bro-blister is not working, sister-blister. Choose. Something. Else."

"It works just fine," Jonathan said.

"Shut up," R & D said at the same time, but not in anger.

Danny sat back in her comfortable lounge chair, whereupon the marpots descended upon her lap, with Tee-Tee nipping at them to keep them off her shoulders.

"Very nice beards, I say again, gentlemen," Danny said smugly, folding her arms. "On all three of you."

Bearded Jonathan stared at bearded Rack and Mamoud, and vice versa. Such full beards in such a short time. And Jonathan noticed that Danny's five-o'clock shadow was becoming more intense by the moment. It was hard to believe some dark magic wasn't involved.

"We look like we've been shipwrecked for ages," Jonathan said.

"In a way we have," Mamoud replied.

Which sobered them all up straightaway.

Crikey showed Jonathan personally to his room a little while later. It was upstairs, a shipshape if spartan space with a bed and an empty bookcase plus a closet and a marmot portrait on the wall over the bed. The tile floor had been swept recently and led to a small balcony looking out on the meadow. The place smelled like floor cleaner and, well, marmot.

No holes here; Crikey and his companions, including a white-furred marmot named Stockton, whom Jonathan thought of as Crikey's lieutenant, had made that very clear—the visitor rooms in the Institute did not connect. Not to one another, and not to the rest of what must be the larger marmot community. A kind of quarantine that made sense to Jonathan. Even if he'd recently had his brains jumbled falling into a chasm for far too long.

Crikey had to bend over a bit to get through the doorway, straightening up into the higher-ceilinged room within. Jonathan noticed a fan above, circled by some pesky nectar deer. Good luck sleeping with all that buzzing. To be honest, Jonathan was rather losing track of whether he was seeing lesser or greater nectar deer, given the size of the flowers.

"This used to be Dr. Lambshead's when he needed some time away," Crikey said. "But mostly, it was Sarah's room. I thought you might like that."

But did Jonathan "like" that, though? And did he like hearing the words from a giant marmot who may have known his relatives better than he did?

Nothing in the room to tell him anything about his grandfather or his mother. Stripped down on purpose? Then it struck him: Sarah had emptied it. Careful as always.

And it wasn't that it was a surprise to hear those names. It wasn't that he hadn't expected some connection. But, still, Jonathan's heart leapt a bit and he struggled to keep his composure. To hide this, he walked out onto the balcony, looked down on the meadow.

There was something profoundly peaceful looking down on the grazing of the marmots amid the freshness of the air up here. Although he had to say that Crikey's presence still made him jump from time to time. The marmot, with his massive muscled bulk and his huge grimacing teeth, would make a formidable opponent if made angry.

Down below, a phalanx of six marmots came down the path, headed for the Institute's front door, dressed in gray robes and with faces hidden by gray masks meant to make them look human, with human expressions. Headed back toward the Pillow Cavern, they each carried a weapon that resembled a spear gun. The masks with smiles and frowns and impassive thin-lipped stares, the eye holes vacant and gaping, startled Jonathan.

"Oh, them," Crikey said, noting Jonathan's discomfort. "Sentry patrol from on high, going on duty. They're how we discovered you— and Crowley's monster."

It explained that glimpse of "people" high on the mountain, staring down as they'd trudged up from Comet Lake.

A stronghold. Of the Order. Of order.

"Why did Sarah come here?" Jonathan asked.

"Well, she was an agent of the Order," Crikey said cryptically. "She was always hither and yon, to and fro. Especially during the War of Order. We were a neutral space during those troubling times."

"When was she last here?"

"Two years ago. After a visit with the Comet Man. She needed a place to think, she said."

"Why visit the Comet Man?"

"I don't know."

"Not even a little bit?"

Crikey hesitated. "She may have believed the Comet Man could be of use against Crowley. Celestial Beasts are a kind of wild card. Hard to control, but they bring all sorts of peculiar knowledge with them."

"Where did she go after?"

"Your Earth, I understand. Via our underground caverns and a door off to Prague."

In a sense, he was still following in her footsteps. Like there was an echo, a resonance. He didn't know if that was alarming or comforting.

So many important questions he wanted to ask Crikey about his family. But he remembered something Sarah said: "Ask yourself: Are the people you talk to secret keepers or secret sharers? Act accordingly." But he thought Crikey might be both and something delayed him from asking further about the body in the way station. He didn't know if he wanted to be a keeper or sharer yet, either. The wrong question could reveal too much.

Instead, he asked, "Where had she come from?"

"Porthfox."

"You mean Poxforth."

Crikey shook his head. "Porthfox Academy here on Aurora, Poxforth back on your Earth."

This jolted Jonathan, and he tried to hide his surprise. What might a mirror academy look like? Might he prefer it to Poxforth?

"Why did she go to Porthfox?"

"I imagine some aftermath of the War of Order. Porthfox was a hotbed of intrigue."

"Why is Sir Waddel Ponder dead and mummified in the way station?"

"Who?"

"The headmaster of Poxforth!"

Crikey hesitated again, looked down on the meadow.

Finally, he said, "That's not the Poxforth headmaster. It's the Porthfox headmaster. And we don't know. It happened at night. One morning he was just lying there."

"And your scouts never saw him before that?"

"No."

"How do you think he got there?"

Crikey frowned. "There have long been rumors of a one-way door into our Alps from Earth. But as you might imagine this would be difficult for us to verify on our side, especially if it were also secret on Earth and used rarely."

A one-way door. The more Jonathan learned about the doors, the more the universe looked like it was made of Swiss cheese.

"And how do you know he's the Porthfox headmaster? He looks just like the Poxforth headmaster."

"Dead bodies fade, too . . ."

Dead bodies fade, too . . .

Jonathan sighed. "Well, surely you've speculated, Crikey. You've had thoughts or theories about it?"

"Alfred Kubin, an agent of the Order of the Third Door, has told us that there is some link between the British Parliament and the body. Some whispers on back channels about a connection between Parliament and both academies. On both Earth and Aurora."

"And that's all?"

Crikey nodded.

"And did my mother say anything else before she left? Anything important? Anything I would need to know?"

"Wouldn't she have told you what she wanted you to know?"

"She didn't have the chance, did she?"

"Perhaps. The War of Order is still fresh, Jonathan. People were being hunted down depending on what side of that they fell on. Outside forces used that to their advantage. Sarah didn't feel safe. If she didn't confide in me, it was to protect me. To protect the Institute."

Jonathan felt a knife's point of unease, a chill.

"This Order of the Third Door. Why can I never seem to find the center of it, Crikey? It's like cloak and daggers and mist and shadows. People keep telling me about it, but it's never quite . . . there."

"The War of Order's to blame. The Order's still picking up the pieces. If . . . when you make it to Prague, you'll see. More of the Order's survived there than anywhere on Aurora. And, of course, at Poxforth and Porthfox."

"There?"

"Yes. Recruitment centers."

Interesting. And yet he'd never seen a hint of it at Poxforth. Had Danny kept him in the dark? And just how precarious and complicated had been Dr. Lambshead's role in all of this? It struck Jonathan for the first time that perhaps his grandfather and mother could have been at odds over the role of the Order.

"And what about the Order and the Builders and . . ."

Crikey, with perhaps a hint of impatience: "Take this. Sarah left it behind."

The marmot handed Jonathan a slim volume titled *A Short History of the Builders.*

"Borrow?"

"Keep. We have many more copies."

"All right."

The marmot portrait was the same one as in Dr. Lambshead's mansion. No doubt it had made his grandfather feel at home. Perhaps it was time to change the subject anyway.

"Who is that?" Jonathan asked, pointing.

"Oh, that's Reggie. Reginald. Dr. Lambshead's old friend. Commissioned the portrait, brought it on one of his last trips through. Best of friends, according to Dr. Lambshead, even if their work meant they didn't see each other as much as they might like."

"Do you know Reggie—Reginald?"

"Not personally. Dr. Lambshead's friend, as I've said. Couldn't get over it. When Dr. Lambshead first visited us, the Order stuck in Reggie's head and not all the fresh alpine water in the meadow could get it out. Took a couple others with him. Thirty years now it's been since we saw Reggie. I hear he's in Paris now, helping with the resistance against Crowley."

Ah! Mystery solved, minor though it might be. Or was it minor?

Jonathan would never be an expert on marmot expressions, under all that fur, but he thought perhaps Crikey was holding something back. There were times, when Crikey turned his head to the side or appeared to be staring at something Jonathan couldn't see, that his cuddly nature disappeared and he seemed cold, almost alien.

And: How long did marmots live anyway? Perhaps magical marmots lived longer than regular ones.

"Was it through Reggie that Dr. Lambshead found this place?"

"Yes. He vouched for Dr. Lambshead, the first time he visited. He came here twenty-five years ago, seeking a rare flower of medicinal value, he said, nothing to do with the Order at all. The silver star, also known as edelweiss."

Jonathan rather thought that had been a cover story, if he knew Dr. Lambshead at all. And if he remembered his childhood comics reading correctly. There'd been a quest for edelweiss in there somewhere.

"What was he like, my grandfather?"

"Oh, a delight. A man of rare taste and distinction. A rare sympathy for the meadow, too. Not much of a magician, but, then, few are fated to be as gifted as you."

"I don't do magic."

The marmot made a huffing, snorting sound with a deep whistle underneath that set the hairs on Jonathan's arms upright. Incredulity? Was that marmot for profound disbelief?

"Well, you are mistaken. You can talk to animals that don't usually talk back. And word has reached us of what you did on the train to Rome."

Jonathan sighed. "This world seems strange and wild and uncontrollable to me. The sensible thing would be to turn my back on it."

"I would disagree," Crikey said. "From up here it looks orderly and compact and sensible."

"Does it?"

"We're not completely isolated up here, Jonathan. We see the world with clear eyes from *up here* not because we're out of touch. But because we have the time to truly see what is happening. And I can see you have a role to play."

Jonathan laughed, but harsh, self-deprecating. "What role? To roam the land looking for a door out before I fade?"

"Can't you begin to guess? To eventually lead the Order. To use your magic in the service of the Order."

"Is that the official marmot position? On me and also on the Order? Your Sprogg and Wallow struck me as having a different opinion."

Crikey looked away, out over the meadow. "We're like any people. A crucible of differing opinions. But, yes, most of us. Especially as it's not just the Order versus Crowley. It's more complicated than that."

"More complicated?"

"Just be aware things can change very quickly. Allegiances, friendships, even, dare I say it, quests. You must be able to bend in the wind."

"I'm not in the mood for clichés."

"I've no better way to say it, Jonathan. Expect the unexpected."

"But *what* exactly?" Jonathan tried, perhaps failed, to disguise his exasperation.

Crikey would not elaborate. Instead, he said, "There's something I need to show you now. It's right about time. The best time. Perhaps the only time."

Crikey stepped hard on one of the floor tiles, and a secret door appeared, outline crack-thin, in the wall opposite the bed. A cramped dark staircase led downward. Barely suitable for marmot proportions.

"After you," Crikey said.

Jonathan stared, dubious. This seemed a bad start to showing a person something.

⁓

At the bottom of the stairs, they came out into a room with a high ceiling and without windows that yet was filled with light . . . and a tiki bar. An enormous tiki bar. Under a canopy roof of canvas, dyed the color of the stones like camouflage. Deluged in vines—and flowers in white, red, and green that glowed brightly enough to give some semblance of daylight.

In the center of the room, in front of the tiki bar, lay an enormous chair, and the chair was covered in a living carpet of marpots and nectar deer. A seething living carpet of creatures that bleated and trilled.

Was this what Crikey wanted him to see? For what purpose?

"You have a visitor," Crikey said, and there came a kind of muddling struggle upon the giant chair. A huge human hand rose from the muddle of marpots and then the other hand, gripping the chair rests.

Whereupon an enormous man arose from a dripping sea of consternated marpots and nectar deer, the deer to hover around his head like a ragged halo and the marpots to bounce and jounce around his person, despite the fact he kept waving them away.

A man in a gigantic reclining chair that looked hand-built. A man rising some thirty feet above Jonathan. In a secret room, protected from prying eyes, from spies circling above. With a beard cascading like a wiry waterfall, itself an obstacle to any expedition to climb the human hill-peak.

Above the beard and the thin mouth, the familiar beak of nose, the worn cheekbones like eroded edges of a cliff. The eyes, though, the eyes not like in photos—the clear blue, but an off-blue, almost a cloudy blue. And clasping the arms of the vast chair, the great knuckled hands with the yellow half moons of unclipped fingernails. The hands so age-spotted and cavernous in their bony detail.

Jonathan's jaw had dropped, and he could think of nothing to say.

For towering there above them was a person he'd long thought dead.

Dr. Thackery T. Lambshead.

A giant.

Alive.

Chapter Forty-Nine
THE SUPERNAL BURGH, THE FAIRY-TALE ROT

Tracking a monster in Prague, Kristýna's adopted hometown, she could not help but be distracted at times. Prague: the place where fairy-tale rot crawled up into visitors' brains, gave them mind-gangrene from undiluted infections of whimsy.

What a dump. What a treasure. Her second true love. This one more than most, for she knew a famous writer from Earth would live a long life in the wall surrounding Prague, hate the place, be poor and desperate there for decades, and yet be forever linked to it. One day, too, everything she loved about Prague would be destroyed. But not here. One day, tanks would grind down these very streets. But not here. This was a stronghold of the Order of the Third Door.

Here might have another problem entirely, and part of that problem was in *not knowing* the exact nature of the problem. Yet.

That would be the tall, bulky figure they followed past the houses like postage stamps of light in the dark. The one who knew about woodpecker tongues. The one she couldn't place no matter how hard she tried.

Spies, spies, spies. Always spies in cities on the brink. She had seen it so many times. Wondered if perhaps this was one time too many. A maze to interrogate, even as they walked through a maze. Granted, many other odd folk had appeared in Prague. Not all of them villains. Mali, Republic, even animal spies, which she hadn't seen for ages. All worse, more complicated, the closer Crowley's army came. The closer they came to siege.

And what sort of siege? Porous or tight? She'd seen all kinds, knew each siege was different, and each siege terrible in its own way.

Too much to sort through to find one Golden Sphere. Among all the vines that needed to be trellised or lopped off. Alfred Kubin's somewhat hysterical missive delivered by a bat through the window of her Prague home had made it clear the Golden Sphere would wreak chaos here if It could. Or, at least, It had wreaked havoc on Kubin. And of this she was wary—wary not of Kubin's information, but of how it had come to be. He had been on the wrong side of the War of Order and even reconciled, apparently, had been known to nudge a conspirator toward a plot. Which is to say, Kubin's hysteria felt a little like play-acting.

Yet . . . she doubted the figure they followed was the Golden Sphere. No, this was something else.

♀

By now, they were quite high. Kristýna always liked to be high—way up above the sullen castle with its crude gargoyles and half-crazed king, up and away from the algae-throttled river of legend, a path that had taken her and her companion through landscapes of eccentric gardens as likely to sticker as to soothe, created by gardeners who had considered their manicured absurdities normal . . . cobblestone streets bordered by fairy-tale houses in pastel shades, roofs dusted with snow, whose walls curved with a delicate grace poor stupid doomed John Ruskin had misdiagnosed as "twee."

Down below, the city roiled, anticipating the siege. Republic soldiers manned the walls alongside local forces employed by the merchant clans. Too many tourists, many of them rich, had risked the journey for annual magic festivals and were now trapped, gumming up the works. Soon to be enlisted in a "volunteer" army if it did not go well.

"Anyway, about the houses, I should explain about the houses," she had been telling Mack, to appear to be casual, because he'd just come to Prague for the first time, after all these years they'd known each other.

Anyway, because no one understood that the point of those curved walls, those slanted roofs, was excellent design for the weather and a wicked comment on fairy tales, not a wish to *live* in fairyland. Even the most whimsical of homes they passed came with mighty doors made of such a stubborn alliance of wood and metal they were unlikely to admit even an intruder armed with an ax. Prague was treacle on the surface . . . and then, underneath . . . became something more wondrous and strange and . . . resistant.

Mack beside her, grunting a reply to her information: I heard you, I have nothing to say.

Mack, and his shadow.

What did Mack see, staring back at her? After all this Time?

And what did the shadow see? Although there was a more important question still.

She left off the banter, asked the question she'd hinted at, only for Mack to deflect, ignore, pretend he didn't understand. But now she was on her home turf, for a little while. Safe enough to ask, given the shadow had seen it all unfold on the wooded footpath she'd chosen to bring them through the forests, through Prussia, and then mere miles to Prague. Or, would've been.

"Did you mean to let him escape? Did you think it would serve some other purpose?"

Five days since Napoleon's disappearance, and nary a hint of where he had gone or how he'd accomplished it. Nothing a tuft could tell her, anyway. Which, perhaps, left the Speck.

Two girls wearing bear masks skipped past.

Mack, trudging alongside, but not breathing heavy like her. "I didn't mean for him to escape."

Two old men holding flowers and hands made it safely past the figure they followed. Not all did.

"Quite a surprise in the moonlight, then," Kristýna said. "For both of us. To see a headless body. Again."

A dancing cat with a singing dog. A dove hitching a ride on a hawk's back. The figure in the dusk paused at these marvels, common for Prague, where magicians had a sense of humor. But they did not of a sudden vanish and the figure continued on.

"Yes," Mack said. "A surprise."

"By now, he could be anywhere. Up to anything."

She'd found a horse for Napoleon. She'd garden-spelled a body for him out of thicket and copse, a stout body of thorned vines shot through with moss and lichen and rotting bark. Something loamy to soothe. A body that wouldn't wilt. That smelled of mint and lavender. To counterbalance the not-so-sweet smell of preservatives and magic augers. With a nice thick carved-out slice of tree trunk, fit to house the head of a military genius.

"And yet it was your watch."

"I saw nothing. I don't know why," Mack said.

Perhaps the shadow knew.

All she'd asked in return from Napoleon was to accompany them to Prague and serve the Order against Crowley. The very Crowley he said he hated. Yet at midnight five days after they'd arranged to pick him up, there loomed the headless body, a thicket without a point, atop a horse they no longer needed. Symbolic of something. Perhaps the state of things within the Order.

"Calm as could be. The horse," Kristýna said. "Not spooked. Not startled. Imagine that."

"Let us concentrate on what we're doing now," Mack said. "And save this for later."

"Right. Mack, no knife and no truck. No truck with questions, rather."

But she laid off him for the moment, their quarry turning a corner, and them both having to quicken the pace without seeming to. She was reminded of ages-old ballet classes, of sidles and sneaks and intrigues so ancient now it made her tired to think of them.

◔◞

The bulky, tall figure had proved adroit at avoiding all sorts of obstacles— sudden cats, dogs, children, old men. Would of a sudden pirouette and be past, almost seeming to invert its shape or to draw in its gut in a spectacular and preternatural fashion. Always sticking to darkness so as to mute the effect. But Kristýna saw it. How the top of the figure's head at times quivered and divided into four pieces, came back together again. Which might have startled a younger soul.

How, too, in the aftermath of this . . . quiver . . . a passerby hugging a stone wall or leaning in an alleyway might have disappeared, never to be seen again. Was it their quarry's fault? Or a trick of the light? Or both?

"Did you know, Mack, that a woodpecker's tongue wraps around its brain?"

Mack said nothing.

"Although this is to say nothing of the local cuckoos," she continued on grimly, "which lay their eggs in the nests of the red-faced imperial nuthatch, laying with them plots against those species' ambitions, and the imperial birds none the wiser as they sit atop eggs that will hatch into babies that do not have the ambition of their own species but of another entirely—"

"Interesting," Mack said, interrupting, because he must feel compelled to say something in the face of so much detail. If only to stanch the flow. Especially as these ridiculous words had also been delivered by the one they stalked, if not as coherent, the past couple of days. And had been known to come from Napoleon's mouth, or something similar, the short time he'd been atop a horse and beside them.

"Tell me, Mack, how do you think this . . . person . . . we're following knew the sign code?"

"Ask Napoleon."

"I can't ask Napoleon."

Mack shrugged. "It is a common-enough saying."

Kristýna opened her mouth, bit her tongue. The "person" had a poor command of Czech, kept talking, when greeted, in specific phrases, including the woodpecker one. Which is how the "person" had been brought to their attention, having talked about woodpecker tongues to the wrong Czech magician.

The figure ahead of them, the one that weirdly resembled a schoolmarm, stopped in front of a wall of posters, backlit by a huge public fountain full of flaming mead. The fountain was surrounded by the balloonicles and floats for a prewar carnival: The next morning there would be a parade of giant red bunnies, porcupines, and bears, precursor to drunken reveries. One last hurrah before getting serious. Children jumped into the honey mead, came out with their cups full, which were given over to their parents. The place was flush with the thick smell of the honey and abuzz with night bees sneaking a sip from derelict cups.

"You Czechs are strange," Mack said, his face on fire from the glow.

"No. We are just very human." She decided not to remind him she wasn't Czech. Not really. Because she was proud of the Czechs, often wished she was one.

"No one is sober around here."

She laughed, but her eyes had never left their quarry. Mack had never understood the Czech tolerance for alcohol. "Later, you will dive for honey mead for me."

The schoolmarm figure had been facing a wall plastered with posters for upcoming cultural events, most of which had been canceled. Now it appeared to disappear into the fabric of the low wall to their left. But they could not quicken their pace, had to walk past as if common citizens of the city.

Yet Kristýna could tell the creature was truly gone.

They walked up to the wall, as if out for a quiet stroll, held hands to complete the illusion, stared at the poster the creature had perused with such intensity.

The Fester Growley Book Club, meeting at the Twisted Spoon Book-shop, midafternoon, in three days' time. The Czechs did have a talent for satire, it was true.

"Can you feel it?" Mack asked. "The residue?"

"Yes. Of course."

The poster exuded magic. Not the magic of animals or trees, but of a Celestial Beast. A Beast could disguise almost every part of its essence, but most were too powerful to be truly invisible.

"Were we tracking a Beast?"

"Or did a Beast put up the poster?"

The idea made her snort. A Celestial Beast putting book-club posters up all over the supernal burgh.

Such fairy-tale rot. Then she sobered.

"The Council must be told about this."

She meant the Council of Czech leaders and their Republic advisers that ruled Prague, given the state of their king. The Prague magicians would spearhead the defense of the city, and they, too, were part of the Council. Kristýna was among the members of the Order who advised the Council . . . on the matter of peculiar doors.

Mack shook his head. "I say no. I say we pursue it ourselves."

"Why?"

"We don't know what it is yet. We don't know where it comes from."

"No, because we *do* know what it is yet, and we must not hide any-thing from the Council."

"At least keep it to the Order, not the Council."

She pondered that, sidestepped for the moment. Mack could keep what he wanted to himself. She was free not to follow his advice. Especially here.

"Shall we attend, then. This book-club meeting?" It wasn't a question.

"Absolutely," Mack said.

That settled at least one issue. So it was time for the next thing. What she'd been putting off.

Appropriate to have waited until on the hill above the castle, where many things banished from the city proper came out to play.

Even the common doors there shared an uncommon resilience out of necessity, lined with spells and varieties of ivy not entirely natural. Sometimes, the ivy in such places seemed to laugh at passersby, a peculiar green laugh, dry and yet deep, as if below the ivy lay buried some plant-beast and the vines were merely its searching limbs. Sometimes, the ivy *scorned* the drunken stumblers spilling out from golden light, bewildered, to the streaking swirl of stars framed by the reaching arms of the trees.

So she meant to use the natural properties of the place for an intervention. But the whole point of intervention was surprise; it allowed for nothing that resembled permission.

Mack in the mead-light stood upon the cobblestone street. But his shadow shone across a thicket of bushes. Such a lush, thick shadow. So intelligent and self-aware and dangerous.

It was a moment's work, but a wrenching, exhausting thing nonetheless.

In the blink of an eye, the thicket's thorns became more than just part of a plant. They reached out, clung to and pierced the shadow, which writhed there in surprise and pain. Like a marmot pooling into black liquid.

While Kristýna pushed Mack away, toward the fountain. Ripping the shadow from him. Ripping it right good off him, in such a way he cried out, which she covered up by drawing him close and kissing him on the lips. Hoping maybe the kiss would replace the shadow in his mind, in such a way that nothing would change.

Out of the corner of her eye, she saw Mack's shadow still writhing in the thorns' embrace. This would not last long. But it would last long enough if she was quick.

She pulled Mack close, as best she was able, stared up at him, stern, unyielding.

"Trust me, my love? Time to run, Mack no truck. Time to run if you don't want a marmot's shadow to find you again."

Mack, in shock. Mack wild-eyed, wrenched out of himself, as if she'd pulled out his spine, not his shadow. The stare he gave her made her wince. Betrayal. Uncertainty. Laid bare to her. Ah, this game was not for the faint-hearted. Not for the weak.

"Mack! Wake up! Wake up now!"

The betrayal faded, and he nodded, and he let her take his hand. There, above the castle, among so many people whose business required secrecy and who lingered in impromptu pubs and beer gardens hidden within mazes of alleys or behind hedge walls, or on the edges of cemeteries with headstones without names or dates.

They ran, together, his rough hand in hers, which was just as rough. Past the fountain and its cheery crowds. Down the quaint cobblestone streets, up high and higher still, gasping for breath in time, but she driven by a kind of mania and sense of loss, Mack by sheer terror. She could feel it. He hadn't known about the shadow. Hadn't understood what his clandestine meetings might mean for him.

Mack shadowless. He shivered uncontrollably as they fled, as if it were cold, which is how people reacted at first when they had no shadow of their own. How they reacted when they learned the "people" they trusted didn't trust them.

Would that be enough for him to tell her the truth?

Chapter Fifty

RETURN OF A KING

Dr. Lambshead. Grandfather. Alive. Much, much larger than life, in fact. Not dead and preserved in an urn back at the mansion. Not murdered by Crowley.

"Why is he a giant now?" A little suspicion in the back of his mind, but it wouldn't come into focus.

"Never mind that, he's lucid now. Go talk to him."

Jonathan should have felt something other than just shock. Relief or joy. But he felt nothing. Nothing but a further hope, a kind of sickness, he knew, this hope, and it was his first question, blurted out without thought.

"Is my mother alive, too?"

"I don't know," Crikey said. "Only Dr. Lambshead might know. But he drifts in and out. He has dementia. We keep him comfortable here. We feed him. We keep him hidden. Not even all marmots of the meadows know he is still here. Not all would approve of the risk. But I am a loyal member of the Order."

"I really must know why he is so enormous. Before I keel over from the shock that he's alive." Holding on to that question for dear life, like a flotation device against drowning.

But Crikey got cranky. "Never mind that, I said. He may not be in his right mind for long. Go talk to him."

Crikey shoved him toward a tall, stout ladder that led up to the coffee table next to Dr. Lambshead. He could just see a huge magnifying glass atop the table, which was more like a dais, at that size.

"So he faked his own death. And my mother came to see him?" It sounded so normal to say those words and yet so weird, too.

"Something like that."

Jonathan opened his mouth, closed it. All right, then, drown it was. He'd climb. But then he hesitated on the steps, looked back at Crikey. Who was looking up, still irritated.

"And what about—"

"*Get on up there.* He's lucid and he's right *there.* Ask him yourself."

Why was he delaying? Perhaps because the gigantic figure was intimidating. Perhaps because until a few seconds ago he had been convinced his grandfather was dead. But Crikey was right. He didn't have time to adjust. Even as now he felt so very, very small.

He got onto the ladder, had one last question.

"Why do I—?"

"So he can see you, of course. So he can see you, naturally! He can't see very well. Shout up at him. He can hear well, but you're tiny. But don't stay under the magnifying glass very long. You'll burn up even with no direct sun on it."

Great. Certainly would not help Dr. Lambshead's mental state to peer down just in time to see a tiny version of his grandson burst into flames.

"And what about—"

"No time," Crikey said, and shoved him farther up the ladder.

Jonathan looked back at Crikey, opened his mouth, closed it again. Time to climb.

Soon enough he was up on the dais and Dr. Lambshead's face was vast and concave and distorted in the lens. He did not seem inclined to notice that Jonathan stood there.

"DR. LAMBSHEAD!" he shouted. "DR. LAMBSHEAD! IT'S YOUR GRANDSON, JONATHAN!"

Dr. Lambshead turned this way and that, then stared down and spotted Crikey. "Is that you, Crikey? Come to visit?"

Good god, but the man's breath was sour and came swirling down like wind, thankfully broken and diluted by the magnifying glass.

"YES, IT IS CRIKEY!" Crikey shouted, from the side. "BUT, DR. LAMBSHEAD—LOOK AT THE MAGNIFYING GLASS. YOUR GRANDSON HAS COME TO VISIT!"

"The magnifying glass, you say?"

"YES, DR. LAMBSHEAD. JONATHAN LAMBSHEAD IS HERE."

The great man's head swiveled down to stare through the magnifying glass. One bloodshot eye shone down upon Jonathan along with the warm wind of his grandfather breathing on him.

"Is that a marpot?"

"NO, IT'S ME, GRANDFATHER!" Jonathan shouted.

"MARPOTS FLOAT AND HAVE FUR," Crikey shouted. "REMEMBER?"

"Oh, quite right, Crikey. Quite right. Foolish old me." Dr. Lambshead drew his shawl around himself and shivered. "Hot but cold. Cold but hot. Can't ever get it right for this old sod. Nothing like the jungles of Borneo and yet exactly like the jungles of Borneo."

"It's me, Grandfather," Jonathan said, not bothering to shout it.

"You're not Jonathan. Jonathan doesn't have a beard."

"It's still me," Jonathan insisted.

But then something clicked on behind that bloodshot eye and Dr. Lambshead leaned over and took a better, longer look, other eye squeezed shut to concentrate.

"That *is* you, Jonathan, isn't it? Under all that . . . beard. I believe it is. What an unexpected and delightful surprise. Goodness, I hope Crikey has been a good host. This place can be a bit blonkers at times, if you catch my meaning."

"OH, I AGREE. IT'S BLOODY BLONKERS. I AM SO GLAD YOU'RE ALIVE."

"Well, not bloody, I hope," Dr. Lambshead said, frowning, and ignoring the other half of what Jonathan had shouted. "That's more the château's style, wot?" His frown deepened, and some of the age fell away from his features. "But what, really, are you doing here, Jonathan? Stimply was meant to keep you safe, and away from all of this. Places like this. No one is supposed to know I'm here."

"TOO LATE, GRANDFATHER. MUCH TOO LATE. I'M IN TOO DEEP FOR THAT."

It was true, and he hadn't really seen it before. But he was. In too deep. Couldn't get out.

"BUT I LOST THE WOBBLE."

"What?"

"I LOST THE WOBBLE."

"Wait a moment, dear boy. Let me get my hearing trumpet. That will make things better."

Whereupon Dr. Lambshead pulled out an ancient, huge hearing trumpet that looked more like a Swiss musical instrument. He tapped it and dozens of nectar deer tumbled out and flew away, then he put it to his ear.

"You were saying, Jonathan? Something something gobble?"

"You'll still have to shout, I'm afraid. That trumpet doesn't work that well," Crikey said.

Jonathan sighed. "I LOST THE WOBBLE."

Dr. Lambshead laughed. "Wobble, my boy. Wobble wobble wobble. Sound a turkey makes in the woods. Or the sound a hunter after a turkey makes. Wobble wobble wobble. Ha ha ha."

"ER, YES, RATHER," and Jonathan stole a glance at a worried-looking Crikey.

But in a moment, Dr. Lambshead was back from wherever he'd gone. "I stole it, you know. Might be people—bad people, not even really people if I'm honest—coming for it eventually. Once they realize it's gone. Stole it from the château, if I'm truthful. Just fine so long as it never comes back." Dr. Lambshead seemed to shudder at the thought.

"THE CHÂTEAU PEPPERMINT BLONKERS?"

Dr. Lambshead looked perplexed. "What other château could I possibly mean? Or did I? Steal it from them, I mean? So long ago now. Well, beware the Blonkers, I always say. Coming into focus, that dreadful place. I can feel it in my bones. Your grandmother always used to say 'What you feel in your bones is the future, not the past.' Quite right."

Questions, what questions should he ask? It had never crossed his mind that his grandfather was alive, so he'd not engaged in that particular fantasy. The one where he had questions. For his mother, questions galore. And the two questions he had to ask his grandfather, he could not ask yet.

"WHO SHOULD I TRUST?" A sad question, really. A question you'd ask a fortune teller. He regretted it as soon as he said it.

Dr. Lambshead laughed. "Is that a riddle? Isn't it clear, my boy. Trust yourself."

"I DO. BUT WHO ELSE?"

"Well, not this bucktoothed wonder here," Dr. Lambshead said, pointing at Crikey and chuckling. "Oh, of course I don't mean that. Crikey's right as rain. Crikey's a good old sod. For a burrower. But don't trust the Wobble. Don't trust the haunted mansion. Don't trust anyone whose name is 'Adolf.' Also, marpots aren't much in the trust department, wot? Adorable as they are. Damned if you do and damned if you don't. But you have all my telephone messages. Surely I've been clear? And the Allies List?"

"YES, I HAVE THE ALLIES LIST. AND WE ARE TRYING TO FIND THE GOLDEN SPHERE, OR WERE, SO CROWLEY CAN'T GET HIS HANDS ON IT."

Dr. Lambshead's expression darkened. "The Golden Sphere's not to be trusted, for certain, my boy. Nor quests around same. Full stop. Stopping being the operative word. Chase your tail or a tale, you might say."

"WELL, I'VE NO CHOICE NOW."

Dr. Lambshead frowned and said, "Sometimes a hamster is a wheel. Sometimes a wheel is a rut in the road. Sometimes you should trust the voice in your head more than anyone."

The voice in his head? Could Dr. Lambshead possibly know about that? Or was it just another figure of speech?

"AND STIMPLY? SHOULD I TRUST STIMPLY?"

"Oh, most definitely, my boy. You must trust Stimply. And Danny. And Kubin. Probably."

How did Dr. Lambshead know about Danny? Jonathan didn't know who Kubin was. Why should he be trusted?

"HOW DO YOU KNOW DANNY?"

"Oh, I suggested to the Order that Danny keep an eye out for you. A good egg, Danny. One of the best. Not like some of those rats at Pox-forth. Those marpots. I never wanted you enrolled there, but Sarah said you'd have to deal with all that mess someday. Better off being mired in it sooner than later. Water under the bridge. You've all moved on. Blah blah blah. No one cares, you know? Not even the marpots. Blah blah blahppity blah."

Was his grandfather already sliding back into dementia again? Jonathan felt a terrible panic. Too soon. He had to ask the important questions.

"WHY IS SIR WADDEL DEAD IN THE WAY STATION?"

"Hmm? Bread in the pay station? Horrible. Need scones. Bad joke. No, poor Waddel. Wrong place, right time. Right place, wrong time. Victim of the War of Order, that much is clear. But the rest is muddy. Sarah was investigating. Sarah knew there was rot at both the poxes, so to speak."

"ROT?"

"Rot and bother."

Dr. Lambshead of a sudden looked under the weather. Fading but not the fade. And there were two more questions Jonathan must have the answer to. If only he wasn't too late.

He took a deep breath, asked the first one.

"WHO IS MY FATHER?"

Laid out naked, revealing more in front of Crikey than Jonathan would have liked. It felt like a secret question. One that should only be said in front of family members.

A sly but scattered look from Dr. Lambshead. "Who isn't your father?"

"WHAT'S THAT SUPPOSED TO MEAN?" Stung. He felt the sting of serious met with clever. Or incoherent.

"Remember the birdhouses," Dr. Lambshead said, unhelpfully. "Stimply's told you about them I hope."

Jonathan sighed. "NO, NOT REALLY. JUST WHAT YOU SAID IN YOUR LETTER." He didn't know if he could ask about his father again, not if he got this same kind of response.

"Everything's there. Stimply's supposed to have told you everything. All the blah blah blahs." Dr. Lambshead chuckled, staring off into space at some elusive memory.

"WELL, HE DIDN'T." Instead, Stimply had tried to smother him in annoying telephone calls from devices that shouldn't work.

A final murmur before sliding off into stupor: "Jonathan. You've started to fade. Not too bad yet. Not so anyone would notice. But . . . you should get that looked at, old bean. Or I could be wrong. Things tend to slip away from me these days, my dear boy."

The lurch and the fade. Sad for his grandfather, even now so remote, so distant from him. It was and wasn't the sadness of distress over the fate of a loved one. Something between personal and impersonal.

Overwhelmed. Overshadowed. Homesick. For Poxforth. For Robin Hood's Bay. For Florida. Anywhere but here. Anywhere he could just be and not have to think. Or think things through.

When he'd climbed back down to the stone patio he felt drained and his voice was hoarse. Crikey was saying things at him he could barely hear.

"That's all you'll get out of him for now," Crikey said. "Perhaps ever. And you cannot tell anyone he is here."

"He's not really here," Jonathan said. "Not all the way."

"Sadly true."

"He left a note for me at the mansion. Do you think he wrote it after or before . . . ?"

"Oh, definitely before. You needn't worry about that. This is a recent development. Although there had been signs."

"And his Allies List?"

"Sometime in-between if I had to hazard a guess. Having seen the list, I must admit. He wanted anyone on the list to agree to being on the list."

"So the squirrel in Salzberg isn't an ally?" Feeble joke.

"Oh, the squirrel's an ally. If in Zurich. Just not the Tether Heads—they were an amateur rugby squad. Back in the day, him and his mates."

"Thank you for taking care of him," Jonathan said, and meant it. What an all-consuming use of resources.

"It's the least we can do," Crikey said. "Considering all he's done for us. For Reggie. Saved us from discovery more than once. Helped us build the Institute building. All sorts of things about this place are down to him."

The dread in Jonathan, talking about these mundane things. Because of the last question he dreaded to ask, had not asked his grandfather. But had to ask, no matter what the answer. No matter how cloudy Dr. Lambshead's eyes.

Dr. Lambshead had snapped out of his nap and was looking around him in confusion, but his eyes were clear.

Jonathan thought he had enough voice left to reach up to those ancient ears. For the only other question that meant a toss.

His voice broke on it, shattered to pieces.

"IS SARAH STILL ALIVE, TOO? IS MY MOTHER ALIVE?"

The cloud across Dr. Lambshead's face, the way his features crumbled inward, told Jonathan the answer even before the words that came down like thunder.

"No, Jonathan. I'm sorry. She died in an avalanche. Not far from here. I'm so sorry."

Back in Jonathan's room, staring blankly out at the meadow, radiant in the sunshine.

"Switzerland is that way," Crikey said from behind him. "Italy there." Pointing pointlessly. Jonathan didn't much care. "But no one wants Comet Land as Man Land." That low whistle of laughter.

Sometimes Crikey was still quite alien, in how he chose his moments. Or maybe he just didn't want to acknowledge Jonathan's grief. He found people rarely did. To be made uncomfortable.

To stop the travelogue, if nothing else, Jonathan asked, again, "Why is my grandfather so huge?"

"Well, my friend," Crikey said, "there is no good way to put this."

"Put it any way you like."

"You've been miniaturized. When you fell through the trapdoor. That's why it took so long. To fall, that is."

"Oh. Is that all?"

"It's the only way we allow humans to enter the Institute and the meadow. A magic Napoleon perfected, to get his troops across the Alps when he was out and about conquering and whatnot. But otherwise, you'd ruin everything, being so much larger than us marmots. Dr. Lambshead's just been here so long he's returned to normal size. As you will anyway, when you leave this place."

A lark. A dream.

Odd, how it seemed the least important thing.

Of all the things now bouncing around his skull.

Chapter Fifty-One
MARMOT CARPET, POUCH AND RELEASE

"All Crowleys and Wretches shall be baked into an enormous pie that is deliberately overcooked and burned beyond recognition hey nonny nonny, yeah! All Crowleys and Wretches shall be dropped into a pit and allowed to fester and fester until they ferment beyond our torment, hey nonny nonny, yeah! All Crowleys and Wretches shall be shoved into an airtight container and dumped in a deep lake, there to drown, hey nonny nonny, yeah!"

—The Speck's decree, as related to Ruth Less, never official or issued

Ruth Less wondered if stinky shiny Crowley had dressed in yet another bear's body in her honor. Was this a naming day? Or perhaps a group-devouring day in their culture.

After losing the last one, he could easily have gotten a worse body, especially given Wretch's mood. But, then, Ruth Less imagined Wretch was very busy these days and it required less thought just to find another bear, which were both plentiful and delicious. If Wretch didn't want her tempted to eat Crowley, then he should give Crowley a gross body instead, like a giant spider body or Wretch's own.

Crammed on top of the war elephant, on the rickety, half-smashed platform, all remains of the grand piano gone. Which Ruth Less knew had been tracked back to the Golden Sphere, which had required Wretch to work up some spells to cloak the origin of his own rabid chipmunks with Crowley faces. Now the grand pianos would drop miles away, on the head of an effigy of Crowley riding atop a scale model of the war elephant.

Crowley held her beloved Speck, standing beside Wretch, the slow one they called No-Name, and a thing made of dead leaves that was called Mange—Ruth Less believed she did smell a faint reek of group-devouring. But Wretch had said it was just a normal meeting, so she did not start the group-devouring. That would not be polite. She would wait for someone else to start, and follow suit if so. After all, this was not her world. Or her meeting.

Wretch was a huge pair of eyes on the underside of a fleshy black umbrella shielding them from the terrible weather, which included lightning and large hail-rocks. Ruth Less would've preferred to absorb the hail-water through her skin as on her own world, but apparently here this would be rude, too. So she just listened to the sound of stones rattling off Wretch's hard exterior.

Not much about this place made sense, and with each day she felt Wretch made less sense, too. Heady had said many things about Wretch that Ruth Less was still mulling. (Mulling was a kind of art among her species. It might take several mulls before determining a course of action. The best mull was a mulled mull and not a hasty mull.)

Nor did Ruth Less much enjoy the shouting, although she joined in, mimicking what she heard.

"What in all the hells! . . . How can this be? This must be wrong. The puddle lies! The puddle lies! The puddle lies!"

Of course the puddle lies. A puddle cannot stand. This was what Heady would've called logic. But when Ruth Less sent that thought the Speck's way, through the glass that trapped it, the Speck just snickered in her mind.

Oh, Ruth Less. You are droll.

Drool?

"Droll" means . . . never mind.

Comet Man drools fire, but is never droll.

The Comet Man is very earnest, it's true. How do you know him?

Ruth Less projected an image of their meeting into the Speck's mind.

Ah. That is terribly devilish of you.

She knew what "devilish" was and disapproved, sent a mental image to Speck of Speck with tiny horns and a tail.

Speck snickered.

Meantime, Wretch was telling her to shut up and they were all looking with horrible fascination at a small puddle that showed an image of another place.

At first, Ruth Less could not tell what the puddle showed, although, most boringly, they had all stared at circles of water back in Notre Dame cathedral, too. If only they'd asked they could've found some of the same pictures inside her pouch. But they never asked. She didn't even think they knew about her pouch or all the things she'd collected there since she'd grown up.

But, in time, cross-referencing with her pouch, Ruth Less realized the All-Seeing Puddle showed a shimmering wave of marmots advancing across tall grass . . . to the outskirts of Paris and that behind them marched a vast army of hedgehog men on roosters and deer folk and badger folk, and while some were of the normal size, many were like Ruth Less: grown huge and fearsome.

"How could this have happened?" Crowley was shouting, smacking at No-Name with his bear arms. "How could you let this happen?"

Wretch, even as a vast umbrella, seemed at a loss. "My lord, it is the old magic. No one can predict the old magic."

Old magic?

Yes, the Speck said, *the old magic. Become new again. The rise of the animals, taking back what was theirs.*

They all look delicious and pouch-worthy.

The Speck just snickered again. It was a master snickerer. No one snickered better.

But it was true. The flowing carpet of marmot fur was golden and glossy. The startling hedgehog men and their dangerous roosters were glorious, although she wasn't entirely sure yet what glorious meant.

"I've seen enough. Get Latrine. Get ET."

Crowley was trying to calm himself by reaching out to the minds of the salamanders inside the war elephant. But both Speck and Ruth Less already communicated with those minds. Such as they were. Salamanders often resided somewhere far distant in their thoughts. But, still, Crowley's hurt and anger and panic came through to Ruth Less. It had not occurred to Crowley that he could lose the actual war, just that Wretch might rule him forever.

Ruth Less didn't enjoy looking into Crowley's brain, even through a veil of salamander thoughts. She didn't envy the salamanders, either. In her culture, Crowley would have been declared "Mooklarak" and exiled to a distant living island, there to be in thrombosis-chloriosis with a klorb until the condition cleared up. But there seemed no such oversight here, or undersight.

Soon, the puddle showed Latrine and ET, both of them with expressions Ruth Less could now read as less than happy. Humans didn't have much facial expression range, so it had been easy to learn.

"The animals are at the outskirts of the city on the east," Latrine babbled. "They're everywhere! They've overrun the guard towers! They've woven spells so that every mecha-animal they meet dies or joins them. Some say they are liberating the animals that power them and swelling their ranks this way."

"Counterattack!" screamed Crowley.

Ruth Less hated his screaming because there was often spit involved, and his spit on the ultraviolet spectrum was a gross black-tinged phlegm, as of something not quite alive. But not all the way dead. Perhaps when the group massacre party began, she should start with Crowley. If only they would get on with it.

"No," Wretch said calmly. "Tell everyone to fall back, use nonmagical troops if you have to. Set the Emissaries on them, and see what effect they have. Remove all mecha-animals to the city center to protect them."

Charlemagne, as if not to be outdone, said, "Make 'em bleed! Bleed 'em out like the meat they are. Make them be like a river of blood. Pour forges into the gap. When they come out of their holes, blast them with your hot irons. Make them beg for mercy with your mania. Stick forks into their rumps. Cut off . . ."

But Ruth Less lost the thread. Mange was hard to understand, and she wasn't even sure she'd heard him right, having to supply words for the nonsense ones she was sure she was hearing. Besides, it was hard to understand him over all the outcry from the pupa in their chrysalides.

She wasn't sure if Mange knew this, but the dead leaves coating him (some would say holding him up) were rife with moth young, soon to birth. Indeed, some of the "leaves" were actually dead moths with chrysalides clinging to them. She didn't know what would happen when they were born, but perhaps Mange would then be nothing but naked bone.

Wretch and Crowley were arguing about what to do about the marmots, while Latrine and ET shouted from the puddle at their feet and the comforting hail smashed down upon Wretch's exoskeleton. Mange offered advice, too, but Ruth Less didn't bother to translate in her head anymore. It hurt too much. She preferred not to know. He was better as a surging throb of moth chrysalides than as a person. Some people were like that, she'd learned.

Ahead and behind, the other war elephants, but from the high hill they currently traversed, Ruth Less could see the city of Prague in the distance: the glint of the wall surrounding it, the golden flecks of sunlight off the fortress towers. Yes, it was sunny in Prague, if not here, and the Speck had told her the hail was a "gift" from the magicians of Prague.

"We must turn the army around and march back to Paris," Crowley was saying.

"Impossible," Wretch said. "Impossible."

"Mixed-use vegetables are zoned for bears," Mange said, or Ruth Less thought he said. "With the meat of nations, we shall prevail in the arena of the stupid. Marmot marmot marmot rooster. Hedgehog."

Ruth Less had liked Prague, found it what Heady would've called "elegant but quack," or was that "quaint"? Sometimes the Speck liked her version of language better, so she didn't mind too much misinterpreting because the Speck's giggle made her happy.

Less likable about Prague: the people who came up to her or followed her around. The ones who approached her she ate, pouched, or ignored, depending on criteria like if they called her "fat" or "ugly."

The pouchable she only left in there for ten minutes or so, which in pouch-time could be as much as a year, and then she set them free, to stumble down the quack cobblestone streets and regain their balance and their lives, utterly transformed.

Ruth Less liked to think that Prague would be a different place in a year, what with all the people she'd pouched and released again. A better place. One she might like to live in, depending on the war.

The small plant woman and the tall man who followed her, Ruth Less would've done the same to, but the woman had an aura about her and a smell that made her a stubborn bite . . . and the other frightened her because she could not see to the heart of him. He had no smell. He had no taste. Did he hide them or did he truly not have a taste, a smell? She would ponder this awhile before they might meet again.

Shall I rescue you from this place, Speck? Ruth Less asked, lulled into torpor by the comforting sound of the hail. It sounded more and more as it intensified like the popping out of the Lorgororstintyrooginstwuth eggs during the sacred month of Oooooooooooe. When out of the holes in the chlorinator beasts bled the fly-babies that rose to slaughter the Babkooksnatbatchpoors. Ah, such a glorious sight, and harbinger of the sixth and final season.

Not yet. Not yet.

They had had such an idyllic daydream on the old war map in the cathedral, she, the Speck, and the Tuft. That they might find a cottage in the forest and live there forever, in harmony. Drink from the babbling brook (although Ruth Less didn't need to drink), chop twigs for firewood, sit by the fireplace in the winter, fish for minnow-giants at the stream in the spring. Although, of course, they would just be fishing to find new friends. None of them needed to eat fish.

But, anyway, it had been such a nice vision. For the Speck had over time less and less affection for the Golden Sphere and no real reason to return to It.

When Ruth Less woke from the trance set by the hail, she caught only the end of what Mange had been saying.

"Hoary old strategy made out of wolf droppings that saturate the canopy with candy. This is what I believe."

From the way they all nodded while ignoring Mange, Ruth Less realized that Wretch, Crowley, and Mange had come to some sort of agreement about what to do, and tasked No-Name with helping carry it out.

That she'd missed the decision didn't much matter to Ruth Less. Another imperative was coming into focus anyway. Soon enough she would be a mother and a father and expel into this world a horde of little Ruth Lesses. Which meant she would soon have to clean out her pouch and whatever was in there would have to fend for itself on Aurora. She didn't mind a full pouch when she wasn't pregnant, but the little Ruth Lesses would need the space soon enough.

Heady had congratulated her on being pregnant, when she'd told him by the roadside where she'd left him. More than most, too, Napoleon had appreciated her pouch. Every once in a while, she'd let a bird out of her pouch, put a message around its leg, and toss it up into the air and tell it to find Napoleon. Sometimes she threw them up too high and she thought maybe they fell down because they'd crashed into the top of the sky. But most of them went on their way.

Heady had said to be careful with all the birds. After all, most of them weren't from Aurora and didn't belong here. And sometimes what she thought of as a bird seemed "outlandish" here, as Napoleon put it. Birds weren't supposed to levitate or have four mouths or twenty pairs of wings or twelve sets of legs and undulate like a dragon. But, what could you do?

Didn't know where she had picked up "what could you do" as a phrase; maybe from No-Name's mutterings to the other demi-mages. But she liked it.

Ruth Less burped long and hard, so long and hard the hail coming down temporarily shot back up from the blast, and Wretch's "umbrella" shot inside out, making him curse her in a language she didn't know and neither did the others, but it sounded dreadful, as if he were eating the inside of his mouth with his face.

Couldn't be helped, though. ("Couldn't be helped" was another phrase she liked, because there were lots of things she did that couldn't be helped, because they were already perfect.)

She'd eaten a couple of demi-urges that she didn't think would be missed. And some nectar deer. And she'd eaten No-Name, but then realized he would be missed and she'd spit him back out and made him promise not to tell. He looked a little paler than before, but she didn't think they would notice. And he was missing an ear. He didn't need that ear. That's why humans had two, she was pretty sure. She still didn't quite understand human anatomy, why they had one of some things and two of others, but pretty much not three of anything. Seemed risky. (Yet sometimes they called each other "four eyes" for no good reason or talked about a third eye—things she'd picked up on the streets of Prague.)

Meanwhile, it appeared from the words writhing and wriggling in Wretch's umbrella mouth that Ruth Less was meant to go back to Prague to continue her search for the Golden Sphere.

Fair enough. She didn't mind too much. Besides, a "book club" she hadn't yet attended. It would be another new thing. Perhaps she would store some "book clubs" in her pouch for a rainy day. Or a hail-y one.

Casually, not so the others would notice, she leaned over enough to whisper in Charlemagne's ear, "The Comet Man says hello."

She didn't find amusement where humans found it, but something akin to amusement made her chuckle in her pouch at his reaction.

How Charlemagne blanched and drew away. How many of his leaf-moths dropped off.

Within her pouch, the Comet Man laughed, too.

What could you do?

Chapter Fifty-Two
BURNING BUT NOT BURNING UP

Rack could feel the fade, ever since they'd entered the meadow. He could feel it coming on in a way he couldn't explain. Like a thinness or stretched-ness that . . . wasn't. An odd beat-beat to his blood. A snake sinuous in his body, hollowing out his bones. Not in his ears, the beat, but close to his skin. A thing he hoped to keep at bay by not talking about it, by ignoring it. Ignoring things was highly underrated. Ignoring many details of his upbringing had saved him. Ignoring details of Aurora had saved him.

Not his normal. Not at all. The joke was more his thing, to hold back the bad. And, for a time, that had been enough. It was who he was, after all. The class clown. Except when he wasn't. The one who turned a bad time into a good time with a classic remark. Except when he didn't want to be that person.

Still, it had gotten him through Rome. But something had changed with the puffins, when he'd drawn the sword cane, and he couldn't quite go back. Not fully. Oh, he'd taken the piss out of Crikey, out of Tee-Tee, but it had felt . . . not light, not good. Almost rote or ponderous. Something unlucky—for him, in the long term. That wasn't the fade in him, but something else.

So he was in a mood he wasn't used to as they got ready for the marmot banquet. Caught between the two places or impulses. Not sure if he was merely melancholy. Not sure if he'd return to the old place or move on to the new.

But Rack tried to be his old self, because, if anything, Jonathan was clearly in a weirder place than any of them. He had come back from his room to the common space in the library sullen, shaken, in his own head to an alarming extent. Enough that Rack had exchanged a meaningful look with Danny and Mamoud. Something had happened, but whatever it was, Jonathan didn't want to talk about it.

Which made Jonathan compete with larf-riot Mamoud for silent. He much preferred Mamoud silly. Or sillier.

And by all the gods, Rack wished their damn foolish beards would fall off soon. Back in his room, he'd ignored their pact and tried to trim it, but the hair was preternaturally strong and resisted the scissors, ruining them. So he was stuck with it.

"We'd best be Punch, Judy, and the audience," Rack muttered to Danny as they were led to the banquet table. "Because these two stiffs . . ."

"Aye aye, bro-blister. Well, I brought my bear gun, which can be used for entertainment, I suppose."

"Bro-blister isn't ripe."

"It is ripe."

"What I meant, yeah?"

"Yeah."

"Tee-Tee says I'll disappoint you again . . ."

"Don't ruin it. I don't care what Tee-Tee says."

"Yeah. Right. True. Whatevahs."

And just like that Rack knew that he was right as rain with Danny and she with him.

Once again R & D.

༄

For the evening feast in the crisp chill of the dark, the marmots had brought chairs from the Institute out to the grass around the firepit, and a couple of long wooden tables on which to place the homemade moonshine that was their drink of choice. It had a purplish sheen in the reused milk bottles requisitioned for the purpose. Rack rather thought milk hadn't been delivered to these parts for quite some time; indeed, they looked much reused and ancient—most prized those with a sobering blue grass growing on the bottom in a thin layer of mud, over which the marmots poured the drink, ladled from barrels. But many of the marmots preferred to partake from bottles woven from a yellowing weed with thick leaves, the thatched weave so tight no liquid trickled out.

Rack decided to be adventurous, tasted it from a milk bottle and winced, proclaiming the taste "Like hay and mead mugged by a wagon full of tequila and then steeped in the britches of a turnip farmer who'd recently pissed himself."

"That good?" Danny asked.

"That good, and so much more."

"I like it very much," Mamoud said.

"Puts hair on your chest, yeah?"

Truth was, only Danny carried off her beard with style. She'd slung it over her shoulder like a scarf, and curled the ends of her mustache. Even without it slung over her shoulder, Danny held herself so straight, never slouching, so no matter how long it got, she didn't trip.

Rack knew from several depressing glimpses in the mirror while trying to destroy his beard that he looked like an unkempt, inept professor of philosophy shoved in some back closet of an office back at Poxforth.

"Look, I'm a man, I'm a burly man!" Danny had become fond of saying. "Now I can be as stupid as I want to be without any consequences whatsoever. Yeah!"

However it tasted, the moonshine packed a punch—just from the sip, Rack was back on his heels, rocking in his not-rocking chair and cooing at the stars above, which had come out, so clear and clean. The entire sky, framed by the white mountain peaks, looking like someone had polished a glass chandelier, wrapped it in thick velvet cloth, smashed it all into beautiful pieces, and then rolled out the cloth for display. Stars stuck to it like crystal shards, somehow sharp and deadly.

Of course, there were also many floating marpots, although to his surprise Rack had soon begun to edit them out of his thoughts, so that now, despite their presence, they didn't ruin the view quite as much as he would've thought.

Crikey sat next to them, and a group of about thirty marmots including Sprogg clicked and whistled and drank their moonshine nearby, not finding it necessary to include Rack in their conversations. Although he thought Sprogg glared at him once or twice. Marmots in all sizes and fur colors, one with an eyepatch and another missing an arm. The latter wore a military hat, like she or he was a war veteran. Still no sign of marmot children, which Jonathan said meant Crikey didn't trust them yet. Might never trust them that way.

"No doubt comparing the virtues of root cellars and remarking on the relative taste of wildflowers and who's got ticks and who's got fleas," Rack whispered to Jonathan, who pushed him away, clearly wanted no part of rudeness, especially with Crikey right there.

"Smells delicious," Danny said to Crikey, perhaps as cover for Rack.

"Yes, we put on a good feast," Crikey said.

Whatever roasted in the firepit beneath the burning coals did smell delicious. It made Rack's mouth water, and Danny fidgeted quite a bit in anticipation—she'd been hearing about the feast for at least a day longer than they had.

But it was an uncomfortable silence after a while, and surprisingly enough it got to Mamoud first, who turned to Crikey with the clear intent of making small talk.

"By the way," Mamoud said, "where did that first door in the way station lead?"

Rack was surprised to see the unflappable Crikey shudder, visible through the thick fur, the face still unreadable.

"Nowhere good. Who knows why the Builders left any doors behind at all. Terrible destructive things. All this moving about for no good reason. It puts ideas in a being's head."

"And yet doors will get us to Prague."

"Napoleon's doing before his defeat, rediscovering them," Crikey said. "He brought his men across these mountains for his surprise attack on Prague using the secret doors underground that you'll use, too. You might even find the remains of his campaign down there. The stray bayonet. Watch where you sit!"

Mamoud just grunted his reply; perhaps he'd had too much of the moonshine.

Rack still thought Crikey wouldn't be comfortable until they'd left the Institute. And it was quite possible the huge marmot had overdone the moonshine, too. He'd drank by Rack's estimation two pints. Certainly there was a glaze to his eyes that hadn't been there before, even discounting the reflection of the flames.

He was staring into the fire now, but as if he was looking somewhere else intently.

"The fade's much misunderstood, by the way," Crikey said to Jonathan.

"How so?" Jonathan said, distant, disengaged.

"It's a friend of peace."

"How so?" Rack asked, to take Crikey's attention off Jonathan, who couldn't have signaled he didn't want to talk more clearly if he'd turned his back on the marmot. "Nothing about the Emissary we encountered in the mansion seemed a 'friend of peace.'" Nothing they'd seen since felt like a "friend of peace," either. Especially not on the train from hell going to Rome.

Crikey gave Rack a look as if he'd been rude to interject, but said, "Not the way Crowley uses them, never lets them be, but commands them, fills them with his evil. No, not like that. But we've had travelers come here from . . . other places . . . to fade. Here at the Institute."

"To die?" Rack, drunk.

"No. Not at first. To study the fade. Imagine—those who are truly sick. Who hear tell of a place in the mountains. An idyllic place. Those who have come too far and merely wish to rest. This was long part of the purpose of the Institute, almost since the days of Charlemagne. So there are ghosts here in the meadow, and we welcome them, and they live among us as part of our history. Our burrows are haunted, in a way, but a haunting can be a good thing. I tell you so you won't be scared."

The darkness beyond the firepit took on a threatening aspect, even though it was the same peaceful gloom as before, with the last birdsong and the rustle of little creatures in the tall, tall grass.

"I don't believe in ghosts," Rack muttered, but Danny shared a glance with him that said she had experienced many a strange thing in her longer stay with the marmots, here in the meadow.

Crikey shrugged, whistled once, twice.

"I highly doubt you believe in Comet Man or talking marmots, either, and yet here we are. Indeed, if all goes well, the Comet Man will, as is traditional, make an appearance tonight, at the end, emerging from the firepit to bless our . . . meal."

"Oh, won't we all be looking forward to that. Will he be bringing any death piggies with him?"

Crikey smiled thinly. "You should be grateful for the hollow world beneath us. You'll be traversing it soon enough, to get to the doors to Prague. And it's Napoleon's abandoned outpost you'll be making for."

"Sounds lovely."

"And now the feast is ready," Crikey said.

The metal cover over the cooking part of the firepit—a rather gargantuan space itself—was rolled back, revealing their feast.

Which was, Rack realized with alarm and no small measure of disgust . . . a whole marmot, looking exposed and shrunken even if a delicious smell now wafted over them, as if a pig had been marinated in its own juices for hours and laced with rosemary and thyme. Surrounded by dozens of similarly prepared marpots, also disconcertingly naked without their fur.

"That's a marmot!" Rack said, erupting from his seat. "And marpots!"

"Of course it is," Danny said, which was just too much, beard or no beard.

"That's a *marmot*," Rack said again, pointing, although now he was more concerned that even this revelation seemed not to have registered much with Jonathan. And perhaps a little unnerved at how the group of thirty marmots nearby had risen from their seats to frown at him.

"Yes, we know," Mamoud said. "Local custom. You should be respectful."

"It's a marmot named Wallow, who you met," Crikey said. "He lived a long life. And now he will serve ours and we will honor his offering."

"That's barbaric!" Rack hadn't liked Wallow, it was true, but he'd not wished him harm. Nor did he have any desire to eat Wallow.

"Oh, come now," Crikey said. "We're far too large to exist as vegetarians and far too civilized to kill anything."

"Except a flower with a face," Jonathan muttered at Rack's side, still seated.

"Wallow died. We're eating him," Crikey said. "And besides, he fed on a good, healthy diet . . . and he's going to be delicious and he wanted not to go to waste."

"Why do you care?" Mamoud asked Rack. "You didn't know him—indeed, you just met him."

"We knew him well," Crikey said, "and we're eating him."

Rack spluttered, waved his arms, felt ridiculous, then felt ridiculous about feeling ridiculous.

"It's just . . . where I come from, eating your own species whether you knew them or not is . . ."

"So you have no problem eating other species?" Crikey asked.

"Well, I don't think that's the point . . ."

"But Wallow was injured. Fighting that monster."

"That killed him? He seemed all right." This rather muffled, because his beard had turned a bit truculent and he'd had to smooth it out.

"Pushed him off a ledge. Or, rather, frightened him into falling off a ledge. Same difference. Internal injuries, though he put a brave face on it. But he was toast."

"So now you want us to eat the poor blighter, insult to injury!?"

"Oh, give it a rest," Danny said, rearranging her beard, and to Crikey, "I'm sure Wallow will be delicious."

"Are you going to eat marmot?" Rack asked.

"Of course not. But I'm not going to whine on about it, either."

"I'll eat it," Jonathan said, looking particularly old as his beard had turned gray for some reason. "I'll eat the dead marmot. I don't care. It's what Dr. Lambshead would do."

Once again, Jonathan's tone was odd, his stare still distant.

"Fine, then," Rack said. "We'll all eat of the marmot and get sick and die in this foreign land."

"We could eat you instead," Crikey said, much to Rack's dismay.

"I'm not a voluntary meal."

"But it would be such a blessing to give you such an honor," Crikey said, showing his teeth.

"Help!" said Rack. "Help!"

Crikey laughed. "Oh, humans. So full of themselves. We wouldn't eat a human unless there wasn't a blade of grass in the meadow. And even then, we'd abstain. Eat, don't eat, but sit there and be somewhat polite. Or at least less fidgety. Nothing I like less than a fidgety human."

"I won't fidget," Rack promised, feeling he'd said his piece and now feeling foolish and angry that he was made to feel foolish about something so macabre.

"Any human customs appropriate for the moment?" Crikey asked with interest. "We're always collecting them."

Danny perked up. "Well, after, we might play my favorite: Marry Kill F—"

"I don't think that fits with this august occasion," Rack said, glaring at her.

"Oh, now it's august, yeah? Just because . . ."

But she trailed off, for the dance of wraiths around the flaming firepit had begun. A willowy, shadowy dance of full-on ghosts. They shimmered and faded and came back into focus down there by the pit, in and out of the flames. In such a way that Rack felt calmer, mesmerized, and would not have thought this would be his reaction. But it was.

It was Mamoud's turn to be discomfited, for he leapt up as the wraiths began to approach.

"Steady there, Mamoud. They're harmless, as I said. No one controls them, least of all Crowley, and left to their own devices they simply wish to live . . . for a while. So we let them."

"No," Mamoud said. "It's not the wraiths. Look."

"Oh, is the Comet Man here already?" And Crikey turned with a delighted look of anticipation on his furry face.

But it wasn't the Comet Man. Not the Comet Man at all. Even Rack could see that.

Emerging from the firepit in an awkward batlike lurch and then taking flight were a dozen huge demonic-looking black leathery creatures.

"Wretches!" Mamoud hissed. "Crowley's found us!"

"Battle stations!" Crikey shouted, and of a sudden the scene became utter chaos.

Already Stockton, Sprogg, and the marmots at the other table had risen, bringing out what looked like bazookas from concealment in peat moss and gravel. Were already shooting what looked like clumps of balled-up wildflowers at the demonic creatures. But wildflowers that exploded on impact, filling the darkening sky with a lurid smell and the taste of burning plants.

Rack drew his sword-cane, feeling helpless. It was useless unless one of these horror shows wanted to impale themselves on it at close range.

Danny fired the bear gun, releasing two bears that ran toward the firepit. She fell down from the recoil, Rack giving her a hand up. Jonathan and Mamoud, gun drawn, unable to look away from the scene, but backing up toward the relative safety of the Institute.

Now the Wretches, as Mamoud had called them, were all in the sky, trying to evade the marmot fire, even as the marpots turned bloodthirsty and also went on the attack.

"Release your shadows!" Crikey shouted.

And just like that, every last marmot's shadow detached from its marmot and flew into the sky to wrestle with the Wretches. Such an unexpected sight, Rack quite forgot to breathe. It was as if a manhole cover had suddenly curled up and become alive.

Although just as disconcerting, Rack noticed that Crikey did not have a shadow to send up in defense of the Institute.

That Crikey, this entire time, had never, as he thought about it later, had a shadow. How odd.

"For Swedenborg! For Reggie! For ourselves!" Crikey shouted at the sky. "Flee, Jonathan! Flee for the underground!"

And so they did.

Chapter Fifty-Three

THAT UNICORN IS JUST A COMMON TERRIER

Early-morning mist wreathed the magical wall separating England from the continent. The mist formed the ghosts of shapes and had a habit of re-creating like a visible echo the events of the prior days. So it faded, broken against the green lichen and moss that drenched the wall, that still muttered and cursed Verne, if under its breath. As if it knew he had won. And yet even as it faded, through those ephemeral glimpses, Verne relived again the desperate last charge of the Burrower, the break-through, the hand-to-hand fighting atop the wall.

All the craziness of battle, the confusion, the fray, being smashed out of the cockpit, dangling by his chain around his waist, bashed against the side of the Burrower, brought close to deranged demi-mage cages, with the demi-mages trying to get him every time he swung close, and then ultimately gravity and his own weight untangling the full length of the chain so that at least he was on the ground, in the scrum, the muddy ground, eye to eye with horrible magical minions, in hand-to-hand combat, hampered by the chain. And when he finally crawled back up, LX still firmly wedged atop his deadman's button. And how figuring out how to disarm the mechanism before LX, at that weird angle, unclenched his arms and buttocks and fell, exploding them all . . . well, it had been a near thing. But it was done.

Disconcerting, how the mist brought such bloody memory back to life for so short a period, and yet also such a wealth of fragrance: lavender and basil and rosemary. Almost as if some English wizard had thought to cast a spell to memorialize the dead of wall battles with scent.

For where would one find flowers or graves? Most of the dead had been swallowed by sarcastic thickets and guffawing ground cover. The wild garlic in particular, which grew mighty as cedar here, had the choicest comments for the vagaries of human conflict.

At least William the Conqueror Eel, in the end, had been no match for the Burrower. Eel remains still littered the landscape: a jiggly, sticky ichor that just wouldn't come off. Wouldn't dissolve into the ground when it rained, nor evaporate in the sun. They'd be wearing particles of William the Conqueror to the end of their days, Verne believed. It had made the demi-mages look even paler than usual.

Of the giant snails, the less said the better. After their writhing displays of sensuality, after all the disaster their wall had provoked, long after Verne had breached their blockade and was on to wrestling with the Eel . . . North Sea griffins had descended to feast upon them before flying off into the horizon.

It was, Verne had decided, some semblance of a cycle of life and should be taken as a hopeful sign: that even this chaotic place had some rules.

Besides, Grimoire R. Grimoire, the wall's librarian, Grimy for short, and he was short, assured them, "That wot was snail, comes back outta the ground, guv'nor. Guv'nor dig deep 'nuf, 'nuf said."

After a pause, Verne had said, "No, not enough said. What do you mean?" He could not tell if Grimy's English was bad or his own English was bad. But he was fairly certain no one was meant to speak the way Grimy did. Or, perhaps, understand someone the way Verne was understanding Grimy.

Grimy lived underneath an enormous pot he claimed had once belonged to an ogre, and had as a pet a unicorn the size of a terrier that snorted and huffed and glared bloody murder at Verne. He was sure the gnat-horse would have trampled him had it only the size to do so. Although he also wondered if it were an ensorcelled terrier that only looked like a tiny unicorn, because it did bark a lot and had not yet flown in Verne's sight, at least. Grimy fed the thing dog food and called it Flappy Spot.

Grimy was decidedly neutral about Verne's invasion, or pretended to be. "Am the 'iberian to all." Which would've made him Spanish, but that was not Grimy's point. "Whosoever ruleth the wall, ruleth Grimoire as well. And Flappy Spot here," motioning at the rabid tiny unicorn. Which also smelled like wet dog most of the time.

Within the ogre's pot, Grimy claimed, was a single book that held all other books about the wall within it. An entire history that Verne wasn't yet ready to examine.

"What to do about the . . . unpredictability . . . of the wall?" Verne asked Grimy.

"'Ad a look once," Grimy said, cryptic. "'Ad a peek at the peak of it. Hee hee. And wot I sawr waren't good, Master Verne. Warn't wot I sawr good a-tall. Good not wot I sawr."

"Yes, I got that," Verne said, although he hadn't.

But Verne hadn't yet gotten much further. Except to note that on the outskirts of the wall, amid the snarled mess and mass of vegetation that lay to both sides of the wall for several leagues, all manner of magical beast poked a head out from time to time. Although not yet venturing farther.

Also, on the interior he'd discovered tethered, no one to man them, a squadron of living blimps grazing the sky above forest and field. They had a vaguely irregular whalelike shape, sans fins, pockmarked and gray like the moon. Grimy told him they had started life as air potatoes on air potato vines, until the magic of the wall had, well, worked its unpredictable magic and turned them into living beings. Ones that were as overgrown with sarcastic plants and shrubs and creatures as anything else around the wall. Verne didn't much fancy commandeering them for military purposes, although LX was keen to.

Thankful at least that the Burrower, which lay now dormant at the wall's base on the continent side, had weeded enough of the opinion-ated plants that a road of sorts now led up to the wall. All his demi-mages were safely atop the wall for now, as he sorted out what to do next.

But what happened next had nothing to do with any of his plans. Or so it first seemed.

For, in the distance, a horseman appeared, fending off the last of the mini-dragons, a stray that hissed and spit only a little bit of fire. The horseman's sword arm was raised high, while the other, held low, carried some kind of . . . package?

A battle in miniature ensued, with the horseman managing to nick the mini-dragon's wing and discourage it. Whereupon the thing flew up into the sky, defeated.

The horseman continued his approach toward the wall and Verne's position. Soon enough, Verne could see that what turned out to be a haggard old man in antiquated armor held a human head under his arm.

"LX—prepare the demi-mages for attack," Verne said.

"I will if they will," Laudinum said. "Much is tired here." Whatever that meant.

"Oh, wise, sir, wise," Grimy said. Either his English was getting bet-ter or Verne's ear was.

Yet once within hailing distance, the old man dropped his sword and lifted up the head, almost as if in tribute.

"Stand down, LX," Verne said.

"Never got up, to be honest," Laudinum said.

Verne did not expect French to issue forth from the head or the hag-gard old man, and yet it did—from the head. The head was, truth be told, haggard-looking, too.

"How fortune shines upon us both, Monsieur Verne," said the head.

"How so . . . Head?" It was hard to rattle Verne after all he'd been through taking the wall.

"What? You don't recognize me. Should I be wearing a hat? Like in the old days. Yes, it is I, much diminished, and yet still: me."

"You!"

"Yes, me."

Napoleon!

Part VI

A LOWER POWER

"You'll be better pouched."

Chapter Fifty-Four

SARK AND JAUNTY BLUE

The sea behind Sark and Jaunty Blue was full of floating bodies, most with horribly anguished expressions on their faces. Sark and Jaunty Blue had been rowing for a long time to reach the shallow seabed just offshore, beneath a sky so bright and blue that had they not been long transformed from mere mortal beings they would have had to squint against its brilliance. The bracing smell of brine permeated the cold air, and it was in all ways a splendid day for both of them.

Sark and Jaunty Blue were full of arrows. Studded with arrows. Pincushions before man and god. But neither of them seemed to mind. As servants of the Builders, or at least some of them, nothing much fazed the two anymore.

Behind them on the open sea lay a sinking galley ship. Its sails lay in tatters, one mast broken in half, the rowing stations empty, smoldering in flames. The clatter of oars foundering one against the other became more and more muffled by the salt water as the ship drowned inch by creaking inch.

"Oh dear oh dear," Sark said, while Jaunty Blue pantomimed gurgling distress. "We're full of arrows."

Jaunty Blue fell over in the boat, dead, then straightened up again.

"The tailor's bill . . . now, that will be astronomical," Sark said, smiling at his longtime accomplice.

Jaunty Blue wore what to the unsophisticated might appear to be a sheet, but it was in fact a Fresian water robe. Jaunty could be quiet, but he could also be fast. And mean. Both qualities Sark admired in a compatriot.

Right now, his "sheet" was torn through with arrow piercings, though. It was only a sarky rumor that Jaunty Blue wore a sheet to disguise the bloody mess underneath, the result of a close encounter with a blunderbuss. Who could tell? Not Sark.

"Quite a dramatic, stirring sight, Jaunty—like a war-torn flag still standing on a hill after battle. Yes, that's right, Jaunty—I compared you to a flag. You should be proud."

Jaunty folded his arms and assumed a defiant position, down on one knee at the prow of the boat, causing considerable rocking and shaking.

But Sark was, as always, unflappable. There simply seemed no part of him that might ever flap. Rage, perhaps. But not flap. For he always looked rather like he ought to have an *h* added to his name just after the *S*—a sharp face anchored by a narrow brow from beneath which remarkable green eyes shone with peculiar force. As if should his gaze ever widen, the world might be in for a bit more trouble than the usual.

Jaunty Blue, as ever, dark eyes shining from pale water robe, appeared to be a little lost ghost, the kind who smelled of baby powder, so you'd invite it into your house out of pity, only to be left headless, you and your whole family, sometime around the serving of bread pudding for dessert.

Bread pudding was always a hit, Sark found, and worth delaying a massacre for, even mediocre bread pudding. Which could be freshened up with syrup. Sark loved syrup. Like some type of pollinating insect or a vicious, bloodthirsty hummingbird, Sark existed almost solely on the stuff.

Jaunty Blue preferred bone marrow, and always ate daintily under his sheet. Although at times it might blossom from the inside out with blood circles and the rich, rich smell of offal.

In truth, there was nothing much left of the original bandit duo of Sark and Jaunty Blue except some affectations and mannerisms of speech . . . but the two who peered out from their eyes had been very fond of the originals. Jaunty had been a handyman become a high-wayman, with a chip on his shoulder and an ax to grind that also was something he used to carry around with him. Of Sark's origins, the less discovered or repeated, the better.

Their heists in this glorious place had been stealthy and their means not those of ordinary highwaymen. For the estuaries had been their life's blood back when they'd been ordinary. They'd silently glided over old, ripple-less water and made landfall with the slightest bump of prow against pier and then docking before proceeding on foot for the next victims, only to sneak away by water unseen after.

Did Sark animate Jaunty Blue, or did Jaunty Blue animate Sark? Who could tell? Certainly not Sark and Jaunty Blue. But it is true they were never seen apart, rarely had a dissimilar thought these days. When they did, it was a matter of grave concern.

It seemed to Sark and Jaunty Blue that their glorious reign of terror had been without end, although they could each remember before, when—

Came then a searing rip and obliteration of the peacefulness of the floating bodies. Came the sonorous fleck-flicker of a tear in the sky before them and a hole forming in a deeper blue. The wind stopped. The stabbing smell of something ancient and stale and dead and yet terribly fragrant and electric. As if the sea had become made, for a moment, of human sweat and tears.

The galley ship behind them crushed to kindling, and the wind rose again across the shallow seabed, likely to smash their boat onto land while they held on for dear un-life and in the subsiding felt both relief and dread.

For still the chaos in the sky ahead lowered and began to conform to a type of shape with which they were most familiar from past summonings.

"We could ignore it, Jaunty Blue," Sark said. "We could go on with our glorious lives in this wonderful place. Raid more ships. Live the good life. With syrup and marrow forever."

But, onward rowing, Sark and Jaunty did go, for there had been a calling and a sending that could not be ignored, even on such a beautiful spring day full of corpses. Across the seabed they had loved so much before they'd been changed.

Ever peaceful they did glide and stride, glide and stroke until finally they reached the door now hovering above the water and prepared to climb through it.

Sark and Jaunty Blue gazed one more time around them.

"Our vacation is over, Jaunty Blue. Our days of simple robbery and slaughter over. Our service begins once more. Alas."

Yet there was a secret satisfaction in his tone. Even a beautiful morning by the seaside could become boring, without the infusion of diabolical plotting, or machinations involving entire worlds.

Jaunty Blue clapped his blood-encrusted hands together like an excited child. For Jaunty Blue would never be able to disguise his delight in returning to the Château Peppermint Blonkers.

"I wonder where we'll set up shop this time?" Sark pondered, for both of them. "And what do you think of the invoker? I'm getting an inkling. Trying to save its own skin. Yes, I think that's it. A worthy cause—none worthier. As for what we can get out of it, I suppose it's hide-and-seek, wait-and-see."

Jaunty gave him a look.

"Oh, Jaunty, you're such a romantic. No one ever escapes from the Château Peppermint Blonkers. The Builders made sure of that."

Together they made passage through the door in the sky, which closed behind them.

There came the terror of nothingness, and the ecstatic glee of nothingness, a cackle of knowledge that nothing ever really ended but was always beginning. Shoals of stabbing light enveloped them, faded into darkness, left needles in their minds from the journey.

Finally they both could see or at least glimpse hints of their destination.

"Oh dear, I remember this backwater. Prague, isn't it? And not even the good part—more the touristy part." Clucking his tongue. "Why not somewhere in Mali or Zimbabwe or the United Iroquois Nations? Well . . . let the games begin, I guess, Jaunty Blue."

Jaunty Blue was still too stuffed with arrows to give a reply.

Chapter Fifty-Five

UNDERGROUND NEVER FOUND

In the vast underground caverns beneath the Alpine Meadows Research Institute, the swaying mushrooms enormous as trees whispered and murmured and hissed while far overhead the blind subterranean cave albatrosses flew ceaseless and wide. Heedless, they would never know the light. But neither would they know the darkness—the maps in their heads were cupped by wing tips soaked in sonar, steeped in the years.

Jonathan knew this without thinking about it. Just as he knew that the enormous pale shapes in the distance must mean they had traveled far deeper than the marmot's burrows. For Sarah had told him this, too, in the stories, and thus he knew she must once have come this way as well.

Now they had come to places deep, deep underground where lived the marmots' darkness-drenched cousins, brethren who foraged on fungi alone and had traded fur for furry scales and whose teeth were gone, for all they must do is numble on the mushrooms with their lips for pieces to break off and become their daily bread.

This was a twilit life, one Jonathan and his friends fled through by no choice of their own, led by a map they'd surveyed only once underground, given to Danny by Crikey.

Of Crikey, they had no word and no way to receive word. Nor of his fellows. Nor of the meadow. Worst of all, what had happened to Dr. Lambshead? Was he still safe? Had Jonathan rediscovered his grandfather just to lose him again?

Four days thus far, to reach the subterranean island where lay the doors that would take them out of the mountains, likely to Prague, and except for the snort of death piggies in the distance, they'd been lucky.

If you could call it luck. It didn't feel lucky. It felt horrible and odd and out-of-body to Jonathan. The creatures that had come out of the rips in the fire were the least of it somehow. No more than a magnification of encountering a caustic carrot, a potato, a giant marmot that was actually regular size.

He'd kept his own council, been relieved no now-giant death piggy had come close, so he didn't yet have to explain to his friends.

For it was . . . too much. Too much, really, for any mind to keep up with. He wanted desperately to be alone, hiking somewhere alone, and yet he had all these companions by his side, who seemed unable to just be silent, even if most of the time they whispered in case of unseen threats catching wind of them.

Worse, Mamoud had said more than once he believed the Institute had been attacked because of Jonathan. Well, not that Jonathan could help being at the Institute. But that he had been the target. Which exasperated him and made him sad. There was nothing special about him. Sarah had engrained that in him, and he rejected any other idea. As pretentious. As dangerous. But sad because if others thought this way, then anywhere he went he would bring danger down upon. Not just on Aurora, but possibly now on Earth as well.

What did that mean for his future? Did he even have a future, except as a hunted animal? Was there perhaps some place so remote and wild it would gladden his heart but also protect him and wherever he lived from harm?

"Yonder through the gloom would come the lights of mushroom cities and of glowworms and of lightning bugs and phosphorescent mice wearing little hats," Sarah had told him.

Well, they'd seen none of that, but the fields of glowing fungi were enough to circumnavigate while not getting lost. They had drunk deep from what Jonathan knew to be pinprick wells, tiny in reality, and used his knowledge of the mushroom world to avoid being poisoned with the little they felt safe to forage.

Small complaint in the face of all the rest, but a final irritation: Jonathan was also extremely sick of how their beards kept growing even now, and thus they all four had had to wind them around their bodies and tie them off around the waist to avoid tripping on them or in other ways facial hair imperiling them. It was almost as if they were all tied up of their own accord, by their own bodies.

Ridiculous, absurd: A lone marpot had followed them below and attached itself to Rack, which thankfully had kept his attention off Jonathan. Who did not want the least bit of attention.

To feel out of place was to not know a place, and Jonathan distrusted how they all marveled at the black light show, the fireworks display, of luminous phosphorescence. At how even his eye was drawn to the unspurling drift of spores and the far glimmer of filaments growing from the ground to the ceiling. How there came in pockets of sublime silence the soft sound of gliding wing above. The murder of the voices of the dead, as Jonathan thought of it.

He couldn't figure out the right time to tell the others they'd been miniaturized. What would be the point right now? It would just unmoor them, unglue what glue still existed between them, set them at odds in some unpredictable way. Even as perversely he resented their comradery as they walked ahead of him, the easy way they had with one another, even as he felt closed off, alone. By his own choice.

There would be the tiresome task of convincing Rack it wasn't a joke and Mamoud's unwavering practicality and Danny's annoying way of turning everything horrible into something positive. And although he found in watching them banter ahead of him that he loved them all dearly, he could not deal with any of that right now.

Sarah was dead. Not hypothetically dead, not trace amounts of dead, but hopelessly dead. And Dr. Lambshead, almost a stranger to him, was alive. And he was no closer to knowing who his father was than before. He'd thumbed through the chapbook on the Builders Crikey had given him, hoping beyond hope for Sarah's annotations, but nothing had been scribbled in it.

Except, he also had a Voice in his head that was trying to convince him both that it was and wasn't there.

The shade in Jonathan's head was in places where it had no right. But when he closed his eyes, he saw it as a black-and-white starfish or jellyfish floating in a cosmic abyss.

Never had it felt more like he was not on Earth than now.

After a time, Jonathan reached out to the Voice, as he did periodically, expecting once again no response.

Voice, I know you're there.

Silence.

I know you're there. Where better than here to reveal yourself?

Silence.

In a softer tone, in his head: *Come out. Reveal yourself. There's nothing to fear.*

Silence.

I can't go on like this. I can't. It will drive me mad. I have to know I'm not imagining it. Please. Give me some sign.

Voice: I am here.

Hesitation. What next? Assuming he wasn't talking to himself.

Is that really you?

Voice: It's really me.

Who or what are you? Why are you haunting me?

(Didn't want to rush in with questions, but was afraid the Voice would leave again.)

Voice: You took me in. In the burning fields of Spain.

The wraiths. I suspected.

Voice: The faded. The fade.

You're a ghost. Haunting my body.

Voice: You absorbed me. Your magic. You have a very specific kind of magic. It stripped Crowley's spell from me but didn't kill me. It bound me to you. Perhaps because you cannot control it yet.

I didn't want you in my head.

Voice: You can make me leave anytime.

I don't know how to.

Voice: You will.

What happens to you if you leave?

Voice: I am no more.

So you want to stay?

Voice: I would rather exist than not exist.

So you pretended not to be there so I wouldn't make you leave?

Voice: When I leave, I will continue to fade and soon I will be like a dead leaf in the wind and then not even that.

You brought me those memories . . .

Voice: I did.

You can control me. You can make me do things.

Voice: No. Enhance. Access. Not control.

What happens if I let you stay?

Voice: I could show you more. I could help more.

Jonathan considered that.

If I'm honest, I can't be sure I can stand a Voice in my head over time.

Voice: It is confusing for me, too, at times.

If I let you stay, you can show me more memories?

Voice: If they exist. I cannot show you what isn't there. I can only draw out things that exist that you don't remember fully.

Who were you?

Voice: That is a much longer story.

Are you a magician?

Voice: No. But I can be whatever you want me to be. I could be Sarah, from your memories.

No! Don't do that!

Voice: I won't if you don't want me to. I can dull your memories of her if you like.

Don't do that, either. Leave me as I am. I don't want to forget her, but don't ever pretend to be her.

Voice: All right.

You're like a prisoner inside me.

Voice: A traveler.

But you know everything about me now?

Voice: Yes.

Do I have any privacy?

Voice: I have my own little space in a corner of your mind. I don't pry. I can show you the boundaries later, if you like. You can make me be in a smaller space. I only see fringes and wisps, though. But, yes, I do know you, Jonathan. We're sharing the same place.

Jonathan stared up at the wheeling albatrosses, trying hard not to stumble, trying hard to absorb it all.

Voice: Would you like to fly with them?

You can do that?

Voice: You can. You just don't know how yet. Shall I show you?

(Maybe the answer wasn't less strangeness, but more, Jonathan wondered, until he was so acclimated to it that it wouldn't register, wouldn't overwhelm, wouldn't be a wave crashing over him, but he would be the wave and it would just be the sea he was a part of.)

Yes. Please. Do that.

(Let me be not myself for a while. Let me be something else, or nothing.)

Voice: Than it shall be so.

Of an instant, he had jumped out of the shell he existed in into another vessel. One that seemed weightless in the glide and drift, and powerful in the expanse of wings and limitless in the workings of the albatross's mind.

The landscape below him was lit up in ways no human could see: ultraviolet luminous trails of voles and the chem trails of beetles in the air and the tracery of the lightning bugs' journey and even the heat-steam coming off the shoulders of the far-distant pale marmots. The grid of possibilities before him, opening up through sonar, which was like a gentle tickling trickle in the albatross's mind, a gentle babbling stream of information that comforted and oriented.

But beyond that, whispers of language and history, for shock of the unknown: Each albatross held a communal memory of the souls of dead explorers, a symbiotic relationship beyond Jonathan. But there it was, within the bird body in which he had hitched a ride: the tales and adventures of human explorers and nonhuman, of a wealth of stories crowded in that space, of all who had come under the albatross's gaze. It was layered maps and layered experience, all coming into his mind through the albatross.

He saw desperate, heroic last stands. He saw acts of kindness and the dying carried on stretchers. The pursued and the pursuers, and how this underground place subsumed them all in the end, and how the albatrosses mapped the bones, so that all that lay beneath the surface of this place was honored and remembered. As they flew tireless.

For the albatross was hundreds of years old, a grandeur that took Jonathan's breath away. The bird had seen so much for so long. So much more than Jonathan could ever hope to experience.

So high. So effortless, looking down on their little expedition. Looking down on his own body.

Came somewhere halfway to bliss, up there in the air, away from it all.

Chapter Fifty-Six
MAKING A HOUSE A HOME WITH A MOAT AND FADE PENS

"All talking animals within the confines of empire must report to factories immediately for identification processing. You will be treated with dignity and respect if only you put down your arms and turn yourselves in. Amnesty will be general and swift. You may return to your old lives as if nothing had happened. All you must do is proceed through the factory grounds for the processing. That is all. Just the processing, the processing of the processing grind your bones to dust you bloody great traitorous stupid beasts."

—Rough draft of a Crowley missive later edited by Wretch

Crowley's war elephant had come close enough to Prague that through his spyglass, he could see the topiaries near the Prague wall if he liked. Deep inside, in his heart of hearts, the place that still retained some love of gardens, Crowley admired the Czech topiaries.

Paris now being a shithole, Crowley rather would prefer to live in Prague awhile. Perhaps a new gleaming capital for his empire, new raw resources for his mecha-beast factories. More fuel for his Emissaries. More everything, perhaps. But mostly: calm. He needed more calm or soon enough he would go off on another larfing jag, and next time, more than the Speck to see it.

Cramped within his war room with the semiuseless map and semiuseless All-Seeing Puddle, it seemed the only option now. He'd ordered, or Wretch had ordered, the room cleared except for the three of them, the three now including Charlie Mange. Let him prove his worth. Or prove worthless. Although, Crowley grudgingly admitted, the raid on the Alpine Meadows Research Institute had been Charlemagne's idea, according to Wretch. Killed a bunch of talking marmots, which was always good, and now in hot pursuit of Jonathan. Also good.

Through the All-Seeing Puddle, Latrine and ET were speaking loudly, in panic-stricken tones, while Crowley tried to ignore how this made his heart beat faster. The Speck had recommended of late that Crowley try meditation, or rather return to it.

He'd been tempted to tell the Speck meditation was impossible when a bloated evil mosquito-bat was sucking the blood out of your head and replacing it every night. But he also felt a little bit of fondness for the Speck, looking out for his health that way. And at least he no longer had a bear body, and not for any reason other than it had begun to fail and Wretch had tired of helping Crowley around. Now he had a strong, young body Wretch had found somewhere on his nightly perambulations into the darkness.

Wretch didn't know it yet, but Crowley had set the Speck loose and it had scamper-rolled off into the forest, squeeing riotously. He had been unable to stop talking to it and even through the containment sphere and with his spells imprisoning the thing, Crowley feared it was beginning to have more influence on him than him on it, with all this talk of "friendship." Nor had he thought it good the way Ruth Less kept looking at the Speck's container. He rather thought Ruth Less's increasingly good and varied syntax resembled that of his mental conversations with the Speck.

Besides, he'd embedded a narsty magical sting in the Speck before he'd let it go—a bit of a hook and stab should Speck and Sphere reunite. Make Sphere go all wobbly, broadcast its location all unknowing.

This intolerable babbling from Latrine and from ET, muddled by the puddle. It gave him a headache. While Wretch listened impassive.

"The animal armies lie on our eastern flank, and within the city and on the west, the garbage mounds have been set ablaze, as obstacles for our mecha-army. There have been sightings of Rimbaud, and a guerilla force has taken and sealed off three quarters of the city."

"Three-quarters or three quarters?"

"Emperor?" A befuddled Latrine. The man could write a blood-thirsty decadent prose poem full of intricate language, but apparently not understand a simple question.

"Surely not three-quarters of the city."

"No, three quarters in the city," ET clarified.

"Very well—hold out as best you can."

"But, my lord," ET said, "some of the demi-mages and mecha-animals for our defense have already begun to leave Paris."

"How curious," Crowley said. It wasn't curious at all. He'd ordered them out of Paris. For one thing, the more demi-mages here, under his control, the more security for him. For another, Paris was now trapped between two armies and both Charlie Mange and Wretch had agreed that they could not easily turn their war elephant army around and get back to Paris with any sort of speed.

No, what made sense was to sack Prague, find the Golden Sphere, and with the powers contained therein make the entire universe of worlds his oyster. Plunder Earth for Aurora, leave them both desolate, and find a world behind the doors that was truly suitable for an emperor of his stature. Perhaps finding a way to consign Wretch to hellfire and a horrible death along the way.

Lately, Crowley had taken to fantasizing about cutting Wretch's head off and putting it on the body of, say, a chihuahua, or a medium-sized rat, and just watching Wretch-rat scrabble on the floor, doing little circles, unable to get much of anywhere. Certainly not able to fly or do horrible things to Crowley. If he decided to even give Wretch a body. Perhaps he would just keep Wretch as a head. Or half a head. Surely Wretch could still exist as half a head. But which half—side to side or top, bottom?

But that would have to be later. In the short term, Crowley had decided on taking a jaunt of sorts that might be relaxing. Away from his minders. One of his old friends from the other Earth lived out here, in the forest outside Prague. Perhaps he'd visit incognito. That would relieve stress. Bring back his friend to the war elephant as an adviser. Get an outside opinion on things.

Latrine in Paris was screaming from the All-Seeing Eye now. Something about abandoning them. Abandonment issues. Well, lucky Crowley had left some powerful demi-mages to help out and to make sure the two didn't flee or do something equally stupid.

"Hold out as long as you can," Crowley said. Maybe he hadn't needed meditation at all. Maybe he'd just needed to see other people panic worse than him. "Over and out."

The All-Seeing Puddle went dim.

"Forsooth, thou hast chosen rightly," Charlie Mange said. "Thou hast no choice but to fortify-eth and create-eth a base-eth."

"Jesus H. Christ on a stick," Crowley cursed. "Can-eth thou learn-eth to speak-eth properly?"

"Perhaps thou shalt one day-eth learn-eth my tongue-eth enough to proper understand-eth it. Mayhap one might hope."

"Children, Abt is here," Wretch said dryly. "Abt is apt and here. Despite still dying of cancer."

"Can't we do something about that? We may need him longer than he actually has left."

"Magic can't cure cancer. Cancer can only cure magic," Wretch said.

"Fair enough, Wretch. Fair enough. Send him in, or should we go up top?" It mattered nothing to Crowley. Up top was just as claustrophobic and frustrating as buried in the bowels of the elephant. Just a different set of obnoxious smells and still no room to breathe.

"Up top, Emperor," Wretch said. "He'll want to see what we've done already."

"Such as it is," Crowley muttered.

⁂

Such a sunshiny day! Almost parasol weather, if not for the gentle breeze and the lovely stitching of swallows in the sky above. Not a cloud up there, just that brilliant blue. Harshing the good vibe, Wretch had, for whatever reason, probably the cramped quarters, manifested as a kind of withered cindered smoldering wreck of a Wretch, barely a wisp of a Wretch, with just one huge bloodshot eyeball glaring at them all. Must be all the nighttime flying god knows where, Crowley believed. That and the toll of refilling Crowley's head every night.

Well, Crowley wouldn't need Wretch once he had the Golden Sphere. Not one bit.

Ahead lay Prague, and all around the war elephant stood other, lesser war elephants, and demi-mages and their underlings busy at a moat around them and around the fade pens also being built and then on the perimeter the lesser mecha-beings that were more mobile and the beginnings of a factory, which had required chopping down a lot of trees, which fact had not discouraged the nectar deer, which seemed oddly drawn, in the absence of shade, to trying to suck moisture off the faces of his men.

But, in short, there was a lot of hammering and sawing and black-smithies doing what they did and people brought up from the rear guard being herded into the fade pens, that they might become Emissaries in the fullness of time. Crowley had brought them from Paris, and now they would serve as the seed for more. Soon enough, if he could summon the energy, he'd create a magical trap that would bring more from other Earths over so they could properly fade and serve him as wraiths. It was a somewhat sad, disgusting process, but entirely necessary. Nothing was faithful like an Emissary, or more reliable, and he'd lost a lot of them in Spain and elsewhere. Hard to throw a proper terror into Prague without more faders drifting down out of the sky.

But Abt, who had been plucked by Wretch late from Switzerland, to which they'd allowed him to return for a time, seemed unimpressed.

"First I am to make it move. Now I am to make it not move."

"Verne made the elephants," Crowley said. "Not you. Don't flatter yourself, Abt."

"He could not have made the elephants without me."

"Just get on with it."

Abt seemed indignant, but put a hand to his chin, and contemplated.

"Well. You've got the moat all wrong. It needs to be deeper and wider. But also you need drawbridges at the points of the compass. Harder to defend, but when you have to flee the Republic or the Prague magicians, you'll be able to leave more quickly."

"Two drawbridges," Crowley said. "And Wretch here is happy to make you a head on a stick if you're insolent one more time."

There would be no defeat here. They had too many demi-mages, too much equipment. And now would build a fortress made of war elephants that would be sung about for ages.

"Your fade pens are vulnerable to attack by flaming arrows."

"Good. They'll fade faster if they're on fire."

Abt, taken aback, said, "Then all I may suggest, Lord Emperor, is that you send men ahead to widen the path to Prague and that you come up the hill to the wall. That is its weakest point and also the most level."

"Oh, possibly, Abt. Or possibly we'll drive some of our war elephants, already aflame, down the hill, so as to breach the wall with their tumbling bodies. I haven't quite decided yet."

"Nor hath I," Charlie Mange said.

"Shut up."

"Both of you shut up," Wretch said.

"What about me?" Abt asked.

Wretch rose up and became wave-large, and this torrent wave with a maw crashed down on Abt, bit him in half, and tossed his legs over the side of the war elephant, splashing blood all over a Charlie Mange and Crowley, who barely avoided being thrown off the turret to the ground below.

"Careful!" Crowley shouted, frowning at the messiness of the Abt torso and head left behind. Abt looked not so much terrified in death as both terrible and fairly surprised. "Are you going to clean that up?"

"Apologies, Lord Emperor," Wretch said. "So much has been so trying of late."

"Well, get it out of here."

"You get it out of here, Lord Emperor. I've been cleaning up enough messes."

"Well, will you *at least* pump some blood into Abt's head double quick so we can get his engineering advice in future."

"What's to get advice on? We're building a moat. We're assaulting the gates. Charlemagne will have a plan. I waited to hear some wisdom from Abt's lips, and none was forthcoming."

"Well, you didn't give him much of a chance," Crowley said. He had little impulse control, he knew, but Wretch was ridiculous. "Are you not getting enough sleep?"

"Never you mind that, Crowley," Wretch hissed.

"Never-eth thou mind-eth—"

"Shut up, Charlie Mange," both Crowley and Wretch snapped at the same time.

Crowley gave Wretch a look and Wretch the same back. So Wretch found the wight tiresome as well. Yet had some purpose for him, must truly believe in his military skills.

On the horizon now appeared a series of flapping dark birds.

"What's that?" Crowley asked.

Wretch smiled, a smile that took up his whole face and revealed once more his vicious teeth and the badness of his breath.

"Reinforcements."

Soon enough, a flock of ragged-winged Wretches circled the war elephant, their cries and jeers no doubt loud enough to be heard even on the streets of Prague.

Chapter Fifty-Seven
A NICE, QUIET NIGHT AT HOME, WITH TRUST ISSUES

No one could see Kristýna's house from the outside. What one saw, high up on the hill, to the east of the old fortress, was an old stone wall drowning in ivy and some vine with a small white flower that if you touched it, it pinched and you forgot where you were going. But especially you forgot anything peculiar you might have noticed about the wall close up. For example, the faint, faint outline of a door in the pattern of the stones beneath the ivy. Or the way the ivy would move even without a breeze in a sinewy, slow, mesmerizing way.

Inside, beyond the secret door, lay a courtyard riotous with flowers, wild and tame, and a little table with a lantern lit by glowworms, and beyond that the two-story house full of plants and curios that Kristýna had lived in off and on for several decades.

But it was there, in the courtyard, that she wanted to talk to Mack. Being in the house didn't matter—it had no memories for them as a couple, was, in a sense, the place she went to be alone, and Mack knew that.

Because she no longer trusted him.

Because it irked her that Mack's bulk beside her, so dapper and indestructible, had made her happy, had made her feel happy. Like she was home. Oddly. But not so odd. And not now.

Mack sat lounging on one of the wrought-iron chairs around the table, so casual she knew it was feigned.

No preamble for her.

"You let it into Prague. What is in Prague now. The old ways."

The marmot's shadow. Which, tethered or untethered, would start to go bad . . . oddly . . . would become more allied to the idea of the darkness than of the light. And, knowing that, she also knew that the animals were willing to take any risk to restore the Old Magic. And how could she blame them?

"It would have gotten in anyway. You know that."

"You don't care that the animals you serve don't trust you?"

"I don't serve them!" Mack, defiant. Good—glad to see emotion. What the shadow dulled.

"You don't know what you've done."

"What about the things you don't tell me? All the secrets you keep from me."

Upset now, so Kristýna knew his mood was dire. Again, good.

"Running a counterintelligence operation behind my back. Behind the Order's back. Using information from the Order."

"The secrets," Mack said, ignoring her. "Secrets about the Lambshead family, for one. From what I can gather from afar. About Earth. About s—"

"You betrayed me." Put it plain.

"I did not betray you! Not really."

Not really. Still parsing the difference, then. Aftereffects of shadow, or just Mack, no knife? And he wouldn't look at her, either.

"Explain it to me, then. How you didn't betray me."

"It doesn't hurt the Order. The animals just want balance. And that serves our purposes, too. And yours—if you'd only think it through."

"Stop defending them! They stole your shadow and spied on you—for weeks!"

"It doesn't change anything. They want a place at the table, so to speak. And that helps my cause."

His cause. Whatever it might be.

"But stewardship of the doors means that—"

"They don't care about the doors. I don't care about the damn doors, either. Pull back from your precious doors. Look at the bigger picture. Do you understand?"

The bigger picture? Did he not understand, even after all this time, the meaning of the doors? Of their impact? Of what could still come through them? The monsters. The deadly echoes of the past.

"Old magic is unpredictable. Other powers stand behind it. It lets in other things. It's only back because Crowley's destabilized Aurora."

"Says you."

"And what about Paris? Have you forgotten?"

"What about it?"

He sounded weary now. Disgusted. Contempt? Could she survive contempt? From him? Kristýna felt very old, like her blood had cooled and slowed. Should she give up? No. She couldn't give up.

"The two who followed us in Paris—I've been thinking about them."

"Why?"

"Because . . . they were too . . . wild. Too different. I don't think Crowley sent them."

"Your spies told us—"

"That he was sending someone after us, yes. And I think that was the demi-mage and the mecha-crocodiles. Not those two."

"Then, who sent them?"

"There's some other game being played here, Mack. One we don't quite see the outlines of. I don't think the animals, the old ways, see it either. Not quite."

"So who did send them?"

"I don't know yet. Someone who didn't like the outcome of the War of Order, perhaps."

"A member of the Order?" Scoffing. "So who is the enemy here? The old magic? The Order? Or do you see enemies everywhere."

"I see opportunity, Mack, which supports ambition. I see a moment in time, in history, where Crowley has created the kind of chaos that . . . well, anything might step into that gap. Several somethings. It isn't simple. It isn't straightforward."

"Or you're paranoid. Or you don't want to admit you're on the wrong end of things this time."

"I'm just pointing out possibilities." Hurt, hiding it.

Mack contemplated that.

"And in all of this, that you've thought about. Have you given any thought about why *I* might be on the side of old magic? As you put it so crudely. You've not asked me yet."

Because Kristýna had wanted to know the answer before she had to ask the question. So she would know if he was lying to her. Again.

"Why, then?"

"Isn't it clear? Why do I need to spell it out? Your doors have made one thing stark. There are too many Earths where Europeans colonize the world. We don't want Aurora, through Crowley or anyone else, to join them. So let Europe be in chaos. Divided. War of all against all. Let war exist here and not on our sacred soil."

"What's coming is larger than that," Kristýna said. So much larger.

"Not to me it's not."

There was so much he did not know, but she dared not tell him.

For example, she had lost contact with Alfred Kubin, and she didn't know why. He chose not to report, as far as she could tell. For example, the Order still didn't know what Wretch meant to let through the doors. For example, the rumors of the Château coming back into play . . .

And there was the phone call from Stimply to this very house. The brief one, in which he'd said, "Don't talk—just listen. This way of contact isn't safe anymore, but I'll be in Prague soon. I need to meet with you. Where can we meet?"

"Fester Growley Book Club," she'd said, and a date, and then the line had gone dead on his end. She thought he'd heard, but maybe not. But it was the only place she knew for sure she'd be, and as public as possible. Who knew who watched even the outside of this place?

"Are we enemies, my love?" she asked. Wanted him to have to say it.

Mack looked away. "No. Not enemies."

They fell silent, long enough to delay what might be inevitable, to reach a truce. Somehow, even silence felt like playing a role. Like, there was the her deep inside and then this outer person who must look the part from some other performance.

Mack, finally: "I don't know if we are together anymore, but we can't be apart for now."

"I still love you."

"And I love you. But that may not be enough."

The sweet, terrible relief that came over her, that made her tremble. It was all out in the open. And he hadn't just run off. That he understood the severity.

"Whatever you've done is done," she said, relenting, even if she wasn't sure she meant it. Because they still had a mission. Because, fatally, she felt she needed him for it. "But you cannot lie to me again. Promise me that. We're at war."

"I haven't lied," Mack said. "I just haven't told you everything."

And that was where they were now: a couple that not only kept secrets from each other, but admitted it. So many times the key was not saying it.

When she made no reply, Mack asked, "Will my shadow return soon?"

"Your true shadow? Yes."

"And I will feel less cold?" Less alone. Less like a speck in the universe.

"You will."

"Will that . . . shadow find me again?"

"It cannot reattach once unattached. Can it seek you out? Yes. But not become part of you again."

Mack slumped in a kind of relief.

"You'll be fine, I promise," she said, reaching out to clasp his hand in hers.

They stared at each other across the widening divide of the table, lit by lantern glow. Not like lovers or friends, but wary. A parlay under a white flag.

It hurt her heart, but she imagined it hurt his, too.

And that was the shame of it.

Chapter Fifty-Eight

THE FESTER GROWLEY BOOK CLUB

Later, Ruth Less felt peeved at how the Fester Growley Book Club gathering fell apart almost before it could come together. She had no experience of "book club," granted, it not being a subject discussed with Heady or the Tuft or the Speck. Or, Wretch, although she much doubted Wretch read many books.

Until recently, Ruth Less had focused more on the idea of "club" as a weapon or as an action, less like a convocation of flargdorneraks, as on her world, with their messy opinions and habit of eating the disagreer. Yet, the Fester Growley Book Club, in retrospect, still seemed disorganized and impolite and not at all pouch-worthy.

Ruth Less arrived early, to get a good seat, and perhaps a good early view of her prey. It had been vexing to make her way to the bookshop. She had eaten many who had called her fat and some who called her ugly. The ones who didn't talk to her, but stared, Ruth Less usually spared. But many needed to be pouched or punched. Including a few who called her a "dirty foreigner." The one who had propositioned her, she had just eaten as soon as she understood he meant a coupling. How rude! Couldn't he tell she was expecting little ones? Anyway, she'd decoupled him and he'd proven a good snack, which only helped the little ones.

In truth, she hoped she might not even have to attend the book club, but stage an abduction-extraction and, leaving the flargdorneraks to their fleemlypflargnak, be on her way. But, just in case, Ruth Less had made the effort to look normal.

That meant human-sized, or close, and a different appearance to her malleable flesh, given rumors were on the rise of a monstrous school-marm prowling through Prague. And some semblance of a suit, because she had decided she liked suits.

Hoping to disguise her mouth-parts, Ruth Less had grown a "hat" atop her head, which was really a thick flap of skin shaped like a hat, with a little red "flower" on it for color. In particular, a farmer's hat with a broad brim. And she'd decided she would look more mannish, although she wasn't in the first place a human woman, but an expert mimic from another world. Nor was her suit actually a suit, but instead just more strategically rearranged skin.

The flower was a third eye, almost like a periscope. Because of some-thing Heady had said about disguises in opera performances, Ruth Less had put on, or grown, an eye patch over one of her two eyes, which she could still see through since it just looked like an eye patch and was not an eye patch at all. All of it hopefully borne with grace.

Not for the first time, Ruth Less wished she had someone to share her cleverness with. She really was a very clever Celestial Beast, but she feared Wretch underappreciated her good qualities and saw only the bad. Because she had yet to pouch Jonathan Lambshead. But perhaps the golden marble would make up for it.

A pipe seemed in order—Abt had liked a pipe before he got splatted—and so, sproing!, a pipe it was.

Her shoes were just her feet, so she made them emerald and curled up at the ends like those of the hedge magician who had stared at her for too long from a hedge and whom she had pouched on principle, long gray beard and all.

Because Ruth Less was both early and a little bored, she cast her vast web of senses around the Twisted Spoon Bookshop, well beyond the sad little circle of chairs in the far corner with the sign in front that read "Reserved for Book Clubs" in Czech.

All those rows of bookshelves filled with tomes loomed over her, almost like walls of a maze, their guts made of paper. She could not avoid them, with their dead smell and sometimes a sharp glue smell or even something like turpentine.

When Ruth Less took a peek out the window, she was surprised to see the two who had no scent right outside on the cobblestone street, in the middle of a heated conversation. The tiny woman and the bigger man! The ones who had followed her. She knew from the Tuft that the woman was called Kristýna, and the Tuft had vouched for her. It was the woman who masked their scent by magic, that no one might track them that way. Which is why they only ever smelled, if they smelled at all, of the plants around them.

Suddenly, Ruth Less felt embarrassed by her suit. Even on her world, looking the same was not recommended, and she checked to see if anyone was looking and then changed it to a kind of tunic pants suit, in stunning greens and blues.

"What if it goes out the back door?" the one called Mack was saying.

"Don't be ridiculous. It's here for the book club."

"You think."

A pause. "All right. We wait a bit and then we go in."

"Have you read the book, Mack?"

"Of course. Have you?"

"No. I've been busy."

Curiously enough, hanging back against the ditch near the ivy-wall at the edge of the street, a kind of large shadow had been trickling along the stone the whole time they'd been talking. A rippling, undulating thing the couple didn't see. With a shape like an elongated . . . beaver? Hog? Bear? Ruth Less couldn't quite place it. On her own world she would have guessed it was a seethrawnikiwaki, a ghost leech that came back from the dead by sucking souls out of the blaghghghghghi underworld. But this shadow had not the courage to get too close to the couple, and hover-lingered in one position.

Ruth Less wondered if it, too, longed to go to the Fester Growley Book Club.

❧

Book club began with introductions. That made sense to Ruth Less. How could you discuss a book if you didn't know who everyone was, although perhaps the opposite made more sense: If you didn't know anybody, there would only be the book, which was perhaps truer to the idea of a book club.

Anyway, as preamble to introductions, the book-club grand leader or emperor, or whatever their rank, repeated the title and author of the book under discussion.

The fearless leader in this case was a harried-looking Czech woman wearing a flower dress. She had long gray hair and the smell of someone who had been drinking beer, and she said her name was Janovka Veraskayaskovask. The book, she reminded them all, was the detective novel *Goose's Way* by Michel Proost. It had been translated into twelve languages and a black-light theater production put on in this very city some years before.

Janovka asked for a show of hands as to who had read *Goose's Way*. Everyone had, although most hands only went up half or a quarter and then quickly down again. Ruth Less had put both hands up, suppressing the natural urge to grow even more hands and cause them, too, to show her polite enthusiasm for both "book" and "club."

"I would note," Janovka then said carefully, in English as a common tongue, but with much deep, suppressed emotion, "that this is the Twisted Spoon Book Club, not the Fester Growley Book Club. Which doesn't exist. This has been the Twisted Spoon Book Club for many, many years. If you are here because of posters calling it the Fester Growley Book Club, I hope you will still stay. And I presume you are. Here because of the posters. Because I see so many new faces. Well, welcome. Please introduce yourself if this is your first time."

Including Janovka there were nine regulars and five "irregulars," four of whom Ruth Less already knew were not the Golden Sphere. The fifth seemed unlikely to be the Golden Sphere for reasons that became clear during the introductions. Which left only the regulars as possible irregulars that might actually be a Golden Sphere.

Ruth Less was unprepared for the possible disappointment of no Sphere, even if the regulars on a deep snuffling sniff smelled nothing like the Speck or the residue on the poster. Besides, she quite liked a good mystery, in book form or in real life. They had no detectives on her world, only what might be called here "mob justice" and the "pounded" and "unpounded" criminals, all of whom were munched on until thoroughly eaten. This made more sense when you realized that without a certain amount of munching, Ruth Less's kind would have overpopulated their world in a matter of decades. Sometimes even noncriminals got munched, but Ruth Less didn't want to think about that.

Onward with introductions! Perhaps because she was so dashing and mannish, Ruth Less found that Janovka latched onto her, pointing and asking her to go first.

"I am an Iberian doctor on holiday who enjoys fishing, hunting, shopping for dresses, doll collection, and sheep days in the big city. My favorite books include wallpaper, omelette, and cheese grater."

These were all things from conversations Ruth Less had overheard or eaten while in Prague, and she felt confident she had used them correctly.

Janovka's smell, which had been a lavender bath wash on top of the beer stench, with an underlying sweat smell like mushroom liquor, now changed mostly to something like baked earthworm. On Ruth Less's world, this smell would have conveyed friendship or sympathy. Here, she doubted it meant either of these things.

"That is . . . interesting. Welcome . . . you did not give your name?"

A name! Ruth Less panicked. She hadn't thought to come up with yet another name! What names of demi-mages did she know?

"No-Name," she said, then saw Janovka's frown. "I mean, my name is . . . Charletta Mange." Then winced, remembering she had dressed like a man.

"All right, then. Welcome . . . Charletta . . . Mange."

Next up was the tiny woman. "My name is Petunia. I am a retired gardener who enjoys reading, gardening, and the simple pleasure of tea."

"Welcome," and this time Janovka's body odor told Ruth Less she greatly preferred Petunia to Charletta Mange. This hardly seemed fair, as Petunia's details had been boring even to Ruth Less.

Mack said, "My name is Mack."

"Anything to add?"

"I like books."

"Very well. Next."

Next was actually a regular who felt inclined to ramble on about book-club rules like no eating, no off-topic questions, no talking over anyone else, and that regulars should be respected given their commitment to the book club. Among many other ruminations that became overlong, and Ruth Less really felt the fellow should have been devoured by the other regulars as a sign of respect to the visitors like herself. But she bit her tongues.

Besides, during this ramble, a curious thing happened: Kristýna, who had been turning quite regular to the window, spotted someone there. More curious still, it was clear Mack, who hadn't looked at the window once, did not expect anyone.

At which point, Kristýna whispered to Mack that she needed some air, which Ruth Less didn't understand because there was plenty of air in the bookstore, if of a mustier varietal than what existed outside. And when Mack made to come with her anyway, Kristýna put a hand on his shoulder to indicate he shouldn't "in case something of interest happens," and she nodded at the group in apology, and walked outside.

To talk to the figure. Who was be-hooded and wearing such thick robes that Ruth Less could not make out . . . features. Like a face. Some sort of . . . mask? . . . was in the way? Bipedal, yes. Human, probably. The smell that came from the figure, who, like all skulkers, hid among the ivy on the far wall, was hard to untangle for Ruth Less. For it was on the one hand sweat, but also . . . stardust? Stardust from very far away. Sweat, stardust, and a stabbing sweetness. Along with trace elements of some pack animal's wool on the robes. Mud. Dust. The usual. And yet . . . yet Ruth Less felt all the smells were a disguise of sorts. Almost as if this person had anticipated a person like Ruth Less smelling him. Peculiar.

The voice from such a protected face came muffled, but still Ruth Less could hear them both. Even as the rules droned on. There was, she noticed, no trace of not-Alice or of the shadow.

"Stimply," Kristýna said. "You shouldn't be here long, and I need to get back in there."

"I won't be soon enough," the one she called simply Stimply replied. "But I had to speak to you. The telephone's not safe anymore."

"So you said. I haven't heard from you in a decade. Phone or no phone. You don't write. You don't visit."

"I'm sorry. So many, many things to be sorry about, but now's not the time."

Kristýna folded her arms. "Agreed. Speak."

"Jonathan is on his way to Prague. But not by the usual routes. And I'm not sure where exactly. The Institute has been attacked by Crowley. Crikey is dead and many of his fellows. Jonathan escaped, we think. It was a raid, not an occupation, but who knows what they ransacked."

"Did they find . . . ?"

"Not as far as we know. They've no clue. For all that helps, which isn't much."

"Is he . . . is he still there at all?"

"He still has moments."

None of which made sense to Ruth Less. These people and their irritating words. She knew "Jonathan" but then that word kept popping up everywhere.

Kristýna was quiet a moment. Ruth Less believed her facial expression was one of distress.

"And what do you want from me? More than I'm doing? This is bad news, yes, but it's already in the past."

"Find Jonathan. Send out tufts. Find him."

"That will take time. Just as we are planning a war."

"Everything takes time. And you're not planning a war by yourself. That's ridiculous."

"Is it now?" Kristýna said in a hurt tone.

"You know what I mean. I'm sorry. No time for the niceties. No time for putting on an act."

Kristýna was quiet again, then said, "You were not to get involved. At all. That was safer. But you got involved. You made *phone calls*, for example."

"There's no time, dear. Paris is about to fall to the Old Magic. There are rumors of the Château Peppermint Blonkers making an appearance. Celestial Beasts seem to be a dime a dozen, underfoot. Kubin's in the wind. Crowley's familiar isn't something he conjured up. At this point, you could practically say it conjured up Crowley, in a sense. It's chaos. It's not the same situation as before. The wheels are coming off, Kristýna. Please."

She considered that. "Noted. You may be right. I've been in this cocoon so long . . . Very well. I'll do it."

Stimply took her by the shoulders, looked her in the eye with . . . his eye or eyes, presumably?

"Be safe. Be well. Remember: We're not doing this for us. We're doing this for so many others. Now, I have to go."

"As always."

A peck on the cheek, a hug, and then the one known as Stimply was gone.

By the time Kristýna was back, eliciting a long stare from Mack, the rules were mercifully over and a woman was introducing herself: "My name's Janet and this is my pet gingerbread man . . ."

She pointed to the little irritated-looking gingerbread man sitting in the seat next to her.

Rules-Maker (Ruth Less had already forgotten his name) asked, "Has the . . . baked good . . . read the book?"

The gingerbread man said, "Up yours. Up yours. Up yours."

Rules-Maker appeared affronted, mouth open, trying to formulate the rule against "up yours."

Janet laughed nervously. "Apologies. He's just recently learned that."

"No, I haven't," the gingerbread man said. "I've known that one forever."

"Let's move on," Janovka said.

⁓

The last to introduce themselves, alas, did so about when the trouble started, when Ruth Less reflected on it later. A sort of last straw, and because of this and because she was still sorting through her own personal situation as complicated by Heady's advice, she neglected to tell Wretch and Crowley later . . . well, any of it except the last bit.

A late arrival had taken up a place, chairless, in the circle, and on all fours, that had Ruth Less's full attention. Crouching there was an all-white cow, one person or persons in a cow outfit. It did not strike Ruth Less as odd in book-club context, but it was odd to her. She thought perhaps the book club had a mascot or some such, but as Janovka turned a bit stiffly toward the cow-man or cow-men, her irritated scent gave her away.

"Oh, me? Moo. I am a forest cow, newly arrived from the forest. Of course. I cannot read, but I like using book clubs to improve my language stills. Moo. Moo moo moo mooooooo! That is all."

But everyone could see it was a pantomime cow.

"And your . . . other half?"

"I have no other half! I am a cow!"

The feeble movements of the other half contradicted this statement, until the upper half—the half with the face—hit the bottom half with the official book-club book and all nether motion ceased for a time.

But Janovka had had enough, could not leave it alone.

"I'm sorry. But . . . you're not a cow. Who or what are you?"

A reasonable question, Ruth Less thought, one as easily directed at her but for her marvelous disguise. Wretch had said there were spies all over Prague and to watch out for them. What better disguise for a spy than an all-white pantomime cow in a city so peculiar it was celebrating before a war.

"I am cow," said the not-cow.

"No. You're not. And you haven't read the book."

"How do you know?"

"I just know."

"I did too read the book. Sort of."

"Tell me about it, then."

"There are murders. And a goose is involved."

"No."

"You'll be better pouched," Ruth Less added, with kindness, but was ignored.

"Oh, let him be a cow. Let us all be whomever we want to," said a new voice.

Standing there, newly arrived, at Janovka's shoulder, was a preternaturally handsome man dressed all in gold thread, from his perfectly fitting trousers to his button-down shirt and blazer. And not showy, either, somehow. For each shade of gold was different, deepening and darkening the effect, with only the gleam of shirt beneath more like the blaze of true gold.

But it all smelled like machine to Ruth Less. It all smelled like marbles and moving parts.

"And who are you?" Janovka asked wearily.

"Oh," said the newcomer. "Introductions, of course. My name's Gob Smack. I'm just a poor sprot from a poor familial unit. Who has become uncomfortably numb. After brain surgery. I now make my holes the old-fashioned way: I squeeze them out. That's a joke, but you won't get it. Hey nonny nonny. I like sea shanties and long walks by the beach. And I read books—like this one."

Gob Smack held up the book club selection triumphantly, like a trophy.

Smelled like the Speck, in fact, except vile.

The Golden Sphere! Leapt up in her excitement, did Ruth Less. The Golden Sphere! Finally!

Several things happened at once, then, and Ruth Less only sorted them into their right order, to make sense of them, much later. It wasn't that she kept a diary, but often when there was conflict and confusion, Ruth Less found it helpful to reexamine the situation, to improve upon her reactions.

True, many of these actions were related to her personal situation and Heady. Some were due to her loyalty to Speck and Tuft.

1. She extended a ruthless pseudopod ending in a fist and smashed Gob Smack into the bookstore wall.

2. All the regulars fled.

3. Ruth Less extended a courtesy to Kristýna by using another tentacle with a face to scream at her, "Squishy says to exit immediately and leave this place! In the name of all the tufts!" Politely and in haste, Kristýna did not hesitate, but fled, taking Mack with her. Perhaps two Celestial Beasts in such a confined space was enough for her. Perhaps a talking tentacle was too much for her.

4. Ruth Less, in stepping forward toward the Golden Sphere, squashed dead the top half of the not-cow, whereupon the bottom half rose half-delirious from the wreckage of the cow suit and shrieked "I'm free!" and fled, too.

5. Janovka made a last stand, screaming, "I just wanted to talk about this amazing book! I just wanted to talk about this amazing book!" She clearly wasn't going to leave so Ruth Less, sighing, extended a third and fourth tentacle, punched a hole in the ceiling with one, grabbed Janovka with the other, and deposited her on the street

beyond, with a little kick from the sudden foot on the end of the tentacle to give her the hint to flee, flee, flee, and forget the book. Which she then did. (Ruth Less was rather sorry to see her leave; in retrospect, Janovka was the only one she would've liked to sit down and share a meal with. Perhaps even talking about books.)

6. Gob Smack pulled itself from the buckling wall, no longer a golden man but a golden sphere, and raced toward her. Whereupon she punched it into the wall again.

7. Giving her time to empty the contents of her pouch onto the streets of Prague, via the bookstore's front door. So many things, with only one left inside for later, per prior agreement with the "thing" in question.

All the things that had been in her pouch! As they left and poured out into Prague in all their magical and nonmagical excess, she sighed in relief.

Some of the things included: bears bears bears. But also, a horse and cart, several dozen cats, a couple of Czech magicians, a few stray circus animals, a few trees, an anvil, a windmill, a wall, a giggly air-breathing sea anemone, a man wearing a bird mask, a thousand red newts, a few dozen confused-looking lighthouse keepers, a giant bird of some kind. Too many things to count or keep track of. Some of them, Ruth Less admitted, were monsters.

There. She felt much lighter, and ready for battle.

Ruth Less turned to face the Golden Sphere in the now-empty, much-destroyed bookshop.

"Squishy for you," she said.

Chapter Fifty-Nine

THE TWO POWERS

The Golden Sphere found the creature known as Ruth Less beyond rude. Beyond any kind of polite decorum—she was unreasonable and uncouth and a terrible conversationalist and in all ways the Golden Sphere despised her and now wished that It had not called a convocation of a book club, but how could It have known that—

"Pow," Ruth Less said after having overturned a table and some chairs and a whole row of bookcases, the Golden Sphere now exposed, at least for a moment.

"Pow, you say?"

In a most surprising way, Ruth Less's head boomeranged at the Golden Sphere and smashed It through the bookstore wall, onto the street beyond.

"The rudeness!" the Golden Sphere shrieked. "Do you know who I am, you wretch!" Except Wretch was the wretch. The Golden Sphere truly had no idea what Ruth Less was. Was running analytics fast all across its vast memory. Looking for a parallel or an analogy or even the Thing itself, whatever Ruth Less might actually be. But finding nothing in the millisecond before Ruth Less burst through the remaining wall, which gave up the ghost, and onto the street next to It.

"Smash," Ruth Less said.

"No smash!" the Golden Sphere said.

But Ruth Less smashed. Ruth Less made two feet into one monstrous foot with clubs on the end, and that foot came down and smashed the Golden Sphere through the pavement, leaving It embedded a few feet below the ground.

All righty, then, if it was going to be like that. It could play the Speck, too. It could be Specky, as they'd learned in Rome.

So when Ruth Less removed her foot and regained her form and peered down into the hole she had made, the Golden Sphere was nowhere to be found. Instead, there was a tiny marble rocking back and forth.

The Golden Sphere waited until Ruth Less was peering down into the pit, then went all spiky and big.

In theory, this should have cut Ruth Less's ugly face to ribbons and sproinged her brains out the back of her skull. But at the moment of spiky, Ruth Less was no longer looking into the pit, but impossibly swift had moved to the side, so the Golden Sphere, braced for the impact of Ruth Less flesh, fell forward farther and faster than anticipated and crashed into the stone wall opposite the bookstore.

First thought was embarrassment. To be caught looking so awkward. But, fortune shone: Not a soul walked the streets. They'd all disappeared for some reason.

Then—It had to work on its reaction times, clearly!—Ruth Less was whispering near an ear It did not have, for the Golden Sphere was all ears and all eyes—and all fists.

For rather than listen to Ruth Less, the Golden Sphere punched out with a myriad of golden fists in all directions. Once again, missing.

What had Ruth Less said?

"Squishy for you, sad buoy. Squishy for you."

And of a sudden, before the Golden Sphere could un-think its own fists, all these soft tentacles had erupted from nowhere good and entangled the fists and the Golden Sphere could not stop from reflexively fighting back and thus the fists became more entangled, but worse, It had not anticipated the larger tentacles that followed the smaller and these tentacles were somehow seeping into its body, into its core self!

"Arggggh!" And the Golden Sphere spun itself around and around ever faster until it was a whirling dervish, it was as a ball of light traveling almost at the speed of light and tentacles flew everywhere and everywhere was splattered with tentacle blood, which was a light green and malodorous and disgusting and the Golden Sphere kept whirling longer than It needed to so It could spray a dose of water across itself from its internal water system that It might feel clean and not icky-sticky.

Before It could change shape again, or size, though, Ruth Less, who had been standing nonchalant while the tentacles icked the Golden Sphere, now slapped It from both sides with hands grown huge and flat and powerful. Slapped It senseless, something vital inside dislodged for a moment, so It plummeted back to the ground, the street, and had an impression of the sun and trees above and a bit of tall wall and the birds flying there were only in its head, It was fairly sure.

"I will pouch you," Ruth Less boomed. "Then you will be good."

"You already punched me, Lug," the Golden Sphere said, still dazed. "And I am good. Already."

"In the pouch you will be better." One huge hand descended on a monstrous arm, like some sort of fleshy crane.

The loose bit rolling around inside the Golden Sphere settled back into place and It went flat, nothing more than a golden shadow on the cobblestone, so that Ruth Less's arm missed and swept past and took out a last bit of wall across the street. Oh, Prague, you will never look the same. They will speak of this battle for . . . at least hours. Until the next thing.

The Golden Sphere as hole had benefits.

"You want to pouch me? ME?! I'll POUCH YOU!" the Golden Sphere screamed, although It didn't really know what Ruth Less meant by being pouched. Poached? Punched? Pooched?

Yet still as Golden Hole, It flipped up, ghost of a manhole cover, and attempted to engulf Ruth Less in the holy hole, the empty golden mean. For the Golden Sphere was mean, and crafty, and bitchy, too, at times, and in flipping up to engulf, the Golden Sphere roared with rage at having been thwarted and put all energy into it and all momentum, became a midnight sun burning across Ruth Less, over Ruth Less, and soon Ruth Less would be sent to another place, the place the hole directed. Somewhere on Aurora, true, and definitely still in Prague, for the Golden Sphere was trapped, but definitely Not Here.

Except the Golden Hole became, upon encountering Ruth Less, a Golden Hula-Hoop, and fell down around her stomach, then her knees, then her horrifying feet, which had clearly never received a pedicure for thousands of years and had little faces staring up from them, and snapping fangs.

By which the Golden Sphere understood that Ruth Less was also a Celestial Beast, no mere creature. And the holy terror of that was in no way matched by the horrifying spectacle, audience or no audience, of Ruth Less clamping onto the sides of the Golden Hula-Hoop and twirling It around her hips, and in that dizzying display, attempting to, at the same time, the Golden Sphere disoriented, tear the Hula-Hoop apart and shove the parts in her pouch.

Was this the end?

Was It to be dismembered and pouched?

Was that to be the last thing in the obituary?

No! It was too cruel, too crass, too . . . stupid-pathetic an end, and so the Golden Sphere went limp, turned to liquid, and fell in puddles and drops to the cobblestone street.

Screaming the entire time, for this kind of dissolution was terrible pain for the Golden Sphere and a kind of temporary death.

And yet *still* the Golden Sphere might not have escaped from Ruth Less if not for the sudden blinking into existence of half a dozen flying Crowley heads, which distracted Ruth Less enough for the last few drops of Golden Sphere to disappear into the cracks in the pavement.

The Golden Sphere had never been happier to see flying Crowley heads in its entire life.

Would forgo sending back a grand piano, as a thank-you.

Chapter Sixty

BEYOND THE DARK SEA

The phosphorescent light show the underground world had put on for them impressed Rack not one bit. Smoke and mirrors. Bits and pieces. Just another slog through a bog.

He was bloody well sick of walking over uneven, rocky ground and through mud. It mattered nothing to him that along the way magical birds soared overhead or that giant mushrooms glowered and glistened, shedding pink-emerald-turquoise light upon them like some kind of bargain-basement version of an amusement park.

Oh, the smells that none of the others in their oohing and aahing wanted to admit to: the stink-stench of exploding puffballs and the unwashed blorg of critters in the night that he didn't even want to think about. The un-phosphorescent beasties hiding in the shadows.

One of the marpots had followed Rack underground and appeared to have imprinted on him, for it floated in his shadow and burbled at him constantly.

"What am I to do about this bloody marpot?" Rack asked.

"Why don't you marry it?" Mamoud said.

Rack glared at him. "You've been in an odd mood, mate, for a bit now." Although not as odd as Jonathan.

Mamoud shrugged. "Odd times call for odd moods."

Worse, despite attempts at trimming, their beards continued to grow, so they'd had to sling them over their shoulders, which made the journey more difficult.

Danny had wound hers like a scarf around her neck, although it was itchy.

"When will this wear off?"

"Once we are through the door, Crikey said," Mamoud told her.

"I wonder how Crikey's getting on," Danny said, wistful.

"The Institute has survived worse," Mamoud replied. "You saw they were prepared. With wildflowers and shadows."

Rack hadn't mentioned Crikey's lack of shadow. He'd begun to believe he'd imagined it. Or rather not imagined it. Or . . .

"It would be nice to know they're still alive," Jonathan said.

"It would be nice to know we're still going to be alive tomorrow," Rack said. "I'd settle for that."

Strange sun, strange light from the ceiling of the cavern. Conspired to look like a sullen white ball of dull light, but couldn't be. Must be some trick of the eye. Some trick like picking the right card out of the deck. Yes, Rack preferred to think of it that way than some other, more majestic way. Keep it all small-scale and it was less likely to freeze your brain.

So what if the arc of heaven, the horizon, gave them a nice view of an iridescent underground sea? Likely, that meant an oil slick of some kind or more of the unnatural magic that everyone kept saying was natural here. Everybody seemed to forget that it was his sword-cane that had to be swung when the hollow reed-weeds that whispered and sang had to be cut down. He didn't much like cutting their voices off midstream, but, then, he didn't like that the path they followed was so overgrown. Truly, no one had trod this way since Napoleon's men.

Well, at least the furless translucent giant marmots grazing on a disgusting banquet of puffballs, tendril fungi, and other not-delicacies had been put in the rearview mirror. They were in uncharted territory to reach their goddamn next set of doors. Which apparently existed inside the tower on the island in the middle of the underground sea. Naturally. Or unnaturally. What less could he expect?

Nor had there been any sign of what Mamoud called "the Wretches."

In short, Rack was in a fine good humor as they took to the dilapidated dead-calm sea, with its ripples and shimmers of shoals of fish beneath the surface, almost like a reflection of the murmurations of starlings, under the dark water. Sparkling murmurations and he almost for a second forgot himself and said out loud, "That's beautiful!"

But he was too wary of more deadly puffins to truly relax, and too aware of how any shift by him or his companions made the rickety contraption shudder and list. Yet it felt good to put his back into rowing, both oars—he'd insisted, after Jonathan's and Danny's help navigating the land.

And by jove, they were out across the sea (or was it a lake?) in record time, oars cutting into that becalmed surface like breaking the crust on some perfect crème brûlée. One that was full of tiny fish inside. He could almost forget the ache as he rowed, the pit of hunger, as they tried to preserve what provisions they had, and the water, too. For to drink from any water source down here seemed foolish.

The scrape of the prow gentle against the rocky shore of the island, the sudden reality of the lighthouse looming above them, with its ridiculous candy-cane coloring, thankfully eroded by time and the common sense of someone's decision not to apply a new layer of paint, perhaps because everyone was dead . . . could not be ignored.

"At least we're there," he groused. "At least I got us there. Me, I, the one least equipped for this mission. Even as I fade. Are you all fading, too? Jonathan—no? Danny—no? Mamoud—of course not."

"You're not really fading yet, Rack," Danny said.

"I think I'll be the judge of that."

"You're in the dictionary under 'famous hypochondriacs,' yeah?"

"Did Tee-Tee tell you that? Well, I'm touched he cared enough to look me up."

The rat was an unkempt guardian on Danny's shoulder, as like to sigh as sneer. When they sang songs about their quest, the rat wouldn't even be comic relief.

"Are the doors supposed to be inside the lighthouse?" Jonathan asked. He was still moody, but at least not of the sort where he was unresponsive. Once they'd hit the sea and the boat, some of his melancholy appeared to have lifted.

"That was my understanding," Mamoud said as they walked up the path, the lighthouse looming like an old-timey monstrous barber's post above them.

"Did Crikey say what else was inside the lighthouse?" Rack asked. "And did he tell you all this . . . gunk . . . would be outside?"

"No, Crikey didn't say," Mamoud said. "I imagine we'll find out soon enough."

By "gunk" Rack was referring to the barnaclelike eruptions that had gathered all around the base of the lighthouse except the path leading up to it. Large as a person's head. Lumped on top of one another. A bunch of closed holes that could open at any moment revealing something dangerous or, at the very least, loathsome. Didn't help the whole island smelled like a spicy cologne and cotton candy, as if an amusement park clown had died going out on a date to the lighthouse.

"Fascinating," Jonathan said as they passed the gauntlet of "gunk" to the door. "It's hard but soft."

"If you say it's squishy, I shall scream," Rack said.

❧

Inside, the lighthouse was very much like any lighthouse, Rack imagined, although he'd only seen them in video games and once near Brighton. The idea of climbing up into one had never really suited his fancy. The ground floor had a gutted kitchen and a space for the lighthouse keeper's bedroom and living room. Not much of anything in it, though. Just a kitchen table with three legs, holding on just barely to the concept of being a surface people put things on. A couple of old rotting chairs. A disturbing brass sign read COELECANTH, INC., like the funicular, and the same >o >o symbols, which seemed destined to remain mysterious. Disturbing (but old) patterns of blood on the floor.

"Do you think that's meant to be artistic?" Rack asked. "The blood, I mean."

"Ancient," Mamoud said. "No one's been in here for a very long time."

"And that doesn't worry you?"

"How so?"

"What if there aren't doors here anymore?"

"I trust Crikey," Jonathan said.

"Crikey ate his friend," Rack reminded him.

"And because you're my friend, I will eat you when the time comes. Don't worry."

Which made Rack chuckle. Which made Danny laugh, and then for some reason that made Mamoud hoot like an owl, and before Rack knew it they were all doubled over laughing hysterically. He tried to manage a comeback, but he was giggling too hard.

"Eat you, too," he finally blurted out.

"Eat you three," Danny said.

"Eat you four," Mamoud said. "With relish."

"Ahhhh," Rack said, and gingerly sat down on one of the chairs. It held his weight well enough. But he wouldn't bet on it in an hour.

"Where do you think the doors are?" Danny asked.

"Up top?" Jonathan guessed.

"In that case, you lot go find out and I'll hold down the fort from here," Rack said.

"I'll stay here with you," Mamoud said, and sat down in the chair opposite Rack.

"We'll be back soon enough, yeah?" Danny said.

The two disappeared up the stairs.

Leaving a marpot floating above two heavily bearded men facing each other across a table. A table with a very large fossilized round of cheese lying next to a rusted knife and some crumbled-into-dust crackers.

"Do you think they're any good?" Rack asked. "Maybe the marpot would like some."

Mamoud turned to Rack, said, "Rack. My beard is too long. You

BOOK TWO: THE MARMOT'S SHADOW

534

must braid it so I too can throw it over my shoulder and not tie it around my waist, which is itchy."

"Only if you do the same for me, mate. I feel like some kind of over-grown moss creature."

And so it began, an epic braiding of the beards in an underground lighthouse by a midnight sea.

"You have very soft hair."

"You're very good at braiding."

❧

Half an hour later, with Jonathan and Danny still up top, Rack had won a hundred pounds off Mamoud playing cards. Their beards no longer getting in the way. Although Mamoud could not explain the exchange rate to Rack.

"Do you mean Earth pounds or Aurora pounds?"

"What would happen if I exchanged Earth pounds for Aurora pounds?"

"You'd be arrested for counterfeiting."

"Not the same faces on the bills, I gather?"

"Not even human faces," Mamoud said. "A lot of hedgehogs, bad-gers, and crows. Ravens. Wolves."

"I could draw animal faces on my bills."

"And then sell them as art."

"You haven't seen my talent for drawing, have you?"

"Is it as good as my talent for jokes?"

"Not even."

Footsteps, then, and Jonathan and Danny appeared. He could tell from the looks on their faces they hadn't found the doors.

"What was up there?"

Danny and Jonathan exchanged a glance. Then Danny said, "A lot of dead Napoleonic soldiers."

"Skeletons," Jonathan said. "Some sort of last stand . . . something must've come in the window."

"Garrison post," Mamoud said. "Interesting. So Napoleon's soldiers lived down here for a time."

"Less interesting than the answer to the question: Where are the doors, then?"

Mamoud tapped his foot. "Under here, maybe? There's a trapdoor. It's a tower and a tunnel."

Rack scowled. "How long have you known?"

"About the time I had lost fifty pounds and stamped my foot in frustration at my poor card skills. Too late to do anything but wait until they got back."

"You mean my amazing card skills," Rack said.

"Your beards look different," Jonathan said.

"You noticed, so you care," Mamoud said, giving Rack a look.

Which is when a telephone began to ring from the living room.

❧

They found the telephone under the rotting lounge chair, which had to postdate any sort of Napoleonic style. Best not to think about that, Rack believed. Best to ignore the telephone and open the trapdoor. But this view was not shared by all.

"I have to answer it," Jonathan said as they all stared down at it like it was radioactive.

"It's just stupid old Stimply," Danny said. "Even Tee-Tee knows he's a fool, yeah?"

Tee-Tee gave her a stern glance. "Oh, sorry, Tee. I didn't mean it. I really didn't."

"She really did," Rack said. "No, Jonathan, you shouldn't answer it."

"We have to know," Mamoud said. "We have to know. Just in case."

"How does Stimply keep finding us?" Danny asked. "I don't like it. And if it isn't Stimply, whoever is on the other end will know we're here if we answer."

"When has it not been Stimply?" Jonathan asked.

"I just want to note for the record, once more, that this telephone has no cord and we have seen no evidence of telephone poles down here," Rack said. "I just want to note that for the record before I pick up the receiver."

He picked up the telephone as Jonathan protested, but Rack fended him off. "No, no, and no. You've answered too many of these calls, and it's taken a toll. Perhaps it's even why you've been so bloody moody these past few days. No, don't protest that, either, Jonathan. We've all seen it. Yes, we've seen a lot, endured a lot, but it's like you've become some kind of zombie. I will not have you become yet more zombified by taking a scarifying call from a fool."

"But . . ."

"No buts. I just won a hundred pounds of some sort. I'm finally ahead on this cursed world, for once. I'm feeling good about things. Let me take the depressing telephone call."

"Someone answer it before it stops ringing," Mamoud said.

Rack turned away from them and picked up the receiver, said nothing.

Silence. Then, a thin, reedy voice, somewhat like what Rack remembered hearing from a distance when Jonathan was on the phone with Stimply. But he wouldn't have testified to that in court.

"Hello? Jonathan Lambshead? Are you there?"

"Meow," Rack said into the telephone.

"Er, Jonathan?"

Rack barked into the receiver, now fending off Jonathan, who didn't seem to think that was funny.

"Stop playing around, Jonathan!" the voice said. "You're in a serious trouble."

That brought Rack up short.

"I'm in 'a serious trouble'?"

Silence again. Then, slyly, "Jonathan?"

"This is Pierre Wainscott Loudwright III, foot soldier to His Excellency's Imperial Army, commanded by our Lord Napoleon Bonaparte."

"Napoleon!" Stimply hissed.

"No, one of his soldiers."

"You're lying. Put Jonathan on the phone," Stimply said. "It's important."

"Jonathan? Who's Jonathan?"

Silence, and a disconcerting growl, a sound like a snapping of jaws or maws.

Then: "I have a message for Jonathan—could you put him on, please? Yes, put on Jonathan. It's his old friend Stimply J. Nightingale, Esquire, with important news for Jonathan, very important news." The voice treacly this time and a tickle of warning in Rack's heart. For the voice was like a question mark becoming an order in his head, and he didn't like how it was also like a hook, caught there.

"There's no Jonathan here, but you can give me the message if you like."

"Who are you, again?"

"I am Pierre Wainscott—"

"YOU ARE NOT! YOU ARE NOT!"

"Now, now, Stimply J. Nightingale, I don't know who you think you are, but that's no way to talk to a member of Napoleon's elite garrison."

"PUT JONATHAN ON NOW OR I SHALL FLAY YOU ALIVE IN YOUR OWN JUICES, YOU—"

But Rack had hung up. He was trembling a bit. As much as he'd tried to be brave, the voice had been so frightening he was glad he hadn't pissed himself.

"I think we need to get to the doors," Rack said, "and now."

"So . . . was it Stimply?" Jonathan asked.

"It was much worse than Stimply," Rack said. "But I have no idea who it was. Or Stimply's gotten very evil in a very short time. Turned into a demon. Eaten some bad chowder. Didn't have his coffee in the morning. Hasn't taken a shit in some time. Doesn't want to—"

Danny shook him. "Snap out of it."

Rack clung to her. "Oh, thank you, sister-blister. Its voice was like a bad spell."

He didn't know why he thought "it" instead of "he," but he did.

Under the trapdoor was a kind of revelation. The small, square room was made of glass on three sides, revealing the same odd twilit scene with fading, slow swallows as the haunted mansion back on Earth. The ceiling was stone painted white, and the far wall had three doors embedded in it. Well, hardly even doors. More like archways for normal-sized marmots—just big enough they could squeeze through them. But not in any way that would make them feel safe.

"Ignore the glass," Mamoud said. "It's a distraction."

"Is it?" Rack asked. "Or is it the point?"

"Not for us," Mamoud said. "The doors are the point."

"He has a point," Danny said.

"Let's just get to the surface, yes?" Jonathan said, and his tone of voice indeed brought them right up to the doors, strange scenes through glass be damned.

That's the real point they were at now. Odd scenes through glass—ignore that. No time for that.

None of the three had been officially marked, but someone had painted words above each in red, with an arrow pointing down. In order, the doors were marked PRAGUE, NOT PRAGUE, and NEAR PRAGUE.

"I do not want Not Prague," Rack said.

"What if it's a trick?" Danny said. "And Not Prague is actually Prague."

"So then Near Prague would still be Near Prague," Jonathan said.

"That sounds quite reasonable," Rack said, "so it's terribly, horribly wrong."

"You can't let death piggies rule your nightmares," Jonathan said. "Not forever."

"Yes, we've encountered so many other things that provide nightmare fuel for me," Rack said, truthful. Oh, for a nice, dependable death piggy right about now.

"If the door is Prague, it's a trap," Mamoud said. "Prague will be closed off by Crowley. No direct doors in or out. And I think we have no choice but to trust the signs. We should choose Near Prague and take our chances."

"Let's take a vote, yeah?" Danny said. "I say Near Prague."

She raised a hand and Tee-Tee raised a paw.

"Tee-Tee gets a vote?" Rack said, eyebrow raised.

"Near Prague it is," Jonathan said, and raised his hand, as did Mamoud.

Rack sighed, deeply. With an exasperation he felt in his bones.

"So if I want to fork off to Prague or Not Prague, I guess I'm on my own . . ."

Strange, unpleasant tearing sounds were coming from above, right about where they'd barricaded the door with the pathetic furniture from the lighthouse.

Near Prague it was, then.

Chapter Sixty-One
SPARE A GOLD COIN FOR A DOWN-AND-OUT GILL-LAD?

The Golden Sphere had never been happier to see any human being than It was to see Kafka once It had reconstituted itself underground. That this had taken hours was infuriating. That it had required so much re-joining and so much irritation and hurt was beyond maddening. To have to share space and commonality with grubs and earthworms and moles grated on the Golden Sphere's last nerve. It did not like Nature or nature—that was not in its ultimately mechanical nature. The ooze and stink, the gelid soft putrescence. Ick and ick. Icky icky icky!

Yet still the Golden Sphere, being tough, had reconstituted. It had taken on the disguise of an entire coach for hire, of the variety that already looked like a transformed pumpkin from a fairy tale, inhabiting also the dead-puppet at the reins and the horses, which if one looked closely in the dusk light were connected by reins and bridles that were long vines of veins and themselves composed of sphere-concentrate and thus as hard as steel.

The Golden Sphere now found Kafka, the salamandary man-lad, guardian of the Prague wall, in resting gill-mode, enjoying a quiet moment in a small squalid pool full of algae-plagued water. No doubt after a long day (well, it was still only midafternoon) of writing protective spells on the wall.

Was that a piña colada in his hand? Surely not. No, it wasn't. Just a glass of water, perhaps. A jug of milk. A decanter of his own pee for all

It knew. The Golden Sphere had lost track of some human customs. It was the Golden Sphere who wanted a strong drink.

The Golden Sphere, about the size of a bouncy ball a child could ride on, sans handles, rolled up to Kafka. It didn't want to waste the energy floating, not right this moment. God, could It use a drink. Even as It could make a million drinks internally and pretend to be drunk all It wanted.

"What a sight for sore non-eyes," the Golden Sphere said to Kafka, who had put down his drink and was staring at It with what the Golden Sphere supposed must be awe. That would account for the narrowing of the eyes and the slight frown and the flapping of the gills in his neck.

"You again," Kafka said.

"Me again. You still can't kill me, so don't start."

"What do you want?"

"As the old sea shanty goes . . . well, actually, I'm a little too scrambled to think of one at the moment."

"Hmmph." Kafka seemed unimpressed.

"Think of us as 'In the Penal Colony,' and I am the Kind Friend and the Wise Old Man both."

"I'm not familiar with that story."

"You haven't written it here, so . . . fair enough."

Kafka lifted himself, naked, out of the pond.

"Whoa! Put a towel on that thing. I don't need to see that after the day I've had."

Kafka obliged, even putting on trousers and a shirt after drying off.

"Now, as to our future plans," the Golden Sphere said.

"You talk too much," Kafka said. "I let you talk too much last time."

"Oh, for shame, Kafka, my old friend. How can you say such a thing when—"

"I am not your friend," Kafka said. "I cannot undo what you made me add to the wall. And I cannot banish you from this place. But I have written something else into the wall. After some delving, I found you in the old books. I found your kind. You cannot stay here. You must go somewhere else."

The Golden Sphere had, until that moment, thought It felt weak from the travails of the day—namely, having been beaten half to a pulp by Ruth Less. But now It sensed the truth to what Kafka said. There was a nausea coming on that was almost human, infecting every pore. Why, It had rarely felt anything quite like this sensation. It was . . . It was . . . most vomitous and vile and curdling. Almost as if someone had filled its delicate mechanism full of runny custard.

"Well, I hardly think that's neighborly, Kafka. After all, I *can* kill you."

Kafka pointed to a golden word glowing on the wall near the pond. "That word says not. That word says if you kill me, you inflict untold damage on yourself."

"You are indeed very Kafkaesque, I'll give you that," the Golden Sphere conceded. "You really should write fiction, you know."

For Kafka spoke true—the word did constrain. The Golden Sphere tried not to panic as Kafka moved his finger and another word appeared on the wall and the Golden Sphere could not speak, was wrapped in silence that seemed for a panicked moment eternal and never-ending.

Then Kafka moved his finger again and the word faded.

The Golden Sphere had no body, but It felt as if It would begin to spew from both ends, from all ends, in just a few moments. It had a headache. It had shin splints. It had a broken leg. It had a concussion. It had a case of malaria. It had dropsy. It had mopsy. It had gout. It had measles. It had consumption. It had irritable bowel disease. It had C. diff. It had . . . well, what didn't It have?

"I . . . I must depart now," the Golden Sphere said. "I am leaving of my own free will, however. I must make this clear. Because I want to."

"As long as you're leaving, I don't care," Kafka said.

The Golden Sphere hesitated, despite its distress. "Kafka . . . don't you ever get lonely, all by yourself. Down here? Couldn't you use . . . a friend?"

In truth, the encounter with the Celestial Beast had sobered the

Golden Sphere right up. Had, at least in part, brought a streak of sincerity bubbling up from its core. And underneath that: a seething shame and regret. The shame of having been made, not born. The regret of being, in the end, by itself.

"I have plenty of fish friends and otter friends," Kafka said. "That is enough."

"Please?"

"The château is almost here. And I hate you for it."

"'For love of a river shanty / I know many / You know scanty / Bullrushes and—'"

"Go!"

The Golden Sphere left weeping, which was only half pretense.

Chapter Sixty-Two

WITHER WANDER; NEITHER A BURROWER NOR A DIRIGIBLE BE?

Napoleon had not much cared for Verne's reception to his surprise appearance, but he had become accustomed to a certain lack of trust in general. Verne had clapped him in irons, so to speak, and had Grimy the "wall librarian" guard both him and Talleygord, holder of his head . . . which was still, alas, all of Napoleon.

It had been exceedingly hard to get across the point that Napoleon had had a kind of spiritual experience while residing in the all-encompassing pouch of a monster controlled by Crowley and Wretch. Very, very difficult. Among the most intricate of the diplomacies Napoleon had undertaken during his long life and un-life.

Yet, in the end, he was back at the parlay table, or at least no longer imprisoned being lectured by the wall librarian Grimy and his not-unicorn. Grimy was tiresome company, but even him Napoleon had charmed with compliments. As much as he was able. But he'd made the effort, for he found Grimy, beneath his seeming harmlessness . . . capable of great harm. There was the wild gleam in his eye of a kind of derangement, which lay beside appetites unknown for mischief.

Nor did Grimy appear to have much knowledge of books.

Now, with grizzled Talleygord by his side, Napoleon rested upon a stone battlement on the wall at eye level, having been granted an audience with Verne, the rather decayed-looking Laudinum X by Verne's side. While Verne appeared uplifted by his experience, in the sense that he looked like a weathered veteran of war, LX looked both worn down and perhaps gentle-fied by the experience. The light in LX's eyes made Napoleon sympathetic. If it meant empathy and understanding, then LX had come out of war better and more uniquely than most.

"You look very ugly," Verne said without preamble.

"This is true. It's been a long, perilous journey with Old Faithful here."

Talleygord grunted in acknowledgment. He was an eloquent man, but hoarded words like magical bullets.

Verne's face had a stern look on it that Napoleon didn't believe fit such a gentle soul. Under all that battle fatigue.

"Go home. Go tell Crowley we no longer serve him! Go tell him we . . . we . . . quit!"

"I thought you might say that," Napoleon replied. "You could say a mote in my eye told me. Well, I quit, too, Jules. I quit. And just like you, I believe I would like to make Crowley pay. Let me not be coy: You need a general. I need a body and an army."

Verne ignored him. "And who is your companion, anyway?"

"Yes, who is the companion," LX echoed, as if out of the need to say something, anything at all. Mostly, he'd been waxing rhapsodic about badgers for far too long, so this was a huge improvement, to Napoleon's way of thinking.

"Oh, you can call him Talleygord. Friend of the family. Bastard grandson of a bastard-traitor. (Look it up, I've no time to explain.) Last remnant of loyalty on the continent. Isn't that right, Talleygord?"

Talleygord nodded, but said nothing. This was tantamount to a friendly hug, in Talleygord's world. Napoleon knew he was overjoyed not to have had to carry Napoleon around the past few days. It had begun to weigh heavy on him. Or at least his arm and shoulder.

"Why should I trust you? At all."

"Don't trust him," LX said. His lucid moments were becoming more common, Napoleon had noticed. Which he appreciated. It meant command-and-control of this dingy army was improving.

"And, for that matter, why should I trust a demi-mage?" Napoleon asked. "He still owes his allegiance to Crowley."

"Because of the wall. The wild magic shorted out Crowley's control. But, locally, here, at least, Laudinum controls the demi-mages. These demi-mages."

"And the Burrower?"

"Yes."

Perhaps Verne was being forthright because he planned to kick Napoleon over the wall into England and let him take his chances there. Or perhaps he was just naive.

"But beyond this wall?"

"Who knows."

"Then—"

"But to Laudinum X's question," Verne said, interrupting. "As to his question of . . . trust."

Napoleon nodded. "It is a good question. It is a vital question. I do not mean to duck it, sir. Or swim under it. The answer is simple: I am a much-changed man, Mr. Verne. I have been devoured by a monster and come out whole and in between I have seen wonders well beyond this world. And I have come to have a great affection for monsters . . . of which I may have been one. Of a different kind, but—"

"So suddenly you're an altruist?"

"Atheist. No longer quite, but close. But that's beside the point. The real point is this," and it was as if Napoleon or the wall or some part of the world that had been blurry came into sharp focus . . . "You've no military experience. Nor your LX here. It's clear Crowley sent you on a suicide mission. A distraction. A way to deflect resources away from Prague, or at least hold the English here."

"And yet we won," Verne said stubbornly. Although he must know Napoleon was right.

"So now you hold a land bridge, or part of it, and a wall, or part of it, and all around dangerous wild magicks still exist, and beyond the wall . . . you think England will not fight to win its wall back?"

"I think that England has more pressing problems," Verne said. "I'm told there is some strange disease running through the Parliament, they say. An odd magic. A peculiar disconnect. The Lords hew to their manors and, bad manners, stay on their lands and appear only through their animal familiars. Out of paranoia. Plots of assassination and land grab and the like. From what I can gather."

"But surely they will come together to present a unified face to an invader?"

"Nonetheless, I will press forward and conquer them." Bravado did not sit well upon Verne; rather, pressed down on him and rendered him small.

"Will you now, sir? Will you indeed." Napoleon nodding at the tired demi-mages on stools and slumped against the wall. Below them, anyone with half a brain could see the Burrower was in significant need of further earthworms. Or snakes. Or whatever looked like a swiggly line and had a pulse.

When Verne did not reply, Napoleon said, "This was *never* your battle, was it? You had no choice. I am correct?"

Still Verne said nothing. Frozen, found out, at a loss. These were all the things Napoleon would have felt in Verne's position.

"And what," Napoleon asked, "what's the disposition of the defenders of the wall? Your prisoners of war? Of which there appear to be many?"

"In the end, to be honest, except for the wildlings that know no master and the ensorcelled animals and the naturally occurring magical animals and . . ."

"And the men?"

"There is a unicorn-terrier and a librarian," LX offered helpfully.

"Yes. I am painfully aware."

"Most were mercenaries trapped by circumstances," Verne said. "Not paid with frequency. Or given raises."

"England? Strapped for cash? A land run by hedgehogs and crows? Impossible!"

Verne gave him a look Napoleon found impossible to read. He had to admit the Inventor had grown, if not all the way up, in the brief span of mind-scarring warfare the man had experienced. In some ways.

"What do you propose?" Verne asked, cautious, as if extending the question might result in his hand being cut off.

"I know you can build me a body, Verne," Napoleon said, smiling genially. "And I've brought a few score men. Seven hundred and twenty-eight to be precise."

Indeed, if Verne looked out from the wall, he could see their bivouac a few leagues distant, safely out of range of the magic, but still visible by the little white triangles of their tents and the smoke.

"Where did you find them?"

"It's what I do. Find men. And women. Who want to fight for a cause. And in this case will hate Crowley as thoroughly as you do."

Up close, it would be more of the Talleygord same: old, grizzled men whose fathers had fought for him, or, among the oldest, his last remaining soldiers. Some were even veterans of his secret miniaturization campaign in the Alps, which had won him Prague. Back in ancient history, now.

Verne still hesitated, and into the gap, Napoleon charged forward, because the wall was so feral and Verne still so green.

"How many times has this wall changed hands?" Napoleon asked.

"Often," Verne admitted.

"And has it ever meant more than ruling a wall? And hasn't it always resulted in the wall ruling itself?"

"This is true," Verne admitted.

"Talleygord here has some knowledge of this place. He says soon the next part of the giant snail life cycle will take place. All the baby snails rising out of the ground, singing ferocious songs and very, very hungry for whatever they can devour."

Verne winced. "I am told this is true."

"And Talleygord here also tells me that the strangling air potato vine some scoundrel seeded here will rise in the summer and under cover of night try to kill your men."

Verne winced again. "I may have been informed that this might be the case."

"Not to mention, but Talleygord has mentioned it, that the manticores are growing out of their buds and sometimes plagues of medium-sized but still ferocious trolls descend and the sea serpents cannot be depended upon to stay in the sea and—"

Verne, who now looked very sad, held up a hand, pleading with Napoleon to stop. "Yes, yes—I have been told this as well."

"And your cheery chappy friend here?" Napoleon asked. "What does he think?"

"Be polite," Verne said, and clapped Laudinum on the shoulder.

A decent-sized wound in the demi-mage's head had been cured by bandage and suture, but Napoleon thought he had rarely seen a face so ravaged or ugly. Defiantly ugly.

"Badgers," Laudinum managed. "Badgers badgers badgers." But in a dreamy, cheery state.

"He means, sir," Verne said quickly, "that we have all heard about Paris being overrun by magical animals."

"Ah, yes. This is true. Paris is no longer in Crowley's hands."

"But no longer in French hands, either."

"Are not some of the animals French, sir?"

"Can an animal be French, sir?"

Napoleon shrugged. "If a terrier can be a unicorn, anything is possible."

But Verne's face had lit up. "Do you mean to retake Paris?"

Napoleon smiled. "Paris is an important part of any attempt to thwart Crowley."

"I should like to return to Paris," Verne said.

"As do I," Napoleon said, smiling again, to encourage Verne. "Sooner than later, one would hope."

Verne looked at LX, then back at Napoleon. "What would you need from me besides a body? The Burrower?"

"Oh, not the Burrower. LX would need that to defend the wall in your absence." That unmaneuverable beast, seen and felt miles before arrival, was not the kind of stealth Napoleon had in mind. "No, I need . . . cavalry, of a sort."

"Calvary?" Verne looked puzzled.

Napoleon stared pointedly at the distant dirigibles. "Now, those would be of use. Many of my men are pilots, you see." Handpicked for that, really. Or at least, many of them weren't afraid of heights.

"Those dirigibles are truculent."

"So are my men. It's a good match."

"And I would go with you?"

"I would prefer it. You could always return to the wall very fast, if need be. Although clearly, LX is competent to hold the wall."

Napoleon didn't believe this, but he'd rather let LX deal with whatever Grim or Grimmer or Grimy really was than Verne. He certainly had no interest in doing so himself. He recognized a deranged lunatic when he saw one.

Did Verne truly believe that the wall had a librarian? And what kind of "librarian" had survived up there for so long, given the wildness of the surrounding magic? No, Grimy would try to cut LX's throat first chance he got. So let LX suffer the consequences, not Verne. Also, let LX bear the brunt should the English Parliament order an attack.

But Napoleon did feel, even from this brief conversation, some sympathy for Verne, and respect. Toughness often had no chance to be expressed, and thus people were misjudged as soft only because they'd never had to be tough. And they could then be tough as nails in one direction and without a clue in another.

Verne nodded. "Very well. I agree." He offered Napoleon his hand, then realized his mistake, and reddening, withdrew it.

Napoleon ignored the faux pas, said, "Good. You've made the right decision. Strange powers move across the lands, as is said in too many novels that end in catastrophe. But here it is true. The Château Peppermint Blonkers awakens. Monsters may turn out to be saints. It's an invigorating time to be half-alive, but you are wise to have strong allies."

He tried to ignore LX's drooling, the sight of Grimy emerging from a kind of overturned cauldron to stare balefully at him.

There had been worse beginnings to vast empires, worse moments to mark the revival of military careers.

But there had been better, too.

Part VII

LOST IN THE MIST

~

"I don't like how you smell."

Chapter Sixty-hic-Four

NOT A MARK, NOT A HAPPY MAN

"Please be advised that weather forecasts call for torrents of blood, but otherwise clear skies. If you begin to see blood-fall, please move inside for your own safety. Some of the blood may come in a form that could crush you. Thank you, forest citizens, for your kind attention in this matter."

—Decree from Crowley, written on a piece of paper and attached with a ribbon to a nectar deer, set free outside the war elephant (never formally issued)

If moving about ponderous in a war elephant had been claustrophobic and, if Crowley were honest, deeply boring, then becoming stationary while having a moat built around one's home ranked high on the ennui scale as well. He hadn't been this out of sorts since losing his body for the first time. The circling presence of the batlike other Wretches, high above, did nothing to help his mood.

Crowley had little control over Wretch, but none over these party-crashers. Wretch acolytes? Were they somehow part of Wretch? So hard to tell what was going on, especially since the Wretch-mob seemed to have arrived to keep an eye on Fort Elephant while Wretch went off on another of his seemingly endless missions.

Where he went, Crowley still had no clue. Lately, Wretch had been much better about keeping him in the dark, even going over military plans with Charlie Mange without Crowley, which meant Crowley had to stand there in front of the demi-mages and pretend that he already knew the strategy. Not that it seemed they were much closer to attacking.

"A week," Wretch kept saying. "A week to ten days. Let Ruth Less do her reconnaissance. Let my spies do their work. Let the Wretches steep and deepen."

Steep and Deepen sounded like a particularly terrible magician duo. Applied to the Wretches, Crowley didn't know what it meant. Although he would sometimes wake of a morning, go to the lookout spot (perhaps he was still a little nostalgic for the halcyon days with Napoleon), and hear the shrieks of sheep and cattle high in the air, for the Wretches kept up their strength by stealing livestock and devouring it whilst hovering in the heavens.

Which meant the land beneath was often subject to a rain of blood and viscera. He had received several complaints from the locals about the stench, those hardy souls still living in the forest. But he had to admit, he didn't much care for this development, either. Nor had he been impressed by Wretch's attempt to mimic the mysterious Stimply for the damned elusive young Lambshead's benefit. Perhaps Wretch should have taken some acting lessons first, for clearly the ruse did not work. Even if Wretch claimed that wasn't the point.

Worst of all, however, was the situation in Paris. It was one thing to resign himself to the impossibility of returning and liberating the city, quite another to bloody well have to endure the day-by-day negativity of ET and Latrine's reports. It put a snarl in his jawline, clenched teeth and bad thoughts.

That very morning, with Wretch gone, Crowley and Charlie Mange had stared into the All-Seeing Puddle to find staring back only ET, no Latrine. Against a dark backdrop that could in no way be the ceiling of the cathedral.

Even as Crowley flinched from time to time, as he caught a glimpse in his peripheral vision of Charlie Mange. Because Wretch, citing expediency, namely that old Charlie was falling apart from moth damage, had given the terrible Mange a full-on brown-and-gray moth body, complete with giant wings, and then just plopped CM's awful head on top. The result a kind of velvety horror show, a glam glossy faux-fur ick-ness.

"But he is more stable now," Wretch had explained.

"He's more hideous and . . . soft . . . now." But, in truth, Crowley was a little envious. Especially of those silent wings. Wretch had already taken Charlie Mange along on an exploratory flight. Without the wingless Crowley, of course.

But Crowley must shake off this latest change in "the situation," as he had dubbed his servitude to Wretch, for Eiffel Tower awaited.

"My Lord Emperor!" she said.

"Where are you, ET?"

"In the catacombs, my Lord Emperor! All is lost!"

"Well, not all, ET—you're still reporting in, not dead with your head on a pike."

"I don't really have a head," ET said.

"Higher levels, then."

Crowley was in an oddly philosophical mood, having seen from the lookout platform half of a whole cow plummet into the empty moat from the Wretch flock circling above. It had smashed No-Name into bits as he inspected the moat work. There but for the grace of the devil went Crowley. These were the times he lived in. That he might one day be grateful to be nothing but a head.

"Rimbaud has captured Notre Dame. The animal army now controls the entire eastern half of Paris."

"Where is Latrine?"

"He took what he could from the factories and some demi-mages and hopes to bring them to you, my lord."

"Good, good." Initiative. He hated initiative, but they could use more supplies. Some rabid animals to shove into war machines would definitely help.

"What are we to do?"

For a scale-model animated version of the Eiffel Tower, ET gave a credible impression of fear across the tiers of what could not be considered a real face. The tensile strength of the magical steel, the rabidity of the chipmunks within, must be remarkable.

"I release thee to pillage," Crowley replied.

"What, Lord Emperor?"

"Get you down to the underground factories and have them remove the growth inhibitor spell and fill you full of more rabid chipmunks." While there were still rabid chipmunks to be had.

"Sir, the factories are on fire now, just after Latrine left. The marmots . . . oh, Emperor, the marmots, the terrible, terrible marmots. All of that is gone. We have just the catacombs and some parts of the old city."

"Well, then, um, I release you to rampage at your existing size with the existing number of rabid chipmunks."

"Lord Emperor, it is not in my temperament."

"Well, it certainly is in the temperament of the rabid chipmunks that animate you, ET! So figure it out! And don't report back again!" The snarling rage had come from nowhere, but he knew it was linked to the claustrophobia and general lack of control.

So. Paris was likely lost. But that still left Germany, Spain, and outposts in various other countries, which he supposed might soon come under attack. For now, he still ruled them. He'd started to build additional war factories in Spain, but they weren't operational yet. Perhaps they could be speeded up somehow.

With a mere All-Seeing Puddle and the forces he'd sent with Verne lost, Crowley couldn't muster much of a counteroffensive. Only hope to hold on to what remained: Prague and the Golden Sphere.

"Nothing to say, Charlie Mange?" Crowley asked, for the wight just slouched there.

"I molt-eth," Charlie Mange managed, in a blurred mumble.

"What, old boot?"

"Molt-eth. Moth-est. Moth-est."

Crowley looked closer. Indeed, Charlie Mange's leaves had all become cocoons or a flutter of brownish wings.

Ah, bloody wonderful. He'd at least hoped for some guidance from the rickety general-emperor.

Well, perhaps his old friend from Earth, this version, would be of more use. A farm in a clearing in the forest. A little cottage. Animal pens. Cheery smoke from a brick chimney. Chickens clucking. Cows mooing. Pigs squealing. He could see it clear as day, had visited with his father a few times on Earth. How different could it be on Aurora.

The Wretches were still busy littering the landscape with animal parts. They'd hardly miss him.

"Hold down the fort, Charlie Mange," Crowley said.

"Mmmmph," Charlie Mange replied, sinking to his knees under the weight of the soft wings of hundreds of moths.

The farmhouse of his friend Mediocre lay a bit closer to Prague than made Crowley comfortable, but still deep in the forest. He had retained a fondness for this patch of woods, with its mighty oaks, lichen, moss, and muffled areas of open meadow with wildflowers. He felt a thrill of excitement as he approached—after all, what if it hadn't been there, here on Aurora? But it was, and this link to his past warmed his heart.

He couldn't greet his farmer friend as "Mediocre," of course—that had just been his father's nickname for the farmer. Or, farmer-philosopher, as Crowley remembered from age twelve. The farmer had had a huge library of books on the occult and had dabbled in spells himself. His wife Belladimma (father's name for her) had been a self-proclaimed witch who healed the locals' ills with mushrooms, magic, and otherwise, along with ointments from crushed roots and leaves.

Once, Crowley had been playing with Mediocre's daughter Shrill-bane (again, his father's moniker) and rolled into some poisonous vine. Mediocre had taken him to Belladimma and she had stripped him half-naked and lathered him up with one of her lotions, which had spread a special glow across his body and perked him right up after several sessions.

The farmhouse with its huge troughs for the pigs, which roamed half-wild beyond the clearing, was just as he remembered it. And out front was Mediocre himself, chopping wood with an old rusty ax! Although he saw no sign of Belladimma—and Shrill would be all grown-up by now.

"Friend!" Crowley shouted out to Mediocre as he stepped out of the tree cover. "Well met!"

Mediocre stopped chopping wood, looked Crowley up and down, spit to the side, resumed chopping wood.

"Surely you remember me? Young Crowley? Aleister Crowley?" Mediocre had called him, alternatively, "Fresh Meat" or "Buttlehead," for some reason. Shrill had called him "Pork Face." Belladimma had called him "Hither." But none of these seemed appropriate ways to remind the farmer.

Mediocre sighed, laid down his ax, put his hands on his hips, looked at Crowley, and said, "Naw, sir. I don't recall." Was it English with a thick Germanic accent or a kind of debased German? Hard for Crowley to tell.

"Summers? Staying here? With my father? Tall man. Brought you books on the occult. Swore a lot. Didn't like mosquitoes. Hated small talk." Was recently torn asunder so he wouldn't thwart my plans.

"Can't say it rangs a proverb ball, sir," Mediocre said.

Crowley almost said "What?" but decided to move on.

"What about Shrill-bane?"

"Shrill? Bane?"

"Your daughter."

"Never 'ad a daughter, sir. Had a pig named Shrill once. Let 'er eat from the dinner table, didn't I? But then 'ad to kill an' eat 'er."

"That wouldn't be the one."

"Well, sir, imp pass."

"What?"

"Imp pass. Means somethin' you can't cross. Ironic-like."

"I know what impasse means!"

"And call off yer wart beasties there. If they a'come tramplin' my clearin' upsetting the chickens an' they don' lay, I lose breakfast."

"Wart beasties?"

"The beasties you use to wage wart, ain't they?"

"Oh, those," Crowley said.

It was true. Although he'd wanted to go off on his own, the demi-mages had protested, and rather than directly face his wrath at their disobedience in not letting him be alone, they had sent five or six war crocodiles behind him at a respectful distance, with Emissaries and demi-mages at their sides. And it was true they'd not only made a dreadful racket, but had ruined quite a bit of forest.

Crowley looked back at them and waved them off. "Farther back, damn you! Farther back!"

They stayed where they were, but came no nearer. The mecha-crocodiles had expressions like sorrowful befanged dogs. They were perhaps the most loyal, being stuffed full at this point, of pieces of deceased demi-mages, having run out of animals. But that fact made them no less off-putting to Mediocre.

Muttering to himself, Mediocre had stepped away from the ax and the firewood and moved closer to the farmhouse, sitting on a stool next to the troughs and using a huge pestle to crush some substance into a pail. Beside him at the troughs stood a ruminating cow and next to the cow, hidden at first by its bulk, a man in a cow suit.

"Hallo," said the man in the cow suit.

"Hello," said Crowley, flummoxed. "Who are you?"

"Tourist from Prague. Farm life, you know!"

"Go away or I shall feed you to my mecha-crocs," waving behind him. Out of consideration for Mediocre, or he would've just killed him with a spell.

The man stood and fled into the forest. For some time, Crowley could see the bipedal white cow moving back and forth into the distance as he threaded his way between the trees. The suit seemed too big, as if at one point there had been two people inhabiting it. The cow man fell often, got up, fell again. Became a white dot.

"Why'd yew go an' do that?" Mediocre asked, staring after the cow man. "Payin' guest. Good milker, too. Milked good." He continued with his pestle and pail.

"Making saltpeter for experiments?" Crowley asked hopefully, and to change the subject.

"Naw—shit from crops."

"You're making . . . shit . . . for crops?"

"Fert'lizer. Myself."

"Ah," Crowley said, and moved a little away from the farmer.

At which point a number of satanic-looking potatoes popped out of the ground, the expressions on their faces enraged, and attacked Crowley. They were everywhere, like cockroaches, except they were potatoes.

He cast a small fire smell and crisped them alive, their tiny shrieks soon fading and their forms writhing and then still on the ground they had popped out of. Potatoes hated him, and he had no idea why.

Mediocre the farmer had risen from his seat and was staring in alarm at Crowley.

"Oi! Yer upsettin' me crop. Crop I'm makin' the shit for!"

"I'm dreadfully sorry, Mediocre," Crowley said, and he was. This reunion wasn't at all what he'd hoped for. It was, in fact, becoming more stressful by the moment.

"What did ye call me?"

"Nothing," Crowley said quickly, sadly. "Nothing at all."

The farmer stared at him a moment, tossed the mortar into the bucket, scowled, and said, "Now, ye listen here to me, strange for-iner. Ahv no recollect of yew. Ahv no recollect at-awl. And yew've not got the right top half or mayhap the wrong bottom half. I've no dear, no wont no dear. Did yew scramble with 'nother gent bottom of yonder hill? Mayhap yew shewd go hence, collect up yer right parts? For yer mind is cut loose."

Crowley was spared a response to whatever Mediocre had said by the heaving of mighty wings, and Wretch plummeted to his side, in a concentrated hawklike form black as night, with but a single huge eye and mighty talons. The sudden physicality of it, that weight at his shoulder, made Crowley recoil and shriek. The smell was the worst thing: seafood chowder gone bad, drowned in castor oil and then set aflame with petrol.

But the farmer was made of sterner stuff, or, at least, must have seen many odd things in the forest.

"What matter of infernal bat be ye?" Mediocre asked, indignant, as if this were the last straw and he needed every bit of hay for the winter.

Wretch opened a mouth that kept growing, roared at the man, "Not the forgiving kind!"

It was clear he meant to swallow Mediocre whole, as the man fell to the ground from the onslaught, and began gibbering and sidling crablike back toward the safety of the farmhouse.

"No, Wretch, no! Don't! He's . . . he's just a . . . badger . . . isn't that right, Mediocre?" Concentrating all the power of his gaze upon the frightened man. "You're a badger. No threat at all. Badger badger badger."

A new light and certainty entered Mediocre's eyes, and he stopped sidling like a crab. Instead, he began digging. Just like a badger. Pathetic. How had his father ever counted this man as his friend?

Then the cow exploded at the trough, covering Crowley and the farmer-badger in offal. Icky, small, rough bits.

When he'd regained his feet, he saw Ruth Less at the trough, which was full of rather disorganized cow parts. The smell would have been life-altering, if Crowley's life hadn't been so altered already.

Ruth Less had slaughtered the cow in a very idiosyncratic way, via explosion, so quickly it had hardly had a chance to moo, the better to eat it, and now was gorging on the body, mouth-parts filthy with blood. Slobber and drool ruined the schoolmarm illusion, as did the opening up of the head to reveal the mouth-parts, tentacles gathering up cow pieces and shoveling them in.

Worst still, Wretch, back to his normal size, joined Ruth Less at the trough-buffet, head over the side, chewing, while behind Crowley heard the unwieldly tread of the mecha-crocodiles approaching.

What a mess.

"Did she have to kill the cow?" Crowley asked the air.

Wretch looked up from his feast long enough to say, "Ruth Less needs to keep up her strength. She almost captured the Golden Sphere. Really, we are so very close. Now she has their scent!"

Wretch, after being almost gloomy the past week, had a kind of maniacal, bright gleam in his eye. Almost gleeful.

"Wot trees 'av come ta dark wood, then yew shall be undone by 'uge monster an' mystery howz." Mediocre muttering at Crowley, looking at him like he was a war criminal. Muttering prophecies?

"There are trees here now, Mediocre."

"Axley m'point."

Wretch nodded at Mediocre. "Did you get the nostalgia over and done with?"

"He doesn't really know me."

"Ahm standin' right 'ere."

"Of course he didn't," Wretch said. "Only I know you. Do you understand now?"

"Understand what?"

Wretch laughed cruelly. "You can't go home again. No one can. No one really wants to."

Ruth Less was sniffing the air with violence, spreading red gore-snot everywhere.

"Sensing something, Ruth Less?" Wretch said in an elevated tone, as if talking to a dog who wanted to play fetch. "Go get it, Ruth Less! Go get it!"

"Jonathan. Danny. Rack."

"Yes, Ruth Less! Good girl! Go go go!"

Crowley had never seen Wretch so maniacally happy. He was even tittering and giggling a bit, which was odd.

Ruth Less went bounding off into the mist.

As if the mist required an equal and opposite reaction to Ruth Less's vast mass smashing into it, the mist disgorged in that moment twelve or fourteen onrushing bears. Along with an odd horse and cart, and a number of other random dangers. Monsters galore. Nothing Crowley hadn't seen before in his mind's eye of a Sunday.

Which was Crowley's sign, spur of the moment, that he wasn't yet done with his wandering, and used the resulting confusion to flee into the mist again, euphoric to escape Wretch's wretched euphoria.

If only for a little while.

Chapter Sixty-Five-ish
I LAUGH WHEN I CRY AND I CRIESH WHENS I LAUGHSH

Such a relief, to escape the Aurora underground, to go through a door that performed as advertised—in this case, deposit them in the forests adjacent to Prague. A clean-smelling, cheery forest full of fox squirrels and squirrel foxes and rabbits and birds unfamiliar to Jonathan, many threading through the canopy, accompanied by song. Even the little abandoned ruin of a castle they came out of, the quaint stone entrance-way that was the magical door, appealed to Jonathan.

So when black bears appeared as they walked through a meadow clearing and Danny had to discharge the bear gun, which only created more bears, and they'd all had to run and gotten more than slightly lost and off course, it still felt different from the claustrophobic darkness, the weight of everything down there.

By the time Jonathan and the others had stopped running, the bears had entered into some kind of growling melee. Jonathan didn't speak enough bear to figure it out; all he knew was they reached some kind of agreement and had forgotten their human prey. Soon enough, Jonathan couldn't even hear the least bit of growl or any other of the ninety-three possible bear sounds. For which, still a bit out of breath, he was immensely grateful.

Danny threw the bear gun to the ground as the rest of them leaned over, breathing hard from the brisk run. "It's out of bears!"

Jonathan stood, leaned over, wheezed, "No—keep it. We'll find some way to reload it later." Honestly, though, he just wanted to be safe somewhere, in a place where a bear gun wasn't necessary.

"Reload it?" Danny echoed. "With what? Where are we going to find more bears?"

"Oh, of course, Danny," Rack said. "That's the real problem. If we can only find more bears, we can reload it. As long as they're okay with being stuffed into that tiny musket muzzle."

"I think Prague is still that way," Mamoud said, pointing to where a much-disused loamy trail led into what looked like ever-darker forest.

"We're definitely near Prague," Jonathan said, even if he didn't necessarily agree with where Mamoud was pointing.

"How do you know? How do either of you know?"

"I only have a feeling," Jonathan admitted. A feeling that they needed to get to their destination soon.

"I've been here before," Mamoud said. "Those birds and bees are humming what I believe is the Czech national anthem."

Danny nodded. "Jonathan's right. Mamoud's right. We're close—and it is that way."

"And how do *you* know?" Rack said, but it was a feeble protest.

Danny shrugged. "I just know."

"Into the *deep, dark* forest it is!" Jonathan said with emphasis. He liked a deep, dark forest. Everyone knew that, and something about his enthusiasm turned Rack jovial again and Mamoud more relaxed.

Perhaps he felt so good because he knew he had been deminiaturized. Something about being big again was good for the circulatory system. Or the internal organs. Which was only a guess.

He was still trying to find the right time to tell them about the miniaturization . . . to tell them about, well, everything.

Before they got to the safety of Prague did not seem like the right time.

But, then, as the forest showed no sign of ending, or revealing a sudden city of Prague, Jonathan found himself in an argument with Mamoud that he hadn't intended, his mood souring. It didn't much seem as if anything about Alice's plotting or Mamoud's role in things had been resolved. And it might be unreasonable, but once he went down that path, he couldn't stop, had to ask Mamoud about Alice, about how they'd come to work together.

"What does it matter, right now? You can ask the Order when we reach Prague—about all of this. Alice, the doors, your haunted mansion. Besides, we have been through a lot together, haven't we?"

Mamoud, trying to take the edge off, and Jonathan acutely aware of that and not having any of it. Thinking of Dr. Lambshead's advice and Crikey going on about intrigues he couldn't see.

But, mostly, perhaps, he didn't like how the Voice had disappeared again despite him asking the Voice to wake up. Nor did he like how despite it being midday, the sky was getting dark and wisps of mist had begun to trail along the uneven ground. The smell was like rain but not, moisture in the air, but there would be no downpour, he was sure of it. It would just linger there, raising the humidity.

"Quite a lot, actually. It matters a lot," Jonathan said. "Because as far as I can tell, the 'Republic' is content to sit back and watch Crowley and hope that he self-destructs. Like the Mali magician—you've not once mentioned Republic military intervention. I think it's just you, Mamoud, working with Alice for a time, and maybe a handful of others. And sometimes it helps you to pretend you support the Order, but in the meantime, someone or some thing—maybe Crowley or maybe not—is picking off members of the Order. But not you and not Alice—neither of you are in danger, because neither of you are really part of the Order. Indeed, given Alice seems to work for Her Majesty's government, you could say you work for her."

"Alice was a mistake," Mamoud conceded.

"Clearly," Rack said, butting in, but butted out again after a stern glance from Danny, for which Jonathan was grateful.

"Is it the Republic that has the same goals as the Order, or just you?"

Mamoud sighed. "I never trusted Alice completely, if I'm honest. But the idea I had, as *both* a member of the Order and a citizen of the Republic, was to feed information to her and see where it ended up."

"Disinformation, you mean," Jonathan said.

"Yes. And to keep her close because, of all of us, I could see her motivations least of all. Something troubled her. She was not herself on our expedition. Not the person I knew."

"Was she supposed to lead me to you?"

Mamoud laughed. "No—I was most surprised when you showed up for tea in the turret."

Jonathan believed him. Felt oddly vindicated, that his own initiative had tossed him into the frying pan, not some intricate deception.

"And where did her information end up?"

"Not determined yet. And now too late. But it was used by . . . the other side. Sometimes. Other times . . . not used at all."

"Is there anything else you're not telling us, Mamoud?" Jonathan asked. "Because I'm at my limit trying to keep up with Aurora and tangled webs and cryptic clues."

Mamoud almost spat out a reply, but, Jonathan thought, with a grudging respect for his resolve mixed in.

"You've only been in Aurora for what? A week? A little more. What do you really know about this place? Do you think it is all idyllic meadows with quaint talking marmots from fairy tales? Did you even know that there is no 'United States' here? That the Europeans never conquered the Americas?"

No Florida. No home. Such a conjoined lurch in his heart, his stomach. What he knew didn't exist here. What he hated didn't exist, either. No colonies. No conquistadors.

But some of this, too, Sarah had told him indirectly in her tales. Mamoud wanted to throw him for a loop, distract him. Sarah had ensured he couldn't be. Not entirely.

"Then why not just leave us? Why do you need us at all?"

"I don't need you."

"Evidence is to the contrary."

Mamoud considered Jonathan for a moment, then laughed, a trifle bitterly.

"Why should I pretend otherwise? You are correct. The Republic doesn't yet see the threat. Not fully. They're content to send advisers and spics over, to harass Crowley where he is weak. Even after losing their foothold in Spain. To occupy Sardinia. To lend aid to Prague—advice and weapons—and to his other enemies. But they don't believe in the Golden Sphere. They don't believe magic can really destroy the world. They fear more that magic will corrupt what we've built in the Republic using science, which is not the same thing. So, yes, I do need you, even as wet behind the ears as you are. Because you are Dr. Lambshead's grandson and that means something to the Order."

"Doesn't seem to," Rack muttered. "Not all that much."

"And wherever Alice is now," Mamoud continued, "she will likely return in some guise just as soon as she confirms from someone more expert that she does not in fact have the real Wobble."

Jonathan felt a lurch in his heart, stumbled over a branch in the encroaching mist.

"What the hell do you mean by that, Mamoud?"

Mamoud reached into his pocket and tossed a black marble at Jonathan, who caught it. Recognized the familiar grooves, the slick-smooth-yet-rough feel. The Wobble!

Danny had sat bolt upright. "That's impossible," she said.

"We're very good at forgeries in the Republic," Mamoud said. "Our operatives do an excellent job of replacing magical objects of military significance to the Republic with fakes. More subtle than destroying them. We've even used what we've learned to experiment with jamming and dissolving Emissaries using radio waves."

Jonathan just clasped the Wobble tight in surprise. "You had it all along."

"I switched it out at the cistern overlooking Rome," Mamoud said.

"I didn't like how Alice looked at it. So there's your proof about my intentions."

"You picked my pocket and you didn't tell me. Bloody smart." Jonathan smiled wryly, with admiration. "Best way to protect it: make sure I didn't have it." Because Mamoud was right: Jonathan didn't know what he was doing . . . yet.

"I meant to keep it secret until Prague," Mamoud said. "But now I find it best used as an act of trust."

"No worries," Jonathan said, and meant it. Just having the Wobble back was a relief.

"Strange way of showing trust—steal a thing and then give it back," Rack muttered.

But Jonathan could tell from the way Rack looked at Mamoud that he found it clever, too.

❧

The mist thickened, reached out tendrils and ghosted over bushes, rising up into the canopy. At times, in the darkest parts of the forest, it felt like night, and the quality of sound became indistinct, muffled. A deer startled nearby, but its panicked retreat sounded to Jonathan as if it came from over the edge of the ravine they were walking through, along a trickling stream. Moss and lichen atop long, low stones.

They had taken to talking about what they would do when they got to Prague, which to Jonathan and R & D meant getting back to Earth.

"A shower. Terrible bathrooms here." This from Rack.

"Just a shower in general," Danny said.

"Concept of a bath," Jonathan offered.

"Concept of a path that doesn't end in puffins." Rack, obscured by mist.

"Do marmots bathe or just groom themselves clean? I don't remember seeing many showers, yeah?"

"The food's been terrible. Let's face it."

"I had to eat a marmot."

Dissolving into giggles.

"You didn't have to eat the marmot."

"I'd love a baked potato."

"Don't say that around the potato folk."

"I'd be curious to eat a flower with a face."

"No!"

"I'd love a phone that works. One not attached to a Stimply."

Even Mamoud laughed at that. "You won't get that back in the mansion, either. Stimply comes attached to all things."

"Wonder how the mansion's holding up?" Jonathan said. "I have this nightmare where we get back and all the junk we moved and hauled away in boxes is back where it was before we started."

Rack shuddered. "Don't say that."

"Pancakes," Danny said. "I miss pancakes."

"They have pancakes in Prague," Mamoud pointed out.

"Scrambled eggs. Any egg at all. A proper breakfast at a proper time." Rack in full reverie.

"They have that in Prague."

"Good coffee," Jonathan said.

"They have that—"

But an unfamiliar voice rose from the gloom, at about shoulder height. Danny's shoulder. A voice with a sharp edge, reedy but loud.

"You know what I'd love? Just personally? Just if I had my druthers? Which I never get to have. If you'd shut your traps. Every last one of you. Even you, Danny. Just the once. Shut your damn traps. Shut 'em. Shut them right up. I am so unbearably sick of hearing your complaints. Your whining. Your inane level of discourse. Every moment. Even underground! Even surrounded by miracles and marvels. Even when there are amazing smells. I have to hear about how you've not had a proper shower. For example. Well, do what the rest of us do. Groom yourself. Groom your damn selves. Any animal can do it. Because there's a war going on, in case you've not noticed. A war of all against all, and here we are in the mist acting like a big ol' bag of fools and there's no time for it!"

"Oh-ho!" Rack exclaimed. "The rat speaks! The rat finally speaks to us."

For it was indeed Tee-Tee, standing up on Danny's shoulder and giving them all the stink eye.

"Admonishes us," Jonathan said. "More than speaking really. I sense a distinct point of view." He felt very punchy by now, perhaps from all the aimless walking.

"Well, at least we rate being given what for, rather than icy silence," Rack said. "Or whispering hateful nothings in Danny's ear."

"Oh, you don't know the half of it," Danny said.

"If I could see you, I'd bite you," Tee-Tee said in Rack's general direction. Which even Jonathan was having trouble discerning.

"If I could see you, mate, I'd bite you right back."

Danny had started to cry.

Tee-Tee's voice became concerned. "What's wrong, Danny? What's wrong?"

"You're so mean, Tee-Tee, yeah? So mean."

Jonathan felt a surge of sorrow, began to cry, too. Soon, Rack was bawling like a baby and Mamoud was weeping as well, loudly.

"What is wrong with you all?" Tee-Tee said, even as Jonathan could tell the rat was crying, too.

"Things are looking up," Danny said, crying even more intensely. "Everything is fine. We'll be in Prague soon."

"Boohoo hoo hoo hoo hoo."

"Ah, sadness sadness sadness." Sobbing great gloopy tears.

"Ahaahahhaahahahahahahaahahaa." Rack now, switching gears, was laughing, not crying, while Jonathan still felt very sad. It felt false even to wipe the tears from his face.

"It's not funny."

"Yes it is."

"NO IT ISN'T."

But he couldn't remember what they'd even been arguing about. Also, what with all the bawling and giggling, it was hard to even tell who was who. They'd been holding hands to protect against being separated in the rising mist, but that had become too dangerous, ground uneven. Too much possibility of stumble-falling and taking the whole chain gang along with.

A cat, a pig, and a skunk tumbled out of the mist, looking surprised, like they'd been caught playing cards. They soon scurried away, out of sight.

This started a laughing jag none of them could stop.

But then Danny started crying about the cat, pig, and skunk.

"They were so happy together and yet we startled them and now they're on the run. Now they can't be happy again. Ever. And we did that, yeah?"

Soon, they were *all* crying again, gasping for breath. Jonathan felt quite light-headed, drunk almost. His sides hurt. His heart pounded loudly in his ears.

"What is happening to us?" he sobbed.

"The cat, pig, and skunk were so happy," Danny said, weeping. "So very happy. Until they met us."

Rack resumed loud weeping at Danny's words. "It's true. It's so true. They were happy. And oh why oh why did my marpot abandon me. Why?" Wailing.

It was true, Jonathan felt sad about the marpot, too. Especially because in the Prague forest it would be an invasive species. He began to bawl. The marpot would possibly find another marpot and breed and then all the native animals would be driven out by an explosion of marpots.

"I would've liked to join all of them, but I have to be on your stupid mission," Tee-Tee said, and bawled like a baby, there on Danny's shoulder.

Then Mamoud started giggling. "I have a blister. I have blisters on my feet. I have so many blisters. I hate blisters. I hate babysitting all of you. I hate blisters." But his words came out a bit garbled, hard to understand.

"Stop complaining," Danny said, but she was laughing hard. And hard to understand as well, slurring the words.

"Do you have blisters?" Mamoud asked, still giggling. Slurring.

"No," Danny said, "but I have the Wobble."

Mamoud gave off a hyena laugh, while Rack wept worse and Jonathan slapped his knee and stumbled even though the ground was level. Nothing could be seen now through the mist, and they stumbled forward like clumsy ghosts, oblong dark shapes against the soft white.

"Of course you have the Wobble," Jonathan said. "I have the Wobble, too! We all have the Wobble!" Was he slurring? Everything felt sloppy and hazy, and that was the mist, surely?

"No, really," Danny wept-laughed. "I have the Wobble. I replaced it with a fake back in the mansion after we met Alice. I didn't trust her. I didn't trust her at all."

Jonathan's thrill of alarm expressed itself as another burgeoning of his tear ducts.

"No one trusts her," Jonathan said, through his bawling. "No one loves her. No one would care about me if I weren't a Lambshead."

"I I I. I did it. Not you. I replaced the Wobble in the Alps," Mamoud said, shrieking with giggles like a cascade of bubbles rising to the top of a deep lake. For they came out muffled and then popped sharp in the mist. Jonathan smelled mint, like he'd just crushed some herb underfoot.

"Jonathan, crush your Wobble," Danny said, chuckling. "Crush it, yeah!"

Lurching a bit, Jonathan took the Wobble from his pocket. Bloody hell! When he grasped it even a little roughly it began to disintegrate. Into crumbs. Like some sort of Wobble-shaped cookie or cracker. Soon it was just a dust he was littering the trail with.

"Oh, look at that," he said, feeling the grainy remains on his hand. He felt so happy-sad, so joyous-melancholy he was fit to burst.

"What was it? What happened?" Rack cry-gurgled.

"Danny's right. It was a fake. Bloody bleedin' hell. Well, no worries. No worries." Now he couldn't stop laughing again.

"Corker," Rack said. "What a corker."

"But what if the real Wobble was just fragile like a cookie or cracker?" Jonathan sobbed. "What if I just destroyed it and the Golden Sphere will go free forever and all the worlds will be destroyed and it will all be because I thought the real Wobble was a cookie-cracker?"

"But it's not fragile. Not like my feelings for Mamoud," Danny said, wailing. "No, not fragile, and that was the fake. I've been to Aurora many, many times. I'm not really that good a rugby player because all the away matches are really me on missions. I'm a top spy for the Order. I've been an agent of the Order my whole life, but I was afraid to tell Rack 'cause I love him and I was afraid he'd never speak to me again, yeah."

The end of that said cheerily, her laughter now like tinkling bells.

Rack was too busy chortling to reply, bent over almost double, leaning up against Jonathan. He was trying to say something through the chortling, but Jonathan couldn't understand what it was.

"I'm a spy, too!" Tee-Tee said. "I'm a spy for the Order!"

Jonathan felt a strong urge to spill beans. He couldn't think of it any other way. Spill the beans. Confess. Tell the truth.

"You were all tiny and didn't know it!" Jonathan blurted out. "And Dr. Lambshead is alive and so very, very large!"

"Dr. Lambshead has dementia!" Mamoud shouted, then gigglesnorted.

Wait. How did he know that? Or that Dr. Lambshead was alive. But the urge to ask Mamoud fell away against the urge to spill more beans.

"I have a Voice in my head that won't go away!" Jonathan felt so liberated saying it. "I have a Voice in my head that was an Emissary, but I neutralized it with the magic I don't have and now it lives in my head. But it's scared of Crowley, so it doesn't come out when Crowley's around and it thought I might destroy it, so it didn't come out for that reason, too. But mostly now I think Crowley might be nearby because the Voice isn't here and that's my story."

"I really wanted to know what marmot tastes like," Rack said. "And sometimes I want to take my foot off and just hit you with it—all of you—for not realizing how much discomfort I go through every day."

"Hit us with your shoe. Hit us!"

"Foot."

From the underbrush, some small distance away, Jonathan thought he heard a voice whisper, "I was born a mushroom and I'll die a mushroom but I always wanted to be a magnificent badger. A moon-blue badger that could fly to the moon. But I'm not. I'm just a fruiting body stuck in a ditch."

But that couldn't be right. He must be hallucinating. Once again the need to tell the truth rose within him.

"I don't think I'm into men or women. I think I'm just not much into romance."

"I hate my father," Mamoud said, "and I don't like how any of you smell."

"I don't like how you smell."

"I don't like how you smell."

"I don't like how you smell."

"I don't smell!"

Weeping, laughing, tumbling through the mist.

Then, at some point, curled up within his own weepy-larfing thoughts, Jonathan felt a new kind of silence. A muffled, fuzzy sense of alarm: He couldn't hear the others anymore.

"Rack? Danny?"

He had more truth to unload on them like a gun full of bears.

No reply, and he had to keep the truths all bottled up.

Revealed by a log, a glowing green salamander the length of his foot stared up at him querulous.

"Do you know where they got to, Amphibian Rex?"

But all the salamander could do was hum the Czech national anthem and munch on a patch of moss.

And that was a kind of truth, too.

Dapp Chapp Sixty-Sixty or Sixty-Seven??!
THE GREAT TRUTH OFFENSIVE

Mist that drooled. Mist that simpered. Mist low to the ground that clung to trees like sheep's wool or seeped through in bunches like milk in paper towels. The kind of mist that smelled like dirty socks and the kind that had no smell at all. The thick stuff that chugged along like the smoke from a train's smokestack. The even thicker stuff with a consistency almost like cottage cheese, droopy and congealed. The ethereal kind like a hundred floating transparent white nightgowns stitched together. Stained with coal smoke or green with moss, pea soup. Friendly mist and creepy mist. The pink-tinged variety that indicated something had gone seriously wrong.

But all the mist—all of it—in any consistency or thickness, whether like walking through clouds or on your skin and shins rough, like cotton swabs or bandages . . . all this mist would make you cry, make you laugh, make you tell the truth.

This last quality had been Kristýna's idea because she continued to believe her "side" held the right way of things and that the other side would not like such a blurting, out of nowhere. They'd all been given the antidote, even Mack. Of course, Mack. What a cruel trick that would've been, to play on him after all her talk of trust.

The beginnings of a beer golem lay before them, its lumpy, thick form dug into the ground like a roughly human-shaped grave. Czech magicians, the scruffy ruffians who Kristýna knew, with affection, might on Jonathan's Earth be dubbed "old hippies," had opened up hundreds and hundreds of barrels of Czech beer to manufacture the mist and a phalanx of beer golems, mixing the beer with the magical tincture that was the truth serum, the "irrational emotion drops" as she thought of them. For it was her concoction, from a certain plant.

Kristýna had thought of the concoction because it was what she feared most: losing control.

The magicians need only keep adding fluids to the beer golem mould-shapes for each new effect to take hold. The beer itself added nothing much, but would make the enemy disoriented and drunk. Not to mention the hangovers of recrimination to follow. Let them all feel awful and pitiable for the next day or two.

Hallucinations, fear, and worse. But not death all on its own. Best not to give Crowley any ideas in retaliation. The Prague magicians rarely fought onside or even within the white lines of the football pitch, but they did not fight *that* dirty. Besides, too, this was clandestine at first, hard to detect. Until too late, and as much distraction and morale-sapping as meant to cause injury. The targets were the lumbering mecha-beasts, to get close enough to disable as many as possible. For troops to get lost in the general confusion, and for the Truth Offensive—for the truth often was offensive—to take hold. Let the enemy undo itself and fester in the aftermath of their truth-telling, while the Prague magicians retreated behind the great wall.

Out went the mist, in came her tufts, reporting back.

No sign of Jonathan.

No sign of Jonathan.

No sign of Jonathan.

Perhaps Stimply was wrong. Or perhaps they'd perished on the journey. No, she could not bear to think of that. She concentrated on the positives: Each tuft brought back something, and what they brought back as a group was a mental map of the forest and all going on within its bounds. That might help, too.

Ever more sappers and other provocateurs from the Czech side crept out with each new beer golem: compact, professional men and women skilled at sabotage. They knew the situation in Paris had cut Crowley off from his main supply lines, but they meant to cause mischief much nearer, make it hard for Crowley to resupply from depots and factories in Germany and Poland.

The beer golem reared up, a ponderous puffball lurching into the dim luminous forest gloom, this time with moss commanders behind. Silent. Sly. Covered in moss. Almost like mist themselves. They would use spells and ambushes to disorient and dissipate Emissaries. Some, too, would lie camouflaged on the forest floor for days after the mist lifted, waiting patient for the approach of Crowley's demi-mages and other soldiers, ready to dispatch them.

This after much effort in containing the chaos disgorged by the monster at the book club, Mack much help, she must admit, in herding all of it to the outskirts of town and then toward Crowley's encampment, to keep him busy as the mist thickened. All of this soured with the disappointment of being so close to the Golden Sphere and yet so far. The helplessness of being witness to two such dangerous Celestial Beasts. It begged the question: How could they control the Golden Sphere? And what mischief was it up to while "lying low"?

Meanwhile, behind them, the Czech magicians were now also busy getting screaming drunk. Which was something, given Czechs drank beer like champions.

Even with all this subterfuge, it was about time to return to Prague, and the safety within the wall. By Kristýna's estimation, the amount of magic they were generating, even so organic, even disguised, muffled, even sowing chaos within the enemy's ranks, would soon bring demi-mages and mecha-beasts their way.

Another beer golem.

Another tuft reporting.

Another moment of Mack being Mack. Saying nothing.

But what was there to say?

They remained together, for now, but it was, at least, for now, a husk.

A kind of ghost or golem itself. A nostalgia for the lost land of trust. And yet, perhaps, in time they might return there.

Tuft: No sign of Jonathan.

Another beer golem. This time the unit meant to sabotage the war elephants followed close behind. These were huge, grim-faced men, and some women: lumberjacks from the north, who with their axes and hammers that would make Crowley's beasts considerably less mobile.

Tuft: No sign of Jonathan.

Tuft: No sign of Jonathan.

Tuft: Sign of Jonathan!

Her heart leapt, but then she frowned. Not much of a sign. Could be misread. A stumbly glimpse of a boot, a possibly familiar hand. A salamander that knew something. Could be any lost boy in the woods. Could be.

Tuft to trust. She gently grasped the tuft from the air, placed it kind and comfortable in a cozy pocket.

It made up her mind, about something important.

"I have to leave now, Mack," she said, already not really there. Sad about it, but also in being resolved a kind of comfort.

"Back to Prague, then," he said, getting up from a stump.

"No. Into the forest. Without you."

"Oh," Mack said.

"Is that all you have to say?" But she couldn't look at his face, to see what emotion lay there.

"It's not sides, Kristýna, I keep telling you. It's not sides like you think." Did she imagine the hurt tone of his voice?

"If you think I don't know how it's complicated . . ." Forcing the words out around the hurt, against the part of her that would have liked to go back with him to Prague.

"Not two sides at least," Mack said, sounding, depressingly, like he'd rehearsed this in front of a mirror. "There are five sides at least, and we're on the same side two or three times. Just not the fourth or maybe the fifth."

Not depressing, she decided. Endearing. That he'd practiced this, that he'd wanted to get it right, for her. Even if it was still wrong. She'd never, ever heard a pleading tone in his voice before. But this wasn't how trust worked.

"I won't be back to Prague right away," she said. "You can take your time finding a new place."

Mack looked her in the eye and she had to return that gaze, to try to tell him something that way even as he said, "We're not done. We're not done yet, Kristýna."

She still felt for him in that moment. She still loved him—leaned up and planted a kiss on his neck as Mack reached down to hug her.

"If you want to try, to help," she said, "then help in the defense of the city. That will be worth something. But I need to go—now."

Because someone her loyalty meant something to needed her help.

Without looking back, Kristýna disappeared into the mist.

Chapper Oh I Feel Funny Sixty-Seven
FELLOWSHIP OF THE THING

The cow had been refreshing, invigorating, even. Ruth Less had forgotten how much pouching things drained her energy and then how unpouching them all at once and having a huge brawl right after, with a Celestial Beast no less, made her fatigued as well. As did maintaining her disguise in Prague, and preparing for the arrival of the little ones. The little ones would be born and then pouched, so that's why she had only left one thing in there. They needed their celestial room. She hadn't pouched most of the bears, just eaten them. There were just a lot of bears to go around.

Cow-full, Ruth Less bounded through the forest as best she could bound, on all fours as she was meant to, energy bursting out of her veins, her arteries, her thrapsases, and her three hearts. Through an ever-growing mist that Ruth Less sensed was unusual and thus grew the membranes over her mouth and many noses hidden around her body that would filter out the bad things.

It was also easier to eat than avoid as she bounded past some deer, a tasty shrub, four rabbits, a porcupine, and several other delicious creatures, guided into her maw by tendrils so that she cut a wide snacking swath through the forest, sampling its many delights. Fungus. Tortoise. Frog. Dandelion. Moss commander? Yes, moss commander is what it called itself, although it seemed mostly human with just a thin layer of moss on top. Into her maw it went.

All in all, Ruth Less did feel very jolly and joyous, not just from the snacking, but the pursuit of her quarry, even as she still had a quandary, in part about the quarry.

The mist helped her sense of smell in such a way that several human scents had become clear and her mission complicated by them. For they were not all in the same place as she might've hoped and the Mamoud scent was already too far—just about at the Prague wall.

Jonathan-stench came from one part of the forest, while Rack-Danny stink came from another part. Meanwhile, by accident or on purpose, Crowley-stench had also entered the forest, which she would prefer to avoid, having encountered it up close for too many hours already. If she were not about to have little ones, Ruth Less would have bifurcated and sent one her after Jonathan and one her after the others. But this was not possible without disrupting the little ones' growth inside her. She could feel them, in their thousands, bubbling and burbling. So very cute and secure.

Even more exasperatingly, Ruth Less could smell the intoxicating lusciousness of a juicy Black Bauble, as attractive to her as a truffle to a hog. Oh how her one hundred and twelve salivary glands flung glistening strands of ooze across the ground as she loped, just from the thought of the Black Bauble. Luscious, succulent Black Bauble.

It was a "blorpepbsikel" in her language, a rich node of nutrients regardless of its purpose as object. For blorpepbsikel and their ilk were mined from blor, a substance so delicious to her kind that to resist was almost fruitless.

Despite Wretch's commands.

For the blorpepbsikel wasn't with Jonathan, but with the Danny-stink.

What now to do, and she slowed her pace, for to veer off left would take her to Jonathan and to veer off right to Danny and the blorpepbsikel. Right would also take her farther from Crowley, who she preferred to meet only with others present.

She ate another deer whole while she argued with herself—a regular deer, not a nectar deer. Then she ate a wild boar hiding near a log, then the frog on the log, and all the millipedes and ants and grubs under the log. Then she ate the log.

Ruth Less hated Wretch, but he had shown her a place full of volcanoes and no food that she would like much, much less than Aurora, which was also more remote from her world than Aurora. Should she ever hope to return. Wretch had told her if she disobeyed or failed him, or kept failing him, which he saw (somewhat correctly) as disobedience, he would send her there.

Ruth Less did not want to go there, even as she knew instinctually that she might as she grew and matured and became powerful enough to snap Wretch's chain and be her own creature again. It was what Heady wished for her, and Speck, and the Tuft.

Usually, that time would be far, far off. Technically, Wretch could hurt her, maybe even kill her, if he wanted to. On the other hand, as Heady had said, "There is the letter of the law, and there is what you can get away with between the letters. Or maybe the letters even form different words than you thought or your enemy thought."

On the third hand, which on Ruth Less was just one of many, so she was physiologically used to contemplating lots and lots of lovely baby options, maturing them in her mind in their separate thought-cribs, "crib" being a baby term from Aurora she quite liked the sound of, even if no child of hers would ever live in a prison like a crib, but roam free in her pouch . . .

But, getting back to this third hand, the Black Bauble was fuel. A lot of fuel. Especially if she pouched it. Then it would be like an internal sun or combustion engine, radiating from within her, shining over her little ones. Whereas if she just ate it, Ruth Less would be quite powerful for a short period of time. Would that period of time be enough to plow through Crowley's army, kill him, kill Wretch, kill anyone else who sought to bend her to their will? She did not know the answer to that question.

She would have to pouch the Black Bauble to bring it to Wretch anyway. Pouching would change it because of the last thing left in her pouch. For a moment, she imagined swallowing Wretch. But he smelled so nasty, like a stinky cheese had had rotted meat shoved inside it and then the whole thing had been dunked in a toilet. She'd have to chew him up and spit him out, unpouched. But unpouched he would likely be, even chewed, vile and terrible. But pouched there was no doubt Wretch would contaminate that sacred space for her little ones.

She shouldn't eat the blorpepbsikel. But she must pouch the blorpepbsikel. The only question being if by doing so she might be beyond Wretch's punishment. Much depended on the quality of the blorpepbsikel. What they called on her world a "sjithidhluou" type of dilemma. You could only find out by doing the thing.

Ruth Less picked up her pace again. Wretch was lost in the mist. His flying Wretches were lost in the mist. But only for a time. She must hurry.

She had made up her mind.

Chap Shixty-Somethin'
A DUEL OR A FOOL, WITH A BLASTED TREE IN THE WAY

There were rather more people in the forest, moving through the mist, than Jonathan had imagined possible, but none of them were Rack, Danny, or Mamoud. He'd called their names at first, as he felt his way through the mist, but as unknown things lurched and grumbled and snuck all around him, Jonathan thought better of it. Stifled to a low murmur, his laughing and crying could give him away.

Both the laughing and crying had subsided somewhat as he'd become more and more . . . drunk? It was a hard sensation to judge, given he'd not been drunk before, had rarely even sampled a beer or glass of wine at Poxforth parties. But the symptoms mimicked what he'd seen in others: a surge of undeserved well-being, combined with a groggy inability to maintain full motor function—for which he groped and finally found a tree limb as a mist-tester and stout stick to hang onto in all his staggering.

Small men in odd hats and carrying tools on their belts, wearing lederhosenlike shorts and tunics, ghosted past in one glimpse bereft of mist and then also the bears again, so many bears, running away in terror from something, one almost bowling him over in its haste.

Once there was a loud clash and crash in the distance and the ghastly outline of a mecha-elephant in some distress, listing to the side, came to him like an overlay of spidery lines against the all-invading whiteness, only to disappear again.

There came, too, the tastes and smells of oil and dead bodies and other sensations that became more terrible as smells or tastes untethered, their provenance an absurd guess.

He concentrated on the smaller details coming to him, to ignore the growing fear, as he tacked this way and that, away from the general direction of the distressed mecha-elephant—deeper into the forest. At least, as he thought must be deeper. North, south, east, west were lost to him as the sun was lost to him. His mirth and his sorrow so routine that he had stopped being surprised by it already.

Instead, the twigs and leaves beneath his boots, that dry crackle, or rubbery hollow sound, or some compromise between the two. The sound of tiny creatures passing all around him, how so many were on the move, trying as he tried to avoid a faceless, nameless enemy. And he came to an abrupt stop, reacquainted with weeping, as he realized many of the creatures were fleeing him in his clumsy, groping progress.

How ridiculous his chain-gang-like progress, the nudge and shuffle, the entry of his precious branch into the murk like stirring a giant cauldron of cloudy soup with a huge spoon. To stir it up as meant to calm it down. He'd be lucky to be found wandering in circles.

That would be the best case, to find his own boot prints, and with the realization a flood of fond memory: on a trail in the wilderness of Florida, one he hadn't walked before, and being caught in a thunderstorm and turned around and lost, seemingly miles from civilization . . . only as the deluge ended to find the road's edge a few yards away.

So Jonathan stopped, finally. Stopped at the center of a small boggy meadow clearly colonized by some small beaver-type animal, and dominated by a giant oak, one that must have been hundreds of years old. He felt the rough susurrations of the bark, looked up through the mist at the vast array of dark branches, took in the relaxing smell of loam and leaves, the sometimes plonk, sometimes rattle, of incidental acorns falling to the ground.

He would stay here awhile, until the mist lifted, and then he would try again, to find his way to his friends or to Prague, where perhaps they would be waiting.

But it wasn't to be that simple, and he wasn't to get any rest or relief from the unknown. For soon enough, staring out from the oak, alert for danger, he spied a peculiar figure at the edge of the meadow.

A man, it appeared, tall, head rather bulkier than his body, likely bald, or had a cowl over his head—hard to tell in the murk.

The frogs had stopped croaking and the katydids, or local equivalent, stopped chirping and even the oak itself, or, at least, the breeze that anointed the oak's branches with motion, had eased for a time.

Jonathan stood still against the tree trunk, trying to will himself to look as much a part of the landscape as possible.

Voice, are you there? Voice, I could use your help or advice right about now.

But still there was silence and still Jonathan was alone in his own head.

The figure approached through the mist, and Jonathan thought to run, to leave the oak and disappear into the forest. Except he'd be as lost as before. Or worse. Except, it was but a single person and everyone told Jonathan he knew powerful magic.

So he waited there, by the oak, and took courage from its bulk and great age, as the figure came clear into view and stood before him.

A ghastly white oval of a head with small eyes and thin lips, a wedge of nose sitting in the middle of the rest. Only a few wisps of hair atop the head that Jonathan at first mistook for more mist. The head wobbled atop a body that gave the confident appearance of being both much younger beneath the cloak and tunic and trousers . . . and much slighter in frame than what it supported. For the head lay atop the slender neck rather like a huge soft-boiled egg perched atop a precarious small egg holder. An ostrich egg where belonged a chicken egg.

"Well met in the mist!" the man said in a raspy, nasal voice. "Well met in the mist!" And started to cry a little, which was only natural.

"You looked like a white blob in a sea of white blobs," Jonathan said. "I thought you were a mushroom," and he cried a trickle, too.

"No one ever talks to me like that," the bald man said, wistfully or perhaps mistfully.

"I don't talk to people the way I'm talking to people in the mist," Jonathan admitted.

"I'm terribly afraid all the time," the man blurted out with a bleat of laughter. "Most of the time." Put a hand over his mouth to prevent another laugh.

Was this man drunk as well? The more Jonathan stared, the more he could see a welter of redness and red veins at the top of the man's head.

"I don't know what I'm doing half the time," Jonathan said. Although, like all the other things he and the man were saying, it came out as slurry, difficult to understand.

"I'm homesick," the man said. "I'm homesick for a place that hates me."

"I don't know where home is."

"Oh boo hoo!"

"I've lost my friends."

"All my sub—my friends betray me or want to."

"I'm sorry to h—"

"Shut up!"

He was quite close now, right in front of Jonathan, and Jonathan felt of a sudden that he needed some space from that presence, that pressure. From the kind of hot breath emanating from the man, from the sight of the red-dotting perspiration on the man's doughy forehead. From the odd line between head and neck, the neck tan, and thus seemingly the head didn't belong even more than Jonathan had thought initially.

The urge had occurred to pull off the man's head to find the real head underneath. Although the longer he looked, the more he felt he'd met the man before, if only in a photograph. But where?

"Why do you back away, stranger in the mist?" asked the stranger in the mist.

"Just tired," Jonathan said, "and I want to sit down against this fine oak."

"It is a fine oak," the man said, and sighed and cried a bit but sat down heavily on some moss between two huge exposed roots, which he used as armrests.

Carefully, and still at a distance, Jonathan sat on a bole in a root that had formed almost stool-like and faced the man. He rather thought in a pinch he could run faster. Although, being both drunk and emotional, Jonathan had no wish to test his boast.

"I sensed you through the mist," the man with the egg head said. "You're a nothing that nothing passes through. That's what gave you away: nothing. Interesting, I thought. Thought I, I'd like to take a look at nothing."

In the middle of soon-to-be war? In the middle of the mist? Jonathan's senses might be befuddled, but ever more of a warning light went on inside.

"Not very polite," Jonathan said, but this time he didn't cry or chuckle, and by this sign and the way the mist was in places wisps and long, low-lying clouds through which he could see meadow grasses and woodland purple violets, Jonathan knew whatever had been happening to them was losing its effect.

On the man as well, for he poked his head around at Jonathan, almost like a snake, body in three-quarters profile, so he was propped up on one hand.

"You're not the Golden Sphere, are you?" the man asked.

"Not even close." Said without thought, instead of "Who? What?" Because he was shocked the man had said "Golden Sphere."

"Ah, so you know the Sphere?" The man's eyes glittered greedily, as if Jonathan had given him some great treasure.

"No." Said with a sinking feeling, as if it was too late to deny.

"But then I wonder wonder little stars just what the bloody hell you are."

"I'm not a star," Jonathan said. He put one hand in his pocket where lay the gently burbling knife.

The man's demeanor had become feral, eyes wild and gleaming, and the hands in the loamy soil closed around it like strangling claws. Jonathan was half-convinced the man was about to attack him on all fours.

"You're not a dirty, dirty spy, are you? One of those Czechs? Or of the Order? Even . . . a Lambshead?"

A blood-cold chill came over Jonathan, and a kind of clarity that chased out the grogginess.

"That's four questions," Jonathan said.

"Then answer them one at a time as we unravel this sordid onion."

"I'm not a Czech spy. And who's asking anyway?"

"We're a quarter way to you being . . . what? A pimple pleasant . . . I mean a simple pheasant . . . Goddamn this mist to hell and back. I mean a simple peasant who wanders this miserable forest gathering mushrooms? Or is it just firewood you father? Ye gods, I could use a real beer."

"Not a peasant," Jonathan said.

"A pheasant, then, after all? About to be flushed!"

"No."

"Still only a quarter way to safety, stranger."

"Halfway if you could count," Jonathan said. "And you've not said who you are."

"A simple farmer. I am a simple shit farmer who raises pigs and until recently, alas, cows and cow-men, one of whom is deceased, I believe, and the other ungrateful bastard ran off."

"Not even close to safety," Jonathan said. "I don't believe you."

"Well, then, I'm a head above the rest," the man said. "I'm an emperor in my own mind, Jonathan."

"Crowley . . . but my name's not Jonathan." He reveled in the ability to tell a lie again.

"Not a Jonathan," Crowley said, regarding him much as a gecko does a juicy fly.

A gecko with a head different from its body. A fly that couldn't take wing to safety.

"Not a Lambshead."

"I think you're a tricky liar," Crowley said.

"I think *you're* a tricky liar."

Crowley leapt to his feet.

Jonathan leapt to his feet, threw the magic pocketknife in Crowley's face. It latched onto his ear and started to bite Crowley. He screamed.

He screamed, but, incredibly, as if the pain meant nothing, Crowley also did an odd thing with his hands and a flash of light, a bolt of lightning or something stronger, surged at Jonathan from above and from all sides.

The light and heat sliced into and through Jonathan so sharp and icy that he couldn't even scream as he fell. Torn apart. He was being torn apart by a magic so cruel and hateful he would feel it in every atom of his being.

He fell, and as he fell and as darkness exploded within him and scarred him, his scream took form and substance.

As he was smashed into the darkness, the last thing Jonathan saw was the sight of Crowley's body on fire, toppling, and Crowley's head, one ear tattered, tumbling end over end back into the remnants of the mist, into the deep dark forest.

Black pit. A dwindling of available light. A glimmer in darkness, then nothing.

Chap (ashprin, pleash) Sixty-Nine
I AM A MOUNTAIN WITH FLOWERS ON TOP

In the end, it was easier than Ruth Less had thought, to bear down on her targets and snap them up. Despite her caution about the one with the bear gun. Ruth Less could handle more bears, but Ruth Less sensed she was at heart more like them than not, and for this reason only she did not like to fight them. The ones in the Alps, she had buried with respect after she'd killed them, rather than eat them.

The Danny-Rack scent separated and diverged, came close again, Rack following Danny in the mist, but the Black Bauble always with Danny. Soon enough, Danny and Rack were a shadow at the edge of her sight, figures framed by the white of mist and the drifting dark shapes of trees. The loam was intense and bright in her nostrils.

There came a clearing in the mist, a kind of air pocket, and within the open space Ruth Less could see Danny and Danny could see Ruth Less.

"Holy shit!" Another incomprehensible phrase.

"Holly sheet," Ruth Less mimicked.

"Bollocks!" Rack screamed, turning to run.

"Ball hocks!" Ruth Less screamed back.

"Get away from me!" Danny said, shouting over her shoulder.

"Got way om mee!" Ruth Less shouted with verve. She could speak more clearly in their language, but found they became more afraid and thus witless when she mimicked them incoherently.

One tentacle reached out—missed Danny, retracted.

"Got way om mee!" Loping after Danny as Rack veered off to the left, tripped on something, fell away into the mist. She could come back for him later.

It didn't take long to catch Danny. The ground-eating strides, delicate over tree roots. The lunge-pounce and her shriek as she fell into the moss and the mist closed over them again.

Ruth Less felt very pleased with herself as she konked Danny with love until she fell unconscious. Just two konks were enough. One to start, and one to make sure. Then she stuffed Danny in her enormous pouch.

Less happy-making: Danny's rat had disappeared and so had Rack. Something about the loam and moss now disguised his scent. Was he underground? Was he up a tree?

She wandered back and forth, sniffing and smacking her many lips. Prowled across that ground several times before giving up.

Then she skipped merrily off into the mist, headed back to Crowley's battle elephant, the one that smelled so comfortingly of the long-gone Speck, but contained the smelly Wretch.

Humming a song she'd picked up from the Comet Man. She didn't understand the words, of course, but she loved the melody. Her kind were very musical in their way.

> *Hug and burn,*
> *Burn and hug.*
> *Shard and lantern.*
> *Urgency for emergency.*
> *Lanterns and ash.*
> *Crumble and cackle.*

Well, she was making up some of the words because she'd forgotten the lyrics, but Ruth Less didn't care. She wasn't fussy about some things. Or most things. Although she wished the chapter headings weren't so drunk.

She would deposit Danny, without the Black Bauble, back at the war elephant, nicely wrapped up in some tentacles, disposable now that she would be changing her form anyway. She didn't think Wretch would mind it was Danny and not Jonathan. Besides, her nose told her that Crowley had already met with Jonathan, so everything was already sorted.

Nor did she feel guilt at leaving Danny with Wretch. She barely knew them.

Wretch would have to accept her "letter of resignation," as Heady had put it. She had already written it, proud of how well she had learned to put sentences together, even if some were Heady's idea. Although some were not, but she put them in anyway.

Dear Wretcher: Here is my tribute. You can make her tributaries. This concludes our business, for this is a much treasured tribute. If you try to find me, I will smash you. I will smash you with rocks and stab you with trees and I will not pouch you and I will also smash and not-pouch all the other Wretches. And I will fight to the last breath against you. And remember: A woodpecker's tongue curls all the way around its brain. Don't harm woodpeckers, for they are miracles. —Your Former Obedient Servant, the former Ruth Less.

Then she would be free to make her way to the outskirts of Prague and find a good place to become a mountain with a huge flower on top.

For she would be the most beautiful and largest flower in creation. The most fragrant. And all the prey would be drawn to that blossom and thus sustain her in her sedentary ways. She would photosynthesize and burgeon with young.

She would find a way to make this world her own.

Chapter (aspirin, please) Seventy
MOTHBALLS AND HEADACHES

"Throughout the newly christened Holy Crowley Empire, shall go out this inflexible decree:
No moth upon any of the Emperor's lands shall be harmed or in any way or method
encumbered with stress or demands beyond its natural life cycle due to the afflictions
of Man. Those who provide succor for moths—food, shelter—shall be exempt
from property taxes for a period of one year, with reduced taxes thereafter.
Penalty for noncompliance shall include seizure of lands, imprisonment,
or immediate decapitation without resuscitation."

—Handwritten by demi-mages on large signs nailed to trees or attached to stakes in
the ground, in Germany, Poland, Spain, and the outskirts of Prague

Wretch looked battered and worn, while Crowley felt fluttery. So very
wispy and fluttery and he felt "thous" and "thees" in his throat like he
had to cough them up, and he did not know why. He pulsed and flexed
his soft, feathery wings, there on the platform of the war elephant and
wondered what had happened to Wretch. It was perhaps better than
wondering what had happened to himself.

"I killed Jonathan Lambshead," he said to Wretch.

"We didn't find a body."

"I vaporized him all right. Epic battle, but I vanquished him."

What Crowley remembered most clearly was that intolerable pocketknife snipping his ear, crawling all over him, until he'd managed to
fling it from him. But also: inflicting terrible damage on the insufferable
Lambshead boy, even if, surprise, the boy had hidden powers of deflection.

Something had not just pushed him back, but moved through him and past him, seeking him in other manifestations.

Namely what he was linked to, like his battle elephant and the salamanders, and he'd had to block this intrusion, if with difficulty.

His own body had been vaporized, and the explosion of their clashing magics had sent him, his head, tumbling forehead over neck through the air, only for him to land in the crook of some oak branches high in the canopy, in a most undignified position staring out through the mist, which had begun to clear. Battered, bruised, but still alive or undead. Whatever Wretch's process had done to him.

He had been there for several hours before Wretch found him—and from his vantage and the cries of panic and surprise gurgling in the throats of demi-mages, the sudden wavelike surges of Emissaries in retreat (how was that possible!)—and took the evidence to mean that the mist had been part of an attack by the Czechs. It was difficult through the foliage, and with wood ants finding his nasal passages a wonderland, for Crowley to concentrate for too long. Especially because of the pain in his head, but further details did, during this prolonged vacation, become clear.

Several war elephants glimpsed in collage through the foliage no longer appeared operational. Some appeared to be slumped over, as if they'd fallen halfway into pits. In the middle distance, meanwhile, he could not be heard in warning from so high up and mist-muffled, as he observed the very moss beneath some of his common foot soldiers' feet open up and the treacherous Czechs hidden beneath pull them down into concealed trenches. Worse, right beneath his perch, requiring eyestrain to see from the downward periphery, there was enacted a conflict drama in which several huge, burly Czech men and women managed to render dead one of the smaller mecha-crocodiles, by application of hammer blows.

Mercifully, Wretch swept in then on ragged wings, an evil, smoldering look in his eyes, and, without a word, plucked him from his crook and airlifted him out of that place and back to the war elephant.

There had then been an extended period of unconsciousness, after which Crowley had woken up on the platform, feeling light and airy and not himself. He had not had the courage to try to look down at whatever new body Wretch had provided for him. But he was thankful Wretch hadn't yet summoned boring old Charlemagne.

"Is it bad?" Crowley asked. "Are we in retreat?"

He recalled seeing from above a half-dozen elephants smoldering, locked in place, singed around the edges, broken, the wheels frozen or blown off, splintered, useless. There was a gash in the side of their own elephant, and much to Crowley's distress, the salamanders had leaked out, disappearing into the cold, the whole system upset, diminished, short-circuited. Demi-mages distracted by Czech sappers.

Wretch sighed. "No. We just . . . I . . . did not expect, well, a beer mist that was also a truth serum and cover for an attack."

Magic was like the air force. Eventually, you had to send in the ground troops. Crowley had no idea where this thought came from; it seemed in part his but also not his.

"What have we lost?" Perhaps if he kept saying "we," Wretch would be more kindly disposed toward his counsel.

"Some mecha-elephants are now small fortresses and will never move again. A large number of mecha-crocodiles have gone to their maker. The Emissaries will need to be gathered and herded back here; something the Czechs did gave them a fright and they are scattered throughout the forest and some seem no longer to recognize our own soldiers as friends. Our supply lines back to Germany are all cut for now, but for one, and small bands of very annoying and determined Czechs hold those roads."

Wretch spoke in a weary way, as if shocked that he had to think about situations he had never envisioned coming to pass. Which made it all the more curious that Charlemagne would not yet be on the platform.

"Anything else?"

"Ruth Less has given up to us a friend of Jonathan Lambshead as prisoner and disappeared."

Clearly, Wretch didn't like having to tell Crowley this.

"When you say disappeared . . ."

"For good, I think. One of the demi-mages brought me a severed tentacle he said she called her 'letter of resignation.'"

Where would Ruth Less get the idea for a letter of resignation? The world was odder sometimes than Crowley cared to dwell on, so he didn't. Besides, he'd never cared for Ruth Less. Who cared if she'd gone off somewhere. Care was overrated. Care could go off and—

"What have we gained?" Crowley asked.

"The prisoner. Currently in the fade pens. Plus some of the sappers and one Czech magician who keeps turning into a frog to thwart our questioning. We also destroyed the staging ground for the mist and have established an outer perimeter closer to Prague."

"Anything else?"

"Latrine has arrived with a few Paris demi-mages and four carts of rabid animals. I have put him in charge of the fade pens for now."

"Well, that's something."

And it was. Good old Latrine. Crowley supposed he should start calling him Lautrémont again. Or maybe not. "What do we do next?"

"We're still a mighty force. We still will prevail."

Wretch said these words in a perfunctory way that frightened Crowley. Much as he might plot against Wretch and hate Wretch, the awful, terrible, gut-churning thought occurred that without Wretch, Crowley was nothing. Less than nothing—he'd be dead in a month, or overthrown. Or both.

The Lambshead boy's burst of wild magic had knocked some sense into his head, had been good for him. He could see that now. The universe was very dangerous, and he'd been pompous, vain, and narrow-minded. Would he rather be back in his old place, unable to work magic, or serving Wretch in this world and helping conquer it?

"Crowley, I need a favor," Wretch said, and Crowley noted the tone of respect and also of intimacy, almost as if trying to indicate . . . friendship? Or comradery?

"What is it?"

"I need you to unbind the Emissaries with our German forces and also those in Spain and Poland. We need a bit of chaos in those places where uprisings are imminent."

Crowley bit his tongue until it bled a little and he could taste salt. He would need to do that a lot going forward, for his first impulse had been to say, "Oh, now you need me, you bollocky clumsy bat. You horrifying blood-recycling *fiend*."

"It will take a little time, but by nightfall, it shall be done," Crowley replied.

"And I will need you to take a more hands-on approach to the mechanics of our war effort. You now have a wealth of experience available to you. Courtesy of the magic of my master."

"I've always thought you served a higher power, or a lower power," Crowley said, and there was a tingle of excitement. Perhaps his claustrophobia in the elephant had also been about a diminishment in the stinging, lashing excitement of the new. Nothing new had happened for ages, not after the initial adrenaline rush of a new world, new power, and, then, so many new bodies and so many beheadings. For if Crowley were honest, much of his behavior also came out of sheer boredom, of how the world turned gray if not roiled up and pushed into motion.

"I have found the ultimate solution to your conflict with Charlemagne," Wretch said. "I have given you his body, and his spirit now exists within you, in specific his military expertise."

This should have been unsettling, but perhaps too much had already happened for Crowley to be too thrown by the news.

His fluttery-ness had a purpose. He had a purpose. He looked down at his perfect new body: the sumptuous and quietly gorgeous cloak of moth wings. How from his head now sprang feathery antennae. How in addition to wings he still retained arms and legs and torso. How he could see like a moth through his human eyes if so wished.

How Charlie Mange was no more.

How the "thees" and "thous" resolved in the back of his skull into a distant shadow of military maps and calculations about use of force and the proper length of supply lines and when to use calvary. Melding seamless with the man who knew very little about any of this.

He'd gotten Charlie Mange in the end, by becoming Charlemagne, in a way.

"Think of it as residue," Wretch said. "Soon enough, what you feel won't even be like a separate person inside you, but just part of your mind. Trust me, I know."

And for a moment, in the haunted look Wretch gave him, Crowley saw not the hideous bat eyes, but the eyes of another looking out, far distant and already receding.

"Perhaps now," Crowley said, "we must needs redefine this relationship. I am not my master, you no familiar. But neither are you my ruler. Shall we stand side by side, bound by dark magic?" Aware his syntax was infected by Charlemagne, but there it was. He was a changed man. Or somewhat changed. He wondered idly if he would lay eggs soon.

Wretch nodded. "Side by side it is."

Who knew if he meant it or was lying, but some semblance of equality was enough for Crowley now.

He stared out at the hillside of Prague, some miles distant, frowned. "What is that?"

For upon the hillside, near the old fortress, to the west of it, there now floated the most peculiar large building, transparent, shifting, so that it was at some times like a fortress itself, others like a château, and then indescribable in the crenellations and other building styles. But, throughout, it remained a vibrant, glowing . . . pink . . . as it hovered and rotated in place.

"What is that? What in all the hells is that?"

Wretch cursed in a language apparently composed of sharp sticks driven into exploding eyeballs.

"The Château Peppermint Blonkers."

"Is it a joke? Some kind of Czech joke?"

"No, Crowley. It is not a joke. It is yet another complication. To deal with in its time."

Crowley nodded. More and more had become clear to him. Thoughts of last stands and heroic counterattacks flickered through his moth-mind.

"We must find the Golden Sphere." He had never said it with such force. He had never meant it so completely. If it took burning Prague to the ground and fighting to the last demi-mage, he must have the Golden Sphere. It was the only way forward.

"Yes, this is true, Crowley," Wretch said, but the urgency in his voice had another source. "But for now, come quickly, it is time to meet my master. It is even more important that you understand all."

Crowley nodded. The Charlemagne inside him understood. The man who reacted in haste to each new thing soon ended in ruin. He'd known for a long time Wretch couldn't be acting alone. Wretch, his un-familiar.

"Lead the way, my dear Wretch," Crowley said.

Wretch nodded and rose in a great flapping of leathery wings, while Crowley followed in a silent and abiding glory of silky soft flight that so gently lapped the air that there was no sound at all, and this was the most glorious thing of all: to make no sound as you traveled through the world, to be so part of the sky that it was as if you were the sky.

The euphoria was unbearable and unending.

And so they ascended into the circling flock of Wretches above, and then, through them, into the circling black-red demon hole in the sky, and as that swirling portal of the unknown took them, Crowley still reveled in the softness of his new self and recoiled at the thought of ever again taking fully human form.

Even as Crowley wondered why so many of his demi-mages down below had odd-shaped shadows and some of them had shadows moving of their own accord.

Chapter Seventy-One

THE CHÂTEAU PEPPERMINT BLONKERS

A crack in the firmament with a weed sticking out. A rip. A fracture. A soundless scream across the deep. And just like that, Sark and Jaunty Blue were back in the Château Peppermint Blonkers, standing inside the entrance.

Staggering to the leeward, legs still accustomed to boats even on dry land: Sark and Jaunty Blue. But other problems, too, even if of the sort they'd become accustomed to.

"Oh dear, oh dear," Sark said. "And you'd just repaired your Fresian water robe. And now we're full of bullets. How did that happen?"

Jaunty Blue made an elaborate "who knows" gesture. His gestures tended to be dramatic so they could be understood through the robe.

"Would be a problem if we were actually here in our skins. Another astronomical tailor bill, though, I'm afraid, ol' Jaunty. Always seems to add up but not yet past due."

Jaunty Blue made a gesture that meant, sardonically, *Haunted by a dark and twisted past.*

"Forever and always," Sark said in an affectionate way.

A long corridor lay ahead, with dozens of doors on either side.

"In my father's house there are many rooms," Sark said. "Although I agree with you, Jaunty, that there are too many animal trophies."

The corridor indeed was crowded with mounted animal heads on the walls. All of which were growling or weeping or snarling or shrieking or screaming or pleading or, in rare cases, chuckling maniacally.

It was, as the clamor rose at their approach, always a tad overwhelming. Such a wonderful greeting to mark their return.

"Yes, my pretties, we're back," Sark said as they walked down the corridor, Jaunty Blue unable to resist stopping at times to pat the head of a particular favorite.

There were several human heads among the rest, but Sark and Jaunty Blue ignored their pleading. Those heads were, after all, there for a reason. Even if neither Sark nor Jaunty Blue could remember that reason.

At the end of the corridor, before it opened up onto a vast hall full of comfy chairs, Sark stopped and looked at Jaunty Blue.

"With or without heads?" he asked.

Jaunty made a chopping motion across what might reasonably be presumed to be where his throat was. Probably.

"Rightly so," Sark said, agreeing. "Minimalist it is."

He reached over to a red lever that appeared on the wall as the heads all began to protest.

"Bye-bye," Sark said, and pulled the lever.

Behind them, circular blades beheaded each trophy, and they all fell to the floor in a cacophony of unpleasantness, rolling around for a time before the floor itself grew tired of their complaining and absorbed them whole.

The silence was most pleasing.

Beyond the great hall lay all the rooms that did not lead to other places. A museum of fused spines. A hall of fashion dummies. A room full of dirt ablaze with wildflowers. A display of outrageous fossils.

The château had never had much respect for temporal-spatial niceties, nor for coherence.

Sark and Jaunty Blue had much respect for the château. In part because they had died trying to rob it, the original, that is. On an Earth far, far away. Centuries ago. Perhaps longer.

On one side of the great hall there was a tall mirror or a doorway—it was all the same in here, and fast-approaching, as if they weren't walking through a château but instead a bird diving down from the sky. Through the panoramic windows swift now a city appeared down below, the corridor become a balcony that had swept them up in its embrace.

"Could this be it, Jaunty? The exact moment of our un-exile?"

Jaunty clapped his begloved hands.

"What do you think of our invoker this time?"

Jaunty made a gesture with his cloak that pulled it off for a moment by mistake to reveal the terrors beneath.

Sark looked away quickly while Jaunty fixed himself. "Quite right. Invoker behind the invoker."

"A worthy cause to someone," Jaunty gestured.

"None worthier, Jaunty. And what shall we get out of it? Another vacation? Escape? Something . . . bigger?"

Jaunty Blue's body language told Sark there was never any escape from the Château Peppermint Blonkers. Besides, it would not do to express certain wishes. The Enemy might be listening in—*was* listening in, probably.

A spy. Tiny. So many rooms. A rat in the walls. So hard to keep the riffraff out.

The voice of the château rang hard in their heads in a most unpleasant way. Time to change the subject. Really, Sark knew better, but every once in a while it was worth testing things. Even if the answer was always the same.

"Tell me, Jaunty Blue," Sark said, to change the subject, staring at the horizon over the city. "Tell me this—why would English dirigibles fly a French flag? Any thoughts?"

Jaunty Blue shrugged.

"No matter." For how could it possibly matter, in the long run. "But now I sense this new adventure may be a story for the ages . . . shall we retire to the bar, for I sense a supplicant approaching, and I've let It in."

The bar in the château was a shimmering gold with hovering soft light above and comfortable stools with backs, curving along opposite a panoramic wall looking down over Prague. At the bar, one could find any kind of intoxicant ever made across most of the worlds.

By the time Sark and Jaunty Blue arrived, the Golden Sphere was already there, having (rather presumptuously, Sark thought) taken golden-man form and seated itself. Currently drinking a huge pint of beer that was spilling through dozens of pinprick holes. Which rather made Jaunty Blue, stuck full of bullets, exchange a glance with Sark that said, "Tribute or parody?"

"Obliviousness," Sark replied.

The Golden Sphere turned toward them, held out its golden hands. "Ah, old friends, if I may call you that. I just feel as if I've gotten to know you on a practically subterranean level superfast. You see, and I'll cut to the chase," and here the Golden Sphere grew sad puppy-dog eyes, "there are unnatural forces afoot in this world that mean me harm."

"Ah, yes, but we find ourselves in a quandary, Old Stone," Sark said.

"Whether to grant me sanctuary as befits my status or subject your-selves to the crude onslaught that is Crowley?"

"Well, Unholy Wheel, it's more that we don't much trust you."

"But . . ."

"Also, a certain, let's see here . . . *Kafka* . . . has lodged a complaint."

"He has not!"

"He has, too."

"On what grounds?"

"Never you mind."

"How did he even—"

"Oh, it could just be Jaunty making something up, but we must still take even made-up things seriously. This complaint. Interference with the natural order. Imposition of unnatural sea shanties—that sort of thing."

"BUT YOU ARE BOTH HIGHLY UNNATURAL."

My, how quickly the Golden Sphere became rattled. It must have "seen some shit," as one adversary had said to them once.

"Tut-tut. It's impolite to bring up Jaunty's having been riddled with bullets. You really shouldn't have mentioned it."

"My apologies."

"Apologies won't cut it I'm afraid."

The Golden Sphere sobered. "I am a Celestial Beast, in all dignity and sincerity apologizing—and seeking refuge."

"Sorry—can't hear you. The bullet holes are very loud and judgmental."

The Golden Sphere pulsed red. "You're mad. You're truly mad."

"Hurtful words. Another demerit."

The Golden Sphere dimmed to a humble mauve.

"Is there nothing you can do for me?" Pleading. "You are only here because of me! I summoned you!"

"Oh, you were the vehicle for the summons, true. But you were not the summoner."

"That makes no sense."

"Few things in this world do. Or in the next. Now, we must ask you to leave."

"I am not sure I want to. I am not sure I don't instead wish to do you harm."

"Understandable. Still, you must. Leave. I'm not at all interested in battling a Celestial Mechanism such as yourself."

"CELESTIAL BEAST." Burning bright once more, like a sphere-shaped tyger in the night.

"If you say so. But, just: go. Your application has been denied. Jaunty Blue has rejected your appeal."

"Who summoned you, then? So I can rip their heart out and feed it to them."

"That would be confidential information. Even as to the matter of whether they have a heart."

"I'm not leaving," the Golden Sphere snarled, sphere once more, spitting fire.

"Bye-bye," Sark said as Jaunty Blue pulled a lever that had appeared next to him.

A door opened in the floor and the Golden Sphere, screaming, was sucked out, to plummet to the earth below. To take its chances in Prague.

"Well, that was fun," Sark said. "What's next?"

Jaunty Blue was oblivious to the question, too intent on finishing off the Golden Sphere's beer.

Besides, they both knew the answer.

Alfred Kubin, the true summoner of the château, waited in the antechamber.

Chapter Seventy-Two
THE HOUSE ON THE RIDGE AND A MYSTERIOUS WOMAN

Jonathan woke to a burning pain in his left side and a shooting pain in his shoulder, but also the aching soreness of strained muscles. He felt as if he'd smashed into concrete from a great height. When he tried to move his left arm, he found it was in a cast, and the cast was in a sling. He was wearing pajamas with cat images all over them. Cats at play and cats at rest. Calico cats, tuxedo cats, black cats.

Well, that would at least indicate he wasn't in the hands of the enemy.

Birdsong. Everywhere around him, it seemed, and so at first he thought he was back in Dr. Lambshead's mansion with the bird-children. Had it all been a terrible dream?

Except the bed felt different, a bit saggy, and the air felt different, too. That expectant, hushed quality before a thunderstorm, charged and humid.

The birdsong was familiar. Red-bellied woodpeckers, cardinals, thrashers, mockingbirds, wrens, and the burry chirrup of the summer tanagers he loved so much . . . and, too, there were other sounds that served as clues this couldn't be the mansion, nor Prague, either.

For one, he could swear he could hear the energetic, clumsy sound of armadillos digging somewhere down below.

Down below?

He tried to open his eyes, gasped, cried out. His head was like a bucketful of nails and the act of trying to open his eyes had made the pail fall over. He waited a moment for nausea to pass, tentatively tried again. His right eye opened proper, revealing a high wooden ceiling above him, with skylights. But he couldn't quite open his left eye. Felt with his right arm, found a numbness there, and a puffiness, and a gauze bandage wrapped partway around his head. But he was fairly sure an eye resided within its proper orbit. So perhaps soon he would be able to open it. Something absurd about his relief that it was only one eye he couldn't open.

Which was another way of admitting he'd expected to be dead.

He looked around with his good eye. He was in a small, bungalow-like room. On a double bed with a nightstand and a closet. A confusing tangle of flowers and herblike plants crowded the nightstand. He rather thought he saw some weeds or more herbs peeking out of the bottom of the closet door. Curious.

The hardwood floors were pine. A few feet beyond the bed, huge window-doors led out onto a small wooden deck painted gray. All around outside were trees—glorious, familiar trees. Live oaks, water oaks, magnolia trees, cypress trees, and . . . it was overwhelming.

He was back in Florida, no doubt about it, and alive. He'd made it out of Aurora, somehow.

Stiffly, weight on his good arm, he rose from the bed. Felt dizzy, felt old.

Unexpected, there came a weight on the bed beside him. A small weight—and a familiar face staring up at him, cheerful. Dr. Lambshead's pocketknife! Not lost at all. It must have stayed by his side after he lost consciousness.

A sudden pang, an upwelling of tears. Good old magic pocketknife. Old pal. He would need to treat the pocketknife better. To understand more about all the magical things. So he didn't take them for granted.

He knew he wasn't fighting back tears because of a pocketknife, but there it was. He felt eviscerated, hollowed out. Like anything could set him off.

Sat on the edge of the bed for a while, then gathered up the pocketknife, which in seeming delight lived up to its name and scurried into his pants pocket.

Then Jonathan shuffled to the window-doors, slid aside the screen door that kept out the mosquitoes, and went out onto the deck . . . there to look upon a heavily wooded ravine with a small clearing at the bottom and a dry creek bed, the area beyond the creek covered in pine straw and loam, in which stood elderberry bushes and an intricate bird feeder station.

There were, indeed, earth pigs snuffling around for grubs in the clearing and, gravitating to the bird feeder, dozens and dozens of birds. He dubbed the armadillos Cutie and Patootie. But he already knew them, or their parents, had called them an assortment of nicknames.

He caught his balance against the deck railing, appreciated the solid feel of cedar under his hand, soft but hard, rough but smooth. Something to hold on to for more than his balance.

For he knew the bird feeder. He knew the ravine. Just, from the other side, the westernmost bungalow and its dilapidated deck a postage-stamp-sized mirage from his vantage.

The little house he'd grown up in. The deck, falling apart, that he'd stood upon so many times, staring out at the many trees. Wondering who lived in the peculiar place that almost looked like a tree house across the ravine.

And now, Jonathan supposed, he would find out.

Oh, Sarah, even exile wouldn't be simple, straightforward, would it? No easy aftermath.

No, of course not.

It was all enough to make his head spin, and not from his injuries or whatever medicine he'd been given.

There were wildflowers without human faces down below, and he laughed with joy to see so many familiar friends: the delicacy of beardtongue, the reliance of Silphium sunflowers, the hardy, tall salt bush and the straggling butterfly weed, swamp hibiscus, and swampier milkweed. With the armadillos, armored intruders but bumblers too earnest and endearing to begrudge them their garden excavations, barreling through, making a riotous mess.

"Hello, chum," a voice said from behind Jonathan.

He turned slow, with care. There, in the doorway, sat his dear friend, in a decidedly non-offensive wheelchair.

"Rack!"

Rack smiled. "In the flesh. It got worse, before it got better, after we were separated, but here we are."

But the "we" rang false and any relief Jonathan might have felt at seeing him, so fit and dressed so proper and Floridian in shorts he must feel were a fashion disaster and a linen shirt he must find very plain, was tempered by the sight of Tee-Tee on Rack's shoulder. Rack taking care of Tee-Tee. Now there was a laugh. But he wasn't laughing.

Rack's gaze was tempered, too, even as Jonathan asked the question to which he knew the answer.

"Danny?" Felt numb, woozy again.

Rack shook his head, looked away. "Missing. We don't know where. Crowley?"

"Mamoud?" Hoping, perversely, that maybe they were missing together. Have at least that hope of helping each other.

"Made it to Prague, helping lead the resistance, last we heard."

"We?" Jonathan asked.

Rack hesitated. "How are you feeling?"

"Better than dead."

Rack nodded. "Very well. Then there's someone upstairs you should talk to—alone—rather sooner than later. The person who rescued you. And me."

❧

Upstairs, even higher in the canopy, was yet another deck that looked out over the vines and trees and more birdsong here, too. The armadillos were little gray oblong dots below, snuffling and snorting.

The top floor of the house, with cathedral ceilings of cedar, lined with long, wide windows. So much light came in, the hardwood floors shone with it. The peculiar asymmetrical living room couch shone, too.

The surreal art on the walls spoke to Jonathan in a specific way, as if he had helped choose it.

Around the corner, the kitchen and the dining room table, with more amazing windows. A small woman in a dress covered in flowers stood next to the dining room table. She had dark brown hair, startling eyes, a small nose, and he couldn't tell how old she was. Perhaps it was a quality of the eyes, which had a directness, an odd clarity, and how she looked right at you and did not look away. She could have been anywhere from her late thirties to fifties. Later, he could not even remember what color her eyes had been.

But he remembered her from the memory the Voice had given back to him while falling. The topiary, the odd tent, Dr. Lambshead taking him on a stroll . . . where? Aurora? So, a member of the Order.

Yet something about her was much more familiar than that. A silhouette, ducking into a hedge. Not Alice. Not Alice at all.

"You were the person I saw when I arrived at Dr. Lambshead's mansion!" It felt so good to have figured that out, even if it seemed like the littlest thing now, after everything else.

"Yes, I was. And I am also the one who found you in the forests outside Prague, badly injured, and brought you here."

"With a stop at the hospital first, I gather," Jonathan said.

"Yes. Rather important. Although I have some healing skills myself."

"The plants on the nightstand."

"Exactly."

"Forgive me getting to the point," Jonathan said, "but what is this place? Right across from my old digs. That cannot be coincidence."

"This place is where the Order kept watch over you, Jonathan. By Sarah's orders," Kristýna said.

"You were across the ravine the whole time."

"Part of the time, yes. Other people other times. Members of the Order."

"And who are you? And why were you spying on me at the mansion?"

She hesitated. "Perhaps you'd like to sit down."

"Just tell me."

"Well, Jonathan . . . I'm your grandmother. Dr. Lambshead's former wife."

"But she died in a car crash!"

"Yes, that was the easiest way to disappear. It was a very dangerous time."

His grandmother.

The room was swimming and the trees were on the inside, not the outside, and the armadillos were up on their hind legs, dancing in a circle with him. He felt quite faint and overcome, and he would have fainted if not for Kristýna shoving a glass of water into his hands. A long drink helped.

She sat opposite him at the dining room table, quiet but watchful, as he recovered.

"Why?" he asked, after a minute. "Why in the blazes have you hidden yourself from me my whole life?"

"It was too dangerous."

"You said that. And now?"

Kristýna leaned forward, would have taken his hand in hers, but he put it down at his side. Which made his broken arm hurt. He winced. She leaned back again, regarding him. He couldn't read her expression to save his life.

"It's changed, Jonathan. It's changed so much. Still dangerous, but less point in hiding it. Everyone knows you're alive."

"So I guess I'm in it whether I want to be or not."

She shook her head. "No. You still have a choice. You've been badly injured, suffered a trauma. You can live here, away from it all, if you like. No one will find you here for years and years."

"And yet, eventually, they will. And meanwhile, my friend Danny's out there, without even Tee-Tee to help her."

"Listen to me," his grandmother said, and there was force to her voice, cutting through his nattering on. "You can have a normal life. You can, if you want. And no one should tell you otherwise."

"I wonder what a normal life would look like now."

He fell silent and she said nothing and clouds took away the sunlight and filled the room with shade. The greenery outside. The sighing of the trees. The whisper of needles from the tall pines. There, on a branch, a nuthatch, doing silly nuthatch things. Hard not to love a nuthatch. He could be so happy here, work in the garden, feed the birds.

It made him sad, though. All of it made him sad. The beauty here, the violence out there. The fact his grandmother, sitting across from him, was a stranger. That he did not feel as if he could reach out to her, embrace her. Even call her Grandmother.

"What do you want to ask me, Jonathan?" Kristýna asked finally. "I cannot stand this silence. You may think this has been easy for me. It hasn't. I can tolerate it if you dislike me, if you dislike the choices I've had to make. But this silence . . . I can't."

"Don't take it personally," he said. "I need time."

"Then ask me questions. Let me help by giving you the comfort of answers."

"All right, then," he said, looking her in the eye. Which took a deep and abiding effort, because she would always have a strength of personality that was hard to look upon direct.

"All right, then," she echoed, a thin smile across her mouth. And now he saw the age lines and he saw the age and he saw sacrifice and he saw . . . he saw that she was his grandmother. He felt it, for the first time.

"Is Dr. Lambshead alive? Did he survive Wretch's attack?"

"Your grandfather? Yes. He's still safely hidden at the Institute."

Jonathan let out a deep sigh of relief. "There's that, then. And the Wobble? Did we lose it? Do we know?"

"It is lost."

"I'm sorry." And he was. It felt a bit like a body blow, after all they'd been through. He tried not to think about what it meant that they didn't know where Danny was, but also knew she didn't have the Wobble.

His grandmother shrugged. "The Wobble was a good plan, solid. One of the better things Thwack came up with in his later years, to be honest. We plan to get it back, if possible, and continue with our initial plan. But if it's off the table, we go on to the next thing."

"And what is the next thing?"

"For you? Go back to Poxforth with Rack. At least, for a while."

"But we have to go after Danny!"

"We don't know exactly where your friend is, Jonathan. And she is in the middle of a war zone, in a situation rapidly escalating. Let those more expert at these things do their work."

"I can't leave her there. Rack can't."

"You didn't let me finish, which I think is a harbinger of things to come . . . Jonathan, the headmaster at Poxforth is not himself."

"Yes—he's dead, in fact."

"Perhaps. It's not as straightforward as that. Things at Poxforth are . . . very strange. Also at Porthfox. It will benefit the Order more for you to be back at the academy, figuring this out."

"After everything that happened?" Bitter. "To be sidelined at Poxforth."

"Not sidelined. Helping. Learning more about your magic. Learning to control it. And investigating a mystery that we need to know the answers to. While you also study more about the Order. There is so much to tell you. To brief you on. Now that I can."

"You'll teach me? You'll explain my . . . powers?"

"As best as I'm able. It's better than plunging you back into this kind of war that's coming."

"What kind?"

"The kind played by fools who think it's a game. It isn't a game. Millions could die."

"Like my mother. Did she die because of this game?"

"My daughter lives on in you. You have her eyes. You are like her. In so many ways. You don't even know."

Were those eyes glistening now, with tears? It must be a trick of the light.

"And my father?" The lurch and dislocation of those three words. But he had to know. She had to know.

She hesitated. "The truth may be difficult for you."

He erupted at that, half out of his seat. "Do you think I care? Everything's difficult. Everything. Just tell me!"

"I'm not that—"

"Out with it!"

"Fair enough. Your father is . . . Stimply. He's your father. And I know that may be a lot to take in. But it's true."

Jonathan sat down, stunned. Everything was swimming, like he was having a stroke. Silly, disorganized Stimply.

Stimply.

"But he's . . . he's . . . ridiculous."

"Jonathan!" Kristýna's eyes flashed. She seemed genuinely angry. "Stimply is one of the bravest men I know! He risks his life for the Order every day."

Stimply. His father.

"How . . . why . . ."

"He's a better man than he seems."

"But he's a fool!"

"He's a muddled man. A complicated man. A haunted man. But he's *not* a fool. There's just a lot on him. He's much harried at the moment, by our enemies. He risked his life to call you all those times, because he loves you."

No all-powerful father to rescue him. No, instead he had . . . Stimply.

"I'll take your word for it. He could've told me anytime." Trying to compose himself.

"No, he couldn't have. Too dangerous for him and for you. No one must know he's your father. Ever."

"Ever."

Kristýna relented. "Or at least until the situation changes—drastically."

Stimply.

He'd been talking to his father for over a year. About stupid things. About silly things. About things that didn't matter. Or did matter. All those sounds in the background. All those frenetic, terrible sounds, while Stimply tried to keep his calm. While his father tried to keep his calm.

Jonathan began to weep. Just put his head in his hands and bawled.

"Jonathan! It's not that bad. As I said, Stimply—"

He raised his head, wiped his nose, tried to stanch the tears. "No, no, you don't understand. It's okay. It really is. I just . . . I just realized, you know—I have a family again. I have a grandfather, I have a grandmother. I have a father."

He reached out his good hand and took Kristýna's in his.

"Grandma," he said, trying it out.

It felt good. But it still felt odd, too.

⁓

Later, Jonathan returned to his room, to the balcony, spent. They would have dinner soon, him and his grandma and Rack and Tee-Tee. They would sit down at the dining room table, and his grandmother would serve him dinner. How miraculous. How unreal.

Everything receded over time. Pain. Loss. Even without Dr. Lambshead resurrected, he had a whole mansion filled with the man's history and belongings. It was almost more real than the man himself.

But Sarah. He had her stories; he would now have her mother's stories about her. But it was harder and harder to conjure up her face. Was that a good thing? Should he let it happen or fight it? Would he still be his mother's son? What would be left of her? In the end, he'd only ever cared about what she wanted for him—a mother who had given him a fake name, who had hidden him from his own family. Had wanted him out of sight. For his whole life? Or only until he could decide for himself?

The nasal pulsing croak of gray tree frogs from the pine trees. A light rain coming down now, and he let it fall down on him. Such a relief. That wet, soaked, humid jungle. He would hate to leave this place, but the memory of it, in his heart, would sustain him through whatever came next.

Jonathan would never be Dr. Lambshead, the eccentric public figure to whom action had come so effortless, who had, before, seemed so decisive and extraordinarily gifted . . . at everything. He was too much his mother's son, and thankful for that.

But Sarah hadn't sat on the sidelines, and he found he didn't want to sit on the sidelines either. Not really. A rising emotion he could not identify overtook him, like the swell of orchestral music. Neither anger nor sadness, but determination. Perhaps this place made him more himself than before, or he'd just experienced so much in such a short amount of time.

All Jonathan knew was that he'd be damned if someone else, no matter how wise, made his decisions for him. If his path led to Poxforth, or even back to Prague on Aurora, that would be his choice. His alone.

"Are you there, Voice?" he asked, out loud.

I am, Jonathan. I am here. Always.

"Good. I'm going to need you."

He was going to need everyone and everything.

There was a Golden Sphere to be captured, by hook or by crook, a deranged dictator to unseat, and a mystery within the Order to solve.

Chapter Seventy-Three

A PARLIAMENT OF CROWS

The hedgehog House of Commons was in session—and in full-throated uproar over something called "Breakfast" or "Brex-fast" as Alice Ptarmigan skulked by the doorway. They were also debating the usurper Jules Verne's attack on the magical wall and not making much progress on that front, either.

She had the right to be there, invited by a member of the House of Lords, and yet still she felt like a thief in the night. Perhaps it had something to do with being neither inside nor outside, the facade of a "room" for the hedgehogs built around the base on the gigantic oak, a good two hundred feet in diameter, that housed Parliament there, close by the River Thames. And the oak itself surrounded by a guardian host of lesser forest trees, stretching a good mile out into the countryside from London proper.

The garrulous hedgehogs were also debating what to do about Verne's occupation of the wall, in squeaks and clicks that few could understand. A hue and cry, as Alice interpreted it, because the magical wall had been taken by Jules Verne—even though England rarely ruled it themselves. So what the hedgehogs really debated was how to return the wall to a kind of impassable chaos. Most government traffic and merchant trade went by sea to avoid the wall. Much better it would have been, for England, if the land bridge didn't exist and they were just an island.

Of course, the hedgehogs were drunk on a special kind of honey mead and pissing and shitting everywhere: side effect of their . . . condition. Thankfully, they were just normal-sized hedgehogs or things would've gotten much dodgier, much quicker.

Alice reached the curving walkway that swept up the oak to its upper branches and the chambers of the House of Lords. The crows would be up there, pissing and shitting as well.

Beyond them, at the very top of the oak: the King and Queen, in their tree-house castle. They were made of living stone and had been encased as king and queen for hundreds of years, to ensure continuity. They made decisions very slowly, so the Houses brought few questions to them, as answer or decree might takes years. By now, the stone monarchs were quite mad from lichen cracks and incapable of rule, cared for by tree-climbing magical lemurs brought in for the purpose. Or so Alice had been told. The monarchs had not been seen by anyone other than, presumably, lemurs, for two decades.

It was all rather too much. An insight into governance that once seen could not be unseen, one that did not imbue politics with much respect.

⤬

Alice was tired. Ever since she'd gone to Dr. Lambshead's mansion, things had become a disaster. She wasn't suited to deception; the rot of it always showed, she thought. Or maybe she'd gotten so used to it—how she must, with each step taken, split the difference. To remain as loyal as she could to the things she cared about, the people she cared about . . . and yet betray them at the same time. To keep Jonathan out of it, and, then, when it was clear her own attempts to keep him out of it had brought him *into* it . . . to try to give him someone trustworthy to rely on, in Mamoud. Even if she had to steal from Jonathan, to leave him at least as well-off as before.

Take something, give something. That's what Alice kept telling herself. Leave the universe the way you found it, on some level. She couldn't do good, not right now, but she could fend off the bad.

Except she'd had no idea Crowley would set an insatiable monster on their trail. Or that there would be puffins. Terrible, horrible, awful puffins. They'd not been in the lake last time she'd had to take that path. Some new legacy? Result of someone else's take something/give something?

It wasn't just the Black Bauble Alice had sought in the mansion. Papers, too. Dr. Lambshead's papers about the Order and the aftermath of the War of Order and how terribly wrong it was all going, which Jonathan would no doubt find out at some point. Who could be trusted, for what side. Perhaps even on what days of the week, so many alliances were fickle.

And in there, the same place as on the Allies List: the Alpine Meadows Research Institute. So why not nudge Jonathan in that direction? Sounding so reasonable. A place Dr. Lambshead considered central to preserving the Order. A place where, maybe, knowing its . . . special properties . . . Jonathan might be sidelined during the coming war.

Safe. Not in play.

While Alice reached into his pocket and stole the one thing she really needed and deserved. The Black Bauble. The thing he didn't understand or know how to use. Contain the Golden Sphere? How naive. Nothing could contain what was coming. She had some hint of that. So did others in the Order, the ones with their ears to the ground, not the higher-ups. Mamoud might ignore it for the Republic's sake, be fixated on Crowley, but Alice already knew Crowley was just a localized problem. Underneath was so much more . . . rot.

Evading the death piggies, evading the Comet Man, evading Crowley's monster. Not exactly fun. Not exactly. But distraction. Definitely that, getting her out of her head. More than a fortnight of eluding various types of pursuit and hiding out in underground caverns until she could get to the right door—and out she'd popped at her destination.

By the river. Near the House of Lords and the House of Commons. Tweedledee and Tweedledum at this point. All stuffed into the awe-inspiring tree.

Courtyards in this place seemed redundant. All the old magic smoldering here, the place a ruin and a dump that influenced the decor and culture of an entire nation. But especially spilled out into an au naturel London that had become at once cosmopolitan and insular, one where you were as like to meet a magical hedgehog in a white wig as a fishmonger.

She much preferred Jonathan's London, filthy though it might be. Even if the pollution made her fade more swiftly, that she must strike out for the countryside every few weeks. Sad but true. True but sad.

No one knew their way through the maze that was the government-in-a-tree. Not really. A little sparkling dandelion sculpted to look like a faery popped up halfway to her destination, because with all the spells of concealment, you'd wander until you died otherwise. Although she'd have to find her way out alone. They didn't care if you got out, the spells, so long as you didn't get in without an escort.

Alice had grown up in the country and knew better than most the state of magic in the country. Most of the actual faery folk had died, when farmers started cutting down the verges and the hedgerows. Turned out faery folks could only live on the fringes. Who knew? Well, everyone now. But did that make a difference?

So what protected the Parliament tree wasn't exactly the old magic. But a kind of nostalgic echo of it, backed up by a kind of cold . . . weirdness. Cleaner, more current. And the main remnant of what had been existed over at the wall, with its air potato herds and its sarcastic shrubbery.

One reason farmers had destroyed the verges was they hated being talked back to.

Nothing worse than a weed giving you what for.

୧୨

Finally, Alice had skirted the House of Lords and its caw-caw-caw, to enter a huge dark hollowed-out bole on the side of the oak. The Lords' private offices. Inside this particular bole, the inner walls were coated in a glow-in-the dark green moss and the high shadowy ceiling illuminated by a trailing ivy of luminous purple morning glories, which shone light down on a thick slab of jutting shelf green-blue fungi the size of a desk. A toadstool stool suitable for a human posterior had erupted in white with red polka dots opposite the desk.

A sickly looking little white crow with blue eyes, one crooked leg, and an unusual upward curve of beak had been fixed to the desk with a dainty silver chain. It cawed, once, twice, thrice, its chain making a glinty tinkling music as it fidgeted.

Alice nodded and crumbled herself into the bole, sat on the cool, clammy stool, which pulsed as if alive. And perhaps it was. The faery folk might be gone, but their residue remained in so many things.

The crow, though, was the work of witches and warlocks, a flesh-and-blood version of an All-Seeing Eye. For no lord from the House of Lords or commoner from the House of Commons came to London anymore. Instead, they stayed home, hovel or estate, and through the arcane remnants of English magic met and debated issues and passed laws through their proxies—the crows and the hedgehogs.

The crow twisted and turned on its perch, the defective beak open in silent protest, the whispering shudder of its wings epic.

Always, these manifestations left Alice cold, frightened her somewhere primal. But she had to keep her nerve. Had to keep her wits about her. Lives depended on it. One life in particular.

The crow settled down as Lord Fenstral's mind settled within it, from afar. There came an added weight to the blue eyes of the crow. The weight of a human consciousness peering out, and the bird's legs for a moment buckled, then recovered, and it stooped there, motionless as if showcased in a taxidermy shop.

From the crow issued forth an odd, tinny voice, full of the static between radio stations. For it was not Lord Fenstral's voice, nor yet the crow's, but something altogether stranger and more ancient. That much Alice knew.

It was also not a friendly voice.

"Alice," said the voice, and she winced. "Alice," said the voice, and it was as if venom had entered her veins. She felt withered and spent, as if only ruin and decay lay before her. "Alice," and she had to grasp the edges of the toadstool with both hands, as if to avoid falling off the edge of the world.

"I have it," she said, before he could ask. The asking could be terrible, too. "I have it. I would have been quick, but I was very far and the circumstances—"

"I don't care," hissed Lord Fenstral. "I don't care for your excuses or your pointless stories or your chatter. Show me. Now."

With care, but in haste, Alice pulled the handkerchief from her jacket pocket. Unwrapped it, held out her hand with the Wobble presented in her palm. She could not say her hand was steady.

The Wobble looked beautiful against the stark white of the cloth, even flecked with death piggy blood: a robust black marble with many a rune and signal etched into its reflectionless surface. The Wobble had burned a hole in her pocket, been such a torment, constantly worried she would rest a moment and find someone had stolen it from her, as she had stolen it from Jonathan.

"The Black Bauble," Lord Fenstral said through the crow, as if it didn't care about the consequences of using the true name. And why should he? He wasn't there. "Black Bauble."

"The Wobble," Alice said. "Yes." Her heart beating hard. So close now. So very close.

"Hold it up to the crow's eyes, feeble as they are," Lord Fenstral said.

Alice did as she was told. The white crow's eyes became cloudy with glints of gold shining through the sudden storm of darkness there.

The crow recoiled from the Wobble, cawed violently, spun on the chain, lunged at Alice, who drew back, cupping the Wobble in both hands to protect it.

"That is not the Black Bauble!" Lord Fenstral cawed. "That is not the Wobble! Not the Wobble at all!"

It was as if Alice had smashed into a block of ice, or her heart had stopped. She felt faint and hot and there was a ringing in her ears.

She heard herself from a great distance, protesting.

"But it is the Wobble. It is! I took it from Jonathan's own pocket. I took it while he was distracted by the monster Crowley sent. I swear. I swear. It is the Wobble. It is!"

It must be the Wobble, for her sister Beatrice's sake.

"No it's not." Said so cold, Alice came back to her senses.

The crow had stopped twitching, and that was worse, and the eyes had not gone back to blue. The stress of that regard was devastating. To have gone through all of this . . . for nothing . . . for worse than nothing. She felt like vomiting.

"It is the Wobble," she said weakly. Oh, Beatrice. Oh, Beatrice. What have I done?

"Open your precious . . . Wobble," Lord Fenstral said in a tone that promised punishment.

"But—"

"Open it."

She pushed the little hidden button at the base of the Black Bauble. It peeled open like an orange.

The inside had all the same inscriptions and moving parts that she remembered when Jonathan had held it.

"I don't see—"

"Look more closely," Lord Fenstral said.

She pushed the one button she'd known, the one that opened up the next layer of instrumentation.

Nothing happened.

"It's stuck," she said, pushing it again, to no avail.

"It's a fake, you stupid cow!"

Betrayed. She felt numb. That was the irony of it all. Someone had betrayed her. Had outsmarted her, had been a step ahead. She should have taken greater care not to show interest in the Wobble. She should've done this, done that, instead. All the thoughts running through her in a panic. But mostly: numb. She was exhausted already, mentally and physically. She had nothing left for . . . this.

"You'll tell me now you were duped," Lord Fenstral said, each syllable like a stab in her back with an ice pick. "Or did you think you could dupe me? Is that it?"

"No, I never—not when you . . ." Could kill my sister.

"Yet here we are. You've failed me."

"I have Jonathan's Allies List. I have all the papers from the mansion. I have—"

A jeering tone, humiliating, from the crow: "Did I ask you to bring me Jonathan's sippy cup? Or his dirty socks? Or his diary? No. I didn't."

"Please." Don't kill Beatrice.

"This is your second failure, Alice. You should have found the Black Bauble at the mansion before the young Lambshead even got there. And then you should've taken it from him sooner than you did. Why did you wait, I wonder?"

Because there was never a good moment. Because as long as she was still on the mission, Beatrice was alive. But if she miscalculated, if she'd failed to steal it . . . and yet here she was anyway.

"I can make it right. I can—"

"Be still! Be quiet!"

Just like that, Alice couldn't move and she couldn't speak and her tongue was thick in her throat and she felt like she was choking to death and she couldn't even scream.

"What should I do with you, Alice?" Lord Fenstral said, much as one would address a spider captured under glass. "We had an agreement. The Bauble for your sister's life. But I have no Bauble, so it stands to reason you shouldn't have a sister."

Still she could not speak, could not move.

"And yet . . . and yet," Lord Fenstral said, considering. "I am not by nature cruel. I believe in last chances. The very last. And that is what I am about to give you. Track Jonathan down. Get me that Wobble. And if you can't get me the Wobble . . . kill Jonathan Lambshead."

"I don't know where he is."

"He's in Florida, of that alt-Earth the Order likes to use to store their valuables. Everyone knows that."

Did they? She didn't.

"He may suspect I'm looking for him." She knew this wouldn't please Lord Fenstral, but she had to say it, had to plead for enough time.

"Everyone's looking for him," Lord Fenstral said, practically spitting out the words. "Everyone knows that. Are you simple? Here's a clue: If all else fails, find a Czech magician named Kristýna and follow her. Or become a shadow at Poxforth—he's destined to return there. Eventually, you'll find Jonathan, one way or the other. If you ever want to see your sister alive again, that is. Isn't that right, Beatrice? You know what I'll do if I don't get what I want."

A scream that raised the hairs on Alice's arms, and then an unmistakable voice, because it was her own voice: "Alice! Please save me! It's terrible here! It's horrible! And they're starving me and I haven't enough to drink and it's dark all the time! And I—"

I love you, too.

Alice slumped on her stool, able to breathe and move again.

Then Lord Fenstral was gone and the crow was just a white, crippled crow again, with blue eyes, flapping its wings in confusion.

Alice had gripped the fake Wobble so hard it had burst into pieces. Flimsy after all, and she had held it so delicate for so many miles to protect what was just a sham, a nothing.

But Lord Fenstral had misjudged the situation.

First, she didn't dare tell Lord Fenstral that the Order might already have told the rank and file to be wary of her, especially if Jonathan had reached safe harbor. Second, Alice didn't think Jonathan had the Bauble, although she had no choice but to pick up that thread first.

Who had taken the real one? Who had done that?

The answer could only be her sometime ally. The one who always thought ahead.

Mamoud.

For a while, Alice lay on the ground, curled up next to the desk. The floor was cool and soft with loam. It was quiet and comfortable. Nothing entered her mind. She needed nothing for a moment. Several moments.

The situation was so complicated. It would have been simple if only Lord Fenstral had actually *been* Lord Fenstral. Under cover of night, before she'd left for Earth and the mansion, Alice had snuck onto Lord Fenstral's ancestral estate. No servants dwelt there. The grounds were overgrown. The many rooms empty. Save for the cupboard with Lord Fenstral's skeleton shoved into it. A musical instrument impaling his chest.

Whoever had kidnapped Beatrice was impersonating a member of the House of Lords, and there wasn't a soul she could tell without risking Beatrice's life.

Another tough chapter in the story of a family half-ruined by the War of Order. Parents dead. Just two sisters now, and it wasn't as if Beatrice were weak. She wasn't. She was tough, and they had often been at odds in part because Beatrice could be stubborn, opinionated. Sometimes, Alice felt Beatrice was a test she could never pass. Always difficult. Always felt she was owed something more. But that made the situation worse, not better. Because Alice felt guilty now for each and every ridiculous argument. How small and insignificant those moments felt now, next to the idea of never seeing Beatrice again.

And she was being destroyed by it, too. Felt like the crumbling facade of a building that had seen better days.

Alice sat up, arm resting on the toadstool. She had another chance, that was the main thing, yes? She looked at her hand, where an outline of the fake Wobble now existed like a tattoo. Whatever it had been made of had stained her skin. Would it fade with time? She wiped at it with her fingers, but it didn't come off. Perhaps some water, later, would help. Or perhaps she would be marked forever. A good reminder.

Although Alice felt a thousand years old, her body as used up as an old dustbin, she lifted herself onto the toadstool once more, leaned over, head in her hands.

Perhaps she would have rested much longer before leaving on her mission, but for the voice that came from the shelf-fungus desk.

"Please, ma'am, may I leave with you? Please?"

She looked over in surprise. It was the crow, of course, talking crow language. One thing she'd become fluent in, growing up in the country. Her and Beatrice on the ancestral farm. Before any of what came next. Before the War of Order.

"Why ever would you leave?" she asked, also in crow language.

The blue eyes stared at her pleadingly. "Please, ma'am, it's unnatural."

"What is?"

"Being possessed. It takes a toll. They keep us in cages in the tree branches, feed us slops and garbage. They discard us quick, with no care. I've been here a year. I had black feathers once, and a foot that worked. My wings . . . I haven't flown in one year. My wings . . . And being that one's voice makes me live in a place with dead things as if I *were* a dead thing—and I am not a dead thing! I am not!"

This last said with an injured dignity at what had been inflicted upon it. The rest said hurriedly, as if she might leave at any moment, and him still chained to the desk.

Tears welled up in Alice's eyes. She couldn't say why she found the crow so moving, but she did. Perhaps because she hadn't considered what it would be like for the hedgehogs and the crows to be inhabited by human minds. Perhaps because a bit of Jonathan's view of animal life had infected her.

What a listless existence, at beck and call. For, in the end, such a frivolous purpose.

"Won't Lord Fenstral notice you're missing?"

"Did he notice the last one missing? Or the one before?"

Alice could guess the answer to that. It'd be like replacing a telephone. Who cared what happened to the old model.

"What's your name?" Alice asked.

The crow cocked his head, said, "They call me Fenstral Voice 343 here. But my name when I was free was———." And he made a series of caws that meant something like "curious blue sky" or "blue horizon diving."

It was folly, but it also felt like a tiny rebellion. An act of defiance. The only one she might be able to afford. Besides, what might the crow know?

"All right, then, you can come with me," Alice said, examining the chain around the crow's foot for the best place to break it. "But if you fly away once we've left this place, I won't fault you. And if you stay, you'll need to learn to perch on my shoulder like a parrot until you're used to the world again."

Now she would have to play a role again. To become the person she was on her mission. Someone she didn't like very much.

The joy on the crow's face was too intense. She had to look away or she would have started weeping again.

EPILOGUE: CLARITY,
NOW WITH HELLSCAPE

Even high up in a dirigible, Napoleon found that the nectar deer were attracted by the moisturizer keeping his undead features smooth, but now he had a mechanical arm to move and a hand at the end of it, and so he shooed them away as he stared through the spyglass down upon Prague and its environs. He didn't much mind them, though. Not now he could wave them away. Their curious, oddly smiling faces. Their quick darting movement. Their grace and their playfulness. Yet he doubted he would have considered them anything but pests before spending time in Ruth Less's pouch.

His dirigible army had arrived just before dusk and taken up a position all around Ruth Less where they had found her: to the east of the old fortress, transformed by the imminent birthing into a mountainlike visage topped by a huge blossoming red-and-white flower with an enormous circular middle and wide flaplike petals. Even from his vantage, he could see animals leaping up the mountainside to jump onto the petals and then slide down into the middle of the flower, so fragrant was its scent, so alluring. So much of a trap.

Lighting up the entire sky stood a flaming figure beside Ruth Less. The Comet Man, just emerged from Ruth Less's pouch. Napoleon recognized him from his campaigns in the Alps so long ago. A Celestial Beast to guard a Celestial Beast. Smart of Ruth Less, if a complication.

But the plot thickened even beyond this incredible sight. For on the other side of the fortress, becoming ever more real, the Château

Peppermint Blonkers floated, low enough to give the illusion it was resting on the hillside overlooking the Old City. A nightmare wrapped inside a silent scream: a place, a thing, that was truly unknowable. What would the château do next? Surely not float there prettily like a bauble. For if any element of this battlefield gave Napoleon pause, it was the château.

Off to the west, in a clearing in the forest, Napoleon could spy the infernal sight of a giant war elephant surrounded by a wide bloodred moat and many hastily erected buildings and some immobilized war elephants beyond as another wall of defense. Indeed, even into the dark, demimages and common soldiers were chopping down trees and waging war against the very forest, that Czech sappers might not use it to attack them from. Crowley and Wretch. Dug in like a huge blood-engorged tick.

A shame.

Napoleon understood the strategic sense, but he'd always admired that forest. Felt that Crowley's men would have been better off understanding the landscape and learning to use it against the defenders than destroying it. Ah well. This was the nature of war, to which he was well accustomed. The stupid coexisted with the subtle, sometimes in the same general.

Above that elephant fortress, a cyclone of crimson swirling light led up to a dense flock of terrible batlike creatures and then an empty orange-lit hole that Napoleon could only think of as a portal. He could feel the heat rising off it from here.

If ever there were a hellscape, some glimpse of what Dante had described, this was it, he feared.

He wondered in passing what had happened to the dandelion and its tufts, the speck. How innocent those days of spying on them with one eye open from his Notre Dame pedestal seemed now.

Verne emerged from an inner room, came out onto the deck. He'd been surly at first when he realized they weren't going to liberate Paris. But he'd come around.

"Bring the English wall to Prague. Cast our lot in that epic struggle," Napoleon had urged. It was war of all against all, and although Napoleon could have gone off in exile or tried to liberate Paris, he was weary of the expected courses of action. He was weary after so much time as a mere head. He wished to effect change as quickly as possible. And, besides, whoever got the upper hand in Prague might emerge invincible, and crush Paris as one did a mosquito.

"My hands are a bit stiff," Napoleon told Verne. The one around the telescope had dented the instrument. He had to grasp it so lightly he felt he might drop it.

"I will make adjustments," Verne said.

He'd also had to adjust to sending emissaries to the animal army holding most of Paris, to parlay and reach an agreement. Neutrality. Safe passage for Napoleon's troops. A common enemy: Crowley. They were even sending some of their army to Prague, where they would reside until deployed within that safe zone created by the two Celestial Beasts.

"It's quite a sight, isn't it, Verne? Who has seen this in any of our lifetimes? Two Celestial Beasts! The Château Peppermint Blonkers."

"Silly name," was all Verne managed, perhaps overwhelmed.

"To speak its true name is to die, for it is an instrument of the Builders, after all."

"But what does it all mean?"

"Ah, Verne," Napoleon said, voice tinged with sadness but also excitement. "It means the end of so many things and the beginning of so many others."

"Will they help us defeat Crowley?"

Napoleon shook his head. "I fear the château has its own agenda."

"I should have abandoned all of this," Verne said. "I could have found somewhere quiet in Brittany. I could pretend I am just a normal person with a normal life again."

"In this conflict," Napoleon said, emphasizing every word, "there is no safe place. No place to hide."

"So you say."

"So say I." And clapped Verne on the shoulder, because he could. Once again.

In the city, from the wall inward, the lights had begun to come on: the lanterns and the candles and the glowing insects used by some establishments. The famous Prague wall a shadow like a snake and, beyond it, the spires and towers of the wondrous city, the ribbon of river running under the bridge. Shining there, below them, the magic city, even now no doubt adjusting with clever, devious plans to this new situation.

That magical beasts lived right above them. That a French invader was on their doorstep along with Crowley.

But shining there in the lights, Prague did not look like a city to be easily conquered or laid siege to. Indeed, few had done so successfully, but only through diplomacy or treachery. And, with any luck, Napoleon had not come to wage war against Prague, but to help defend it.

You could not drive them out through thirst, for the river refilled their reservoirs and aquifers. You could not count on starving the defenders out, for there were farms and gardens even within the city walls, and the city elders, no matter Prague's current allegiance, stocked the grain silos and cattle pens with an eye toward desperate conditions.

The terrain made it difficult to throttle Prague as well, for you could not cut the city off from the outside world without great discipline. The forest, the hills, the river, meant you must needs devote the greater part of an army just to checkpoints and to severing vital arteries. But even then you might not succeed.

Nor was it wise to ignore the wall itself. For legend had it that the wall was alive—that should Prague be in utter peril, the wall, under the influence of the most powerful magics, might come alive, revealed as stone wurm or mighty dragon, and lay waste to even the most formidable enemy.

It might be myth only, but Napoleon had come to believe that myth held potent metaphor and warning. Regardless, the wall was not what it seemed and could confound an attacker just as a wall, no matter how many defenders stood upon its ramparts. Certainly, Verne no longer believed a wall was just a wall.

In addition, there was the matter of the magic doors leading in and out of Prague, not all of which were yet known to Crowley—this much was clear—and thus not yet secured. Even if the number of undiscovered doors numbered only one. It would be hard to lay siege to a city from which agents could freely travel great distances without detection. Nor was it clear what aid the Republic might extend to Prague . . . if only Prague decided to accept the Republic's help.

Nor what the Republic might think of Napoleon's presence.

Yet arrayed against Prague and its allies would be a growing army of Emissaries, a legion of mecha-elephants and other bio-mechanicals, the demi-mages that helped control them, a huge number of potentially unreliable mercenaries, a small host of coerced allies, and what might be termed "nonmagical weapons" like cannons, crossbows, rifles, and muskets that would be a nuisance to the Prague magicians, but were mostly sacrifices to misdirection and subterfuge. No one much thought they would be a factor. Nor his paltry cavalry, the "horsies." Not after the catastrophe in the Crimea, where the Russian cavalry had been turned into horrifically fused centaurs that had gone down in twisted heaps of broken legs and general madness and confusion. Not a one surviving. Perhaps Crowley would turn his cavalry into temporary centaurs to begin his offensive, Napoleon mused, but he was not about to suggest it.

Then there was the question of Wretch's masters, and thus Crowley's. And the other unknown in the equation: What acts might desperation drive a man to? For Crowley would be frantic to find the Golden Sphere now, and bend it to his will. As the only sure checkmate of his opponents.

All this Napoleon pondered as the night deepened and Verne took it all in, silent at his side. No doubt he worried about LX and the wall. No doubt even more so after Napoleon had voiced his doubts about Grimy.

Nor had Napoleon yet informed Verne that the English Parliament had finally decided to send an army to the wall. So perhaps LX and the Burrower would earn some glory sooner than later. If Grimy let them.

So it goes. So it went.

The hard part was ahead, the easy part behind.

It was an uncertain time in which to be an undead head. Even with a new mechanical body. That was all Napoleon knew for certain.

"It is pretty," Verne admitted. "Even if monstrous. The sunset."

"Yes, it is that, Verne," Napoleon said. "But this is our cue for much labor, alas. And without a view."

"And several representatives are waiting for us inside."

"'Mack,' he says his name is, yes?"

"Just 'Mack.'"

"And who else?"

"A shadow of a marmot . . . and no love lost between Mack and shadow."

Napoleon considered that. Was there a rift in some alliance?

The shadow of the marmot lay heavy across Europe already. What had been invisible had made itself known: The animals were not content with their lot. Was 'Mack' now not happy with his own lot?

"And . . . is that all?" He rather felt it wasn't.

"There is a magician from Mali here to see us, on a related matter. And, now, that is all."

Napoleon smiled. "We're of a sudden popular, aren't we, Verne? It is good to be popular. It tells us we are powerful. It tells us me have some measure of control. Very well. To work it is."

He took one last breath of fresh air, then retreated into the inner rooms. This latest peculiar peril of a parlay was just the first of many. In the morning, they would meet with the Prague council, and Napoleon was prepared for mistrust yet again. If not open hostility.

Whatever happened, Aurora would never be the same. The animals would never be the same. Napoleon was sure of it.

Paris? Such an obsolete objective. Defending Paris had never gotten Napoleon anywhere but last stands.

But Prague? Not one, not two, but three Celestial Beasts in play— and the château?

Now, *there* was both a challenge and an opportunity. An opportunity to crush Crowley, for one thing.

He would see Crowley's head on a stick or become a head on a stick again himself.

Avaunt! It was time for battle.

THE COMET MAN BOOK CLUB QUESTIONS

If you would like your score acknowledged and tabulated in our ledger of how satisfied we are with our readers, please painstakingly handwrite this questionnaire on a piece of parchment, fill it out in this new form, put your worst enemy's name on it and their hometown, fold it in half, write your favorite river shanty on the outside, and give it to a stranger, asking them to "Send it on to the Château Peppermint Blonkers." We will receive it due to the power of pure luck and ill-fortune.

What is one of the major themes of Book Two?

A. Marmots are people, too.

B. Humans are marmots, too.

C. Not helping your friends is the best way to live a long life.

D. Gravity works everywhere in the universes.

E. Being chased by monsters decreases the chances of romance.

F. Love conquers all, if by "love" you mean hedgehogs riding roosters.

Which would you like more of in Volume Two of the series?

A. Car chases.

B. Explosions.

C. Page-long descriptions of how magic works.

D. Beard-braiding.

E. Soliloquies from minor characters like the surly carrot man.

F. All of the above.

Do you hope the lost Wobble is also intelligent like the Golden Sphere?

A. Yes.

B. No.

C. I would like fewer things to talk in Book Three, thank you very much.

ACKNOWLEDGMENTS

Dear Reader: Some things are original. Other things have been pilfered for your pleasure. Sincerely, Stimply J. Nightingale, Esq.

Rack's quoting of a Poxforth professor saying "A thesis on the curve became a dog turd on the curb," attributed by Rack to a Poxforth professor, can be found in the introduction to the 1994 Exact Change edition of *Maldoror* by the Comte de Lautrémont.

The bear gun is the creation of, and used by permission of, Adam Mills.

Dracula's testicles belong to Horia Ursu, who provided the idea, for better or worse.

The subterranean compass exists, a creation of the artist Angela DeVesto, and is referred to by permission. DeVesto is also a rat aficionado and was of use with regard to Tee-Tee.

The brief reference to "church tanks" is a nod to artist Kris Kuksi's church-tank sculptures.

Rack's feverish description of a funicular is taken from the Wikipedia entry on funiculars.

Quotes in the death piggies scenes are from William Hope Hodgson's public domain novel *The House on the Borderland* (1908).

The term "rage and flap, flap and rage" from the Golden Sphere's hand puppet stint is a joint composition of VanderMeer and the artist Abinada Mesa. The "flap" may have been created by VanderMeer, but the "rage" was concocted by Mesa.

The stilts used by the giant marmots to navigate steep, uneven mountainsides were a gift from the demented mind of Jonathan Wood. Even if they didn't make the final cut.

The term "Circus Meat," used by Sprogg at the Alpine Meadows Research Institute, was first brought to the author's attention by the blonkers artist Jeremy Zerfoss (who also created the illustrations for this volume).

Dr. Lambshead's mentioned quest for the silver star, otherwise known as edelweiss, is a nod to the comic *Asterix in Switzerland*. (Which is not, one might add, an accurate representation of Switzerland. Or Gauls.)

ABJECT THANKS

My everlasting thanks to Wesley Adams at FSG Books for Young Readers for embracing the screwball weirdness of my creation and for being on the same page in general. Thanks also to my wife, Ann, for taking away the router so I could have peace and quiet to write (among other kindnesses). Additional thanks to my agent, Sally Harding, especially for field-testing the Ruth Less suit, and Ron Eckel for international adventures.

For those intrepid explorers at FSG BYR who accompanied Jonathan on his misadventures and went behind him sentence-by-sentence correcting his and his friends' mistakes and helping his story get out into the world, my thrilling and heartfelt apologies for the length of the journey and the lack of appropriate accommodations: Senior Designer Aurora Parlagreco; Production Editor Taylor Pitts; Copyeditor Patricia McHugh; Proofreaders Janine Barlow and Mandy Veloso; Assistant Editor Melissa Warten; Assistant Production Manager Celeste Cass; Associate Marketing Managers Teresa Ferraiolo and Melissa Croce; Executive Director of Publicity Molly B. Ellis; and Executive Director of Subrights Kristin Dulaney. Special thanks for keen and useful observations: Ann VanderMeer, Jonathan Wood, Jackie Gitlin, Jeremy Zerfoss, Aeman Ansari, and Alex Blaszczuk.

Apologies to the bird-children in the backyard for bouncing so many story ideas off them during this process. I know it became tiresome, especially to the wrens (who had better things to do). But I appreciate the tip about puffins.

Finally, thanks to the summer tanagers for peeking in my office window from time to time, out of concern for my well-being while I was working on these novels.

"*I am mighty now . . .*"